BLACK SUGAR

J.B. Levert

BLACK SUGAR

A novel

In Bran Harkey
Jan. 15, 2005

Ira Brown Harkey

This book was printed in the United States of America.

To order additional copies of this book, contact:
Xlibris Corporation
1-888-795-4274
www.Xlibris.com
Orders@Xlibris.com
21511

FRONTISPIECE PHOTO COURTESY OF IRA BROWN HARKEY COLLECTION

In loving memory of my mother,
Marie Ella Levert Gore Harkey

Papa is a benevolent sort of man who wants to help people
out of their financial problems; he just buys them out—
Stephanie Marie Eulalie Levert

Jean, you are a very rich man. It's just time
for you to begin giving something back—
Colonel John Louis Bush

I should begin this story with the events of the devastating hurricane that slammed into our plantation house in the middle of the night fifteen years ago, just as my Mother went into labor with me, and especially since she nearly died giving birth to me. My Father told me about that terrible September night many times. He never let me forget it, and due to his repeated accounts, I can recall details of the worst hurricane ever to strike Iberville Parish. It destroyed everything in its path. Listening to Father tell about the storm and knowing that the experience almost drove him from sugar farming forever, was very hard for me. So many times, too, he told me there was something about the coincidence of my birth and the passing of the hurricane—an omen, perhaps—that stirred peculiar feelings in him, feelings he couldn't explain then and I can't explain now.

Jean Baptiste Levert

1854

CHAPTER 1

AUGUSTE LEVERT WAS awakened by the hurricane that came in the night, driving its crushing force against his six hundred acres of sugarcane fields on Golden Ridge Plantation. As he stood on the second-floor gallery outside his wife's bedroom, *Madame Levert* went into labor with her sixth child, her pains rising in intensity and rhythm with the wind gusts that slammed into the walls of the Big House.

By the powerful wind gusts Auguste knew that the storm measured several hundred miles across. Lighting flashed, followed by roaring thunder blasts and heavy rain. Suddenly he felt cold; the temperature had dropped. Having ridden out other hurricanes, Auguste recognized a wind shift. For most of the night it had blown in a northerly direction from the Gulf of Mexico, the weaker flank of the storm; now it seemed to turn more northeast and gain intensity. Thick oak and skinny pine tree limbs snapped and crashed to the ground.

Finally in the early-morning, the wind stopped and Auguste left his wife in the capable hands of Mammy Bébé. He hurried to the stables to meet his overseer, Jacques, who had waited for him. Auguste mounted Thunder, his blue-black stallion, and the two men rode out of the barn at a gallop and headed for the cane fields.

But the sounds of the frightful night had not prepared Auguste for the destruction he saw when he and Jacques reached the fields after sunup. Auguste sat forward on his horse and stared through the lightening haze at the awesome work of the hurricane. He leaned on the pommel of his saddle and fought back tears. "Oh, my God, Jacques," he said hoarsely, "I'm ruined."

Little of his crop remained standing. Thirteen-foot stalks lay collapsed on the soggy earth, swept haphazardly by blasts of winds and flooded by waters pushed upriver in tidal surges that overflowed the banks of the Mississippi River. The cane had lain for hours in the foul-smelling waters, a dark slush that was now lowering slowly, trickling back into the bayous and marshes.

Auguste jerked Thunder to the left to better see the damage; his Cajun overseer followed him on his mule. "Oh, My God," Jacques murmured sympathetically. "*Mon dieu. Mon dieu.*"

The men stared for a long time at the apparent ruin of Golden Ridge's nurtured fields. In Iberville Parish, called Sweet Iberville, were the most productive plantations in Louisiana. A fine loam, the pride of Auguste's six hundred acres located on a bend in the river, was rich and black, producing some of the world's best sugarcane. Now, the fields resembled a mass burial ground. Cutting a wide swath, the storm had torn magnificent oaks out of the earth, exposing enormous root systems never meant to see the light of day, now washed raw and red by last night's slashing rain. Other oaks, left standing, had lost stout branches that were hurled like projectiles into the weathered walls of the house. Magnolias, pines and other smaller trees were stripped bare, and appeared starkly naked. Bodies of animals were scattered along with those of chickens and guineas.

Auguste uttered a prayer and continued to stare at his once-abundant fields. "We were days away from one of the best harvests we've ever had, Jacques, only days. This crop was going to be better than the banner year before. Now look."

The sun had risen higher and now glinted on the wet and littered wreckage. Auguste tugged at his khaki trousers, then pulled the brim of his brown straw hat down sharply to shield his eyes. Thunder snorted and tossed his head up and down as he guided him under a mushroom-shaped oak undamaged by the storm, its long beards of Spanish moss still there.

The row of slave cabins on the river banks remained standing, but was heavily damaged. Its occupants, Auguste's field hands, had taken refuge with milk cows, sheep, and work mules in the sturdier barn behind the house; both cupolas had been blown off the barn's roof. Windows of the Big House were shattered, shingles loosened. The planter knew that hundreds of poisonous snakes had been washed from their lairs by flood waters, and they must be watched for in open boats and on the galleries of the Big House. He shook his head, wondering at the pleasant day—the skies were now clear and blue.

"All this destruction in only a few hours," said Auguste. "You know it's going to take several growing seasons to replace what I've lost, and I don't have that much time." Tortured by the threat of another failed crop, he added, "Recovery will be slow and very expensive."

"Jes don give up, Meester Augus. De water, it won stay round too much longa; see, it already drain off right fast, yeah," Jacques told him in his thick Cajun accent. "Bet we cain save lotsa dis cane, yeah." Maybe if . . ." The overseer twisted on his horse and looked out again at the cane fields. Auguste looked at him, sensing what the Cajun, an experienced sugar farmer, was thinking. "What do you mean? You mean you think we could . . . are you thinking all the roots of the cane might not be ruined? Is that what you're thinking?" Hope crept into his voice: "If they're not, it's possible we could salvage some of this cane."

Jacques sat taller on his mule and gazed at his boss. "Meester Augus, jes let me round up de nigras, dey huddled in de big barn. Ain't none of dem hurt, just scairt. We go out and try to set de stalks up, prezz dem roots back down, let de cane dry, yeah. De sun'll pull dem stalks up straight, you see. Dis land gonna drain, yeah. Member, you got lotsa hands so let's jes work at it stalk by stalk and hope and pray."

But Auguste had slumped in his saddle again. "If we can't, I'm ruined, and I can't take another failed crop, not after the hard freeze three years ago almost ruined me and everybody else down here. I know no other work, Jacques. My father taught me everything I know about cane. That's all I've wanted to do, and to teach my sons." He took out his watch. He felt he just got in Bébé's way, but knew his wife would want him nearby.

Again the planter seemed overwhelmed. "I just don't know about this hurricane . . . my father settled down here in St. James Parish and turned a dried-up piece of land into cultivated productive ground that made fine healthy cane and a good income. But damnit, Jacques, I'm thirty-six years old, and farming's all I've ever known, ever thought of doing." He put his watch in his trouser pocket and turned Thunder toward the Big House. "Come on, we've got to try to save some of this crop. Get moving, I'll be with you."

*   *   *

"Mister Augus! Mister Augus! Wait!" shrieked the Negro boy as Auguste turned his mount toward the Big House. "Queeck! Miss Eu'lie want you, hurry!"

"What's the matter, Rufus?" his master shouted, reaching for the rope bridle. "Steady mule." Wide-eyed and barefoot, with overalls rolled halfway up his skinny legs, the sixteen-year-old boy was smiling as he broke clear of spraying water churned up by his mule. "You and Miss Eu'lie got another boy, fine boy, yeah. Fat, too. Bébé tell me de Misses fine, for you don worry. But hurry, Misses want you back!"

Sitting straight as a cane stalk in his saddle, Auguste did not answer Rufus right away. Immediately he felt the fears and threats of the past six hours wash away—loss of the crop, provision for his growing family, borrowing more money from his sugar broker to finance next year's crop, all of it. A wide smile replaced the gloom on his face. He felt alive again. News of the birth of his fifth son filled him with a surge of confidence. A strange optimism took hold of him, lifting him out of his thoughts of material loss. He didn't understand what was happening to him, but he knew that he'd never forget the early hours of September 14, 1839, and the birth of his new son.

"Come on, Rufus," he shouted, leaning over the neck of his horse. "Let's be gone. *Madame Levert* needs us."

By the time Auguste and Rufus jerked their mounts to a stop at the stables behind the Big House, almost a mile away, Eulalie Levert's painful, twelve-hour labor and delivery were well over.

"*Cher, cher*, look at your new son," said Eulalie weakly, as her husband burst into her bedroom. Auguste looked from his wife to his newborn son, a well-formed baby, he thought, with a round face and plump rings of flesh at his wrists. Still breathing hard from his gallop, he leaned over Eulalie and kissed her on the cheek.

"You already seem to be recovering from your ordeal, *ma chèrie*. Look! Our new son is kicking, has good color and appears well. From the sound of his cries, he has strong lungs. Listen to him!"

Auguste knew he was raving like a madman. He was also eager to tell Eulalie about his strange feelings at the moment Rufus brought him the news of the birth. "There is something about the timing of his birth and the passing of this devastating hurricane. I can't explain it, *chèrie* . . ." But then he stopped, remembering his wife's weakened condition. He noticed her smiling at him, her soft brown hair framing her pale face on the high pillows.

"Bébé, I don't need to tell you to give Mrs. Levert every attention she needs. She's been through so much. You know better than anyone else how to care for her, and you've been here for all of our babies."

"Don worry none, Mister Lavair, I do all I cain to help *Madame* till she git back up." She smiled. "No, no, don you worry none, yeah. I been wid *Madame* too long to let anything happen now." Auguste knew it was Bébé more than anyone else on Golden Ridge who had pulled his wife through her grief and heartbreak when her first-born son, Augustin, died in infancy nine years earlier. And he was certain that Eulalie could not have survived any of her children's births without "Bay Bay," the family's chief house servant and mammy.

Gently, Auguste rose from Eulalie's bedside and walked to the gallery outside her room. As he stared out at the hurricane's destruction, he felt again that something good was about to come of all this. While his family and the house servants had survived the storm, he knew every man who survived must now do his duty to help whatever widows and orphans it might have left in its wake. "Some of us have much to be thankful for," he muttered to himself.

And from the cradle, Auguste heard the new baby emit cries, loud and lusty. He hit the balustrade firmly with his fist and smiled. *This boy was going to be special, strong like the winds that blew in with him.*

CHAPTER 2

"'ON THE BORDER between the English Colonies and New France is my native Acadia. It's very cold in winter and heavy snows cover the ground much of the year. My Acadia is not at all like your land, diversified by its gentle hills and covered by thick carpets of green grass . . . I mourn and grieve for my native home with its heavy snows, because I have left my heart in the tombs of those I loved so deeply . . . '"

Before seven o'clock on the early October evening, Auguste Levert stopped reading and laid his mother's small, quill-written journal on his lap. His eyes moistened, and he choked back tears. The journal was filled with accounts written many years before by Anna Comeaux Levert about her forced exile by the British in the late 1700s, of the frightful experiences she endured during her journey to freedom and new life in French Catholic country around New Orleans.

"Children—children, these descriptions of *ma Mère's* ordeal are always too sad for me to read. Wouldn't you rather I tell you stories more amusing?" asked their father, after regaining his composure.

"No, no, Papa, we feel close to *Grand-mère Levert* when you read to us from her journal." Jean Baptiste's blue eyes beseeched his father. "It's the only way we can learn about our people, what they did, where they came from." Jean knew his revered grandmother through the words of her journal, and he was determined to record his daily life as she had.

Jean had asked his father to read from his grandmother's journal. Jean, sister Marie Euphrasie, older brothers Joseph and Auguste, Jr., called Augie by the family, and baby brother Amèdèe sat around their father's tall rocker in the parlor at Golden Ridge Plantation, less furniture in the room than was customary, thought Jean, and the colors paler giving an illusion of light. Jean knew his father felt deeply reverent toward his parents, that he grew emotional about his mother's difficult migration to Louisiana whenever he read to his children. And he knew he'd had a powerful influence on his father since he was seven years old.

"I wanted to read Mama's words this evening, since it is the anniversary of her arrival in the Louisiana wilderness more than fifty years ago." Again Auguste's voice faded. He threw back his shoulders, stopping the rocker's slow motion. He stared through long windows which overlooked his sugarcane fields. Jean looked at him with sympathy; he was certain his father was thinking of the two older children he had lost. Cholera had taken his favorite sister, Marie Aimeè, several years before, and only last summer his brother Eloi had died in a riding accident.

Jean, his sister and brothers drew closer to the rocking chair; no one spoke. The planter frowned slightly, then continued reading in his resonant voice: "'My people were not allowed to lead a life of idleness or laziness. We all had our place in the order of things: Men tended flocks and tilled fields; women tended to household chores, spinning wool and cotton and making clothing, all forming a single family unit, this village of Port Royal in Acadia, not a community of separate, diverse families.

"'From the time the British ordered us to either disown our Mother Country of France—give up our religion and become exiles—or to sign the king's oath of allegiance, we began leaving our homes, becoming estranged from our land, without family, friends, money—bound for distant, unknown lands. We wandered about in despair, crying, cursing our red-coated tormentors.'"

Jean watched his father's face brighten, even a shining expression, then push his gray, bristly hair off his forehead. Inheriting a pleasant blend of traits from his French-Canadian father and Acadian mother, Auguste was very handsome. He read for another hour until Euphrasie, Joseph, and Amèdèe fell asleep near his chair. At nine o'clock he put the journal on the table.

"That's enough," he said softly. "Morning will come mighty quick. Besides tending to the '55 crop just planted, we have many days of hard work ahead bringing in the '54 harvest." He gazed at his children. Jean looked at the sickly Joseph, who had never displayed the interest in farming that he and Augie did. Euphrasie, Joseph, and Amèdèe rose, said goodnight, and went to bed.

Muscular in body, with an enthusiastic manner, Jean, however, insisted: "Please go on, *Père*. You may not be able to read again for awhile, certainly not till after the '54 crop is harvested and sent to market." Jean, who dreamed of becoming a well-to-do planter like his father, with a fine house and a lovely wife, knew that his father's farmland in the flat lowlands of the Mississippi River—with grasses that rolled like sea swells and spread out with an evenness that had few equals—was the best farmland in the Union. That his father was one of Iberville Parish's largest sugar producers. "Can't Augie and I hear one more letter tonight? Augie loves learning about farming from you just as much as I do. And what about poor Grandpa Joseph?"

Jean noticed his father looking at him with eyes shaded by thick brows and lashes so dark as to seem black. "All right, son, a few more minutes. What I tell you, though, will be from my memory." He stood tall and straight, lighting his pipe before continuing.

"Well, Mama was forced to leave Acadia when she was only nineteen. She and Papa planned to make the long, dangerous journey together to southern Louisiana after Papa sold his wheat farm near Montreal, but—"

Mama crossed herself and prayed, but when the British soldier started reading the oath document, she lifted her head—she'd bow to no Britisher! She began to cry, felt hopeless. She panicked, pushed her way through the crush of Acadians to the rear of the church where she was being held prisoner . . . after three days she and the others were marched single-file to one of the small sailing vessels, frenzied with despair, clinging to each other for comfort and strength . . . it wasn't enough that Mama was being separated forever from her parents,

that older family members like her parents began to die, losing
the will to go on . . . .

"Then what happened, Papa?"

"I—I am sorry, son, my mind was wandering . . . well, Mama was able to escape from an overcrowded, unseaworthy vessel, jumping over the side and almost drowning trying to swim several hundred yards back to the shoreline of Port Royal. She was trying to meet up with Papa in Montreal, but the British found her, after she reached shore, and deported her again . . . eventually, she made her way with other exiles to Tennessee in a covered wagon, then she floated down the Tennessee River to the Mississippi on a raft. Then on down here to St. James Parish."

Auguste told Jean his mother had given his father up for dead, that she didn't see him for so long she thought he'd met somebody else to love in Montreal; that his mother had married a planter named Berard, inheriting his plantation when he died. "Later your *Grand-père,* who was one of the settlers of St. James Parish about 1801, found her and they were married."

Jean's father rubbed his eyes with palms of both hands. "Papa loved Mama very much." He tried to suppress a yawn. "When he found out where she was, he risked his life and left the security of Montreal for the wilds of Louisiana."

Jean watched Augie, who was eight years older and four inches taller than him at six feet, with hair touching his shoulders, go to bed. He and his father climbed the curving staircase, side by side, and Jean snuffed out the candle. Auguste put his arms around the boy's shoulders before they went to their separate bedrooms and said wearily:

"What your grandmother suffered through, losing her parents during their wretched journey into exile, history will never let us forget. Her people endured. They brought a new culture and way of life down here to Louisiana that is as much a part of our existence today as sugarcane."

CHAPTER 3

"JEAN, JEAN, TIME to git up! You got big day in de fields. Mister Lavair, he need you, all his boys today. If you don git up, I gonna come and git you up, yeah!" Jean heard the deep, powerful voice reverberating from the bottom of the stairs. He knew he wouldn't get any more sleep this morning. It wasn't quite six o'clock. "I'm up, I'm up," he answered in a manly voice. He rubbed his eyes. "Be downstairs as soon as I can."

Bébé thundered back to the second floor: "You know betta dan stay up half de night listenin to Mister Lavair tell bout your *grand-mère* life. Your brothers ready so you git ready, yeah. Dis day too impo'tant to stay in bed all day."

Jean walked barefoot across the cypress floor to the long window. He shielded his eyes against golden sunlight streaming into his bedroom and glowing on the white walls and dark mahogany furniture. The antique patinas gleamed like red wine. He looked out at the flat, lush green lawn, with its rows of peach and orange trees. Fall was approaching but the October air felt thick, steamy to him. From his window Jean could smell the fragrance of late-blooming magnolias. But this morning he had no desire to lean on the broad sill and contemplate nature. He was anxious about the '55 crop, but even more anxious about bringing in a healthy, profitable '54 crop.

"Come on!" shouted Bébé. Jean, Auguste, Augie, and Amèdèe looked up from the breakfast table in the pantry to see Bébé's large brown hands unloading a tray: Smoked ham, large yams covered with butter, and a seven-inch stack of buckwheat cakes dripping cane syrup. The boys finished in minutes, but their father laid down his fork. "I can't eat today," he told Bébé. "I'm worried."

They sat at the table where food, silver, and china were stored. "Success in sugar is as much a gamble as betting on a throw of the dice," Auguste said, staring at his plate. "If this year's crop proves to be a bad one, we'll have to borrow more money to pay the notes. Those brokers in New Orleans, including mine, Albert Desmont, sell their money at the highest rates they can, sometimes as high as 25 percent. You know if we have three or four bad crops in a row we could be ruined."

"Listen, you gotta eat, Mister Lavair, yeah," declared Bébé. "You gotta eat and dat dat." She stood straight and put her clenched hands on her wide hips. Bébé means business, thought Jean, for she frequently ran the Levert household. "It do all you good. Need strength cause you work hard today. And you gonna eat eber bit a dis food . . ."

Bébé's voice trailed off as she walked out the long open passageway to the kitchen. Jean smiled. Bébé had her way of letting her owner know where she stood on certain things. When she returned to the pantry, Jean listened to his father and Bébé air their minds; and he studied the tormented expression on his father's usually serene face.

"Our neighbors may lower their debts in a year's time, but often they enlarge them," said Auguste, looking straight into Jean's eyes, clenching his fists. He frowned. "Many planters risk everything and pledge their crops to their brokers, or factors, long before the crops are even marketed."

Auguste watched his sons eat a second helping of buckwheat cakes. "We've had some setbacks and some good years," he continued. "It's God's will that fortunes turn for the best or go sour. I feel confident about this crop, but I am depending on you boys more than ever to help with cutting, with hauling cut stalks to the sugarhouse for processing—anything you can do. He leaned forward, speaking in a more urgent tone. "I hope the favorable weather conditions we've had in the last weeks of September have ripened the crop and enhanced sugar content. Boys, I don't need to remind you that if we have another failed crop, we could be in very deep financial trouble." Jean smiled at his father. Despite Auguste's gloomy thoughts, Jean rejoiced in the prospect of making a larger crop than usual— he felt success in his bones. Having to borrow more money always dampened his father's normally buoyant spirit.

*   *   *

From the back gallery, Jean saw Salem Bibb standing on the porch of the overseer's house having an early-morning stretch. The new overseer lived in the four-room gray house behind the Big House, and was treated by his boss with courtesy. But Jean was sure his father's slaves looked upon Bibb with contempt. Grouped several hundred feet behind Bibb's house, in a strange confusion, Jean thought, were storerooms, washrooms and other outbuildings. A little farther on were neat stables for the saddle and carriage horses.

It had been several weeks since the ditches on Golden Ridge had been cleared, choked by vegetation for most of the summer and early fall. Auguste had ordered Bibb to take Isaac and a couple of the older, stronger hands to inspect them again. From a distance of fifty yards, Jean, standing on the gallery steps, watched Bibb plop his large body into a rocking chair as his father stepped upon the overseer's porch. Moments later he heard rising voices.

"Mr. Bibb, I am talking to you. Damnit, did you hear me?" Jean knew his father was growing impatient with the man he paid a dollar and a quarter a day. He already knew his father was thinking of discharging him for insubordination. "This day's too important, and the ditches have to be maintained at all times, even after planting, so they can drain. If not, there is a good chance next year's crop will not fare well. You should know that, Mr. Bibb. Standing water, next to frost, is the most destructive threat to cane."

Auguste obviously was tired of repeating this. "I need experienced hands out there, and Isaac's one of the most reliable ones I have. So get moving and check things like I asked. Understand?"

After a long silence, Bibb shrugged, his sallow, unshaven face flushed red. His eyes went wide. "Oh, okay, I'll take Isaac and three others to check the ditches, make sure they're clear for draining. But Mr. Levert, suppose we should dispatch another gang to make sure there're no problems with the current harvest, that things are off to a good start?" The overseer stood with his arms at his side, peering smugly at his boss. "My gang could go ahead and make sure the ditches get cleared out."

Auguste nodded curtly to Bibb. "Very well."

Auguste with his three sons mounted to ride out. He turned abruptly to Augie and Amèdèe. "You boys go along with Bibb and his gang and help inspect the ditches and dikes." As he and Jean headed into the plantation's miles of dirt roads, Auguste said, "I am glad you boys ate well this morning. It'll be some time before you eat again. Jean, you almost didn't get to breakfast on time."

Jean grinned. He enjoyed being alone with his father, watching, listening, learning, and he appreciated his eagerness to teach. As usual, Auguste talked, describing the growing process as though Jean had never heard it before: Cane didn't reach its full height, under ideal conditions, in less growing time than twelve months, and it did not grow from seeds like other crops. Stalks had a series of joints and each joint had a bud. When stalks were planted and covered with soil, the buds sprouted, producing a new crop. Cane did not have to be planted every year. When one crop was harvested, another crop grew back the following year from the same roots.

And Jean did not mind his father repeating himself: Three annual crops of cane were usually harvested from one planting in Louisiana; cane that was planted one September was first harvested the following October; cane was vulnerable to cold—a moderate cold not only shortened its growth cycle, but disorganized it so that the qualities of its sap were changed; cold rendered it almost valueless for sugarmaking; great care had to be exercised to protect the crop during the growing time, to keep open at all times a system of drainage ditches to allow water to flow into the river. "This is very hard work, it takes constant labor," he often said to Jean. "Water is our greatest enemy."

Jean helped his father plan his crop operations in the plantation journal like a general plans a battle campaign on his map. He and the slaves had helped him dig parallel ditches about two hundred feet apart to drain Golden Ridge, dividing the plantation by main ditches and roads dug into sections called cuts, each section subdivided by shallow ditches into fields of twenty-five acres. Jean knew his father always had maintained a constant check on drainage within his fields, and that this meticulous effort for drainage, which had no direct result in the production of cane, required a great deal of money.

Jean and his father reined their horses in the south field to observe three separate gangs, two consisting of women and one of men. The gangs were busy working some of the furrows with plows that had not been uncovered, as Salem Bibb had ordered. The seed cane had been buried in the furrows since the previous fall, and Jean and Auguste, besides inspecting the '55 crop, wanted to make sure the hands were uncovering them. Many of the men were virtually naked, with cloth strips attached to waistbands in front and behind. Several of the women, removing the seed cane with iron hooks and loading it onto carts, wore rags and were bare-breasted.

"What happens to this cane?" Jean asked abruptly. He was looking at the women's bare breasts. He never looked at his father.

"Well, the cane that's been resurrected is carried on these carts to where the ground has been prepared for planting."

Jean turned away when he noticed some hands were working in three sections. "Why, *Père?*"

"A female gang takes the stalks and drops them in heaps alongside the furrows. The planter gang follows and places the canes in the furrows, and still another gang of women covers the furrows." He told Jean that he had planted more than four hundred acres of cane by the end of September, and "I hope we'll realize six tons of cane to an acre."

CHAPTER 4

AS JEAN BAPTISTE sat with his father in the parlor later in the afternoon, going over the '55 crop planting records, he looked up to see Bébé's helper, Piksie, standing in the double doors jumping up and down and flapping her long, skinny arms like a pelican exercising its wings before flight.

"Mister Augus, sorry to bother you, but a Mister Desmont from de big city a New Orleens now here," she said in her shrill voice. "Won me to let him in?"

Auguste rose. "Yes, yes, of course, Piksie, please show him in," her master replied.

Rising with his father, Jean inquired: "Who is it, Father?" Usually his father went to New Orleans to tend to business— order supplies or to borrow money. He didn't know that brokers came to see planters at home.

"His name is Albert Desmont," said his father. "I've been expecting him. He wrote several weeks ago that he was coming upriver this month to talk business with some of his planter clients, and that he would stop to see me."

When Desmont entered the room, Jean quickly took in the man's distinguished appearance—strong features and extraordinary height and posture. Jean watched the broker hand his cape and hat to the reedy Piksie. *Beaux yeux*, thought Jean. Good looks. Fine eyes.

"Come in! Come in, sir!" The two men shook hands formally but with warmth. "Allow me to present my son Jean Baptiste." Jean politely shook the hand offered him.

"Mr. Levert, I compliment you on your beautiful landscaping. The giant oaks give you such shade! Your crape myrtles still bloom this late in the season! A brighter pink than I've seen in the city." He raised his heavy eyebrows very slightly. "And your rose and hawthorn shrubs, with their pink flowers and red fruit, edge your gardens and orchards perfectly."

"Thank you, sir. The crape myrtles are a longer-blooming variety. The shrubs do add something to the grounds, don't they? I must give my wife your compliments. The grounds are in her charge."

As the men discussed architectural details of the Big House— twelve-foot ceilings, plaster walls, wide galleries, traversing halls— Jean gazed about the familiar room with renewed appreciation. *My favorite room.* His eyes explored the chandelier, with its Austrian prisms that glittered with every flicker of its candles; a soft, inviting sofa in the center; portraits of his grandparents and his mother hanging between arched French windows at the rear of the room.

"How long have you lived on this fine estate?" Desmont gave a twisted smile.

"I bought the property a few years before Jean was born from a Plaquemine widow. She was in a hurry to sell to help pay some debts owed by her late husband's estate. I got it for a very good price—nineteen thousand." He told Desmont the farm equipment was included in the deal: Cultivators, rotary harrows, plows, rakes, corn planters, stubble diggers, water carts for hauling sustenance to the field slaves. "The whole estate, all seventeen hundred acres, including slaves, is worth a hundred and twenty-three thousand dollars, now."

"It appears that you have made many additions to the main house."

"I had no choice. As my family grew I had to add bedrooms. I also built stables and other outbuildings, because I kept putting more and more acreage into cane production. Of course, as I enlarged my fields I had to buy more slaves, mules, horses, oxen."

Now Desmont, as he brought news of the world to Golden

Ridge, told Auguste that because of the expected bumper sugarcane crop, he should get his '54 crop to market as quickly as possible to take advantage of the anticipated high selling prices. Something set Desmont apart from any man he had ever met, thought Jean. Was it his mysterious face? Was it that he knew enough about the sugar market to upset the commercial world?

As Desmont turned his talk to include him, Jean found that great knowledge of the sugar business wasn't required to join the conversation. He made Jean feel at ease, even flattered, and the boy became aware that the broker wielded an important influence in the sale of the Golden Ridge sugar crop. He sensed that the business Albert Desmont had chosen for his life's work—sugar brokering—contrasted acutely with that of a sugar planter's. And he was fascinated by the contrast.

*   *   *

Jean leaned his aching body over the iron kettle of cold water behind the Big House kitchen. Sweat glistened on his flushed face, and his tongue felt parched. He saw his face in the water, then beside it he saw Bébé's, both their features rippling slightly on the surface. Jean splashed his hot face and turned to look at Bébé. He could see she had something to talk about. "I'm hot and tired, Bébé. This must be God's hardest labor." He took a deep breath. Jean had spent three sleepless nights helping his father fertilize the '55 crop after planting and helping Augie and Amèdèe haul this year's harvested stalks to the sugarhouse to be manufactured into brown raw sugar.

"How it been dese pass few days, Jean?" said Bébé, in her deep voice. "You couldn be learnin farmin from no betta, kinda person dan Mister Lavair. Dese last days of plantin de cane and workin de fields impot'ant, considerin what your father suffa in past years."

Jean dunked his head into the kettle of cold water again for relief from the October heat and humidity that had settled over him like a heavy net. Bébé, short with a soft bosom and round behind, sat down heavily on the green wooden kitchen steps. The kitchen was separate from the Big House to avoid fires, and now a light breeze wafted through the connecting passage. Shaking water from his hair and face, Jean looked at two cooks on benches under a giant pecan tree, cracking crab claws and peeling shrimp. A basket of oysters sat near them.

"Gombo," said Bébé, as if to forestall a question. Then she laughed. Her laugh, like the sweeping gestures with her hands and arms, was nervous. Bébé laughed often, and Jean liked how she made him laugh when he least felt like it. The mammy continued, "I feel dat closeness between you and Mister Lavair day you born, I hold you in my arms, and he run into *Madame* room and lay eyes on you de first time, after dat bad hurricane. I feel dat special bond, yeah."

To Jean, the sixty-year-old Bébé was like having a doting aunt around. She interceded with his mother and father for him, punished him herself for misbehaving, told him fascinating stories of her hard life and how she became part of the family. Jean realized her influence on his thoughts, language and character was inestimable. Bébé, the only servant who sometimes slept in the Big House, had no doubts he would be a success in life if he put his mind to it. "If you won to be like Mister Lavair, then be it," she drawled to Jean, "but be it cause you won it, not cause he won it or spect it."

Jean heard Bébé but he was thinking about the rigors of planting and growing cane; for already he felt the same pressures that his father suffered:

Rain and drought, cold and heat, all were prepared for with the greatest of care. The tender plant was nursed from day-to-day by plowing and hoeing. At the first sign of growth in early spring, rank weeds and grass threatened his father's '54 crop. If weeds and grass were not subdued, they would choke the cane. If the weather was cold, dirt was pulled up over the roots to keep them warm. If rain packed down the sod, a plow was used to loosen it. If water stood in the furrows, shallow trenches were dug to allow the water to run off. Every two weeks, for half a year now, every part of Auguste's cane fields was worked over until the whole place had a garden-like neatness.

"If I git to talkin too much bout early times, before I git to Plac'mine, hope you don mind. I don know when to stop sometimes," said Bébé. Jean laughed and again splashed his sunburned face with water.

Jean's friendships with Bébé and Isaac, his childhood Negro companion, held no social implications for the young white boy. He and his father often had intervened to prevent Isaac and other slaves from being punished by Salem Bibb, and Jean preferred the company of Isaac to that of many of his white neighbors. But Jean's exposure more and more to the cruelties perpetrated upon his father's slaves, especially Isaac, led to disillusion and confusion regarding the Negro. Jean had become less able to tolerate Bibb's use of the whip. He had begun to reason that there was more to be gained from kindness and understanding than from brutality. He looked at Bébé with fondness. Of course, he knew that she never experienced the cruelty suffered by field hands.

Bébé left the steps to check one of the two cisterns in back of the kitchen for a leak. Finding none, she returned to her perch. Jean shifted position to ease acute soreness in his lower back. He sat straight on the bench in the passageway. He did not take his eyes off of Bébé, although they were growing heavy from exhaustion.

"I member we leave St. James few months after Mister Lavair and Miss Eulalie marry and we git to Plac'mine two weeks to Chris'mas. Miss Eulalie had much patience and kindness as young girl. I work so long for her folks, begin when I bout ten. Seem I always been wid her, yeah. When dey marry she ax me to come wid her. O, I been through some good times with dem. If Mister Lavair pass to glory before I do, I know I won see nice times again. Mind if I tell you one more story and den I go in kitchen and start suppa?"

Jean nodded slowly. "Fine, fine, go ahead. I want to hear more."

"Servants eat meals after Mister Lavair and *Madame* eat same tings. Dere was plenty on de table for all de house servants. Me and Piksie was cooks for dem big meals. And no time do I member Mister Lavair people eber hurry. He neber say to git to work and no boss overseer eber say it, too. O, no, we neber hurry back in dem days. And he neber git mad wid hands for bein late to work. But I feel tings changin now, Jean. I don know what makin me feel dis way, but I do . . . feelin in air, rumblins goin round, yeah, wild talk I and Piksie and Isaac and others hear now."

CHAPTER 5

"YOU BASTARD, YOU goddamn sonofabitch!" Jean screamed, standing on Salem Bibb's porch steps. "What the hell you think you're doing using the lash on Isaac? He's a few minutes late one morning during four months of working like a dog on this crop, and you take out your goddamn rawhide whip!" He controlled his anger with difficulty.

"My assistant, Davis, says Isaac's been slack in his duties lately," barked Bibb, who had come out onto the porch when Jean banged on his front door. Tall, bald, and potbellied, the black-booted overseer appeared groggy from his afternoon nap. "Davis permits no loud talk or quarreling among them niggers, but he tells me Isaac's been mouthing off about other niggers threatening to run away, like he almost done hisself. I had to show Isaac who's boss, to set an example for the other hands, to keep discipline among them niggers. I'd do it again, Mr. Jean, whether you like it or not. I took to the whip, to remind that nigger what his place is."

Jean's and Salem's threatening voices had attracted the attention of slaves milling about the slave cabins, which were grouped like a tiny European village and clustered along both sides of a long dusty lane quarter of a mile behind the Big House. Some older slaves baked in the hot sun; some mothers nursed their babies; a score of naked children played under the eyes of an old mammy, who sat on a stool knitting.

Jean was aware that Isaac had been late for work two days earlier to help prepare Auguste's cane fields. Since early spring he'd been going into the fields before sunrise, working until sunset.

Isaac had been cutting trees, pulling fodder, grubbing, scraping top soil with his hoe to control weeds and grass to keep it pulverized and loose so that the roots of the current crop could get air and moisture for continued growth.

Now, the serenity, the comfort Jean had found in the Big House earlier in the morning was gone; it was though his privacy had been violated. He shook his head, his stocky body rocking on the steps. "My brother Augie tells me you gave Isaac about twenty licks, because he was late by thirty minutes. Damnit, Bibb, you could have killed him."

"Think that brother of yours is going to tell you why he got them licks?" Bibb stifled a yawn then swaggered down the porch steps, but only halfway. Any farther and his shiny head would have been below the level of Jean's eyes. He jabbed at Jean's stomach with his truncheon, trying to rouse and frighten him.

"Now, you, Mr. Jean, are surely smarter than that to understand. All Isaac's good for is just what he's doing, has been doing all along. Nigger work."

"Isaac's no animal," Jean said hoarsely, raising his hand to his face to conceal the revulsion he felt for the man.

"Isaac's a nigger and he's expected to work like one—hard—to do what he's told, break his back if called upon. And you, young man, should mind your own damn business and stay up there in the Big House where you belong. You keep snooping 'round this part of the plantation and you . . ."

"Shut your goddamn mouth, you—you sonofabitch!" Jean had never been so enraged, had never heard himself curse like this before. His voice had become high-pitched, his round face flushed red again. It was Bibb's insulting manner that angered him most. Suddenly, like a furious ram, he lowered his head and butted the overseer in the stomach. Then he tried to punch him twice in the face. But Bibb, a full head taller, grabbed Jean's fist in midair before it struck its target.

"Don't think you want to continue this way," he warned Jean. He stared contemptuously at Jean. "You taking this nigger's side, are you? I'm going to keep him busier than ever, Mr. Jean. An extra task or two every day till he straightens hisself out to my satisfaction, till he learns some respect for who is boss and knows his place."

"I just want to see him treated fairly, Bibb, that's all. Everybody says Isaac's a real hard worker, one of the best my father's ever had. I'm not saying that because he's my friend. Bébé says that, my father says that, and I have no reason not to believe it."

Bibb slapped his truncheon menacingly in the palm of his hand. "Want some of this?" Then he added: "Got any more you want to say about this matter?"

Instead of answering the overseer, Jean grabbed a straight-back chair leaning against the house and crashed it down on Bibb's head and shoulders. Bibb staggered and fell down the steps. He lay flat on his back, out cold.

Jean felt that Bibb's manner had been resentful for the past several months. He had grown to hate the puffed-up arrogant Yankee, who had come to Golden Ridge the year before with good references from several plantations, including two in Mississippi—first for his insolence and cocksure attitude toward his father, now for his senseless cruelty toward Jean's companion and friend. Jean could sympathize with Isaac's reasons for trying to escape, but he could not understand Bibb's cold-heartedness and the flogging. *Didn't Bibb realize that he didn't have to whip or scare the hands half to death to get a decent day's work from them? Father's told Bibb how he prefers his slaves to be treated. How does Bibb dare not to follow his orders?*

Bibb began to stir on the ground. He opened his eyes, shook his head. "Where's your Daddy," he snarled.

"He's in New Orleans," snapped Jean. He turned and headed to the Big House before provoking another loud harangue or giving Bibb time to retaliate.

*   *   *

That evening Jean sat at the head of the supper table in his father's absence, sipping oyster soup Bébé had made especially for this night. But his mind was still in turmoil over the news about

Isaac, the twenty-three year-old slave his father had purchased five years before for eight hundred dollars. *What a terrible time for Isaac to be late reporting to the fields, if that's what really happened, then trying to escape. Especially this year, when so much is at stake for my family. Hardly any offense could have been worse.*

Worried about what Isaac's escape attempt and subsequent flogging would mean—not only for other slaves on Golden Ridge, but slaves on other plantations—Jean lifted his eyes from his soup plate and gazed in his mother's direction for solace.

"It was terrible, just awful, Mother, what Augie told me Bibb did to Isaac. The fear, pure hell of the ordeal—after being whipped, Isaac became so afraid and angry that he wanted to escape if only for a few hours."

"Jean, dear, please listen to me," Eulalie Levert interrupted, putting her spoon down and touching her mouth with a napkin. Her eyes lit with a flare of interest as she regarded his sunburned face. "Bébé has just informed me that Isaac's in his cabin. Perhaps there's more to this incident than either you or your brother are aware of, son. Do you know if this is the first time Isaac's been late for work in the fields, the first time? Are you certain his complaints were not a subtle way of inciting his fellow workers?"

"No, Mother," Jean shouted, not ready to drop the matter. "But did Bibb have to resort to heavy flogging?"

During discussion of the confrontation, Marie Euphrasie, Augie, Joseph, and Amèdèe remained silent, eating their meal of mutton, yams, snap beans, and vanilla custard. After they were excused from the table, Jean remained seated. His mother went to her bedroom to read.

As Jean waited anxiously for his father to return from negotiations with his sugar broker in New Orleans, he looked about the room. Everything was in its place: Heavy mahogany table and sideboards, mantel clock, two silver trays, colorful rugs on the shining floor. A comforting spacious room. But his father was not present yet.

Then Jean turned in his armchair to glimpse a long line of white-clad field hands with hoes and machetes over their shoulders. The hands were projected upon a background in the downing sun— silhouettes—singing and making their way home from the fields. Staring through a window as if hypnotized, he thought back five years to when he was ten. He had recorded in his journal:

> *After school some friends and I saddled our ponies and started for home. Today on the ride home, I suddenly fell into the swirling Mississippi, and it could have been very bad had it not been for an alert slave I'd never seen before. When the stirrup on my saddle snapped I fell headfirst into the swift currents . . . the negro, riding home from town, saw my waving hand, jumped off his horse, dove in the water, and swam to me. I was no match for the river! As I bobbed in the water, realizing I couldn't last much longer, the negro man grabbed my hand and managed to pull me to the nearest bank of land . . . with the help of my schoolmates on the bank, I grabbed a long pole and was pulled back to dry safety. Then the negro laid me down on the levee with my head down so the water would run out of my lungs. Later, my scared friends were ready to race back to Golden Ridge. Tonight, Père told me his name is Isaac.*

Jean felt a hand grip his arm and he jumped, shattering his thoughts, bringing him back to the present.

"You all right, dear?" Eulalie asked, her expression compassionate.

"I'm fine, *Mère*." He kissed her goodnight, thinking how beautiful she was as she returned to her bedroom.

*   *   *

Upstairs Jean paced in his bedroom. He was too tense to sleep after his confrontation with Salem Bibb. He gazed into the black night from his window—he imagined mellow, mature sugarcane stalks ready for harvest. He still couldn't get out of his mind the pain poor Isaac must have felt when that monster Bibb found him and beat him to near collapse for something not worth the punishment. It made him sick at his stomach to recall what Augie told him:

Bibb trailed Isaac for more than a mile, then made dogs pull him out of a tree near the swamp where he was caught. The dogs bit him badly and if that wasn't enough, Bibb resorted to his rawhide whip to teach him a lesson . . . the long whip was applied with dreadful power and precision. Every stroke brought away strips of skin that clung to the whip or floated to the ground while blood welled in the wound. The poor man shrieked and writhed, with each overhead stroke of the lash, pleading with his attacker: "Oh, spare me! Don't cut my soul out!"

What the hell does all this mean? More slaves causing problems for their masters, more runaway attempts, slaves possibly looting Golden Ridge? I thought the slaves were happy, contented. Bébé tells me they're thankful they have what they have. Father cares for them when they are ill, when medical attention is needed. Why did Isaac try to run away then? Where could he go? I understand trying to escape the whip or total neglect by an insensitive master, but Father is not insensitive in that way. At any rate I'm glad Isaac's safe in his cabin. Frustrated because of his naïveté about certain plantation realities, Jean hoped he would never have to spend another night like this. He was a precocious boy, but at fifteen he knew the situation was too cruel and complicated for him.

Jean wouldn't allow himself to believe that Bébé, Isaac, and the other hands and servants might be miserable. He knew they all enjoyed simple amusements of their choice on rest days, and his father provided good food, clothing, shelter, because it was good business. It was stupid to mistreat and not care for expensive slaves. Did these abolitionists exploit Negroes for their own purposes, as father believed they did?

Father wants me to go to college, pursue my own destiny, learn the ways of the world, and he believes New Orleans is the best place to start. But Father also needs me to help with harvest and grinding of this year's crop. I could delay college for a year or two—Golden Ridge and Father can't wait. Mother and Father would be disappointed if I didn't go, but I don't believe I have any other choice but to delay college, with so many things at stake: Need to bring in a good crop, keeping the hands from growing more discontented, preserving our way of life . . . .

CHAPTER 6

AS THE 90-FOOT, triple-deck steamboat left Plaquemine wharf, heading for midriver, Jean waved to his father, who stood with Isaac on the dock. Isaac had carried Jean's trunk and several boxes up the gangplank. Standing beside Auguste, the slave waved his old felt hat to Jean.

Jean gripped the rail as the steamboat blew its whistle. He hastily swallowed the lump in his throat as he watched Isaac turn the carriage around and head for Golden Ridge. Soon, a young man joined him at the rail and introduced himself. His name was Alexander Hamilton Kent, son of a planter who had moved to Baton Rouge from Indiana. He, too, was on his way to New Orleans to enroll in the University of Louisiana.

Together, the boys watched lush semitropical scenery glide by as the twin-stack steamboat *Cotton Blossom* rode the eddys and currents down the muddy Mississippi River. At one in the afternoon the white vessel was about seventy miles upriver from New Orleans.

"You have any interest in history and geography, Jean? You seem so serious," said Alex.

"Of course I do," said Jean. "My family has an interesting history. My *Grand-mère*, my father's mother, was thrown out of Nova Scotia because she practiced a different religion from the English—Roman Catholicism." He lifted his head with apparent pride that was not lost on Alexander. Feeling Alexander's appraising stare, he went on: "My Father always brings back stories of New Orleans' unique past and flavor of life. Part Spanish, part American, more French than either." He looked at his new friend with large fine eyes that could have come from either parent.

Alexander seemed bored. "Oh well, I suppose some Kents, my family, have had similar hard times and experiences. Our family isn't much for keeping records; the Kents are not ancestor worshipers." He tossed back his heavy black hair, which fell again over his forehead. At seventeen, he had a thin black moustache. He shrugged and changed the subject. "But Jean, did you do nothing but work in your Father's cane fields? Don't you have time for girls?"

Jean's face reddened. He was surprised at Alexander's directness. They had just been talking of taking a room together in New Orleans; now Jean wondered how tolerant he would be of someone so plain-spoken. "What's wrong with working in my Father's cane fields, Alexander? On several occasions I served equally with my older brother Augie managing our plantation in my father's absence. Besides there's nothing wrong with being serious. You better be serious if you want to make it through the first weeks of college. They're the toughest. This is an important moment in our lives. It certainly is for me." Jean had agonized over the final decision to go away to school, leaving his father without his help, which Jean was convinced was his best help. His brothers worked hard too, but they did not have the natural competence in all matters, particularly the business aspects of producing cane.

Alexander put on a sober face. "I've never been to a large city before, never met a woman of the world. Even in Indiana I lived on a farm. But you're right, probably. I don't mean to, but I give people the wrong impression sometimes—serious when I should be light-hearted, airy when I should be solemn."

Both boys turned their attention to the passengers about them. All day they had heard the older people talking politics, about divisions between North and South; particularly crude references to a controversial book published two years earlier—the Yankee lady Harriet Beecher Stowe and her *Uncle Tom's Cabin*. The fiercest talker was a thin, fiery-eyed little woman who expressed a fervid hatred for all Yankees and a desire to have bits of northern abolitionists to pitch to the gulls that followed behind the steamboat. Shifting her ruffled umbrella to better shade her wizened eyes, the woman concluded from time to time: "They are devils. They are devils."

From their imposing vantage point on the hurricane deck, the boys watched the Crescent City come into view. In bending to the right, the river formed a curve or crescent in the recess of which lay New Orleans. Rows of warehouses and commercial establishments appeared, extending for three miles along the river, a scene with which Jean was familiar through maps, much reading, and accounts of his father. In front of the warehouses and other buildings, and close to the levee, was a forest of sailing vessel masts rising above the docks. The levee was about a hundred feet wide and extended protection along the city for nearly five miles. It followed the river's curve that gave New Orleans its sobriquet.

The *Cotton Blossom* had slowed, accommodating river traffic as tugboats and ferries chugged among the steamboats angling for a berth or crossing to and from the town of Algiers on the west side of the river. Jean looked back at the sights and approaching wharves. "Look at those steamboats over there. They're fantastic. Look at the gaudy colors." He was excited by the noises of the river traffic, as the pilot maneuvered the *Cotton Blossom* against the strong current into Poydras Street Landing. Close by, flocks of pelicans flapped heavily over the river, dropping to scoop up fish in their bucketlike beaks from the teeming schools near the shore.

On shore, Jean noticed that business was in great motion; he was inspired. Docks were piled high with goods and produce; mountains of cotton bales stacked ready for shipping; rows of hogsheads filled with sugar; bags of rice in huge heaps—the magnificent produce of Louisiana's lowlands. And dock workers ran about; Negro children danced for pennies; vendors sold oysters from their stands; blind men played their fiddles.

He pointed. "Over there, Alex, look at all that stuff, ready for export to the world."

"I see them, Jean." Alexander waved to the merchants, clerks, ship captains, customhouse officers, sailors, and porters who were busy on the docks.

Two girls the boys had met aboard ship were among the first to debark. They waved back, laughing. Jean courteously doffed his light-colored hat to them. He was not eager to know the giggling girls. His thoughts were on what lay before him in New Orleans. He was overwhelmed with what was becoming a reality so fast—everything big, everything rushing, all the opportunities the City offered him. One of his first duties must be to call on his father's broker, Albert Desmont, and extend another invitation to Golden Ridge.

CHAPTER 7

ABOUT A HUNDRED miles northwest of New Orleans in Plaquemine, Auguste Levert was roused by a riotous chorus of mockingbirds at five o'clock in the morning, an hour earlier than usual. After his customary bath of river water, brought in by Celestine, the old Negro attendant, the planter walked to the back gallery on the first floor of the Big House. He swatted at whining mosquitoes that were already advancing in force, driven out of the swamps by a thunderstorm.

For Jean's father, everything was riding on the '54 crop. Could he continue growing cane after suffering more failures than successes in the past decade? Would he have to get out of agriculture altogether? Could he retire some debts? Everything depended on the judgment of Albert Desmont. Auguste always worried at this stage of growth. And he missed his favorite son.

Augie joined his father. "Have one of the hands saddle my chestnut, will you, son?" said Auguste, stepping off the gallery. His twenty-three-year-old son disappeared into the barn. "Try not to worry about the crop, Papa," Augie said later, handing Auguste the reins to his horse. "We've managed in the past, despite some real bad years, and we'll manage again. We always do."

"Maybe so, you're probably right," his father replied. "I appreciate your concern and support." Feeling better, he adjusted the stirrups and continued: "A good broker can look at a crop in any of its growing stages and tell whether it's going to be a failure or a sugar-producer and moneymaker. This one appears to be one of the best crops we've ever had—rain at the right time, dry at the right time." He pulled down the wide brim of his straw hat, as he settled into the saddle. "You're welcome to join us, Augie. I think you'll find Mr. Desmont as fascinating as Jean did. He's passing through on a social call. Maybe one day I'll take you to the city to see Mr. Desmont at work in the financial district. Where's Amèdèe?"

"He's coming," said Augie, who had a sparse beard and a ruddy complexion like his father's. Soon ten-year-old Amèdèe, five feet six inches tall, slightly plump with curly hair like Jean's, joined his older brother and father for the ride through the dewy fields. The fields had assumed a green glow as growth advanced during much of the summer. The cane had slowly increased in height, its leaves growing wider and longer until they cast their own shade about their roots, soon taking entire possession of the surrounding earth and flourishing without a rival in the fields.

After a routine inspection, Jean's father took out his watch. "Quick, boys, we've got but fifteen minutes to meet Mr. Desmont." He flipped his reins to turn his chestnut around. Wearing lightweight khaki trousers, knee-high riding boots, and straw hats, the three of them headed for the riverfront at a gallop.

Desmont was waiting for them there, along with Salem Bibb. Auguste wanted his broker to see this section of cane first, because it was his specimen acreage, yielding from one to one-and-a-half hogsheads of sugar per acre, or about three thousand pounds. Here he directed cultivation with special care. The smartly dressed Creole was watching the field hands working on the riverfront.

"*Bon jour, Monsieur Desmont.* So good to see you again," Auguste said. "Happy you could visit with us on this important day—important for us anyway. I want you to meet two of my other sons, Augie and Amèdèe." The Levert brothers greeted Desmont cordially, extending their hands in formal handshake.

Desmont was mounted alongside Bibb, who slouched on his lanky pony, whip in hand. After a curt salutation to the gentlemen, the overseer rode off to another field. Auguste, agitated, steadied his horse. He had told Jean several times before he left for college: "The man's arrogance has worn thin my patience, especially after that run-in he had with you over Isaac. Is the man getting tired of his responsibilities?"

Desmont, with Auguste, continued watching the field hands. Strapped to plows and running through furrows between cane rows, the hands talked only to their mules. Three gangs were armed with several carts containing casks of water for the hands, a bucket of molasses, pails of hominy, and enough pannikins from which the slaves could eat. Other vessels held material for their breakfast, which included dried fish. The hands put on weight during harvest, because their diet was supplemented to keep up their strength.

Female members of the gang were more noticeable than males; shoes, ponderous and ill-made, had worn away their stockings, which dangled in fringes over the upper leathers. Coarse straw hats and bright cotton bandanas protected their heads from the sun. The women were silent, as they cut the cane to be hauled to the sugarhouse in large mule-drawn carts. The only sound was the swishing blades of large machetes on the tall yellow-gold stalks.

Behind the cutters stood Davis, armed with a heavy thonged whip. As a display of courtesy, Pompey, one of the cutters, was called out by Davis and came immediately to ask his master's visitor, Mr. Desmont: "How you do?" Then he quickly returned to his labor. But the females scarcely looked up from under their flapping *chapeaux*.

"Much of the planting, cultivating, and cane-cutting depends upon the wise use of labor," said Auguste, as if Desmont didn't already know this. "I can hardly exaggerate the importance of experience in directing it, either." He said he knew it was better to wait until late October to start cutting the cane, for it constantly sweetened its juices, but there was always a big danger of frost, bad storms, even hurricanes.

"I understand your eagerness to get the crop harvested and processed," said Desmont in his heavy Creole accent. The broker's head jerked to one side, distracting Auguste and his sons for a moment. "I truly sympathize with your concern about the weather."

"I used to live high and well," Auguste said, changing the subject. "I used to buy and sell land, raise cane, experiment with cotton and rice, and grow many of the supplies necessary on this estate. But I was also careless, paying more attention to family matters than to my financial affairs. Constant buying of real estate pushed me into serious indebtedness, and I had to depend more and more on profits from my cane crops to cover my obligations."

He told his broker that when he first started planting cane many years earlier, he'd spend money before the crop was ever sold or borrow heavily when he could from banks against follow-on crops with no idea that it would be a successful crop. "Now I am more cautious in my older years."

On the way to the Big House for breakfast, Auguste took Desmont to the sugarhouse to observe the harvest being processed. At the sugarhouse, Salem Bibb, seeing them coming, yelled at the slaves: "Hush! Be quiet! We have visitors. Be working." Bibb raised his hat with the handle of his whip. Auguste noticed the overseer leaning against a post; he didn't change his position or his insolent expression. The slaves, shirtless and wearing coarse cotton trousers, had stopped their soft singing, but they continued to unload cane stalks onto conveyor belts that carried them into the sugarhouse for processing.

After Desmont asked Auguste a few perfunctory questions, the men rode on to the Big House for Bébé's elaborate breakfast; another thunderstorm was gathering overhead. The long early morning ride had made Auguste and his sons hungry, and Auguste was eager to offer the hospitality of his table to Desmont. They sat in the dining room, and Bébé and Piksie began the breakfast by pouring strong, steaming coffee into Eulalie's most elegant bone china cups. They ate scrambled eggs, pancakes, cane syrup, ham, grits, biscuits, and fig preserves.

"You know full well, Mr. Levert, a successful crop depends on many conditions coming together just right, one of which is escaping the frost," said Desmont, placing his empty coffee cup on the saucer. "If you can go until December or early January without any cold nipping the juices and the cane, your crop is

increased in value each day." Desmont's dark eyes looked over the
fields in the direction of the rich riverfront section of the plantation.
He clipped a pince-nez on his nose, took a small black book
from his coat pocket, and placed it on the polished table by his
plate. He wrote down everything he could recall about his
exchanges with Salem Bibb—tour of the sugarhouse, field hands
at work, even Auguste's ramblings; all of it helped him to put
things in perspective. After several more doodlings, and while
Auguste's fork remained poised over his plate, Desmont continued:
"It appears that you should escape the damaging frost, too,
particularly if you send all your cane to the mill before late
December." He flipped more pages of the notebook. "If I remember
correctly, you wish to borrow four thousand to buy some two-
mule plows, a rotary harrow, plant seed for the '56 crop, and to
help meet this year's payroll. We'd also discussed my giving you a
small amount now with the rest payable within twelve months."
He closed his notebook and removed his glasses.

Finally, Albert Desmont said the words Jean's father had been
waiting to hear since the mockingbirds had awakened him three
hours before: "Yes, yes, Mr. Levert, under the circumstances, there
should be no trouble advancing you the necessary money against
next year's crop. Your fields appear to be in excellent condition.
I'll have the papers worked up for your signature before I leave
today, and I'll leave a check and you may expect the balance over
the next twelve months. Is that agreeable with you?"

Auguste did not answer. He stared at Desmont from across
the dining table. He clinked his coffee cup against his saucer; his
heart had been pounding from nervous anticipation. Now he let
out a deep sigh of relief. He laid the white damask napkin beside
his plate, walked around the table to the broker, and extended his
hand, smiling broadly.

CHAPTER 8

SOON AFTER SETTLING in at Amelie's Boarding House on Baronne Street in downtown New Orleans, Jean was feeling homesick. He tried to overcome it by recalling why he had come to the City. He tried to convince himself that he had not made a mistake by deserting his father when he was needed to harvest the '54 crop. He felt pangs of guilt. Anyway, he thought, the university offered him the best chance to get what he wanted: A career in the sugar commission industry, a chance not only to control his own destiny, but destinies of others. To have it all, the best of both worlds. To control the fortunes of other planters as a broker, like Albert Desmont, and to be a shrewd, successful planter and plantation owner like his father.

Later in the day, while standing in front of commodious university buildings on Baronne, Common, and Dryades streets to register, Jean remarked to another student: "Why is admission to this school so regulated? Hell, until recently there was almost no college at all because the state didn't want to support it. You'd think we're trying to enter a professional school or the military academy at West Point. Exams are required in Latin and Greek and geography!"

After two days devoted mainly to registration, Jean decided to get a letter off to his family. He wasn't sure when he'd get another chance once classes began.

New Orleans   *October, 1854 Thursday*

Ma Mère and Mon Père,

I write because I know your solitude. I got here safely on Tuesday last; people here are most hospitable. Oh, I met a nice boy on the steamboat, named Alexander Kent of Baton Rouge. His family moved there from Indiana; tired of the winters. We hit it off right away and talked about becoming roommates, but I decided to room alone, at least for now. I did as you instructed and found a boardinghouse close to campus. The rent's $10 a month and includes breakfast and a hot supper. I must say the room isn't very large and there's not much furniture. Just an armoire for my hanging garments and two drawers for toiletries and other belongings. Probably have to live out of my trunk.

The university is located at the door of about 225,000 people—almost a third of the state's population. The city offers many cultural advantages such as the opera, balls, a thriving theater. The second night here a professor convinced me to attend the French opera. I enjoyed the performances and music. Oh, I have paid a call to Mr. Desmont, and he said he enjoyed his visit to Golden Ridge.

Before I close, the total annual expense for classes will be $175, and this price of tuition must be paid for each term in advance. I have decided to pursue some general courses this first term, including science, language and literature, ancient geography and history, exercises in writing Latin and Greek, French speaking. Hope this is not too heavy a load.

I will write later when I am settled. Please let me know how the crop is doing. I miss all and I hope to be home for Christmas.

Love to all from your affectionate son

Jean had trouble going to sleep after finishing the two-page letter. As tired he was, he lay awake in the strange room on the second floor of the boarding house, on his thin, hard mattress that rocked on bare springs. For what seemed like a long time, he looked beyond two brass candlesticks on the narrow mantel out at the dusky sky. Surely he had not made a mistake coming to New Orleans. His father had insisted that he enter college if that was what he wanted to do.

What Jean wanted was not to work in the fields, always with an eye out for weather—rain and drought. Albert Desmont's visit at Golden Ridge had inspired him and brought him to the City. The man's cool aura of power and confidence filled Jean's mind with possibilities of which he had never dreamed. *I want to be a rich and powerful man*, he was thinking when he finally fell asleep.

CHAPTER 9

THE MORE NEIGHBORING farmers saw of the kind of life that Jean's father lived in *le maison grand*, the more they admired him, his hospitality, his charm, his power. For Philippe Auguste Levert guarded Eulalie and his children with extreme care. He was hardworking, firm in exercising sway over his household. He considered his home charming, because of Eulalie's presence, her grace as mistress and hostess. Her taste and warmth were evident at the dinner table, in the food, decor, furnishings, and especially in her bedroom—with its high mahogany four-poster, shell pink cotton hangings, and mosquito netting tied to eight-inch-thick posts, with its walnut dresser with a flat slab of white marble on top. He provided a beautiful setting for Eulalie, and he was drawn to her bedroom by her presence.

Outside, wild pink roses sprawled over the whitewashed cypress fence, and long white wooden gates were usually open wide to Golden Ridge, a sure sign that neighbors were welcome. Looking across the broad green lawn, through orange and pear trees, camellias, and azaleas, Auguste's neighbors—smaller farmers, the backbone of the sugar industry—could see the impressive row of slave cabins far in the rear. Much less affluent farmers could, for a moment, forget their own reality and enjoy the scene.

Jean's father rested his head against a cushion on his favorite rocking chair in the parlor and gazed sleepily at the wall. He was reflecting on his most immediate good fortune—the success of the '54 crop. And on his house, material evidence of the high position he held in Iberville Parish and in the town of Plaquemine,

French for persimmon. The town was named after groves of persimmon trees that grew in the backyards of its largest plantations and along the banks of Bayou Plaquemine on which it was settled. He was assured of keeping his family comfortable for the time being. How lucky he was.

Suddenly he bounded from his rocker. "I must write dear Jean and tell him how well we have done this year. He'll be so happy to hear that money for his schooling is no problem for the year ahead. I have been too concerned with my own problems to answer his long letter of three months ago." At his roll-top desk he picked up a pen and in the soft glow of an oil lamp wrote:

Plaquemine, La
December 15, 1854

Mon cher Fils—

Even though I was on the lookout for your letter, I apologize for not replying right away. I know how you get when others aren't punctual—responsible, you say—about letter writing. We should realize a hundred seventy-five hogsheads, or about three hundred thousand pounds of sugar from the '54 crop. Most ever, and it came at a time we most needed it. However, there is distressing news, news we could only pry away from Bebe after much persuasion: Isaac has apparently run away! Hasn't been seen for about two weeks. Poor Bebe, who raised him from a pup, is beside herself. Try not to worry, though, Isaac's strong, can take care of himself. Let's pray we hear from him soon, that he's safe.

Your brothers and I have worked extra hard on this crop. We've really missed you. But your life has taken on new direction and purpose with your schooling. I've ordered that no-count bastard Salem Bibb off the plantation. Gave him his notice after grinding ended. I know you are happy with that news! Anyway, things have a way of working out for themselves so don't worry *yourself about the crop. Just keep your nose in the books, work hard, and write any information you obtain of a disturbing nature—about abolition talk or slave uprisings against their masters. And I never will understand why Isaac ran away. I'll let you know something.*

Goodbye, dear son,
Your affectionate Père

Postscript: gave orders for $200 to be forwarded to your bank in New Orleans. This should provide you with a surplus over your budget estimates. A surplus which may allow you to bring a gift to your Mother for Christmas.

*   *   *

Auguste woke to find Eulalie at the window of their bedroom, staring into the darkness.

"What's wrong, dear? Don't you feel well?"

"I'm all right," she replied. "Can't sleep. I'm going down to Bébé's cabin and see if she's heard anything."

"It's after midnight. Don't be foolish, *chèrie*. Can't this wait until morning?" He didn't want Eulalie to go out in the cold black night alone on Golden Ridge. But he knew she was determined.

"I'll go with you." The sugar planter pulled on his trousers. "What makes you think Bébé's heard anything? It would take days for the news to reach us. I don't understand why Isaac ran away. Well, I do and I don't. I thought he was content. He was close to the boys, particularly Jean, and Bébé has been like a mother to him." As always, Auguste trusted Bébé. Often on his way home at midday, he dismounted at her shanty in the slave quarters to talk and laugh. He depended upon her to inform him of problems among his slaves. He stuffed his shirt tail into his trousers and followed his wife from the house.

Auguste knew the heat, even in early fall, often was too unbearable for the acclimated white people in the swamps. No

one but Negroes braved the noxious smells that rose from stagnant
water and organisms. It was to a place like this, a few miles from
Golden Ridge, that Isaac had fled in pursuit of freedom to await,
in a shadowy hideaway, help of food and as soon as possible
delivery to the underground railroad to Canada and safety from
slave catchers, who were paid to return runaways alive to their
masters.

"Freedom is a powerful thing," Auguste said, trying to
rationalize the incident and lessen the terrible fears Eulalie had
harbored since Isaac ran away.

"I never heard of this underground railroad system," she said,
hurrying through the dark. "But I'm not forgetting that this Negro
boy saved our son's life. He pulled Jean out of the Mississippi."

"Don't think I don't remember." Auguste pounded on Bébé's
door.

"Oh, Misses, Mister," Bébé screamed as she threw back the
door to her one-room cabin. Separated from the field hand cabins
by wooden pilings, her hut had windows but no glass; wooden
shutters kept out rain and wind. "What we gonna do? Poor Isaac
been shot, I tole, yeah. Shot by dem bad men on lookout for
run'ways. Dem who go out lookin for em."

"Bébé, is he dead?" Eulalie, who hardly ever showed alarm,
was frantic.

"I don know, I don know. But I fraid somethin like dis goin
happen to him. Isaac come and talk to me de other night. He was
hurtin, lost. Shoulda spected he do somethin like run'way."

"Why didn't you tell us sooner, let us know this horrible
thing had happened?" asked Eulalie, in a firm voice now but with
kindness. Her servant's eyes and face were swollen from weeping.

"What in hell's fire happened? How did you find out he's been
shot?" Auguste asked, cutting off his wife. "You know how all
this has upset you, Bébé. Think what it will do to Jean."

"I don know much, Mister Lavair, only what I hear from other
nigras on plantation. I ax dem to tell me everthin," Bébé began
again, stumbling over some of her words. Her voice quaked and
then broke.

"Steady, steady, settle down, try to calm yourself," pleaded Bébé's master. Eulalie and Auguste removed their coats and hung them on the only two nails in the wall, then sat on the edge of her crude bed of padded tickings stuffed with dried Spanish moss.

"All I tole is dat right before Isaac to meet wid people who hep him move up Nawth, while he hidin out, guess one slave catcher spot him. Not even out state yet, not far from dis house. As he begin to . . ."

"Go on, go on, Bébé," urged Auguste. He placed his hand on Eulalie's arm.

"O, as Isaac go way from where he hidin, I tole gun shots ring out over his head. I guess to warn him. But he keep runnin for his life in dem woods, dem catchers give chase on hawses, and dem bloodhounds, too, and more shots fired to scare him, I guess. One dem bullets acc'dentally hit him in de back. All his dreams to be free gone. I don know why he won to go up in dat cold land. Dangers big, yeah. Bet Isaac got no idea where Can'da is. I don know.

"My friends also tell me Isaac look bad when he lef. Guess he skinny, lost much weight, neber smile. Bet dey ain't one nigra in hundred who try dat. Isaac neber make it out de woods alive. Know somethin else, I bet he won be welcome up in de Nawth if he make it. Bet he find no work, yeah."

Eulalie and Auguste left her to her grief. As they walked back in the cold early-morning light to the Big House, they heard Bébé's heavy sobs.

CHAPTER 10

IN NEW ORLEANS, Jean Baptiste watched secession fever burn during the summer and fall of 1858. His father's fears of a slave uprising frightened him. To gain their freedom, would the slaves burn the Big House, injure or kill some of the servants, do harm to his family? Years before, his father had warned of issues affecting his economic interests—the bank, protective tariff policies of the Union on behalf of his crops, drainage. "There is great excitement in the Congress of the United States. The North is meddling with slavery . . . it could eventually cause us to secede," he had told his family.

Meanwhile, Jean criss-crossed the downtown campus of the University of Louisiana whenever possible, listening to members of the plantation aristocracy who advocated a separate Southern government. He learned that Louisiana's leaders were convinced that separation from the Union was essential to preserve slavery and prosperity of the South. He attended a slave auction in the French Quarter, but the experience depressed him and confused him. He absorbed as much as he could on both sides of the issue that he thought could split the Union. Jean realized that the South would have trouble surviving under any national political party. The only solution to maintaining Southern rights lay, he felt, in secession. He recorded in his journal: "Our state's political machine is now in the hands of the secessionists. Hotheads have decided to act. Cooler heads both in the North and South have attempted compromise, but foundered. One reason for their failure, I think, is that compromise would weaken the South for the future."

In his small room at Amelie's Boarding House several weeks later, Jean made this entry: "The South is reeling like a drunkard. If the situation leads to war, God forbid, one battle probably would end it. I bet every young man would rush to volunteer before the battle ended just to be able to tell his grandchildren that he fought in a war."

Month by month, he watched the clouds of war darken. Abraham Lincoln had won the Republican Party's nomination. The platform adopted at the party's convention, an outgrowth of the Dred Scott Decision of 1857, stated that Congress now had no authority to promote slavery by permitting its expansion, as southern states wanted. The platform stated that slavery could exist only where it had before the decision. The slave Dred Scott was a citizen of neither Missouri nor the Union and, therefore, could not sue for his freedom in federal court. That court decision, Jean believed, inflamed North and South, and it was a major factor leading to civil war. When the Republicans and Lincoln stood firmly on this platform, Jean and his family, like most southern whites, sensed that Abe's election would guarantee war.

CHAPTER 11

WHEN JEAN LEFT New Orleans to enroll in Mount St. Mary's College in Emmitsburg, Maryland, he headed into the Blue Ridge Mountains, into the blue mists of the rugged highlands, a complete change from the flat lowlands in southwest Louisiana. Throughout this change, Isaac's cruel murder had made him aware of increasing unrest in the Union. Although he was not present when his childhood friend was captured and shot to death, not far from Plaquemine, images from his father's graphic descriptions haunted Jean. Newspaper stories in both North and South, describing political fights and debates, had become more commonplace, and times had become more troubled.

Jean had been graduated from the University of Louisiana in June, 1858, and for the first time in four seasons, he had helped his father harvest the cane crop at Golden Ridge. After the '58 crop had been marketed the following winter and spring, he began readying himself to enroll for graduate studies at the Maryland school. He wanted more education in economics.

At the Emmitsburg railroad station, Jean and other southern students boarded the Mount St. Mary's carriage and rode on a narrow branch road farther into the mountains toward the college. Rich in Catholic heritage, Jean thought the school sat above him like a holy city. The college and seminary provided courses that fit the students to be priests, farmers, economists, businessmen, even good Catholics. Mount St. Mary's was called the "cradle of bishops" due to the great number of prelates produced there.

At the door, Jean and the other students met a broad-faced, smiling priest, who welcomed them and led them to an elegant drawing room. There the rector, announced by the soft jangle of his rosary beads, entered and in a clear voice assured them: "Welcome, my sons, welcome to Mount St. Mary's, the oldest private Catholic college in the land."

Again, Jean settled into scholastic life. Although struck by the mountains and by the differences in climate and speech, he found that arguments about slavery continued much as in Louisiana.

*   *   *

Down the hill from the college at Quincy's Tavern, a long-haired man slumped over his shot glass spoke up: "Don't think we'd be looking at even the remotest kind of skirmish if it wasn't for them niggers."

"No it ain't, George. You're dead wrong. It's them Southerners threatening to pull out of the Union that likely would start something. Not the darkies."

George Peabody, a two-hundred-pound putty-faced man with bad teeth, was contemptuous. "Even so, I'd fight for the Union flag before I'd risk my neck for them niggers."

Behind the tavern's tinted glass doors, another regular declared: "I'm with you, Peabody. The goddamn Southerners will split the country right down the middle. But I see it another way. Best solution to this whole goddamn mess—this festering sore—would be to shoot all the darkies dead."

Jean, seated in a secluded corner of the dimly lighted tavern, rubbed his overworked, burning eyes. He had spent most of the night and day before translating the history of Rome into French and studying prosody, the science of poetical terms; cramming for examinations to end the third quarter of his second year at Mount St. Mary's. He listened to the steady drone of voices, oft-heated and shouted sectional jokes, loud songs, of irrepressible college students enjoying a break from the classroom. Jean recognized two students from his Latin and economics classes. Exchanges blaming both North and South for the division in the Union generated loud agreement from others.

Jean made no comment for a long time. He had insulated himself from arguments about slavery, the same arguments he'd had with Yankee classmates at the University of Louisiana. He was tired of Yankees who could never understand life in his beloved South, in Louisiana cane country. During his four years at the university and three quarters at Mount St. Mary's, he had learned to listen to both sides of an argument before speaking his opinion. When he spoke, he commanded attention. Jean gulped a whiskey. He feared for his family's safety; he doubted that his way of life could be preserved, but he was determined to fight to preserve it if it came to that. *So far so good, but if these sectional feelings ever spill into war, God forbid . . . no man in this tavern who has had his eyes open for the past five years can deny that abolition fever is getting worse.*

"We're on a collision course with the damn Yankees," Jean called from his corner, breaking his silence. "Reasonable men discuss the need for compromise, but nothing seems to be getting done here tonight. If anyone is responsible for pushing Southerners toward an independent government—"

"Is what you're saying, sir, that you want a separate independent government?" interrupted George Peabody, still standing at the bar. Peabody pivoted to see the person addressing him.

"No, mister, I am just saying that I think it's coming. But let me finish what I was about to say. I think that madman John Brown has done as much as anyone or anything to provoke the wide divisions between our sections that could lead, yes, to an independent government."

"Come on, man, don't be so goddamn naive." Peabody shrugged, looking at Jean with a steady gaze. "You know that whatever precious way of life you want to keep is rotten through and through. A life of ease and pretense built on a foundation that recognizes—what? Bondage!"

Jean countered: "Listen, Peabody, are you aware that the North is regarded as the cradle of slavery, that the first colony to practice it was Massachusetts? Some prominent families in New England are engaged in the slave trade, making huge fortunes in the process. Did you know that, Peabody?" Growing frustrated, Jean waved irritably at a waiter to order another whiskey. After taking a few sips he glared at the man from his table. "Now, I believe the real reason the North's itching for a fight to preserve the Union is not to get rid of slavery in the South, but greed, yes, fear of economic loss."

"Hell, man, what are you talking about?" Peabody swayed, then put a hand on the bar to steady himself. Jean noticed the old, wizened bartender standing for long stretches of time without moving, except to serve Peabody another round. He saw that Peabody was getting drunk; he was slurring his words.

"In my opinion, Peabody, if the South were a free, independent nation, the North probably would suffer great economic loss, because it likely would lose its control of trade to the states along the Mississippi. Tariffs from the wealthy plantation class could no longer be collected."

Jean shivered with anger. What upset him most about such men as Peabody was their lack of intelligent, evaluative thought. No matter how worthy the cause seemed, the issues were somehow twisted to suit one's prejudice and personal considerations. In the end, the slavery argument, whether at Quincy's or in private conversations in a plantation house parlor, always took on an existence that Jean never understood completely. He had hardened his view of northern abolitionists, disliking them more than ever. He wondered how many of them, including these tavern regulars, were more concerned with confrontation than resolving the problem through sensible dialogue and compromise. How many preached hate and anger instead of common sense. Clutching his coat, he stormed out of Quincy's into the damp night. Unless sane minds and understanding hearts took charge, he felt that his precious Southland would be shattered to pieces over the slavery issue.

CHAPTER 12

CHEWING ON AN unlighted cigar, Jean arrived at the sugarhouse on Golden Ridge before dawn. Powerful in physique, he mounted a narrow, raised platform to check the open kettles, arranged in a straight line. He was sweating, panting a little. Temperature in the sugarhouse, with the sun barely up, was ninety degrees. Now smiling, Jean was pleased that everything needed for harvest and for grinding his father's '60 crop was moving at full tilt:

Workers seemed energized, as if touched by fire. Mule teams pulled rattling carts of freshly cut cane from the fields to the sugarhouse. Windows and doors of the sugarhouse were thrown open. The carrier shed was full of women and children. Tall chimneys belched smoke, once-idle machines came alive. When enough cane was gathered in the carrier shed, rising in large masses on every side of the sugarhouse, a laborer sounded a steam pipe whistle. As the cumbersome conveyor moved, cane stalks tumbled between rollers, and sweet juice was pressed out, spilling into receivers.

A few minutes later, Jean was joined by his father. Together they bent over a rickety, wooden railing, the only barrier between them and the cast-iron kettles boiling the cane below. As Jean glanced at the kettles, his mind wandered. *There is so much wrong on both sides, North and South, that has encouraged our sectional bitterness . . . abolitionists of the free states ought not to have agitated the slavery issue, making slave masters react harshly.*

From morning until night, Jean and his father had become indifferent to sleep. They hung over the open kettles to see what the cane juice promised in color and sugar content. But there was a threat during this grinding that was worse than any Auguste had ever experienced: The possibility of losing his favorite son to war. Disillusioned about the condition of the Union, Jean had come home from Mount St. Mary's in the summer after more than a year of graduate study, to get his father's advice, to help harvest the crop. He hadn't slept well for days. He had known Plaquemine to be a friendly and hospitable town when he first left home for New Orleans and college. He had left Mount St. Mary's seeking a happy return to Iberville Parish. But when he returned home he sensed an air of suspicion, even hysteria. Dinner guests at Golden Ridge talked of little else than secession and their intense hatred for Abraham Lincoln.

As Jean and his father walked to the Big House for the noon meal, Jean said that he feared dissolving the Union would be the worst thing that could happen to the country and to the human race. "I fear for the South, this plantation, our way of life," he added, hitching up his baggy trousers and wiping sweat from his face. "And because of the motives of these damn northern abolitionists. I can't bare to lose what we have if our differences explode into war, *Père*. Because we have everything to lose, I can't just turn my head as if nothing is happening."

"Jean, *mon fils*, what would you choose to do then?" Auguste looked at him with stern, questioning eyes.

"I don't know. I really don't know."

*　　*　　*

Because the '60 crop had been large and sugar had sold at good prices, Jean, Augie, and their father celebrated their good fortune in the dining rooms of the great St. Charles and St. Louis hotels in New Orleans. At Antoine's Restaurant in the French Quarter, they watched beautiful women wearing elegant gowns and sparkling jewelry fill out the saloons. Jean knew the French opera was in full season, and that money was abundant, the banks filled with accounts of successful sugar planters like his father.

For weeks, dancing and reveling continued at the hotels and the opera attracted large audiences. Jean and his family could not believe that war would really come; they could foresee the desolation that could cover the face of the plantation South. When the holiday season finally ended, a rude awakening awaited Jean, his family, and other people of the South. From quivering lips came these words:

"Louisiana has seceded!"

CHAPTER 13

ABOUT TWO WEEKS after escaping the battlefield, Jean Baptiste waked lying among briar bushes somewhere in Iberville Parish, Louisiana. He didn't know exactly where he was, but after inhaling some familiar smells, he felt that he wasn't far from Plaquemine. It was the only decent night's sleep he'd had since he left the Tennessee battlefield, made his way across half the state to Memphis in a rented carriage, and boarded an Illinois Central train for New Orleans.

Abrasions and bruises on his body and blood on his trousers reminded him of the battle of Murfreesboro at Stones River, near Nashville. *At least I'm whole. Oh, God knows, I'm still in one piece.*

Jean had volunteered for service in the Confederacy on August 26, 1861, at Camp Schlater outside Plaquemine. He had been ordered to Baton Rouge and assigned to Captain Calvin Keep's company known as the Ed Moore Rangers, which eventually became Company A of the First Louisiana Cavalry, or Old First. During the following year, from September to December, 1862, Jean's Company A had participated in confused marching and countermarching through central Kentucky and Tennessee. On October 8, Union forces had struck the Confederates at Perryville, Kentucky; the battle was a draw. On December 31, the armies had clashed outside Murfreesboro in one of the most bitterly fought battles of the war. It seemed to Jean another Shiloh, a battle in which his Company A, under Colonel John S. Scott, had participated earlier in the year. Three days later, on January 2,

1863, the Rebels, under General Braxton Bragg, commander of the Army of Tennessee, had been shattered at Stones River in their futile attempt against the Union forces commanded by General William Rosecrans.

As Jean stood up, he thought of Oscar Babin, his friend from White Castle, Louisiana, of Captain Jonathan Bramlett, and other officers and friends, who were lying in the meadows and woodlands around Murfreesboro. "Who won the battle at Murfreesboro?" he muttered to himself. "Who took possession of the town?" *In my mental and physical condition, I don't know nor do I give a damn.* For Jean had survived not only the futile attack on the enemy on January 2, but he had also survived his risky escape from his outfit to come home to help his father and brothers decide about land purchases and sales.

Jean rejoiced and felt well after two days' rest and much delicious food at Golden Ridge, and he was pleased to be heard on the land deals by his father and brothers. Aggressive as Jean had become about land acquisitions, he advised that they not buy land until the war was won. He also was flattered to be invited to the council on the estate of Gideon Octave Dupuy, a respected sugar planter and landowner from St. Gabriel, who had been murdered by a roaming outlaw on his plantation. Jean had learned from his father that Dupuy arrived home on a dark night and was surprised by a thief stealing saddles and bridles from his stable. As the planter ran for his home and safety, the outlaw shot him in the back, orphaning his only heir, a young daughter named Stephanie, who Jean's father told him was now twelve years old.

*   *   *

"Hello, I am Louis Joly," the man said, standing on the front gallery at St. Gabriel Plantation house, across the Mississippi River from Plaquemine. Joly grasped Jean's hand as the twenty-three year-old soldier stepped down from the black, squeaky barouche. "I have met your father, son, but I don't believe that I have had the pleasure of meeting you. You are the living image of your mother, I might add."

Sporting a close-trimmed grizzled moustache and fresh clothes, Jean smiled politely at his host and said, "Glad to meet you, sir." Joly appeared sickly looking, with sagging shoulders.

"Thank you for coming here to help us try to resolve a matter of significance to the Dupuy family, especially to the twelve-year-old minor child, Marie Stephanie," said Joly, offering his hand to Jean's father. Joly had been entrusted by the Iberville Parish court, three days after the murder of Stephanie's father in 1858, to serve as tutor and guardian in the child's best interests.

"I want you to meet Duhamel Dupuy, my assistant and brother of Stephanie's father," he said. A tall man, in his mid-forties, his dark hair thinning a little, Dupuy left the gallery and walked briskly toward them. He shook hands with Auguste and Jean.

"Over there, boy. Tie the carriage to the fence post closest to the house," Joly called to the house servant.

"Let me say, Mr. Joly, I brought my son along because he may be able to help resolve the succession matter you outlined briefly in your letter of two weeks ago." Auguste and Jean preceded Joly and Dupuy from the wide gallery into the parlor. The Dupuy maid served *café au lait* and small éclairs, Jean's favorite pastry.

"Jean arrived home a few days ago from the battlefield in Tennessee," Auguste said after they all sat down. "There are some family matters involving the sale of certain properties we own. I depend a great deal on his judgment. His brothers wish to sell some land we've held for a long time, hoping to get the highest price. But I wish to keep the tracts a while longer. I hope Jean will help us come to an agreement before he has to return to his cavalry unit."

Auguste, almost sixty, brushed his gray hair off his forehead. He told Joly and Dupuy that Jean had been privy to negotiations between him and his sugar broker that were profitable for both. "He's been an inspiration and ally to me from the time he started thinking for himself."

"We welcome him," responded Joly skeptically.

Sunshine broke through gray clouds on the mid-January morning, casting long shadows on the white walls of the house and over the green oaks and camellias. St. Gabriel house was beautifully proportioned. Jean admired its simple architecture inside and outside, its arches and concrete masonry construction and few ornamental appendages to mar its classical lines.

Jean had been told by his father that after the Catholic church at St. Gabriel was built on part of a Spanish land grant, Iberville Parish decided that the church property, totaling five hundred and thirty-five acres, was too large to maintain. Several years later, the church parish sold what became St. Gabriel, or Dupuy, Plantation to its first owner, Ignace Babin, for seventeen dollars.

*   *   *

"Well, now, who might you be?" Private Levert inquired, smiling broadly. He was stirred by the face and figure of the pretty girl who had entered the parlor.

"Stephanie Dupuy," she replied softly. Jean studied the green eyes, luxuriant blonde hair, willowy grace of the French girl. She seemed to have a strength of will in her face. Behind a large wing chair, Stephanie stared up at the visitor. Jean slipped past the others and leaned forward to greet Stephanie. He thought she looked mature for a girl of only twelve.

"Her name is Marie Stephanie. She has been an orphan for nearly five years," Louis Joly said with a frown. Jean tried not to stare at the precocious child. *I don't blame him for being nervous about her,* thought Jean, who had to tear his gaze from her face to avoid staring.

"Stephanie, this is our neighbor from Golden Ridge, Jean Baptiste Levert," Joly said impatiently. "Jean is home on—well, we won't go into that. He's home from the war to help his father and brothers settle some family business."

"Marie Stephanie is a beautiful name—old Greek," Jean said. "I understand it is undergoing a revival." He knew he was babbling.

He was shocked to feel his blood rush through his body when his eyes met her's. He thought she was the loveliest thing he had ever seen. He bowed and turned away to join Joly, Dupuy, and his father across the parlor. He was dumfounded at his reactions. *What savage beast inside of me, what lust, God forgive me, has been released, seeing this young girl with golden hair?*

"I have explained to Jean why we are meeting today," Joly said. "His father thought he could help us resolve the matter of the plantation sold to Mr. Henry Biegel. I know you don't always like it, child, but the court has ordered that your Uncle Duhamel and I arrange consultation in estate matters that have a bearing on your future."

"Yes, Mr. Joly, I remember, I know," the girl responded obediently. She didn't understand at all, thought Jean.

Jean interrupted Joly before he could answer: "If I may be presumptuous, sir, I think it would be in the young lady's best interest, to the estate itself in the long run, if the plantation formerly belonging to her father's succession—what's it called? Willow Glen?—were reclaimed. I understand that this Biegel fellow was sold the estate from the Dupuy succession so Stephanie's guardians could pay off some debts left by her father. Now that this gentleman has defaulted on his payment, I believe the plantation ought to be reclaimed and held for the heir's benefit. She might command an even greater price than she received from Biegel, should she ever decide to sell."

Jean looked at his father. "I apologize for speaking out like this, but I have a habit of doing it, especially when I feel strongly about something. When something is on my mind . . ." He walked toward Stephanie.

Louis Joly, Duhamel Dupuy, and Auguste Levert, sitting around Stephanie's father's rectangular desk, were silent. They all stared at Jean standing by Stephanie.

Suddenly Joly jumped up, red-faced. "I believe this meeting is over, gentlemen. I am sure Mr. Levert and his son are anxious to be on their way." Of Duhamel, he demanded: "Make certain the house servant has their carriage ready out front."

Jean smiled, his blue eyes gleaming, and replied: "Not at all, Mr. Joly. We're in no great hurry. I would like to tell Marie Stephanie some stories of the war and some of the places I've been and seen in connection with it."

Joly nodded curtly. Jean knew he would be regarded with suspicion by the guardian as long as he was in the neighborhood.

CHAPTER 14

BEFORE DAYBREAK, IN a brick farmhouse outside Shelbyville, Kentucky, Jean bolted up in bed. Sweating, disoriented, he rubbed his eyes and stretched. He had been dreaming of Annie Blanton, the nineteen-year-old war widow who lay beside him. "What's the matter?" asked Annie, shaking Jean gently. "Oh, oh, nothing, nothing." He slurred his words; he was about to fall back into dreamy sleep again.

Annie and Jean lay still in the dark. Last night they had made a supper of fried fish, bread, and coffee and then talked for hours, kissed, caressed, made love—and made love. It was always the same whenever they found rare moments of privacy. Whenever Jean was with her he could forget all the madness of nearly three years of fighting, arguing, sickness, death. He had tried to find something of worth, something to believe in, for four months since Company A, First Louisiana Cavalry, rode into Shelbyville in late February, 1863, to join General Bragg's Kentucky campaign. The only cause he had come up with that seemed worth anything was Annie. They had met for the first time right after Jean had rejoined his cavalry unit in Shelbyville.

Jean thought he would never forget her running down the farmhouse steps in the fog, wrapped in an old nightgown to greet him after dark, as she did last night. Thoughts of holding her in bed, of stroking her soft white skin, of running his fingers through her dark hair before they made love. He could not get her out of his mind, and he didn't want to. Annie Blanton satisfied his every desire.

During Bragg's Kentucky campaign, Jean's unit was stationed at Shelbyville, not far from Annie's two-story farmhouse, which was surrounded by tall sugar maple and sycamore trees. But Jean did not see her often. He had become acquainted with her during one of General Edmund Kirby-Smith's sojourns outside Shelbyville. He thought she must be one of the handsomest women in Kentucky.

"It's not going well, Annie," said Jean, holding her hand and kissing it. "Papa says some neighboring plantations are stripped bare of sugarcane and cotton; houses are burned to the ground. Thank God nothing has happened to Golden Ridge." He told her that his father was worried the Yankees would come to Golden Ridge, that the war would not give him and other planters enough time to repair their damaged cane fields trampled flat by galloping artillery batteries. "My father is now in the midst of war."

Jean told her he had learned that Union General Benjamin Butler had been placed in charge of New Orleans and surrounding parishes after the fall of the South's largest city, and that the heart of sugarcane country was in Yankee hands; that Union armies, led by General Nathaniel Banks, had moved west of the lower Mississippi River, Louisiana's sugar bowl, and seized plantation animals, especially mules, and burned plantation houses and sugarhouses; that Federal soldiers chopped fences, wagons, and carts for firewood; that plantation Negroes, who regarded Union troops as their liberators, were bewildered.

"All these conditions make cane growing at Golden Ridge impossible," he explained. He gently kissed her hand again. "But the single worst blow to Papa is the loss of his work mules. There is no way for him to grow cane without his mules, and he spares nothing in his search for the animals to keep his plows and carts moving. Damnit! Damnit to hell! My father plants and plows acres and acres of cane and an hour later the goddamn Yankees ride across them and he has to begin all over." Seeing tears in his eyes, Annie squeezed his hand.

"I believe I understand your concern about your family, the future of your precious way of life," she replied, "but . . ."

"I am certain my family is living in a hellish nightmare." Jean then told her some men in his outfit were convinced the war had turned sour for the South. "It doesn't matter how brave you are if the other side outnumbers you. All the bravery and courage aren't going to change a thing."

Suddenly Jean felt a cold air blast through the raised window in Annie's second-floor bedroom overlooking the gardens, billowing the curtains out into the room. "I'm cold. Is there an extra blanket?" He rolled over on his stomach, cupped his hands and put both arms together underneath his shivering body. Annie quickly put another blanket over them.

"Annie, I am worried about you here. It would be safer if you went to stay with your family in Louisville until things calm down. My unit manages to enjoy itself occasionally—sing songs, attend religious services, indulge in horseplay. But this fighting in Kentucky could last a lifetime and you're in constant danger from the Yankees. Being away fighting all the time all over this state, I'm not worth a plugged nickel to you as far as your safety is concerned."

"Stop this kind of talk, Jean. There's nothing for you to worry about. You're exaggerating the danger. Besides, I don't want to run away to Louisville. Shelbyville's been my home all my life."

He was silent. Annie raised up and lowered her naked body onto his. She kissed his eyes, stared through the dim light at his sad face. He felt her mouth and hands moving across his face and body, stopping where they would, as he became caught up in their discovery. All Jean knew was that she was not close enough. Then he held her closer, pressing his body against her with a tense insistence. His body tightened, thrusting against the length of her. He cried out in ecstacy, as the first shudder ran through him.

Finally Annie spoke: "Sometimes I don't know why I love you. I wouldn't let my feelings go for the longest because of the war. I was so afraid, never knowing if I could survive this war-torn place."

"No, no, no, Annie, enough," Jean said in a comforting voice. "You are only tormenting yourself. There is no need now. I am here . . ."

He stopped. He knew he couldn't be with her no matter how badly she needed him. He desperately wanted to be with her, but the war made cruel demands. Thinking he might never see her again, Jean rolled Annie over on her back and tightened his hold on her. He stroked her thighs, moving over the silk-soft curves of her body. An instant warmth radiated from her. She stirred under him, sighed, moaned, as his palms covered her warm nipples.

"Oh, God, you feel so good," he gasped. "You are so beautiful . . . your eyes, mouth. You're so . . ." He bent to kiss her breasts, then to kiss her stomach . . . .

His passion frightened him. He loosened his grip on her body and kissed her softly again and again.

CHAPTER 15

NEAR TEARS ON this muggy morning, sipping chicory coffee with Eulalie and Augie in his small office, Auguste Levert lamented the winds of destruction blowing harder toward his beloved Golden Ridge. Scanning the March 31, 1864, issue of the New Orleans *Times*, he noticed a list of recent war prisoners at the bottom of the front page: " . . . J. B. Levert, 24, received at Fort Delaware, Delaware, March 4, 1864 . . . Amèdèe Levert, 20, received at military prison in Union-occupied New Orleans, March 26, 1864 . . . ."

"Oh, God! Oh, God! I was fearful I'd see something like this in the papers. I wasn't sure what had happened to Jean," said Auguste, turning to Eulalie and Augie. "I remember reading one of the New Orleans papers several months back about some Rebels on a mission being captured in Kentucky, being overwhelmed by Yankees at some river. I knew Jean volunteered for this mission. The paper said for weeks that there was no word about survivors or whereabouts of the troopers. But I didn't expect this news about Amèdèe. I lost track of him for a long time."

Frightened upon hearing the news, Jean's mother, staring blankly at the wall, did not reply for a long time. Augie made no comment at all.

Jean and a hundred other officers and troopers, including their leader, Lieutenant Colonel James O. Nixon, had been captured in late August, 1863, while on a secret mission near Irvine, Kentucky, south of Lexington. Following five days and nights of incessant fighting, being outnumbered, exhausted, starving—with rations consisting of green apples—the expeditionary force had been swallowed up by a horde of blue-bellies at the Dix River assault. Jean's eagerness to strike a blow at the Yankees, despite pleadings from Annie Blanton not to volunteer for the dangerous mission, had won out over reason and common sense in the end. After capture, Jean had spent several months at Camp Chase, Ohio, prison before being transferred in March, 1864, to Fort Delaware Prison near Wilmington, Delaware.

"The economic base of the plantation system is collapsing," continued Auguste. He looked at Eulalie who remained silent. "The Confederacy is bleeding inside. Because of the damn naval blockade soldiers are deserting, and it's hard for us to move our crops to market." He said the whole Louisiana coast has been closed for two years, because the blockade cut the South off from its resources and cut the Confederacy off from the factories and supplies of the world. "Hell, all the Confederacy has left are the leadership and patriotism of heroic generals and brave soldiers. The Union has all the arsenals and factories."

The sugar planter, stooped and wrinkly with age and worry, sipped more of the strong brew, then looked at Augie who was slumped in a chair. Eulalie, as always dressed fastidiously with her brown hair secured neatly in a bun, laid her hand on her husband's arm. After a few more sips of coffee, Auguste set his cup on the table. He coughed. "I think we're suffering from a kind of moral blockade, too. This slavery thing has been turned into a morality crusade. Yes—yes, it has been glorified into a crusade, and the Union armies are pushing deeper into Rebel ranks, unlocking chains, they think, from the wrists and ankles of the slaves."

Jean's father knew that much of the South's military strength had caved in following the decisive defeats at Gettysburg and Vicksburg. Nevertheless, he knew high hopes had been replaced by resolution. "The South is in a virtual state of siege, even though many Southerners will not admit it," Auguste said. He said it was a terrible blow when the Vicksburg loss gave the Yankees control of the Mississippi and cut off sugar crops from the Confederacy.

Augie sat silently looking at his father. Connected to the second division of the Louisiana state militia, he had been engaged at Plaquemine when Union troops came up the Mississippi to capture and occupy New Orleans. But after that he had spent the war near the town looking after the safety of relatives of soldiers at the front and caring for the slaves on his father's plantation.

"Well, son, I know we are more fortunate than many of our neighbors. While most slaves ran away after Lincoln's proclamation, more than half of ours remained out of loyalty. They are true Southerners, as devoted to this land as we are, and they still love the old ways that the invaders are threatening to take away. Furthermore, I believe that one of the reasons the South has survived this long is due in no small part to the heroism of women like your Mother."

Eulalie Miro Levert, descendant of Esteban Rodriquez Miro, fifth Spanish governor of the Louisiana Territory in the mid-1700s, had inherited from her father her courage and compassion for others. She had sent three sons to war and, at the same time, sacrificed her luxuries and comforts on the plantation to give her time to those less fortunate than she. On occasion, she had nursed the wounded in a ghastly Confederate hospital in Baton Rouge.

"We have the brown sugar from two crops of cane hidden away in the outbuildings near the slave quarters, but little good it does, Augie. We've always been able to sell our sugar and buy the things we cannot produce. But nowadays, we can do neither. Still, no life is more independent and rewarding than that of a southern planter—before the war. I'd rather remain a planter on this plantation than be president of the Confederate States of America. I—" Auguste knew he was rambling, now.

"Enough, dear, enough. Stop tormenting yourself. The Yankees haven't reached us, not yet. We've been very lucky so far, dear." Mrs. Levert, nearly sixty, rarely discussed politics, sugar operations, business of any kind. This evening, after a supper of smoked ham, sweet potatoes, French bread, and warm bread pudding, she tried to lift her husband's spirits, to give him all the comfort in her power, despite her worries about Jean and Amèdèe. "Of course, you know best about such things, *mon cher,* but all is not lost, cheer up!" He looked at her fondly; his eyes brightened. "We should be grateful for what we still have, dear. Many of our friends have been made orphans by this terrible war. Some have been robbed and burned out of their homes."

But later that evening, after going to bed, Auguste whispered to Eulalie, his voice hoarse with sorrow: "These times, *ma chèrie*, are no longer normal times. Most planters are in the same predicament as we are. Cane production has dropped by millions and millions of pounds during four years of war, and only a few plantations even produced a crop after the first two years of the war. I am afraid recovery of our industry is going to be very, very slow. No, *chèrie*, war has smashed not only our sources of credit, nearly ruining Albert Desmont in the process, but one by one our plantations and dreams as well."

CHAPTER 16

"A COMPANY OF Yankees led by General Banks closer to home than we liked had encamped in a field above Plaquemine . . . most of the blue-bellies looked like dregs of the world, scarcely in uniform . . . when the keys were not produced right away, some pried open the locks of the wooden doll trunk that belonged to your sister Aimeè, God rest her soul; it caught the eyes of one of the bullies. 'Don't break the doll trunk,' I pleaded, when the key couldn't be found. I remember the bully saying, 'It's big enough to hold my pistol,' as he ripped the top off."

Jean strained to make sure he had read his father's letter correctly, hadn't missed a single meaning in it. He wadded the letter into a ball and threw it against the wall of the three-story, graystone prison building on Pea Patch Island in the Delaware River. Fury and worry clouded his blue eyes. How in God's name could he sit here on this cold, rat-infested island. He might go mad with frustration and fear for his family; for Annie Blanton who continued to be in his thoughts. He retrieved the wadded paper from the floor, the second letter he had been allowed to read since he was imprisoned at Fort Delaware Prison a month earlier. The first told him of Bébé's death on a December morning, one month almost to the day—November, 1863—after slaves in territories conquered by the Yankees were freed. News that grieved him still. In that letter Auguste had told Jean that Bébé, according to the doctor, was a victim of "old age and a lonely heart," stemming, in part, from the loss of Isaac to slave catchers and that she missed Jean, confiding to Jean's mother shortly before her death: "I don't think

Jean ever get out de bad war still livin when he fightin all de time, yeah, close to dem murderin guns."

"A broken-open desk revealed some love letters from your old girlfriends, son, and they were amusing to the Yankees. They found the wine cellar and drank 'till they were drunk. The leader of this foray announced he had come to hang your father on the nearest tree! One blue-belly waved a whip over your mother's head because she tried to restrain the drunken fellow . . . these fellows were drunk enough to do anything; one even said Piksie was about the age for his lustful pleasure. I guess, son, we've been living within the battle lines and didn't know it! I feel we can no longer stay on the plantation . . . oh, one more thing: I understand Amèdèe is quite ill with typhoid in some forsaken prison in New Orleans or Landry upstate. I forget now where he is. The prison hospital sent word the other day; I don't know whether to believe the hospital . . . ."

Jean turned blood-red and jumped to his feet. "Goddamn it! Oh, God!" he said under his breath. He let the wrinkled four-page letter slip from his hands onto the filthy damp floor. For a moment he looked at the tall, narrow barred windows, then put his head on the knapsack he used for a pillow and repeated a vow over and over—until he fell asleep about two in the morning:

"I'll survive this place, I'll survive this goddamn hellhole. Whatever I have to do to survive, I'll do it."

*   *   *

Jean knew that the only time he had to compose his thoughts and put them down in his tablet was late at night when there was no moon. For as a Yankee prisoner, he wrote mostly in the dark, sitting against the prison room wall with the tablet on his lap or knees. He feared having his tablet confiscated.

March 21, 1864—I've tried to keep my mind off my ordeal by thinking about my family, about Annie. A letter from Annie awaited me at the compound when I arrived to let me know someone on the outside cared, cared a great deal. She sent soap, writing tablets and pencils, pipe and tobacco, even some money, but a guard confiscated the money.

May 2, 1864—Finally met the commandant of this hellhole prison, a Colonel Jud Wilkinson, a mean disposition . . . appears younger than his years, high voice that better fits someone in another line of work . . . our quarters are so crowded that none of us has any space. Hard floor, holes in the walls of the building surrounded by a moat . . . much of the island is below water. Rations are irregular, sometimes two ounces of meat, sometimes none. Soup is served at times, but such stuff my robust stomach couldn't take for long . . . consequences are that a large proportion of the men are reduced nearly to skeletons . . . this compound is so unhealthy I believe I would have a better chance of survival fighting in the army.

May 9, 1864—We lost two by death . . . arteries burst, bled to death . . . we had nothing to eat today. I think they mean to starve us to death! . . . I bet I've already lost twenty-five pounds since entering this hellhole. I've lost all interest in everything, my spirit has been dulled . . . a few prisoners try to read to kill time and escape insanity, but I no longer find reading enjoyable.

As bad as anything was the monotony. To turn tedious hours of prison life to some account, Jean continued to write his thoughts in the tablet. He hoped to transcribe them after the war.

June 10, 1864—Catching and eating rats that live on the island is very common among the prisoners . . . whiskered officers, grown men lurking, club in hand, near breathing holes which rats have cut in the hard earth—waiting to strike a blow for fresh meat and rat soup for dinner!

August 6, 1864—We're fighting for freedom, for hearth and home, ready to resist to the end. I suspect letters I have written have been burned or dumped into the Delaware River.

October 3, 1864—My fingers are so cold I can no longer hold a pencil. I coughed for several minutes; think I have a bad cold. One doctor says prisoners die at a rate of a hundred and fifty a day . . . dysentery is the most fatal disease; men lie on the ground in their own excrement . . . it is dreadful.

November 23, 1864—It rained again—all night. Felt sweaty, weak . . . cold getting worse . . . feel sick, but don't want to go to hospital . . . incompetent nurses, inadequate supplies—chances are better if I stay away from them!

November 29, 1864—I will survive this place and the sadistic commandant as well. I will survive this goddamn place!

*   *   *

By early January, 1865, Jean believed that the South was worn out, for it seemed to have lost its strength and will to fight. From his prison room he was thinking:

The Confederate army is failing, and there's not much hope in Louisiana . . . Union armies now control the southwestern part of the state. Rebel forces aren't strong enough to attack them . . . southerners are dispirited, soldiers are deserting and going home— for good! Of all the problems besetting the South, I've heard the one that most worries Lee is the shortage of troops . . . the army is running out of soldiers, and the Confederate states have so few men to replace them.

The Union Army of the Potomac had recovered from its terrible sacrifices of the previous spring and summer, and by early April, 1865, the gloom that pervaded the Union ranks after the failure to take Petersburg turned to optimism.

On April 9, 1865, Lee's army of ragged, exhausted soldiers surrendered to General Grant at Appomattox Court House in Virginia. The other Confederate armies surrendered shortly afterward.

*   *   *

After the surrender, Jean wrote his first letter to his parents in three months; then he wrote Annie Blanton in Kentucky. He felt guilty for not writing to Annie for more than a year, not since her letter greeting his arrival at Fort Delaware. He hadn't seen her since before his capture at Dix River near Irvine, Kentucky. Jean realized a letter to Annie was not going to be easy to compose and send if, in fact, it ever left the prison compound.

Fort Delaware
May 1, 1865

My dear Annie,

I again sit down to the pleasant task of writing to you. But in doing so, I realize the task of this particular writing is to be unpleasant for me. I also feel deep inside that I write you with a firm conviction that it is for the last time as a prisoner, the last time as a soldier, for this war is all but over. Two thousand of us have orders to be in readiness to leave at any time for the South. You can best imagine my feelings at this moment. Many of our boys are not going back with the joyful expectation of meeting the smiles of their friends and sweethearts, having died in this terrible place.

Forgive me, but I destroyed this very morning all your precious letters written to me before my imprisonment. It was a painful task, as I would have treasured them in afterlife. It may be that once I am released, I may never have an opportunity to write you, may never see you again. But please rest assured whether in camp or on the field of battle or in the field of sugarcane—wherever I may be— my deepest thoughts will be of you, my cherished hopes to see you again—soon! Remember me to all of my kind friends and believe me.

Yours always and forever,
J. B. Levert, Private, Company A, First La. Cavalry

Chapter 17

Golden Ridge
May 10, 1865

Dear Jean,

We now have endured much since 1862, and more since you last heard; it was finally the ransacking of Golden Ridge by General Banks' blue-bellies that drove us away, and we did not see home for many many months. What kind of people are these damn rotten Yankee soldiers to trespass on other people's property and lives this way? I know this is terrible news for you, for I know you feared this. But let me say to begin with, this account has a happy ending.

To save your mother's life as well as Euphrasie's and Augie's, I took them and some loyal house servants to hide out in Bayou Plaquemine swamp. We were joined by Amèdèe, who had by then been released from prison. We all feared that in our absence the marauding Yankees would again ransack Golden Ridge, even burn the house to the ground.

When, finally, we set out in our rickety wagon to try to go home, we all feared the worst. I tell you every one of us imagined our house and all our possessions gone or destroyed and our fields in ruin. We passed burned-out shells of our neighbors' homes in shambles, and at every bend in the river road we expected to see a blackened skeleton of Golden Ridge. So, imagine our joy when the dear old house hove into view beyond that last curve, almost its old self. You should have heard our shouts of joy and relief. Augie and Amèdèe jumped off the wagon and ran the last hundred yards. Your mother and I hugged each other when we stood in the front of the wagon and thanked God. One of the servants raised her head and hands to the heavens to rejoice. I can assure you I have never been so humbly grateful to our God.

Most of our nine hundred acres of fields look bad. They haven't burned the crop completely, and our soldiers won't need it any longer. The cause is dead. You and I know a burned over cane field is not necessarily a ruined field. Yankees don't know anything about sugarcane. They did ransack the house, stole about $800 in Confederate money, most of your mother's silver, but she found some pieces in that little hidden closet under the back stairs. As you would expect, she was brave and courageous through everything.

I told the family there's too much to do to waste time celebrating war's end in New Orleans, that there's still time to reap something from the soil. I know restoration and rebuilding will be endless, though. But our spirits are high, son, even knowing that the sugar industry might never recover the golden age of Louisiana, when wealth wrenched from the planters' soil by slave labor was poured into the lap of New Orleans, making it a great commercial and cultural city. You remember Golden Ridge rose from dirt to riches on sugar. Now I will have to raise a rich plantation again out of the ravages of war. When I look at this estate, Jean, in its slightly damaged condition, I think I know why wars are fought. They're fought for land, for grand white houses, for rich black soil that is ours and will someday belong to my children and your children.

We need you badly, and trust you will be coming home soon. We send our love and we pray for your good health.

P.S. Before we start rebuilding we plan to visit the cemetery to

honor the memory of Aimeè, Joseph, and Eloi and to place
wild flowers on their graves. I know your thoughts are with
your twenty-three-year-old brother Joseph, who just didn't
have the strength to win his long battle against consumption!

The letter fell from Jean's hand onto the prison room floor. He was feverish with dysentery, and the letter made him feel more ill and useless. He could do nothing to help his family.

CHAPTER 18

*Wilkinson stood over Jean with a long stick, packing a side arm
. . . Jean was too weak from his escape attempt and was suffering
from nausea and loss of appetite. Wilkinson's blow to his face
stung him, causing him to fall. Jean clenched his fists, tears filled
his eyes, blood ran down his lip, sharp pain shot through his body
like an electric current—his pain, nausea grew worse. Wilkinson
jabbed him in the back with a bayonet as they marched outside
in a light drizzle, down to river's edge. Wilkinson tied his hands
and feet with a rope, then tied him to a birch tree so if he tried to
escape again he'd roll down the embankment into the water and
likely drown . . . Jean coughed and coughed, pain shot through
his entire body again; he was left tied to the tree in a contorted
position, curled like a ball, in freezing cold . . . hours seemed like
weeks to him; chills changed to fever and sent him raving into
hysteria . . . .*

WHEN EULALIE LEVERT entered Jean's upstairs room at Golden
Ridge this November morning, she interrupted his nightmare. She
already had called Dr. Artemas LeBlanc, the family physician, because
she was worried about her son's mental state, his dull response to
family and friends without his old spirit and energy, his occasional
melancholy. The doctor's visit gave her renewed hope.

"What can we do, Doctor?" she asked, running her hand through
thick graying hair. She sat down at the foot of Jean's bed as Dr. LeBlanc
examined her son. Two candles provided dim light. "He's been
through so much, but we haven't seen much improvement in his

mental outlook. My husband is so worried. I'm really confused by his nightmares about prison." Her voice broke. "If I get my son again, Doctor, I'll bless you to my dying day."

After Jean had been released from Confederate service and returned home in June, 1865, he told his parents that he thought his ordeal at Fort Delaware Prison was more debilitating and left a far worse impression on him than war itself. For five months he suffered periodic bloody evacuations and high fever. He had almost died from dysentery.

Eulalie stood up, smoothed her black dress and removed the ribbon around her neck. She cleared her throat and said, "Jean doesn't care to get out, to travel, to go to town, visit friends, even go to Mass. It's not like him to brood like this."

Stroking his long gray beard, the plump Dr. LeBlanc said, "Have you invited him on your social evenings—to change the scenery, get his mind off his problems?"

"There have been several socials at the church since he came home in the summer, but he refused to go."

"Have you tried involving Jean more in daily operations of the plantation? Giving him some responsibility?"

"No, actually, because he gets so little rest. He's been having nightmares nearly every night since he came home."

Dr. LeBlanc pondered this information. He pushed his spectacles up the bridge of his nose, then fingered his pocket watch. "Please, I urge you to be more forceful with Jean. He needs constant human contact again to help draw him out of himself. The longer this is allowed to work on his mind, the harder it will be for him to conquer his deep depression."

Jean watched his mother stare out of the bedroom window. "You're right, Doctor. We need to help pry Jean away from his brooding. I'll try, Dr. LeBlanc. I think I might help him now that you've talked to me." She smiled with more confidence. "Jean can be awfully stubborn and moody at times," she added as she handed the doctor his long-tailed coat.

"You and Mr. Levert and the whole family must be supportive and encouraging," said Dr. LeBlanc, as he stepped out of the front door.

*   *   *

Jean bolted up in a cold sweat. He rubbed his eyes, trying to shut out another nightmare: *Rolling into the river, hands and feet tied, sinking beneath the water, clawing against the current to reach the surface—and failing . . . .*

He locked his hands below his pulled-up knees and tried to force out the image of the ruthless Jud Wilkinson. His knowledge of the man's wickedness made Isaac's shackled suffering all too real to him. *Nôtre Père, qui sont an paradis, que ton nom soit, sanctifie', ue votre segne arrive, ton volonte' soit fait . . . .*

Jean's mind had been a tempest for most of the night, and his thoughts were still confused. He knew, like his father, that Louisiana now was in chaos, that it faced basic problems of restoring its government, rebuilding its agriculture, redefining a place in society for the newly freed slaves. As distraught over destruction of his homeland and the sugar industry as he had been over the horrors of prison, he put his elbows on the table next to the window, cradled his head in his hands, and tried to reflect in the darkness.

There are fewer homes for many returning soldiers to repair, fewer cane fields to furrow, fewer seeds to plant, fewer plantations to even go home to. War saw to that . . . rich land Papa held before the war brought fifty dollars an acre, now it's selling at three to fifteen an acre. Soil remains but there's a scarcity of tools, livestock, plant seed, labor—especially labor. The freed slaves are confused. Jean knew that many of the slaves traveled in bands like gypsies to the North and many of them had died up there from want. *Our Father, who art in Heaven, hallowed be thy name, thy Kingdom come, thy will be done, on earth as it is in Heaven. Give us this day, our daily bread, and forgive us . . . amen.*

Jean's anxiety seemed to be easing. The Lord's prayer helped him. He lighted a candle to look at a clock—a few minutes past one o'clock. The only sound he heard through the open storm shutters was wind whipping oak branches outside his bedroom. At that moment, a small click sounded in Jean's mind. His instincts of self-preservation began to take over, rallying his thoughts of what course to take his life back. For he knew he must get on with his life. He had known that all along.

He believed his most daunting challenge was going to be helping to rebuild all that had been destroyed by the war—a task made somewhat more attainable by its own necessity. Jean was certain the wave of rebuilding in south Louisiana would give him the opportunity that he had dreamed of: To convince fellow planters and others that his theories for reviving the sugar industry were sound; they could all make money—big money.

Too much damn blood spilled the last four years—and for what? Federal troops occupying our towns. Some damn Yankee radicals capturing public opinion up North, imposing upon our land concepts of morality—who the hell do they think they are? The Yankees want to erase our class distinctions and launch voting rights for all; they are so goddamn hypocritical!

Jean continued questioning himself. Finally, he laid his tired head down and stared at the ceiling. He breathed deeply and was able to relax. He must relax, and he must rest. But now his imagination was stirred. In a rush of clearheadedness the idea came to him:

There is a way to reorganize the industry of the South, especially cane and cotton cultivation. Enterprising, intelligent planters have turned disaster into success before and they can do it again. But they will need help. If not help from banks, then from whom? Let's face it, Louisiana is the only inhabited place in the United States with the climate and other conditions needed to produce the quality of cane required in commerce. Could the South get all the capital it needed to revitalize and reorganize its sugar industry? A great want then is the certainty of credit or advances. Not merely the certainty of credit but cheap credit. Arrangements will have to be made for advances of cash to planters for field equipment, seed cane, mules, even to meet payrolls. If not banks, then help must come from private capital. That has to be it, private capital.

His mind had slowed down and his muscles were relaxed. He fell into a normal sleep.

CHAPTER 19

THERE WAS AN expression in her glance across the dance floor that thrilled Jean Baptiste. *Who is she? When—where have I seen her before? That face, those green eyes, that golden hair? Where?* Six months after his return home, Jean had pulled himself out of despair. He was listening to a fine orchestra from Baton Rouge. The music filled the hall of the cypress Catholic church at St. Gabriel across the Mississippi from Plaquemine, and glad feet moved in graceful waltz and merry polka. It was Christmas.

Jean, seated against the wall in back of the church, continued to watch the exquisite girl. She turned away and spoke to two older Creole gentlemen. She looked like a young girl; her mouth and eyes showed that she was not older than fifteen, sixteen. The face seemed faintly familiar, but he could not recall where he had seen it.

Who could she be? Jean was frustrated now. He stroked his moustache and leaned over to ask a friend if he knew her name but changed his mind.

Jean realized that the girl was watching him, now. She wore a costume that suited her well: A green silk dress trimmed with black velvet. Black satin shoes laced high up her ankles showed her well-shaped feet. Her fair neck and finely molded arms were bare, without jewelry, and her blonde hair was dressed without ornament.

Jean was in a most elegant costume newly purchased in New Orleans, thanks to Albert Desmont: A full-length black coat with wide pointed lapels, gray trousers, and low-cut waistcoat that buttoned to the side, allowing full view of a white ruffled shirt, a gift from his mother. Wrapped around his high collar was a long, burgundy kerchief tied neatly in shape of a bow. He was standing with two friends from secondary school days, whom he had not seen since leaving Plaquemine for the University of Louisiana eleven years before.

Not agile at dance, not interested in dancing, Jean was about to begin the polka for which he had not practiced one minute— until he saw the charming girl. He felt sure she had more invitations to dance than she could possibly accept; she seemed to relish the triumph of being a belle in the presence of older, better-known young ladies. She was attracting stares of nearly every young suitor in the church hall. Later, his eyes made contact with her's on the dance floor. She gave him a quick smile.

Jean thought the decorations gave the hall the appearance of a large leafy temple. White walls were draped with evergreen. Holly swags hung overhead, and wax candles in crystal holders twinkled in the four corners, illuminating the hall softly. He smiled. The fair daughters of the sugar planter class appeared to advantage amid the fairy Christmas scene. He had never seen so many elegant young ladies in one place as they promenaded the dance floor on the arms of their escorts.

"Jean, my son, Jean. How have you been?" asked the tall, bearded priest. "It is so nice to see you up and around again."

After a fleeting look of embarrassment, Jean smiled and said, "I didn't know it was you, Father Paul. Please forgive my manners. How have you been?"

Father Paul St. Pierre, church pastor, who had celebrated Mass at Jean's christening, was a chaperone. But Jean's mind was on the beautiful girl, and soon Father Paul moved on. Jean was dizzy with infatuation. He envisioned two perfectly matched people finding each other. *She must, she must be mine, at any cost.*

A few minutes later, she waltzed within a few feet of him, and Jean felt a consuming warmth rush through him. He had felt this mysterious thrill one other time in his life.

Mon dieu, it is Marie Stephanie Dupuy!

CHAPTER 20

IN EARLY FEBRUARY, 1867, Jean traveled to New Orleans with his father, Augie, and Amèdèe. Jean knew his father needed to talk to his broker about an advance on the fall sugarcane crop, and he wanted to show Jean and his brothers Albert Desmont at work in the financial district. He knew their visit was to be a proper celebration of the family's hopeful new start after the war.

There continued to be many problems, both in financial recovery and in the unsettling, sometimes violent, threats to civilian peace in Louisiana. Still, Jean believed that it was in the best interest of Golden Ridge to familiarize him and his brothers with the business side of agriculture, which was fully as important to a successful operation as were the daily ups and downs that nature imposed; that his father expected his sons to have a good time, enjoy the luxury of a fine hotel, and the French cuisine.

Augie, Jean, and Amèdèe, though sons of a privileged class, were still country boys whose knowledge of civilian life off the plantation had been limited to their schooling when they were barely grown. So, when they disembarked the steamship late in the afternoon on the cold day, at Poydras Street Landing in New Orleans, a singular adventure began for them and their father. Jean's first trip by steamboat to enroll in the University of Louisiana flashed through his mind. They rode by carriage to Hotel Girod on Canal Street. Jean had not been to New Orleans since before the war, and he expected to see some damages of war, weeds in the streets, general ruin. But he saw a city in good repair. They were surrounded on Canal Street by bustling business, barouches in shaking hoops of black fabric, horsecars, two-seat chaises, dray wagons loaded with barrels and furniture. Men in overcoats stood under clusters of stovepipe hats; some men wore dark business suits and starched collars, discussing business and politics; other men carried canes. Jean couldn't help but think what a waste of life the war represented. And delighted with this scene, he immediately fancied himself in such a milieu.

Jean and his brothers were even more excited by Hotel Girod. The Canal Street doors, through which they entered, were marked by polished brass and gleaming glass, a fitting portal for the great lobby with its gilded ceiling and crystal chandeliers. The young men stared open-mouthed at rich decorations of brocades, oriental rugs, and heroic scenes depicted in tapestries and paintings. There was no evidence of war damage that Jean could see. *How had the Girod survived the marauding Yankees? Apparently Union occupation of the City was not without benefit.* Well, Jean was glad, for this elegance appealed to him instantly. He was in a world to which he knew he wanted access.

While his sons surveyed their surroundings, Auguste went to the lobby desk. Quickly a uniformed attendant sprang to take the Leverts' traveling bags, and all mounted the grand staircase to the second floor and their suite. Auguste smiled with the satisfaction of providing the treat for his sons, though of the three, Jean was obviously more impressed with the luxurious accommodations afforded them.

Although their rooms were less flamboyant than the lobby, they were almost as comfortable as those at Golden Ridge. By the time they had hung up their coats and washed after the long steamboat ride, a Negro porter appeared with a cloth-covered tea cart. The porter lifted the white damask cloth revealing a tray of sandwiches and a coffee service.

"Yes, indeed, boys," said Auguste, "let's have a bite, for we have an appointment at two o'clock with Albert Desmont over on Factors' Row." Jean began to pour coffee for them, and all drank and ate hungrily. They had boarded the steamboat at five in the morning in Plaquemine.

"I'm eager to see Mr. Desmont again, *Père*," said Jean. "It's been a long time since we met him at Golden Ridge, hasn't it? I learned then what an interesting man he is, and you know I was fascinated by his business."

"I know you were, son." Amèdèe passed the sandwich tray around again. "Aren't these delicious?" he said as he stood before Augie.

"They're wonderful," said Augie, with his mouth full; he peeled back a slice of French bread. "Look at this stack of thin-sliced beef. It's so spicy." He took another bite.

"Eat another sandwich, Jean," said his father, "we won't have dinner for hours. It's almost time to go to Mr. Desmont's office."

"Can we walk?" asked Amèdèe.

Auguste took out his watch. "We'd better take a carriage if I can get one quickly. We don't have time to walk."

Down on the street the Girod doorman hailed a carriage.

Jean thought business was thriving on Factors' Row, a line of unique six-story buildings that began at the corner of Carondelet and Perdido streets in the financial district, several blocks from the Girod. The name *Factors Row* appeared on a railing along the edge of the balcony above a wrought-iron cornice. The windows on each floor showed elaborate French ornamentation.

"These buildings house the middlemen," said Auguste as they entered the second building. They walked up a long flight of stairs to Albert Desmont's suite of offices. His secretary, a tall thin young woman dressed in wool, with dusky red hair and a pince-nez clipped to the bridge of her long thin nose, rose to greet them.

"Good afternoon, Mr. Levert. Please be seated. I'll tell Mr. Desmont you're here." Jean watched her back and thought of Stephanie. *Hmm. There were women and there were women.*

She reappeared. "Please come in, gentlemen."

"Auguste!"

"Albert!"

The men shook hands enthusiastically though with great dignity.

"You remember my sons."

"But of course!" Albert replied in his deep voice.

Pleasantries exchanged, Jean glanced at the commodious office as they were seated on the leather couch and chairs. He looked up at the arched fanlight window overlooking a courtyard. He watched Desmont return to his roll-top desk close to the fireplace. Perhaps Desmont preferred the freedom of space to pace in his office.

"Now, my friend," said Desmont to Auguste, with a cordiality that Jean knew was welcomed by his father. "How may I be of service?" As was his habit, Desmont's head jerked to one side after he finished.

Jean noticed Desmont had lost weight, aged since he last saw him. His high collar sat looser around his neck. His face was gaunt. No doubt the war had been hard on him. But, as Auguste began talking to the broker, he's still here. While so many sugar brokers fell to the exigencies of war in the South, Albert Desmont had survived in style from the look of his handsome offices. He had managed to survive because of his large clientele and a considerable inheritance. Jean was certain his father had wondered if his broker had cooperated with the Union occupation forces.

Auguste was reading from a list of supplies that he wanted Desmont to advance money for and ship from New Orleans. Jean was familiar with the list. It included mechanical parts for machinery in the sugarhouse as well as items for household consumption: Seven barrels of sulphur, one barrel of coal oil, five shovels, a coil of cotton rope, one cask of bottled Milwaukee beer, five gallons of lard oil, three sacks of wheat bran, two barrels of flour, olive soap, fifty pounds of chicory coffee, and twenty-five pounds of smoking tobacco.

"I'm afraid some of the supplies aren't available now and others may take longer to ship," said Albert. "But I'll do my best, of course." Desmont explained that efforts of many brokers to provide their clients with supplies after the war were difficult, because southern railroads were worn out from war use and because of the choking power of the Union naval blockade on the Mississippi.

Amèdèe and Augie sat silently side by side on the couch. Amèdèe discreetly suppressed a yawn behind his hand. Augie stared across the room at a seascape on the wall that included a many-masted ship. Jean thought his brothers did not care about this end of the sugar business; they're too immersed in the growing. It occurred to him that it was just as well, because he would not be at Golden Ridge to help much longer.

As Jean heard his father talk about the costs of necessary materials, about the risks of nature and circumstances, about interest and repayment, he was reminded of how sophisticated a planter Auguste was, and he was proud of him. Auguste handed the list to Desmont and smiled. They rose and shook hands. They had made a deal. Again.

Albert Desmont shook hands all around and bade them good afternoon.

"Come to see us when you make your calls in late summer, Albert," said Auguste cordially.

"Thank you, my friend Auguste. I look forward to that."

As they left, Jean gazed at the secretary, giving her an appreciative smile for so long that she turned pink and her pince-nez dropped from her nose to the silver filigreed pin on her shoulder.

Chapter 21

JEAN CALLED ON Stephanie Dupuy before he moved to the sugarhouse on Golden Ridge for the fall '67 grinding. He had fallen in love with her and had paid court to her through the year since the memorable Christmas dance where he had rediscovered her. With his nerves wound tight, he approached the side entrance to her plantation house at St. Gabriel. He was again reminded that it would be his last chance to see her for weeks, a gloomy thought. But before he had time to fret, the door swung open and there was Stephanie.

"Jean!" she said, her green eyes dancing. "I've been watching for you from the bay window."

His heart leaped at the sight of her. *How lovely a young thing she is, how melodious is her low soft voice.* He wanted to reach for her, but he restrained himself. He had learned that Stephanie was shy, and if he showed much ardor, she darted away.

"Steph, *ma chèrie.* May I come in?"

"Yes, of course." She stood back, swinging the door wide. "Please do come in." Her servant, behind her, moved back with Stephanie like a shadow. Jean wished she would go away. During courting, he had taken her for rides along River Road in her family's cabriolet and for nature walks, but always accompanied by one of her ubiquitous servants.

He followed Stephanie into the drawing room with its yellow walls reflecting sunlight over pale blue brocade upholstery. He thought she looked like a pale butterfly in her white summer frock. Her long blonde hair swung over her shoulders.

"Would you like coffee, Jean?"

"But certainly, *merci*."

Stephanie asked the servant to drip coffee for them, and the woman disappeared.

At last, thought the lover, as he quickly took Stephanie's hand. "My dearest Steph. How I have missed you!" He lifted her hand to his lips.

But Stephanie drew back as if alarmed. Jean raised his eyes in bafflement. He looked behind him, expecting to see another servant come in to assume guard.

"Steph! We are to be married, aren't we? Surely a man can be allowed the favor of a small kiss. Or several!" He was exasperated, but he was determined not to show it.

Stephanie gazed out the window. "We are moving too hastily, Jean." She looked about the room then back at him and smiled hesitantly, turning her head to one side most endearingly. Her timid smile told him that his touch had been sweet to her. He was about to go to her again when the servant brought in the coffee tray and began to pour. But Steph said, "Never mind, Lily, I'll pour."

Lily's head came up in surprise. She paused a second, perhaps two, and set the small silver pot back on the tray. Then she turned and walked barely across the threshold into the foyer. Jean looked after her and was disappointed to see her stay so near.

"Stephanie," said Jean, in a low tense voice. "Are we never to be alone? We must talk about our wedding plans. After tonight I shall be confined for weeks with sugar production at Golden Ridge. Then I'll be going to New Orleans in search of a position and a place to live." He again laid his hand on her arm, careful not to grip it too tightly. When he felt her tremble, he decided to take another tack. He removed his hand. He sat on the edge of the French loveseat and took the small cup of thick black coffee she had poured.

"Tell me about your Father, Steph. We have never talked about him much. I do know that you loved him very much." He smiled gently as if acknowledging the sensitivity and intimacy of the subject he had broached.

"Well," she said, taking her coffee to the matching loveseat facing Jean. "You know he died when I was a small girl. I did love him. He meant everything to me, for I had already lost my mother." She sat down and set her coffee cup on the table between them. "All the things he talked to me about were the things a father says to a very young child. We had no conversations about, well, adult things. He never talked about courting. My upbringing was always tied to the needs of the house and family. My Father was a wonderful, wonderful man. He taught me to ride my pony. I remember that."

"And what about your Mother. I've heard that in her day she was one of the handsomest women in the parish, that she turned many a head?"

"How beautiful, indeed, Mother was. But God took her from me when she was only twenty-one, after giving birth to my sister Marie Octave. I was only two years old when she died. My Father never talked much about her and I never asked him why."

"Can you talk to your grandmother?"

Stephanie seemed startled. "About what?"

"Well, about getting married and being a woman."

At that she became very shy again. Jean tried again to take her hand. "Steph, my darling, I love you . . ."

But she stood up quickly. "Oh, dear, look at the time. You must go now."

"Go? I just got here."

"But Jean, I must dress for a party my Uncle Duhamel is having for my favorite cousin, Rachel. Why don't you come to the party with me?"

"No thanks," he said. *How was he ever to get this girl to settle down?*

"I'll tell you what," she said brightly.

"What."

"Stay here and eat supper with me before you go."

"Very well, *chèrie*. Whatever you say." This was the most he could hope for tonight, on the last night he could see her for so long.

So Stephanie and Jean moved to a table in the bay window, and Maurice, an elderly house servant, brought supper to them. Lily had disappeared at last, leaving them alone. Jean sat quietly on his side of the table and they watched the red sun go down, its glittering reflections in the swirling currents of the Mississippi.

*   *   *

When Jean stepped upon the gallery at Golden Ridge later that evening, after the ferry ride across the river, he found Augie sitting there in the shadows. Jean sat down heavily beside his brother and sighed deeply.

"Is that a lover's sigh?" said Augie. "How is the fabled Stephanie Dupuy?"

"More beautiful every time I see her. I believe she loves me, though maybe not as much as I love her. Yet."

"I hope so since she's agreed to be *Madame Levert*. Have you set a date yet?"

"No, I can't get her to agree on a date. She is skittish. Still young, you know."

"Yes, she is. But you know how these French girls are raised from the cradle to the obligations of motherhood and household duties. She'll make a good wife. But, Jean, you have to think of Stephanie's life—no mother, no father since she was a tiny child. Of course, she is leery of a twenty-eight-year-old man. You may be young and dashing, but to Stephanie you are an older man." He paused. "She has probably never heard the term *facts of life*."

"Oh, yeah. I'm constantly aware of all that. She has only old Joly and her grandmother and all those Negroes. She has girl cousins, of course . . ." He stood up and stretched. "Well, I'll go up and get the rest of my things together. I'll be moving into the sugarhouse first thing in the morning."

"I don't envy you."

"I know, but I really look forward to it. It'll probably be my last time. If things go as I wish, I'll be working in New Orleans early next year. I'm going to tell Mother and Father of my wedding plans and that I plan to go to the city to look for an apartment after grinding is over." Jean walked to the front door.

Looking down the long, wide hall, he could see Eulalie sitting on the back gallery fanning herself. He walked back to bid her goodnight. He knew it might be many days before he would see her again.

"Did you see Marie Stephanie, Jean?"

Jean smiled broadly, "Yes, I did, *Mère*. Goodnight."

*   *   *

After he had moved into the sugarhouse, Jean became indifferent to sleep and rest, throwing his energy into supervising harvest and grinding—thriving under the taxing activity. He visited various sugarhouse departments, kept an eye on the steam engines, hung over the new vacuum pans to determine what the expressed cane juice promised. After working day and night, he was pleased that the power steam engines still pumped with energy—man and machine alike heedless of fatigue.

Since the end of his postwar convalescence, Jean had spent many nights from October to December keeping the plantation journal for his father, recording daily operations, describing the weather. At sixty-three, Auguste was turning over more and more daily operations to him, Augie, and Amèdèe. Sitting in his father's cramped ground-level room at the sugarhouse, Jean made his first journal entry on October 30, 1867:

> October—Rain on the 11th. North wind on the 12th.
> Through hauling wood . . . weather cool enough for
> winter clothing. Began cutting cane for processing in
> the sugarhouse. Sugarhouse thoroughly examined on
> 16th and 17th; each department underwent rigid
> repairs—the steam engine wanted several screws; the coolers

have opened their seams; the large casks were not all made;
and poor Father found that the work of leisure summer hours
now crowded into a few already too-many occupied days.
Everything was hurry and bustle . . . began grinding on 28th.
Very heavy rain on 29th and white frost on 30th. Frost so
thick it could be scooped up by the handsful at seven o'clock in
the morning.

He spent what was left of the last night of October thinking of
Stephanie before fatigue set in, forcing shut his blood-shot eyes.
He had started several letters to her but not sent any of them.

November—Began expressing juice of the cane on
the 3rd by passing it twice between rollers. Stopped
grinding on the 6th; heaviest rain seen in year on 7th,
flooding ditches and ponds. Resumed grinding on the
10th—one of the boilers leaking! Weather too cold on
the 11th to complete repairs on third boiler. Making
only four hundred pounds of sugar per day! On the
15th immense pressure brought on mill broke it asunder!
New Orleans closest place for repairs—delay in
grinding, as the invalid roller is packed on boat. Father
paces, watching flatboat leave Plaquemine wharf for
the city . . . by 25th, expressed juice strained into vessels
heated at 140 degrees F, when clarified by application of
lime. Cane juice reduced by evaporation to syrup—
boiled in vacuum pans. Stopped grinding on Sunday, as
custom . . . six hundred pounds of sugar made on the
28th: Syrup reached concentration by the 30th, drawn
off into vessels and remained 'til granulation.

Jean knew the sugarhouse, 570 feet long by 75 feet wide and
35 feet high from floor to ceiling, was the most important structure
on Golden Ridge. He'd always been impressed by its size, and its
elaborate workmanship made it appear to be more for ornamental
display than for practical use. His father spent twenty thousand

dollars after the war to repair the damage wrought by Yankee marauders. Auguste had spent thousands every year, in fact, with northern and western artisans, paying them to improve upon the machinery and mill used to crystallize sugar: After the cane juice was extracted from the stalks, it ran through gutters into receivers in the purgery, a place for vacuum pans and where impurities in the juice were removed. Then the juice, boiled to the point of crystallization, went into coolers in the cooler room, and from the coolers to the purgery where the molasses was drained from the sugar. From the purgery, it came out as unrefined brown raw sugar.

Jean knew the mill, vacuum pans, wagons, steam engines, and wrought-iron molds mostly were produced in the North. He understood that hundreds of families in Louisiana depended on these artisans for their living as much as his father did for the successful cultivation of his crop.

> *December—Finished cutting cane on the 4th. Began plowing on 7th. Weather little warmer. On 8th stopped grinding, having made three thousand pounds of sugar! Twenty-three acres of cane yielding more than ten thousand pounds. First all-day rain on 9th . . . roads and fields in bad condition. Rain again on 10th . . . before daybreak, on 12th, realized sixty gallons of molasses per hogshead of sugar produced . . . sugar now raw and brown—unrefined . . . raw sugar improved by filtering through animal black on 13th and 14th, same way liquors are "fined." Cloudy on 15th and 16th. Cleaned ditches on 19th . . . sold and shipped all the sugar made on 20th. Crop yielded one hundred fifteen hogsheads, selling at eight cents a pound; with molasses, total was twenty-two thousand . . . expenses for year: Nine thousand sixty-eight, leaving profit of little more than twelve thousand.*

For the first time since he began making entries in his father's journal, Jean added a postscript:

> The novelty of sugar-making passed away in time, for the whole affair assumed a business sameness. Each person, by experience, became familiar with his duty and things continued on with a nice smoothness . . . I moved back into the Big House permanently . . . mules now pretty worked down from hauling thousands of pounds of cane stalks from the fields to the sugarhouse for grinding. The hired labor calculated when the finish will come, and as January approached, weather became unsettled; rain fell hard and roads badly cut up . . . the last load of stalks, as it was carried to the mill, was greeted with wild satisfaction!

I agonized for weeks over my decision to leave Golden Ridge and my family and move to New Orleans, leaving my Father without his best help in the cane fields. But I knew in order to take advantage of the opportunities for personal enrichment and investment of my resources, I had little choice. I figured the Big City was the best place for me to realize my dreams of becoming a shrewd, accomplished sugar broker like Albert Desmont, controlling the fortunes and destinies of planters, and of becoming a successful planter and plantation owner like my Father. I was fortunate to find a position with a reputable brokerage firm in the City, and I know I will be an asset to this firm, that the experience will help me realize my dreams, dreams I've had since boyhood growing up on Golden Ridge and learning about farming from my Father.

Jean Baptiste Levert
December 1867

CHAPTER 22

IN LATE DECEMBER, after grinding was completed, Jean traveled to New Orleans to look for an apartment. Without much difficulty he found one in the *Vieux Carré*, a brick building with floor length windows on a balcony overlooking Royal Street. The courtyard, which was large enough to admit a barouche, captivated him. A graceful stair curved up to a balcony that bordered two sides of the courtyard. There was a profusion of elegant ironwork—acorns and oak leaves. He entered and was pleased to find four ample rooms, well lighted by the large windows.

"How much is the rent?" Jean asked the flirtatious, attractive French landlady. He noticed her looking him over as intently as if she planned to paint his portrait.

"Twelve dollars a month, sir," she said. She had large brown eyes and dark hair held back by a Spanish-style comb. He watched her move about the apartment in her dark dress that did not hide her voluptuous figure. She agreed that Jean could move in on December 28.

Jean paid her, bowed, and stepped out onto Royal. He felt that he was somehow escaping.

Amid the clop-clop of hooves, rumble of heavy wheels on cobblestones, and vendors' melodious chants as they hawked their produce, Jean smiled contentedly. He recalled his visit with University of Louisiana students to a slave auction nine years before, a few doors down the street. Well, all that was past.

After a brief stop for coffee and beignets at Cafe du Monde in the French Quarter, he returned to his hotel, a more modest accommodation than Hotel Girod, he thought. In the room he thought of writing to Stephanie, but realized that he would likely see her before she could get the letter. So, feeling somewhat smug over the state of his business affairs, he lay down on the bed and pictured in his mind what Harry Groeble's sign on the office building would say:

Harry Groeble   J. B. Levert
Harry Groeble & Company
Cotton Factors and Sugar Brokers and
Commission Merchants
No. 65 Magazine Street, New Orleans

Earlier in December, after two trips to the City and some help from Albert Desmont and his father, Jean had found a promising position with Harry Groeble & Co., a highly respected brokerage firm on Magazine Street in uptown New Orleans.

"I know I'll be losing an unusually capable assistant, but I did help you get the job," his father had told him, after reading the letter announcing Jean's hiring effective the first of the year. "I think this is a good opportunity; it'll be great experience. And your Mother is rejoicing with me, although she's a bit sad that you'll be leaving home. New Orleans after all is not far away and we shall see you often."

Groeble had, in fact, surprised Jean at the interview. He asked him few questions about his education or his knowledge of sugar growing and manufacturing. He was interested only in his war experiences. He had pictured his boss as a big man, someone like his father; he figured he was forty-five, forty-six. He wore a dark business suit that needed pressing, a pince-nez, and seemed somewhat preoccupied.

He had told Groeble at the interview: "Like most Southerners, I was carried along on the wave of patriotism that swept over the state. But patriotism started to decline at home and in the Rebel armies after the first year. I thought the war would last a year, at most, and that if I didn't get to the front at once, the fighting would end before I had a chance to take part.

"After the first year, my unit, the First Louisiana Cavalry, joined the Army of Tennessee. And we seemed to be fighting all the time, all over Tennessee and Kentucky, until I was captured while on a special expedition . . . I was in some of the big battles, too, such as Shiloh, Perryville, Murfreesboro, and I came close to being killed many times."

Jean thought Harry had been pleasant enough, and he assumed that the recommendations of Albert Desmont and the word of Auguste Levert, whose reputation as a major planter was well known, were enough. Jean had no doubts that he'd be a major asset to Harry Groeble's company. He had a natural confidence, as if he were sure enough of himself and his beliefs that he had no need to thrust them upon anyone else. He was now even more impatient to be married to Stephanie and to have her as his wife in New Orleans.

* * *

Jean returned to Plaquemine on a Saturday for a last weekend visit with Stephanie and his parents before beginning work. Stephanie and Jean attended a dance that night at the Catholic church in St. Gabriel. They spent most of their time together talking of their wedding plans, about their life together. He knew she wanted to be married, too, and he had already made up his mind about the kind of house he wanted to live in with Stephanie. .

"We are going to live in a two-story house in New Orleans, chèrie, with a big open fireplace, young trees, and roses growing at all the windows—peeping in to see how happy we are," Jean said, as they strolled along the river near tall golden cane stalks behind the plantation house.

"Ah, but how I wish we had the house now," replied Steph.

Jean, tightening his arm around her, said, "But we will. Very soon, too."

"How soon?"

"What would you say to later this year? I am doing well with Harry Groeble & Co. and I'll get a raise in salary soon—a big one. That's what I came to tell you this weekend."

Stephanie smiled. The hem of her skirt brushed his shoe as they walked. "How wonderful, Jean. I'm so proud of you." But when Jean began to talk of a wedding date, possibly before the end of the year, she demurred. "Oh, Jean, I don't know. I do love you, dear. But we cannot order everything as we please. We cannot rush these things."

"We most certainly can, Steph," he insisted. "No one can interfere now. You are eighteen and your own mistress. You are of age to do of your own free will without interference. What is to prevent our going to the priest after we clean up some of your family affairs, as soon as I can find and furnish that big white house?"

He picked up small rocks on the bank and began to toss them, watching them skip over the river's surface. *What's got into this girl? One moment she is enthusiastic, the next she seems frightened.* Then he remembered something he thought that might help convince her. "It might interest you that I received the kindest letter from Mr. Henry Browne, your new legal guardian, on your behalf. He commented when I asked him for your hand in marriage: 'It affords me great pleasure . . . I know of no one to whom her future could be more safely entrusted than to yourself.'"

Jean asked her if she wanted a piece of cane from the fields; she said, "Yes." He jumped over the ditch and crossed a couple of rows until he found what he thought was a good stalk, then came back to where she was waiting for him. He sliced off the last two joints and threw them into the ditch; he didn't think they looked sweet enough. Jean peeled the third joint and tasted it—*very good.* He cut off a round and gave it to Stephanie. She chewed it, the juice running down her chin the way it would a small child's. Jean cut off a round for himself and chewed it—*very soft, very sweet.* They chewed cane stalks and walked along the river for at least half a mile.

Jean noticed that Stephanie still was uncomfortable so he walked her back home to the side entrance of the plantation she preferred when they courted. He took her two hands in his, in farewell, and whispered: "Goodnight, tomorrow is Sunday. I'll come at one o'clock and we can have luncheon together before I return to the city. Perhaps we can go for a horseback ride and then go . . ."

Stephanie stopped him. "No, *mon cher*, don't come tomorrow. I want to rest. Besides, I have work to do and I cannot spare time for you in the afternoon."

Jean's face showed how disappointed and confused he was. Why? He wondered if she was unsure of his love for her. Or could it be their age differences. Jean knew that in Stephanie's innocent mind, he was a man of the world. He only said: "I am very sorry I cannot come tomorrow afternoon. But if it will make you feel bad, I should be a brute to complain."

She went through the door and Jean waited until one of the house servants closed the door. It was all right. But, oh, how many weary hours, days, even weeks, before he could see her again. If she had doubts . . . He stood at the entrance for a few minutes after the servant bolted the door. He had no doubts.

He had never doubted Stephanie was his woman. The seed had been planted deeply where he was concerned. With other girls he felt no more than passing physical attraction. He thought of Annie Blanton occasionally but never as someone with whom to spend the rest of his life.

Jean left the house to catch the ferry back to Plaquemine, there to await the lonely steamboat ride back to New Orleans.

*   *   *

His face the color of bleach, Jean Baptiste rushed into Harry Groeble's office on Monday afternoon.

"Mr. Groeble, sir, I'm ruined, I'm a ruined man!" He unrolled a paper while he spoke. "The sheriff of Iberville Parish was just in my office and served this claim on me. It's for a security debt. This is all I need now in my life, after starting a new job!"

"What on earth are you talking about, Jean?" Groeble drew his dark eyebrows together in an expression of puzzlement. With a small mouth and thinning brown hair parted in the middle, he said, "What could be so bad as to render you a ruined man? What's this sheriff business?"

"I'll try to explain as best I can, Mr. Groeble." He told his boss that a trusted friend, Oscar Babin's older brother, Ethan, asked Jean to put his name as security on some bank papers for a thousand dollars—to help the young sugar grower from White Castle get back on his feet. Jean saw no danger in helping Ethan, whom he had met at war's end, so he signed. Confident of his friend's honor, he gave the act no more thought.

"Then the sheriff shows up, scares the wits out of me," Jean said. "I am determined to pay back every dollar. But to do that I need time."

Groeble leaned forward close to Jean's ear, as if ready to tell him a secret. "I would like to offer some financial aid if I may, Jean. What are we talking about? How much would you need?"

Jean politely refused the generous offer. He was against borrowing from his boss.

"I realize this may not be the right course, but have you given any thought to taking the benefit of the bankruptcy law?" asked Harry. "I realize that this would not be a light step to take."

"No," Jean said. "I allowed this to happen, and I must take on the burden of repaying it." He shook his head. "Never again, never, never."

"Well, son, if you will not accept any financial help, surely you'll accept my invitation to join my family and me for dinner this Friday. I've been meaning to have you in our home since you joined the firm. Perhaps we can discuss your predicament further if you like. You may even change your mind about my offer to help."

"I'd be honored, Mr. Groeble," replied Jean, with a smile. "I look forward to meeting your family."

After Jean left Groeble's office, he spent the rest of the afternoon staring out of his office window. The betrayed trust was the sourest drop in his cup, he thought, but he would not let it get him down. He realized he might have to give up most of the commission money he would earn for a time, royalties from his land properties, too. But the one thing he couldn't bear was the thought of him and Stephanie being deprived of comforts, particularly the white house they dreamed of. He was determined to tell her nothing until the whole matter was settled. Now he was certain of one thing: He had learned his lesson.

Later that evening, after he returned to his apartment, his dejection quickly went away when on the stairway his landlady handed him a letter addressed in French.

Iberville Parish   *January 6, 1868*

My dear Jean—

I have been waiting impatiently for a letter from you and I have been pleasantly surprised in seeing the magnificent presents that you have kindly sent to me. I congratulate you on your good taste. God is too good to punish two hearts which long for each other and which nevertheless their happiness he won't forget. Since your departure a few days ago, despite our apparent disagreement, I have died of boredom and the hope of seeing you soon supports me with a little patience. It seems impossible to refuse you of anything that you ask of me. Mr. Henry Browne has received your most recent letter and quickly passed it on to me. Thank you so much for the presents.

Devotedly yours,
Stephanie

Jean quickly began a letter to Stephanie:

My beloved Steph—

Here I am far from you, chère amie, but near in heart. I am miserable in happiness; it is bliss, indeed, to feel that you will be mine, mine in the eyes of God! Yet, I am miserable, miserable! Because I cannot be with you. I miss you, if possible, more than the first time. I thank Him for giving me such an angel of Virtue and Goodness to make my happiness in this world. My dear Stephanie, I wish you could concur with me in that there is no plausible reason for postponing the consummation of our nuptials till September this year . . . besides, I would like to take you traveling this summer, and September is too near the opening of the business season to think of it then. Would not the 17th of August be equally convenient to you? I do hope so! I have decided to send you the ring, the harbringer of all our cherished hopes. I can see a sweet expression on your countenance. I can see you in the parlor entertaining a few selected friends with grace. I can see you presiding as head of the table, the proudest, happiest, dearest little wife on earth.

*   *   *

On Friday afternoon, Jean left his office about four, caught the mule-drawn St. Charles Avenue streetcar, and got off at Canal and Decatur streets. Wanting some exercise and to think, he walked the remaining several blocks to the Groebles' residence in the upper Pontalba apartment building in the French Quarter.

Steph's tired of courting, mainly on dance floors and seldom being alone with me. I know she is. I'm tired of her aunts and uncles questioning me about my family and financial and social assets; it annoys me like hell . . . then they want to know about my ancestors . . . family skeletons. And that damn cousin of Steph's, Emilie Dupuy, thinks I'm after Steph's money, she's trying to drive a wedge between us. I know Grandmother Dupuy thinks our match is one of deep affection and devotion. I'll never forget what Steph told Emilie when she had doubts about being in our wedding, because of my motives: "Do as you please, cousin, but I would rather marry a good man, a man of mind, with a hope and ambition and bright prospects ahead for position, fame and power, than to marry all the gold in the world."

Upon arrival, Jean glanced upward at Harry's second-story, corner balcony that overlooked Jackson Square before climbing the long stairs. He admired the long windows, the chimneys and doors repeated in a line on both levels. Two identical buildings, the upper and lower Pontalbas, each a row of sixteen connected, brick sections, filled an entire block on either side of the square. The apartments had iron columns that supported wrought-iron balconies. A Negro maid answered the doorbell.

"Good evening, I'm Jean Levert." He handed her his topcoat. "Would you please announce me to Mr. and Mrs. Groeble."

Harry's wife greeted Jean, and led him to a long sofa where they sat down. The table in front of the sofa was covered with New Orleans newspapers and business publications. Barely five feet tall, Jean thought Mrs. Groeble was striking in a long green evening dress with sparkling jewelry at her neck and wrists. "It's so nice to meet you, Mr. Levert," she said softly. "I've heard many kind things about you from Mr. Groeble."

Then Harry came in briskly, kissed his wife on the cheek, shook Jean's hand, and took a seat in a wing chair opposite them. He noticed his boss still wore the dark-vested, loose-fitting business suit he had on at the office.

"I am admiring your lovely apartment, the many antique pieces," Jean said.

"Thank you, we enjoy it, it serves us well, plenty of room. We thought about buying in the Garden District uptown, but wanted to stay close to the French Quarter, the opera house, antique shops, restaurants."

Jean's financial predicament never came up. The three of them enjoyed a meal of roast beef, assorted vegetables, yams, and vanilla ice cream, Jean's favorite flavor.

In the living room for a demitasse and cigar later, Jean mentioned the Pontalbas. "I've admired them since I moved to the city. But until now I've never been in one. They don't appear to be very old."

"They aren't, Jean," replied Harry. "They were built about fifteen or sixteen years ago by Micaela, the Baroness Pontalba, a famous

person, as you may know. First apartments of their kind in the
United States, I believe."

"I am especially interested in them, sir. I learned only recently
from the young lady I'm courting, Stephanie Dupuy of St. Gabriel,
and her guardian, that Stephanie is distantly related to the baroness
on her father's side of the family. Stephanie's a descendant of wealthy
land owners and sugar farmers from Grenoble, France."

Harry then gave him a brief history of the apartments: The
baroness's father, Don Andres Almonester y Roxas, New Orleans'
first great benefactor, had built several buildings that flank St. Louis
Cathedral on Jackson Square, including the Cabildo, home of the
Spanish government that controlled the Louisiana Territory in the
1700s. Not to be outdone by her father, the baroness later received
permission from the City to build other buildings, equally
imposing, on the square, on property that she had inherited. With
the Pontalbas, she helped restore the *Place d'Armes* to its former
grandeur as the heart of the French Quarter.

"I love to tell this bit of background," he said.

CHAPTER 23

AS RAIN PELTED the roof of the wooden Catholic church at St. Gabriel, Marie Stephanie Dupuy and Jean Baptiste Levert took their marriage vows on Saturday, August 17, 1868. In making their final and somewhat hurried plans because they were so long setting the date, the couple made sure that there would be minimal fuss. Only their families and closest friends attended—twenty-six guests in all. When the couple stood before Father Paul St. Pierre, dressed in a floor-length white linen alb with tapered sleeves, Stephanie was eighteen and Jean was one month away from his twenty-ninth birthday.

Jean was fully aware that it was not altogether the kind of wedding Stephanie might have dreamed of, for she missed the presence of a mother and her well-remembered father. She would have had them there to see her become Mrs. Jean Baptiste Levert.

He thought the small church near the levee, which was built by exiled Acadians who had settled the river town between 1765 and 1775, was well adapted to such an occasion, especially since it was there he had rediscovered her at the Christmas dance. Green smilax and white amaryllis, Shasta daisies, and ginger lilies were arranged in almost every available space, the scent of the ginger lilies perfuming the air. Stephanie looked stunning, thought Jean, in the white silk brocade-and-beaded dress her mother had worn at her wedding almost twenty years earlier. A wreath of fresh orange blossoms and white rosebuds confined her simple tulle veil.

Jean's blunt fingers fumbled with the ring, a ruby mounted in a yellow-gold setting, engraved *My Love to You Is Eternal*. As he slipped the ring onto Stephanie's finger, he saw a sense of fulfillment in her face.

Jean overheard some members of the Dupuy family saying to each other: "Stephanie is scoffing at her family traditions by committing herself to a man of the world . . ." *How absurd.* Jean had assured his family and her's that he fell in love with Stephanie the first time he saw her when she was only twelve, and he was home without leave from his cavalry unit during the war. He had convinced the Dupuys that his family was delighted with their new daughter-in-law.

After the ceremony the couple, along with his parents and witnesses, signed the church register and hurried through the rain to carriages that took them to St. Gabriel Plantation for the wedding tea. Sally and Maurice served food from the long dining table, which was covered with a white linen cloth embroidered in turtledove design; and the cake was still warm when the bride and groom cut the first slices.

Stephanie and Jean slipped away from the party in the afternoon after final toasts, and Maurice drove them to catch the ferry to Plaquemine, where they boarded the steamboat *Belize* and headed downriver to New Orleans. As they floated down the Mississippi aboard the steamer, oblivious of the rain pounding the decks, their courtship was crowned by the delight they found in each other.

CHAPTER 24

HIS MIND FILLED with hopes and ambitions to make a success of his responsible assignment, Jean boarded a steamship in New Orleans for the eight-hundred mile, three-day journey upriver to St. Louis, Missouri, the second trip for his firm to the old city in the three years since his marriage to Stephanie. The voyage against the Mississippi's redoubtable currents was arduous and exhausting to him. Aside from its economic lure, Jean liked St. Louis, for it reminded him of New Orleans. It was settled in 1764 as a fur center and it was French. As a river city and hub for shipping by water and rail, St. Louis was a vital center of commerce.

Harry Groeble had sent Jean to meet the sugar merchant, William Clarke, one of the company's most important clients. Although Stephanie wanted him given more responsibilities and improve his capabilities as a broker, Jean knew that she dreaded his long absence, particularly now since Marie Aloysia, their twenty-month-old daughter, was sick with a cold. The night after his arrival in St. Louis Jean wrote to Stephanie:

January 28, 1871

Beloved wife, I have been extremely busy with this fascinating assignment, yet I cannot refrain from writing a few words to you tonight, if only to drive away the depression. Yesterday I would have told you I liked St. Louis. Today, I am sick of it because you are not here. Mr. William Clarke took me "on chance" this morning,

*where I formed the acquaintance of some of the leading
commission merchants from this place. "On chance"
means mercantile association where all business of
consequence is transacted. In other words, the
marketplace. There you meet hundreds of men in pursuit
of their interests, representing their merchandise. The
weather continues very disagreeable, dreadfully cold
and windy. Clarke is a thorough gentleman, friendly
toward me. He has invited me to his home tomorrow
afternoon. Perhaps I shall write more of that tomorrow.
I would like to hear that you and Aloysia are well. Let me
press you to my heart and say goodnight! Your Jean.*

Jean had felt much sympathy for Stephanie having to go back
home to St. Gabriel Plantation to live after their marriage and
romantic honeymoon on the steamer and at Hotel Girod. But he
had insisted that his French Quarter apartment was not a suitable
place for his wife, and that he needed time to build up his income
during his continued apprenticeship at Harry Groeble & Co.; he
wanted to buy their dream house. As his apprenticeship
progressed, he had traveled increasingly out of the City
interviewing sugar growers throughout southwest Louisiana,
lending money, and on the alert for purchases from those whose
mortgages had ruined the owners beyond saving.

He was pleased that Stephanie had settled in at St. Gabriel and
resolved to be patient. She had told Jean before they married that
she would be content to live on his income, mainly in response
to her cousin Emilie's insinuations that Jean was interested only
in her money; the couple was not likely to be in want living on
Jean's annual income, which was a thousand dollars and
commissions, plus an income from land investments that his
father had given to him and his brothers after the war.

Mr. Henry Browne, who had been administrator of her father's
succession since the death of Louis Joly before her wedding, had
provided Stephanie with an inventory of her properties made at

the time of her father's murder; he had estimated their value to be nearly one hundred thousand dollars. Jean had learned from Browne that her holdings were now worth significantly more. Willow Glen Plantation, an eight-hundred-acre sugar estate near the Dupuy place, had been reclaimed from Henry Biegel at a recent foreclosure sale.

She had found herself pregnant soon after her marriage, and she and Jean were extremely happy by the birth of Aloysia exactly nine months after the honeymoon voyage down the Mississippi on that rain-drenched and romantic night. Jean was pleased that his wife named the baby girl after her mother. Jean's mother sent Sally from Golden Ridge, a freed Negro who had chosen to remain with Eulalie after the war, to assist Stephanie and serve as Aloysia's mammy, for Sally loved Aloysia and was a great help to Stephanie.

Jean loved his baby daughter and showed a father's pride in her, but he realized that he did not have the enthusiasm for babies that she had. On visits home he was still more eager to be with Stephanie or to go across the river to talk of land deals with his father.

* * *

Jean rang the doorbell of William Clarke's suburban home, a tudor-style mansion, on the afternoon of January 29. A butler admitted him, took his wraps, and announced him at the door of Clarke's study. The merchant, dressed in corduroy trousers and soft suede jacket, was standing at a large bay window watching the winter shadows dance over the broad lawn.

Stout with bushy hair and eyebrows, Clarke turned to welcome Jean, taking his hand in a firm handshake. Immediately Jean was struck by the man's brilliant blue eyes. He felt assured that Clarke had got over his initial doubts based on Jean's youth and his experience. Used to dealing with the more mature Harry Groeble, the principal of the company, Jean sensed that the gentleman was impressed with his significant background in all phases of the sugar business, with the fact that his father had been a planter all his life, his grandfather as well, and that Jean was brought up in a sugar atmosphere.

"Good afternoon, Jean." Clarke smiled and motioned toward the lawn edged with birch trees. Jean noticed a woman galloping a horse in a circle over an expanse of wintry grass. Though dressed warmly, she was stylishly turned out in her habit, including hat and close-fitting veil. When she came by the window where they stood, William waved to her. Jean was stunned by her beauty and her youth; he had never observed a more graceful horsewoman. She waved back and flashed white teeth in her smile.

"I must say she is a spirited young rider," said Jean.

"Yes," said William. "She is my wife."

Silently, Jean thanked God that he had not asked if she were his daughter. When she did not reappear at the large window, the men sat down near the fireplace and began to discuss the business of buying and selling sugar and some back payments that Clarke owed Jean's firm.

Soon there was a tap at the door and the rider came in. "Am I interrupting?" she asked. Jean tried not to stare at her stunning beauty and perfection of her tailored clothes. Her heavy jacket and hat now gone, she appeared elegant and self-possessed.

Both men rose at once. "Adelaide, may I present Mr. Jean Baptiste Levert of New Orleans." Clarke rolled off the French names with a special flair. Jean saw her smile brighten when she heard his somewhat exotic name. He bent slightly over her proffered hand. He felt himself transfixed.

*   *   *

Soon after Jean returned to his hotel in Gas Light Square, the section that reminded him of the French Quarter, he received a telegram from Stephanie. Their little Aloysia's cold had worsened. She was dead. Dazed, Jean immediately penciled a reply: *Leaving here immediately STOP Am grieved beyond words STOP I love you STOP Jean Baptiste Levert.*

Almost crazed with shock, he asked the hotel manager to book passage for him to New Orleans on the next departing steamer. But there was much ice on the river, and no passage could be granted for twenty-four hours at best. Jean notified William Clarke; he eschewed Clarke's offers of help. There was no help. Jean was beset with guilt, for being so far away when his beloved Stephanie, still weak from the delivery of their second baby, a son, in December, was in such grievous trouble. *If I had been with her I might have made a difference. Somehow, I'm always gone when she needs me. I'm too seldom at her side, traveling to St. Louis, Chicago, anywhere to pursue this obsession of mine.*

In grief, he began to pace in the hotel room, then sat on the bed. He put his face into his hands and mumbled, "Oh, my poor darling baby. Gone. The person in all the world I'd have laid down my life for." He rose and resumed his march back and forth, his mind keeping step and, like his pacing, leading nowhere. He wiped more tears from his cheeks. Finally, he lay down on the bed and tried to sleep, but only stared blankly into the darkness for the rest of the night.

After more than a day's delay, he finally boarded a steamer in freezing rain and snow and headed south. After three more tortuous days and nights, he stepped off the boat at the Plaquemine wharf. After crossing the river by ferry, Jean paid the hired hack at the gate; later he burst into the side entrance of St. Gabriel Plantation house, where he clasped poor Stephanie sobbing in his arms. By now he felt more composed, able to face her, to beg her forgiveness. But he had been delayed too long. Aloysia had been buried that afternoon in the cold, wet cemetery at St. Gabriel church.

Now, he tried to comfort his wife, stroking her beautiful hair and kissing her streaming cheeks. He could hear Sally and Maurice moaning and weeping somewhere in the Big House.

Chapter 25

FINALLY, THE DAY of departure had come, and Stephanie Dupuy took her eight-month-old son Albert Octave to board the Texas & Pacific train for the overnight trip to New Orleans. Her servant Sally stepped up behind her into the carriage, and Maurice drove them to the riverside in the village of St. Gabriel, where they boarded the ferry to cross the river to Plaquemine. Sally carried Albert and Stephanie carried her large handbag filled with baby supplies. Maurice followed them up the steps into the wooden train car with a heavy basket packed with chicken, fresh-baked bread, boiled potatoes, and coconut cake. By the time they were settled in their first-class accommodations, it was after noon. Stephanie held Albert in a standing position at the window so he could wave to the people on the Plaquemine depot platform, as the train hissed great puffs of steam and the engineer blew the screechy whistle.

As the train began to move, they waved to Maurice, who had returned to his driver's seat on the carriage and was lifting his hat up and down on his head, his eyes glistening. Stephanie smiled and waved Albert's tiny hand to Maurice until the servant disappeared from view. She and Sally and the baby rode in silence as the sun went down.

Jean had told Stephanie that it was not going to be an easy move, because she had to select furniture that she wished to move to the new house that Jean had purchased for them at 1530 Third Street. Then she had to arrange for it to be shipped downriver a month ahead of herself, so that Jean could have it in place by the time she and their son arrived. Stephanie had sorted and packed all of her clothes, linens, and her baby's clothes; then she dealt with saying goodbye to her beloved *Grand-mère Dupuy* and the house servants whom she was leaving behind. As her last act she visited the grave of her baby daughter, Aloysia, in the St. Gabriel church cemetery. As Jean had requested, Stephanie had remained at St. Gabriel plantation house for three years after their marriage.

The train rattled through the Louisiana swampland, occasionally blowing its lonesome whistle into the black night. Stephanie was disappointed in the amount of time Jean was able to spend with her and his baby; Jean understood her disappointment. His absence when Aloysia died had hurt her deeply, more especially because the infant was buried by the time he got home to her. But he knew the circumstances caused fully as much pain for him as they did Stephanie.

Nevertheless, Jean was aware the marriage they had entered into with such passion had become quite another relationship, that they had been together very little as man and wife. Jean knew his work as a broker was the culprit, for it presented a routine of traveling a circuit that not only kept him on the rails and in carriages throughout Louisiana, but also to St. Louis, Chicago, Memphis, and other cities. When he settled down for a few days, it had been more likely in his French Quarter apartment than in St. Gabriel plantation house.

Stephanie and Sally passed the baby back and forth between them through the night on the train, sometimes laying him down on the seat beside them to sleep to the rocking rhythm caused by the undulating roadbed.

Late the next morning of September 19, the train pulled into the depot at Annunciation Street. As Jean had instructed Stephanie, Albert, and Sally remained in their seats until most of the passengers were off. Then Jean came aboard with a porter to handle all their luggage. Jean kissed his wife and took his son from her arms, and with the silent Sally they left the train and climbed aboard the new four-seat carriage that Jean had recently purchased. Steph looked it over admiringly and said to Jean, "Yes—yes, we must have a carriage, a large barn for the horses and a carriagehouse."

The horses' hooves clop-clopped smartly as they rode out St. Charles Avenue, Jean talking about the handsome houses that were being built far out beyond Canal. Everything looked lovely to them in the September air. Soon they turned left off the avenue onto Third Street, then the carriage stopped before a lovely, white, two-story house. Stephanie stood up and gazed at the house and lawn. "I love it, Jean, I love it."

"I'm glad, *ma chèrie*. So do I." He spoke to the new driver: "Drive around to the back, Daniels, and put Mrs. Levert's things into the big bedroom."

"Yes, Mister Levert," said Daniels, and he lifted his cap. Holding a long cigar between his teeth, he bowed and smiled as the four passengers walked up the steps to their new home.

*　　*　　*

Stephanie, already two months pregnant with their third child, woke late after her first night in her New Orleans home. She stretched her body on the silky sheets and slid her hand to Jean's side of the bed. She felt the hollow in his pillow, where his head had finally fallen last night. Jean had left at dawn for the office, his custom. They had made love and talked of their future and made love again. They had fallen asleep with no doubts that they would lead a charmed life in New Orleans.

Stephanie sat up to look at the Dresden clock on the marble mantel, one of many gifts Jean had brought to her during their courtship. Daniels had helped hang the silk draperies and tassels that covered the large front windows of the spacious room. Jean had seen to getting his wife's own elegant furnishings well placed. Nothing, he had reported upon their safe arrival, had been damaged. Or stolen, he'd added, which was remarkable considering the lawlessness rampant in postwar New Orleans.

Eleven o'clock! She got out of bed and hurried to the bath to do her toilette. She hummed as she brushed her blonde hair and fastened it back with a green satin ribbon. After she dressed in one of her frocks, she surveyed herself in the long mirror in the bedroom. Though only twenty-one, Jean knew that his wife was ready to be welcomed as the newest resident in the Garden District, that she had waited a long time to assume the role of mistress of her new home by his side. She didn't have servants to look after her in ways that she was used to, but she had been reared by her aristocratic *Grand-mère Dupuy* to be a gracious hostess. Her household was provided with appropriate and elegant appointments—her silver, fine French china, European glass, and linens that she took for granted but fully appreciated.

Jean had decided to settle in the Garden District because he wanted to participate in its expansion and because of the opportunities it offered for investment. The district was the residential section of the City's American colony, with crisply painted Greek revival and white wooden houses, all in stark contrast to the brick French Quarter houses inhabited mainly by descendants of French and Spanish settlers, the Creoles.

Stephanie smiled at her image in the mirror, then went downstairs to find her son. She found Albert laughing as Sally danced him around the kitchen, but when Stephanie put her arms out to him he eagerly leaned into her warm embrace. She hugged him and continued the dance toward the pantry and into the dining room, where they circled the table and laughed together.

Sally followed them and handed an envelope to Stephanie, a message from Jean saying that he would be detained at the office too late to have supper with her, their first real supper in their new home. Stephanie sighed with disappointment; Jean knew she would be disappointed. She resolved to wait up for him no matter how late he was. But today she planned to hire a cook, a Negro woman who could prepare their meals and serve them and also do some of the housework.

She found Daniels in the lot behind the carriagehouse-barn brushing and currying the horses. "Daniels," she ventured.

"Yes, Madam. Good mornin, Madam." Bow-legged, he smiled through cigar smoke and removed his cap. She asked his help in locating a cook and housekeeper. "Someone clean and honest," she added.

"Well, Mister Levert, he done mention that to me, and I tell him my wife Vic just about fit your need. He think you might want us to move in above this carriagehouse. He not tell that to you?"

"No, he didn't, but that sounds like an ideal arrangement. I'd like for Vic to come and talk to me right away. Bless Jean, he thought of everything, but I guess he just forgot to tell me last night." She smiled to herself. "I must see to furnishing the room."

"Madam Levert, Vic never stole nothin in her life, I reckon. She be here early in the mornin. She want to work for you all bad. We don't have chilrens now, and we can moves right in. Thank you, Madam."

For the rest of the day Stephanie played with Albert and sorted small items to be stored in their proper chests and closets. That night she and Sally ate smoked ham and cake from St. Gabriel that had been in the basket they brought on the train. Tomorrow she planned to ask Daniels to take her to the uptown produce market around the corner on Prytania Street, where she could lay in a stock of fresh foods.

She brought her petit point bell pull into the drawing room and turned up the lamp. She opened the draperies before she settled down to do her needlework and wait for Jean. It was still daylight. A horse and rider passed their home, and at such a stately gait that they stirred up scarcely any dust; there were no carriages or other conveyances. Two elderly ladies strolled by carrying parasols, shading themselves against the sun that had sunk low. She kept an eye on the grandfather clock that had been her father's.

Soon after the clock struck nine, a barouche stopped before the front gate, and Jean was soon letting himself in at the front door.

"*Chèrie!* What are you doing up so late? And down here all alone in this big house!" He clasped her to him.

"I saved you some ham, and we have wonderful cake."

"But darling, I have eaten. We ate this wonderful filet of snapper, with shrimp and sautéed mushrooms, at Antoine's where we had our meeting. You shouldn't have bothered, and you should be in bed. You'll have to get used to my long hours."

"I sat here hoping to see some neighbors. I saw two nice-looking ladies walking past at about seven o'clock."

"What? Ladies out on the streets of New Orleans so late? They are very foolish indeed. Our streets are no longer safe. Promise me you will not leave this house without Daniels when I am not home."

He put his arm around her waist, and as he guided her to their room, he said, "Our rotten black state government, the corrupt carpetbag policies of our incumbent Governor Warmoth, and the despicable Yankees have all destroyed the peace and calm of our city. Unless something's done soon to overthrow Warmoth's policies and the Negro presence in state politics, our white citizens will have no freedom left."

Chapter 26

. . . Mistress Delphine Daigle, widow of Isadore Daigle of West Baton Rouge Parish . . . for the purpose of cultivating and working a certain plantation . . . of planting, gathering and selling the crop thereof requiring advances of money in the amount of ten thousand dollars, has applied to Harry Groeble & Co., commission merchant of New Orleans, which has consented to make the said advances . . .

FEELING INFERNALLY HOT in a fawn coat and breeches and billowing brown cravat, Jean Baptiste arrived at a point where River Road along the Mississippi met the moss-hung lane leading to a great house. He had also arrived at a point in his carefully plotted and ambitious career at which he was determined to acquire as many of Louisiana's grand war-worn plantation houses as possible through foreclosure. Here was one of the grandest, and the widowed owner needed a loan. If he had been less exhausted from the boring seventy-five-mile carriage ride from New Orleans, a few weeks after he and Stephanie had moved into their new home, he would have laughed. For Jean was at St. Delphine, a twelve-hundred-acre plantation on the West Side near Baton Rouge.

For two years, he had been planning to begin acquiring once-great manor houses like this at bargain prices by means of mortgage and subsequent acquisition; his dream could be coming true with the gaining of this prize. A small cigar, the last he had, went out as he stared admiringly at the house, large, square, and relatively simple in its architecture. He counted twelve square masonry columns rising two stories and supporting a deep cornice under the slate roof. A thick picturesque wisteria vine climbed one chimney on the east wall. Getting down from his carriage he rehearsed aloud, "Good morning, Mrs. Daigle. I wish to speak with you. It has been three months since we last had dealings of a business nature together."

Mrs. Daigle, watching Jean's approach, was dismayed as he knew the seventy-year-old widow would be. She couldn't understand why Groeble dispatched Jean on this important mission after she had complained to him about Jean's rudeness and insensitivity at their meeting earlier.

"I saw you coming up the lane," she said politely, firmly, "but I am surprised to see you, Mr. Levert. What do you wish to say? What do you bring in the way of news concerning the matter of advancing money and supplies to take care of the current crop needs here?"

Jean ignored the implications of her surprise. He paid no attention to her remarks about money and supplies, either.

"Well, Mrs. Daigle, as you might have guessed, I am representing my firm on Mr. Groeble's behalf, so I must do what is in the best interest of the firm. That is, work out the best possible way for both parties to be served. Furthermore, advances of money may be too late in your case."

Chilled by his remark, the small, whitehaired Mrs. Daigle cut him off. "What seems to be bothering you, Mr. Levert? You seem far away, like something's tugging at your heart. Why the coldness in your voice? I realize you are a hungry, ambitious young man. I learned that from our previous meetings. But you seem to have this uncompromising way of dealing with clients—doing it your way or not at all. Why?" When Jean didn't respond, Mrs. Daigle led him into the parlor. "Why did Mr. Groeble send you? Did he have no one else to send to represent the firm?"

"He sent me because I know the situation. You have had some hard times managing St. Delphine and the mill since your husband's passing. We understand your need for money and supplies to bring in the current crop."

"Actually, Mr. Levert, the war ruined plantations, credit houses, brokers like yourself, and made financing of another crop next to impossible for a long time."

Impatient with hearing what he already knew, Jean interrupted her. "Yes, the inability to obtain needed money from banks delayed the recovery of the entire sugar industry." His voice hardened. "There were too few brokers with sufficient money to back crops where banks couldn't or wouldn't."

Beads of perspiration had appeared on his face. He unfastened the buttons to his coat for relief from the humid heat on this Friday in late September. He was determined to advance the necessary money to the widow Daigle—take a mortgage on St. Delphine and the '71 crop at the highest rate he could extract. When gentlemanlike tact seemed to fail with her, Jean turned coldly businesslike, determined to do whatever it took to undersell his competition, even at a loss to himself and his firm. But the first time he heard his own greediness, he felt surprised and guilty—surprised at how easily the lie sprang from his lips and guilty as he realized what he was doing. Jean had little doubt what his father would say about unfair business practices, especially by a broker toward a sugar grower. His father would be hurt and probably rebuke him. Jean also realized he must balance his reputation as a risk-taker with a cautious side lest their house—Harry Groeble & Co.—fall apart.

On Magazine Street in New Orleans, Jean appreciated being known as the *Gravedancer*, the ghoulish nickname that had been given to him only a few months after he joined the sugar commission house; it delighted him. In his view, it suggested an opportunist who profited in the name of tough, strict business practices made possible by the folly of those whose properties ended up on the auction block; they couldn't pay their taxes; they lost their credit.

Jean took a lengthy document from his coat pocket. "I'll

appreciate your looking at these papers, reading them carefully. I drew them according to the wishes you expressed at your earlier meeting with Mr. Groeble. If they are in order, please sign them; if you wish, your agent or attorney may be present."

Mrs. Daigle took the document from Jean and read it carefully, slowly. "I don't believe it will be necessary for my agent or attorney to be present," she said, watching the expression on Jean's face turn to surprise. "I am familiar with its contents, Mr. Levert. As I understand, this is but a formality; these are the terms agreed to between your firm and myself several weeks ago."

"That is correct. Now, if you will affix your signature," Jean said, with the same hint of impatience as before.

> . . . Mrs. Delphine Daigle has furnished four prom-
> issory notes endorsed by her; one for four thousand
> dollars, one for three thousand, one for two thousand;
> and one for one thousand, all payable to Harry Groeble
> on the first of October, 1872, with interest at ten per-
> cent per annum until paid . . . to secure full payment of
> said notes, Mrs. Daigle declares that she does mortgage,
> affect in favor of Harry Groeble & Co. and to ensure
> use and benefit of all future holders of said notes, all of
> which are accepted for the company by Jean B. Levert,
> representing the firm, a certain plantation called St.
> Delphine, together with all buildings and adjoining tracts
> of land, horses, cattle, farming and agriculture imple-
> ments, that Mrs. Daigle shall be bound to cultivate said
> lands as a sugar planter to the best advantage, and to
> shop and consign to Harry Groeble & Co. all the crop
> and produce of said plantation . . . in addition to the
> mortgage Harry Groeble & Co. shall have a lien and
> privilege on the crop raised during the current year of
> 1871 . . . .
> Act of Mortgage from Harry Groeble & Co.
> New Orleans, September 25, 1871

* * *

"Jean, Jean! Please step in my office before you leave for the day." Harry Groeble's admonitory tone startled him, interrupting his thoughts of Aloysia. Groeble was holding a letter he'd just received from Delphine Daigle, a disturbing letter that he didn't particularly like or understand.

"What's the meaning of this? I hope I haven't been wrong about you. Mrs. Daigle is complaining again about your attitude, abruptness at times, at your recent meeting at her plantation. She's so hurt. I can't believe it." Harry rose and stalked the office, then stared out to the street at brokers making their way home for the day. "Good God, Jean, can you explain any of this?"

The office in which Jean stood was small. It seemed too small even for Groeble's slender hand that clutched the edge of his desk, motionless. He glared at Jean. Embarrassed, Jean still couldn't look him in the face. "I was so full of enthusiasm at your prospects here," said the soft-spoken Harry. "When I hired you I was so impressed with your attitude, knack for selling, eagerness to learn. I was thinking of turning over to you some of our more influential, credit-worthy clients. I realize people have bad days. Something may be bothering them. But I must know why, son."

"I mean to write to Mrs. Daigle and apologize for my haste and rudeness that day and at earlier meetings with her," Jean finally said. "She has to know why. She's so valuable to our firm. I realize this more than ever, now, Mr. Groeble. I've just been having some bad days lately, for several months. It's just—I don't know, I really don't know what to say. It won't happen again, sir."

"I'll count on that, son. We all have our bad days."

Feeling he needed to further explain his recent behavior, his irritability, Jean thrust a hand into his shirt pocket and pulled out a newspaper clipping from *The Daily Picayune* he had carried for about six months. He stood looking at Groeble as he read the worn piece of newspaper:

"On February 4, 1871, at 2 o'clock in the afternoon, Marie Aloysia Levert, aged one year nine months, first daughter and firstborn of Stephanie Dupuy and J. B. Levert of this city . . . the friends of the family are respectfully requested to attend a special funeral Mass this evening (February 5) at 4 o'clock. . . ."

Groeble removed his pince-nez clipped to his narrow nose, and shook his head. "I'm sorry, Jean. I'm so sorry."

CHAPTER 27

AT MIDNIGHT, VIC entered the spacious drawing room at Third Street and announced to Stephanie's and Jean's guests: "Suppa served in the dinin room."

Jean was bursting with pride as he watched his wife reigning over the party, elegant-looking in a white satin dress embroidered in silver threads, its artfully designed bodice and full three-tiered skirt—not concealing her advanced pregnancy, but enhancing her beauty. He thought she floated among her guests. He felt assured that there was no more gracious and winning a hostess in all of New Orleans than Stephanie.

Tonight Stephanie and Jean were entertaining their families and a few friends at a Christmas dance, three months after his meeting with Mrs. Daigle. Eager to show off their new home, Stephanie and Vic and Daniels had decorated the house with great pains to display the reception rooms at their best. Jean's parents and his brothers and their wives came; so did Stephanie's *Grandmère Dupuy*, her Uncle Duhumel and several of her cousins. All traveled down together by steamer and took rooms at Hotel Girod. Albert Desmont, his father's long-time broker, also came with his wife.

Jean glanced at the heirloom crystal chandelier, a gift to Stephanie from her grandmother, glittering beneath a plaster cartouche in the center of the drawing room. Its flickering hundred candles sparkled in Stephanie's eyes when she entered and beheld the beauty her grandmother had contributed to her home. Furniture had been pushed to the walls to clear the way for dancing, and music stands were grouped at one end of the room near the tall Christmas tree laden with decorations.

Stephanie and Jean watched Daniels, dressed in a white shirt and black tie, as he opened the door to admit guests, the last of whom were Harry Groeble, his wife, and a gentleman Jean had never met. Jean's colleague had asked if he might bring a sugar broker of importance whom he wanted Jean to know. "I believe your father would enjoy making his acquaintance also," he said, by way of explaining why he would ask to bring a stranger to what was essentially a family party.

"May I ask who the gentleman is," said Jean.

"Colonel John Louis Bush," replied Groeble.

"Ah," smiled Jean, recalling that Bush was one of the signers of the Ordinance of Secession ten years earlier. "I was fortunate to have been in the capitol building in Baton Rouge on that day with my father and Augie to witness the signing. What a momentous occasion! Yes, Colonel Bush is welcomed warmly in my home. I know his reputation well as a former legislator and much admired Louisianian. He's been an asset to the local mercantile community ever since he gave up his successful career as a Thibodaux attorney."

Now, Jean saw the two men approaching. He greeted them formally but cordially, bowing over Mrs. Groeble's hand.

"Colonel Bush, sir, I have long been an admirer of yours," Jean said, turning to Bush. "And I of yours, Mr. Levert. I very much approve of the way you are handling some of the state's important negotiations of sugar planters." Colonel Bush, a graying man Jean judged to be in his middle fifties, exuded a restrained charm. His head was clustered over with waxy dark brown hair; he had a neat dark beard. His teeth were straight and white, his snappy hazel eyes had a cool glitter in them. Surely his smile was winsome. A perfect Creole gentleman. Jean had heard as much, and now he believed it was true. Jean and the gentlemen joined Stephanie and the other guests entering the dining room.

In the dining room the guests exclaimed over the heavy silver pieces laid out on side tables, most engraved *G.O.D.* in French flourishes for Gideon Octave Dupuy. Vic and Daniels served the guests from sterling trays and flatware brought from the Dupuy Plantation. Stephanie had found a florist to arrange large bouquets of hothouse flowers and ferns in her silver baskets and vases. Candles glowed flatteringly over the women and romantically over everyone, as they sat down to turkey, ham, roast, steaming rice and gravies. Later, Vic and Daniels brought in trays of desserts— custards, pies, charlotte russes of homemade sponge cake, spread with raspberry jam and served with a blancmange of whipped cream that was dotted with red cherry stars. From their opposite ends of the long table, Stephanie and Jean leaned to one side of the centerpiece to see each other and exchange congratulatory smiles, as the guests spared no words of praise.

After the main courses had been served, Jean stood and held his glass high to first toast his wife for her brilliant success with the party, then he toasted Auguste and Eulalie and Albert and thanked all the relatives for coming. Then Auguste raised a glass to the happy couple, expressing pride in Jean's success. The ladies clapped their hands in a proper way, and the men shouted, "*Très bien, bravo!*"

In his rather self-effacing way, Harry Groeble offered the last toast, surprising everyone with what amounted to a little speech: "I wish to toast Jean Baptiste Levert, my associate and friend." Groeble paused, pulling at his high starched collar as he looked at the chandelier. He continued, "Young Jean, whom I hired actually as a favor to your father, you quickly have succeeded in this volatile, unpredictable business where many have failed. Your services to me these past three years have been invaluable, both your efforts generally and your quick attention to details. If I ever had any doubt about your staying power, I do not have any now. For someone relatively young and coming to this business in unnatural times, you have made your mark on Magazine Street and along Factors' Row. Thanks, thanks, and to you, too, Mrs. Levert, for this wonderful gathering tonight. Mrs. Groeble, Colonel Bush, and I are grateful to be allowed to join your family party."

He nodded to Stephanie and to Jean at their opposite ends of the table. All glasses were lifted. Colonel Bush said nothing but he rose quickly and lifted his glass to Groeble's remarks.

The party broke up at near daylight, after there had been more music, dancing, *café au lait*, and oyster gumbo to help sustain the out-of-town guests back to the hotel before they boarded a return steamer to Plaquemine. To a person, Jean and Stephanie were proud that the guests left filled with enthusiasm and exuberance about the resplendent night. After many kisses and embraces, Jean closed the front door. He thanked Vic and Daniels who were cleaning up the last vestiges of pleasure in the kitchen and pantry, and he and Stephanie went to their bedroom, quite tired but pleased beyond measure with their party.

CHAPTER 28

AS JEAN WALKED to work a few days after the party, he saw a well-dressed white woman alight from a barouche not far from his office. She dismissed her driver and walked in the direction of St. Stephens Cathedral at the corner of Napoleon Avenue and Magazine Street. Suddenly, two tall, heavyset Negro men blocked her way.

As he hurried to assist the woman he waggled a finger in the air to get the men's attention. But the men did not move; they both glared down menacingly at Jean. Several suited men passed Jean in the street without looking or offering to help him. Jean didn't know what kind of trouble he might be in for. Fortunately, two uniformed policemen came around the corner at that moment. They carried billy clubs, and one of them wore a side arm.

"Sergeant," Jean called, "would you officers be of service to this lady? See that she is escorted to safety. These hooligans mean trouble, I'm afraid."

The policemen poked the two Negroes with clubs and kicked them hard in the shins. To Jean's relief they ran for an alley.

"Sir," the lady said breathlessly, "I'm grateful for your help. I would hate for you to have been harmed on my account."

Jean did not fail to notice her stunning face and her melodious, warm voice.

"Ma'am," he said, "I apologize for the inconvenience these ruffians caused you. A lady is no longer safe on our streets."

She smiled. "Thank you again."

Jean touched the brim of his hat and watched as she resumed her walk to St. Stephens.

* * *

That evening Jean slammed the kitchen door. He was stamping his feet and shaking the rain off his clothes as Stephanie hurried back to meet him. It had started to rain hard moments before he stepped down from his carriage at Third Street.

"Dear! Give me your coat," and she hung his greatcoat on the rack near the door. Jean plopped down on the bench in the pantry. Stephanie handed him a towel and at the same time kissed him on the forehead. "Would you like some coffee to warm you, darling? You seem upset about something."

"Yes, my dear. Thank you. Blacker the better."

Stephanie handed him a large cup, and he took a few sips of the chicoried brew. He looked at his wife thoughtfully before he spoke.

"Steph, I rescued a lady in distress this morning on my way to the office, right down on Magazine. Two huge Negroes, obviously from the North, down here to do nothing but cause trouble."

"Jean, what on earth happened?" Her expressive face showed alarm. "Please tell me."

Vic appeared and announced that supper was ready to be served.

"Tell me, Jean!"

"I have to get upstairs for dry clothes. I'll tell you later." He set his cup down in the kitchen and hurried to the bedroom.

They were alone at supper, for it was late and one-year-old Albert had been put to bed. Over roast chicken and green salad, Stephanie reminded Jean, "Tell me everything about what happened to you today. You frighten me."

So, he told her of the episode. "My dear, you and the children must not go out unaccompanied by a strong male. We are under siege. As surely as if armed Union troops marched through our streets. Negroes are on top of us, and behind them are Yankee guns and bayonets.

"Without as much as a warning we could all be killed. You and other ladies in the Garden District could be attacked and very probably killed. Nothing would be done about it. It would be ignored, forgotten about, I'm afraid. And if you tried to avenge such an act, perpetrated on you, or anybody else, you would likely be hanged by the Yankees. Probably hanged without benefit of a trial."

"My, God, Jean, what in heaven can we do?"

"That's what I'm telling you, Steph. There seems nothing we can do. The Yankees are never going to let the South get back on its feet. I am lucky to be a functioning member of Louisiana commerce, though you may as well know it's more difficult daily. New Orleans is the principal battleground of this damnable Reconstruction." Stephanie was almost in tears.

"Let me tell you that *The Daily Picayune*, for one, is muzzled. Absolutely muzzled, and it can raise no protest against injustices to innocent citizens. I hate for you to have to know all this, *ma chèrie*, but these are bitter and dangerous times . . . any complaint levied by a Negro that a white man is surly to him can land a citizen in jail, and Negroes can always be found willing to accuse white folks, true or false. So the only possible hope may lie with one of the secret organizations . . ." He stopped. Stephanie, who could do nothing, looked terribly frightened. "I'm sorry, my dear, this has been a hard day."

Stephanie rang the bell for Vic to take the supper plates and serve their vanilla ice cream and demitasses.

*　　*　　*

In their bedroom later, Jean could tell Stephanie was having trouble sleeping, no doubt because of what he had told her at supper. He knew she was becoming increasingly concerned about his safety as well as her family's. She continued to lay awake in the dark, the only light from a bright moon. As she turned on her side the daguerreotype of her parents' wedding day caught her eyes. If anything, seeing her mother's serene, girlish face—the same age in the picture as Steph was now—caused her spirits to sink even lower.

Several hours later, as night drew toward daybreak, Stephanie finally fell into a deep sleep about four in the morning. Jean had fallen asleep at midnight, soon after his head hit the pillow.

Chapter 29

JEAN BAPTISTE TRAVELED with his young family to spend Christmas, 1872, at Golden Ridge. It was his first such visit since he and Stephanie had set up their household in New Orleans. "We want to spend Christmas with you," Jean said in a letter to his mother and father. Eulalie immediately began to make plans for her grandchildren, Albert, two, and Mathilde Marie, eight months.

"We must have a large tree for the parlor," she said to Auguste. "We'll have Ned and Celestine go out and cut one. I've been watching a lovely cedar down past that old log house beyond the cane fields. It has a lovely shape and will fit in the space beside the fireplace beautifully. I think Albert is old enough to enjoy a tree, don't you?"

"I suppose so. He's mighty young, but yes, I'm sure he'll like the candles and the ornaments. But don't you overdo, my dear. Let these Negro girls do the work. You just sit down and supervise. I don't want you to be too worn out to enjoy the children, Eulalie." He patted her shoulder.

"You're right, dear. You're absolutely right, and I'll try not to get carried away."

But as the New Orleans Texas & Pacific train pulled into Plaquemine station just after dark on the 23rd, their son was not thinking of Christmas. His real motive for the trip was business, specifically an advantageous disposition of St. Delphine Plantation, on which he and Groeble had foreclosed in October, just as Jean had intended. The buyer he intended to capture was his father. He clenched his fist on the arm of his seat. It made such good sense. The family holdings would . . . The train jerked to a stop.

"Albert, darling. Wave to *Grand-père!* Look, look!" Stephanie held both children up to the rain-beaded window.

Suddenly brought back from his reverie, Jean realized he was looking down into his father's face. By the light of the station's wall lamps, the face looked old and worn. Jean waved and smiled. Then he waved at his twenty-six-year-old sister Euphrasie standing next to his father. Euphrasie, unmarried, still lived at Golden Ridge. Jean stood up and gently lifted the baby from Stephanie's arms and assisted her to her feet while she took Albert's hand and walked toward the exit. Jean gathered up their several bags of baby supplies and other travel necessities and followed his wife down the steps to the station platform.

His father was already embracing Steph and lifting Albert into his arms. "Come to *Grand-père*, young man," he said. Seeing Jean, he managed to hug him and Mathilde and Albert all at once. He settled Albert on his hip and said, "You've grown since we saw you! And you've just had a birthday!" The driver took their two large valises off the baggage wagon and stowed them in the back of the carriage.

"Come, come, all of you. Let's be on our way. *Grand-mère* is waiting at home with all kinds of good food for our supper." He sat Albert on the floor before climbing in himself. Jean helped Stephanie up the step and handed the baby to her after she was seated. Jean was glad to get out of the fine mist that was collecting in his moustache. He felt a twinge of nostalgia and some guilt as the driver flipped the reins and the horses settled into a trot down moonlit River Road. It was a route so familiar and unchanged, and as always his devoted mother awaited him at the end of it. Now here I come, he thought, with wife and children. He swallowed and felt the wheels crunch in the sandy ruts of the old road.

"How is grinding this year, Father? Is Augie in full charge? Getting plenty of help from Amèdèe? How are your profit estimates looking?"

"Oh, fine, fine," Auguste said, plainly more interested in Albert, who sat on his knee, and Mathilde, who gazed at him intently with round eyes from Stephanie's lap. He shook the toe of her little shoe. "You've grown, too, little sister, since we attended your baptism back in June."

"Who is this new driver, Father? I haven't seen him."

"His name is Ned." I hired him three weeks ago to drive and do other things. He's good help."

"Oh. Well, I'm sure you are cautious about whom you hire. Louisiana is like a powder keg with the northern white trash and rebellious Negroes running wild in the legislature and all over the countryside. New Orleans is unsafe. We don't let our wives and children on the streets unaccompanied by a strong male."

As the carriage entered the drive to the plantation house, Ned stopped and took the lantern off the post and set it on the floorboard at his feet and clicked to the horses to move on. Eulalie was waiting on the gallery. Lamps on the walls behind her reflected on her hair and on her beautiful green silk dress. How elegant she looked, thought Jean. He was proud of her. She embraced him first, then hugged and kissed Stephanie and kissed the baby. Then she led Albert into the wide hall, which was aglow with candlelight from polished brass sconces along the walls and dancing with shadows that flickered on ceilings so high that they seemed far away. Mistletoe was tied to the sconces with red ribbons.

"Oh, how lovely," smiled Stephanie, as she entered. "You've outdone yourselves." She turned to her mother-in-law. "It reminds me, I have brought you several boxes of candles I found at the French Market last week. They aren't easy to find."

"How wonderful, Steph. I feared I didn't have enough to get through Christmas night. We are using oil lamps where we can, to save the candles." She beamed obviously delighted to be so remembered by her son's wife. "Excuse me while I go to the pantry and let them know we'll be ready to eat right away. You all take off your coats and wash up. It won't be long."

Almost immediately a young Negro woman in a black dress and long white apron came out and spoke softly to the children,

charming them with coos and wooing them to go with her to the
large pantry where young children were fed at a table of their own
in the old highchairs and, Jean recalled, the same old bibs that he
and his brothers and sisters had used. He glanced after the servant,
admiring her slender figure. He'd never seen such a light Negro
around here. She was very pretty, he thought, for a Negro. She
might have come from New Orleans. Such creamy *café au lait*
skin and a slender nose . . . .

Eulalie came beaming from the dining room. "Come now
and have gumbo and bread just out of the oven. I want you to eat
your fill. We think our gumbo is as good as Antoine's."

"Much better, *Mère*," said Jean, easing his mother's chair under
her as she sat. He noticed she was wearing her diamond barpin. It
seemed to underscore her cleavage that disappeared under the ruching
of her green silk gown. She was looking older, and it reassured him
to see her so splendid as she certainly was tonight. Two beautiful
women, he thought, as he watched Stephanie being seated by his
father. Her traveling dress was cut with a high neck, he noted
somewhat ruefully. Few things unrelated to the sugar business pleased
him as much as the sight of his wife's creamy bosom. Tomorrow
night she would be wearing her new Christmas dress, which had
much more feminine lines. It too was green, to match her eyes.

He noticed Stephanie looking over the room, seemingly
admiring it. It was a mix of sophisticated elegance and country
charm. Eulalie had made a centerpiece of dark glistening magnolia
leaves and the earliest-blooming camellia japonicas. The chandelier
was hung with fresh holly, and boughs of mistletoe were bound
with red ribbons to the high backs of the dining chairs. Silverware,
Austrian crystal, and fine French china gleamed under the candles.
The four of them crossed themselves and murmured, *"In the name
of the Father, Son, and Holy Spirit, amen,"* and Auguste said his
familiar blessing over the food. Eulalie lifted her soup spoon to
her lips and smiled confidently at her loved ones.

"I can't imagine a more beautiful dining room," Stephanie said.
"You're so fortunate to still have your lovely things after the Yankees
came." She lifted a delicate goblet appreciatively.

"Somehow we were able to carry all these things, all the silver we own, china, glassware, linens, to the storage space at the back of that big closet under the backstairs," Eulalie explained. "That little door doesn't look like a door; it looks like the wall, it's dark and I guess they simply missed it. I dread to think where all these things might be tonight if they had stolen them. The Yankees didn't seem to know the value of the things they took from us." Eulalie changed the subject. "*Père* and I don't want to keep you children up late tonight. You must be very tired after such a long day on the train. So after we finish here, everyone do feel free to go right on up to bed."

"Thank you," said Stephanie. "It's true, we are tired, but this wonderful food has restored us. And having your new girl look after the children makes such a difference. She must work some magic over children. They were both content to go right up with her."

"I can almost promise Scilla will have them asleep when you get up to bed." She looked at Auguste. "Now what time are the boys and their families to arrive tomorrow, my dear?"

"Before noon, they said. Jean, we plan to have the big meal no later then one, then we'll all decorate the tree and have a good time so they all can be home before dark. I hope Albert will enjoy playing with his cousins." Augie and Amèdèe, now handling most daily operations at Golden Ridge for their father, planned to come from beyond Plaquemine.

"Yes," said Stephanie, "they don't get to see each other often." She stifled a yawn.

After a dessert of oranges and cream, the Leverts rose and climbed the curving staircase together. Steph's hand rested heavily in Jean's elbow, and she was again thankful that the children were in bed. She tiptoed into the room, leaving Jean at the door talking with his father.

"I have a wonderful business opportunity I want to talk to you about, Father." It had been difficult for Jean to sit all evening through the supper chatter. When his father showed no interest, he said, "If you are too sleepy tonight, we can wait till tomorrow."

Auguste smiled wearily. "Very well, son, but let's not talk too much business. Remember, this is Christmas. Your mother and I want to enjoy our grandchildren. With Auguste's four, we'll have six here tomorrow. And you know Amèdèe and Ernestine are expecting their first child."

Jean wasn't to be put off. "Of course, sir, but I'm sure we can find a moment while Amèdèe and Augie are here. We'll talk tomorrow." He kissed his father goodnight and entered the dimly lit bedroom.

Stephanie was already asleep, her clothes piled over a chair in unusual disarray. He could see that she had laid out his nightshirt on the bed. The children slept silently in the old baby bed that had held all the sleeping Levert children. Bébé had established Jean there soon after his birth and had pulled her cot up and slept beside him until she was sure he was safe alone. Now, the pale light from the window limned the sprawled, relaxed bodies of his little Leverts. This room had been witness to the developments of all his life. He stretched out beside Stephanie.

He thought of the nights of his boyhood when he'd lain here planning to be a sugar planter, then, discovering the better life of Albert Desmont, had begun to dream right here of becoming a sugar broker, the most successful one in New Orleans. He recalled how he had languished in this bed, depressed, after the war and the horrors of the Union prison camp until his mother had finally succeeded in getting him up and out among people again, which took him to the church dance and his rediscovery of Stephanie. That was the luckiest night of his life.

He looked at his wife. She had released her long hair, which lay like a pale cloud on the pillow. By the light of the guttering candle beside the bed, he could see how beautiful she was. After all she'd been through in four years she looked so young. He leaned over her and stroked her body hungrily, wanting her terribly, wanting to slip off the ruffled garment so he could clasp her to him. But she didn't respond. So he kissed her hair and fell back on his pillow. Poor girl. He hoped she was not pregnant again.

Until he fell asleep, he lay on his back and let random thoughts pass through his mind. He thought of St. Delphine Plantation, which he and Groeble now virtually owned and which he was determined to have his father buy. He could visualize Auguste and his three sons becoming the most powerful landowning men in Louisiana sugarcane country. The house at St. Delphine was more elegant than Golden Ridge, a house his mother could grace to perfection.

Drowsily, he imagined the creamy exotic face of Scilla leaning over the children's bed in the morning before he fell into a deep sleep.

*   *   *

Jean was on the gallery of Golden Ridge at daybreak. He had had a quick tub bath in cold water and he wore fresh clothes. He had found a newly dripped pot of hot coffee in the kitchen, but had as yet seen no living soul. He hoped his father would not sleep late, because he wanted to get a chance to speak with him about St. Delphine before the children and other family members were about. It was plain his father was interested only in his grandchildren and would have to be pursued in earnest. What had happened to the man? Could he be getting senile? It was natural for him to love the children, but to let them absorb all his attention was something Jean could not understand.

The December scent of freshly cut cane and honey-sweet aroma of cane juice in the sugarhouse tickled Jean's nose. As he sat there absently savoring the familiar scents his father came out onto the gallery carrying a cup of coffee. Jean stood immediately.

"Good morning, Father. I am glad to see you up bright and early. We can visit before the household begins to stir." He took the cup and saucer from Auguste's hand and set them beside his own on a small table between the two rockers.

"Good morning, Jean. My, but it's good to have you here. I'm glad we are having this warm weather for Christmas. We can all enjoy sitting outside, and the children can play on the lawn. What time does little Albert usually wake up? Scilla is ready to bathe and dress him when Stephanie is ready for her to."

"It will probably be a while. It's only seven." He took a sip of coffee and cleared his throat. "Father, I have something I believe strongly you will be interested in. A piece of property in West Baton Rouge Parish that ought to be worthy of your consideration. A sugar-producing plantation, beautiful house, sugarhouse, rent houses, and a general store—all in good condition. It's St. Delphine Plantation. Groeble and I foreclosed on the widow Daigle. Did you know . . . ?"

"Of course I know. Everybody on the West Side knows all about that. And I expected you to have that business on your mind, son. You have a one-track mind, son—business—wherever you are, whatever you're doing. Is business more important to you than being with your family and reliving past memories or reclaiming old acquaintances?"

His father's impatient tone surprised Jean. But he went on, "I would like for you to go over the official papers pertaining to St. Delphine, give them your complete attention and consideration."

"Really, son. I hardly think I can deal with this . . ."

"Father, I am not asking that you give Groeble and me your decision now. But the proposition is something that ought to be considered by you and my brothers. If you are serious, as you have indicated in the past, about expanding your land holdings, diversifying your interests, heaven knows, Father, here is your chance. With your know-how you could turn St. Delphine into a real moneymaker. Have you seen the mansion? The whole place is a bargain."

"But . . ."

Jean refused to stop. "Hell, if there comes a time to put all our holdings—yours, my brothers'—under a single style, such as A. *Levert & Sons*, what better time than right now? Why, your opportunity is fabulous!" He bounded from his chair, leaving it rocking by itself. Auguste stared at his son. This son whom he had loved almost unrestrainedly, who at thirty-three was a hard-minded business dealer, a broad shouldered man with slightly graying temples. A different person.

"My God, Jean, no wonder you can make sugar growers and little old ladies do your bidding. I have never felt so ordered about in my life. And certainly not by one of my own sons."

"Then you will do it? You'll purchase St. Delphine?"

"I didn't say that. I must learn every detail of the matter before I can make a commitment. After that and only after that will I give you my answer."

"When will that be?"

"Jean! I will not be coerced! Is this the way you treat your clients? Am I to believe that you are a selfish, calculating man? Are you completely motivated by profitable gain? Give me the papers. I will read them over. I want Auguste Junior to examine them. And Amedée if he wants to." He picked up his cup and saucer. "My coffee is cold." He went into the house.

Jean was not intimidated by his father's brusque response. *If I were not so deeply interested, I should enjoy this negotiation for St. Delphine with my father. Nothing puts me on edge more than finding myself up against baseless resistance because of fear of taking a chance, giving something a try, risking something. They'll thank me later.*

CHAPTER 30

JEAN RETURNED TO his office in early January, eager to get back to work after what he considered a successful Christmas holiday at Golden Ridge. Now that he felt that St. Delphine Plantation was theirs—his father had signed the tentative purchase agreement for the plantation—he wanted to seek out new moneymaking challenges and deals. He knew the stability of the sugar industry in New Orleans was severely threatened by high taxation of brokers and growers alike at the hands of an irresponsible legislature.

As he moved among the brokerage houses on Factors' Row with confidence, he found comfort and encouragement in the clangor of clerks' sharp voices reading off late price quotations from the leading markets of the world. Jean knew what was afoot, but he seemed fearless, challenged. On the other hand, he thought Harry Groeble, who was watching the market with more trepidation, seemed preoccupied; something was bothering him.

The sugar market did collapse in late summer, as Jean had feared, and by the time the dust had settled, two-thirds of the brokers on Factors' Row, excluding Harry Groeble & Co., were gone—victims of dwindling clienteles because high taxes had plunged many growers into bankruptcy.

As the firm had grown in profitability and reputation, Jean and Harry continued to advance thousands of dollars to sugar planters just on their personal word—no security for advances was needed and only a brief memorandum to witness the amounts involved was required. This unique basis of agricultural credit had been established between the firm and its clients over the past five years, and, Jean believed, the relationships had remained close. So, the partners committed themselves to this optimistic business approach, but not without full awareness of risk in the bad political climate.

By November, Jean was taking inventory of his assets. He personally had not been threatened with ruin as he knew he surely would have been had he not owned the resources given him by his father right after the war when land was cheap. And he knew that Stephanie's holdings were invested in safer places than in the sugarcane fields; her large inheritance was not only safe, it was productive and growing.

*   *   *

On the twenty-second of December, Jean Baptiste knocked on his partner's door.

"Come in," said the barely audible voice. Groeble sat slack in his leather chair. "Thank you, Harry." Jean shut the door behind him. "May I sit down?"

Groeble stood up then, politely, and said, "Of course, Jean, do sit down." And he dropped back heavily into his chair.

"Harry, may I say that I have grown concerned about you lately. You've grown almost silent, rather depressed. I know we have had the most serious business difficulties this year, most terrible, in fact. And of course I do not know just how you are suffering, both momentarily and—uh—spiritually, but this market crash does seem to have dealt you quite a blow, gotten you down much more than it has some others. Uh . . ." He looked into the poor man's face and into his eyes more directly than he had in weeks. Groeble's eyes were hollow, with dark circles. Obviously he had lost weight. He looked like a haunted man. "I just wonder if I can be of any help to you. In any way. Is your family all right?" Jean felt that he should try to talk to Harry, who was not as well off financially as Jean, to make himself available for a discussion in which he might be of help. As a friend. Like everyone who knew Harry, he regarded him as a rock, so he was not completely comfortable in the role of counselor.

Harry Groeble, the man of iron, so highly respected among his peers for his honor and unshakeableness, so respected for his business acumen, clutched his hands on his desk, then dropped his head into his hands.

"Oh, God! Oh, God!" he groaned. It was all he could say.

Jean leaned forward over the desk. "Oh, really, Harry. I had no idea you were so, so sick with this whole collapse. Can't we talk more about it? I believe we are going to be able to pick up and go on. Look man, we have survived! Besides, we already helped to re-create a thriving market in the city, with sugar once again the main staple trade, as strong as before the war."

"It's not the collapse! The collapse is the least of my worries!"

Jean sprang to his feet. "Then what is it? In the name of God, what is wrong? Are you ill?"

Harry laid his head back against his chair, his face filled with anguish, his gray eyes staring at Jean. "I'm being blackmailed!"

"Blackmailed? Blackmailed? You, Harry? For what? By whom?"

Groeble stood up and walked to the window and looked out at the wet New Orleans winter afternoon. It was almost dark. He rested his hand briefly on the glass. Then he took his handkerchief from his breast pocket and patted his face with it. Jean could not tell if he was weeping.

"It is a long, awful story. I—I don't know if I am up to telling you the whole story. You will soon need to be going home to your family. I don't want to keep you here." He replaced his handkerchief and returned to the desk. After a moment of silence between the two men, Groeble sat down again.

"I can't talk more tonight. Perhaps tomorrow . . ."

"Of course, I understand, I'll be here." Jean stopped at the door and turned back toward his partner. He wanted to say to him that Christmas was near, that he could take cheer from the season with his family. But he decided better and said only, "Goodnight."

He returned to his own office, filled his briefcase with papers he wanted to look over after supper, put on his overcoat and hat, and stepped into the outer office. The secretaries were gone. He looked briefly at Harry's door. There was no sound and Jean felt sure that his partner still sat in the darkness brooding over his problem. Whatever it was. There was no point in intruding on the man again tonight. But he would speak with him again tomorrow. Jean shook his head worriedly as he walked to the stairs.

Outside, Jean met an unusually cold December evening for New Orleans. The wind off the river whipped his coattails and those of pedestrians still on the streets. He looked at the sky and thought the heavy clouds dimly visible did not bode well for Christmas, only two days away. For a moment he thought of Christmas a year ago; he and his family were alighting from the train at Plaquemine at about this time. He waved to an approaching cab, and the driver reined his one-horse vehicle at the curb.

Jean sat back in the darkness of the cab and smoked a cigar as he rode home through muddy streets. Rain had fallen off and on for several days and the ruts on St. Charles Avenue were deeper than usual. He stared into the night with narrow eyes and wondered again what could be wrong in the apparently perfect life of Harry Groeble. Blackmail! One usually thought first of a woman. That seemed out of the question; not Harry Groeble. But the thought did give one a turn. He felt a slight shiver. One had to be careful; one never knew what kind of riff-raff was lurking, spying. Such a thing had never occurred to Jean Baptiste Levert. *I guess I am still innocent of big city dangers.* He flicked his cigar out into the mud and thought warmly of getting home to Stephanie and a candlelit supper in the warmth and comfort of their dining room. The cab's wheels crunched to a gravelly, sliding halt before the Third Street house.

Supper with Steph was indeed a softening pleasure, and they enjoyed an end-of the-day talk. Stephanie had had a caller in the afternoon, a lady friend, who spoke to her almost in terror about fears of a race riot. Jean knew he must soon talk to his wife about the very subject because of his growing fears for the safety of the white people of the City and because gentlemen were arming themselves. He hated to expose her to the truth; he still thought of her as a country girl of extremely rarified rearing. He much preferred to keep her that way. But if he decided to join an organized effort to bring peace to the City, she would have to know about it. But not tonight. He steered the subject to Christmas and recollections of last year's trip to Golden Ridge. He inquired about the children who were already in their beds. He told her that she looked very pretty tonight.

After a demitasse he removed himself to the small parlor he used for business, and as was his wont, began work on the papers he had brought home. Stephanie retired for the night while he lost himself in studying two projected purchases. Harry Groeble did not cross his mind again that night.

*   *   *

On the morning before Christmas eve, Jean arrived early at his office. He was bent upon leaving early, too. He had some shopping to do—one gift to buy, and that was for Stephanie. He had seen earrings that he liked at a small shop on Bourbon Street owned by an importer of fine jewelry from France. They were small beautifully etched panels of gold with several drops of diamonds and pearls. Stephanie had a small chest of beautiful jewelry, gifts from her father and her grandmother, things that had belonged to her mother, but Jean couldn't believe that she would not like to add these elegant baubles to her collection. He imagined the gems dancing and twinkling close to her lovely face.

Now, however, he must make himself available to Harry Groeble. He hoped to get to the base of his partner's problem, and perhaps between them they could find a way out for him.

In the outer office he dropped his umbrella in the stand and hung up his top coat and hat. The secretaries had begun their holidays today. He sat at his desk only a few minutes before he heard Groeble's door shut. He tapped his fingers on his blotter a few times, then began to tug his moustache nervously. He could not rehearse what he would say, for he had no idea what he would need to say; he had almost no idea of what he would hear. He got up and walked to Groeble's door and knocked.

"Come in, Jean," said Harry in the same dead voice he had spoken in yesterday. He didn't rise or even look up when Jean entered. Jean looked around the office briefly and sat down facing Harry as he had last evening. He felt as though he had never left, almost as if his time at home overnight had not happened.

"Harry, if you want to talk to me about this problem you have, I assure you that it will be confidential. But I am completely in the dark. You say you are being blackmailed. I can't imagine why." He sat waiting.

"About six months ago I met a young woman—" Harry stopped and looked toward the window. "I didn't meet her, I—she—I never even learned her name." He cleared his throat and took a deep breath, lifting his head as if trying to come up for air. "I had crossed Canal and was walking home. To the upper Pontalba, you know. I was walking along the river. I saw this poorly clad girl—she was just a girl, eighteen maybe, very poorly clad. She was standing outside one of those shabby tenements. She had a beautiful young face, rather ethereal. She seemed distressed. I don't know. I stopped. I asked her if I could be of assistance.

"Suddenly, she was looking up at me. Her little face was almost saintly." Groeble's voice became more animated; he was reliving those moments when he had experienced the initial discovery. "She was small, didn't come up to my shoulder. She had dark curls. Her eyes were large and dark, like a Raphael virgin."

Jean was embarrassed at his partner's maudlin disclosures. But he did not interrupt or show any emotion.

"She allowed me to give her a few dollars to get herself some decent shoes. Her's were coming apart . . ."

"Did someone see you?"

"Why, I don't know. I didn't notice. There was nothing to hide. She was just a poor child I stopped to help."

"And that's all there was?"

"No, no, I found her out on the bankette the next afternoon. We talked a moment. She showed me her new shoes, and we took a little walk along the river."

"And no one saw you?"

"I tell you, Jean, there was nothing to see!" His voice rose in anguish. "I wasn't doing anything! Just taking an innocent little walk."

"Was that the end of it?"

"No, it wasn't. She began to wait for me every afternoon. I— I began to watch for her. Then I discovered what a miserable little room she occupied in that tenement. She told me her father was a drunkard, that her mother was dead. I gave her money to make it more livable. I gave her . . ."

"You went in there with her?"

"Yes, I . . ."

"That's when you were seen, of course. Were there other times, Harry?"

"Only a few. I only . . ."

Jean jumped up and stood looking down at Harry. "Only hell, man. You laid yourself wide open." Jean could not believe that this apparently sophisticated man could have been so naive. Stupid. Jean said, "Have you told your wife any of this, I mean about trying to help this girl?"

Harry sagged deeper into his chair. "My wife! Certainly not! I couldn't tell my wife." He looked up at Jean with incredulity. "It would kill her."

"Well, Harry," said Jean, sitting down again, "who is making this trouble for you?"

"A vile creature. A nasty wretch of a human being accosted me one afternoon last week on Decatur Street. He was fat, filthy. He brushed against me most impertinently. He said he knew all about us. 'I seen you visiting this house,' he hissed at me. 'All I want,' he said, 'is a couple of thousand.' For that he said he would keep silent. If I refused, he would go to my wife. I was dumbstruck with the shock of it. And frightened at the threat of a scandal that would ruin me. It will ruin me. You know that. My wife will be

scandalized. Of course, I could never expect her to understand."
His voice was rough with emotion. "You know that I am a ruined
man."

"I do not know any such thing, Harry. Don't you know that
half the men in New Orleans are having illicit relationships? Did
you give the rascal money?"

"No. I told him I had no such sum on me. I didn't want to
give this filthy wretch money. I hadn't done anything. I am
innocent. I—I never touched that girl."

"Have you seen her again?"

"No. Strangely, she seems to have vanished. I feel sorry for the
poor girl. But Jean, I hope I never see her again. What in God's
name was I ever thinking of?" He put his face in his hands again.

"That's it, Harry. Don't you see? They're in it together, this
blackmailer and poor girl. He sends her out to entice a gentleman,
then he springs the trap. How long did he give you to pay him?"

"Till Christmas eve. He told me to be in Jackson Square, just
outside St. Louis Cathedral about eleven. There'll be a crowd there
then for midnight Mass. He said he would find me. I took two
thousand dollars out of the bank yesterday morning. It's here in
my wallet." He touched his breast pocket.

"Harry, let me go in your stead. I'll confront the blackguard.
Better still, I'll take a constable with me. We'll pitch this fellow
into Orleans Parish prison. That should put the fear of God into
him." Jean warmed to his idea of a confrontation.

"Oh, no. I can't risk that; he'll get out of jail and he'll talk. You
are never free of a blackmailer."

"Well, you must know that if you pay him, he'll be back for
more as soon as he has drunk it all up. You simply can't begin
that. He'll bleed you dry."

"Don't you think I know that? I've known that from the
beginning. You see, there is no way out for me. I'm facing the loss
of everything, everything that I have worked so hard for. So very
hard. Oh, I know the collapse of the market and loss of so many
fine brokerage houses hasn't done us in. We could come out of
that; it would just take time. But this is something else. I've ruined

myself. In every way. My life as a respectable citizen of New Orleans is over. You must leave this firm now so you will not be tainted by my indiscretion, Jean."

"This is ridiculous." Jean walked around the desk and laid his hand on the older man's shoulder. "You must pull yourself together. You are hysterical. Now, believe me, you can do nothing until you calm yourself. You must remember that you are a man, a strong man, a capable man." He gave the shoulder a little shake. "Listen to me, Harry. Do not go to meet that blackmailer. Just don't go. Defy the bastard. Stay in on Christmas eve with your family. Sing carols with them. Just throw yourself into the spirit of the season for now. If he comes back, we'll get a discreet lawyer and go to the police. I'm betting you'll never hear from him again." Jean stole a quick look at his watch. The jewelry importer in the French Quarter might be closing early.

Harry lifted his haggard face to Jean. But he didn't look at him. "I wish it was that simple."

"I never claimed to think it was simple. I wish I could do more to help you. I will gladly confront your tormentor if you'll let me." He turned to the door.

"No," said Harry. "But thank you. You have become more than a business associate, Jean. You are a true friend. God bless you."

Jean attempted to smile. "Go home, *cher*, now, before noon. Surprise your family." He closed the door. He could not bring himself to say Merry Christmas.

CHAPTER 31

"*MON CHER!* SO wonderful to have you home early. It's only six o'clock," said Stephanie, as she entered the drawing room at Third Street. She stepped close to him and he kissed her on the forehead.

Jean had come home early from the office because he wanted to tease Stephanie a bit with the mystery of his Christmas gift for her. But he did not intend to give it to her until late tonight or perhaps Christmas morning. He had placed the beautifully wrapped present on the mantel in the drawing room, half hidden in the greenery she and Daniels had used in profusion to decorate the fireplace. It occurred to him that she might have something for him, though he did not see anything. If she did, he wanted them to enjoy exchanging alone. Not with the children, of course, just the two of them.

"Oh, I almost forgot, dear, these came today." Stephanie handed him two letters.

Jean looked at the two envelopes, one from Golden Ridge, obviously from his father. The other was from Baton Rouge. *Who do I know in Baton Rouge?* But he opened his father's letter first and sat down by the fire to read it. The first few paragraphs were about his father's health and possible surgery to relieve piles. "Don't be uneasy," Auguste wrote, "the doctor says it will make me ten years younger. That certainly sounds good to a man of my age." Then he got to the subject that Jean was waiting for:

> *About the offer for St. Delphine Plantation, you win! If the offer still stands, I accept your firm's price of twelve thousand dollars—four down and the rest to be*

paid according to the success of my crops. I am sorry it has taken me so long to arrive at my decision—almost a year, but I needed time to gather some cash. I do think your interest rate is a little steep, but believe I can manage. Son, I feel your asking price is a bit unfair for these times, too. You drive a hard bargain. After all, the plantation has not had a marketable sugar crop in several years, because of the war and the state's discouraging political condition. I'm hoping this purchase will have several advantages. We have talked of putting our holdings under a single corporate style or name, and the St. Delphine purchase might be a good time to begin, calling it A. Levert & Sons. Suspect you have the final papers all ready for my signature and the parties gathered soon to close the sale. I trust I'll hear from you soon in this regard.

All are well here and send their love. Your mother is pleased about St. Delphine, I think, though she never has come right out and said so. But I can tell she is. Maybe we'll send Augie to manage it for us.

Yours truly,
Auguste Levert, Sr.

Jean smiled and folded the letter neatly and laid it in his top desk drawer, a ritual he had practiced since he first had received a letter from his father when he was a first-year student at the University of Louisiana. He smoothed his moustache. While his father's acceptance of St. Delphine required hardly any arm-twisting or dickering, he was relieved to have the final firm acceptance. Harry would be, too. Perhaps it would cheer him up.

With curiosity, he slipped the letter opener into the envelope from West Baton Rouge. The handwriting was feminine. He unfolded the pale blue vellum.

Dear Jean Baptiste,

I don't really know how to begin this letter. I took a great chance in sending it, not knowing how you would react to it. I wrote to your home address that you gave me during the war

*and requested your present address. Your brother was kind
enough to send it to me. I hope that you do not mind my
sending this to your home in New Orleans. How many years
has it been, Jean? I've often thought of you, wondering what
you are doing, if you are married and have children.*

*I was married three years ago to a fine man from a
distinguished planter family. His roots go back to the
Randolphs of Virginia—Edwin Kleinpeter. We live now
at one of his family's sugar plantations near Baton Rouge.
Jean, I also felt obliged to tell you that Edwin and I had a
son whom we lost in infancy last year, God rest him. I
named him after you—Andrew Levert. I hope you don't
mind and that it does not cause any embarrassment. But
you and I were very close, and I will never forget our
happy days and nights together during the war.*

*If my writing you upsets you in any way, I apologize.
But if it is at all possible, I would like a note from you,
telling me about yourself, when it is convenient. I eagerly
wait to hear from you again, Jean.*

Truly yours,
Annie

Jean was not often taken by surprise, but this letter did indeed
catch him off guard. He folded it and put it in his pocket. He would
take it to his office. *What must the father of this boy think*, thought
Jean, *naming a son after me?* Perhaps he would answer it one day.
There was no hurry. Annie Blanton occupied a remote corner of his
memory. Seeing her handwriting did not stir him at all, only that the
coincidence of her marrying a Louisiana sugar planter seemed notable.

*   *   *

On Christmas eve Jean and Stephanie received several callers
who paid brief visits to Third Street and left gifts of foods and
wines. Jean thought the small children, who were among the
visitors, proved pleasurable for Albert and Mathilde as well as for

Stephanie, who loved children, even other people's. Vic passed through the drawing room several times with trays of tiny glasses of cordials and delicate cubes of fruit cake and petit fours for the adults.

At five o'clock Vic came to Jean and quietly told him a policeman had come to the door. She had shown him into the small parlor.

"He look right severe," she said. "I hope I did right to let him in?"

"Of course, Vic." Jean entered the small parlor in puzzlement. He was staggered by the uniformed man's quiet announcement. Harry Groeble was dead—a suicide.

"I'm sorry, sir. I felt you must be notified immediately."

Jean steadied himself. He felt as if the wind had been knocked out of him. "Of course, officer. Of course. Thank you. When? How? Does Mrs. Groeble know?"

"Sir, we felt that we should notify you first. We found this letter on his desk, so we thought we should tell you. We will go to his home after you have identified the body. We thought you might want to go with us. We just weren't sure . . ."

"What happened? How did you know? Tell me what you know, officer." Jean rubbed his hand over his mouth and sat down abruptly in his desk chair. The policeman remained standing, clutching his hat.

"Well, sir, the policeman on the Magazine Street beat actually heard the shot. He was walking almost directly in front of your building when he heard an unmistakable pistol fire. He blew his whistle several times to attract any other officer that might be in hearing distance and mounted the stairs to Harry Groeble & Co. The door to your outer office was open so he walked in and on into what we took to be Mr. Groeble's private office. And there we found him, sprawled across his desk, gun still in his hand. He had just blown his brains out, sir. I mean they were scattered about the office by that bullet."

"Yes, I understand." Jean put his hand up to stop further details. He looked at the plump sealed envelope in Harry's hand. "*Mon dieu!* Was there any other letter?" Surely Harry would have some message for his wife. "My God," he said again. The fact was becoming clear to him. At first he was too stunned for it to sink in. *My God, Harry! I should have thought of this. I should never have left him.*

"What time did this happen? How long ago?"

The policeman looked up at the wall clock. "It's been over an hour, now. I'm the officer that heard the whistle from half a block away. I ran toward the sound; I blew my whistle, and Officer O'Toole came out and called me up. We know you sugar and cotton gentlemen on the street, we who walk the beats of the finance neighborhood. I haven't even reported to the precinct captain."

"Do you have a cab?"

"Yes, sir. At your gate."

Jean stood up a bit shakily. "We'll go at once. I'll inform my wife, and I will join you immediately."

"Right, sir. I'll just wait for you at the cab, sir." He left by the front door while Jean turned to find Stephanie. Stephanie! What could he tell her? Great God! It would ruin her Christmas. And what of Harry's wife? He stopped at the closet and took out his coat and hat.

Stephanie was in the butler's pantry putting away some fruit cake after the last caller departed.

"My dear."

"Yes, Jean." She smiled. "Hasn't this been a lovely afternoon? I am so happy you have been here with us."

"Steph, *chèrie,* come into the parlor with me. I have something to say." He led her by her hand and sat her down in a chair by the window. "Stephanie, I have had some bad news. Some shocking news."

"Jean? Is it *Grand-mère?* Is it your *Père? Mère?* What has happened?" He saw her eyes searching his face fearfully. She pressed her fist to her mouth.

"It's Harry Groeble, my dear. I'm afraid he is dead."

"Mr. Groeble? Was he in an accident?"

"Perhaps. I—I am not sure. I cannot say for sure. A police officer is waiting with a cab to take me down—to where Harry is. I will be back as soon as I can, but it may take a while. It is sure to take a good while. Mrs. Groeble does not know; we must go tell her. It is terrible."

Stephanie rushed wordlessly into Jean's arms and buried her face in his shoulder. He held her a moment then pushed her gently away.

"I must go. The policeman is waiting."

He hurried back to the kitchen. "Vic," he said, "I have been called out on an emergency. Your mistress needs you badly. Stay with her as much as you can until I return. I'll probably be late. Get Daniels to help you."

*   *   *

How empty Magazine Street is. And dark. The only vehicle Jean saw was an ambulance in front of Harry Groeble & Co.'s door. The horse was white and even in the dark obviously unkempt. Its head was down near the muddy street, and it did not come up when the policeman's cab pulled to a stop behind it. The policeman told the driver to wait. Jean led the way up the stairs. At Harry's door, Jean could smell the blood, several hours old now. Already that awful rotting smell. That and the sight of Harry's body, face down on his desk, transported Jean to the battlefields of Tennessee and Kentucky. He had not looked upon death in ten years and now almost never thought of the grotesqueness of violent death. Seldom since those days and nights after coming home from Fort Delaware Prison had he had to fight desperately to shut out the terrible images of scattered bodies in bloody and broken disarray on those southern battlefields.

Goddamn those Yankees. Irrationally, in his shock, he associated the sight before him with the current climate in New Orleans that underlay the minds of men like Harry Groeble. The connection was vague, but it hung there in the foul air as he stared at Harry's thick gray hair stiff with dried blood around the horrible hole in his head from just above one ear to just above the other.

"Do you identify this body as that of Mr. Harry Groeble?" the coroner asked.

"Yes, it is Harry Groeble."

"All right, men, haul the corpse to the morgue." He gave Jean some papers to sign, and two men, not in uniform, came from the outer office and stretched the body out on a litter. Jean heard one say as they went down the stairs, "Keep your end up, Kennedy, or he'll shoot right off ahere."

The policeman said, "Better leave things like they are, sir. Lieutenant O'Bannon will want to have a look."

"All right. Cleaning people come in weekly to sweep and dust. Perhaps they could wash . . ." Jean walked into his own office and lighted a lamp. The two policemen followed him. He motioned them to be seated, and he sat down in his own desk chair.

"Well, sir, there don't seem to be much doubt, here. The gentleman did himself in. Down in the dumps, lately, was he?"

Jean ran his hand through his graying hair. "Yes, he was. He has seemed rather depressed lately."

"Would you be knowin' what his demons might be?"

Jean looked at the pair of men for a long moment. "No. No, I can't say that I do. He just seemed blue." That would be it. He was not obliged to tell them more. What difference did it make? Harry was dead. Now, he had to go with these officers to tell Mrs. Groeble. Poor, wretched woman. What would he say? Her children would come to the door with her. What would he say? He stood up, and in a voice that surprised him in its strength and authority, said, "Well, men, we had better speak to the widow."

As they rode into the French Quarter, Jean found that he could not remember Mrs. Groeble's first name. He had seen her only twice—that night they had him to dinner and when she and her husband attended the Christmas dance at the new Third Street house. Harry seldom spoke of his wife; when he did he referred to her as Mrs. Groeble. But all gentlemen did that.

The Pontalba apartments had wreaths in the second-floor

windows and some had candles. The facade of St. Louis Cathedral glowed from its tall doors, its inner light spilling out into *Place d' Armes*. In only a few hours Jean knew worshipers would be streaming into the cathedral for midnight Mass, and in the crowd a vile man would be looking for Harry Groeble.

Jean pulled the bell, and Mrs. Groeble sent a manservant down to open the ground-floor door for them. He bowed slightly and led them up the stairs to the apartment door where Mrs. Groeble admitted them. There they were, the two children with their mother. Were they expecting their father? He couldn't tell.

"Why Mr. Levert." Then she saw the uniformed officers, and her hand went to her throat.

Mrs. Groeble's sister, who was with the family for Christmas, took the children out of earshot. The servant disappeared. When Molly Groeble heard the news her face showed shock, Jean saw, even horror, but she held herself amazingly well. Like Jean, she said only that her husband had seemed somewhat depressed but had made no threats. While she talked with the policemen, Jean walked to a lamp and took the letter out of his pocket. With his back to the others he opened it, intending to take a quick look. To his surprise there was another smaller envelope inside. On it was written, *For my wife*. Leaving the letter to himself in the larger envelope, he put it back into his pocket. He walked back to Mrs. Groeble and handed her the letter addressed to her.

She looked at it hesitantly before she accepted it. "Thank you. I will read it alone if I may."

"Of course, Madam," said a policeman. "But if there is any information that you believe the authorities should know, Madam, please inform us. Lieutenant O'Bannon will call on you."

Jean offered to assist her, to make funeral arrangements, to help her in any way possible during the next few days. He thought her self-possession remained almost unbelievable. She would send a telegram to Harry's brother who lived in Mobile and who could come immediately and handle everything for her.

"Now I must see to my children," she said, near to breaking

down, if Jean could judge.

Jean stood before her and bowed stiffly. "We will leave you then, Mrs. Groeble. Let me say that I held your husband in the highest esteem. He was a noble gentleman, honored by all who knew him. I will always be grateful to him for what he did for me." He cleared his throat quietly. "If we can be of no further service tonight, we will take our leave. I will speak with you again tomorrow. And in the meantime, don't hesitate to call on me if I am needed. You have my address, I'm sure."

"Thank you, Mr. Levert." She managed a wan smile. "My husband was extremely fond of you." Molly closed the apartment door behind them, and the servant escorted them down the long stairs to the street. He said goodnight and locked the door. Jean was thinking of the lady's remarkable composure as he walked to the cab. Suddenly, from the rooms above, the rooms they had just left, came a long ragged scream. And another. And another. All three men turned and looked up at the lighted windows. Then they stood back looking at each other in silence, seemingly uncertain whether to go back or to get into the cab. Finally, Jean stepped in the cab and the other men followed him.

"You see," said one of the policemen, "them that try to hold it all in sooner or later got to let off the steam or they go crazy. I seen it many a time."

The cabbie had been ordered to go to the station house on Canal Street. When they arrived there, Jean assured the officers that he was at their disposal regardless of Christmas. He thanked them sincerely for their services, for he felt that they had performed their duties in the best possible manner. Then he ordered the driver to the Third Street address.

On the ride home he sat in the dark depths of the cab, as he had only two nights before after leaving the distraught Harry. He felt that he should have been more sensitive, more discerning of Harry's despair, in preventing his friend from taking his life. All the way home he kept his hand inside his coat touching the letter from his partner.

Jean stepped out onto the paved square before his gate and

paid the driver. He was glad that Daniels had left the gas lamps burning on the veranda. It occurred to him that if all colored people were like Vic and Daniels, all this trouble in the City would not exist. He entered the house quietly and removed his hat and coat. He walked quickly to the small parlor and lighted the lamp on his desk. Holding Harry Groeble's letter under the glow, he read the message scrawled beneath the engraving on the firm's letterhead:

"Dear Jean Baptiste, It's too late and I simply cannot go on. After living a good life untouched by taint or scandal for fifty years, I have stumbled. What I did to bring my whole world down was done with the purest of motives, and that makes my doom all the more bitter . . . My wife will never know, and though I can hardly bear to think of the shock that my act will bring to her, it is better this way. She is a stoic if one ever lived, and she will go on. I wish that my poor children would never have to know of my cowardly way out of my despair. Thank you for your friendship and for the hard work you have put into the company. You will have the will and the intelligence to go to the very top, and I know that you will achieve all that you have dreamed of. Try not to judge me harshly. And may God forgive me for what I am about to do. Your obedient servant, Harry Groeble."

Jean's hand, clutching the letter, fell to the desk. He was aghast and incredulous. Harry Groeble, the iron man, was a naive fool. He just blew this thing all out of reason. Jean didn't care whether Harry had had the girl; he had hardly thought of that aspect of the man's dilemma. Who cared? He was tempted to believe Harry though he couldn't see the point of his trailing around with this girl just to be charitable. *The wicked creature was a tramp, a poseuse. The whole business was a horrible mistake. It didn't have to happen. Goddamn.*

He pounded his fist on his desk. He had misread Harry. Had he been more observing, more caring, he would have foreseen the possibility of such an outcome yesterday morning. *It made no sense, none of it. A bright, wise businessman, who should have been knowledgeable of the ways of the world, who should have known his strengths, including the belief and support of his family*

*and friends, a man who if he had indeed done nothing wrong should
have been eager to storm the evildoer. But here a fifty-year-old man
went haywire when confronted by what he perceived to be a threat to
his good name.*

Obviously, when his situation called for self-confidence Harry's
cupboard was bare. Jean put his face in his hands and wept. Oh,
oh, oh, how sorry he was about Harry, who gave up his life out of
confusion. That was it. Harry's mind fell into a vortex of confusion
that sucked him away.

Jean took out his journal, released the gold clasp, and began
to write all these thoughts down. He hadn't written in it in nearly
two years, since Mathilde had been born lifeless and Stephanie
nearly died giving birth to her. He filled several pages; it helped
him to articulate on paper the thoughts roiling in his mind. He
wrote for more than an hour, until he knew that what he was
writing was no longer making sense. But he felt some relief; the
journal had always done that for him. All through the war he had
managed to keep some sort of paper to write on, even in Fort
Delaware Prison. He closed the leather-bound journal and clicked
the clasp shut.

Jean rubbed his eyes. He wanted to write his father tonight and
tell him about Harry. He knew his father would be shocked and
saddened; he was so pleased to have Jean in business with a man of
Harry's reputation. Jean picked up his quill, then put it back in the
inkwell. It was nearly three o'clock. He was exhausted. He must go
back to the Groeble apartment by midmorning to help with the funeral
arrangements. He had to get some sleep. He must also inform
Stephanie of the true cause of Harry's death. He feared she would be
terribly shaken. He stood up and turned out the lamp. Nothing was
left but the smell of burned oil and the silent darkness.

In their bedroom he undressed in the dark. He put on his
nightshirt and crept as quietly as possible into the high four-poster,
careful not to disturb Stephanie. He lay awake awhile, wanting to
think no more but to be asleep. Finally, the comforting rhythm of
Stephanie's breathing helped him to sleep.

CHAPTER 32

"FELLOW CLUB MEMBERS and citizens, the urgency and importance of organization and action most certainly, I believe, are on the minds of every good citizen who has at heart the salvation and regeneration of our unfortunate state. We all know that turncoats have elected stupid and ignorant men to state offices. And worse, these turncoats have bartered their own birthrights and betrayed the principles of their race, and their country."

Jean Baptiste Levert's earnestness took the audience by surprise. He was pleased for he had recently been elected a member of the Pickwick Club of New Orleans, an elite men's club. With no hesitation in his manner, he continued his address on this March evening, 1874, at his club on Canal Street.

"I want to thank you gentlemen. This is a great honor you've given me—to one so new among your ranks—to address you on such a serious matter. The feeling of alarm among all our people is growing stronger. All because of a bill helped to passage by our so-called state legislature composed of Negroes and carpetbaggers that authorized formation of a brigade of metropolitan police now controlling this fine city . . . I'll do whatever it takes to preserve our way of life that seems to be sliding into oblivion."

Jean stared into the audience of about two hundred for a moment, his cheeks flushed. The press of bodies of Pickwick Club members, the upper crust of New Orleans male society, made the hall feel stuffy despite the chill outside, and in the smoky light of oil lamps he saw the gloss of heat on every face. Some members stood in the aisles and at the rear, while others leaned against the surrounding walls on which were portraits of the club's first officers of 1857. A large bookcase held current books on the Civil War and pamphlets describing the relationship between the club and the Mistick Krewe of Comus, the City's oldest Carnival organization; both club and krewe were founded the same year by the same citizens.

Colonel Louis Bush had arrived early enough to capture a seat on the front row, and he seemed to be holding the seat beside him, which was vacant. Jean noticed the Colonel watching him. He had nodded recognition when the Colonel had sat down.

Jean continued: "A series of bad sugar crops, havoc of yellow fever epidemics, financial panic of last year that crushed our sugar commission industry, stagnation of commerce, all have spread despair over our downtrodden city. Intelligence, honest industry, and rights of property are without representation in the ignorant, corrupt state legislature still operated by the Federals here in New Orleans. Scandalous fortunes that are being made with no other capital than a carpetbag have dried up the service of vital credit and emptied the public treasury." Pounding his fist on the lectern, he asked his audience: "Who should take the responsibility for the ambitions of the Negro voters? State officeseekers who cower at the feet of a counterfeit governor by the name of William Pitt Kellogg?"

Jean and all the Democrats present in the hall regarded the radical Republican Kellogg as a usurper. He knew Kellogg, who had been inaugurated governor in early 1873 at the Cabildo in New Orleans, had alienated sugar growers like his family, because of the Republican Party's crushing tax program that combined fraud with liberal social legislation and depended on the Negro vote for passage. Most white citizens, former Confederates, were still not allowed to vote. Some white citizens had devised a scheme they called Unification, which, according to Jean, intended to bring together the better elements of the Democratic Party, the white man's party, and to help reduce the dangers threatening them under the federally controlled state government. Louisiana Democrats, especially Jean, felt that they could no longer live under these intolerable and ruinous circumstances.

Jean paused to sip some water and looked again over his rapt audience. He recognized an elderly gentleman entering the hall, a tall man who met Jean's gaze as he was ushered to the front and seated in the chair next to Colonel Bush. The two Civil War veterans greeted each other warmly, then both nodded approvingly toward Jean. Jean smiled as he waited for the two distinguished guests to get comfortable. The new arrival was General Alexandre Étienné DeClouet of St. Martinville, who had been the Whig candidate for governor, barely losing, when Jean was about ten years old. But Jean had heard of him and his family from Auguste and in the schoolroom. The General's father, who had established the military Attakapas Post, which became St. Martinville in 1817, was killed in a duel, adding to the family mystique. Most recently, General DeClouet was gaining attention for having spearheaded formation of one of the first White Leagues in Louisiana at St. Martinville. The unexpected appearance of such a personage inspired Jean to greater fervor:

"Fellow Pickwickians, we cannot close our eyes to the fact that a black league is in full operation and that its object is to overthrow the last defenses of our dearest rights as citizens." His voice became more impassioned. "Are we fallen so low as to bend our necks under their yoke? Are we prepared to surrender our manhood to give the lie to the superiority of our race—the white race—and bequeath to our children the shame of a disgraced country? NO!" Jean's fist hit the lectern again. "A thousand times no!" He leaned over the lectern and in a lower but intense voice ended his speech: "In the face of a common danger, let us forget for a moment our personal ambitions. We trust all Pickwickians and Louisianians will respond to our appeal and join in with the organization of a White League for New Orleans."

As Jean, wiping his damp face, stepped down, Colonel Bush came forward and shook his hand. He introduced General DeClouet, who wrung Jean's hand and congratulated him enthusiastically. The noisy crowd clapped and cheered as they pushed forward to speak to Jean, and also to try to meet the visiting general.

Colonel Bush deftly steered Jean out of the crush, and they stepped out of a side door and onto the street. "Mr. Levert," he said, "let me first extend my consolation in your loss last December of your business partner and close friend, Mr. Harry Groeble. I held the gentleman in highest regard, and I am sure his departure from this life continues to be a source of grief to you."

"That is true, Colonel Bush. I am still quite hard put to handle the business without Harry Groeble's presence and expertise." Jean inhaled the fresh, cool air. "Let me say, sir, that I was delighted to have you introduce me to General DeClouet. Perhaps we should have called upon him to say a few words."

"I never thought of that. But yours was a powerful speech and needed no further comment. The General is in town to visit his broker."

"By the way, Colonel, didn't the General lead a loud cheer after the secession ordinance was signed for Louisiana to leave the Union? I seem to recall something like that."

"Absolutely, and you have a very good memory, son. His cheer really got everybody stirred up."

Before Jean could inquire further into the subject of General DeClouet, Colonel Bush said, "If you would like to escape the heat and noise in the hall, let us take a short walk along Basin." The two turned and strolled slowly away from the Pickwick Club. "If you will forgive me for speaking of business in such an informal way, I have been thinking of approaching you about a possible business alliance between you and myself. I have been most favorably impressed by your finesse as a broker and as a gentleman since Harry took me to your home several years ago when you and Mrs. Levert entertained with a Christmas dinner." He paused and cleared his throat. "Could you confer with me in my office on Thursday afternoon and allow me to talk further with you?"

Jean was careful to conceal his delight at the Colonel's invitation. "I should be happy to call on you, sir. You may expect me on Thursday. Will four o'clock suit your schedule?"

"Yes, sir." Suddenly, the Colonel laid his hand on Jean's arm.

"Look," he said, gesturing toward a house directly across the street. They paused in the dim light of Basin Street, known to have an increasing number of houses of ill repute. A young woman had walked out of the house and down the steps with a gentleman. She clung to his arm and kissed his lips until he gently loosened her hold and climbed into a waiting vehicle. As Jean and the Colonel watched, they could see a sadness in her movements and even at that distance in her beautiful face. She wore a revealing rose satin dress, draped around her shapely hips into a bustle. The décolleté would have been shocking in any other setting. Jean was mesmerized by her voluptuousness; he had never seen such a woman. Without noticing the two men, she wrapped her arms around herself against the chill and walked slowly up the steps and into the house. Inside, Jean could see a brightly lit, gaudily decorated room before she closed the door.

"Shall we go back?" said Colonel Bush. He politely nudged Jean's elbow.

"Yes. Yes, yes, of course." Jean looked back over his shoulder, half hoping that the beautiful creature would reappear.

Colonel Bush shook his head. "A sad plight for a young woman. Don't you agree? Who can guess what her background might be. It pains me to see these girls of the streets. But then we cannot solve all the world's problems, can we?"

"No, we cannot. But this one was lovely looking. She obviously cared for that man. I think she wanted to go with him in his red-wheeled barouche." Jean took one more quick look back. The light still flickered on the porch. He and Colonel Bush, both wearing fashionable frock-tailed coats and modified top hats, walked slowly.

"Basin Street evolved from a narrow lane through woods and swamps into an important thoroughfare back in the Thirties, becoming a fine residential district with imposing mansions. But it is in a direct path walked by the prostitutes near Canal and toward the river where brothels sprang up before the War." Colonel Bush appeared to know New Orleans well, thought Jean.

When the two men arrived at the Pickwick Club, they shook hands and took separate cabs to their homes. Settled in the cab, Jean continued to think of the girl they had seen, her long black hair, her shapely body. He found himself wishing he were her lover. What would she be like if he could hold her. Somewhere in the recesses of his mind came the voice of Harry Groeble on that last day, describing the beautiful saint who had captured his fancy. Poor Harry. He was a fool. Jean lighted a cigar.

So, the Colonel considered him a likely business associate? Jean was pleased but not with the surprise or humility he might have felt several years earlier. Certainly he wanted to talk with the older man. He did need someone to help maintain the New Orleans office, someone who could make it possible for him to travel out into the sugar parishes more often and also to other cities where marketing was done. He already knew of Colonel Bush's impeccable professional and social credentials in New Orleans, and his previous law practice was an added qualification.

The tip of the cigar reddened occasionally as Jean settled back and closed his eyes and enjoyed speculative thoughts until he arrived at the Third Street house. If a partnership were to be formed, he intended to take with him acquaintanceships with an increased number of planters from outlying parishes—St. Martin, Iberville, Lafourche, and others. He did not want to waste time as the panic of the market collapse ebbed and business hopes rose. Timing was everything in business—securing a competitive edge. It was especially true of sugarcane, establishing relations early with planters was more critical than in any other business.

Recalling the association between his father and Albert Desmont, Jean wanted his relations with the planters to be similarly close and confidential, lifelong when possible, socially and personally. He wasn't sure to what extent the close relationship between his father and Desmont had affected plantation policy at Golden Ridge. But it had been significant, and Jean wanted his advice and counsel to carry weight in the affairs of his prospective clients.

*   *   *

At their meeting the following Thursday on Factors' Row, Jean and Colonel Bush agreed to become partners, and they signed the partnership papers:

> *That on March 16, 1874, by and between Jean Baptiste Levert, originally of Iberville Parish, and Louis Bush, of Orleans Parish, the following agreement and covenant was entered into: Said parties hereby form from this date to expire October 1, 1875, a partnership for transaction of a general commission and factorage business, principally in sugar, cotton, and molasses, to be domiciled in New Orleans under the name of Bush & Levert . . . each partner shall furnish on or before April 1, 1874, in cash, the sum of twenty-five thousand for establishment of the house . . . main thrust of the house shall be to set a safe, sure and reliable business, selecting customers with great caution and not extending the business for the sake of business . . . should other ventures be undertaken, each partner shall furnish his quota of one half outside of the capital of Bush & Levert, and such ventures shall be kept separate from normal business . . . this covenant, to be renewed and extended every two years, shall not be affected by the death of either partner, but the survivor shall continue the administration of affairs until separation of this contract. Should either partner have died before liquidation is completed the survivor alone is vested with the liquidation . . . partnership by consent is renewed and extended to the first of April, 1876, when it is contemplated by Bush & Levert to admit Reuben Bush, son of Louis, as a member of the firm . . . .*

Chapter 33

JEAN REALIZED THAT the time had come when he must talk to his wife about the Crescent City White League and his commitment to its plans to rescue the City from carpetbag government. He had put it off for as long as he could because he did not want to alarm her. This was man's business, and wives and mothers had other responsibilities—children, households, social affairs—and should not have to be troubled with politics and its tangents.

"Steph," he said in a low voice at supper; they were alone. Vic had just left the dining room through the swinging door. "Steph," he said a bit louder. "There is something I need to talk to you about."

Stephanie raised her eyes to his face. "Yes, what is it, Jean?"

At that moment, Vic reentered the room, carrying the dessert tray and coffee. Jean shook his head negatively and looked down at the silver left at his place. Stephanie looked puzzled, but Vic's reentry had forced him to stop whatever it was he wished to say. As soon as Vic left them again, Stephanie rose and walked to Jean's end of the table, carrying her dessert and demitasse, and sat down.

"What is it, Jean? You look so serious. Is anything wrong?"

"I'm sure you know that I have become interested in the founding of the White League in the city. The organization is now prepared to take steps to defy the corrupt carpetbag government that has held this city hostage since '62. My dear, William Claiborne and Andrew Jackson wouldn't recognize this once-proud city as I am sure you know."

"What do you mean by 'take steps,' Jean?"

"I mean do whatever it takes to regain our state government. Take up arms, if necessary, fight them in the streets, if necessary. Negroes and rotten Republican whites must go; we must break the back of their administration, if you want to call it that. They are a pack of renegades, traitors, plundering politicians, and ignorant Negroes drunk with power and ambition."

Now, she looked alarmed, as he knew she would. She pulled the heavy chair closer to his.

"I am sorry to hear that you plan to involve yourself in all this. After all, you are a family man with many responsibilities—a wife, young children, your business. What do you, personally, expect to accomplish? But I have feared something like this since you came home that day and told me about the Negro bullies and the white lady on Magazine Street. I feared it but I didn't say anything."

"Oh, Steph, there is so much more to it than simply a single event. That is only one incident among hundreds. It is a general and pervasive situation, as old as the war. It is a matter that has concerned my father and my brothers and thousands of other responsible white men. It is, after all, for you and our children more than anything else that I have committed myself to participate in the actions of the White League, whatever steps the organization must take."

At that moment, Vic pushed back into the room carrying a tray with the coffee pot.

"Oh, thank you, Vic. Just set the tray down here and I will pour for us. You may go on to settle down for the night with Daniels. Mr. Levert will take the things back to the kitchen. You've been on your feet enough for one day. It's getting late." Stephanie smiled warmly at the faithful servant.

"Yazzum. But now you know I glad to look after things late as you need me."

"I know you are. But not tonight. Thank you."

"Good night, Miss Stephanie. Good night, Mister Jean."

"Good night, Vic," said Jean without looking up.

For a few minutes Stephanie sat in silent resentment. Finally she turned to her husband. "I'm not convinced you are justified in risking your life. I'm still very weak from two deliveries and two difficult pregnancies—Mathilde's and Freddy's. What about my feelings? I presume I have a choice here: Facing the risks of destructive government or facing the loss of my husband? Anyway, the thought of anything happening to you is unbearable."

Jean understood perfectly how she felt. But, as usual, he was well prepared with arguments to convince her to think his way. He said: "Our way of life is being drained away from us, largely through fear. People are afraid of going out about their business. Since coming here you have not enjoyed full freedom of moving about the garden district, much less the city. Look at the opera, our marvelous opera. It is failing because citizens have too little money to support it, they cannot get the best artists to come here, they're afraid to go out at night—take their womenfolk out at night to attend performances. That is just one example. Had you thought of that?"

"Jean, I have thought of more than you think I have. What I do not understand is your determination to take up arms—and I guess that is what you propose to do—and go into the streets to do battle. Am I wrong in thinking that is what it may come to?"

Jean looked thoughtfully at his wife. It was obvious she had been doing more thinking than he had given her credit for.

"Why haven't you talked about this to me before?" she asked.

"I wanted to have everything ready. I was not ready before, that's all."

"But you waited so long . . ." She said no more. It would do no good. She believed in Jean, and whatever her fears, he was doing what he believed was best for New Orleans and all its decent citizens, including his own wife and children.

Finally, she said, "Please set the tray in the kitchen, Jean. Perhaps you should empty the coffee pot and rinse it with water." When Jean stood, she pushed her chair back, and he helped her. The matter was settled, neither of them displeased with the other now. When he came back, they ascended the stairs to their bedroom where their infrequent disagreements usually were put to a satisfactory end.

*   *   *

Greatly relieved after telling Stephanie of his plans, Jean hurried to work the next morning to complete negotiations for purchase of several hundred acres of undeveloped property in uptown New Orleans for construction of rental houses. He planned to have lunch with his bankers at Antoine's to discuss a loan.

"Morning, Mr. Levert," said Alice Mead, as Jean entered his new office at No. 31 Perdido St., near Baronne and Poydras streets. Miss Mead, his new secretary, was tall and slender, in her late twenties, and a stylish dresser but he didn't think she was very attractive.

Jean asked her if there were any messages from Colonel Bush, who was in London on business. "No, sir, just the usual messages. Nothing from the Colonel, though." Then she handed Jean two notes, one from Amèdèe requesting food commodities to be sent to Golden Ridge; the other from Augie. "Oh, I—I almost forgot. This telegram arrived for you earlier this morning. Unfolding the yellow paper, she started to read, "To Mr. J.B. Levert : . ."

Without thinking, Jean grabbed the paper from her trembling hand. He feared it was bad news from home, that his father was ill, that the Colonel had met with some tragedy overseas.

"Are you all right, sir?"

"Yes, yes, thank you." That will be all, Miss Mead." Jean unfolded the telegram and read:

March 25, 1874

St. Louis, Mo.
    To Mr. J.B. Levert . . . note sudden passing of Adelaide Clarke STOP pneumonia STOP with deepest sympathy.
                      J.B. Brocklefurst
              Manager, William Clarke & Co.

The news stunned him. Aside from an occasional tryst while in St. Louis on business, he had not seen or heard from Adelaide in many months. He crumpled the telegram in his hand and pressed it against his chest.

*   *   *

Four months after Jean's speech at the Pickwick Club, the Crescent City White League came into existence. Jean knew the most prominent white citizens of New Orleans joined in the movement, including members of the Boston Club, and the league's platform was approved by the conservative press. Its first officers included General Frederick N. Ogden, president, and Colonel William J. Behan, first vice-president. Then members met at the Pickwick Club and signed a pledge declaring that, "the right of the people to keep and bear arms shall not be infringed."

Dr. Samuel Choppin, an orator and president of the Boston Club, helped to arouse the people with an emotional address, and the pledge attracted a tide of signatures, including those of Colonel Behan, Colonel Louis Bush, and Jean Baptiste Levert.

CHAPTER 34

MADELAINE WAS HER name. Madelaine de la Croix.

As much as Jean Baptiste had on his mind—his family, concerns with the new sugar brokerage and his alliance with Colonel Bush, not to mention his promised participation in a race war on Canal Street, in which he expected to be on the frontlines—he had never gotten the sight of her face, her eyes, hair, the shapely body out of his memory since his speech at the Pickwick Club. Quietly, secretly, he was obsessed with finding her. His fantasies of becoming her lover were highly imaginative.

So, he had begun to look for her, whenever he went out into the street from his office and back, to the Pickwick Club, to the several restaurants he frequented with his gentlemen friends, to the tobacconist. Often, he had turned to look into a passing face that was so worn and unbeautiful, so desolate of all youthful sport that he was embarrassed, and he looked away.

It seemed a long search; actually it was not. He saw her entering the house at 21 Rue de Basin late one afternoon. Only the briefest glance, but he was certain—the walk, the swing of the hips. It was the girl. After making sure that no one saw him, he went into the house, hoping to find her. The gaudily decorated front parlor was empty when he closed the door, but an older woman came in and smiled at him.

"Come in, Mr. Levert. What can I do for you?" She smiled cordially.

Jean was startled. *Mr. Levert? How does this woman know my name?*

He removed his hat. "I am looking for a young lady who entered this house a few minutes before I came in. I do not know her name, but I would very much like to speak with her." He went on before the woman could speak. "May I ask how you know my name? I do not recall making your acquaintance, and I have never been in this place before."

The woman smiled again. "Why Mr. Levert, we ladies know all you fine gentlemen of the financial district, all you busy, rich gentlemen rushing about." She bared her bad teeth in another wide smile and looked him up and down. "And I might add, handsome . . ."

"May I see the young lady? She has long dark hair . . ."

"That would be Madelaine. Madelaine is my prettiest girl. So refined and educated, too."

Again the face wrinkled into an intimate smile that made Jean increasingly uncomfortable.

"Where is she?"

"Up the stairs, third door on the right." She backed out of the small parlor through an arch hung with long tasseled velvet panels.

Jean lost no time. He bounded up the narrow stairs and quickly went to the third door. He stopped, feeling a tingling on the back of his neck. He was here, this close. The girl was on the other side of this door. He knocked softly.

"*Entreé.*" The French was unmistakable, floating like a light river breeze through the door. So her voice was as lovely as her face. Jean felt another tremor as he turned the knob.

His eyes widened in amazement as he entered; he'd never before seen such a room. He assumed it was typical of a boudoir in a bawdy house: Finely carved marbletop table next to her bed; glass-door armoire with shelves on which were linen wear and bedding; next to the armoire was a damask sofa and over the mantel a French mirror with a gilt frame; a profusion of velvet curtains; on the walls were several oil paintings, including a nude. Her access to money was apparent in many of the garish furnishings. And he saw her standing near a window that permitted light to glow through the flesh-colored peignoir that draped in soft folds to her small bare feet. The dark hair fell heavily over her shoulders and down her back. Her skin was flawless rich cream, and her eyes were dark and long, fringed with thick lashes. Jean was transported by her perfect beauty. He moved his hat from one hand to the other.

"May I take your hat?" she said in her low voice. When she did not reach for it, Jean walked across the room and handed it to her. When she laid the hat on the chair between them, her peignoir fell off one shoulder, revealing one full round breast and a bright pink diamond-hard nipple. She made no move to cover herself. Looking directly at him, she said, "Do you want to spend some time with me?"

"Yes."

Easily, she stepped close to him so that her body was near but not quite touching his. Jean slowly pulled the peignoir off her other shoulder, looking down at her taut breasts as he did. She untied the loose sash, and the garment fell to the floor. Jean laid his hot palms over her nipples, massaging them, his fingers caressing, enveloping the beautiful breasts. She moaned, lifted her lips to his hungry deep kisses, then deftly, slowly began to remove his clothes, his coat, his waistcoat, his shirt, slowly laying studs and cuff links on a small table by the bed. Her deliberateness of movement was so erotic that Jean thought he might faint from delight. She was incredible. He was mad with the touch and the smell of her. Finally divested of his last piece of clothing, he allowed her to press him back onto her bed.

For the next hour, Jean could not have named any woman he had ever made love to. His mind was totally void of any cogent thought about anything or anyone except this perfect unstoppable creature. And he did not have to think about her. He absorbed her. When it was over and he was dressed, he put her peignoir around her and tied the sash for her. He felt some call for decorum with which Madelaine was not bothered. He held her body close for a few moments before he told her that he must go.

"Why must you? Are you tired?"

"Aren't you?"

"No. I could love you all night." Jean smiled at that.

"Will you come back?"

"Do you want me to?"

"Yes."

"Then I will be back."

"When?"

"Soon."

"Will you come back often?"

"Often," he promised.

Downstairs, the uncharming madam appeared through the velvet hangings. Expressionless, she mentioned a figure, and Jean laid several bills in her hand, then departed, thankful that she was no longer so garrulous.

Darkness had fallen, and Jean glanced up and down Basin Street. Relieved to see no one, he turned toward Canal and the Pickwick Club.

He breathed a deep sigh. He had found her. And now he was overwhelmed by her beauty and her knowledge of lovemaking. He had never had such a lover, no never, never. He felt certain that he would never make that kind of love again with any other woman on earth. Not even Madelaine herself.

CHAPTER 35

HOW COULD I ever forget the power and conviction of Colonel William J. Behan, thought Jean. On the September Monday morning the Colonel was addressing the Crescent City White League assembled on Poydras Street in the New Orleans financial district, not far from Jean's office:

"You men, listen up! Men—QUIEEET! We are drifting fast toward a conflict that only the white men of this state must settle, if justice and fair play will ever rule instead of federal violence. A conflict the decision of which we would gladly remit to the votes of the radicals, to any body of civilized men in the world." Square-built, red-faced, Colonel Behan twitched his handlebar moustache, waiting for the five companies of his command to assemble before he continued: "This is also a conflict between virtue and perversion, between enlightenment and thickheaded ignorance, between civilization and barbarism . . . ."

Jean and members of White League organizations from Louisiana, along with unaffiliated local citizens, had joined Behan's Crescent City White League on Poydras Street. Jean understood why Colonel Behan, ex-soldier and war hero, had been chosen by General Frederick N. Ogden, League president, to command the troops; he was aware of Behan's reputation as one of the top three officers of Civil War commands.

About an hour later Jean's company, Company C, armed with Winchester rifles, muskets, and several twelve-pounder Napoleon guns, mustered at the Henry Clay statue at the foot of Canal Street, maintaining all the discipline of a well-drilled unit. Most of the White Leaguers, dressed for the most part in rag-tag uniforms, were on foot, but a few rode horses. While Jean stood with Colonel Louis Bush and some enlisted men, Behan's chief scout galloped up from Metropolitan Police headquarters on Canal and shouted:

"Armed men advancing, sir."

"How many, private?" Colonel Behan shot back.

"Doesn't know for certain, sir, but I venture several hundred or so. Looks to be a right strong body."

Immediately Jean felt his stomach churn. He thought of Stephanie. *Have I been a fool? What have I done now, leaving her and the children, risking my life like this?* His hope for no fight suddenly took a hard tumble; he had never seriously expected a battle. The weather—drizzle and driving winds off the river—had become nastier, which didn't help his sudden gloom. He buttoned his faded Confederate private's coat, covered himself with a scarf, and pulled down his ruffled gray trooper's cap, with a rattlesnake rattle on top, against the rain and wind. Colonel Bush quickly snapped the buttons of his old Confederate officer's coat.

But the overturned streetcars, horsecars, and makeshift barricades erected at intersections along Poydras Street were proving effective as a line of defense should a retreat ensue. More important, Jean noticed that the steamer *Mississippi* had docked at Canal, carrying a cargo of arms intended for the conservative Democrats. Deployment of Kellogg's metropolitan policemen away from the barricades and toward the foot of Canal and the river, Jean saw, was to prevent the White Leaguers from getting the much-needed guns and ammunition. The policemen thus held off, it was the Leaguers' chance to charge.

About four o'clock, Colonel Behan turned his five companies, supported by three twelve-pounder Napoleon guns positioned along the levee, against the main column of Kellogg's police brigade near the Customhouse. Jean thought he saw fire in Behan's eyes. Canal Street reminded Jean of a military camp, with sentinels standing watch in all directions from the Henry Clay statue.

"Where the hell we going?" Jean shouted, his heart racing, as Company C stormed the Customhouse, bullets whizzing past his head. No one answered him because no one apparently had heard his question.

While Colonel Behan was arranging the White League troops into position, Jean watched nervously as the enemy took its place on Canal near the Customhouse. Famed Confederate General James Longstreet commanded the Metropolitans, consisting of five hundred policemen and many Negro militiamen; General A.S. Badger, commanded the other Kellogg force; and a third brigade guarded the governor's arsenal at Jackson Square, several blocks away in the French Quarter. Suddenly General Badger and about three hundred policemen, many dressed in flannel shirts and trousers with baggy behinds, opened fire with one Gatling gun and two twelve-pounder Napoleon guns on Colonel Behan's defenses on the right.

But Jean and the Leaguers received the policemen's fire without flinching, continually charging the enemy. Jean and some Leaguers never fired a shot. He believed that the surprise attack of the Leaguers at the river's edge, combined with a charge from the front, caused the Metropolitans to scatter and rush back toward the Customhouse; then they retreated to Jackson Square. After Jean, Colonel Bush, and the other White Leaguers captured the arsenal at Jackson Square and other Kellogg-led units, the governor took refuge inside the Customhouse, and General Ogden withdrew his league forces to the original position on Poydras Street.

To Jean's relief, order was restored quickly after the short, sharp battle, and by five o'clock the City was quiet again— barricades gone, streetcars and horsecars righted and running again, and commerce resumed.

*   *   *

That evening, after Stephanie, little Albert, and babies Mathilde and Freddy were in bed, Jean decided to enter some thoughts in his journal about the battle at the foot of Canal Street. In his home office, he wrote:

> *September 14, 1874*
> *10:45 p.m.*

> We won! We won! But I feel so sad for the families of the 16 Leaguers who lost their lives and the 45 who were wounded . . . and without doubt a friendship has been forged between myself and Colonel Behan! How the hell could I ever forget the way Behan commanded the White Leaguers, and on my 35th birthday to boot . . . what a fool that damn Kellogg's been! I hope he's learned his lesson and begins responding to the wishes and rights of the citizens under his charge, and carries on government with less arrogance . . . as I predicted the carpetbag machine declined very fast after our League was formed. I think Reconstruction will end quickly now that the governor's policemen have been defeated . . . what a damn waste of a good business day, of engaging in commerce! . . . it shouldn't have come to this . . . actually I never really thought Reconstruction was an apppropriate term to describe the postwar South; hell, nothing has ever been done, little rebuilding has even been attempted!

As a postscript, he added:

> My dear Steph was right, after all! I could have been killed! I was kind of crazy to participate in this race war. But something had to be done to stop Kellogg's people, somebody had to do it. I know it was a risk, but I believed in the cause and I couldn't just turn my head as if nothing was going on.

CHAPTER 36

Perhaps nothing has had a more favorable influence on
the mercantile relations of the city than the sugar, cotton, and
rice trades, and certainly no house in that trade exhibits more
energy and enterprise than Bush & Levert

Advertisement, The Daily Picayune
March 17, 1874, announcing partnership

ARMED WITH CONFIDENCE and intricate plans, Jean traveled by train in late fall, 1875, to make several business calls in southwest Louisiana. He took the opportunity to go first to Golden Ridge to visit his parents, to look at the grinding prospects there, and to learn firsthand about family operations now being handled by Augie and Amèdèe. Colonel Bush had suggested that Jean see General Alexandre DeClouet at Lizima Plantation near St. Martinville, but Jean, knowing something of DeClouet's reputation as a flagging planter as well as a revered war hero, had been planning such a visit.

Satisfied the family businesses were going well, but sad that his mother and father were aging noticeably, Jean left Golden Ridge in a carriage he'd rented at a Plaquemine livery stable for the forty-eight mile trip to St. Martinville. *It's critical I get off on solid footing with General DeClouet . . . my first extended business trip outside New Orleans since the Colonel and I became partners, and it's my chance to impress him. I know DeClouet's situation as well as any broker—his history as a farmer is not so notable as his military and political record; he's not clever at business or farming. I'm*

more interested in these things about the General than all the battlefield
heroics and the political platform . . . I'm so determined to build my
holdings and finances at all costs, letting nothing stand in my way—
what better time to begin than now . . . hell, DeClouet's property just
might be for sale.

Jean's heart beat faster as he arrived at the grand white-columned house at Lizima. He stepped down from the buggy; the old war veteran's enthusiastic cheers and support after Jean's speech at the Pickwick Club last year flashed in his mind. He looped the bridle over an ornamental hitching post, walked across the wide gallery, smoothing his khaki trousers, and rapped the door with the handle of his whip. A manservant admitted him and announced him to General DeClouet, who sat drinking coffee and nibbling a cigar at the back of the parlor. He seemed to Jean as wooden-faced as a cigar-store Indian, a little tense. The General greeted his caller with formal politeness but not with enthusiasm; he was already late for a meeting with his son Paul and his overseer to discuss progress on the current crop.

Jean removed his brown straw hat, thrust forward his hand, and complimented DeClouet: "Your plantation, sir, pleases me. It is tasteful and productive, and you, General, are evidently a smart man in your special field." His sudden bellow of laughter made him feel rather stupid.

"I beg your pardon, Mr. Levert." A frown sending a sharp message to Jean spread over the General's bearded sixty-three-year-old face. He seemed puzzled at his guest's familiar and unsolicited compliments. "Of course Lizima pleases you, it pleases everybody. It pleases every hungry broker in New Orleans. And what gives you the idea that my plantation may be for sale or that I may be seeking additional capital from you or any brokerage house? Your presumptions, sir, are offensive, to say the least."

The General's unfriendly reaction surprised Jean, but it should not have since he was admittedly testing DeClouet as a potential client. What appeared to irk the General was Jean's cockiness and unsubtle flattery. "Your comments alarm me. Somebody must have supplied you with false information, or perhaps you desired to toss a fishing line in my direction, hoping that I would nibble your bait." DeClouet did not bother to conceal his anger. "The gall of you . . ."

Without completing his statement, the General stormed out of the parlor and into the long wide hall that divided the plantation house. A few minutes later, Jean watched him enter one of the two *garconnières* that flanked the Big House. Jean assumed it was the one that DeClouet used for his office. As he stood at the tall window, studying the elaborate architectural details of the *garconnière* and the boxwoods and roses in the formal garden that surrounded it, he stroked his moustache thoughtfully. He realized that his own clumsy behavior had gotten him into trouble again. The widow Delphine Daigle flashed through his memory. Of course, he should not try to cajole the General into revealing his plans, if he had any. The man had every right to regard his business as private. Jean gathered his courage and headed for the *garconnière*. It never occurred to him to retreat before DeClouet's anger.

Finding the General standing at his long plantation desk, Jean, his face sober and guileless, said: "Permit me to say, sir, that your plantation is beautifully secluded, out of the way from city noises and large crowds. You have wonderful privacy here. Also you have room for expansion, should you ever wish to add outbuildings. You have plenty of surrounding land available to cultivate more cane. The mansion must surely be Louisiana's most beautiful. Your possibilities seem to have no end."

General DeClouet looked at Jean and smiled in a friendly fashion, for Jean knew these kind and perceptive remarks about Lizima pleased him. "I am glad that you have taken the time to study our land here and that you appreciate the Big House," the General said.

Despite their unfortunate beginning, Jean's knowledge about farming drew the older man's respect. Jean explained that the actual reason for his visit was to sell his firm, to explain the nature of his business, to distribute catalogs advertising his firm's services, which ranged from furnishing funds and supplies to acting as agent to sell plantation products.

"Our firm's strong financial position allows us to help growers rebuild their shattered fortunes as a result of the war and Reconstruction troubles," Jean said. "You might say Bush and myself are part of a new breed of investor, or risk-taker, on the plantation landscape. We make our money from production commissions or high interest repayments from foreclosures." Jean told him that because banks still are hesitant to extend the long-term credit for operations that planters want, his firm helps planters to meet their payrolls, to buy field equipment, seed cane, livestock—in return for a share of the profits. He said Bush & Levert's capital and accumulated holdings in land, rentals, warehouses, and sugar plantations in New Orleans and in several parishes have made all this possible. "Our commissions may be high, but so are our risks."

Jean already knew that the master of Lizima had a contract with another New Orleans sugar brokerage, a firm that had been staggered by the market collapse of the sugar commission industry two years earlier, and, though still operating, did not have enough capital available to enable DeClouet to expand his sugarhouse.

Jean left General DeClouet on the gallery with a friendly handshake and almost certain conviction that the old gentleman was the latest client of Bush & Levert. *I've never accepted the creed that others had the right to stop me once I set a goal for myself, and I don't plan to start now.*

At the end of the drive, he reined the horse pulling the carriage. He gazed back up the lawn at the Big House framed by live oaks, bearded with Spanish moss. He thought he must be viewing the most beautiful plantation house in Louisiana. Visions filled his mind in which he lived in the house, saw its graceful white columns, tall windows; he saw carriages drawn up, ladies and gentlemen visiting, laughing.

*   *   *

The sugar broker called at a few more plantations in the Bayou Teche sugar district before he returned to New Orleans after a two-week absence. At the Perdido Street office the day after his return, Jean told Colonel Bush that he expected the firm to benefit from his outing, and he pleased his partner with his reports.

"Never has the country seen such growth in processes and methods flourishing now in the North, discovery and invention thriving up there," the Colonel remarked, turning the discussion to include the business of the country in general. "We here in Louisiana are still suspended in the aftermath of war. We're antiquated. Just look at New York City. As you well know, it has begun an electrically powered streetcar shuttle service and installed the country's first electric lights. San Francisco has cablecars running."

"'I know, sir, but our industry is far from being at a complete standstill. We are seeing some vital changes in field operations. I mean mechanical tools for crop cultivation—think of the plow for the hoe, the row cultivator for the gangs. Think of the cost reductions for field hands once required to cultivate cane, Colonel."

Colonel Bush smiled at Jean's analogy. "Never lose your optimism, Jean. Your positive way of viewing things is a large item on your resumé."

Still, there were other matters that did give Jean satisfaction— almost as much as chasing a client into a cane field on horseback to seal a deal with unlimited profit potential or seizing a plantation at a tax auction. On August 5, 1875, Stephanie gave birth to the couple's fifth child and third daughter. He was proud that they called her by the names of his mother and his wife: Stephanie Marie Eulalie.

CHAPTER 37

AS HE LEFT the office on this Thursday in mid-October, Jean was chilled by a cold snap with piercing winds and rain that changed quickly into sleet. The snap had ended a sultry summer that included a yellow fever siege in New Orleans, which had experienced thirty epidemics since the turn of the century. But in terms of lost lives, human suffering, and loss of production, this '78 siege was the worst on record; thousands perished in the City.

Jean and other brokers and merchants on Factors' Row, like many Orleanians, who shivered when the temperature dropped below sixty-five degrees, went straight home from their offices at the end of the business day, eager to get to the parlor fireplace or a steamy kitchen to warm themselves. But he decided not to go directly home on the day of the cold snap. Instead, he walked to the two-story brick house on Rue de Basin to visit Madelaine de la Croix.

Madelaine's house had become a refuge for him in which he unwound from the rigors of a hard-dealing day on Perdido Street. He couldn't seem to get enough of the black-haired girl, of talking to her, watching her, reveling in her sensuality. He left his inhibitions at the doorstep when he went in to be with Madelaine; she added a dimension to his life. He tried to figure out why he ever got entangled with her. Was it her knowledge of lovemaking? Was it simple hunger for a woman's company? He didn't know; he did know she fascinated him. Jean called her a close friend but he knew their relationship, including an occasional tryst, never interfered with or had any bearing on his love for and life with

Stephanie. Still, he was not without guilt feelings that sometimes threatened to torture him.

Nothing mattered to Madelaine, Jean realized. She welcomed him with enthusiasm and without reservation anytime he chose to be with her. She told him he was different from the other men she had known in her life and that she broke a rule with him she had adopted and applied early in her career: Never kiss a man on the mouth lest you become emotionally involved. The first thing Madelaine did when Jean arrived this evening was to kiss him on the mouth—a long, deep kiss. In almost metaphysical order, after she had first kissed him on the mouth, she had fallen in love with Jean.

Over savory seafood gumbo, Jean told Madelaine about a recent business trip to St. Louis. He described the city and its attractions, saying they reminded him of New Orleans. He explained how fortunes were made and lost in minutes on the floor of the New Orleans Cotton Exchange. He told her about his experiences as a prisoner of war.

She shuddered at his description of Fort Delaware Prison. "God in heaven, Jean, how did you get through that hell alive?"

Looking up from his gumbo, he gave her a quick answer: "By faith and a lot of praying." He ate a final lump of white crabmeat and placed his spoon on the underplate. Madelaine was seated across from him at a small French "two-table," just large enough to hold two place settings. A servant had brought the food up from the kitchen to her sleeping chamber.

Later, after making love, Jean told her about managing his family's cane operations at Golden Ridge when he was only fifteen at the time his father was ill; how he feigned death on the battlefield in Kentucky to avoid capture by Yankees. After talking of such experiences, he grew self-conscious at what he saw as his impulsive revelations. As his mood changed, guilt fell over him like a mantle. Guilt was the price he paid after such relieving talk and other pleasures he enjoyed with Madelaine. *So far I've been able to manage the guilt.*

Jean did not share with Stephanie word of hard financial times or any threat of failure in business. He believed such worrisome admissions to one's wife were unseemly, just as unseemly as making the kind of uninhibited love with Stephanie that brought him to Madelaine's boudoir. He scarcely thought of such a thing. Certainly, he never yearned to unburden himself about business matters with her. He assumed that Steph would be alarmed or confused or both.

But Madelaine? Her sympathetic attention made him want to share every facet of his life except, of course, his life with Stephanie, which, in the labyrinthine circuits of his reasoning, Jean held sacred. At the same time, the occasional thought of someone discovering his affair with Madelaine aroused fear in him. That, too, he managed to hold in abeyance, that is to say, he managed to keep such thinking aside.

Madelaine snuggled closer to Jean, instantly rekindling a firestorm in his heart. She stroked his brow, passing her hand down his cheek, over his lips, and back up to his forehead. He gazed at her soft beautiful face and eyes. He knew he must tear himself away. Now. After he dressed to leave, shortly after midnight, Madelaine kissed him on the mouth again, twice, then murmured: "Please come back soon, will you? Please come . . ."

"I will, I will try." He saw that the lack of resolution in his reply didn't escape Madelaine. "I must go home to Plaquemine early in the morning. There is some business with my father that I need to discuss, then I'll be off to Chicago on business. "But when I return to the city . . ."

Jean did not finish. He clutched Madelaine's small soft hand tightly and kissed her fingertips, then left her second-floor sleeping chamber, descended the stairs, and went out into the dark, damp cold of Basin Street.

*　　*　　*

To Jean's shock, near disbelief, Daniels was waiting for him outside Madelaine's house.

"Mister Levert, please, sir. I come to fetch you. I sorry, no offense meant, but your baby girl is sick, bad sick. Madam, she need you. I lef her with Vic and the doctor."

He opened the door to the fashionable new buggy, recently bought for Stephanie.

Jean said only, "Take me home, Daniels, as fast as the horse can go." Fear for his child's life, sudden realization of spending hours with Madelaine when Steph was at home with a sick child, Daniel's knowledge of his affair, altogether stunned him. He felt a hard rush of shame and guilt, but it was overridden by his enormous concern for tiny Marie Lucie, his eighteen-month-old daughter, and for Stephanie, his poor beloved Steph. His throat was painfully tight and his tear ducts burned. The evening just passed in Madelaine's arms, which he had thought he could defend against the world, now seemed sordid.

Jean found Stephanie, eight months pregnant with their seventh child, and Dr. Anton Fortier bent anxiously at Lucie's crib. They were trying to cool her fever with wet cloths, mopping her face and small dimpled hands, hoping to reduce her temperature which had shot to 106 degrees earlier in the evening. Her face still flushed, the baby tossed from side to side as if in pain.

Finding Jean at her side, Stephanie threw herself into his arms and broke into sobs; it was as if a dam had burst. She screamed, "Oh, God, Jean, our baby has yellow fever! Why in God's name can't you be here when we need you? Look at our precious little girl, our happiest, smilingest child." Still weeping bitterly, she turned back to the crib where Lucie continued to be restless, her eyes glazed and blank.

"Dr. Fortier, is our baby going to die?" Stephanie clutched the sleeve of the man with massive shoulders and a wiry beard.

"Mrs. Levert, we have used every measure known to the medical profession of this city. All we can do now is try to cool her temperature and pray."

Jean felt completely useless. He also felt as much fear for Stephanie's survival as he did for poor little Lucie's. Stephanie looked gaunt and thin, making her distended belly appear grotesque. Her skin had no color, and fear burned like a sickness in her eyes. The loss of Aloysia at St. Gabriel, her critical illness at the deliveries of Mathilde and Freddy, and Freddy's delicate condition at birth, had worn down her twenty-eight-year-old body. Jean wondered if she could bear the loss of another child. She adored the children; they were her life. Her care of them was as complete as he could imagine—their health, their comfort, their amusements, and so much love, everything. Yes, they were her life. He tried to comfort her, and he found her trying to comfort him.

"Poor Jean," she said over and over.

Dr. Fortier, skilled in the care of yellow fever patients, instructed them before he departed to call on other victims of the epidemic: Keep trying to lower her fever and keep her body covered against draft. Although the disease was not contagious, he told them to keep the other children away from Lucie as much as possible. Lucie had been thoroughly purged with calomel. Stephanie and Jean kept vigil for the rest of the night and into the next day.

At eleven o'clock the next morning, black projectile vomiting seized Lucie, and Jean and Stephanie knew that their little girl was dying.

"Lord, oh, God! Have mercy on us!" Stephanie's anguished screams emitted from the upstairs nursery at Third Street. She reached for her child, as if she had hope of pressing life into the small, dying body. "Please, Lord, please have mercy on us." She clasped her hand in prayful mien. "Oh, merciful God, why—why?"

Jean thought his heart would burst with pain as he watched Stephanie gently lift her baby from the crib and sit down in the rocker in which she had so happily rocked all her babies. She handed Lucie to him, and he held her tenderly for a few moments. Then he gave her back to Stephanie and called Vic to bring in their other children, Albert, almost eight; Mathilde, six; Freddy, four; and Stephanie Marie, three. The children stood, heads cast down, around their mother's chair looking at the pathetic form of their baby sister.

Their mother said, "Each of you kiss Lucie for God's blessing and everlasting peace and then kiss her goodbye for yourselves."

In silent awe they did as they were told and then quickly filed from the nursery into the care of the faithful Vic.

Jean could not suppress his tears. "This is too hard. I can't take any more of this."

For the rest of the afternoon Stephanie sat by the window, holding the baby in a sunlit spot, as if she hoped that the sun's warmth might restore her. The parents cried together and tried to comfort each other as they waited for death. Death was slow coming.

*   *   *

Jean and his family bowed their heads in submission as Marie Lucie Levert was laid to rest at sunrise on Saturday, October 19, in Metairie Cemetery beyond the city limits. Formerly Metairie Race Course, the six-year-old cemetery had attracted governors, senators, and the business elite to participate in the carnival-like madness of horse racing.

At home after the funeral, Jean and Stephanie were touched by the warmth of the many sympathy messages they had received from their friends in the Garden District, associates on Factors' Row, business friends in New Orleans and surrounding Louisiana—the Behans, Bushes, LeBlancs, Molly Groeble, Harry's widow.

*   *   *

The Leverts welcomed a third son a month after Lucie's death. He looked so much like Jean that Stephanie smiled at him and her family with some of her old cheer. "We must name our new son Jean Baptiste, Jr.," she said to her husband and children, and they all heartily agreed.

But Jean and Stephanie knew they would never get over the loss of Lucie. Jean began bringing work home from the office and continued to do so for months after Lucie died. On rare occasions, he visited his properties in the City and outlying parishes. He and

Colonel Bush continued to work in close harmony, the Colonel having great sympathy for the grieving Jean. Jean showed no emotion, outwardly. At home he was smiling and cheerful with Stephanie and his children. He became acquainted with his new son in the intimacy of a home atmosphere that he had never had after the births of his older children. He supported Stephanie with more love and compassion than he had exhibited before in their marriage, and he sensed that she loved him for it.

Stephanie maintained a slight smile most of the time, Jean saw. Her manner with everyone remained kind and gentle, as it had always been. But Jean could see none of the old sparkle that had so charmed him since his first sight of her during the Civil War when she was only twelve years old. When he and any of the family at Third Street came upon Stephanie, they could almost always see that she had been weeping, and seemingly powerless to stop.

Jean saw Madelaine de la Croix only once again, to tell her that he could not see her again. He was convinced that Lucie's death was God's punishment for his being with Madelaine the night that the baby became so desperately ill. Jean did not know how Daniels knew about his philandering, but neither he nor Daniels ever mentioned it again.

CHAPTER 38

"OF COURSE, GENERAL DeClouet's broker, Thomas Brierre & Co., is near bankruptcy and cannot possibly finance the extensive maintenance and improvements needed at Lizima. We both know that," said Colonel Bush, tapping a bit of ash from a newly lit cigar. At Antoine's, seated across from Jean at a wooden table covered with a crisp, white tablecloth, the Colonel pulled the heavy glass ashtray toward himself as the formerly dressed waiter set demitasses of fresh black coffee before them. "Maybe it's time one of us paid the old gentleman another visit. We might be his only hope."

Jean blew smoke to one side. "Oh, yes, I'm watching the General. He didn't like me very much when I called on him at Lizima Plantation four or five years ago. But he may have little choice now. I figure we should let him play out all his cards any way he can. He needs thirty or forty thousand, and we both know few houses can risk that kind of money these days, especially to a man who is as poor a farmer as he is a businessman." He told the Colonel he had fallen in love with the plantation house that day, a beautiful house with an ampleness and elegance that would be hard to match, yet with a roomy informality that charmed him. "Colonel, you should see the galleries, upstairs and downstairs, front and back. And the most intriguing staircase tucked away midway in the wide central hall, almost hidden until one mounts the first few steps. The *garconnières* . . ." He looked down, smiling, somewhat embarrassed by his own effusiveness.

Colonel Bush smiled broadly, for he had heard Jean rave over Lizima more than once. "Why Jean, anyone might think that you covet the General's house."

"I would hate to be asked for an honest answer to that notion." Jean sipped his coffee and placed the demitasse on its saucer. He watched a waiter arranging flatware and polishing crystal drinking glasses at the next table.

"Well, which of us should make the trip to St. Martinville?" The Colonel looked Jean in the eye with mock seriousness for a moment, then burst into laughter. "I couldn't be so cruel."

"I'll be glad to go. You know that I am eager. But let's wait until after Mardi Gras. Things are piling up. After the big event is over, I'll be happy to make a quiet trip that way, probably make a few other stops in the western parishes."

The partners had spent nearly two hours at their favorite French Quarter restaurant, eating, talking about the coming Carnival season several weeks off; about the likelihood of the city council forming a new park commission to operate a park on several hundred acres of the old Foucher-de Boré properties; both men supported the movement underway to provide a public park in that part of the City. Jean knew this large acreage, bounded by St. Charles Avenue and the river and bisected by Magazine Street, was the site of the first commercial sugarcane crop on Étienne de Boré's plantation in the mid-1790s, which gave birth to the modern sugar industry in Louisiana. He knew that the acreage had a scandalous history under the corrupt Kellogg administration and that it was of great importance to all real estate speculators.

For a moment Jean's thoughts wandered to Stephanie's health, and how Lucie's death cruelly had marked the end of their first ten years together. "My God, Colonel, poor Steph's aged so much under the strains of sorrow and from her closely spaced confinements . . . the glow that I saw in her face only a few years before has been dulled by—by a physically and psychologically burdensome existence." He cleared his throat. "Mourning over Lucie has taken nearly two years out of her active life. She has no heart for social events, especially the opera. But lately I've fancied her in a leadership role in restoring the city's opera."

Jean and the Colonel sat quietly for awhile, relaxing, smoking, drinking the strong, hot coffee, enjoying the midday retreat. Hand-pulled fans circulated air from the high ceiling on the sticky day. They watched their waiter deftly rake into a small silver dustpan crisp crumbs of French bread that lay scattered over the white damask cloth. The Colonel shifted slightly in his chair, punctuating a change of subject.

"Jean, I saw a feature story in the newspaper last night that reminded me of your famous speech at the Pickwick."

"Oh?"

"Yes, do you recall that we walked a little way down Basin Street to cool off that hot night after your speech? We had a look at the houses occupied by the ladies of the evening. You've probably forgotten."

Jean's head came up in surprise. "No. No. I haven't forgotten. I remember quite well."

"We saw a young girl. Quite a young beauty. Had black hair, a beautiful face, really. So you recall her?"

"Oh, yes, I remember. I remember the girl. Yes, a dark-haired beauty. Yes." He traced a small sharp wrinkle in the table cloth with his finger. "What about her?"

"She killed herself."

Jean stared at his partner. He was speechless. *Madelaine! No!*

When he found his tongue, he said, "Oh, really. My goodness, how sad." *My God, Madelaine.* "What? How? How did she do it? I remember her. She was very pretty." *Pretty . . .*

"Oh, the paper didn't have much. Apparently it happened more than a year ago. This was just a human interest story. I think they call it that, about the city's cribs and brothels, slavery, and so on, the plight of young girls who fall into this sort of life. But they had a large sketch of her that was easily recognizable, quite good, and the house, too, and the number on Basin."

"How did she . . . ?"

"How did she do it? She cut her wrists. Blood all over everything. Poor little creature. Beautiful little girl." The Colonel shook his head and opened his hands on the table in a gesture of resignation. "Oh, well, forgive me for ending our lunch on such a note. I just thought you might remember that evening after your great speech at the Pickwick. That was quite a night for you. Remember DeClouet was there? He was mightily impressed with you." Bush slid his chair back, and a waiter stepped forward to help both gentlemen leave the table.

They walked onto Bourbon Street. Jean drew a heavy breath of humid city air into his lungs. He didn't think of Madelaine often, but occasionally that beautiful face, the large soft eyes, the long black hair passed across his mind's eye . . . he hadn't actually forgotten any exquisite part of her.

"Wonder what made her do it?" he murmured.

"What?"

"The girl. I wonder why she killed herself."

"Oh! She left a note. That's what caught the writer's imagination. She wrote, 'Never kiss a man on the mouth lest you become emotionally involved.' She had tucked it into the bosom of her dress. Perfect for the yellow journals, eh?"

Bush, his cane over his arm, lifted his hat to a passing acquaintance as he and Jean turned toward Perdido Street.

* * *

Jean left his office during the afternoon to visit his tobacconist, and when he returned Colonel Bush had laid the paper on his desk. When Jean saw the small wrinkled paper, he recoiled as if it had been a snake. He did not want to read the article, and he most certainly did not want to look at the illustrations. He rolled the paper up tightly and put it into his waste basket for the cleaning people to take away. He realized that his partner was innocent in placing it there. He had no idea. Or did he? After all, Daniels knew. Jean decided Bush did not know anything about his affair with Madelaine. *He'd have come forward, probably would have cast me out of the firm and denounced me. No, he didn't know. If he had, he would not have placed the paper there. Teasing was not his style.*

Madelaine's name was never mentioned between the two men again. In fact, Jean never heard her name again under any circumstance.

* * *

That evening Stephanie greeted him with a kiss on his cheek and after supper urged him to come into the bedroom. Her gown for the Comus Mardi Gras ball had already been completed and delivered by the *couturiére* that afternoon. It now hung on the open door of her armoire, a green velvet creation, trimmed in a paler green and white silk ruching, with bustle and train. Stephanie's green eyes became greener when she stood near the dress.

"Hmmm, *chèrie! Trés élégant!* You will be the most beautiful lady at the ball, and I shall be so proud of you." Jean imagined the décolleté, her still lovely neck and bosom. He was tempted to ask the price but held his tongue, for he had urged her to have what she most desired. On the bed were long white kid gloves, soft stockings, ruffled handmade undergarments, and a silk fan that Stephanie had spread out to display Oriental paintings of yellow and white chrysanthemums, accented with gilt and green foliage that would blend beautifully with the dress.

Like Jean and Stephanie, Colonel Bush and his wife, Celeste, loved music. As the shadows of Stephanie's sorrows had begun to lift, the Bushes suggested not only that the two couples attend the opera and theater together, but attend the Comus Mardi Gras ball in February, 1880. To Jean's surprise and delight, Stephanie had agreed to these plans with enthusiasm. Immediately she began to talk of clothes and all other preparations to attend the brilliant affairs, and Jean insisted that she "spend whatever the occasion demands" for her various gowns, wraps, and accessories. It seemed that their relationship had never been better.

By the time Jean had assumed a more normal work schedule

at his office, after months of working at home following Lucie's death, he and Colonel Bush had established a close relationship. The Colonel was thoroughly sympathetic with the problems of grief and stress. Jean had never experienced such a kindly friendship with anyone, and he considered himself blessed to have such a partner. His aggressive, often ruthless approach to business deals was tempered by Bush's more deliberate manner. Though never chastised by the obvious contrasts, Jean could not fail to see that Colonel Bush brought as much gain to the partnership with his lower-key overtures to sugar planters and brokers as Jean did with his high pressure tactics. It did not convert Jean's personality, but it affected him.

"So, you are all prepared for the ball months ahead of time," Jean continued. "So efficient! Now all you need to do is sit back and look to the big night."

"Yes, I feel accomplished. Dressmakers will get busier with every passing week. I might never have engaged *Madame Bourgogne*, and she is the finest in the city. Some of the ladies will order their gowns from Paris . . ."

"I cannot imagine a more beautiful gown than this, *chèrie*. Now, if you'll excuse me, I must get to my work."

"Oh, Jean, can you possibly spend a few moments with the children before they go to bed? They haven't seen you for several nights. Just a moment, dear, a brief word with each of them?"

Jean was tempted to shrug off the request, but he did not. "Of course, Stephanie. Send them into my office. I'll delay my work."

Vic brought the children into Jean's downstairs office where he sat with some appearance of indulgence. They filed in front of his desk, all beautifully dressed in night clothes, hair combed, and all with some apprehension on their faces. Aside from being devoted to the maintenance of the Levert household and being excellent and faithful servants, he knew together Vic and Daniels were equally capable of executing a formal dinner or bathing and dressing five growing children to bandbox perfection every afternoon for a stroll along St. Charles Avenue. Jean wondered who felt the most maneuvered, himself or the children.

"Goodnight, Papa," they chimed in unison.

"Goodnight, children," Jean nodded solemnly. Then on impulse he arose and, walking around his desk, he kissed each on the forehead. He paused briefly to look closely at little Jean, then gave him a light tilt under his chin and nodded to Vic to hustle them off to their beds.

For nearly three hours Jean bent over stacks of real estate papers, the light of the desk glistening on strands of disheveled hair, on the white shirt clinging to his shoulders because of the unseasonably high humidity, the shirt's folds suggesting the stoutness of his body. He worked on Stephanie's own inheritance, which he carefully invested. He protected her principle with no thought otherwise, ever to risk losing it; he reinvested her yields with equal diligence. He also studied notes about possible purchasable land before he put out his lamp and went to bed with Stephanie, where he slept peacefully until seven the next morning.

Chapter 39

IN EARLY JANUARY Jean received a long letter from General Étienné DeClouet announcing his plans to attend Mardi Gras in February, 1880. "I have never been to the Mardi Gras in the city," he wrote, "and since I shall soon be sixty-nine years old, I think that if I am ever to witness the spectacle, it should be now. I intend to bring my son, Paul, and his wife, Celeste, and their son, my grandson Paul, Jr. We shall be stopping at the St. Charles Hotel." He went on to recall "with pleasure the visit from Mr. Jean Baptiste Levert" several years earlier, and said he wished to discuss the likelihood of Bush & Levert becoming his broker for future business. "We shall arrive on the day before Fat Tuesday and would like to meet with you on Thursday. I have been told that no businesses function the day after Fat Tuesday, but I trust that you can see me the next day. I must return to Lizima and my responsibilities here, and in fact we have train reservations to return early Friday morning."

Jean and Colonel Bush had spent the fall and winter responding to reports on the '79 cane crop and sugar production. They felt their clients' fortunes were varied—weather conditions similar throughout southwest Louisiana; temperatures were about the same, but rainfall heavier near the coast; flooding at the right or wrong time could be welcomed or feared according to the stage of growth or cutting; hard windstorms destroying cane and damaging acreage to different degrees within the sugar parishes. Jean knew a lot depended upon the wits of the planter, who must be both farmer and businessman. The partners felt that the season just

past had been a favorable one for planters, with one exception—
General DeClouet. The brokerage had heard directly from the
General before Jean could carry out his intended visit to Lizima
Plantation.

Jean went into Colonel Bush's office and handed him the letter
from the General. He stood silently while Bush read it. "Well, the
mountain has come to Mohammed. You won't be going to St.
Martinville, after all."

"Not anytime soon, anyway," said Jean, smiling. "Eventually
I'll be going. Whatever the General borrows, he won't be able to
pay it back."

"Now, Jean, don't be greedy." Colonel Bush stroked his dark,
graying beard. "Poor man, you can be sure we are his last hope.
Brierre told me his firm couldn't bail out a small skiff, let alone
DeClouet's leaky ocean liner."

Jean digested his partner's metaphor. "DeClouet may be the
chief cause of the bankruptcy of Thomas Brierre & Co. They have
pumped tens of thousands into Lizima. We have to remember
that, Colonel."

The Colonel nodded. "Brierre also told me that DeClouet could
not even pay the wages owed the manager he hired to bring in the
'79 crop." He shook his head in sincere sympathy. "He never has
been able to make all those machine repairs to his sugarhouse."

"And they are absolutely essential to a productive and profitable
operation. DeClouet is no farmer. He is a war hero, a politician,
a—a—an aristocrat! He doesn't even know how pretentious he
can be! If we know we can come out ahead eventually, I think we
should lend him what he needs. We must find out how much he
does owe, and we need our most ironclad agreement." Jean's hand
gripped the edge of his partner's desk.

"Well, he's all yours. You know our ship sails on Friday
morning, and I won't be available for this interview." He smiled,
folding the letter, and handed it across the desk to Jean. "While
you get ready for the old boy, my wife and I will be spending our
last day at home before the great Mediterranean tour. It's our second
trip to Europe, you know. This will be better than before. We're

older and can appreciate the old countries and their antiquities
and natural beauties." He looked at Jean with affection. "You should
take Stephanie on such a tour. She would be so at home in France.
And so would you."

"It's too expensive. France would be cold in February." Jean
yearned for no such luxury.

"Jean! I'll wager you have the first dollar you ever earned." He
shrugged. "Don't wait too long. Travel is strenuous. You won't be
able to do it forever. This will be a warm vacation. We're docking
on the toe of Italy, won't go farther north than Milan. Of course,
we wouldn't cross the North Atlantic in early February."

It was Jean's turn to shrug. He picked up DeClouet's letter.
"I'll get a reply off first thing in the morning."

"Why don't you take the DeClouets to dinner?"

"That would be too expensive. Remember we aren't catering
to him; the General wants our favor."

"Very well, Jean." Bush chuckled. "I know Bush & Levert is
not about to lose one cent with you at the bargaining table." He
stood up, taking his hat and coat off the tall walnut rack. "Speaking
of restaurants, let's walk over to Tujague's on Decatur for lunch."
He reached back for his gold-headed cane. A gold-headed cane
like the Colonel's was a little luxury, an ostentatious little luxury,
that Jean wanted.

"I'll get my coat," said Jean. As they walked down Perdido
Street, he ventured, "You know, Colonel, I really admire your cane.
I wish Stephanie would think of getting me one for my birthday."
His face was serious and he looked straight ahead.

Bush looked at him surprised, then laughed. "Well! I'll pass
that hint down the line."

"We are looking forward to *La Traviata* and to the Comus
Ball," said Jean, after the men were seated at a small table in Tujague's
located near Jackson Square. Jean spread a large white napkin
over his lap. "I must say Stephanie has gathered up a stunning
wardrobe for the winter affairs. My children are as pleased as their
mother over the coming festivities."

Jean said again that his wife had lost almost two years during which there was little light-heartedness. Her newly kindled pleasures over the opera and the ball pleased him; he regarded them as therapy for her. Also, he anticipated his own pride and fulfillment in Stephanie's style and beauty. He looked at the calm relaxed face of Colonel Bush. *Bush is so damned confident, so comfortable about himself, about everything.* Celeste was at least fifty-five. She was neither beautiful nor young, yet Jean knew Bush loved her deeply. She had great quiet dignity. She probably had not bought a new gown for years. Jean leaned forward as chicoried coffee was served. As sometimes happened, he thought of Madelaine. Her face seemed to appear on the glistening surface of the black coffee, her black hair swirling in his fantasy. He loved Stephanie, and he knew that if she behaved during lovemaking as Madelaine had he would not be comfortable with it.

The Colonel told Jean that their first trip to Europe had been on their honeymoon, after a big New Orleans wedding in St. Louis Cathedral with most of social New Orleans present. He said he and Celeste had talked of a return visit to Europe during their entire married life. "This Mediterranean tour is to be a dream come true. We plan to see southern Spain, France, Italy, and Greece."

"I am sure you will have a splendid time," Jean said.

After plodding through the excellent meal of seafood jambalaya, imported draft beer, and coffee, the two men discreetly loosened their belts and left the restaurant with their coats buttoned. Jean returned to the office to compose a letter to General DeClouet and Colonel Bush said he was going home for the afternoon.

* * *

Dear Sir:

Colonel Louis Bush and I are in receipt of your letter informing us of your visit to New Orleans and your wish to call upon us on Thursday, February 8. Colonel Bush will be on an ocean trip to southern Europe, that is Italy and other countries on the littoral. But I shall be here and I shall make myself available to you and your son on that day. All business

*in New Orleans is usually shut down for the rest of the week
after Mardi Gras, but in consideration of your wish to make
the long trip from St. Martinville to New Orleans, I will be in
my office . . . Unless I hear differently from you by letter, I shall
expect you in my office at No. 31 Perdido Street at 10 o'clock
on Thursday, February 8.*

Your obedient servant

Jean read over the letter and was satisfied with the polite, noncommittal tone. He tore it out of his notebook and took it to Miss Mead. "Have this ready to go off in the morning mail pickup, please."

She nodded, her square jaws and prominent teeth seeming grotesque to Jean. In ten minutes, she laid the perfectly executed copy on his desk for him to sign. He read it and made no corrections. He handed it to her as he left for the day. The popular Creole style of *table d'hôte* dining and the fine beer he had drunk at Tujague's had made him sleepy.

"Good day, Miss Mead."

"Good day, sir," Miss Mead croaked. "Shall I lock up?"

"By all means." He just couldn't enjoy any sort of exchange with a woman as homely as Miss Mead, yet he realized it could be disastrous to have a pretty secretary.

Instead of going home, he dropped in at the Pickwick Club. He sat in a leather chair by a big window and nodded until six o'clock.

*   *   *

Jean walked home on the January evening after leaving the Pickwick Club. It was a long walk, but he felt rested after the eventful day. The short nap by the window at the club had refreshed him. Temperature was a pleasant 65 degrees, and there was an unusual lack of humidity in the atmosphere. He felt a certain satisfaction knowing that he had now almost certainly set up his firm's eventual acquisition of Lizima Plantation. The loss to General

DeClouet scarcely crossed his mind. After all, the General owned at least two, maybe three, other plantations near Lafayette. At his age, the old gentleman should be relieved at last to be rid of Lizima. No, Jean knew better than that. DeClouet loved Lizima. His wife had lived with him there and had died there. He wanted it for his heirs.

Bush & Levert decided to prop him up through another season, make sure that the necessary repairs were done on the sugarhouse, support the hiring of a decent manager, and wait to see what happened. In the unlikely event that the plantation could be restored to profitable productivity under DeClouet, then certainly the firm wouldn't stand in the way of the General's survival and enrichment. If he could make a rich harvest, pay off a fortune in old debts and, of course, new debts, the firm would rejoice with him. Jean smiled at such fanciful notions.

On his way home, Jean glanced at the glow of gaslit shops and homes that lined Magazine Street. A butcher was rolling into his small shop bins of sausage that he had displayed for the day. The strong smell of boiled shrimp wafted through the double doors and tickled his nose as the butcher bumped his wares over the threshold. The crudely painted window sign said: OYSTERS 25¢ PER GALLON: LIVE HENS 35¢ EACH. *Prices haven't gone down since the official end of Reconstruction.*

He had his own chickenyard within a tall board fence behind the horse barn. There was a small chickenhouse with a roost made of bamboo poles and hay boxes where the six White Leghorns layed almost enough eggs for the family's needs, and a small flock of Rhode Island Reds that included a handsome rooster that crowed at daybreak. Jean found pleasure in going out most evenings that he was at home before dark and throwing handfuls of corn on the ground for them. They lowered their heads and ran for the corn, pecking it up kernel by kernel. He watched them drink water from a round water pan, dipping their beaks into the holes over its top and tipping their heads back to let it roll down their long throats, their round eyes blinking, alert. Occasionally, he suggested that Vic or Daniels select a hen before she got too old and tough, wring her neck, and make dinner from her. He didn't regard his flock as pets. He had never dealt with chickens as a boy on Golden Ridge, though there was a large flock kept for eggs and meat for the Big House and to help feed his father's slaves. He never pondered his interest in chickens. He did think of one thing, as he glanced at a row hanging by their yellow waxy feet on the butcher's counter in the dim light of an oil lantern: Anyone of his well-fed chickens cost more than 35 cents.

Jean turned the corner onto Third Street. As he approached his iron gate, he heard the clip-clop of hooves on cobblestones, horses drawing a streetcar on St. Charles Avenue. The gate handle pivoted in his palm as he swung the wrought iron gate closed. He climbed high steps toward a flickering wall lamp, and Daniels opened the front door for him.

"Come in, Mister Levert. Have a nice day? Yes, the chilrens all in bed. If they not asleep, they tucked in for the night." He walked solemnly to the coat closet. "Madam Levert in the parlor."

Jean stepped into his office and laid his full briefcase on the rosewood top of his desk. He went into the bath and washed his hands and splashed his face. With a soft white trousseau towel he patted his face dry. Refreshed, he joined Stephanie in the parlor where she sat working on her petit point.

"Jean, you're home early!" She looked at the grandfather clock, which struck the first note of seven. "Have you had a nice day?"

Jean tugged gently at his waistcoat. "Very nice, my dear. Very nice, indeed. And how about you?" He leaned forward and kissed her forehead. He sat down in his chair, upholstered in dark red brocade that matched the French settee where Stephanie sat. A circle of light from the lamp nearby cast a soft yellow glow over them.

"I must tell you, dear, that little Jean gave me quite a turn this morning. I feared he had broken a bone."

"What happened?"

"He fell. He climbed up in that chinaball tree in the corner behind the chickenyard, and he fell and hit the ground very hard. It knocked the wind out of him. Mathilde screamed, and all of us rushed out. Daniels picked him up and slapped him on the back until he gasped and sucked air into his lungs. I was terrified. I've begged him not to climb."

"Is he all right?" Jean asked her with compassion, for he knew she was haunted by threats to the lives of the children.

"Yes, he seems to be perfectly well. But I wish he would not give me such a scare."

"My dear Steph, boys will be boys. I know it is hard for you, but I hope you will be less terrified as time goes on. We have a long time to go raising these children through all the hazards they must encounter." He leaned forward and covered her hand with his. But he did not ask to see young Jean for himself.

Stephanie took a deep breath as if she were about to say more, but Vic came in and announced supper. "Good evenin, Mister Jean. You all come in for suppa. While it hot."

"What have we, Vic?" Jean said, taking Stephanie's arm.

"I made you all some fine shrimp stew. With fluffy rice. And some apple pie for dessert."

"Oh, Vic," said Stephanie.

"I set your place down here at Mister Jean end of the table," said Vic.

"That is fine, Vic," said Jean, seating Stephanie on his right.

"Yes, we can talk better here together," said Stephanie. "Thank you." They sat together while Vic brought in soup plates of the thick, rich stew with a generous heap of rice. She set a bowl of toasted bread between them and poured water in their goblets.

"Can I get you all anythin else?"

"This will be fine, Vic. You can bring the dessert and coffee at the bell." Stephanie smiled at the servant, who pushed through the swinging door into the pantry.

The Leverts lifted large soup spoons to their lips, murmuring over the steaming food and over the delicious taste. Both liked fresh seafood. Jean mentioned the oysters he saw on Magazine Street.

"I'd like to have an oyster stew soon," he said. "This is a fine time of year for fresh plump oysters. Vic knows how to make an excellent oyster stew, full of butter and salt and pepper. That is excellent wintertime fare. Don't you agree, my dear?"

"Oh, yes, indeed." She paused and laid down her spoon. "Jean, I have been reading about the opera today."

"The opera?"

"Yes, Jean. The opera. *La Traviata*, the one we will be attending on the twenty-seventh. *La Traviata*. You know, Giuseppe Verdi's great work is based on Alexandre Dumas' three-act play, *The Lady of the Camellias*. Of course you've read the novel. In French, I mean."

"Oh, yes, a sad story, bitterly sad. I do know that. But I'm glad you are studying the opera for both of us. I probably won't know what is going on. It is in Italian, isn't it? I know almost no Italian." He took the last half spoonful of stew into his mouth and lifted his napkin to blot his lips. "I just want to see you enjoying the opera. I know you have long wanted to see it. Now that the political climate is more calm in New Orleans, perhaps we can have more fine productions. I would like to have you see every opera you have ever read about." To himself, he thought that the hero's name was Armand—in Dumas' novel—but he was not certain, and it didn't matter.

Vic took their plates and silver away and returned with dessert, plates of apple pie with a small wedge of yellow cheese to eat.

"Hmmmm," murmured Jean, "*Délicieux*."

"*Oui, monsieur!*" said Stephanie, smiling, for she loved to speak French with Jean.

After his demitasse, Jean pushed back his chair and left his napkin loosely folded by his plate. "Well, I have had all the pleasure I can afford for tonight. I must get to my desk and study some important papers."

Despite her protest, Jean knew Stephanie understood his immersion in work at home. She had accepted it, and she was grateful for whatever time he could spend with her. She did not mention the children, for she did tire of his failure routinely to say goodnight to them. She smiled and folded her own napkin.

"Goodnight, Jean. I'll go to bed and read about poor Violetta."

She smiled as he pulled her chair away from the table.

"*Bon soir, ma chèrie.*"

Jean retreated to his office, where he sat down and bent his chin over his high stiff collar. This painful-looking nightly practice seemed a sort of discipline that surprisingly had never cut off his breathing. He neither unbuttoned his waistcoat nor took off his coat. He pulled out a number of papers describing a piece of property on Camp Street where several investors were known to be struggling to erect eight large warehouses, but who, it seemed to Jean, were likely to be in desperate straits for money. The eventual owner who could afford to see the development through stood to make a fortune on rentals. He began jotting figures on a clean sheet, stopping every now and then to stroke his moustache and narrow his eyes as he speculated on possibilities. He worked until nearly midnight, then returned the papers to his briefcase and wrote several pages in his journal. He was now into his eleventh volume.

*   *   *

On the night of the twenty-seventh, Jean thought Stephanie looked magnificent in her gold silk taffeta gown, it's décolletage and bustle subtly trimmed in metallic braid. Her hair was piled elegantly high, and she wore some of her Grandmother Dupuy's most spectacular jewelry, which was fetched from the bank box for the occasion. Jean was resplendent in his formal attire. His wavy hair was as thick and handsome as ever, and his well-tended moustache was now grown quite large. He took due notice of Violetta. He wondered how much of her full inexhaustible soprano tremoloi was owed to her fat stomach and enormous breasts. From his vantage point, he could see glistening perspiration surfacing through heavy makeup.

Jean enjoyed the aria, and he appreciated the entire production. His greatest pleasure, however, was in seeing opera glasses raised by the women of New Orleans Society to allow them a better view of Stephanie Dupuy Levert, who sat gracefully in her husband's box beside him, barely moving her silk fan below her face. He was sorry that Colonel and Mrs. Bush were not present. Especially since it had been Mrs. Bush's idea that they should attend *La Traviata*.

CHAPTER 40

ON THURSDAY MORNING after Ash Wednesday, Jean waked at six o'clock, anticipating his engagement with General DeClouet. After dressing, he went to the kitchen where Vic already had a fine-smelling pot of coffee dripping on the large wood stove. A heavy smoothing iron sat heating on one cast iron eye of the stove. Several cups sat in saucers on an unbleached domestic cloth that covered the square table in the middle of the room. Jean smelled an acrid odor as he poured himself a cup of coffee. Vic came from the laundry room behind the kitchen before he could look for the source. She was clutching another heavy iron in the folds of a thick cloth.

"Mornin, Mister Jean." She set the iron down beside the one that was heating.

"What do I smell?"

"You smells sovvent."

"What's that?"

"It cleaner. I cleanin up your long-tail suit."

Jean blinked, then smiled. "Oh! You mean solvent? You're cleaning my formal clothes from the Comus Carnival ball. Well, good. I hope you can get that smell out."

"I let it air out in the back yard, all day if it take that. It smell fine, I put it up in the big closet. I got Miss Stephanie fine dress all done yes'day. Made a big bag for it out of an old sheet. We got keep those things nice and fresh so when you need em again they be ready. Let me fix you some breakfast, Mister Jean. I got grits. Got ham, and I just bring in some eggs from the chickenhouse. Just laid." Vic looked at him expectantly.

Jean looked at her for a moment. "No, Vic. Go on with your cleaning. I'll get some of that bread you made yesterday and spread it with butter." He looked up at a shelf and took down a jar of fig preserves. "Did you make this?"

"Yazzum. Figs come from trees on Miss Stephanie old homeplace last summer. Hold up to the window and see how clear and pretty they is."

"You sure they didn't come from Golden Ridge?"

"That cousin of Miss Stephanie bring em when she come down here last summer to do all that shoppin. Oooh, that lady do some shoppin. She bring a big bucket of figs all the way on the train. Daniels and me met her at the station, and he had to go on and bring em out with her other stuff. Great big bucketful."

"Oh, yes," Jean shook his head. "That would be Cousin Emilie Dupuy, Miss Emilie Dupuy, still Miss. Never found anybody good enough to marry a Dupuy. Did I ever tell you Miss Emilie didn't want Miss Stephanie to marry me. She didn't think I'd ever amount to much. She thought I was after Miss Stephanie's money."

"Bless my soul, Mister Jean, nobody got as much money as you?"

"I was just a young war veteran starting out." Jean had finished assembling his breakfast on a plate, which, along with his coffee, he carried through the butler's pantry into the dining room. The heavy door swung behind him.

He set his food down and walked out to the front porch to pick up *The Daily Picayune*. The grandfather clock chimed 6:30 as he sat down to eat and to read the paper. The house was silent except for an occasional thumping from the kitchen area. Jean liked peace and quiet at home. He enjoyed a little chat in the early mornings with Vic and sometimes with Daniels. It reminded him of his boyhood and the easy exchanges with Bébé and Isaac. There was hardly anyone with whom Jean could have as casual, even amusing, conversation as Vic. Daniels was thoroughly respectful, but he was more reserved.

*　　*　　*

At ten o'clock, Jean heard the outer door to his Perdido Street office open and close. He rose from his leather desk chair and walked out to greet General DeClouet and his son. He shook hands formally with both of them, and made a gesture with his arm toward his office that ran across the front of the second floor of the three-story building.

"Do come in, gentlemen, and have a seat." Paul DeClouet sat down immediately as if, thought Jean, he was used to taking orders. The General's forty-two-year-old son was taller than average, but with a slender neck and shoulders, and wore a dark business suit. The General remained standing, his thumb in the watch pocket of his waistcoat. Then fingering the heavy gold watch chain as if it were a rosary, he gave the office a critical look.

"Did you enjoy the Mardi Gras, General? I'm sure it was a relief to have a quiet day yesterday." He knew he wasn't in the mood for small talk for long.

"It was a spectacle, Mr. Levert. There must be nothing like it anywhere else on the face of the planet. Streets were filled with costumed merrymakers, masked and not masked, pushing, shoving, shouting. It was a spectacle!"

"Indeed it was," agreed Paul.

"I feel these revelers and floats pulled by muleteams help to define the character and tastes of the city's past and present inhabitants," the General went on. "The tableaux showed best in the evening by torch light. The city, especially the narrow French Quarter streets, was packed with people of all walks from poorest to richest—men, women, children, Negro, white, all shamelessly mixed in this Mardi Gras spirit. They rang bells, beat drums, blew penny whistles. Oh, the noise and color and giddiness and near or total inebriation."

"Yes, indeed . . ." began Jean.

But the General, who seemed determined to give a full description of his experiences on Fat Tuesday, was just getting started: "We found an excellent spot from which to watch the Rex parade right at the corner of St. Charles Avenue and Canal Street. On a mounting block there, my daughter-in-law and my grandson stood for a spectacular view of the parade. Just as they got safely settled, there was a shout: 'Pickpocket! Catch him—catch him!' A large man in a red devil costume and carrying a pitchfork, crashed through the crowd, yelling. He almost knocked my family and others down into the street. It gave us all a fright. A shot rang out, and a policeman gave chase.

"Sir, your Mardi Gras is not all laughter and festivity, I'm afraid. Merrymakers need a full forty days of Lent to recover from this strenuous spectacle. Oh, yes? Men were dressed as women, and women as men. A masked woman, I think, in doublet and hose kissed everyone in sight and within reach. Men on stilts threw flowers. When Rex, King of Carnival, arrived at the corner where we were, he waved his scepter and drank from a silver goblet . . ."

"Sir . . ." Jean tempted to interrupt.

"I tell you, sir, the sights we saw from the streets and from our balcony at the St. Charles Hotel were thrilling. But to hard-working, sober people as me and my son here, such revelry and tomfoolery, if prolonged, could become worrisome. Still, I enjoyed the commotion. My grandson enjoyed everything, but I would not want him to assume that all this is right and proper."

"General DeClouet . . ."

"We have found the St. Charles Hotel to be comfortable and accommodating, surely the handsomest hotel in the city. I studied the exterior architecture and found the handsome white marble with its striated Corinthian columns to be quite . . ."

Jean stood up, for a moment towering over the General. "Sir—"

"Much finer than the Girod, where I stayed back before the battle at the foot of Canal Street . . ."

"Sir," insisted Jean in a stern voice, "sir, we must get to the business we met here to discuss. Believe me, General, I am glad to hear that you enjoyed our parades and all the rest of it. But we must get down to business. Please tell me what you would ask of Bush & Levert." He looked from father to son and back to the father. Paul DeClouet cleared his throat but said nothing.

Jean waited, unwilling to open the subject with a statement that might suggest any sort of offer on his part. From his desk drawer, he took a file folder and laid it on his rolltop desk. He looked across his desk, where an coal-oil lamp stood, and at the sleeping sofa in the corner of his office. A large mirror hung on the wall nearest the window. The folder contained all the information on Lizima Plantation he had been able to assemble over the years, a ready reference for the discussion. Both General DeClouet and his son looked down at the packet as Jean laid it down like a lead weight; Jean saw they feared what they might expect from its contents.

"Mr. Levert," began General DeClouet, "we are sorry to have missed Colonel Bush. It is indeed a disappointment to me that he cannot participate in this discussion. I trust he is enjoying his outstanding holiday."

"I am sure he is," said Jean, impatient to stop talking around the subject at hand. Still he sat quietly, waiting for his adversary to begin his plea. For Jean felt that DeClouet was the adversary; he felt sure that the old man still resented him from his earlier visit to Lizima and he was determined to make a point of it, subtly or otherwise.

After a moment, the General was forced to begin. "As you know, sir, Lizima Plantation is one of the outstanding sugar plantations in Louisiana with perhaps the handsomest manor house in all the state. It without question has the potential of earning handsome revenues and producing record cane and sugar."

"I would be quick to agree," said Jean.

DeClouet let that settle for a moment. Realizing that Jean in his own mind emphasized potential, he hurried on: "Unfortunately, we have, for several seasons, had bad fortune at the hand of nature and at the hand of some hired management that have left us with a bit of red ink in our ledger books."

Jean decided to let this poor misrepresentation pass without comment.

The General cleared his throat. "So you see, sir, we, my son and I, have discussed our situation, and we decided that we will very likely do well to seek a brokerage firm of the finest reputation for judgment and experience to participate in our renewed determination to once again lead Louisiana in production." He paused and took a deep breath.

Oh, for God's sake. Who did this old man think he was fooling. Jean said, "Well, General, I would like to see your ledgers for the past six years. I will have to study them with great care. Also, I must see a statement of your outstanding debts, whatever they may be for and to whomever they may be owed. This is simply routine, I'm sure you understand." He explained that Bush & Levert was one of the strongest sugar brokerages in New Orleans, and had been for several years. But it was still standing because it abided by the strictest rules of the industry. "We are unerringly fair, and we must also be unerringly cautious."

General DeClouet remained silent, his eyes on the folder, which held the answers that Jean wanted. Jean knew he was playing a tough game with his quarry, a highstakes game with increasing skill and calculation. He pulled out a sheaf of papers and tapped their edges even on his desk. He was ready to read aloud a few paragraphs from the contract when Paul DeClouet broke his silence.

"Mr. Levert, do you think you can help us?" His father looked at him reproachfully, and Jean was surprised at Paul's subservient tone. Paul took a small packet from his pocket and spoke again before Jean could answer:

"Do you have some tobacco, please?" He pulled a cigarette paper from the packet. "I would like to roll myself a cigarette."

Jean reached to the tobacco table behind his chair and brought out a humidor which he set before Paul. The younger man deposited a pinch of the aromatic blend of Turkish and Bright tobacco in his narrow trough of paper, moistened the edge with his tongue, and formed the cigarette while Jean watched with some distaste.

"May I pay you, Mr. Levert?"

"It will be twenty-five cents, please," Jean said without hesitating. The General watched, his face showing incredulity. Jean knew what the General was thinking: *Jean may be a well-to-do young man, but he reminds me of a person on the cheap side.*

Paul DeClouet took some coins from a small leather purse and laid them on the desk, then struck a match on the sole of his shoe and lighted the cigarette. It seemed to relax him instantly.

General DeClouet half stood, then sat down again and said, "Mr. Levert, we need at least twenty-five thousand dollars to get a fresh start at Lizima. If you are interested in financing us for the coming seasons, we would like to hear your terms."

Jean opened the file and took out the top papers. "General, I shall be glad to read from our contract. You and your son may feel free to ask questions, and I will answer to the best of my ability." He tilted the papers for better light from the window:

"Interest rates vary with time, place and existing economic conditions, usually ranging from 8 to 12 percent . . . the current rate is 9½, the rate you will be charged as the funds, or $24,560 advance are drawn for your use . . . customary brokerage fee of 1 percent to be added to the interest charge. To the price of supplies purchased there will be an additional commission of 4 percent for selling your plantation products . . ."

Jean lowered the papers and explained that these charges are the few items of profit open to the broker in a transaction such as this. There was another charge that helped make Bush & Levert attractive to planters, notwithstanding the risks involved, and Jean started reading again from the contract document:

"There is a penalty commission feature of advancing contracts in the business, incident to the repayment of loans in kind rather than in money . . . the fundamental consideration inducing extensions of credit, should that be necessary, will not only be interest on the funds advanced, but for control of large volumes of a great commodity—sugar in this case—that holds a high position in the mercantile world."

Paul choked on his almost finished cigarette as he stood up abruptly. "But I think the four percent commission charges added to both buying and selling our products are a bit unfair, sir." He turned to his father for support but did not get it. "Can there be any adjustment there?"

Jean anticipated objections, but he thought they would come

from the General. Jean replied, "It may not sound fair, but it is business, Mr. DeClouet. Now, what I have told you is what we feel that we are able to offer. Of course, you are free to reject our plan and seek funds elsewhere, but in all truth, I must ask you to make up your minds. I have no more time after noon." He took out his watch and looked at the dial.

Jean's blue eyes kindled with a genuine bargaining fire now, as he faced the DeClouets. Lizima represented the largest account to date for the firm. And besides Lizima, the General's family owned Magenta and St. Clair plantations in the Lafayette area not far from St. Martinville, and Jean already anticipated some business from them. He was as ready to battle relentlessly now as he ever had been; he must be careful, firm but not overly aggressive.

"But Mr. DeClouet," he went on, "I think we can find a way to help you make money as we provide you with funds and terms that you can live with." He was trying to allay doubts the General might be having concerning the ability to repay the loan. He adjusted his neck in his stiff collar and continued to encourage: "The more growers who haul their crops to your mill, a mill centrally located in the parish, the more money you will earn and will have for other plantation operations, of course. But, as you say, it will require remodeling the mill first, and that takes money, lots of it. The potential, as I view it, is excellent in a situation like yours, gentlemen, if all is handled wisely, I—"

Paul interrupted, turning to his father, "Now, Papa, do you feel that we can live with this loan and the terms Mr. Levert has outlined?"

Jean saw the old war hero's shoulders sag; the General had no choice. He shook his head toward his son who stood between him and Jean. "We have no choice, Paul," he said in a low but audible voice. He stood and addressed Jean: "Mr. Levert, I think we'll manage just fine. We simply have to have more money and at least two decent crops in a row. Unlike the past three or four years, God needs to smile on us and allow us good luck for a change. We accept your terms although we do have reservations about certain commission charges." His blue eyes still beamed with the brilliance of youth. "May I see the entire document, please?" He smoothed his gray beard.

Jean handed him the seven-page contract. The DeClouets sat beside each other and began to read each page. Jean tried not to watch them. He knew a sad situation when he saw one. But he gave not even a perfunctory reminder, let alone a warning, to the father and son about what a high-risk trap they were setting for themselves. Surely an experienced man such as General DeClouet knew risk when he came near it. Surely, the old man knew what he was doing. He had done it before.

When the preliminary papers were signed, Jean accepted the sheaf from the General, who stood with military erectness and proudly shook hands with Jean. He was determined not to walk out a beaten man, Jean saw.

"When can we expect to begin our mill restoration, sir?"

"I shall visit you at your plantation within two weeks, General, and we can make specific plans for deliveries of parts and for labor. You will receive a letter from me, which I shall mail to you on Monday." Jean looked directly, unblinkingly into his blue eyes. "I wish you well, sir. I believe your"—he almost said chances— "outlook is favorable. Colonel Bush and I will be eager to be of service. He will be back in this office the first week in April."

He opened his office door for his guests. Étienne DeClouet bowed and walked politely past Jean. His son followed, his face a study in anger and frustration. He made no such genteel gesture as his father had mustered. Jean shrugged as he closed the door.

Jean looked at his watch and nodded to himself contentedly. He had a luncheon date at an excellent small restaurant in the French Quarter, where a delicious casserole of steamed white lumps of crabmeat, dressed in drawn butter with fresh lemon, was served. He was meeting his friend Colonel William Behan.

CHAPTER 41

JEAN BAPTISTE RODE the Texas & Pacific train toward St. Delphine Plantation in West Baton Rouge to consult with Augie about that farm and about Golden Ridge, for which Amèdeè, assisted by Augie, had assumed major responsibility now that his father was nearing eighty. Amèdeè also had become manager at Willow Glen at St. Gabriel after Auguste, Sr., had purchased the plantation, at Jean's insistence, from Stephanie's estate in 1874.

Jean blew a bit of the train's soot from his French cuff. His haberdasher in New Orleans had just outfitted him in fashionable new clothes. He admired his new black silk hat on the seat beside him in his first-class compartment. It had arrived from New York at the New Orleans shop and been delivered to Third Street only yesterday; he was eager to wear it. He wore a new black silk frock coat tailored with pinched waist and a skirt that flared to a length just above the knee. His slim-cut fawn-colored trousers, held taut and wrinkleless by the strap under each instep, matched his silk scarf. He had seen how much taller and more slender he appeared in these clothes in the pier mirror that hung in the foyer at Third Street; it was equally true of a handsome new coat tailored of soft sheer Peruvian alpaca that was of the same cut. Today, he felt warmly dressed for the heat of late September, but there was a special reason to be dressed up. Jean was to make a call in East Baton Rouge before crossing the Mississippi River to visit with his brother. He had decided to accept Annie Blanton's invitation to stop at her plantation.

He wasn't sure how he felt about seeing Annie. His decision

to see her had been a hesitant one. He didn't pretend to have the feelings for her that he had experienced nearly twenty years before. He admitted to himself that he was curious. She had been a striking young war widow; he had had his first real love affair with her. He could still remember those rendezvous with her in the farmhouse her parents had fled as the war came closer. He was thinking of Annie's great passion with him when the train jerked to a stop, shattering his nostalgic musings—she was now Annie Blanton Kleinpeter.

Jean gathered his hat and valise and left the car. From the steps of the train he paused to observe the State Capitol. The strange gothic-style building had been reoccupied by the Louisiana state legislature only six months earlier. Jean was surprised to see that James Dakin, who designed the newly remodeled Capitol, had had it painted a dark color. Jean had only seen it white, but then it had lain in ruin for twenty years. It also seemed to Jean that Dakin had made it noticeably taller. Jean stepped down, thanking God that the Reconstruction bullies did not now occupy the Capitol. He knew they had left the state four years earlier, in 1877, when President Rutherford B. Hayes withdrew Federal troops from New Orleans and the state after the longest occupation of any southern state. The wartime seat of government was no longer in New Orleans, but back in Baton Rouge where it belonged. Down the slope from the Capitol to the river, Jean saw the ferry pushing away from the bank where he planned to cross the river later.

On the station platform he hired an open buggy to take him to the Kleinpeter plantation. While waiting for the driver to hitch horse and carriage, he thought briefly of his fortunes rising in the early Eighties and throughout the decade, of Bush & Levert's continued success in post-Reconstruction Louisiana while many brokers and other professional people struggled to stay afloat or failed outright. *How lucky I've been.* Business, good or bad, held his attention ever increasingly, and though his funds were seldom liquid, he was never unable to make an investment that he strongly desired. There were times when he invested alone if he had high hopes for a property that Colonel Bush did not agree was a sound purchase for the firm. Not that the Colonel lacked money; he was getting older and did not have the drive by which Jean seemed consistently propelled. Recently, he had invested some of Stephanie's funds in more real estate. He'd never lost money that he had borrowed from her or his parents. He never suggested borrowing from his brothers, because as planters they operated on narrow margins; knowing the status of their finances, he presumed the right to be consulted about all the family-owned plantations.

"That is the ferry I should get for the ride to the West Side, isn't it?" he asked the Negro driver after climbing aboard the buggy.

"It is, Boss. You from New Orleens?"

"Yes," said Jean.

"Don't know bout Baton Rouge?"

"Not a lot."

"This a good town. Waw kinda tow it up." The buggy rattled along a rutted street past some pretty white frame houses with green lawns, still colorful in the lowering sun. "That is the big Cath'lic church, way over yonder on the right. Gunboats fired on it. Ain't it fine, though? Little ways up here I show you the baarks."

"The what?" Jean felt that he must have come upon the local historian.

"The baarks! The baarks! Where they kep all them soljers."

"Oh, barracks! Yes, well . . . How far are we from the Kleinpeter home?"

"It ain't far, right up the road, here."

Finally, Jean stepped down from the buggy and paid the driver. "Will you come back for me in an hour? I'll need a ride to the ferry in about an hour."

"Yes, Boss. For hour, I set here and wait."

"Oh, very well. I just don't want to have to wait for you."

Jean walked along a shell drive that led through an elaborately wrought iron gate that swung under a similarly designed arch. He stepped upon a bricked gallery floor of the two-story, white-columned house, noticing as he did a movement of draperies at the window. He rapped the door knocker. Was Annie there at the window watching for him?

The door was opened not by Annie but by a short plump servant. With a hint of a curtsey, she took his hat and the silk scarf and indicated the parlor off the wide hall. Jean entered the room, quickly noting its rich furnishings: A fire burned in the high fireplace, wrought iron lamps with painted globes, a grandfather clock, and a side table on which lay several books by Poe and Hardy. Edwin Kleinpeter left his widow well-housed, thought Jean. Glancing at the face of a bearded man in the portrait over the marble mantel, he was wondering if it was Edwin Kleinpeter when he heard a rustle behind him. He turned and there stood Annie. He was for some reason startled. She was still pretty, perhaps prettier than in 1863.

She came to him quickly, and Jean thought she might embrace him. She stopped short of that, but he immediately knew that she was more than a little glad to see him. Annie glanced over him, his face, his attire, and she did not hide her favorable impression. She ushered him across the room and asked him to be seated on the velvet sofa. Then she sat down beside him, surprisingly close to him, all the time clucking soft little comments about how nice it was of him to come by to see her, as if it had not been her idea that he come.

Annie wore a green velvet dress with a tight bodice that Jean thought was contrived to display a youthful, full figure. She continued boldly to look him over—the breadth of his shoulders, the luxurious moustache. Suddenly, he recalled how she used to say to him, "I love those blue eyes." Jean nervously touched the edge of his moustache, and smiled, weakly he knew, for the intimacy of her look and her words made him feel not similarly intimate, but strange.

"You've changed so little, Jean. Just as handsome as ever. I've wondered all these years if you ever thought of me and the old days during the war."

"Yes, of course, of course I have, Annie. Many times." He

smiled and looked over the room again. "Mr. Kleinpeter certainly provided a fine home for you, Annie. Yes, very beautiful. How many acres do you cultivate? Is it all in sugar?"

"Oh, we alternate. Most of our land is farther upriver. Right now we are mostly in sugar except for the . . ." She was interrupted by the approach of a young man. "Oh, Jean, allow me to present my son, Jean Baptiste Kleinpeter. Son, I want you to meet an old and dear friend who shares your name, Mr. Jean Baptiste Levert of New Orleans. He has dropped by for dinner on his way to visit his brother on the West Side."

The boy stepped forward and accepted Jean's hand in easy cordiality. Jean stared at the youth; he must be about fourteen, fifteen, certainly too young to be the offspring of—of himself and Annie. Recalling the last time they were together before his capture during the war, Jean could not help but consider such a possibility. In an earlier letter, Annie had mentioned she had named her firstborn son Andrew Levert Kleinpeter; he died in infancy. But she had never mentioned another son that she had named Jean Baptiste. Her son looked like a charming fellow, but Jean felt increasingly alien in this place. He could not remember being more uncomfortable. He looked at his watch, then at the two of them.

"Really, Annie, I do apologize. I simply am not able to stay and visit with you as I would have liked to. I'm afraid I must be on my way. I asked my brother to meet the ferry at nine o'clock." He looked at his watch again.

"Why, Jean, we expected you to have supper with us. We have food all ready to serve. Are you sure you can't stay just a little while?" He could see that she was disappointed as he began to move across the hall toward the entrance.

"May I have my hat and scarf, please?"

The plump maid appeared and took his things from the closet. Jean took Annie's hand. It felt small and dry in his large moist hand. She looked at him, her eyes sad and questioning. He gave the hand a little shake and dropped it. Jean Baptiste Kleinpeter stood to one side, merely polite.

"Goodbye, Annie, I am happy to have seen you again. You are every bit as young and pretty as you were twenty years ago. I don't know how you do it. I . . ." They were out on the gallery. He saw her face as she became aware of the buggy waiting, the driver standing beside his horse. Her face showed that she took it all in, that he never intended to stay, not even for supper. She stopped at the edge of the gallery and said nothing more. Jean looked back at her and hurried down the shell drive to the waiting buggy. He stepped into it and settled back.

"Take me to the ferry," he told the driver.

"Okay, Boss. We get right down there." He tapped the rump of his horse lightly with a whip and tugged the reins sharply back to the left, heading down the lane toward Baton Rouge.

Jean was frustrated and put out. *What did she expect? What had he expected after all the years? Some sort of flirtatious evening? There was a time . . . but tonight with Annie, the prospect of a romantic encounter now sounded like something between a bore and a fright. At best tedium.* He shook his head. *I must be getting old,* as the buggy rattled down the road along the riverside. Between clumps of growth, Jean glimpsed splashy silver reflections of a pale early moon on the rippling river in its endless surge toward the Gulf of Mexico. On how many youthful nights had he contemplated such a scene from the banks at Golden Ridge. He sighed deeply. There was often something stifling about these rural sorties he had to make from time to time. Relief could not be found along the way; it came only with returning to New Orleans. The old saw that you couldn't get the country out of a country boy did not apply to Jean. He was a city man. He had been since his first job in New Orleans.

Upon arriving at the ferry landing, Jean stood up in the buggy and paid the driver. He was relieved to find the old tub moored and ready. Carrying his own bag, he walked to the boat on long wide planks over wet gravel and mud. Already on board was a wagon loaded beyond capacity with sugarcane, no doubt intended to be at the head of the line early in the morning at a West Side sugarhouse. The Negro driver had tied his mules and was already sprawled atop the cane for a nap. Jean walked gingerly among scattered cane stalks on the wet deck. Mindful of his new clothes, he laid his leather valise on a damp bench and sat on it under an oil lamp, its chimney made dim by coats of grease, bugs, and dust. He heard a thousand frogs under the willows laughing at him until the ferrymen pushed off into the muddy and stubborn currents of the Mississippi.

*   *   *

Augie had sent a young plantation worker down to meet Jean's ferry, and although Jean was more than an hour early, the man was there. He placed Jean's valise aboard the carriage and they headed down the river road toward St. Delphine. Although there was little moonlight at eight o'clock, Jean thought he recognized the old carriage as his father's. He felt around on the horsehair seatcover and the shape and details of the floor and sides; he was almost certain. He estimated that the old carriage was nearly thirty years old. He remembered Isaac and his father taking him to board the paddle wheel for New Orleans and college when the carriage was new. He and his parents rode in it to the church on his wedding day. It still provided a comfortable ride. He approved of Augie's economic preservation and maintenance of property; it was typical of his brother's careful operation of St. Delphine.

When the carriage turned into the drive toward the house, Jean could see the wisteria clinging to the east wall, cloaking the tall chimney in the dim light. It was a landscape design that had captivated him on that first visit to St. Delphine. He recalled Mrs. Daigle with all her patrician armor and fragile beauty. He shook his head. The war ruined Mrs. Daigle, not he, he reasoned. Now, he clearly saw a man carrying a lantern coming to meet them. It was his brother. The carriage came to a stop, and he climbed aboard, motioning the driver to move on.

The brothers shook hands and embraced each other after Augie hung the lantern on the side of the carriage. Immediately they began to talk about the coming harvest. At the front gallery, Augie dismissed the driver, who clucked to his horses and drove on toward the rear of the Big House.

Inside the lighted hall, Augie gasped at his brother. "*Mon dieu, Jean!* What are you dressed for? You look like you've gotten yourself up for a city wingding! I hope you brought some rough clothes. What's this all about?" He squinted through his glasses at the silk coat, and he held the hat gingerly until he set it on a marble-top table.

"I paid a call in Baton Rouge this afternoon, and thought I'd wear some of my new clothes. That's all. I do have suitable clothes for tomorrow." He looked at his valise.

"Was it by chance the Mrs. Kleinpeter who wrote me for your address?"

"That's who it was."

"Is she trying to sell some of her land?"

"Hmmm, I don't think so. I never thought of that. I was just there a few minutes."

"Come on back in the pantry. Have you eaten? We have saved things for you from supper." He looked back. "But here, give me your coat. You're likely to get something on it."

"Auguste, I'm used to eating in a coat. I am hungry, though. I ate the food Vic prepared for me at about noontime, and that's all I've had today." He realized he was very hungry. They sat down at a round table where a white cloth had been spread over the odd shapes of bowls and plates of food. Around them, the pantry shelves were lined with dishes, glassware, and foods. He sniffed the dried herbs, garlics, onions, peppers, and other useful produce from the gardens at St. Delphine that hung decoratively on both sides of the window facings. A brass oil chandelier hung over the table.

Augie removed the top cloth from the table, uncovering the food. "Look here, Jean. Take a plate and help yourself. There's sliced turkey and dressing. Good bread. That's one of the things that our cook, Tess, does best. *Ooh, cher.* Just have a slice; here's butter. The last of our snapbeans, squash, fig preserves, and strawberry jam. Just help yourself, *cher.*"

Jean ate the home-cooked, mostly homegrown food. "This is good. Hmm! The bread is excellent. *Délicieux!*" He ate for a while, then, "Augie! Wasn't that *Père's* old carriage your boy met me in?"

"*Oui, Frère!* I wondered if you'd recognize it."

"In the dark, even! I'm amazed. That old buggy has taken this family many a mile up and down the river. It must be thirty years old."

"Twenty-seven. I don't mean to keep it. I was down at Golden Ridge awhile back, and I borrowed it because I had some bulky things to bring back. I needed a two-horse conveyance. Didn't want to drive a wagon. Once I got it up here, I decided to fix it up. Actually, it didn't take much. I greased it good, washed it, and even painted the spokes red. That's what they were originally. *Père* took good care of it."

"How are *Père* and *Mère?* I haven't seen them since early in the year when I went over to Lizima Plantation. I stopped by to see them. They seemed to be in good spirits, but they are looking old, of course."

"They are old, Jean. And neither of them is well. *Père* can't do much of anything anymore, and *Mère* doesn't have any energy. She still gets up and dresses herself beautifully every morning, always looks elegant. But she looks thin, poor color."

"Well, I hope she can build herself up somehow. It worries me to see them decline." Jean drank from his glass of milk. "I know I have not seen as much of *Mère* as I should have over the years since I moved to New Orleans. I think of her every day, but I should write to her more often. *Père* and I write to each other . . ."

"You and *Père* were always so close. Amèdeè used to think you were far and above the favorite of our father. I was older and did not notice as he did, being the little brother, the baby. But you were unusually close. Are you still?" Augie looked serious and not very young himself, peering through metal-framed glasses and stroking his chin whiskers. Aside from graying whiskers, Jean thought his brother, now fifty, looked as slender as a willow shoot, slenderer than he'd remembered.

Jean hesitated. "I feel close to him, but I stay so busy, I am so wrapped up in my business, day to day, just don't have time to keep up. He probably has other things on his mind, too."

"I am certain that he would love to hear from you often. I don't know how many times he has told me the story of your birth, how you were born during the great hurricane of thirty-nine, while he and the overseer were out surveying damage to the crops. He took your birth at that time as some sort of omen. He believed you would do great things, and he and the slaves went out and propped up the cane, stalk by stalk and succeeded in saving the crop. A visit from you gives them both a lot of pleasure. I don't mean to . . ."

Jean put up his hand. "No, I understand. I have always admired our Mother greatly. She has always epitomized grace and dignity to me. I don't know why I haven't been more attentive . . . I will try to do better."

"I have an idea," said Augie. "Why don't we drive down to Plaquemine from here, perhaps tomorrow afternoon. You can leave from there for New Orleans. I need to return the carriage; I have a saddle horse down there to ride back home."

But Jean was shaking his head. "I am sorry, but I cannot do that this trip. I must leave here tomorrow right after noon to catch my train directly from Baton Rouge. It will get me into the city tomorrow night. But I'll be there the next morning, on hand for an important appointment. I appreciate your suggestion."

"I'm sorry, too, *cher*," said Augie. "Can I get you anything else?"

Jean wiped his mouth on a white napkin. "No, thank you. This has been delicious. Thank you." He stood up and began to cover the table.

"No, no, don't bother. Tess is back in the kitchen. She'll put all this away." He walked to a door and called across the back gallery to the kitchen. "Tess! Oh, Tess! Come on, she'll be here."

As they walked through the dining room together, Jean said, "Where are Aurelie and the children?"

"They're upstairs in the sitting room. They want to see you. Come on up." He picked up Jean's valise, and together the brothers walked up the curving stairway softly candlelit by wall sconces. Jean thought Aurelie had maintained a charm and beauty at St. Delphine equal to those of the former owner.

*   *   *

Seated in his train compartment on Tuesday afternoon, Jean leaned his head back and closed his eyes. Upholstery notwithstanding, the seat felt hard and the pile of fabric harsh to his touch. Despite the heat, he closed the window to avoid flying soot. Vic would have to have a go at the new trousers. They hadn't gotten as dirty as they might have, but there were some specks of clay and soot.

Jean felt good about the crop at St. Delphine. The cane was tall and lush, and Augie was a good farmer, better than Jean ever expected him to be. There was little cause for worry about loss this season; indeed, weather cooperating, the brothers agreed there were good reasons to expect a good profit. His two successful seasons proved something. For Jean, one thing it proved was that an experienced man was much more capable of running a sugarcane plantation than a woman. Mrs. Daigle failed completely under wartime conditions and did no better during the hard times after the war, but somehow Augie was overcoming the inherited problems at St. Delphine. No doubt much of his facility came from growing up a pupil of their father, who Jean still regarded as possibly the finest sugar grower in Louisiana. Furthermore, Augie was obviously becoming the operator of two plantations, including St. Mary's, located near St. Delphine. Jean's father had purchased the four-hundred-acre estate at an auction. Gazing out at the passing swamp grasses, Jean hoped his brother was capable of doubling his work load.

Jean was not so confident in Amèdeè's management of Willow Glen and Golden Ridge. Amèdeè worked hard, apparently, but he was not far-thinking, and he lacked the judgment and imagination that Augie seemed to have in abundance. So far, he had kept both plantations in black ink, but Jean was doubtful from season to season. One of Amèdeè problems was that he did not like to take Jean's advise, and Jean believed that could one day prove a mistake.

Jean took down his valise and got out his business schedule. He could not write because of the swaying of the train, but with effort he read and jotted rough notes on the days and weeks ahead. His mind was filled with a number of ponderables.

For a long time, he and Colonel Bush had been thinking of and talking about the need for a Louisiana sugar exchange. Since Bush had returned from Europe in April, they had been able to concentrate on their project and draw up specific proposals, a tentative constitution, and by-laws. Many planters and brokers were eager to be a part of the organization, for unity throughout the entire Louisiana sugar industry, from planter to the most outlying broker of a sugar product, was essential to keeping the revenue-rich industry at home. *Organized unity*; those were the bywords for preventing a takeover of sugar by East Coast industrialists. The threat had become more menacing during and after the war. But Colonel Bush and Jean were ready to lead the way, if called upon, ready to attend meetings of the Louisiana Sugar Planters Association, of which he and the Colonel were active members, and meetings among his colleagues in the months ahead.

Of course, the partners were listening for General Étienné DeClouet's production reports, as the growing season at Lizima came to an end. Until now they had heard nothing of misfortune regarding the General's 1881 crop. Jean had made the necessary improvements at his sugarhouse. It seemed to Jean that the Lizima sugarhouse was ready to make money, and grinding was already beginning. DeClouet and his son, if they knew what they were doing, could chalk up some profits in grinding. Jean and the Colonel prepared to go along with him for a second season—that was their pledge.

Jean's two spring visits to Lizima Plantation had been pleasant. He thought the plantation was beautiful at any season, the house especially enchanting, but the cane fields in early growth were the most graceful sight to see anywhere—endless rows of yellow gold-arching young plants in black soil made fine and crumbly by the tools dragged behind mules. That was what would tell the tale—the cane.

CHAPTER 42

AS AUTUMN SETTLED over New Orleans and the far-south sugar parishes, and as he prepared himself for whatever awaited him in business and politics of the City and region, Jean Baptiste received upsetting word in a letter from Augie stating that their mother was seriously ill with pneumonia. Immediately he put aside all concerns and rushed to his mother's bedside at Golden Ridge.

Upon arrival at the family home Jean raced across the gallery, through the windrushed center hall and up the stairway, into the bedroom his mother had given birth to him during the howling hurricane forty-two years before. But he got there too late. Eulalie Miro Levert had died less than two hours before he arrived winded and desperate to speak to her, to spend some time with her. Augie and Amèdeè stood in the doorway while he buried his face in the sheet that covered her on her high four-poster.

"*Mère! Mère!*" He was too late to try to explain why he had stayed away so long at his pursuits in New Orleans.

Jean found his father, sister Euphrasie and brothers in shock over the passing of the woman who had been such a model of strength and unselfishness for him, for all of them. Jean joined them in their sorrow, and he fell into his own private furrow of regret and guilt. *Why did I not come back with Augie from St. Delphine for a final visit with Mother and Father? Business, always business.* Because he was so wrapped up in convincing other New Orleans brokers of the necessity to form a sugar exchange from which the industry could function and keep business and profits in Louisiana; so determined to be ready for whatever challenges came along and to stay up on developments after he had returned from his business trip to East and West Baton Rouge parishes, he had refused to see the need to visit his mother. Now it was too late—forever and ever all chance was gone.

Jean held his father's arm as they walked down the aisle and sat a few feet from his mother's bier at St. John the Baptist church in Brusly Landing, north of Plaquemine. As had been their way long ago, they sat huddled together almost excluding the others. The old man leaned heavily on Jean, weeping for his wife, while his other children, middle-aged and appearing somewhat shut out, sat on the pew behind their father and brother during the eulogy. As they left the church, Jean noticed that the sanctuary was filled with saddened friends and relatives. Among the colored people in the back of the church, Jean saw Sally, who had returned to Golden Ridge after helping him and Stephanie get settled at Third Street, sobbing into her hands.

Jean sat up late with his father. When at last the old gentleman stopped talking and fell into exhausted sleep, Jean pulled a soft old blanket over him and turned down the lamp wick, then he blew out the last small flickering flame. Moonlight streamed into the darkened room from large windows that looked out across the stubble cane fields. He stood at the window a few moments before he walked down to the gallery to talk until midnight with his brothers.

"I had tremendous love and respect for her," he said to them. "I always looked upon her as a tower of strength and dignity."

The brothers nodded, their faces solemn. They had been here through all the years, attentive to their mother as she grew old. No doubt, Jean realized, they thought he had neglected her, though they did not say so or imply it in any way. A cool breeze came up from the river on the strange warm November night in 1882. Then it hit Jean: For the first time in his life his mother, seventy-eight when she died, was not moving about in the Big House looking after him and his family's every possible need.

Early next morning, Jean caught the train back to New Orleans. He was full of resolve not to neglect his father during his remaining years. He vowed to himself that he would return to Golden Ridge at frequent intervals for the warm chats that he knew the old man longed to have with him. And he would write to his father often.

*   *   *

Back in New Orleans, Stephanie and the children met Jean with tender solicitations. He truly appreciated their sympathy, but he soon convinced them that the best healing for him was to get back to work. Mourning could not be allowed to absorb one's whole mind and heart, he believed. He never told Stephanie of the morbidity that enveloped him while he was at Golden Ridge, where the mood of death had taken him back into the heavy-hearted grief he had known after Lucie's death. It wasn't the first time he had been pulled back down, but the loss of his mother to the dictates of Death caused the worst return to smothering depression that he had known since his child had died. The memory carried too many complications of guilt and regret for him to be cast off easily.

If Jean was expecting solace from his return to work, he was more than disappointed. True, the first two weeks back at work went well; Colonel Bush welcomed him with his typical quiet expressions of sympathy and support. Even that was somewhat shadowed by his partner's appearance of fatigue; his posture seemed to sag, and Jean was discomfited to be reminded that the Colonel was much older than he and was now vulnerable to the many failures of aging. On top of that the Colonel looked worried, the usually calm face marked by signs of stress. Something was worrying him.

*   *   *

Two weeks after Eulalie Levert's burial, Jean was publicly rebuked in *The Daily Picayune*, castigated for improperly conducting his business affairs. To win new accounts, the article charged, "Jean Baptiste Levert dealt with cane growers in distress with manipulative, underhanded, and deceitful cunning . . . ." What Jean acknowledged in his dealings as shrewd and, yes, sometimes hard-boiled, relentless tactics, the paper construed as mean and dishonest. Such treatment by the press angered and bewildered Jean, especially since he was in the midst of doing his best to benefit his profession. For nearly fifteen years he had benefited the cane industry by strengthening his own personal practice as a broker and those of two highly respected partners.

At first, in his own mind, he wavered between denial and some admission to guilt. Added to his dilemma was his virtual certainty that Bush & Levert was approaching a showdown with the admired Civil War hero and former state legislator, General Étienné DeClouet, an act that he knew would bring hellfire down upon his head, and probably the Colonel's, too. Consideration of the hard facts of the DeClouet case led him to toughen his response to the condemnation these damned newspaper people had hurled at him. *What the hell did they know about business?* He and his partner were sugar factors, not alms givers. The hard look made him feel that he was ready to talk with Colonel Bush about the unfortunate affair.

Now, he knew the source of Colonel Bush's worry and anxious face—he had known that Jean was in ill favor among some of their fellows, and he feared such public rebuke. Jean wondered how long had this been simmering? How was he to greet associates in the street? Ignore the insult? With apology? By public letter to the paper? Should he mention it to Stephanie? Stephanie so proud that she assumed without question her own invulnerability. If she read the financial news, he did not know it. Perhaps she would never hear of it; he should not create anxiety for her. He slammed his hand on the open newspaper that lay on his desk.

The next morning Jean went into the Colonel's office and told him how sorry he was to bring any embarrassment to Bush & Levert, but he laid out a simple defense of his business conduct. He did not offer a denial of dishonesty; he felt that accusation did not merit defense.

Colonel Bush was silent for what seemed longer than it was; he stroked his whitening beard, and Jean realized that his partner's eyes were glistening. Jean's plight, and Bush's, too, had moved the Colonel to tears. This in turn struck at Jean's emotions, forcing him to swallow with difficulty.

"Colonel . . ."

The Colonel raised his hand in a gesture to silence. "Jean, you have been having some hard times lately. Actually, beginning with the loss of your baby Lucie. I've watched you struggle with that; then you lost your mother. And now this." He looked down and shook his head. "I wish I could help you in some way." He waved one hand aimlessly, then glanced behind Jean at the wall. "As to the newspaper, try to move ahead of all that. Frankly, I would not respond to the paper. I would be ready with a reply to anyone else. By that I mean one of our colleagues or a client who expected some sort of explanation—a friend, maybe. But I believe I would not make more of it than is necessary. We will probably hear from patriots if we have to foreclose on General DeClouet . . . ."

With considerable support of Colonel Bush, Jean found no need to speak to anyone about the incident, and he took as good advice the Colonel's counsel to be quiet about it.

In wake of the troublesome events, Jean did not find the right moment to speak to his partner or to his brothers about one matter: He had borrowed five thousand dollars from his mother in 1879 for his share of the down payment on several thousand acres of wilderness land in St. Martin Parish near St. Martinville, Bush & Levert's first venture there. It was an opportunity too filled with potential profit for him to pass up. He'd already made up his mind to mention it to Augie and Amèdèè and repay the loan to Eulalie's estate.

CHAPTER 43

JEAN BAPTISTE SMILED with pride and shouted approval with the enthusiastic crowd as Colonel John Louis Bush addressed the opening ceremonies of the new Louisiana Sugar Exchange on June 3, 1884:

"No one here today doubts that the sugar trade in our city has been gradually leaving us, lured away to other cities on the Atlantic coast. So it is important that our crops be marketed right here in New Orleans, as they were during the flourishing days before the war . . . we believe all Louisiana planters with significant acreage will be pleased to once again send their cane to this fine city."

Again Jean and the crowd applauded. Colonel Bush raised his arms as a signal of success and beamed his best smile over the large hall located at Bienville and North Front streets near the river. Despite his obvious pleasure in his acclaim among his peers, Jean noticed that his partner's stoop seemed more pronounced than usual. He was sixty-three, he was suffering from an ailment unknown to Jean, some vague disease. The Colonel paused to fan away a mosquito near his face, then went on:

"We planters and brokers went to work with a strong will after the war, settling our debts as best we could. We launched our small barks once again, if you will, onto the sea of commerce despite crop failure after crop failure, more than one might expect the planters of Louisiana to endure. Yet, our planters weathered the storm; to have given in would have meant inevitable ruin . . . I am proud to say that relatively few growers fell completely by the wayside."

Loud applause and whistles erupted from the crowd of planters, merchants, and brokers. Jean looked into the Colonel's face for a long moment as together they acknowledged their success in the establishment of the exchange in 1883. He knew the Colonel's influence and popularity among sugar men had won him the presidency in the exchange's first year of operation. In fact, Colonel Bush had recommended that the Louisiana Sugar Planters Association sue the city-chartered New Orleans Sugar Shed Company for mismanagement and price-gouging, and it had won. The company had held a monopoly on commodity sales. Later, the New Orleans City Council had granted a charter establishing the exchange.

"The years after the war and all of Louisiana's Reconstruction troubles have taught us a hard but valuable lesson," concluded the Colonel. "Those years taught us, I suspect, that our new reliance must be on the integrity, industry, and sensible management of our own sugar trade in the future, that arrangements must be made to ensure and encourage our growers to send their crops to this new exchange."

Jean, Colonel Bush, and other planters, factors, and brokers had met a few nights before the speech at the Louisiana Sugar Planters Association building on Baronne Street to complete formal organization of what they called the "palace of trade." They had finalized provisions of their charter, pledging to protect competitive prices through brokers in the marketplace; to provide, maintain, and regulate suitable accommodations for the sale of sugar and molasses; to set fair and uniform prices that would govern all transactions among exchange members.

Jean and the Colonel had been instrumental in setting the capital stock at one hundred thousand dollars, which the shareholders paid for in full, each member holding one share of stock. Act of incorporation took effect when ten thousand of the total capital stock was subscribed; incorporators of the exchange included Edward Gay, sugar planter, St. Louis Plantation near Plaquemine, E. M. Scott, sugar trader in sugar only, Colonel Bush, and Jean. Twelve directors were nominated from a list of eighteen planters, brokers, buyers, and dealers. Jean was nominated to the board to lead the exchange in its first year, but not elected. The loss did not seriously disturb him; he was confident of his turn. For several years, his involvement in the exchange had been so intense that he found himself glad to be able to look around at other developments in the City.

Other facets of post-Reconstruction revival encouraged him. Mississippi River traffic, for example, was thriving. The French Quarter produce market, located between the river's edge and Decatur Street, was a commercial success; it had become one of the busiest spots in the City, rivaling its renowned counterparts in Europe. For the produce market was clean, always stocked with produce of all kinds—a lavish, artistic display of fresh and colorful vegetables and fruits, nuts, and grains, but also a great variety of meats, fowl, and fish and shellfish freshly caught from the river and from the Gulf of Mexico. Jean particularly liked the stucco building of colonial design, the roof of its long, busy porches supported by deep capitals and Doric columns reminding him of Caribbean structures.

At sunrise on Sunday mornings, the market reached the height of its activity and charm as noisy cooks and housewives filled their baskets from heaps of lush greens, piles of melons, fruits, and brilliant pyramids of tomatoes, eggplant, bell peppers, squashes, and purple onions. Tubs of ice held drawn fresh poultry and cuts of red meats. Moving along with bustling lines of fishmongers' benches, eager customers might gather shrimp, live crabs, redfish, speckled trout, sacks of unopened oysters—the whole scene rendered more enchanting, thought Jean, by the mingling aromas of fresh pineapples, citrus fruits, heavy stems of bananas, green and ripe yellow, which came off boats docked within sight of the market.

And the year 1883 especially had been a year of important events for Jean, not the least of which was the birth of his tenth child, Marie Stella. Jean realized his business concerns had occupied most of his time and his thoughts throughout the year, but he tried to find time to show fatherly pride in the new little daughter. He tried to comfort Stephanie, who again had had a difficult delivery and a slow recovery, just as she'd had with her son Lawrence in 1880 and her daughter Anna Beatrice a year later. Each birth had taken its toll on her, and her doctor looked quite serious when he discussed her health with Jean. Doctors, Jean knew, were reluctant to discuss intimate matters of health concerning their female patients, even with husbands, but her doctor implied that Stephanie should not try to bear more children.

Chapter 44

STILL BRIMMING WITH pride over Colonel Bush's well-received speech and the opening of the sugar exchange, Jean arrived at Lizima on a Thursday night in October on a lathered horse that was half dead from exhaustion after the twelve-mile ride from the New Iberia train depot. The broker roused the DeClouet household long after it had retired, and Paul DeClouet took Jean to a guest room, assuring him that his father wanted to talk with him early Friday morning. A servant led the horse to the barn where the spent creature was given a rubdown, water, and oats.

Jean slept soundly and was up at six o'clock. He joined General DeClouet at the appointed breakfast table on the sun-washed back gallery. Looking over the table with its display of heavy silver flatware, immaculate linens, and elegant centerpiece of late summer flowers, Jean smiled and shook his head. *There is no other way for him to show hospitality to a visitor no matter his straitened circumstances.*

The General rose from the table and extended his hand. "Good morning, sir." He motioned toward a chair. "Do join me for breakfast. You must be famished after your strenuous trip last night. We have grillades on grits and omelet with ham. Our cook's specialty is these little dollar-size biscuits."

"Thank you, sir." A grizzled Negro servant pulled out a chair for him and gave it a proper push to seat him. Jean spread a large napkin across his lap, and the servant half-filled his cup with strong, aromatic black coffee, then added hot milk for a perfect *café au lait.* Jean knew from an earlier visit to Lizima that he was drinking a chicory coffee blend called Mellow Joy, found only in St. Martin Parish. Upon swallowing the first sip, Jean regretted that he was duty-bound, very likely, to bring about an end to this old aristocrat's charmed existence.

"I don't believe any court in the land would give us enough money to make up for what those swindlers did to us," he told Jean. "And I am not certain I would not take the same chances again if another situation came along that gave me hope. I will do anything, anything honorable. Lizima has been in my family for more than fifty years, not for me to be swindled out of it through some scheme, but for it to remain for my children and my grandchildren. Now, I have lost four thousand dollars to two New Orleans swindlers, so-called financiers I had contracted to help me overcome my problems." He paused to look out at the gentle swaying of the oak trees, overhanging Bayou Teche, in the stiff breeze. "Those bastards ran off with the money instead of helping me, damnit, so I should have some recourse, right?"

Jean, who felt some sympathy for the General, had heard rumors and read accounts of colorful charlatans perpetuating outlandish schemes among struggling planters, but the General was the first victim he had come face to face with. Reckless and naive as DeClouet's dealings with the crooks had been, Jean did pity the man, for he knew four thousand dollars would have gone a long way in the expenses of harvest and grinding.

"Apparently fraud of this magnitude is getting out of hand in rural Louisiana," Jean said. "Banks are partly to blame because they still refuse long-term credit for cane operations. It makes farmers vulnerable. These fellows are unconscionable. And you are right about the courts. They can't get your money from these crooks; the crooks are in jail; they spent the money long ago, and they have nothing. No, there is no recourse there."

The General squirmed in his chair, and Jean knew the old man felt foolish; he had said enough. Preaching at this point would do no good, probably never would have with General DeClouet.

"As long as I have anything to say about all this, we will not just give up and walk away from our financial problems," said the General. "You don't fold up the family plantation like you would a tent."

Bush & Levert had secured a mortgage on General DeClouet's 1884 sugarcane crop and on his plantation properties, including Lizima manor house. Jean knew DeClouet already had spent the thirty-five thousand dollars advanced to him over four years by the brokerage, paying his most pressing debts and making major renovations at his sugarhouse. Jean and Colonel Bush had told him they could not extend his credit beyond June, 1885, credit that he badly needed to buy supplies and to pay off more long-standing debts; they had gone as far as they could with him.

In the long process, Jean had grown more sympathetic with the planter, despite the man's apparent arrogance and obvious lack of judgment as a farmer and businessman. Jean felt that he no longer coveted the beautiful house at Lizima, though he admired it not a whit less; that he and the Colonel would have done anything sensible to help DeClouet retain his plantation.

The General had become desperate to prevent loss of his house and land, and his desperation led him to seek outside loans from sources that turned out to be fraudulent. His back now to the wall, the General had requested that Jean or Colonel Bush come to Lizima.

Before Jean departed soon after a sumptuous lunch, he spoke briefly about DeClouet's obligations to his firm; he offered a tactful reminder that the big day of reckoning was in June, eight months away. He assumed the General had invited him to get some reassurance, some hint that there was some way to extend further credit, but Jean could do nothing about the losses to the thieves who had gotten away with the money.

Jean mounted his rested horse and headed for New Iberia and the long train ride home. At Lizima's gate, he looked back and waved to General DeClouet, wondering at the war of pride and desperation going on in the old man's mind.

*   *   *

On June 1, 1885, a letter went out from Bush & Levert under Louis Bush's signature.

> My dear sir:
>
> What I have to say, General, will take a few pages; let me know if you would prefer that we meet in person to further discuss the situation. We have examined the memorandum presented to us by your agent, Charles Mouton, relative to a modification of the existing mortgage contract entered into with you a year ago in May, and hereby submit our reply. We wish to say we are anxious to lend ourselves to accommodate everything that would be agreeable to you. But there are certain requirements which you propose that we feel would nullify our present contract and to which we cannot agree. If we extend your indebtedness according to your outline, we would be assuming all the risks. Thus, it is preferable that we remain just as we are under terms of the present contract. To grant any further extension would impair the agreement, we feel, lead to confusion, and we think it is to the best interest of all parties to avoid such an extension, given your present financial situation, General DeClouet. We have no choice, General, but to demand payment of said indebtedness now, which exceeds seventy-six thousand dollars.

CHAPTER 45

JEAN, OUTGOING PRESIDENT of the Louisiana Sugar Exchange, was saying at the annual shareholder's meeting in January, 1886:

"The business of this sugar exchange was handled with faithfulness and care last year. Revenues have been collected and dispersed wisely and properly, and the credit for this good work is certainly not mine alone. It is shared by you gentlemen." Elected president the year before, and pleased with his service, he added: "We have carried our burdens well in the early years of existence, overcome hardships associated with rebuilding our industry after the war, particularly . . . we should rejoice that able and faithful men are waiting to carry on the business of this fine institution. I see this exchange expanding and growing in power and honor and usefulness to the sugar trade until it shall become one of the leading exchanges in the land." Then he raised his hand in a salute and concluded his extemporaneous remarks: "Remember, gentlemen, this is your exchange, and its prosperity will benefit you for all time to come."

He stepped from behind the lectern at the sugar planters building on Baronne; he bowed slightly, acknowledging enthusiastic applause of the audience of a hundred members. The meeting was held at the planters building because the exchange hall was being remodeled to accommodate a growing membership. All seemed to want to shake his hand, and he felt quite rewarded by the surprising, if embarrassing, fervor of the crowd. Then he noted that a stranger was stretching his arm between two members, obviously determined to speak to him. Finally, as he clutched Jean's hand, pumping it up and down, the man spoke over the noise in the room:

"Mr. Levert, Mr. Levert, I wonder if I might have a word or two with you? I much enjoyed your remarks, and I have heard many good things about the work of this exchange. I think it is sorely needed, if planters such as myself are to receive a fair deal in the open market for their products."

Retrieving his hand, Jean looked at the man's face, then at the marquis diamond stud in the lapel of his imported brown worsted suit, and replied, "Certainly, I'll speak with you briefly." He took out his watch. "You do know that the evening is late." He had promised Stephanie that he would be at home as early as possible. She had not felt well since the birth of Ella Marie six months earlier, and his late arrivals seemed to distress her. But he guided the stranger to one side of the room, out of the loudest sounds of voices.

"My name is Emile Ulysses Morvant of Lafourche Parish. I am here as a guest of one of your members who suggested that I speak to you. I had hoped to do business with an established commission merchant in New Orleans. I traveled here at some expense and inconvenience, sir, but if you are not interested or don't have time to hear me out, I'll . . ."

Caught by the word *business*, Jean decided he had better listen to what Mr. Morvant had to say. He smiled and nodded hospitably.

"I am a sugar planter. My family owns Webre Plantation near Thibodaux," said Emile Morvant.

Jean's face brightened. "Webre! Webre! Do you have any connection with Jean Webre who served with the Louisiana militia in the War of 1812?"

"He was my father-in-law. Webre Plantation has been in the family for sixty years now."

"And your wife?"

"My wife is Emilie Webre, Jean Webre's youngest daughter."

"Isn't your wife's sister Aurelie Webre Levert?"

"Of course, Mr. Levert. My wife is your brother Auguste's sister-in-law." He beamed, for most French south Louisianians enjoyed claiming family kinship by blood or by marriage.

Cordially, Jean motioned toward a chair, and they sat down at a table. Most of the crowd was leaving the hall. "May I call you Emile?" He studied Morvant more closely. "I know about Webre Plantation, but I have never had the pleasure of knowing Aurelie's family."

"Well, there are many of us. Aurelie has nine sisters and brothers."

"Well, Emile, what sort of business did you have to discuss with me?"

"Some of our Lafourche Parish planters have had good dealings with you and Colonel Bush." As an aside, he added, "They did warn me that you can drive a hard bargain, but . . ."

Although he definitely wanted to talk with this new acquaintance, Jean realized this sort of meeting could last until well after midnight. He politely interrupted Morvant: "Emile, please, are you staying the night in the city? Surely you don't plan to take to the roads or rails at this hour. Why don't we meet in my office tomorrow, where we can take our time, be more deliberate? How about ten o'clock? Could you manage that?"

"Why, yes. Perhaps that would be best. Yes, I will be there promptly at ten. My train doesn't leave until afternoon."

Jean rose. "Excellent. I hope you can meet my partner, Colonel Louis Bush." The men parted outside the hall, and Jean hurried home, hoping to arrive there before midnight. He settled comfortably in the cab, and as the horse trotted through the familiar, dim nighttime glow of the New Orleans streets, he relaxed, resting his head on the back of the cushioned seat and directed his thoughts to his family.

The house on Third Street, while not quite the center of the universe for him, was surely home where Stephanie always was there for him. He had no idea how it might be without her. And it was where he preferred to be at the end of his long days of concentrated effort as a sugar broker. But on most nights, either riding in a cab or walking, which he preferred, he paused to think about his wife, children, household. The house had filled up with a stairstep row of little Leverts, some of whom looked very much

like little Dupuys. Handsome children, those in school reasonably
dedicated to their studies though showing no evidence of brilliance.
They behaved well at home, at least within his sight and hearing.
Stephanie, with no small amount of help from Vic and Daniels, ran a
happy, efficient home. Jean demanded peace and quiet after a long day,
and he was grateful to Stephanie for being accommodating. He looked
out at the corner gas lamp as they turned from Magazine onto Third
Street. He didn't tell her often enough, of course, but she never showed
any pique at not being constantly thanked or praised. The rich little
girl from St. Gabriel Plantation had become a staunch woman and
a fine lady. He loved the children, but he admitted to himself that he
was relieved, as he unlocked the front door, that they were all sound
asleep. He hoped.

He found Stephanie in their bedroom, standing at the side of
tiny Ella Marie's crib. The shadows from the bedside lamp
emphasized the shadows under Steph's eyes. *Dear God, don't let
her be pregnant again.* He held her shoulders lightly as he kissed
her forehead.

"My dear, why is the infant's crib in our room? I thought you
had settled her in the nursery."

"She was agitated, somewhat. I feared she might disturb little
Stella. You know dear Jean that two-year-olds have to have their
sleep, too." She smiled wanly and patted his shoulder. "You look as
though you need some sleep, too."

"And what about you?" He looked at her figure. "Steph, I must
say that I hope you are not *enceinte.* You are far too weak to . . .
for . . ."

Stephanie smiled again. "*Non, non, mon cher!* I am happy to
tell you that I am not."

"I am glad, my dear. We must think of your health. Dr.
Gonsoulin frowns on your pregnancies."

"Yes, I know." She laid her face against his chest. "He suggested
that we should have separate bedrooms."

Jean felt a sudden anger against Dr. Emile Gonsoulin, the family
physician. He held Steph back, frowning, but he found an impish

smile on her face. Almost to his dismay, he thought she looked like a girl again, the evidences of aging wiped away. He clasped her to him. "Oh, *Madame Levert*, did you tell him that your poor husband finds you irresistible, that he is helpless at the sight of you?"

"Yes, that is what I told him."

"No, you didn't."

"No, I didn't. I just said . . . I just didn't answer him." As she turned away from him, the lace shawl collar of her pale blue dressing gown parted, revealing her bosom. *After all those babies*, thought Jean. The sight of her like this erased all other thoughts. He rubbed his eyes and determined to change the subject, which was unlike him, for thoughts of making love to her when they were alone, or almost alone—he glanced at the sleeping baby's placid little face, its eyelashes lying in charming dark arcs on its cheeks—were likely to lead to shared desire. He dropped Stephanie's hand, moved away, and began to remove his collar.

"I met a man tonight named Morvant from Webre Plantation at Thibodaux. It turns out his wife's sister is Aurelie, Augie's wife. I was dumbfounded. Did you ever know the Webres over there at Thibodaux?" He dropped his cuff links into a Servre's bowl on the highboy and sat down to remove his shoes and hose.

"Oh, yes, I believe I do know the family. At least I've heard of them." She was in the bed. "Well, isn't that interesting. Is he a sugar planter?"

"Yes, and I have an appointment with him at ten tomorrow."

He slipped into his nightshirt and got into bed. He leaned over and kissed Stephanie's cheek, resolved to say goodnight and mean it. But with the slightest, subtlest movement, she turned her face toward him, and his kiss landed on her incredibly soft lips. Now the warming wave of passion that possessed him washed away all doubts and fears. Such longing, he thought, must be savored.

*   *   *

When Emile Morvant entered Bush & Levert brokerage at ten o'clock the next morning, he took a chair in the waiting room along with three other men. He sat quietly for a few moments pondering his situation, then he stood up abruptly and approached the secretary, Alice Mead. "I thought I had a ten o'clock appointment with Mr. Levert. Why are these other men here? Surely Mr. Levert did not forget. I am a relative of his; he is eager to see me before I leave the city in a few hours."

Miss Mead looked at him without expression, showing no intent one way or the other. As Morvant simmered impatiently, Jean's door opened a crack. The secretary looked that way and said, "You may enter, now, Mr. Morvant. Mr. Levert is ready to see you."

Morvant went into Jean's office, his annoyance quite evident. He took off his gray worsted suit jacket and folded it over the back of a chair. Only seconds after he sat in the chair, he jumped up, muttering, "Now I have crushed my verbena. I should have watched what I was doing."

Jean looked up from the papers before him. "What, what? What did you say?"

Despite his apparent bewilderment, he knew what Morvant had said. He felt that such a flower in one's buttonhole was an affectation, and diamonds worn there were ostentatious. Eventually he discovered that the verbena was not an affectation in Emile's mind, and that he loved verbenas and most other flowers, and he did not feel fully dressed without a sprig for his buttonhole.

Finally, Jean laid aside the papers that had occupied him. "Mr. Morvant, are you ready?"

Impatiently, he added, "Need anything? Coffee? Tea? Beignets?" Morvant shook his head.

"Well, then. Suppose you begin." By now everyone who had done business with Jean knew that his sometime eccentric behavior over business bordered on rudeness. Morvant was learning, thought Jean. Jean watched him shuffle his feet, in black shiny shoes, this way and that. Morvant took out a sheaf of papers, all in his own handwriting.

"I have some two thousand acres under cultivation at Webre Plantation. Being far from New Orleans, I have a costly problem of getting my cane, once it has been ground and manufactured at the sugarhouse, to the New Orleans market. I want a more direct line to the primary market to get a better price for my products and more buyers for them."

"In other words, you need a broker, an agent to move your cane?"

"That is correct, sir. As a farmer living in the country, I have only the vaguest knowledge of the demands of the market, how I could benefit from it, since I am so far away from it."

"I see no problem with that," Jean assured him. He explained that a broker received consignments from sugar producers, who live away from the City, and disposed of them at a predetermined rate of commission on the selling price. He said that there was a high degree of risk involved in such business. In fact, most brokers commanded a commission in proportion to the amount of cane harvested, and that the cane was handled without incurring any liability concerning the quality or safety of that harvest. He offered as many details as he thought a prospective client needed to make a decision. He wished Morvant asked questions, but he did not. Jean noticed a twitch in the man's neck.

"Fine, fine. That's what I am looking for, a broker to look after my interests," said Emile eagerly. "Perhaps we can do business together."

Jean stared at Emile. The man's eagerness and his failure to ask probing questions signaled to Jean that he was in danger of his own imprudence.

"I must be honest with you," said Jean. "Such an arrangement can place the producer—yourself—at a great disadvantage. You would be represented at a distance of about seventy-five miles by this firm in transactions that you will not be able to scrutinize regularly."

He explained that until another avenue to the primary market was opened, the present one—the sugar exchange—would have to do. He told Morvant there was no speculation at the exchange, no daily calls, no dealing in futures, and the business purely buying and selling. "Most of the products are disposed of at the exchange by the brokers representing their clients, the growers."

Morvant showed no response; he stared out of the window. Jean watched the twitching in his neck gain in rapidity and believed it was a sign of anxiety. Here was a man who could be taken advantage of; business did not appear to be his skill. What irritated Jean most was Morvant's failure to ask questions. Jean guessed that the man still preferred to do business the old-fashioned way, as before the war. He probably knew little about production technology; he appeared not to be aggressive. He awaited some reply from Morvant, but Morvant still said nothing; the explanations elicited no apparent doubts. Finally, Morvant said, "I have to thank you again."

"Does this mean you want our firm to represent you?" Jean looked out and saw that a dense morning fog had burned off. He looked back at the Thibodaux planter.

"Yes, I think it is the thing to do," said Morvant.

"The fog has lifted," Jean remarked, wondering if Morvant recognized the metaphor. He stood up and smiled. "Listen, Emile, I have several more appointments this morning, so unless you have something more to discuss, questions to ask, I will have to bid you good-day and a safe journey home."

Now Morvant looked a bit put off. Jean knew he wanted to stay longer, but that was out of the question. Jean had things to do. He rose and walked around his desk. "My secretary will draw up the necessary papers within the next day or two, and she will send two copies of the contract to you. Just sign the original for us and keep the other copy for your records."

Morvant smiled, looking more confident. "Yes, yes," he said, "I shall look forward to receiving the contract, and I'll return it promptly."

"By the way," said Jean, "I shall notify my brother Auguste that I have made your acquaintance. He and Aurelie will be interested in that. My father, too, will be interested. He has lived at St. Delphine Plantation with them for several years now, ever since my mother's death." Jean extended his hand, and the two men shook hands warmly, considering Jean's opinion that their interview had been a bit strange. "Emile, I hope that our association will be a good, long one."

"Yes, yes." Morvant paused at the door. "It's been a pleasure to make your acquaintance."

*   *   *

That evening when Jean arrived home, he found a letter from Augie.

October 13, 1886
St. Delphine Plantation
West Baton Rouge, Louisiana

My dear Jean—

*   I don't like sending bad news, but Father is ill! The doctor isn't sure what's ailing him other than old age. His eyesight is getting worse all the time, the effects of glaucoma, and his hearing is pretty bad. We have to practically yell to get him to answer. Father asks for you to come here as soon as you can. He wants to talk to you. I don't know what else to say except that we all want you when it is convenient. Haven't heard from Amedee yet but he knows Papa is ill.*

Yours truly,
Auguste Levert Jr.

Jean put the letter on the dresser in his bedroom. Its tone frightened him; it was shorter than his brother's letters usually were. Augie wrote rambling letters, even with an order for supplies for St. Delphine or St. Mary's; he always included news of the family and inquiries about Stephanie and the children. Jean knew he must get up to see his father within the next day or two.It was too late to talk to Steph tonight; he would discuss it with her in the morning. He fell asleep thinking of his father, thanking God that he had kept his resolve to visit him oftener after Eulalie died.

CHAPTER 46

DIED,

On St. Delphine Plantation, West Baton Rouge, on Saturday, October 16, 1886, at 7:30 o'clock a.m.,

PHILIPPE AUGUSTE LEVERT SR.,
age 83 years.

The relatives, friends and acquaintances of the family are respectfully invited to attend his funeral to-morrow (Sunday) morning at 11 o'clock, from his late residence (St. Delphine Plantation), whence the procession will proceed at St. John the Baptist Church at Brusly Landing.

JEAN BAPTISTE RUBBED his palms over his graying temples and looked across the sizable crowd of relatives and friends, who had gathered in the garden behind St. Delphine Plantation house to pay their last respects to Philippe Auguste Levert. Notes that he had written for the service were in his coat pocket, but which he realized he would not use. He felt too deeply moved to read words that must come naturally from his heart, so grieved that when his brothers approached him he had told them that he didn't think he could deliver the eulogy.

He cleared his throat and swallowed, hoping that he could get through the next few minutes without breaking down. He felt the same agony of sorrow he had experienced when he buried Marie Lucie and when he tearfully said goodbye to his mother. He had stood vigil near his father's coffin in the parlor of Augie's home until buggies, carriages, and wagons filled with farming families of all economic levels from up and down the river, began to arrive on the wide front lawn. They all lined up on the wide gallery to file past the bier for a last look at the well-known planter.

Jean had been further depressed by the sight of his father's body, pitifully wasted and shrunken in death, the once-robust six-footer hardly recognizable. It was one of many pictures of his father that he knew would always stay with him, projecting it on a mental screen and watching it, unchanged, for as long as he desired. Feeling that he could scarcely bear another minute of his grief, he was glad to go outside into the brilliant October morning sunshine where oak trees, rich shrubbery, and late-blooming flowers waved in a river breeze that cooled the air. The setting rendered a funereal occasion bearable; it also struck a tender cord in him that made death all the sadder.

"The urge to sustain the memory of one we all loved, to make enduring the memory of the man who has just passed from our daily lives and beyond further affection, is one of the oldest cravings of the heart . . . Auguste Levert, *mon Père, mon maître, mon ami,* I know of nothing harder to understand and to bear than the sense of loss—sudden, mysterious . . ."

Jean paused in his French and English comments and unbuttoned his overcoat. "Our minds are all brimming, I dare say, with wonderful memories of him, none more crowded, of course, than my own. So, in the days to come, let us draw upon some of those memories and try to comfort each other as best we can . . . I always wanted to be like him; I respected his grasp of all matters of sugar farming, his prowess as a planter and his approach to the duties and cares of parenthood. The most persistent image I have of him is that of a vigorous, youthful planter instructing his young son of ten or eleven.

"I also recall the keen relish with which he read aloud to his children from the pages of his revered Acadian mother's diary, which brought to my brothers and sister and me much inspiration. I never knew my *Grand-mère Anna Comeaux Levert*, but I felt I had come to know her well through the words in her diary . . . I know it now, though of course, I did not know it then, it was our mammy on Golden Ridge, Bébé, who discerned the strong bond between *mon Père* and me, a bond that will not end with his passing . . ."

Jean realized he was rambling; he could not go on. Perhaps these people knew enough about grief to understand. Tears flowed over his cheeks and down to the corners of his mouth. Before him sat Augie and Amèdèe and their families. He turned to his left where Stephanie, her face etched in sympathy, and his five oldest children—Albert, Mathilde, Freddy, Stephanie Marie, and Jean, Jr.—were seated, pale-faced city strangers to this scene of the country sugarcane origins like those from which he had sprung. Auguste's long-time sugar broker, Albert Desmont, seventy-three and in declining health, sat next to Stephanie. Seeing Desmont, Jean recalled his great fascination with him the first time they'd met. Occasionally they ran into each other at lunch at Jean's favorite restaurants. Fondly, he remembered his sister Euphrasie who could not attend her father's funeral from Plaquemine because of crippling rheumatism. He saw all the faces swimming before him. Who among them fathomed his emotions as he struggled on?

"Philippe Auguste Levert was *l'homme le plus grand que j'ai jamais connu*, the greatest man I ever knew. I never knew a kinder man, the embodiment of stern tenderness, truth, and wisdom. He was a loving husband . . ." Jean knew he must stop. Perhaps his face revealed the ache in his heart. He looked at Augie. Yes, Augie knew, of course he knew, for he was with his father every day. He missed him in a special way.

"Thank you, all of you, for coming." He remained on the platform until the crowd had dispersed, most going into the house where a priest pronounced the final words of benediction. Jean made the sign of the cross with his head bowed in silent prayer before entering the house.

The priest's tone was nasal, " . . . the Father, the Son, and the Holy Spirit, amen."

Jean and his family watched Auguste's remains entombed alongside Eulalie's in the above-ground concrete vault at St. John the Baptist church cemetery at Brusly Landing. Jean and his brothers went back after the interment with a mason, who sealed the tomb in the fading light of the autumn afternoon. The rasping sound of the trowel and the dappled shadows on the wet cement meant closure to Jean.

*   *   *

A month later, Jean and his brothers took possession in equal shares of their father and mother's four working sugar plantations: St. Delphine, purchased in 1873, and St. Mary's, purchased in 1880, both located in West Baton Rouge Parish; and Golden Ridge, purchased in 1833, and Willow Glen, purchased in 1874, both located in Iberville Parish.

Still in the shadow of grief for his father, Jean realized that his dreams of empire-building were coming true. Through inheritance of the four plantations with his brothers, in addition to his ownership of Catahoula Plantation in St. Martin Parish and the forthcoming foreclosure on Lizima, he could now afford the security and freedom he cherished. He could now go into other kinds of investments. His already considerable wealth grew far beyond those long-held dreams, and well before his fiftieth birthday.

CHAPTER 47

"HOW IS JANUARY sugar?" Jean wired the telegraph clerk.

"Last sale of plantation sugar late yesterday four cents a pound," the clerk wired in reply.

"Then sell 12 January in New York higher than the market price."

Sitting at his long wooden desk on the first floor of the Louisiana Sugar Exchange, Jean was trading on behalf of his new client, Emile Morvant. The Thibodaux farmer stood near the desk on the damp, hazy January day, thirty minutes after the exchange doors had opened to admit scores of brokers, merchants, and growers, and a bell had rung to open the day's trading. For a moment Jean stared through a large plate-glass window at the yellow sun that gave off the kind of glow he could look at without hurting his eyes.

From his desk, positioned next to several long tables used to display samples of sugar growers' products, Jean looked up when he heard a broker, in bold checkered suit, shouting and waving his hands trying to sell plantation sugar to merchants clustered around him. He saw another broker, in dark suit and top hat, leaping up and down braying bids for sugar at any price.

He turned away from the scene to send more instructions to the clerk at Glover & Odendahl in New York, bargaining with him to raise the price of Morvant's sugar to four and a half cents. A few minutes later, the clerk advised him: "We have sold 12 January at four and a half cents." Jean turned to Morvant, a stout, broad-shouldered man with a face shaped like a full moon, and nodded.

Morvant, wearing a fine worsted suit with a sprig of verbena in the lapel, nodded in return and smiled.

Jean was pleased that Emile had made a special trip to the City to observe for the first time daily operations on the exchange floor. He glanced up as Morvant moved closer to his desk. The glance seem to say that Emile's visit meant that the grower was serious about learning the brokerage business.

"For your information, Emile, twelve or thirteen people in widely separated parts of the country handled that order for us, and still the transaction was completed in a short space of time." He said that negotiating a good, fair price for a client's crop, as he had just done, happens many times during a trading day. That there was no comparison between this system and the method of a few years ago, when there was no commercial house in the City where growers could obtain price quotations. "In the old days the poor grower never knew what price he would get for his cane until it was delivered and, as a result, a grower often took less for his sugar or molasses than they cost to produce. The bulk of sugar trading, Mr. Morvant, used to be handled on the levee or in a saloon." He explained that there were no headquarters where cargoes of river steamers that bore produce from plantations to New Orleans were exhibited for inspection, where brokers displayed their samples to tempt buyers, even where the receipt of goods and sales each day could be documented.

"If you walked into Glover & Odendahl right now, Emile, you'd think you had stumbled into a house of madness." Jean was warming to his subject, which he knew as well as anyone in New Orleans. "Exchange officials direct how goods upon the floor are bought, sold, and delivered. They fix penalties for failure to comply with sales contracts and they arbitrate all transactions among exchange members." He told Morvant they help to settle disputes over charges for brokering, weighing products, drayage, or conveying products in small carts, and warehousing. Pointing to the product sample tables, Jean said, "An entire crop from Louisiana growers is sold from these tables."

"How do you work with all this noise going on around you?"

"What noise?" replied Jean. "You should have been here when the doors first opened this morning. Talk about barely organized chaos. But it does take time for a broker to learn how to do a decent job for his client. We just have to know what we are doing. Misinterpreted orders cost money. Remember, the broker has to make good on all losses due to errors he makes in handling his client's orders. Service is our job, always, and service simply must not suffer—ever."

After Emile Morvant arrived, Jean had given him what amounted to a brief history of the exchange: Built for fifty-two thousand dollars, the triangular exchange hall was a hundred feet long and fifty-five feet from floor to ceiling; a skylight twenty-three feet square provided ventilation through a cornice; large plate-glass windows provided light on three sides; noisy public telegraph offices and salesrooms on the first floor, all faced the levee; excellent acoustics; porches or overhangs covered all hall entrances, where millions of barrels of sugar had been bought and sold since the exchange was opened three years before; a library, reading room, several lavatories, and two committee rooms dominated the ground floor; and a portrait of Étienne de Boré, first mayor of New Orleans after France took control of Louisiana in 1800, hung on a wall in the lobby. Jean told Morvant that de Boré had helped pave the way for cane growing and the development of sugar-making on the rich lowlands of southwest Louisiana that had attracted his *Grand-père Levert* and his father.

Jean decided to remain at the exchange until half past five after Emile left at mid-afternoon to return to Thibodaux. He loved a day like this on the floor, and he wanted to stay longer but Stephanie had planned a dinner party for some of their friends who lived in the Garden District. Between December and March, when the cane harvest was ending and the buying-selling of raw sugar and molasses on the exchange floor were at its height, Jean and Colonel Bush worked night and day. It was exciting, stimulating for them. But when the exhausting time ended in the spring, Jean escaped the sweltering City for vacations on the Mississippi Gulf Coast, a few hours from New Orleans by train.

*How fortunate I've been in business all these years,
especially since Colonel Bush and I became partners.
I'm blessed to have him for a partner: My relentless,
often hard-boiled approach to business deals is
tempered perfectly by his more deliberate manner. I've
always been able to make an investment I really desired,
and sometimes I invested alone if I had high hopes for a
piece of land or an apartment building that the Colonel
felt was not a sound purchase for Bush & Levert. Not
that the Colonel was short on money, but that he was
getting older and didn't seem to have the drive by which
I'm consistently propelled.*

*Lizima Plantation would not only represent the largest
account to date for our firm, but represent the foundation on
which to start building my holdings and finances at all costs,
letting nothing stand in my way. And if I ever own Lizima
outright I will devote the rest of my life to making it a model
sugar producer and moneymaker.*

Jean Baptiste Levert
Mid-1888

CHAPTER 48

JEAN BAPTISTE AND Colonel Bush arrived in St. Martinville in late May, 1888, amid wild celebration, as wild a celebration as a town of two thousand could bring about. For the Southern Pacific train was making its maiden journey across southwest Louisiana marshes to the town, and the two brokers enjoyed being present on a historical occasion that was obviously of great importance to these Louisiana Acadians. Jean noticed people staring at them as they walked toward the new yellow station, thinking they might be judging him and the Colonel to be railroad officials come to celebrate the extension of their rails.

But they had come on their own mission, itself historic considering how long they had been propping up Lizima Plantation. It had been eight years since they took the first mortgage on General Alexandre Étienné DeClouet's plantation. They had supplied additional loans and had given him several more extensions for repayment than either of them believed was prudent business practice. General DeClouet, who had continued to live in fine style, had never had money to repay Bush & Levert anything on the debt of more than seventy-six thousand dollars. They had notified the old gentleman that they must have their money or else seize his property. And in his typical observance of gentility, DeClouet had replied promptly, inviting them to visit him and spend a day in his home and partake of his excellent cuisine.

Jean could not be surprised at the General's cordiality, for he had dealt with him enough to know that this was his manner. But seventy-six thousand dollars, by anybody's measure, was a great deal of money. He knew their firm was strong, but not strong enough to carry debts of this size indefinitely. He and Colonel Bush had made a vow—no further credit accommodations.

Suddenly, a small black man called to them from his box seat on a four-wheel barouche: "Excuse me, but is you M'sieu Lavair and de Col'nel? My name is Edward Hypolite." He pronounced it Poleete. "The Gen'ral say for me to meet you and bring you back to de Big House."

Hypolite, shiny black, almost blue, stepped down with agility and swept his hat off. "You gen'men step right in my buggy and I be glad to drive you to Liz'ma."

"My goodness, Jean, he has sent someone to meet us. Now isn't that just like him?"

Jean and the Colonel took facing seats. "I'll remember you to General DeClouet for your courtesy and prompt service," said Jean. The stooped servant tipped his hat to them. He shook the reins and told the horses, "allons." They traveled a short distance from the train station through a freshly graveled street and three miles down the dirt lane to Lizima.

Jean knew that the Bayou Teche sugar area had not recovered from the war; after more than twenty years, some of its richest land was still not in cultivation. One reason the townspeople had been so jubilant over the railroad was that the first-ever train service was a solid step toward progress and new growth. Jean, too, was pleased, for he expected to be a major landowner soon in St. Martin Parish as a result of the foreclosure. Constantly, in his own mind, he tried to separate his exulting anticipation of ownership from his true sympathy for General DeClouet's plight. He told himself that DeClouet had other plantations where he could live what life he had left in comfort and in his inimitable style. He could not, however, imagine that DeClouet owned another such manor house as the one at Lizima. Jean wished he could expect DeClouet's son or his son-in-law to handle properly the remaining sugar-growing lands, relieving the General of management, something at which he had never excelled or even eked out small success. It was, in fact, an unexplainable wonder to Jean that he had not lost everything years earlier.

On the other hand, Jean had forgotten nothing he had learned about successful farming at his father's side. A businessman par excellence, and barring natural disaster, he felt confident of making Lizima a model producer and moneymaker. The manor house was an imposing *contrée demeure* for his large and growing family. He hoped that Albert, after his education at Mount St. Mary's College in Emmitsburg, Maryland, might show an interest in being a successful planter. No young man could ask for a finer plantation to show what he could do. Jean enjoyed these musings, as the barouche rode through high stands of maturing sugarcane stalks, then made a right turn into the magnificent grounds that would soon be the property of Bush & Levert.

"Good God, Jean! No wonder you are infatuated with this place. Just look at it!" The Colonel's head turned in both directions as he tried to see the entire area of green lawns and enormous, spreading live oaks, their drapes of Spanish moss nearly touching the grass in the breeze. The lush perfection of flora under the bluest of skies seemed almost unreal to the partners, and the great white house, seventy-five yards through the trees, was an architectural gem that looked invulnerable in its classic dignity. "I have great pity for this poor old gentleman, pity for his sad lack of horse sense that could probably have saved all this for him and his heirs." The Colonel shook his head. "I've known him a long time, you know."

"I feel as you do. I tell myself that his sad *dénouement* was inevitable. But if he had not lost out to Bush & Levert, it would have been some other brokerage, and long before now. There is one thing about it, this property is going into loving hands," Jean said with emotion that caused his partner to turn and look at him. "If I can own it outright someday, I'll devote my life to keeping it beautiful and productive."

"Well, Jean, as I have said before, we can surely expect to work out a deal that will enable you to assume full ownership. None of my children, as you know, is the least bit interested in farming or running an estate of this magnitude. I will feel better about selling the firm's other half ownership to you than I would trying to get a just price for it on the market. In fact, we couldn't hope to do it. If I were twenty years younger . . ." He lifted both hands and dropped them into his lap again.

The barouche glided over a packed gravel oval before the wide gallery and came to a stop before the front door. Hypolite jumped down from his box and lifted his old hat to the two guests. If he had heard gossip about their mission, thought Jean, he did not show it. He seemed to have no doubts about his future or that of his employer.

As they stepped down from the barouche's springy step, General DeClouet came out the door, his right arm extended. "*Bienvenu, mon amis.*"

Colonel Bush shook his hand. "General! Let me be candid. You show no distress or tension on this occasion. Let me say that we do feel great distress."

DeClouet shook hands with Jean. "Ah, *Monsieur Levert*. I trust you gentlemen had a comfortable ride with Hypolite. And how was the new *machine vapeur*? Quite a *joyeux* for our parish, eh?"

"*Bon jour, General*." Jean could not bring himself to be so *joyeux*. It seemed false. The man was about to lose his prize possession, for God's sake. He sighed. Perhaps DeClouet was right to pretend. Jean wished it was over; he wanted to get back on the train and return to New Orleans. The partners were considering an offer to purchase a small plantation called Davis in St. Charles Parish, forty-five miles southwest of New Orleans. Jean had scheduled a meeting for the day after tomorrow at Davis, and he wanted time to prepare for the negotiations with Ezra Davis, the owner, and his business manager. Davis could no longer pay taxes on the property and Jean knew that he was selling it for far below its value. *Thank God the train is coming back through, heading east, in the late afternoon.*

DeClouet and the Colonel were talking as Jean followed them

into the central corridor of the house, which seemed longer and wider each time Jean saw it. It was decorated with handsome pieces—French chairs upholstered in red velvet, carved mahogany tables, unusually tall stands overflowing with graceful ferns that brought inside, in a charming way, the outside so visible at front and back. Jean had never looked closely at these furnishings before. He and Stephanie must call on the dealers in New Orleans for furnishings and *objets d'art*. He knew these tapestries were Flemish. The General had told him so on a previous visit. Jean thought them rather stodgy. But the portraits of DeClouet's ancestors were enviable, and Jean was taken with a painting of the plantation house itself, dated *1861*, and signed *A. Persac*. Well, it would take some time to adopt a new name—the name Lizima meant nothing to Jean—and decorate the interior with comfortable furnishings suitable for the best kind of Creole living. Stephanie should enjoy furnishing the house.

"May I offer you some refreshments, gentlemen?" asked DeClouet. "No? Then let us remove to the *garconnière*, my office, and settle this business." Jean followed the other two men onto the structure's front gallery. He thought the *garconnière* had the added charm of a view of Bayou Teche in back, where several *bateaux* were tied to a short pier. From the south end of the gallery, the men walked through a formal rose garden and into the office. There they found the General's son, Paul, and the family's attorney, Charles Mouton, along with Bush & Levert's St. Martinville attorney, Robert Martin.

"Gentlemen," the General announced, his voice quivering slightly, "this business of ours should not take long. Please sit down. I don't wish to detain you. I know you want to return to your places of work as soon as possible. So now I will turn over the meeting to my attorney, Mr. Mouton."

The presence of the attorneys on the warm day added some formality to the assemblage, and, Jean felt, more tension. Still, it was a relief to have the lawyers do the talking. He was painfully aware now that the General was about to lose what must surely be his dearest possession, his heritage from his father. It had been nearly three years since Colonel Bush wrote General DeClouet telling him that Bush & Levert was going to foreclose on his mortgage. Because his debts had not been removed from the books by June, 1885, the General had to turn over certain properties during the next three years to the brokerage firm as payment.

Charles Mouton was reading: "Whereas Mr. Alexandre Étienné DeClouet, Sr., had declared on June seventh, eighteen hundred eighty-five, that he was still indebted unto Jean Baptiste Levert and Colonel Louis Bush in the sum of $76,985 . . ." Mouton, a short dapper figure, his bright round face as red as a boiled Gulf crab, adjusted his pince-nez. "In the event that said Mr. Étienné DeClouet, Sr., is unable to pay in money his indebtedness, he has given, in part payment, the following described properties to Bush & Levert . . . firstly, Chrétien Plantation with buildings and improvements on Bayou Teche . . . secondly, Lizima Plantation, located on both sides of Bayou Teche . . . the dwelling, sugarhouse, sawmill, thirty-six mules, twelve oxen, cane cultivators, carts, harrows, plows, stubble pickers . . . ."

*   *   *

When the painful interview had ended, the men proceeded to the oval driveway where the lawyers continued to discuss legal matters. General DeClouet asked again if Jean and the Colonel wanted coffee before going back to St. Martinville and a long wait in the new train station. Gratefully anticipating escape from the stressful business, Jean stepped into the barouche and left the final amenities with DeClouet to his partner.

Just as Colonel Bush settled himself on the facing seat, sudden loud screams startled Jean, as a red-faced, enraged man rushed out of the house, hurdled four gallery steps, and landed flat-footed on the gravel drive beside the carriage. "You—you conniving, heartless sonofabitch!" he yelled at the top of his lungs. "How could you do this? How could you keep kicking a poor old man while he is down? Why must you destroy what pride and self-esteem he has left?"

Jean and the Colonel looked at each other in alarm and puzzlement. The man was addressing Jean only.

"That is Charles Berard, the General's son-in-law," Bush said quietly. "He is a firebrand." Berard shook his gold-tipped cane in Jean's face, causing Jean to lean away from the open side of the barouche. *Less than half an hour after passing the title to this plantation and this madman might pull his revolver on us. On me! He seems to blame me for all of it. Damn! Why doesn't Hypolite, or whatever his name is, get us out of here!* But the barouche sat there while Jean watched the General, on the gallery, rebuking his son-in-law with gestures.

"You used deception and arm-twisting to coerce General DeClouet into taking on more debt. Oh, you did a thorough job, smooth, clean!" Berard was trembling with rage. "That final one-year extension was nothing more than a way to collect more interest. You knew damn well there was no way he could repay his debts in that time! I can just hear you! Telling him, 'There will be no problem making payments despite the existing promissory notes.'" Berard's tone was mocking. "Your greed has ruined a noble family."

Finally, Colonel Bush began making downward movements with his hands as if to hush the furious man. "Mr. Berard. Mr. Berard. Listen to me. Please! Extension was granted because of our long association with your family and deep respect for General DeClouet. Unfortunately, sometimes business doesn't work out the way we hope it will. Mr. Levert deserves none of your condemnation."

"A damned lie! A damned lie!" screamed Berard, his fury out of hand, again. He moved toward Jean, but his father-in-law signaled to the driver to leave, and Hypolite flicked the reins, quickly getting them on their way. The barouche raced down the drive too fast. The top was in place now not only to spare Jean Berard's rage and gold-tipped cane, but the dust of a swift journey from Lizima. The buggy swayed as it poked over the main gate's cattleguard. Jean felt his heart beat quicker. He'd slept restlessly the night before their arrival at the plantation, but now he was nervous. Jean was thankful to get out alive, but he was embarrassed to have Colonel Bush witness such a vulgar display.

"My God, Colonel, am I that bad?"

The Colonel shook his head. His admiration of Étienné DeClouet, Jean knew, was war-related, an almost religious basis for comradeship among Confederate veterans. "Charles Berard is married to the General's daughter, Blanche. I must tell you, in all due respect for DeClouet, that both are spoiled beyond reason. As far as I know, Charles has never worked in his life, and Blanche has a reputation for being a—well—a brat. If, in the war, General DeClouet had disciplined his men with the laxity he has his children, he would never have become a hero of the great Confederacy. Pay no attention to this boy. He is probably drunk. He is from one of the richest families in this part of Louisiana. He knows nothing of business or real life. He is, in fact, a fool."

In St. Martinville, Bush gave Hypolite a generous tip, and both men thanked him for his courtesy. Then they sat down in the paint-smelling, small waiting room of the yellow train station, and Colonel Bush told Jean more about the DeClouet family. He knew more about the family than Jean had realized.

The Colonel said the wild-living Charles Berard, DeClouet's handsome, lazy son-in-law, had never known any life but that of privilege and imagined *royauté*. His flighty wife, Blanche, was of the same cut; and her father wanted her thus, to be a princess, never to assume any persona other than that. For the old man considered all of them the elite, the chosen. Berard's grudge against Jean had begun eight years earlier, as soon as the General had contracted Bush & Levert to become his sugar broker during Mardi Gras, 1880. Berard became suspicious of Jean's methods then, and the Colonel's, too. The tough lending demands and contractual terms that Jean had presented were made when the General had no choice but to accept them, when he was believed to be at the end of his rope. When Bush & Levert had extended the loan four years later, in 1884, Berard was convinced that Jean coerced the General into mortgaging his prize holdings—mainly Lizima—as collateral.

Besides, Charles Berard simply did not like Jean. The more he thought of Jean and what had happened—the title transfer—

the angrier he became. Obviously, Paul had told Charles of that first meeting in Jean's office when Paul had felt that they were not treated with respect. He often recounted the unacceptable reception during the Mardi Gras visit, the failure of Jean to provide invitations to the ball of his krewe, the outer office wait at Bush & Levert, like common people, and generally rude treatment.

"Charles has schemed since then to get back at the firm, Jean, you in particular," the Colonel said. "He's dreamed of all sorts of ways to provoke you, to embarrass you, to expose you and your manner of business conduct for what he thinks it is, shadowy and suspicious."

Jean was surprised at all this, but he was more shocked when Bush said he suspected Berard of being behind the hurtful criticism of Jean in *The Daily Picayune*. "And how do you know all this?"

"Gossip, Jean. Talk. Talk, talk, talk. I keep my ears open at Antoine's, Tujague's, the Pickwick. One listens and one picks up these bits, pieces, trends. One draws conclusions: Charles Berard is your enemy, son. It's that simple and that complicated. My dear Jean, you have broken no laws, and none of your moves should have broken any hearts. Nevertheless, Berard is not through tormenting you, because you are his whipping boy, his excuse for amounting to nothing himself. So prepare yourself for more words and threats, but do not fear serious wounds. A charming old war hero has lost a battle to you, perhaps his last, but in the final analysis it is of his own doing."

Later, aboard the new train bound for New Orleans, he told Jean that the General had returned to Lizima shortly after the war to rebuild his shattered dreams and fortunes. For awhile he enjoyed a life of ease and quiet happiness, employing his leisure hours in literary pursuits, croquet on the front lawn, and social company of many friends. But after the adoption of the 14th and 15th amendments to the federal constitution had invested newly freed Negroes with all the rights of citizenship, including the vote, the General became alarmed. He stressed in speeches before citizens of St. Martin Parish and throughout the state that "the freedom of the white people of the South is now threatened." He then left his self-imposed retirement on Lizima and tried to unite and aid the white people of the South against Reconstruction, against the state's carpetbag government led by William Kellogg.

The Colonel also told him that personal problems beset him early: The panic of 1873 and subsequent collapse of the New Orleans sugar commission industry drained his savings set aside to restore Lizima to its antebellum grandeur. The bumper crop he had counted on a year later was destroyed by the worst frost in Bayou Teche history. Two years later, a flood drowned his entire one thousand acres of cane and cotton and damaged his sugarhouse so severely that he could not afford to harvest and grind for the next two years. Property taxes on the plantation went unpaid for the next two years. DeClouet's failure to reduce his indebtedness and his steadfast optimism about the next year's crop, and the next year's, contributed to his inexorable slippage toward bankruptcy and his growing dependence on the sugar brokerage Thomas Brierre, Tucker & Co., in the beginning, and Bush & Levert in the end.

"So you see, Jean, his decline was not wholly due to mismanagement."

Still, there were certain expenses that the General would never reduce, he told Jean, especially the cost of hospitality. He could not tolerate the idea that anyone considered him a skinflint. In the dining room of Lizima, he often abstained from the outlandishly fine meals to which he treated his guests; this also applied to his beloved French wines, so he could serve his friends and his many kinfolk who for so long had looked to him for the best food and drink in southwest Louisiana. These expensive indulgences proved a considerable drain on his dwindling resources, yet he never turned away any visitor without offering something from his famous table.

Colonel Bush gestured with his hands, palms up. "And Jean, his concerns with indebtedness bordered on obsession. It was the most grating of all the anxieties afflicting him in these years since the war. He not only feared being considered a skinflint, but a poor credit risk." He explained that debts the General had incurred with Brierre, Tucker, for example, still were unpaid five years later. Smaller debts to family members from whom he had acquired property, including Lizima, dragged on for years.

The Colonel stared out the train window for a moment; rain was coming down in sheets. "I believe the General's habit of excessive indulgence began in his relations with the Chevalier de l'Hommes, his aunt and uncle and adoptive parents after his father was killed in the duel. He could never bear the thought of being labeled a stingy parent with love or with money. Why he needed to borrow money from us remains a mystery to me. I have since been told that there was money available from wealthy family members at no interest."

Jean had no answers, and remained silent. He was determined not to feel guilty for his part in the General's ill fortunes.

"The loss of Lizima does not remove completely the threat of more misfortune or the possible loss of the two other plantations that he owns near Lafayette. I only hope that he loses nothing more." The Colonel looked at his watch in the fading light. "The General is scheduled to be grand marshal in St. Martinville's railroad parade tomorrow, and I will bet you good money that he will be there on his white stallion leading in his grandest manner."

"I had no idea you knew so much about him," said Jean. "But all this makes no difference, does it?" He knew it was a rhetorical question.

"No, it doesn't. But as the new master of Lizima, you should know all the lore of its previous owner. Is it not so?"

"Of course," said Jean.

CHAPTER 49

SOON AFTER RETURNING to New Orleans from St. Martinville, Jean set out for St. Charles Parish to inject the interests of Bush & Levert into the distress call of another plantation—to offer to purchase Davis Plantation. Exhausted from the trip to foreclose on Lizima, Colonel Bush returned to New Orleans unable to pursue business for the firm with Jean and eager to retreat to his home on Coliseum Street in the Garden District. Jean had become accustomed to his partner's increasing inability to last through prolonged days of stressful business.

With no manor house involved and without the personal complications that he sometimes encountered at other plantations in distress, Jean came to a tentative agreement with the Davis business manager on an offer of twenty-one thousand dollars for the eight-hundred-acre farm. He offered to pay half down in cash and the balance over three years. Jean returned to the City satisfied that the firm had acquired another propitious, productive sugar plantation, and he was eager to apprise Colonel Bush of the uncomplicated matter.

Alas, a letter from the maddened Charles Berard shattered his calm before he could recount the matter to his partner.

August 1, 1888

J. B. Levert
No. 31 Perdido St.
New Orleans, La.

Sir, I challenge you. I propose to meet you at such place as may be agreed upon between us three weeks from to-day, at 6 o'clock (dawn), the weapons to be chosen. Dress to be ordinary fall clothing and subject to examination by both parties and their seconds. Furthermore, each party may have on the grounds, besides his second, a doctor and a few friends. General DeClouet, the poor soul, had never really recovered fully from the ravages of the war, the broken fortunes suffered by himself and his close friends. Now, this takeover of Lizima, cutting out his heart literally, was the last straw! It almost broke my heart to see him feebly call his family together and announce it would have to remove from St. Martinville to his St. Clair Plantation outside Lafayette. I trust the terms of this challenge meet with your approval, and I look forward to a response and our meeting.

Your obedient servant,
Charles M. Berard

Dismayed, Jean threw the letter on his desk and dropped into his desk chair. After only a moment of brooding, he jumped up, infuriated. "Damn the brashness and gall of this fool," he shouted aloud. "Who the hell does he think he is, accusing me of deception, of lying. Goddamit, I am no thief. The insolence of this man!" He scarcely knew how to respond to this irresponsible action by Berard, but he knew he must defend his honor. *My God, this is 1888. Dueling is against the law.*

Jean paced the length of his office several times, rubbing the back of his neck, stroking his moustache, cursing under his breath. *Of all the damned foolishness.* He didn't have time for it. Calming himself, he realized that he must make a serious decision about Berard no matter how absurd the whole business seemed. He must talk to the Colonel. He took his hat and coat and left the office. Tomorrow was Saturday; he would try to see Bush and talk over the matter with the older man. He locked the door behind him, descended the stairs to Perdido Street, and hailed a cab.

*   *   *

On Saturday morning he sent a messenger to Colonel Bush's home asking for a brief conference at whatever hour was most comfortable for his partner. He did not wish to tire the Colonel or interfere with his regimen of rest and quiet. The reply urged Jean to come for a light lunch at noon.

Precisely at twelve, he handed his hat to a manservant inside the foyer of the two-story mansion on Coliseum Street. The house had become familiar to Jean, for occasional conferences here had become necessary since the decline in the Colonel's health. Jean admired the elegant house and its purely classical embellishments— the heavily beveled molding, the Greek key, acanthus leaf, striated Corinthian columns, dormer windows, and open space at ground level for four barouches. Inside, the reception rooms were aglow with polished floors and richly colorful oriental rugs. Sculptures, marble mantels, beveled mirrors, and bookcases containing the best literature in ornate covers adorned the rooms. Choices of draperies, paintings and tapestries by Celeste, the Colonel's wife, pleased him. Since the foreclosure on Lizima, he had a renewed interest in such things, and even found himself looking for ideas and inspirations.

Bolling, the heavy-set servant, led him to the large, bright parlor where his partner waited, half reclining on a chaise near a desk. Bolling bowed slightly and left the men alone.

"Jean! Come in. It's mighty good to see you. Do sit down. Pull the chair closer and tell me the latest news on the street."

"I'm very glad to see you, sir." Jean accepted the Colonel's thin hand and shook it lightly before he settled into a comfortable chair. "Well, I have more than one thing to talk to you about. I completed our mission at Davis Plantation, and I have brought you a written report describing my visit there and also a copy of the proposal, of course. It's pretty much as usual, but there are a few variations I'd like your opinion on. No hurry. The business manager and Mr. Davis were agreeable, and I feel assured they will accept our offer. Mr. Davis has wanted to sell for some time; he's getting up in age. Besides, he could no longer afford the taxes on the place. Things are not terrible there. Yet."

Colonel Bush took the papers and laid them on the desk beside him. "Is it all right if I look at all this later?"

"Of course. There is no terrible rush. I'll come back, or perhaps you'll feel like going to the office next week." He said it with a hopeful tone in his voice.

But the Colonel frowned and looked down at his hands. "I fear you must not count on that, Jean. I am showing no improvement." He sighed. "But we shall see. You really don't need me, Jean. Thank God you are fully able to carry on . . ."

"Oh, Louis! Don't talk like that. You are looking stronger today . . ."

He raised his hand to brush Jean's words away. "Now, Jean, we have always been honest with each other. I look more like a corpse every day." He waved his hand again. "But what other matters did you want to talk to me about? More decisions with our clientele?"

Jean withdrew Charles Berard's letter from the inside pocket of his jacket. He felt some regret to be bothering a sick man with such a problem, but he knew that the Colonel would have some bits of advice and wise counsel. He handed the letter to his partner without comment.

Colonel Bush attached his pince-nez and read the challenge from Berard through before he commented. Finally, he removed the spectacles and dropped them into his breast pocket. He shook his head and rubbed his eyes, as if fatigue and circumstance were almost too much for him.

"I'm sorry, sir. I shouldn't have . . ."

"Oh, no, Jean. No, no. I'm glad you showed it to me. It's just that . . . how much more must you contend with? Why must this spoiled, witless boy pursue a nonexistent affront and make trouble in your life? Have you drafted a reply? Have you made a decision?"

Jean took the draft of his letter to Berard from his pocket. "Yes, I have," he said before handing the letter to Bush. "I can assure you I have no wish to kill Berard. Indeed, I have not fired a pistol since the war. I don't even own a gun. But I don't want him to kill me, either." He handed the letter to Bush.

"I should say not—a man with a wife and ten children can hardly take his safety lightly." Bush returned the spectacles to his nose. "From that point of view, the whole thing is patently absurd. You can't go out somewhere and get yourself killed or maimed; what on earth would Stephanie and all those children do without you?"

"It's a matter of honor, Colonel."

"Honor! Jean, what could be honorable about deserting your wife and children? I'm sorry, but I can't remain silent about this. I would like to see you write to Berard and remind him that both of you have responsibilities, that these are modern times, and that dueling is against the law."

"Well, sir, I appreciate your frank opinion. But, please, don't let me make you ill with this rubbish."

"That is exactly what it is."

Bolling knocked discreetly before more could be said, and opened the door to announce luncheon. "I brought plates on the teacart, Mister Louis, like Madam Bush ax."

"All right, Bolling. Just roll it right up to the chaise, and pull a side chair up for Mr. Levert."

As Bolling followed orders, the Colonel sat up straight on the side of the chaise, and Jean sat down in an armless wicker chair. The teacart was set with fine bone china on a white linen cloth and centered with a small bouquet of roses. The men pulled napkins across their laps.

Jean tasted fresh fruit salad, apples, pears, pineapple, and grapes. "Hmmm," he murmured, *Délicieux.*"

"Yes," said the Colonel. "Would you like some crackers?"

"Thank you."

Presently Bolling removed the salad plates and brought soup bowls of cream crab chowder. "Such fine lump crab!" said Jean.

"Yes," said Bush. "Bolling cadged this recipe from Henri, the chef at the St. Charles Hotel. Celeste and I like it very much."

As the men ate, they commented only on the food, which Jean believed to be as good Creole cuisine as one could get in New Orleans. After clearing the table again, Bolling brought a tray bearing a small silver coffee pot and two demitasses.

"I believe you like sugar, Mr. Levert."

"Please, Bolling."

After Bolling had removed the last cup and saucer and had left the men in private, Colonel Bush looked at Jean. His gaze signaled to Jean that something might be wrong. Anticipating further lecture on the madness of dueling, Jean remained silent. He stared through the open casements onto the walled garden at a pair of mockingbirds fluttering in a shallow stone birdbath, spattering drops of water in all directions. When the Colonel spoke, the birds flew up in a frenzy of wet plumage and disappeared into the dark foliage of a magnolia tree; as if the sound of his voice bode danger to them.

"Jean."

Jean turned his gaze from the small nature display to his partner's face. He was startled at Bush's painful expression. "What is it, Colonel?"

"I am dying, Jean."

Jean stood up abruptly. "Dying? What do you mean, sir?"

"Sit down, Jean." Colonel Bush looked very tired. "I should have talked to you sooner—especially after being out of the office so often during the last year or so. I—I just haven't known how to talk about it. I have until recently had some hope of regaining my health, enough to continue our partnership."

"I am shocked beyond—beyond all words, I . . ."

"I'm sure you are. Celeste and I are both very sad, for it means the end of a very happy marriage. My daughters and sons seem broken-hearted. For you and me it means the end of a very amicable business association. It is a bad time for us all, eh?"

"Yes. Yes."

Many questions came to Jean's mind, but they were all questions that seemed inappropriate to bring up at this time. Always ready to look out for himself, he was wondering if Bush would sell out to him. *Bush's son Reuben had wanted to rejoin the firm; what of that? How long had doctors projected Bush's life to last?* Jean was genuinely grieved over Bush's announcement, but business was always uppermost in his mind; he could not suppress it. Be that as it may, he said nothing of it. He continued to express his concern to Bush; he assured him that Stephanie would be equally sad to hear this very bad news.

"Colonel Bush, sir, I don't want to appear impertinent, but can you tell me what malady is causing you this terrible, this frightful prognosis?"

"Bright's Disease. It's a kidney disease. The kidneys just refuse to do their job, and their perfect function is absolutely necessary for life. Jean, I can tell you that I have had the best of care. Actually, it was diagnosed in France when we were there, and I have seen some of the best kidney specialists in Europe and in this country. I'm afraid we have exhausted further treatment. Some day, scientists and physicians will no doubt solve the mysteries of kidney malfunction. But, unfortunately, not in time to save me."

"I fear that I have worn you out, Colonel. I will leave now and let you rest. I pray that I have not unnerved you with my problems. If I had known . . . I want to stay in as close touch as possible without imposing on your comfort. I hope Mrs. Bush will call on me for whatever assistance I can give. Please do not bother your mind with this silly Berard. I will settle that. Please give Mrs. Bush my regards."

"Yes, I will; she is having lunch at her club over on the Avenue. Since you were coming, she felt that she could leave me a little while. She has great admiration for you and Stephanie. Try not to worry, Jean. We will talk more soon about my retirement. I am eager to leave you in the best possible circumstances to continue the operation of Bush & Levert." Suddenly, his voice broke, and he shook his head and waved Jean out of the sunroom. Bolling was quickly present to show Jean out.

As he walked slowly down Coliseum Street toward home, he thought, with a heavy heart, of losing Louis Bush. He deeply admired his partner, whom he found to be intelligent, honorable, and an altogether sympathetic friend. Time and again, he could recall a ready kindness and support from the Colonel through all the stressful times Jean had encountered in his work and personal life since they had become partners. At this moment, Jean, the cool business operator, felt a need for a warm comforter. He thought of going to the Pickwick Club where he might see a friend who could lift his spirits. But that had little appeal at this time. He stepped up his pace and hurried on toward home.

He thought this was one of those times when the Third Street house and Stephanie answered his gloom. He could never tell her how much he needed her, yet more and more he depended upon her, and she seemed to know, to be ever ready with her love and support. He could admit to himself that he had never yearned for the presence of his children. But he could also admit that babies, who seemed to arrive at the most frequent intervals possible, were part of the warmth of his home. He had, in fact, lately become attentive to his eldest son, Albert, who was approaching eighteen. Albert, who came to New Orleans as a babe in arms under the devoted care of Stephanie and Sally, Sally who had been "on loan" from Eulalie at Golden Ridge. The boy, in Jean's mind, was tied to the past in Iberville Parish. He was, after all, the grandson of Auguste Levert, Jean's idol among sugar planters, and he was interested in sugarcane farming. From the scant time that he had given to listening to Albert, Jean had learned that. Based on this skimpy knowledge, Jean's plan for the boy after college was for him to become the eventual manager of Lizima, which Jean was now thinking of privately as St. John Plantation.

All these thoughts, mixed with the grievous news of Colonel Bush, were stirring in his mind as he lifted the heavy latch on the iron gate at home.

Chapter 50

AT DAWN JEAN climbed atop the Mississippi River levee at the end of Napoleon Avenue, not far from his old office on Magazine Street, within view of some magnificent plantation homes on the banks of the churning, brown Mississippi. The twenty-foot-high levee served as the only buttress against attack from floods. Jean had accepted Charles Berard's challenge.

Attendants of both camps talked quietly waiting for Berard to arrive. Jean talked to his close friend, Colonel William Behan, who stood with Jean's attendant, Gilbert Radolin. Behan had brought along a physician. *I've never before participated in a duel, hell, I've never even held a dueling pistol.*

"Will you please give your version of the cause of this problem between the two men?" Radolin asked.

Rupert Kane, Berard's attendant, retorted, "It does not matter, sir. We are here to fight."

"Well, now. But brave men don't fight like children for nothing. We wish to know what we are going to fight about," declared Radolin, his tone growing contemptuous. "If we are wrong, we may apologize." Irritated, he added: "What we are proposing to do, you know, is against the law."

Kane answered sarcastically, "You know as well as I, sir, that the *code duello* is widely practiced despite Louisiana law." He turned from Radolin and walked a few feet away without saying more.

Jean Baptiste knew that in spite of their continued efforts, the attendants could not settle his dilemma. He could not avoid the fight unless he wanted to seem cowardly. Of course, saving his honor and face, he might lose his life. That's exactly what made the *code duello* so idiotic to him. Jean mumbled to himself: "Mr. Berard saw so much dying in the War Between the States that I didn't think he would regard death so lightly this morning."

"Wait!" yelled Rupert Kane. "We see Mr. Berard!" Kane hurried to assist Berard up the steep levee. A narrow worn path covering about sixty yards suggested that there may have been other duels fought there. Still, Jean thought it a bit strange that Berard had selected a levee on the river as the place for the duel and not the more famous dueling oak at City Park.

"You could be killed, Jean," said Colonel Behan.

"Mr. Levert has no business fighting duels," insisted Radolin, after he was rejoined by Kane. "This Berard fellow is experienced." Then he added: "I have heard Mr. Berard referred to as a wastrel, famous for his supper parties, even more famous for his losses at the gaming table." Jean had learned that Berard kept himself in shape for duels by making regular visits to Lafayette's pistol ranges.

Off went the two attendants to their places on the levee. Shortly, Jean and Berard were beside them.

Radolin, trying every means to get Berard to change his mind, said, "Apparently there is no possible way of arranging this matter in a civilized manner. Suppose both parties approach and shake hands without a word. Just the same, will you talk to Mr. Berard and tell him our proposition of settling the argument in some other way. I would appreciate it."

More animated discussion and gesticulation followed between Radolin and Kane, but both men refused to give in. Jean wondered if reconciliation was even within reach. They returned to their principals, remaining by their sides for about ten minutes, before announcing, "Jean Levert says Charles Berard ought to apologize, then shake hands."

During the exchange between Radolin and Kane, parts of the letter Jean had received from Berard three weeks earlier challenging him to a duel kept flashing in his mind. He often thought of the proud General DeClouet, his wrinkled face that day his attorney began reading the notice of foreclosure, followed by the voluntary transfer of title. Jean had not lost his respect for the venerable gentleman planter, politician, diplomat, Civil War hero.

"Then, I guess it means a fight," Radolin said finally. "So, go and load your weapon. We will do likewise . . . twelve paces, single ball, fire when the signal is sounded."

The line of fire was a ten-foot wide, flat stretch of ground atop the levee. Nearby stood Colonel Behan, Jean's physician, Berard's friend who was not introduced, and the attendants; Jean knew that duels were kept as secret as possible. Berard, contrary to advice and the rules laid down, wore white trousers and an alpaca coat, making him a dangerously conspicuous target. Jean wore black evening dress, with white gloves, white ruffled shirt, and black tie. The attendants, also in elegant evening dress, loaded the pistols with care, and the command was finally given: "Gentlemen, are you ready?"

Jean bowed and Berard nodded. They stood back-to-back before pacing off from each other. Jean, who was facing upriver, as a few steamers and multimasted sailing vessels slid past in the fog, answered firmly, "Ready!" He kept his eyes looking steadily down the barrel of his cocked pistol. Berard, affecting a nonchalant pose, threw his head to one side, his pistol dangling at his side, and replied in a lazy tone: "Ready."

Then the attendants yelled: "Fire!" Jean whirled around and raised his weapon parallel to the ground and discovered that his adversary was still facing in the opposite direction. Berard, his right arm held above his head, pistol cocked, remained perfectly still. In a few seconds, the initiator, the experienced duelist from Lafayette, deliberately lowered his arm to his side. Jean recocked his weapon with his right thumb—to be prepared in case Berard changed his mind and whirled around to fire at him. But Berard's pistol barrel hung a few feet above his shiny black riding boots.

"Foul, foul!" shouted Radolin, realizing what had happened. The shot that Jean knew probably would have killed or wounded him was never fired. Berard kept his pistol at his side. According to agreement between Radolin and Kane, if either party was badly wounded, or confusion followed, or if it appeared either man called off the duel, one of the attendants would cry, "Foul, foul!"

Berard, now sobbing silently, standing in the same spot he had been when the order to fire was given, bowed his head. "What's wrong with me? What's happened to me?" he said aloud. "True courage has nothing to do with fighting. True courage is associated with a perception of right and wrong; it will exert itself only in a good cause. What almost happened today—wounding even killing an innocent man . . . the foreclosure wasn't Mr. Levert's misdeed; it was plain business. I realize now that this duel was a very bad idea. I have lately heard nothing but good things about Bush & Levert. After all, it was the town fathers in St. Martinville who recommended the brokerage firm to the General."

Surprised that Berard didn't turn to fire, Jean slowly lowered his pistol, still cocked, to his side. *Why did he not see this fight through to the end? Good God, I could have been killed!*

Berard, Rupert Kane, and Berard's friend declared themselves satisfied, and what had begun as a fight to the death ended in minutes. Charles nodded and gave Jean a half-gesture of apology. Standing on top of the levee, Jean watched the towering Creole make his departure down the grassy embankment.

I hope Colonel Bush never hears of the episode.

CHAPTER 51

JEAN AND ALBERT traveled to St. John on the Southern Pacific train on a chilly December morning. It was Albert's first visit to the plantation where he wanted to make a career as a sugarcane planter—if he could meet his father's exacting expectations. Jean was watching his son closely from the moment they turned into the long, oak-lined drive, where Albert got his first view of the house.

Albert's eyes were wide. The nineteen-year-old city-bred, college-educated young man was not unfamiliar with large, fine homes; there were many in his own neighborhood in the Garden District, and they were still abuilding there. But his son was not quite prepared for the magnificence of this place, not just the size of the house, but the simple classical perfection of the architecture in its expansive setting. Albert lifted his rangy body up in the buggy to get a better view; his mouth was open as they rode down the avenue of spreading oaks and pines toward the house. Usually loquacious, he seemed at a loss for words; he was clearly impressed. Jean smiled and paid the driver, who clicked at his horse and drove away, his buggy wheels crunching on the fine gravel.

"Papa, I had no idea! I mean your descriptions were fine, but frankly I was not prepared for this . . . this beautiful place. Just look at it! You want me to manage all this? Do you think I can handle all this?"

"I'm counting on it," Jean said seriously, then added in a lighter tone, "but not the first day. Or the first week or the first month or even the first year. I have good experienced hands here who will teach you, and I have had a competent overseer looking after things until you and I made up our minds. And son, remember I was reared on Golden Ridge, and I'll have a hand in everything. Do I think you can do it? I certainly hope so. Remember, Albert, you are the grandson of Auguste Levert, sugar planter *sans pariel*. Your Uncle Augie has made great successes at St. Delphine and St. Mary's, not to mention your Uncle Amèdèe at Willow Glen and Golden Ridge. You are part of a proud tradition."

He laid his hand on his son's shoulder, which was slightly higher than his own now. He cleared his throat. Not given to physical expressions of affection or even fatherly intimacy with his children, Jean gave Albert a pat. Albert responded self-consciously, giving his father a shy smile.

"Oh, good morning, Mr. Boudreau." Jean turned to shake hands with the approaching thick-bodied man with shaggy gray hair and piercing eyes. He was dressed for the fields. "Let me introduce my son, Albert. Albert, this is Ramon Boudreau. He has been keeping an eye on everything here at St. John while we prepared to get over here."

"How do you do, sir." Albert shook the man's hand. "St. John, father?" He shook hands politely with Ramon Boudreau, but his attention was divided—the house still had his eye, he was interested in meeting Mr. Boudreau, and he had suddenly heard for the first time the plantation called St. John.

"Well!" said Jean enthusiastically. "Let's begin our tour of the manor house and the sugarhouse, Mr. Boudreau. Come, Albert. You have much to see. First, the sugarhouse, then we'll see the Big House, your new home. You might spend the rest of your life here, son."

The men walked rapidly round the back of the mansion and a hundred yards farther to the sugarhouse, which was located about halfway between the Big House and Bayou Teche. The sugarhouse stood between the Teche and surrounding cane fields to divide as evenly as possible the distance between cane hauled in mule-drawn carts from the fields and the packaged product loaded aboard railcars for shipment to market. *ST. JOHN* was painted vertically in black letters on the tall red brick chimney. A black pitched roof covered the structure 500 feet long, 200 feet wide, and 70 feet high from dirt floor to ceiling. While his father was describing the sugarhouse, Albert turned in all directions, trying to take in the immensity of the structure.

"It's huge, Papa, but it seems so, so dead. There's nothing going on in here."

Jean laughed. "Just wait, Albert. The rush is just over here. At the height of the grinding season, this place is a beehive of activity."

Boudreau added, "Sugarhouse de vitality and heart of dis whole plantation system, yeah. Come here, young man."

Jean took Albert's elbow and nudged him toward the grinding machinery where the cane was ground into juice that was boiled to become syrup, then brown raw sugar; he began to describe the whole process to him: The product passed through different rooms, including a place for vacuum pans, presses or crushers, and the mill. The different places and machinery were all connected by gutters that carried cane juice from the mill into receivers that supplied the pans. Presses consisted of several iron rollers three feet in diameter and five feet long that sustained great pressure when cane passed between them. Each stalk came out of the press crushed into almost dry fragments, while the extracted cane juice flowed down into vacuum pans for boiling. There it was crystallized into granulated sugar . . . attached to the sugarhouse was a carrier, an eight-foot-wide band of chains and crossbars of wood running upon iron rollers. The carrier, which transported stalks from carts outside up into the sugarhouse, extended a hundred feet beyond its walls and was fed cane continuously by the workers.

Jean continued: "Albert, about mid-October, the presses begin to turn, extracting juice, filling the vacuum pans to the brim. It gets very stuffy in here, hot and very sweet-smelling. It goes on night and day for two or three months, sometimes longer, extracting and boiling, extracting and boiling. I used to move into the sugarhouse at Golden Ridge, and I stayed there throughout the season. You will very likely do the same here."

Listening to Jean, Boudreau added, "Yeah, yeah, Albert, crushin and boilin go on in all dem pans at one time til juices concentrate so dey gran'late when cool. Tons and tons a de cane and gallons and gallons of de syrup, yeah." He pointed to the bagasse burner in a corner. "That make more dan enough steam to run de mill. Bagasse is cane after it part with much a de juices as de mill can extract. You got to be here, Albert, when dis place really git busy to appreciate what goes on. Yeah, nuttin like it." He paused, obviously enjoying his role. "And when grindin over, you see dis place—everybody rockin, shoutin. Wild, yeah. You see soon enough, yeah, when you go through your first grindin, you see."

"I can't wait to be part of all this, to live it for myself. Mr. Boudreau, you must surely miss the excitement. I don't see how you could give it all up." Boudreau laughed and lifted his worn broad-brimmed hat to father and son, and in his thick Cajun speech excused himself, but he assured the Leverts that he was available to assist them all day.

Jean and Albert went into the Big House after Boudreau left them. Again, Jean felt pride as he watched Albert look over the broad well appointed center hall. The youth walked down the middle of the room looking right and left. When he came to the staircase, which had charmed Jean from the first, he swung abruptly to the right on the polished newel post, and looked back at his father. "Papa, it is beautiful." Then he spun back around and continued through the hall to the rear gallery. He returned and said, "It's almost as long and broad as the front gallery. My goodness! And the view of the gardens, the bayou, the fields, even the mill! I don't know what to say . . . ."

They toured the rest of the house with Albert now at a loss for words. On the upstairs back gallery, a duplicate of the one below, the freshly painted name *ST. JOHN* on the sugarhouse chimney was in prominent view.

"Papa," said Albert, "I've wanted to ask you since we first got here this morning about the name. I didn't know you had changed the name. I certainly don't blame you for getting rid of Lizima; it was ugly to me. But how did you choose St. John? Is it the Americanized version of Jean?"

"Certainly not! I haven't canonized myself!" But Jean did not seem seriously offended. "You are right about Lizima. I didn't care for that; it has significance to the DeClouets, but not for me, for us. No, I thought about naming it *Twelve Oaks* for the trees General DeClouet planted along the drive long ago."

"Perhaps it is the name of the church cemetery where your parents are buried that inspired you, St. John the Baptist at Brusly Landing."

But Jean, his eyes growing moist, made no reply.

They walked together into the parlor, where Albert surveyed the big room, examining the views from each tall window. He walked to a petit point bell pull that hung near the mantel and gave its silken tassel a curious pull. Jean was amused. They had such a bell pull in the parlor at Third Street. He thought Albert found every appointment new and special at St. John.

But immediately a servant entered the room with a silver tray bearing coffee. Albert looked at his father in surprise. "Did I do that?"

"Of course, I kept some of the servants who worked for the General. You may want to keep some or all of them once you take up residence. This is Dottee."

Dottee gave Albert a dazzling smile and asked in her barely understandable Cajun dialect, "You won cream and sugar, *M'sieu Albert?*" She pronounced it Ole Bear.

"Neither, thank you," Albert said hoarsely, carefully taking a cup and saucer, dumfounded by the girl's beauty. While she babbled away with his father, Albert looked at her closely. Her skin was light-light, and she had an incredible dimple in her chin, with her nose and lips pert and exquisitely formed. Her figure was lithe and slender with a tiny waist and full breasts, all fitted neatly in her rose cotton frock, its edge swinging prettily about her ankles. Jean was watching Albert even as Dottee talked to him. He smiled; this was a servant that his son would keep. *Oh, to be young again.*

Jean smiled contentedly. Letting Albert leave Mount St. Mary's College before graduation had not been a mistake. Albert's response to everything at St. John was just what he hoped for; his son was fascinated by everything he was shown today. He thought somewhat wistfully: *What a joy and pleasure to be so young, just beginning life. My son is about to embark on a life that in my heart I feel is right for him. And right for St. John and for me. But I shall be a landlord in absentia.*

Jean and Albert remained at St. John for two days. They parted with Albert telling his father that he was eager to begin his internship under the guidance of Jean, Mr. Boudreau, and the experienced sugar workers on the plantation.

*   *   *

Since he felt his son should know, Jean told Albert on the train ride back to New Orleans why he had decided to become an absentee landlord, that it was not unusual for wealthy plantation owners.

"Cane cultivation spread very fast across southern Louisiana in the early 1800s, then it appeared on the banks of Bayou Lafourche near Thibodaux and Bayou Terrebonne around Houma, and before long here in Bayou Teche country." Jean told his son that the sugar region, before the war, stretched south all the way from the Red River near Alexandria, including Lafayette and the Mississippi River and extending almost to the Gulf of Mexico, and that the Teche area was thought of as a new frontier by many sugar men, including himself. By the Nineties, he explained that many small farms in the Teche district were combined into great plantations, and some of the wealthy owners who acquired those already had established names and standings in their own communities, and they didn't want to leave all that. "So they decided to operate their great holdings in absentia, as I plan to do with St. John."

CHAPTER 52

JEAN INSTRUCTED ALBERT to get his possessions together so they could return to St. John in two weeks. Meantime, Jean planned to check into his office and at the sugar exchange, then leave for St. Louis and Memphis on business. But he discovered upon arriving at the exchange that he was again the subject of unfair gossip in New Orleans sugar circles, in fact, untrue criticisms of his methods of doing business. Most discouraging to him, he did not speak to anyone about it or try to investigate the source.

Jean gave his secretary a note to Colonel Bush and asked her to send it by messenger to the Coliseum Street address. Jean needed his counsel again, though he did not want to cause the Colonel harmful distress. The response came back directly: "Come tomorrow morning at eleven." So, on Saturday morning Jean rang the doorbell at the Bush home.

Mrs. Bush admitted Jean and greeted him warmly. She smiled. "I miss you and Stephanie, and how are all the little Leverts?"

"Everyone is fine, thank you." Jean bowed and laid his bowler on a marble-top chest in the foyer. "Believe me, I do not intend to wear the Colonel out with my business. I shall speak to him briefly and be on my way."

He followed Celeste Bush down a long hallway toward the sunroom, listening to the pendulum blade of the grandfather clock cutting through time with soft metallic ticking. Mrs. Bush walked ahead to her husband's chair and carefully added another pillow behind his neck. Then she smiled and left them.

"Come in, come in, Jean," said Colonel Bush, extending his hand. "I'm glad to see you this morning. My wife will send us in some coffee. Would you like something to eat?"

"No, thank you, Colonel," replied Jean. "I've had my breakfast. I eat early, you know. I've also had my walk along St. Charles. The weather's nice. Now, Colonel, I won't stay long, don't wish to tire you. I'll get right to the point." He sat down facing him. "I have been hearing criticisms about my business methods again, since I returned from St. John. I'm worried—I am afraid that if they, or whoever is doing it, do not stop, it could do damage to the firm."

The Colonel repositioned himself in his chair, trying to ease the pain in his back and midsection. Getting more comfortable, he said, "Remember, Jean, you have never been accused of oppressing your rivals, hurting their business by securing unfair rates of interest, or going into a frenzy in your office to get them to honor their obligations. You've been irresponsibly accused in some newspaper editorials and nagged by sugar exchange gossipers, but never in a court of law. And I dare say you never will be. In my opinion you have every reason to maintain your confidence."

As he continued, the expression on Jean's sunburned face relaxed. The Colonel's voice was surprisingly cheery, and it lifted Jean's spirits.

"I've heard you accused of building up your holdings by pulling down those of others—piling your holdings on their ruined lands, cane fields, plantations, that sort of thing." He reached for a glass of water. "But you and I both know that your dealings are the exact opposite; these stories are plainly lies circulated by the unscrupulous. It's a shame that you must be distressed by gossip. Wonder if that scoundrel Berard has something to do with it?" He shook his head in frustration.

Jean remained silent. He was sad to witness his friend's obvious pain—this remarkable man who had risen to the rank of colonel in the Civil War, who had been a state representative, practiced law, and then made a success as a commission merchant. Some of

Colonel Bush's ancestors, like Jean's, were of French descent and had gone into cane farming.

Jean was about to speak when Colonel Bush continued. "Once a man enters the brokerage business, he usually is pursued, spied upon, and eventually his business, if he's not careful, is overtaken for a fraction of its true value—that's the impression left in the minds of some where it concerns you, I am afraid, but it's not the whole truth. We both know it's not."

"I know, I know, sir. I tell myself that few people really understand the nature of our business. Am I right? The public doesn't understand that our dealings require shrewd practices—quite tough at times. Our competitors and clients often don't understand all this. When we foreclose on a plantation, some people invariably assume that we have dealt dirty or misrepresented our position as brokers."

Jean paused to inhale the fragrance of late roses and asters drifting through an open window. The lawn was bordered with lush mounds of dark green violet plants and beds of colorful lilies, all accented with the aromatic scent of tall sweet olive bushes and other sweet-smelling shrubs.

"I could never have achieved true success by the means my detractors credit me with—by squashing people. Capable men who do things in a big way cannot be squashed. Oh, we may suffer a setback or two—who doesn't?—but it would be only a short time before we'd be back on top." Jean's tone became more defensive. "I've made every effort to become friends with big men, to cultivate them, no more for the firm's benefit than for the good of the sugar industry. I've tried to join up with big successful men; of course I have."

As he finished, Jean watched the Colonel swallow two teaspoonful of Stomach Bitters, then try to wash away the obvious bad taste with another glass of water. He knew it was the only medicine he had found to treat his pain, probably laudanum.

"Of course you're right," the Colonel said, laying down his spoon.

Jean appreciated his partner's assurances and advice. He never wearied of the Colonel's judgments. He also appreciated his obvious faith. But as noontime approached, he feared the Colonel might be tiring from this conversation. Jean rose.

"Really, Colonel, I feel that I am causing you too much exertion . . ."

"No, Jean, no. Sit down." His voice was kind, but he sounded firm. Jean looked at him. "Sit back down, Jean. There is something I want to talk to you about. I think it is very important. If you do not agree with me, now, please give my words some serious consideration before you reject them altogether."

"Of course, Colonel, I . . ." He sat down and rested his hands on the arms of the chair.

"Jean, I want to pass on some advice to you. You be the judge of its wisdom." The Colonel took another sip of water. "We have been wonderfully successful in our partnership. As we begin the Nineties, we find ourselves rich men. Both of us! We own more than 30,000 acres of rich productive land in five Louisiana parishes—most of it under cultivation, some in wilderness. Think of our real estate holdings in the City—warehouses, duplexes, apartments. My advice to you is to take it easier, now, in your business pursuits." He told Jean he had more money than he'll ever need, and it will just keep growing. He reminded him of his interest in St. Delphine, St. Mary's, Golden Ridge, and Willow Glen plantations with his brothers and now he had St. John, Davis Plantation, Catahoula. "Don't forget, son, the exchange was reorganized last year as the Louisiana Sugar and Rice Exchange, and you and I will become much richer. Our clientele will only increase now that we'll be handling rice crops as well as sugar crops at the exchange. Jean, you are a very rich man. It's just time for you to begin giving something back."

Jean listened intently. He had thought of these things, but hearing the Colonel's words gave a new concrete meaning to his own passing considerations. The Colonel added before he could respond: "Find a way to give something back to the towns and parishes in which we've done good business, perhaps donating land for schools or churches. It's important to repay society. Promise me you'll give this matter some careful thought."

Jean smiled warmly into the Colonel's eyes as he rose to shake the older man's hand. "I shall indeed, sir. You can count on it."

Now, when Jean left Colonel Bush, he always had the uneasy feeling that he might not see his old friend again. The feeling continued to dog him as he walked home to Third Street, pondering Bush's advice.

Two days later he departed New Orleans by train to travel far up the Mississippi Valley. He stopped to do important business in several cities, including Memphis and St. Louis. He had not been on the Illinois Central train since the war, when he had deserted his cavalry unit, and he was anxious to see the new passenger terminal at the corner of Howard Avenue and Rampart Street. Throughout the important tour, two concerns remained in the back of his mind: The Colonel's condition and the return to St. John with Albert.

*　　*　　*

When the travelers returned to St. Martinville, after Jean's protracted business trip, Albert was eager and ready to establish permanent residence at St. John. Freddy and Lawrence pulled Albert's three bulging pieces of luggage from under the seat of the rented buggy and carried them to the gallery of the Big House. Two young Negro boys ran out and carried the bags into the house, whereupon Freddy and Lawrence raced back to the buggy, their eyes round with awe. They were clearly excited, Jean saw. "Marvelous structure," shouted Albert, as he stepped down with his father. "Just like I remember. Nothing's changed. The house is just as it was. The *garconnières* still stand guard."

"What the hell did you expect to find, Albert, no house? Fields choked with weeds? A shell of a burned-out house?" When Jean saw the stunned reaction in Albert, he realized how cruel his sarcasm had been. Albert made no response, but walked on to the house in silence. Jean knew that the easy-going, happy Albert had no way of understanding such a sudden outburst of bad humor. Jean himself did not fully understand, but he wondered if he was jealous of his son, so young, so excited, so fortunate. Jean had these thoughts for only seconds, and did not think of them again.

Inside he found the boys rushing about, shouting to each other about every discovery in the big rooms on the first floor. He walked in and sat in a comfortable chair in the parlor to rest his back and legs, stiff from the long buggy ride from St. Martinville. He heard Albert calling to his brothers.

"Lawrence, Freddy, have you discovered the stairway? Look! It's tucked in here on the right side of the hall. Come on! I want you to go upstairs. You won't believe the views we have from the galleries!"

Jean heard young feet running up the steps. He sighed and closed his eyes as he rested his head on the high back of the chair. "*Dieu tout-puissant!* God-almighty! It makes me feel good everytime I come here." He sat there relaxing and quiet until the boys came back down the stairs, still talking animatedly among themselves.

"Papa, sir, I would like to live here, too. I could have a horse to ride and swim in the bayou. Wouldn't you like to live here, Freddy?" Lawrence gripped the arm of his father's chair. "Oh, no, Lawrence," Jean said sternly, "Albert is now a man. He is here to work. Work hard. He wouldn't have time to look after a little boy. But you can come back to visit in the summertime."

"I think that would be splendid," said Albert.

Jean thought Albert sounded oddly timid. He cleared his throat. "Let me tell you boys about the previous owner of this grand house." Jean told them that General DeClouet was a great hero in the war; that he came home determined to devote all his energies to regaining his fortunes shattered by war; that the General and his family established this plantation. The original house had burned to the ground in the 1830s, Jean said, and the General had it rebuilt in the 1840s to look the way it does now. "I've been told that before he left here for the last time, he stopped and pressed his lips to the bole of each of the twelve oaks he had planted along the front driveway. It was his last farewell."

"Why did he leave, Papa?" asked Freddy.

Jean pressed the fingers of both his hands together and looked at the fireplace, musing a moment. "Well, the General was not a smart businessman, wise and fine as he was in other ways. To try to get the plantation producing again he borrowed heavy amounts of money to rebuild. But no matter what he tried or did, his plight was never relieved. It went on for years. He lost this plantation because he could not meet his debts. To our firm."

Freddy and Albert looked at each other, but remained silent. Then Lawrence piped up childishly insisting, "I want to live here."

Jean showed no sign of hearing his son. He continued the story: "Did you know that the General was the Whig Party's candidate for governor of Louisiana in 1849? He lost by a thousand votes, I believe. He and Colonel Bush served at the secession convention and both signed the Ordinance of Secession for Louisiana to leave the Union, though both gentlemen vigorously opposed it."

"Then why did they sign it, sir?" asked Freddy.

"There was no other way, Freddy," said Jean, rising and walking to the carved mantel over the fireplace. "There was no other way out." He shook his head. "The war was a subject that would always be a sad one."

Suddenly, and in a more cheerful tone, Jean said, "How would you all like to spend Christmas here? *Mère*, all of us. Even Uncle Auguste and Uncle Amèdèe and their families. We could have one giant Christmas house party. Lawrence, you could hang your stocking on this mantelpiece."

Lawrence clapped his hands, and Albert came alive. "What a great idea, Papa! What a wonderful, wonderful idea! I will be the host, won't I?"

"If you wish, Albert," said Jean, who was thinking of himself as the reigning Christmas host at the great Levert estate. He smiled good-naturedly and repeated, "If you wish."

*　　*　　*

Jean Baptiste, while on his extended business trip, had received distressing news from Colonel Bush. His partner's telegram had reached him during his overnight stay at the Palmer House in Chicago:

January 26, 1891

General DeClouet died at the family-owned St. Clair Plantation near Lafayette with his children at his bedside STOP services and burial in St. Martinville STOP

Although ailing himself, having retired from Bush & Levert and sold his half of the business to Jean, Colonel Bush had represented the firm at the services at St. Martin de Tours church, and conveyed to the DeClouet family his and Jean's deepest sympathies. The General, who was seventy-eight, was buried in the church cemetery next to his wife, Marie Louise St. Clair, for whom the family's St. Clair plantation was named, and his father, Étienné Chevalier DeClouet.

Besides family, Jean had learned from the Colonel that hundreds of people from St. Martin and Vermilion parishes— local and state politicians, bankers, retired legislators with whom DeClouet served in the House of Representatives when Louisiana seceded from the Union, sugar farmers, even former slaves and free laborers who'd worked for him, including Dottee—had paid their respects to one of the state's war heroes and finest gentlemen.

CHAPTER 53

AFTER SETTLING ALBERT in at St. John Plantation, as grinding was coming to full operation, Jean Baptiste returned to New Orleans with Freddy and Lawrence. His sons didn't want to leave, but he reminded them, "We must get home. We do not have long to get everything ready to come back for Christmas. *Mère* is already shopping for gifts for everyone, and she and I must get everything organized. This will be a great undertaking." Jean, with a party of fourteen, including Vic and Daniels, was used to large undertakings. But he thought this effort exceeded by far anything he and Stephanie had ever attempted; they must include Amèdeè and Augie and their families, accounting for as many as fifteen guests.

He had talked to Dottee, and she seemed unfazed by the prospects of such a house party. "Brought all dem fokes on in here, *M'sieu*," she told Jean, "an we give dem de bes party dey eber been to, yeah!"

Knowing Albert was full of plans for making everything festive, Jean left St. John confident that such a crowd could be managed.

* * *

By the time Jean arrived at the Third Street house, Stephanie had filled a corner of the parlor with gifts wrapped in bright red paper. Clothing for a four-day stay had to be sorted for packing. Daniels had shopped for French champagne and Spanish sherry at the vintner Pedro Cordoba's on Baronne Street; he collected special foods—salt mackerel, anchovies, cheeses, olives, chocolates, and other treats—at Solari's on Royal Street to add to the delicious but less exotic fare to be found in the kitchen at St. John. To make things comfortable, even grand, extra linens, china, silver, and glassware had to be transported on the train with the family. Even Stephanie Marie's harp. Jean protested this, but he relented and had the harp packed in its wooden crate and shipped.

Jean imagined his brothers and their families' impression of his beautiful sixteen-year-old daughter, with her extraordinary talent, seated at the harp playing Christmas music. This would indeed be the *pièce de résistance*. Yes, by all means, he thought, bring up the crate and pack the harp. *I should have engaged an entire private car.*

Early on December 23, amid chatter and laughter, Daniels and the driver of the hired mule-drawn dray loaded boxes, bags, and crates. Then Jean and Stephanie took seats side by side in one of the two carriages parked in front of Third Street that Jean also had hired. They seemed to like each other's dress for the long trip: Stephanie in dark blue bombazine traveling dress with large matching hat, its turned-up brim filled with feathered birds and scrolled ribbons; Jean in dark brown alpaca coat, fawn trousers, and, of course, high stiff collar with cravat. Vic, in her Sunday clothes, sat with the younger children, and Daniels, his derby straight on his head and cigar between his teeth, rode backward beside the dray driver, his hand resting on Stephanie Marie's harp.

Thus, the pilgrimage proceeded to the Southern Pacific station at Esplanade and Elysian Fields avenues on the mild, clear day. Jean wondered, as they boarded the train, how often the porters and conductors hosted such a large family. When everyone was reasonably settled, the train's whistle signaled for departure and the party was on its way to St. John. During the afternoon family members brought out baskets filled with fried chicken, potatoes, cold tea, and cakes for a lunch. Vic added favorite tidbits for the children to eat. Then she took ample food to the colored car for her and Daniels.

By the time they reached St. Martinville, the food baskets were empty, pleats and creases wrinkled, and white collars and cuffs smudged, but the family was still happy and eager. Jean noticed that Stephanie appeared quite tired, though she did not complain. He watched the porter give her full assistance as she descended the train steps. Jean had arranged with the livery stable owner to have carriages and drayage ready to transport his family and possessions to the plantation. A large carriage with a middle box seat had been produced; it carried twelve passengers. The older children thought it was a lark to ride in the open wagon that carried the boxes and luggage. Down the narrow dusty road lined with colorless dry weeds of late autumn they bounced, the children and Vic and Daniels incongruously singing "Jingle Bells." Jean was pleased to see many dried cane stalks, fallen from overloaded carts, strewn along the roadside to St. John, for that meant the sugarhouse was grinding more cane than the production from its own fields. *We are making money!*

Jean knew through wires and letters from Boudreau that the plantation was busy with its own bumper crop of cane and also grinding cane for other plantations throughout St. Martin Parish. The ambitious owner of St. John could hardly have been more satisfied. He had been informed that Albert was absorbing the teachings of Boudreau and the hands. Boudreau told him Albert had moved into the sugarhouse; he rose before daylight and worked until darkness ended the day's labor; he could not seem to get enough of the entire operation, and he showed judgment and initiative beyond his years and experience.

As they drove down the oval drive to the gallery steps of the Big House, Jean and his family exclaimed aloud, not just at the handsome house and grounds; the doors and windows of the house and *garconnières* were lavishly decorated with wreaths of fresh red-berried holly and draped with dense green garlands of mistletoe. Even the horsehead on the hitching post had a small wreath of holly laid over the iron curls in its mane.

"Oh," said Stephanie, "How beautiful, Jean! How perfectly beautiful! Do you suppose Albert did all this?"

"I wouldn't be surprised, *chèrie*." He smiled.

Albert came running out the front door to greet them,

whereupon a new burst of shouts erupted from the children. Several workers came out and began carrying the boxes, crates, and luggage into the house. Albert hugged and kissed his mother; he shook hands with his father and with Freddy and Jean, Jr. He greeted Vic and Daniels with warmth. He grinned at Vic, "Did you bring your black silk dress?"

"Oh, yes, Mister Albert!" she said. "And Daniels' white serving coat."

"Great!" said Albert. "We'll have some elegance out here at St. John, won't we, Papa?"

"You should have fifteen more guests," said Jean. "Can you sleep everyone?" He stepped onto the gallery.

"I have had wonderful good fortune. In the *garconnière* we don't use I found twenty folding cots and wool blankets marked *CSA!* We got them all out and unwrapped them; they've been sunning and most of them seem to be in good shape." Albert looked at Freddy and Jean, Jr. "All the boys who are big enough can sleep on them in the *garconnières*. This means all the ladies and girls can be very comfortable in the Big House. What's this! Sister's harp! My goodness! This is wonderful. I have the perfect chair for her, a little gilt one I found in the closet under the attic stairs. It yielded quite a few nice things. Please! Do come in, *Mère, Père. Père Noel*, please!" He led the way in.

Stephanie exclaimed on the beauty of the long hall and the parlor and dining room. The interior was decorated with holly, magnolia, pine, and mistletoe. Red candles filled the sconces, candelabra, and chandeliers.

"Thanks for the big box of candles, *Mère*. They'll make a big difference at night."

"It will be beautiful, son."

The children scattered over the house and galleries while Albert led his parents to the first-floor bedroom at the back of the house, which Jean had claimed for his own use as soon as he became owner of St. John. "Bring their things in here, Justin. Hang things in the wardrobe." The doors stood open.

The soft resonant voice of a Negro called to Albert from the hall.

"Excuse me, please," said Albert.

"I would like to lie down, Jean," said Stephanie.

"Of course, my dear. I'll send one of the girls in to help you. Look, the steps are on this side of the bed. Just sit in this chair until Mathilde or Stephanie Marie comes in to help you." Jean thought Stephanie looked exhausted.

Jean took Vic and Daniels out to the kitchen, where he found Dottee taking a whole ham out of the baking chamber in the brick wall. She was having trouble lifting it. Daniels sprang forward to take it from her and put it on the cutting block in front of the oven. Jean pronounced introductions between Dottee and his New Orleans servants, who had always lived in the City. He observed the response in this dignified pair in their fifties as they acknowledged the light-skinned, flirtatious Dottee. They showed no flicker of reservation as they nodded politely and said, "How you?"

As for Dottee, she thanked Daniels primly and disarmed both of them with her warm welcome and talk of the nice cabin *M'sieu Albert* had arranged for them near the Big House.

"We want do anythin to help," said Vic.

"I can use some hep, yeah. I got dis kitchen awganized pretty good. We got tings cooled in de root cellar. Tings nice 'n cool down dare. We got turkeys, got dis big ham, got lotsa paddiges, all ready to fry for Christmas mornin breakfast. Serve em wid milk gravy, grits, eggs, biscuits, all dem good stuffs, yeah. And *M'sieu Albert*, he done put de wine down dare on de ice." Dottee switched her pretty hips as she was wont to do and said, "Scuse me, *M'sieu Jean*, I take dem to see where dey gonna stay at." She flashed him her seductive smile. *My God*, he thought wistfully.

"Of course, Dottee." Jean smiled and nodded, glad to be dismissed. He didn't know whether Vic and Daniels could understand her Cajun *patois*, but he thought they all work well together, that the older two would like Dottee—he was sure Daniels did. And he was certain of one thing: If Vic did not like working with Dottee for several days, no one would ever know it. "We

brought fresh cranberries from the French Market," Jean called
back, and entered the house.

In the living room, he sat in one of the four large chairs he
had had shipped from a New Orleans store. For a French design,
he thought it was very comfortable, and it was much nicer looking
here than it had been in the store; the rose velvet seemed softer.
The harp had been set up near the piano. The small gilt chair had
been supplied; it had a thin, soft cushion. Jean thought he had
never been in a more festive and tastefully appointed room. Albert
had thought of everything. It was amazing. A year ago, he barely
noticed this boy.

His fingers stroked the polished rosewood arms of the chair.
Suddenly, he thought of Eulalie. He wished for her. How delighted
she would be with this house, with him, with his family. He
could visualize her seated across from him, facing him from the
other side of the fireplace. He could see her, poised, lovely in one
of her beautiful dresses, wearing some of her fascinating jewelry,
her hair in a bun. The memory of her face was perfectly clear to
him. He also wished his father could see the plantation, the sugarhouse
at work, see Albert, who had set his star beside his *grand-père's*.
Were he here, Auguste would see all of his living sons gathered, all
successful planters. How pleased he would be. But Jean thought he
would be most rewarded by the turn his grandson Albert's life had
taken. There were long periods when Jean didn't think about his
father at all, but he always came back into his mind.

The house seemed quiet to be so full of children. They had
disappeared quickly after arriving. Oh, well, they would be all
right. How could they get lost on five acres of land around the
house? Jean closed his eyes for awhile and relaxed, his chin resting
on his tall stiff collar.

Childish shouts filled the house, rousing Jean from his nap.
All of the younger ones came in, excited. "Papa, Papa, we have cut
a Christmas tree! We all went down into the woods and Edmond
cut us a big fir tree. Look! Look!" Jean had never seen his children
so noisily animated.

Albert and the old Negro servant, Edmond (Edmawhn), dragged in a full green fir tree that must be ten feet high. They set it up in the space behind Stephanie Marie's harp. They put the trunk, which had been trimmed of lower limbs just so, into a nail keg and filled it with sand. They steadied the keg with bricks, and the tree stood within a foot or so of the twelve-foot ceiling. Another Negro brought in a tall stepladder and set it up close into the tree. He disappeared and came back with two buckets of water, which he set behind the tree.

"It's magnificent," conceded Jean. "What will you use for decorations?"

"Mother brought a box of things from home, and she bought tree candles at Solari's for us. Tonight after supper, we can decorate the tree and everything else we have. It is going to be a splendid Christmas tree." All the children cheered.

Jean assured Albert that he was impressed. He stood up and added that he wanted to "look in on *Mère*." Perhaps she would want to come in presently to see their tree. He walked a bit stiffly as he left the room. He believed that today had given him the most prolonged exposure to his children—all of them—that he had ever known. Awkwardly he rubbed the back of his neck and smiled to himself. He suspected they did not know that he had left them.

Supper was ham sandwiches on buttered homemade bread. Vic set out a bowl of large olives and a tray of assorted cheeses. The children ate as fast as they dared, then began decorating the tree.

"May we light the candles tomorrow night, Papa?" asked little Ella, six, leaning against her father's knee.

"We'll see," said Jean, standing. "But now we all need to get to bed. We have a big day tomorrow."

"Yes, children," said Stephanie, taking Jean's arm. "Let's get some sleep. When we wake up, Ella, it will be Christmas eve."

*   *   *

Of course, the children waked early on Christmas eve, eager to continue their adventures in the country. They ate big breakfasts of oranges, ham, sausage, eggs, grits, biscuits, fig preserves, muscadine jelly, and quince jelly. They drank mugs of fresh milk drawn by Edmond from the cows in the big barn. The adults ate, and they drank *café au lait* and black coffee. The children begged to leave their table immediately so they could rush outside to examine everything they were permitted to climb onto or burrow into. Jean left all safety measures to Albert and Daniels, who seemed happy to take the responsibility for maintaining the preservation of life.

After breakfast, Albert attached a strip of lath to the edge of the parlor mantel with small brads tapped into it; on these he hung an assortment of men's and women's stockings, ready for a visit from *Père Noèl*. Jean assumed that Albert had purchased fruit and candy to fill the stockings; it turned out he had. Now there seemed to be nothing left to do in preparation.

Soon after noon Augie and Aurelie arrived from St. Delphine with four of their eight children—Octave, Mark, Aurelie, and Julia. And soon after they were greeted by Jean and Stephanie, another carriage rushed up to the gallery. From it stepped Amèdèe, his wife Ernestine and five of their nine children—Amèdèe, Jr., Emily, Omer, Hilda, and Victoria.

"Such a gathering of Leverts!" said Jean, greeting each guest warmly. Stephanie smiled with genuine hospitality as she welcomed her in-laws and their children. She turned all comers over to Albert and his servant helpers, who directed them to their places in the house. Jean was pleased to see that his brothers and their wives seemed delighted to be there. They all appeared prosperous, well, happy. Augie and Amèdèe reported good crops, which was the best news Jean could hope to hear. Coats and bonnets were left in the bedrooms. Jean was especially fascinated as he watched the girl cousins and the boy cousins fall easily into chummy groups, talking and laughing. The newcomers piled more gifts around the Christmas tree, adding to the heap Jean and

Stephanie had brought from New Orleans. The keg, which was not pretty, had long disappeared behind bright-colored packages of many shapes and sizes.

Vic and Daniels passed silver trays through the afternoon laden with delicious treats from New Orleans' finest importers that elicited many exclamations from the country gentry. The short, round Vic, who reminded Jean of Bébé, wore her black silk dress and white apron. Daniels wore his usual dark trousers, white coat, white shirt, and black bow tie. The brothers talked of Golden Ridge and their endless store of family memories and customs, recollection of their parents, the church, the schools, floods, storms; and, of course, the wives found much to say to each other. The children, from the oldest to the youngest, began to beg Jean to "do this every Christmas." Little Robert leaned against his father's knee and said, "Please Papa, please." Not used to such intimacy from one of his children, Jean awkwardly patted Robert's curly head, and said, "I think that would be a very good idea, young man." Jean saw Stephanie watching him, smiling. Two servants began lighting the candles on the tree. When it was done they stood behind the glowing fir with buckets of water in case of fire.

At five o'clock, Daniels appeared with a silver tray with small glasses. The fine wines drew many compliments. Jean did not approve of drunkenness, and Daniels knew not to serve much alcohol to anyone. However, Jean was surprised to see Albert go back to the tray for a second glass of champagne and then a third. He drank the third glass as he stood close to Daniels and walked away with a fourth in his hand. Jean was displeased and shocked. He had never thought of his son caring so much for alcohol. He rose and walked over to Daniels. "Make sure Albert gets no more to drink," he said. "When we return to the city, take all the wine that is left back with us and lock it up."

"Yes, Mister Levert," said Daniels. "I understand, I do it."

At that moment, Stephanie Marie entered the room and seated herself at the harp. The room, which had now filled with the family, elders comfortable in easy chairs and children, many of them seated on the floor around the musician, seemed as expectant as a French Opera House audience before the curtain rises. Jean and Stephanie felt great pride in the scene before them.

Stephanie Marie, dressed in pale blue silk with a deep Bertha off her shoulders, her blonde hair, so like her mother's had been at this age, bouffant around her face and fastened with a blue satin bow behind, began playing "Adeste Fidelis." Each familiar selection drew sighs and murmurs of approval and fascination from her audience. Many had glistening eyes in response to her beauty and talent. There was no applause, of course, for the sacred music. But when she played, "God Rest Ye Merry Gentlemen," everyone sang along and finished with enthusiastic applause. Albert, now relaxed and rosy of face, went to his sister and hugged her.

After the music, Vic and Daniels brought in more trays of food. Stephanie rose and walked among her guests, spending some time, showing genuine interest in each person, whatever the age. *She loves children,* thought Jean. *She is a true lover of children. But she is tired. All this social life in New Orleans is wearing her out.* But Stephanie lasted the entire evening and did not go to bed until the guests had left the room and the servants had come in to take away all vestiges of the party and make the room ready for Christmas morning.

*   *   *

"In the name of the Father, the Son, and the Holy Spirit, amen."

Early Christmas morning Augie conducted a brief religious observation when the large family gathered in the parlor after breakfast. He and Amédée said prayers of praise for the Christ child and asked blessings for the descendants of Eulalie and Auguste Levert. Jean missed the prayers because he was getting into his *Père Noel* costume, a handsome red velvet suit trimmed in white cotton, made by Stephanie's dressmaker. He wore shiny black boots, and a shiny black belt encircled his waist which was made fat with a large pillow. Albert had devised a snowy white beard from cotton, and, in the mirror, Jean noted that his own hair was turning white enough to blend in well. His ample moustache, a source of great pride to him, was even whiter and lay gracefully atop the full cottony beard.

Jean burst into the parlor to the surprise and delight of everyone. His own little ones—Beatrice, Stella, Ella Marie, and Robert did not recognize him. Robert, in fact, who was four, seemed frightened. But Santa calmed everyone down, and, while Stephanie looked on in amusement and amazement, her husband began to pass out gifts, reading each name and calling the youngest recipients to his knee. Such a large pile of gifts required hours because Stephanie insisted that each person open a gift and show it around. By the time the last present had been opened, the family was knee-deep in wrapping paper, and everyone walked out onto the galleries for more talk and play.

At noon, Dottee came out with a gong, which she pounded as she called, "Christmas dinna served! Christmas dinna ready! Yeah!"

Miraculously, it seemed to Jean, Albert had provided a seat for every guest. The banquet table seated all the grown people and ten of the older children. Small children were seated at a side table that was decorated just as the large table was with holly and red candles. Then food began to arrive—golden brown turkey, ham, cornbread dressing with oysters, jambalaya, white rice, giblet gravy, candied yams, snap beans, asparagus, peas, fruits. And more. Jean could not eat the pecan pie with whipped cream. The feasting, he felt, was at an end. But, Dottee told him later, the guests consumed five pies.

Early on the morning of December 26, Jean and Albert stood on the gallery and bade the visiting Levert brothers and their wives and children off in their carriages. Horses bobbed their heads and snorted in the cool air as the men shook hands and the ladies and girls embraced. Baskets of lunch had been stowed in the carriages, and lap robes were spread across knees as the horses took off at a trot. Jean heard youthful voices floating back.

"Goodbye, goodbye, goodbye, Uncle Jean. Goodbye . . . ."

Chapter 54

"TWO GENTLEMEN TO see you, Mr. Levert," announced Agnes, stepping just inside his office. "They came during lunchtime while you were at your Pickwick Club. They left when they found you gone, but now they are back. I didn't tell them you would see them after lunch; they have no appointment."

Jean looked admiringly at Agnes Townsend, his new secretary. The unattractive Alice Mead had taken a higher-paying job with another sugar broker. Slim, rather tall, with the figure of a woman much younger than her age—forty-two, Agnes wore a black skirt tailored to the curves of her glorious backside, and a white shirtwaist, tucked in front, with a high lace-trimmed neck. A pencil pierced the smooth auburn surface of her unswept bouffant hair. *Mon dieu, beautiful women seemed to be everywhere one looked.*

"I might as well find out what their business is, if any. I just returned from a festive holiday at St. John with my family and brothers' families. I couldn't be more proud of the way things turned out and I couldn't believe everybody got along so well. I'm really in no mood to accept visitors yet, but since they're here, please show them in, Miss Townsend." His satisfying look at his secretary lifted his spirits and made him more receptive than he might have been after coming in from a hot and humid walk on the New Orleans streets. He hoped the callers might bring news of one of the clients with whom he was trying to make a lucrative deal in Orleans Parish.

He sized up the two men as they came in and stood before him. They were well dressed and seemed dignified and sure of themselves. He rose after only the briefest hesitation.

"Well, gentlemen, what can I do for you?" He took his gold watch from the pocket of his waistcoat and gave it a significant glance before replacing it.

One man was tall and thin; the other was rather short and plump. The short one spoke as they stood. "Mr. Levert, I am Henry Breaux, and allow me to present Mr. Alcide Duvall."

Jean extended his hand to each of them politely but not cordially. "Will you sit down?" he said, indicating two chairs as he returned to his desk chair. He did not know the men, but they did look somewhat familiar. Breaux had a red face, and Jean thought he smelled brandy on him when they shook hands.

"Mr. Levert, we know you are a very busy man, and we hope you will forgive us for impulsively appearing at your office without an appointment. We'll get right to the point of our visit. We are associates of Mr. Alfred Soniat, head of the Anti-Lottery Democratic Party. As you may know, our party was recently joined by the state's Farmer's Alliance and the New Orleans Anti-Lottery League."

"I've heard as much," said Jean curtly.

The men looked incredulous. "Then surely, Mr. Levert, you know the facts about the state lottery company—born of evil, sustained in corruption, and it has blighted the lives of decent, hard-working citizens."

Wary of a sermon, Jean said, "I am not sure what you gentlemen are after. If it's money, I must tell you I am already overcommitted to good causes. What can I do for you?"

Duvall, who was as bald as an egg, then gave Jean a brief history of the Louisiana lottery's unsavory past, leading from its roots in the Civil War through its flowering corruption during Reconstruction and into its current money-and-power age of manipulators, cheats, and thieves.

"Of course! I know how evil it is, and I'll tell anyone that. But beyond my opinion, what has all this got to do with me?"

Jean sensed the men were frustrated. Whatever dramatic speeches they had been prepared to make, Jean didn't want to hear anything but exactly what their business was with him.

"We want you to be our standard bearer, to be the anti-lottery party's candidate for the state senate in the general election of 1892."

Jean did not blink. Like most conscientious citizens, he was indeed well informed of the perfidy of the lottery. He despised the injustices and mockeries imposed on Louisianians in the name of valuable revenues and every sort of benefit that was boasted by lottery promoters. He could probably have given these two men detailed information that they had not heard of, but he did not make any such claims. He thought it was quite odd that he was intrigued with the idea of entering politics; he, Jean Baptiste Levert, financier, son of a planter, a Louisiana gentleman with as much romantic family history as any living citizen of the state. His mouth quivered. Surely he was not nervous. A challenge? Hell, he thrived on challenges. He thought of the Colonel. The Colonel had not mentioned elective office as likely public service for Jean, but Jean was already summing up what a well-managed political office might do for his reputation and fortunes. It would surely attract more business. Then he thought of Steph; could she be expected to stand by while he took on another major challenge, one that would take him away from home more than ever? He realized that he thought of her last. Still, how could he say no to an opportunity to serve his state; the need was no less dire than it had ever been. Steph would want him to do his part to rid the state of the menace that the lottery presented.

"Gentlemen, I'll give you an answer when I give it to you," said Jean hoarsely. "At this moment that is all I can say, I'm afraid. I can say no more today. Forgive me, but I am very tired." He rose. "Let me say that I will meet you gentlemen at eleven o'clock on Saturday at the lottery hall on Decatur Street in the French Quarter, where I will witness firsthand a lottery drawing, a unique experience for me."

Breaux and Duvall rose; they seemed not bothered at all by his abruptness. These politicians were men of the world—the world of Louisiana politics. Perhaps there was no more greater combat between humans in the world than the contest over the lottery in New Orleans in the Nineties. Jean was thinking this as he bade the two men good-day, and he felt sure that they were of like opinion.

*   *   *

Jean kept his date with Breaux and Duvall on the rainy Saturday. He stood with them among a throng of gamblers for the final lottery drawing of the year on the last day of December. In Jean's opinion, it was a strange-looking setting. Strong wind gusts blew into the hall from open windows, causing kerosene lamps fastened to the plaster walls and hanging from the ceiling to gutter and almost go out. The faltering lamps did little to brighten the dismal day or the large damp room. Perhaps the most undoing part of the experience for him was the appearance onstage of two of the most idealized local heroes of the Confederacy—Generals P.G.T. Beauregard and Jubal A. Early. Jean winced at the sight of the two men, Early in his gray uniform and Beauregard in a black suit.

There had been much talk of the circumstances and renumeration of the generals, Jean knew. Beauregard first accepted the position as a commissioner, and he asked Early to join him in supervising the drawings. He first asked Wade Hampton, but Hampton was elected Governor of South Carolina before he accepted. Beauregard, like many veterans, was short of funds, but Jean thought getting on the payroll of the Louisiana State Lottery Company, where he had remained since 1868, had tainted the heroic image of him and of Early.

Jean likened the lottery to a giant octopus, its tentacles creeping over and into everything. The lottery had controlled nearly every legislature from 1868 to the present; it controlled most of the New Orleans newspapers. Its basis of control was money and its large deposits kept the City's banks under the lottery's thumb. The French Opera House was its charity along with many other good causes. The lottery had even built a sugarhouse for the sugar planters. He knew that he must accept the sponsorship of the anti-lottery party and endeavor to become a senator in the legislature of Louisiana. Once he made up his mind, he was possessed of great determination to win.

He departed the lottery hall. He planned to notify the politicians Breaux and Duvall tomorrow, and send a letter to Colonel Bush informing the sick man of his plan.

*   *   *

In his final campaign speech two days before the April 4 election, Jean Baptiste stood on a high platform at the corner of St. Charles and Jackson avenues, a few blocks from his home on Third Street. He looked out over what he estimated to be hundreds of people filling the intersection below, many standing not ten feet away; many more stood behind him. He noticed that the intersection was becoming too crowded in front of him, and thought of cautioning against crushing but decided against it. Finally he loosened the cravat around his high stiff collar and with passion swung into his main theme:

"I oppose the kind of gambling the lottery company promotes. No good cause comes from such money-producing activities as lotteries. No amount of money can make up for the evil they do to this city, the state and to society as a whole . . . I give you my solemn pledge that if I am elected I shall vigorously support legislation to control present gambling opportunities . . ."

Electric lights mounted on tall towers of iron lattice work produced a soft glow where Jean was standing on the warm early evening. He smiled broadly as the crowd gave him loud applause and cheered after nearly every line of his speech.

"And I shall fully object to extending the charter of the lottery company . . . we all know that the charter never should have been granted in the first place. We must, and we will, rescue our fine state from this pit of evil."

By now, Jean was punching the air with both fists. He spotted a reporter from *The Daily Picayune* furiously scribbling in a notebook. Pleased, he paused to wipe his brow, then for a moment looked around at some large galleried houses along St. Charles

Avenue, the enormous city mansions with halls running through their centers that he had come to admire in the Garden District. The houses were surrounded by green lawns, banana and orange trees, large beds of lilies and roses, and great glistening magnolia and oak trees. Most of the lawns were bound by handsome wrought iron fences—fine artistic creations, he knew, by a number of outstanding black artisans in New Orleans.

He raised both arms to silence further applause. As he had done during other campaign speeches, he informed the crowd of the "treachery of the lottery" and how the lottery has "blighted the lives of decent, hard-working Louisianians . . ." Then the crowd erupted into applause. With roars ringing in his ears, Jean stepped down from the platform and into the crush of voters who wanted to shake his hand.

Jean felt he had run a hard campaign for the Louisiana state senate, and to his surprise it hadn't taken him long to find competent people to help him run his campaign. He had savored the cheering of supporters and well-wishers, and large crowds had pushed to his speaking platform on the corners of busy New Orleans streets. Despite his hard work and the enthusiastic response, Jean thought there was little hope of winning the election. He had no machine, and he feared he did not have enough political experience to judge how his campaign was really going. He felt that he was not well enough known outside the immediate business world of New Orleans to make it to the senate hall of the turreted statehouse in Baton Rouge.

CHAPTER 55

TO CELEBRATE HIS election to the state senate, Jean and Stephanie attended the performance of Saint-Saen's opera *Samson and Delilah* on a balmy New Orleans Saturday afternoon in early May before the summer's heat had settled in. The overture was already beginning when they arrived in their box in the second-level gallery of the gleaming white French Opera House on Bourbon and Toulouse streets.

Jean, in formal dress, noticed many eyes were turned toward the five-foot-tall Stephanie, who, like the other ladies in boxes and orchestra seats, wore her best jewelry. He thought she looked handsome in a Paris gown and long white kid gloves; she carried a fan and a bouquet of miniature fresh flowers with hanging ribbons of pale blue satin. But elegant as his wife might look, Jean knew she was not her usual buoyant self. He had noticed this earlier but remained silent, preferring to believe it was merely a mood. Jean had become a staunch and generous supporter of the opera, and he had learned to appreciate opera after years of accompanying Stephanie and joining her enlightened response. He knew that the opera's future in New Orleans was no certainty—foreclosure had been threatened several times. This was especially painful for him, because the French Opera House, with its massive exterior arranged to give the audience a full view of the stage from almost every point, had replaced the small, cramped Théâtre d'Orléans as the "center of opera" in the City. He believed it was in New Orleans that opera had been established as an art form in the

United States and that there were probably more music lovers and appreciators of opera in New Orleans than in New York.

Stephanie seemed to love *Samson*, and her lips moved, framing the words of the chorus. She smiled and leaned toward Jean. "I know it all by heart." He was glad to see her absorption seem to clear away her anxieties, those typical of a mother and wife, and the general fatigue that plagued her of late. Jean smiled as he saw her pat her feet and silently clap her hands, for she had inherited her love of music from her *Grand-mère Dupuy*.

Despite his pleasure, Jean grew restless in their box. Sitting for long stretches wore his patience these days. He shifted in the small gilt chair and murmured to Stephanie without looking at her. He repeated his comments about the opera, and when she still didn't respond, he looked more closely at her. Her eyes were closed, and there was no brightness in her face.

Stephanie had fainted.

Shocked and alarmed, Jean impulsively swept his wife up in his arms and carried her down the marble staircase that curved into the lobby. He laid her on a velvet settee and began to pat her hands and fan her face with his handkerchief. Before he could summon aid, a voice of authority spoke beside them.

"I am a doctor, sir," said the tall, whiskered man. "Allow me to be of service to you and your wife." And he began to lift Stephanie's eyelids and to feel for her pulse. Jean stood back in relief as his wife began to regain consciousness. As soon as she realized her predicament she looked at an intermission crowd collecting around her. She was embarrassed. She tried to sit up, but the doctor and Jean restrained her.

"Please, madam, I am Dr. Hebert. You have fainted, and we must be sure that you are able to get on your feet before you attempt to stand."

Stephanie looked at Jean in alarm. "Jean . . . ?"

A male voice said, "Ladies and gentlemen, please move on. The lady only fainted. Please do not crowd *Madame Levert*. A doctor is with her. Please!" The operagoers withdrew in orderly fashion.

"Doctor! What seems to be wrong with my wife?" Jean looked worriedly at Steph.

The doctor patted Stephanie's hand and stood up. He shook hands with Jean. "Mr. Levert, is it? I am Henri Hebert. Your wife has just fainted. Her pulse was racing when I first took it, but it has slowed sufficiently for you to assist her to your carriage." He smiled reassuringly toward both Jean and Stephanie.

"I wonder what on earth caused this," said Stephanie in a weak voice. "I felt nothing before I suddenly . . . just faded out . . ."

"Dr. Hebert, have you any idea?"

"Possibly a passing problem of minor origin," replied Dr. Hebert. "Perhaps you should call in your family physician." He assisted Stephanie to her feet. "Let me walk on one side of you, Mrs. Levert, and we'll get you a cab."

"Oh! Our own carriage should be here. Jean! Isn't Daniels due to come for us?"

Then they saw the faithful Daniels holding the horses' reins at the curb. When he saw that his mistress was being helped by two men, he stamped out his cigar and hurried forward.

"Mister Levert, is Madam Levert sick?" He hurried back to open the carriage door.

"I'm all right, Daniels, I'm all right." She turned back and thanked Dr. Hebert and gave him what Jean was relieved to observe as a dazzling smile, her green eyes bright. He saw that she was comfortable before he addressed Dr. Hebert.

"I don't know how to thank you, sir. You have given us much comfort. Here is my card. I shall expect your professional statement." He extended his hand. "Thank you, sir. Thank you again." Jean stepped into the carriage and sat beside Steph.

"All right, Daniels, take us to Third Street."

*   *   *

Despite heavy campaigning in winter and spring for the state senate seat, Jean's mind was much concerned with Colonel Bush. He hadn't seen him in nearly a month; he knew the Colonel had gone to Wisconsin for special treatment—a last resort. But the duties of a freshman senator—laboring hard against the state lottery as well as learning to juggle his busy business schedule with his new political dedication—occupied more of his time than he'd ever expected. He knew the Colonel understood how this was, and that he would be proud of his public service.

But news finally did come, in a front page story in *The Daily Picayune* issue of August 11, 1892: "Announcement comes from Madison, Wisconsin, that one of the foremost citizens of Louisiana, whom her citizens had trusted in council and followed in battle, died after a long, painful illness . . . ."

Sitting at his desk in his office, Jean put down the newspaper, lowered his head in his hands, and wept. He expected the news, but he wasn't prepared for the death of his partner, who was seventy-two. After there were no more tears to shed, Jean fumbled in his desk for his journal to write his feelings about this loss while they were still fresh in his mind:

"The news brings much sorrow and gloom to me and a host of friends in the city with whom the Colonel's life of usefulness and honor had always been the subject of pride and admiration . . . his leading characteristics were integrity, high sense of honor, natural ability, sound judgment, quick perception. Courtly and commanding in his presence, he was a fine type of native Louisianian."

He put the journal back in the drawer. He glanced around the office, seeing nothing. *Colonel would have been proud of me . . . how I wish he could have been with Stephanie and me at the opera celebrating my winning the senate race.* Jean remained at the office for another hour, reflecting, thinking about his old mentor and friend, about Bush's widow Celeste and their four surviving children, their long, productive, profitable partnership. *God, I'm going to miss him.*

While staring out of the window at people on their way home from work, he began to worry about Steph; her fainting at the opera still concerned him. He flicked off the desk lamp and left for Third Street. This time he rode the streetcar instead of walking, but he got off at Coliseum Street to leave his card at Colonel Bush's home.

*   *   *

Jean stayed late at the office on Perdido the next day to prepare contract papers for new clients and to catch up on work he'd put off for days. He gave some thought to a new partner, although he still wasn't sure that he wanted another—go it alone for awhile, perhaps. Still he couldn't get the Colonel off his mind.

At midnight, after Stephanie and the children had been asleep for hours, he set a cup of chicoried coffee on the cluttered desk and looked about his Third Street office for a moment. The room was now decorated in a vaguely oriental style, with an ornate built-in bookcase covering an entire wall, expensive antique pieces among the books, some housed in glass cases. Except for daily newspapers and some sugar industry trade journals piled on his desk, the study was uncluttered, thanks to Jenny. On Dottee's recommendation, Jean and Stephanie had hired Jenny, Dottee's older sister from St. Martinville, to assist Vic. To help get his mind off the Colonel, Jean wrote some final thoughts in his journal, entitled, *The Colonel I Knew*:

August 12, 1892

He knew his Bible well for a man who never took part in church activities. The basic problems—life and death—I could see, were constantly on his mind. He sometimes spoke to me with admiration of his wife's church work, though not often . . . he took no pains to conceal that he himself did not like all the sermons of priests . . . a true Democrat was the Colonel. I never heard him speak wrongly of another man. His servants idolized him . . . there was an optimism and enthusiasm about him that won over a person. His love and knowledge of poetry, especially Shakespeare, was both touching and startling; he remembered jingles his Mother sang to him when he was a boy no older than six . . . I never met a man, I believe, who had a more wise view of the worldly things of life. He served his day and generation, his family admirably. His achievements will never be fully appreciated.

Chapter 56

JEAN RECEIVED STEPHANIE Marie Levert's telegram shortly before he left St. John to catch the train back to New Orleans. He had been visiting Albert and inspecting the planting of the '93 crop. Such visits had become a ritual for Jean since his son had became manager of the plantation. The message was terse:

Come home right away STOP Mama's taken ill STOP

Carrying a small travel case in one hand and in the other his blue cord jacket that he'd removed because of the oppressive heat, Jean dashed aboard the Southern Pacific train the moment it stopped at the St. Martinville depot. He cleared two steps at once.

The train seemed to poke along interminably, slowing for every byway and side road, as if it would stop, then chug on toward New Orleans. After he'd found a dusty seat, he felt panic closing in on him. He pressed his forehead against the window and stared through the rain at passing cane fields and rows of shanties. Perhaps he should have allowed Albert to come home with him. But it was at the height of the planting season, and they decided he could telegraph Albert to come if it seemed advisable.

He had trouble breathing the stuffy air. He thought he might die before he could reach Stephanie. Usually, on this train ride to and from the plantation, the abandoned fields still scarred by old Civil War battery emplacements stirred in him vivid memories of his beloved South the way it was before the war. But on this trip Jean thought only of his wife. "Oh, God, not my Steph!"

*　　*　　*

Stephanie Marie, just turned seventeen, Beatrice, eleven, and Lawrence, now twelve, had been waiting at the Southern Pacific train depot for nearly two hours for their father to arrive. Expressions on their faces, seen through the dirty, rain-streaked window, did nothing to ease Jean's fears.

"What is it? How serious is your Mother?" Jean said, almost shouting, as he stepped down from the train. He hurried with his children toward the Levert carriage parked nearby. Daniels helped Jean with his bag, then assisted the children. After climbing aboard, Jean looked at his children seated across from him, their hands in their laps. They smiled at him with sympathy and understanding in their eyes.

"What is it? Is she . . ." Did the doctor tell you anything?" Jean couldn't complete his thought. He didn't even want to think of the possibility—critical illness, even death. *Not my strong-willed Steph, mother of my twelve children, my strength, my comforter.*

"Oh, no—no, Papa," said Stephanie Marie. Jean thought his daughter was mature for her age and had her mother's emotional strength and plucky resolve. "She has not left us, thank God in heaven. But I believe she's awfully sick."

"What seems to be wrong with her? When I left a few days ago she seemed well, in good spirits. Did she fall?"

"No, she didn't fall. The doctor is with her now at home. She was having trouble breathing when I telegraphed you, and she's been quite dizzy. The doctor has ordered her to bed for complete rest and quiet."

Jean found no comfort in her words. "Does Dr. Gonsoulin know anything yet about the cause? Anything?"

"I've told you everything I know, Papa. It's all any of us knows."

After nearly an hour, the four-wheel barouche, a gift to Stephanie from Jean's father two years before he died, rattled to a stop on Third Street. Jean and his children stared apprehensively at their home before alighting. The home sheltered them through all their troubles and triumphs. Jean had had the large attic converted to a full third story four years after he purchased it, making it almost a third again as spacious as it had been. The facade bore eight floor-to-ceiling windows and the balconies were supported upstairs and down by fluted Corinthian columns. A handsome home, fully satisfying the dream Jean had when he bought it for Stephanie about the time she moved to New Orleans three years after their marriage. Now Jean recalled how Stephanie had loved the house from the first day she saw it. Daniels met them at the wrought iron gate.

As the four of them entered the foyer, Daniels took the carriage and horses to the barn. Jean made straight for the stairs, heading for the bedroom door.

"No, Papa, not yet. The doctor's in with her now," said Mathilde from a bench in the hall. Jean's twenty-year-old daughter had been in Bay St. Louis visiting with friends when she learned of her mother's illness, and she had arrived home shortly before Jean.

Sweating from anxiety as much as the scorching temperature, Jean shed his stiff collar and cravat, a rare display for a man who seldom was in the presence of his family without coat and necktie. "Your Mother's better, isn't she, Mathilde? Please say something, girl." Mathilde, about to make her debut into New Orleans Society, ignored her father's desperate remarks.

"I—I still can't believe this is happening," he cried, loud enough for all his children to hear. "Is it something I did or should've done? Is God punishing me now, at this instant, for being away from her so often on business? When little Aloysia passed away?" He covered his eyes.

Finally, Stephanie's door creaked open, and the family physician, Dr. Emile Gonsoulin, stood quietly before Jean and all his children except Albert. The doctor looked at all the young faces—Mathilde; Stephanie Marie, Beatrice; Freddy, Jean Jr., almost fifteen, Lawrence and Stella, ten, Ella Marie, eight; and Robert, the youngest, five. The physician's goateed chin sank gradually to his chest.

"Mr. Levert, your wife would like to see you now, but stay

only for a few minutes. She requires rest and quiet, understand? Then, if you don't mind, please gather the children and yourself for a brief conference later in the parlor. I'd like to discuss what I believe to be wrong with Mrs. Levert, and I may have some suggestions regarding her care from now on."

"I won't be but a few minutes, Doctor," said Jean. "I just want to see her."

Jean opened his wife's door. "How do you feel, *ma chèrie?* I got here as fast as I could from St. John. Albert sends his love." Stephanie's green eyes, dull when he entered, focused on his when she heard his voice, and she smiled. As their eyes met, tears welled in him. His stomach felt hollow. He saw her thinning, pale form propped up against large pillows, her arms crossed on her chest. She appeared weak and frightened.

"I'll be fine, dear, you must not worry yourself so, for the children's sake," she said softly. "We must not upset them."

Jean gently smoothed her pillows and laid his hand on her brow. "Don't talk, Steph. It will tire you. You need rest. I'll look in on you later; and Vic will get you some broth. I understand you haven't eaten all day. Maybe later, if you're feeling like it, I'll allow the older children to come in. Now, try to rest. Doctor's orders." As he turned to leave, he glanced over the luxurious bedroom, its walnut four-poster brought from her childhood bedroom at St. Gabriel, other familiar objects they took for granted. They had shared this room for more than twenty years.

Outside her door, he stood with his hands over his face, trying to erase Stephanie's sharp signs of illness. Through his disbelief, he felt a visceral fear. Her eyes had no glint; they seemed waxy and yellow, and she looked surprisingly aged. He had left the room sooner than he intended.

*   *   *

Jean and six of his older children were waiting for Dr. Gonsoulin when he entered the parlor. Jean had not lost hope for a good prognosis for Stephanie.

A large man with black hair beginning to grizzle and recede, Dr. Gonsoulin looked at him directly. "Are you feeling better, Senator Levert, now that you have seen Mrs. Levert?" He sat in a chair facing the Leverts. Jean sat between Mathilde and Stephanie Marie on the chintz-covered sofa in the large bay at the end of the room. The other children stood behind the sofa. "Much better, thank you," said Jean somberly. His children nodded in agreement, all eager, if somewhat fearful, to hear the doctor.

Jean noticed Dr. Gonsoulin looking at him and his children, then glancing at the bookshelves along a wall of the sitting room. It made Jean curious but he said anything.

"Have you felt well since your return this morning, Senator?"

"Yes, indeed, Doctor. But I had conducted my affairs with my son Albert and was ready to return to the city when my daughter's message reached me. Actually, not very well, now that you ask. Business travel tires me more than it once did. But unfortunately, being a sugar broker requires that I travel a great deal. I've tried to reduce my travels, especially since Mrs. Levert's fainting episode at the opera last spring."

Concerned about Jean's health, the doctor said, "You really should not go to bed while you are in such a state of mind. I generally insist that a person should fall asleep only with pleasant thoughts." He leaned forward from his chair and began what the family was waiting for, but dreaded:

"Mrs. Levert definitely shows one of the early symptoms of heart disease—shortness of breath, perhaps the cause of her fainting at the opera," the doctor said, choosing his words carefully. "As far as I can determine, activities that she has been able to carry off without trouble may now be beginning to leave her breathless." He stopped when he noticed a paleness in Jean's face. "Do you wish to say something, Senator?"

"I'm sorry but I—I simply am amazed and surprised this has happened to my wife; no history of heart problems that I ever heard about." He smiled faintly, as if remembering a happier time. He couldn't continue and turned instead to his children, looking at them one by one, as if he expected one of them to come up with an explanation. The children were staring soberly down at the floor.

"Oh, she had some difficulty giving birth to several of our children, but we all thought of that as a passing difficulty." Jean was seeking reassurance from the doctor with this last remark, but he got none.

"As I was saying, your wife's shortness of breath may indicate heart trouble," said Dr. Gonsoulin, resuming his diagnosis. "She may even have had a mild heart attack during the night. Mrs. Levert did wake from a deep sleep last night with a kind of choking sensation. Do you know if she had scarlet fever as a child?"

"I've already told you I know of absolutely nothing in Stephanie's past to indicate any kind of heart problem," said Jean hurriedly, spacey, obviously frustrated. "I've known her since she was a young girl. The subject of her past health has never come up."

"Do not blame yourself, Senator. Sometimes the sign of a defective heart does not appear until a person reaches middle age. This is obviously a case in which neither you nor anybody else could have done anything, even if you had known of something in her history. I am not certain all of this was not brought on by a congenital defect of the heart, regardless of her history."

Dr. Gonsoulin, who often faced a family like this when a parent's health was in question, changed the subject to how best care for Mrs. Levert. He first mentioned a change of scenery— away from the noise of a large city to the quieter life and the cleaner air of a small town. "I am not sure but it's highly possible that the stress of labor," he glanced at the children, dubiously, "during the delivery of twelve children could have complicated Mrs. Levert's overall condition. Pregnancy, you know, imposes a heavy, predictable burden on the heart. No question about that."

Jean spoke before the doctor finished. "What you're saying then is that it would have been helpful to know if there was any history of heart problems. That all of this could have been avoided?"

"Not entirely. It may have helped, though. If there had been problems, when you and Mrs. Levert were building a family, we could have recommended not having any more children after a certain number."

Jean smarted with what sounded like a reprimand given in the presence of his children. He remembered quite well the warnings from Dr. Gonsoulin at the times he delivered her last three children. He immediately thought of the night when Stephanie told him the doctor suggested they sleep in different beds, different rooms, even. Jean had been indignant, Steph apologetic. They had solved their dilemma by making love. That had assured Jean that Stephanie had taken the doctor's caution no more seriously than he did.

Jean said, "What can we do then—what can I do? What do you suggest as a way of getting her well again—as quickly as possible? Please, we must know. And should I send for my eldest son?"

Dr. Gonsoulin rubbed his chin. "I would say not yet." He looked away from the Leverts through the long front windows toward Third Street as several different-size carriages glided by. Then he said, "I want you to give some thought to finding a place away from the city, where she can be free from the stress of her social and family activities from time to time. An escape to a less congested area. Perhaps one with a better climate than New Orleans. What about the Gulf Coast of Mississippi? It is becoming a popular resort area, I'm told."

Jean didn't answer right away. He had taken the family on more than one holiday to the summer homes of friends at Bay St. Louis and Biloxi. He knew the children loved going there. So had Stephanie. But now the children said nothing. Jean hooked a thumb under his chin and rested his nose on an index finger while pondering the doctor's suggestion, for he thought it made good sense.

"I will give the Mississippi Gulf Coast serious thought, Doctor. If such a change of scenery and a lightening of responsibilities is what you recommend, there is absolutely no question about it. Her health is our first concern, now."

The doctor rose to leave. Jean retrieved his black medical bag from the marble-top console table in the foyer and handed it to him. He shook hands with the man and thanked him on behalf of himself, his children, and especially Mrs. Levert.

"I'll check in on her tomorrow. Just remember, plenty of rest and quiet," said Dr. Gonsoulin, opening the leaded glass front door. Daniels met him there with a lantern and escorted him to his black buggy and untied the horse's reins at the hitching post.

CHAPTER 57

THE MAGICAL DATE, February 6, 1894, finally had arrived, and all day the entire Levert household was in an uproar. Jean Baptiste figured all the partying in connection with Mathilde Marie Levert's debut and presentation as queen of the Comus Mardi Gras ball had exhausted everyone.

Because Dr. Gonsoulin had imposed limitations on Stephanie's activities, Jean made sure that Mathilde had been fitted with a Paris gown of white satin heavily beaded in pearls and brilliant stones on the bodice and exaggerated leg o'mutton sleeves; the dress served as underdress of the royal purple queen's cloak when she appeared later on the arm of her king. That his daughter's wardrobe had included formal gowns, wraps, and appropriate attire for teas and luncheons in some of the City's most elegant homes.

Jean was happy that his wife was feeling better after rest and confinement, despite her constant protests, and that she wanted to participate in every event in Mathilde's social whirl. She had accompanied her daughter to only a few luncheons during the Carnival season, and Dr. Gonsoulin had grave reservations about those and particularly the tiring schedule and her plans to attend the ball later tonight. Stephanie often had told Jean, "New Orleans Society must be unique."

Jean rented an extra carriage to accommodate bouffant skirts of his wife and daughters. He left the care of their transportation to Albert, who was in town for his sister's bow and who had, to Jean's surprise, found himself in much demand as an escort. He

ordered a special carriage to take him and Mathilde and Vic to the
French Opera House promptly at seven-thirty, a full hour ahead
of the rest of the family.

Jean was amused, but pleased at how naturally Mathilde
adjusted to the role as queen—sitting perfectly straight in the
carriage, and when they alighted on Bourbon Street, stepping down
with queenly composure. *Suddenly she is a woman of elegance,
beauty, charm. There is a certain sang-froid . . . Look at how she
walks to the door of the opera house, her lips slightly parted in a
half smile for the crowds lining the walks. I can scarcely believe
this is that little girl. She isn't as talented as Stephanie Marie, but
she has*—he groped for a word—*she has presence! These people
do not know they are looking at the queen of Comus.* He and Vic
trailed behind the queen to the opera house door, when Jean
handed Vic the case filled with the queen's personal grooming
items for her *cabinet de toilette.*

Turning away, he was pleased to see his friend Colonel William
Behan, who was there for his niece's presentation. He hurried over
to greet the Colonel, who could, Jean believed, give him some
information about a block of rental property Jean had heard was
for sale at a good price. The owner, he had heard, was in desperate
need of cash.

At nine o'clock, Stephanie and the nine children, in front-row
balcony seats, watched the presentation of the debutantes,
appearance of the king and queen, and finally, revelation of the
queen's identity. Moments later Jean stepped out on the ballroom
floor resplendent in his formal attire, escorting Mathilde. The
Leverts gave an audible sigh of awe as their father and twenty-four
other fathers paraded their daughters before the audience. Robert,
sitting next to his mother, whispered loudly, "Is that Mathilde
with Papa?"

"Yes!" said Stephanie, staring at her daughter and husband on
the polished floor. When Jean and Mathilde had danced the first
waltz, he released her to a young man, then invited Stephanie to
the floor, where they danced just enough steps to make her wish
for more. But Jean dutifully returned her to her seat, knowing he

must not unduly exercise her. He was glad he had, for as he seated her he found himself looking into the stare of Dr. Gonsoulin not ten feet away. Jean nodded solemnly at the doctor, and led Stephanie Marie to the dance floor.

Stephanie and Jean had not told the children that their sister was the lucky girl. Beside Mathilde, her parents, and a select few in the Mistick Krewe of Comus, the only other persons in the household who knew about it were Vic and Daniels. He and Stephanie had agreed the servants, because of their discreteness, should be told. Vic and Daniels had helped the children dress, combed their hair, polished their shoes—got them ready to offer a united front at the opera house.

Jean and other gentlemen gathered in the lounge to smoke cigars and sip brandy during an intermission between the debutante dance and the arrival of the king of Comus and his queen. Jean heard over the big plush room: "Who is the old boy's queen? Hasn't anyone heard? It has been the best kept secret in the history of Comus!" Jean was amused, but he was tired, and now his thoughts had been interrupted by information he had obtained from Colonel Behan. *On Thursday, I must get busy on matters of portent.*

A bell rang, and the men put out cigars and downed a last dram of brandy. They hurried back to the ballroom and took their seats before the orchestra began a prelude to the king's arrival. Diamonds and pearls, with a generous range of rubies, emeralds, and sapphires, glittered from the ladies in the opera house, Jean saw. Past queens wore tiaras as symbols of their former glory. Jean, who had attended most of the Comus balls, was certain he had never seen a more gorgeous assemblage; he hadn't expected to feel so exultant.

Suddenly, the prelude came to an abrupt end, and the orchestra sounded the first chords of the processional. The crowd murmured as one, "It's the king! The king! Who is the queen? Who is she?" Tears rose to Jean's and Stephanie's eyes. She reached for his hand, and they held onto each other as one after other voices were heard to say: "It's Jean Baptiste Levert's daughter? It's the Levert girl! It's Mathilde Levert! Ah! Isn't she lovely! Look! Look! It is Jean Baptiste Levert's daughter. Jean Baptiste Levert . . ."

"Is that Mathilde? Is that really her?" said the Levert children almost in unison. Then they all clapped hands and squealed with the thrill, exhausting themselves with excitement. Stephanie Marie, who sat on the other side of her mother, holding her other hand, beamed. "*Mère, Mère,* I didn't really believe it. I have been *stupide! Stupide!* I should have guessed." She dabbed her eyes with a lace handkerchief. "Oh, *Père! Felicitations!* This is an *honneur,* too, *Père!*"

Jean thought Mathilde was dressed as elegantly as any queen on any throne. She wore a cloak of royal purple velvet with jeweled tiered sleeves over her white satin gown and a choker of latticed diamonds that had belonged to Grandmother Dupuy, jewelry that had lain in the Levert's bank box until tonight. Pear-shaped diamonds hung from her ears—also from Grandmother Dupuy's collection. The sweeping fifteen-foot train of purple velvet was lined with finely pleated white silk and widely bordered in jewels similar to those on her gown. She appeared as comfortable as if she were strolling on the second-floor balcony outside her Third Street bedroom.

Jean leaned close to Stephanie's ear. "Was there royalty in your family, *chèrie?* She looks like a real queen."

"I never heard of any, but I am going to get some of that jewelry out of the box and wear it. Doesn't it look splendid?"

"It certainly does; keep these pieces out and wear them at every opportunity."

Stephanie Marie said, "Look at her hair. Isn't it exquisite! Vic did that and she tucked the violets into her hair over her ears. Oh, *Père,* I wish you would have her portrait painted in this gown."

"*Halte, ma chèrie!* Your poor father has not a cent left in his pockets."

Reluctantly, Jean had allowed Mathilde to join the coterie of *jeune filles* as a debutante and to make her bow on the night of Fat Tuesday at what he considered the most brilliant event of the New Orleans social season. As a member of Comus, he had the privilege of presenting his daughters to society at the annual Comus Mardi Gras balls. His wife's health continued to worry him, and he was afraid all the activities associated with Mathilde's debut might make her condition worse.

While there was no other honor to exceed that for a daughter and her family, Jean knew debutantes from elite families in the City often were presented to society at great financial hardship to their fathers. Faced with heavy expenses of a New Orleans debut, some mothers sold jewelry and fathers borrowed wherever they could; some even mortgaged the family home to make the envied splash in Old Society. Of course, while Jean realized presenting Mathilde to society did not require great financial sacrifice on his part, he did not look upon the expense of his daughter's debut as frivolous. Indeed, it bespoke his own attainments to present his daughter. Only men of elevated station, financial or social or both, were so identified in the community. So, while he was pleased for Mathilde and for Stephanie, who loved Society, the main and basic recognition—the honor, actually—was for himself, and nobody questioned this fact or faulted a father for it.

Jean believed he had never been so busy, either. With all the requirements on his time in his legislative duties and even as the Carnival season deepened, he was as occupied as ever with business deals—buying, selling, negotiating over property, including the hoped-for purchase of a house on the Mississippi Gulf Coast. He even had entertained the notion of approaching Emile Morvant about a partnership or some sort of formal business association. He knew that Morvart had money, and he was definitely interested in investing.

Now, Jean was certain that Stephanie wanted to enjoy the reception that followed the pageant until midnight. But he ushered her and all the children except Mathilde, Stephanie Marie, Freddy and Albert, out to Vic and Daniels at the waiting family carriage before it was over. He was determined to get her home and into bed before she could be enveloped in the crowd's well-meant congratulations. Vic climbed onto the seat beside Daniels. Jean knew he could depend on the servants to get all six of the younger children safely home, and on Vic to help Stephanie prepare for bed. The older children had been coached as to their responsibilities of getting the younger ones to bed promptly. Jean wished he could feel as sure of his children as he did Vic and Daniels. *Surely Mathilde, Albert, and Freddy would observe Mass early on Ash Wednesday morning. Surely.*

After seeing the family carriage off, Jean returned to the ballroom to talk business to several important men. But champagne had been passed to every one at least three times before he could get to anyone to whom he had anything to say. Constantly hailed for congratulations and hearty pats on the back, he gave up. He made small talk as best he could and tried not to notice Albert and Freddy, who never seemed to let a waiter's tray pass them by. To his disappointment, Mathilde, too, had apparently acquired a taste for the French grape.

About eleven, after enjoying a great deal of flattering attention on his night of nights, Jean sought Mathilde, Albert, and Freddy to join him and Stephanie Marie for the traditional toasts by the courts of Comus and Rex at midnight. He found Mathilde but Albert and Freddy were nowhere to be seen.

"I am assuming Albert and Freddy are together, with friends perhaps. Surely they will be back to the opera house in time for the toasts. Besides, they will need to be home early enough to rest before early Mass to properly begin Lent." His eyes narrowed and he shrugged.

"They went to a party at the upper Pontalba, Papa," replied Stephanie Marie. "They'll return in time. Don't worry."

"I certainly hope so. After all, Mathilde would be disappointed. By the way, weren't you invited, Steph?"

"Yes, I was invited."

"Why did you not accept the invitation?"

"I am too tired, Papa. I am ready to get quiet. Let's get home and go to sleep after the toasts."

"I think we feel the same way, my dear. But wasn't it grand?"

"It was perfectly wonderful. I have never beheld such gorgeous clothes. *Soeur* was just splendid. And Mother was never more beautiful."

"I agree. I agree. But what about you, *ma chèrie?* Are you not eager to make your debut in such style? Has this spectacle made you want to do all this? Maybe next year?"

"No, Papa," she said.

"No? I'm surprised."

"I want to do something else."

"Something else? And what is that, my dear?"

"I want to go to France and study the harp under Rene Moret; he is a student of the great Sebastian Erard. Nothing could mean more to me than to be his pupil at the harp."

Jean should have known, for he had heard her talk of the great teacher before. Still he had not realized that his daughter had such serious resolve about training with Moret in Europe. Now that he was hearing the determination in her voice, he felt that the die was cast.

Finally, Stephanie Marie, Mathilde, Jean, and Albert and Freddy, who had returned from the party, climbed into a cab and rode away through the fog on St. Charles toward Third Street, none of them speaking again until they arrived home.

Promptly at 6 o'clock the next morning, all the Leverts, including Queen Mathilde, Albert, and Freddy, were kneeling among other celebrants inside the dark Romanesque Church of the Immaculate Conception on Baronne Street. Jean knew that Catholic Jesuit priests had introduced cane cultivation to Louisiana about 1751, when they planted seed canes from Santo Domingo on their land on which the Jesuit church now stood, on land that became Baronne Street and areas near Canal Street and the Mississippi River. Jean noticed that many of the celebrants were still gaudily clad in their Mardi Gras costumes and appeared strangely subdued and prayerful.

Chapter 58

ON A FRIDAY afternoon in March, Jean caught the Louisville & Nashville train to Biloxi, hoping to see new color in Stephanie's wan cheeks or a sparkle in her eyes. As he did many weekends since Stephanie had become ill, Jean rented rooms for his wife and children at the plush Montross, an L-shaped, two-story hotel with columned porches overlooking the Mississippi Sound. On occasion he had rented a house on the beach, but the family liked the Montross and Stephanie benefitted from the lack of responsibilities.

It was unusual for Jean to refer to the coastal waters as the Sound; all water in sight was called the Gulf, though the Gulf waters actually began beyond the barrier islands—Horn, Ship, Petit Bois—sandy cays several miles out. He thought it was a delightful view for a seaside resort frequented by visitors from all over the country.

Always in March the sun warmed the rows of rockers on the Montross porches. Upon his arrival, Jean was pleased to see Stephanie sitting outside in the sea breeze, her head protected by a hat, a robe over her knees, and enjoying the children fishing and crabbing from the hotel's two-hundred-foot pier and playing on the yellow sand.

"I was so anxious to get here to see how you are doing, my dear," said Jean excitedly, kissing her forehead and taking a rocker next to her. He rubbed her hand gently. "And dear, I believe I do see improvement in your color and a sparkle in your green eyes. Dr. Gonsoulin certainly knew what he was doing when he suggested we bring you to the clean fresh air of the Gulf Coast for rest, far away from your city routine."

During this transitional period, Jean, never far from his business, had brought the prominent Lafourche Parish planter, Emile Morvant, into the Levert company as a partner, and in 1896 they had purchased Rienzi Plantation near Thibodaux from the heirs of the Louisiana jurist and artist, Richard Allen. Soon after sealing these two deals, he had traveled to be with Stephanie, to tell her about them.

Later, in their hotel room, he began to describe details of the Rienzi manor house to her; he sensed she was delighted with the picture he painted in words: A Greek revival style with a hint of the Caribbean, wide eaves, tall windows, and high ceilings. Then he read passages from the abstract by lamplight:

> According to legend, Queen Maria Louisa of Spain ordered her personal representative, Juan Ygnacia de Egana, to have the house built as a possible refuge in case her husband, King Charles IV, was defeated in battle in the Napoleonic wars and they had to flee Spain . . . perhaps Rienzi was built for a favorite lady-in-waiting, who desired voluntary exile because of a failed love affair, or perhaps it was built for the queen's suitor, Duke de Rienzi, as a rendezvous for their trysts, or taken from a character in fiction. But the most intriguing and romantic legend was that the queen was so enamored with Duke de Rienzi that she had the plantation and a horse named after him . . . Juan Ygnacia de Egana obtained title to Rienzi about 1800 and lived there on two different occasions for about twenty-five years . . . the house passed through other owners, including Henry S. Thibodaux, founder of the town of Thibodaux, Governor Thomas Bibb of Georgia, and Richard Allen who bought the plantation in 1861 and lived on it for more than thirty years—

"I'm so happy for you, *cher*, in your triumphant purchases of real estate, especially when they include beautiful houses," said Stephanie, interrupting Jean's reading. "Is it as beautiful as St. John?"

"Oh, my dear, they're different. Rienzi has a certain formal delicacy in its details. It has an exquisite double staircase to the upper gallery. There are fine banisters, and they curve," he curved his arms, "like this, like an embrace."

Stephanie clapped her hands. "I hope I can go with you to see this elegant Rienzi!" Then he saw her eyes slip away from his face and look wistfully at the horizon.

"Of course you will, *chèrie*. We will go soon by train to Thibodaux. Rienzi has beautiful gardens that should be at their peak in another month or so."

Stephanie smiled more brightly and looked again into his eyes with the warmth and good cheer that he longed to see. He got up from his chair in their room and stood in front of her, his back to the Gulf.

"Ah! And listen to this! Steph, I have found a fine large house just a few lots east of this hotel that we can rent for the entire summer beginning the first of May. I have rented a buggy for tomorrow to drive us there if you feel well enough . . ."

"Oh, yes, Jean . . ."

"Yes, *chèrie*. It is known as the Judge Brown House. It is owned and in the winter occupied by a Wisconsin judge, Edward Brown. It is not an ordinary-looking house. They rent it out during the hot months. Oh, yes, my dear, I think you will like it. I have not been inside, but from the road I can see that it is surely large enough to accommodate our whole family. And Judge Brown's asking price is not unreasonable—only eighty-five hundred dollars."

"Jean, I believe you are almost as excited over the house as you are over Rienzi. I can hardly wait to see this place."

Silently, Jean rejoiced to see a flush rise in Steph's cheeks. On the Montross porch now, he sat down beside her, and together they watched Jean, Jr., Lawrence, and Robert, half way out the long pier, pulling up heavy crabnets, hand over hand.

"Can you see if they have some crabs?" she asked.

"I can't see what is in the nets from here, but I'm sure they do. There seems to be no end to those big blue crabs, heavy with meat. What do they do with them? Throw them back?"

"Oh, no *cher.* They take them to the hotel kitchen in a washtub. They sell them to the cook for a penny each."

"Very enterprising," said Jean. He smiled at Steph. He and Stephanie sat rocking in the lengthening shadows on the porch, watching their boys, barefoot, their trousers rolled up to their brown knees, their hair whipping about their heads in the strong wind.

"It is getting cool. We must send someone to bring them in to bathe and put on their shoes and stockings," said Stephanie, pulling her hat down around her head.

*   *   *

Next day after lunch in the Montross dining room, where the Leverts maintained a table for eight, Jean and Stephanie stepped into a buggy, and Jean drove them along the shell beach road from the hotel. In less than half a mile, he turned the horse into a drive lined with blooming camellia japonicas and yellow daffodils.

"Whoa," he commanded the horse. Stephanie laid her hand at the base of her neck and stared.

"My goodness, Jean! This is quite a house."

They sat staring at a sprawling gray, single-story house. The front and sides were bound by porches with gingerbread woodwork; on the lawn were mature live oaks streaming with Spanish moss; a shoefly had been built around the trunk of one oak, its structure and lattice sides painted white. The floor was at least eight feet off the ground and was accessed by a staircase that curved around the tree trunk. A dozen people, Jean figured, could gather there and watch the waves and whitecaps comb the shore.

"Isn't this remarkable, Jean? I've never seen such a shoefly. I remember one at the Landry plantation in St. James Parish, years ago, but it was nothing as elaborate as this. Won't the children love having a shoefly!"

Again, Jean felt a surge of hope at Stephanie's enthusiasm. He stepped down from the buggy and looped the reins through a ring in the nose of an iron horse hitching post. Then he helped his wife alight, and they walked slowly up a long, curved brick walk. "I arranged yesterday for us to see the interior." He held her elbow as they climbed wooden steps. A colored man came out and held the screened door open for them to enter. Inside, they stared, then looked at each other. The sitting room occupied the wide center hall that ran the entire depth of the house. Doors to three large connecting rooms along each side were framed in dark, fancy woodwork and decorated with heavy brown cut velour draperies, panels, and fringes. The wallpaper was dark red and deeply embossed in a chrysanthemum pattern.

"This is indeed ornate for a summer home," said Jean. "Just look at the oriental carpets."

"Well, you know we're seeing this style in many of the city mansions at home. I must say it is a bit strange. To us, I mean, with our plantation backgrounds and more . . . ," she paused and smiled, "more simple, conservative tastes. This reminds me of a picture in *Godet's* magazine I saw recently of reception rooms in the White House."

It reminds me of that bordello on Twelfth Avenue in St. Louis. Such a recollection, unbidden, made Jean uncomfortable, but there was a certain similarity. It was those cut velour hangings and those thick tassels ending in balls covered in shiny gold silk and finished in heavy gold fringe. He cleared his throat and smiled tentatively at his wife.

"Do you think you could live with this, dear?"

"Well, let's see the rest of the house before we make a decision." And they walked through several large rooms all of which were ornately decorated. The dining room had a brass chandelier over a long table that bore many curves and curlicues. But Steph said she rather liked it. She called it "odd" and "amusing." The kitchen was large and airy, with tall windows and spacious work areas.

There were two unusually large pantries, each with big iceboxes commensurate in size.

"Fo fish!" the colored man said, smiling, as he opened the back door for them to see a screened porch. "Beside servant quarters, that's extra bedrooms," and he pointed to a separate two-story building behind the house. It was a plainer structure that Jean thought looked ample for housing a number of people. Behind it was a large cistern.

Stephanie sat down on a tufted horsehair sofa near the front door while Jean inspected the servants' quarters. She was tired from the effort to get to the house, then walk through most of it. Jean joined her, then thanked the man, who locked the door behind them.

On the porch, Jean waved a hand toward the Sound. "A breathtaking view, my dear. This property's more than two hundred feet across the beach front and a thousand or so feet deep. There's no telling what it would sell for some day. I don't know how we can say no to Judge Brown's agent."

In the buggy ride back to the Montross Hotel, Jean assured Steph that she could be quite comfortable in Judge Brown's house, adding that he felt the whole family could be happy there during the coming summer months.

"The children can invite their friends. Goodness knows, we can accommodate a crowd. We must bring Vic and Daniels with us, of course. That's the only way. We must get more help for Third Street, to see after you during the week. Perhaps we should buy certain housewares rather than bring all the needed things for such a big house. What do you think, dear?"

Jean smiled at Steph's enthusiasm. "Yes, yes, of course, chèrie. We shall do just as you say. Just promise me you will not try to do anything yourself. You must promise all household responsibilities must rest on the servants and me. We shall have all the help we need to do absolutely everything for you. I want you to enjoy those big rockers on the porch. You can just sit there and look at the water and bathers and sailboats." He pushed his windblown hair off his forehead. "If you wish, we can take you out on the pier. As you can see, it has two decks. Quite unusual. It is one of the longest and finest residential piers I've seen on the Coast, and the platform looks large and comfortable. I'm told it has a good roof, and we can take canvas chairs out there. All the children will enjoy that pier, don't you think?"

"Oh, yes. Yes, indeed." Stephanie sighed and let her head rest on the back of the buggy seat.

CHAPTER 59

JEAN BAPTISTE STOOD on the front gallery of St. John Plantation staring across his eleven hundred acres of sugarcane fields. He heard wind whistling through the branches of live oaks and sky-reaching pines near the Big House. The oaks trailed Spanish moss from their limbs. Long swaying leaves of golden cane stalks dripped dew. Toiling men, women, and animals in shrouded fields loomed in exaggerated heights against the gray sky. Outlines of fresh green limned the cypress treetops.

The sound of cane-cutting began before daybreak in early October, and grew loud and sustained; thirteen-foot stalks crackled as they fell to the ground. Jean thought of the time of year simply as grinding, or what he, Albert, and French-speaking farmers in southwest Louisiana called *roulaissant*. He watched scantily clad field hands slashing stalks with gleaming machete blades—swish, swish accompanying the timpani of mules' hooves on the rich black loam. Swarms of field hands, most carrying hoes, were running inside and outside the cane rows. In the distance he could see cart drivers, barefoot and shirtless, slapping leather reins on the backs of the subborn animals, as they guided their carts, overflowing with stalks, to the wooden sugarhouse located two hundred feet behind the Big House. Negro children were playing and dancing in place around a long line of carts that waited to be unloaded.

When he heard footsteps he turned to see Albert joining him on the gallery. Albert handed him a cup of steaming chicory coffee from Dottee's kitchen.

"Morning, son."

"Good morning, Papa. Up mighty early, aren't you? It's barely daylight."

Leaning against the rail, facing the fields, Jean smiled. "Couldn't sleep. You know how excited I get this time of year . . . farming, grinding, all the details of running a plantation have fascinated me, well, since I was ten years old. You know this. Every season I used to watch your Grandfather Auguste's slave women open furrows for plant seed, ride on his water carts, carry his hoes, do anything to learn about being a planter like your grandfather was."

Jean looked out at the fields; he smelled a storm in the air. An eerie darkness had fallen with unusual swiftness, turning morning into night; low-hanging clouds looked threatening. A rumble of thunder told him the clouds would soon spill their moisture, and in minutes rain was pouring over the eaves and crawling diagonally in streaks down the tall windows of the Big House. Tree limbs snapped and crashed to the ground, frightening him. He and Albert noticed birds of many species scurrying for safe roosts. Thinking it might herald the approach of a hurricane, Jean braced his hands against the gallery rail.

"I don't like the looks of this storm, Albert. It came up too fast. I can't stand the thought of another bad storm." He gulped his coffee and set it on the rail, then pushed his thick brown hair off his forehead. His manner showed strain. "I think we should call all the hands in from the fields and herd the livestock into the big barn for safe cover. Let's get Dottee and the other servants to close the windows and shutters and bolt all the outside doors."

Albert could only say, "For your sake, Papa, I just pray to God this is nothing more than a late-summer thunderstorm."

Jean remained silent for a long time. Now, sitting in one of the tall rockers lined up on the gallery, he gazed blankly at the nurtured fields. He tried to grasp all the implications of what could happen if another hurricane were to strike. Finally he said, "God, Albert, I can't afford another failed crop, not after all the failures we've had recently and the hard freeze that ruined us and our neighbors two years ago.

Unless this '97 crop is a decent one and the selling prices are good, we could . . ." He couldn't complete the thought; his eyebrows went up. "Your grandfather taught me everything I know about growing cane. I've dreamed of teaching you and your brothers what I know."

Jean told Albert he had always prided himself on being able to make do in the worst of times, but if this was another hurricane coming—"I just don't know, son . . ." He gave a deep sigh and looked down at his riding boots, his eyes and mind out of focus, as if he were in a fog. Then he added, "Another storm could ruin me, us. Son, I'm almost sixty years old."

Jean knew the white-columned house had survived twenty-two hurricanes, including severe ones in '93 and '95. But now he feared wind gusts, which he figured to be sixty miles an hour, might shake the house from its foundation. Although the gallery columns had iron cores, each anchored to heavy stones below the ground, he and Albert were alarmed, until finally, around midmorning, the gusts subsided.

As he drank from a fourth cup of coffee, he noticed the clouds breaking up and moving away, the rain slacking, the sun beginning to peek through the clouds. He leaned back in the rocker, looking as if a concealed smile were to push away the tension on his face. The storm front flew on eastward.

"Oh, thank God! Thank God that damned storm is moving out of here." Jean's mouth held a hint of a grin, now; there was a sparkle in his eyes. He glanced from Albert's face to the cane fields, shaking his head with the ardor of a schoolboy.

Jean Baptiste had arrived at St. John the evening before. He had planned only a brief crop inspection with Albert; in two days Albert would make the customary move into the sleeping room at the sugarhouse for grinding. Both men had predicted that the '97 crop would be better than the year before, when about two hundred and fifty thousand tons of sugar, or about five million pounds, had been produced in Louisiana. They knew favorable weather conditions— moderate rain, dryness during the last weeks of September and early October—had hastened ripening and added to sugar content.

Now this storm, thought Jean, as he stood with Albert atop the widow's walk to survey the damage. *Goddamit, I'm tired of having to rebuild, tired of the loss of healthy crops, of the enormous monetary losses—tired of everything associated with these goddamn storms, no matter if wind gusts are sixty miles an hour or a hundred miles an hour.* "I was so upset and frustrated after the '93 and '95 hurricanes that I seriously considered selling . . ."

Albert responded before his father finished: "I hope you never will sell St. John, Papa. I pray you never will."

Jean drained his coffee cup of the dark, strong brew and gazed heavenward, as if saying a prayer, before descending the widow's walk and mounting to ride out with his son to check the extent of the damage. Jean looked keenly at Albert. He realized he had achieved at least part of his dream; perhaps the most important part.

* * *

Jean left the plantation early next morning, trusting that Albert could direct the start of cleanup. He feared the costs he faced and the loss of this most promising crop. But he needed to take care of several important business matters in New Orleans before he caught the L&N for the Mississippi Coast with most of his family.

He arrived in New Orleans too late to see Stephanie. He let himself in at Third Street as quietly as possible. He set his bags on the floor of his office and walked back to the dining room where Vic brought him a hot plate of baked red snapper.

"Vic," he said, placing a napkin across his lap, "I see you have made up my bed in the office. Thank you. Now tell me about *Madame*. How is she doing?"

"Well, she look about same. Dr. Gons'lin, he come yest'day. We told him we take her back to the Coast, and he say good, good. He say air here just too much, not good. Say it all right to take the chilren long as I'm there to keep em in line."

"Tell me, how does she look to you? Any problems with the children?"

"She look very well. Never as good in New Orleans as on the Coast. Tires easy, you know. She always so much better when you round, Mister Jean. Chilren fine. You know, since Mister Freddy come home from college at Spring Hill, he a big help to me and Daniels." She took a deep breath. "I have everybody ready to go to Biloxi when you ready. That is where we goin this time, ain't it?"

"Yes, I have a nice house. But we couldn't go anywhere without you, Vic. By the way, how are my chickens?"

"They doin fine, Mister Jean. Layin good. Got five fine eggs today. Daniels keep em fed, watered. Rake up fertilizer yest'day, and put it in the rose bed. Best thing for roses, you know."

"Good."

Vic disappeared through the swinging door. Jean looked over the evening paper as he finished a glass of tea and a slice of coconut cake.

* * *

The following night Jean came upon three of his children sitting together in the dim parlor. He hadn't intended to eavesdrop, but something made him stop. Beatrice sat with her arm around nine-year-old Robert on the sofa. "I think you are right, Robert," she was saying, "to say we hardly ever see her anymore."

Freddy sat on the edge of the chair nearest the sofa. "Of course we can't see much of her. You both know Dr. Gonsoulin's orders. Mother must be quiet—very quiet—if she is to recover."

"What does he mean, if?" said Robert, lifting frightened eyes to Bea's face; she had dimples and a round nose.

"What he says is true, Robert. She cannot deal with any sort of trouble. It could cause her heart to fail. Any of us could cause it without meaning to."

Jean was about to go in and offer further explanation to Robert when the child replied to his sister. "What about Papa? He goes in to see her whenever he wants to."

"Yes, when he's here, but he's hardly ever here," said Bea, smoothing her hair tied back in a bun.

Freddy jumped up, glaring at his sister with steely eyes, his cheeks flushed. "Father is great. And Mother's awfully proud of him."

Bea shrugged. "That's where I believe you could be wrong, Freddy. Papa may be at the bottom of Mama's illness. I think the strain and loneliness of being left here without him so long and so often have taken a toll on her. She has needed him so many times when he was out gallivanting around the country, buying and trading. I know Mathilde believes this and I think Stephanie Marie does, too."

"Beatrice, you should be ashamed of yourself. Papa loves Mama with all his heart. And do you ever consider that you are a very well-off girl because of Papa's hard work? Day and night he works to give us all everything . . ."

"Oh, stop it, Freddy, Papa was rich enough years ago. There's no telling what all he owns."

Robert interrupted. "I don't know about all this. I just want to see my Mama. So do Ella and Stella. They are tired of being told they can't go in Mama's room. They say she's not even in there anymore . . ."

"That's ridiculous, Robert," said Bea. "She came down to lunch yesterday. You just weren't here to see her."

Jean turned away, silent and saddened by what he had heard. He felt nettled. He had no idea that his children would speak so disrespectfully about him. He could not imagine him or Augie and Amédèe having such a conversation about their father. Times had changed, but Beatrice's words disturbed him. Of course, the girl did not know what she was talking about. She had not the faintest notion of what it took to run a household like this. And Mathilde? Where was Stephanie Marie?—in Paris with her golden harp, studying with possibly the finest teacher of that instrument in the world. He yawned and turned toward his office.

Getting comfortable on the sofa, he turned his thoughts to Stephanie and how she always improved in the salty air of the Mississippi Gulf Coast. He imagined her out on a pier surrounded by all her children, basking in the sunshine, her cheeks ruddy. It was his last thought before he wakened to the aroma of Vic's rich black coffee.

CHAPTER 60

THE BUSY PLANTER-BROKER returned to St. John Plantation three times during the weeks following the severe thunderstorm. It was difficult for him to assess the extent of damage just as the crippled grinding season got underway. But with Ramon Boudreau and Albert, Jean concluded on the third trip that his losses were not so devastating as they first appeared. On that last night he went out to the sugarhouse and gave Albert some assurance. "I shall leave very early in the morning. Your buggy will be back here by midmorning." They shook hands and said goodnight.

Jean stopped by Hotel Bienvenu on the town square before the Southern Pacific train arrived in St. Martinville. It was not unusual for him to go into the hotel barroom to wait for the train, conduct some business, or to socialize with a client or fellow planter over a whiskey. On this occasion, he needed something to ease his mind as it settled down following his most recent worries. He found this country bar with its multicolored stained-glass windows to be something of a retreat, an interesting change from the sophisticated restaurant bars of New Orleans. He removed his coat and loosened his tie, a rarity for him.

Seated at a corner table near the bar, the resilient Jean did some deep breathing and began, with relief, to think positively again. He was pleased with the way his partnership with Emile Morvant was developing; they had bought more land adjacent to Rienzi Plantation and planted two hundred additional acres of cane. Also, whatever the daily situations with his family, he felt assured about the effects of the Gulf Coast on Stephanie. Dr. Gonsoulin warned him not to expect miracles, but the doctor agreed that Stephanie was a different patient in what he called the "bracing atmosphere of the beach."

The last thing Jean expected in this small, dimly lighted barroom was a fight. But he heard rising voices, and there emerging from a far corner in angry argument were the prominent St. Martinville sugar grower George Banker and Claude LeConte, St. Martinville's leading banker. Jean guessed the source of their argument—Banker was threatened with losing his plantation to LeConte, who held his mortgage.

After the first serious blow was thrown—by LeConte, who had been insulted—Jean stood up and called to Angelique, the buxom barmaid, "Angelique! Serve these gentlemen a glass of your best whiskey!" With a passionate look, Angelique winked and turned to Emile Webre, owner and bartender, who filled two shot glasses with redgold liquor and slid them across the bar toward Angelique. She held high one glass and began to flirt outrageously with both of the irate men. Her appeal worked, Jean saw, and Banker and LeConte lowered their fists and turned to the bar and the free drinks. Jean joined them and asked for a drink for himself. He raised his glass toward the men and then to blonde, green-eyed Angelique. The two men thanked Jean civilly, but LeConte excused himself after downing the whiskey.

"Well, Mr. Banker, the last time I saw you was in this very bar, and you mentioned then that LeConte was threatening you. Are you still having problems with the bank?"

The plump, balding planter banged his glass down on the table, startling Jean. Banker was in his early forties, Jean figured. He recalled that he rarely discussed his personal affairs, especially business. "That bastard foreclosed on me this morning. Everything I own will be auctioned off. The sheriff's already notified me. Even my wife's beautiful piano that came down the Mississippi on a raft before the war." Banker's voice broke.

"Listen, I've been in your position myself. I know well the feeling. One day you're high because some investment you've made works out. The next day you're contemplating doing yourself in or selling out because a hurricane ruins your dreams of profit and riches."

After finishing his drink, Banker crushed the brim of his felt hat and put it on his head. "Well, Mr. Levert, I must be going. Thanks for your concern and the drink."

Jean Baptiste smelled blood. Banker Plantation's twelve hundred acres abutted on the front border of St. John Plantation, separated by a curvy dirt road. He adjusted his tie and put on his coat. Laying a bill on the bar, he winked at Angelique.

"I'll see you soon, *Mademoiselle*."

"But *M'sieu*, you did not finish your dreenk!" giggled Angelique in her exaggerated Cajun accent.

"I don't need it, *ma chèrie*." Jean hurried to board the train, which was blowing clouds of white steam from its great engine into the November air.

*   *   *

"Ladies and gentlemen," the swarthy man shouted, "I've got some things, quite elegant things that will interest every one of you." The auctioneer pointed toward the corner of the stage in the St. Martinville auction hall, his shirt dripping sweat in the midmorning heat and humidity. "This exquisite square piano is in splendid condition. Look at the carving. Look at the inlay, the excellent condition of these pure ivory keys! It's the kind of piano that music-minded people would like to see in their parlor. You would be partial to the fine tones of this instrument, which was only recently tuned to perfect pitch."

A well-dressed man raised a hand barely visible, his gray moustache twitching ever so slightly. He was one of fifty or sixty people standing in a clump near the stage.

"I have four hundred," barked the broad-shouldered auctioneer. "Do I hear four-fifty? Five hundred? Six hundred?" He raised the price until the gentleman who had opened the bidding offered seven-fifty.

"Sold to the gentleman. I guarantee this mahogany Victorian glass-door armoire. Behold this incredible English walnut four-poster . . . a dream for *madame's* boudoir . . ."

The well-dressed gentleman in a gray suit again made his discreet gesture for the required number of times. "Sold to the gentleman . . . Thank you, sir! We will now pause an hour for lunch." Typical of a small group of itinerants known in their argot as a *courtier de commerce*, the smooth-talking auctioneer sold or acted as agent for everything in stores or doorways, on street corners, in town halls. "We shall convene promptly at two o'clock at the plantation house as directed on your paper."

Promptly at two, the chanting auctioneer began: "And now, ladies and gentlemen, the former owner of this plantation house required me to satisfy myself that every buyer is financially responsible. I plan to do that with the largest offering of this auction, this single-story cottage that once housed the pieces sold today."

He announced that the first bidder to show him at least one-half of the purchase price, in cash, with the balance, if any, at one year's credit, would get the pretty, well-cared-for house located at the end of Oak and Pine Alley east of St. Martinville. He then gave a detailed description of the interior . . . "I now have four thousand, six hundred."

The well-dressed bidder in gray suit and starched collar barely nodded his head.

"Thank you, sir, for your generous bid. Do I hear four thousand, eight hundred? . . . Going once, going twice? The single-level house is yours, sir."

In two hours, several weeks after the frightful storm, Jean had purchased not only the charming four-bedroom house known as Banker Plantation, but the choicest pieces of its furnishings for about six thousand dollars. All twelve hundred acres of the estate. He was not sure what he would do with that piano, but he could see Stephanie Marie's harp positioned beside it.

*   *   *

"Oh, afternoon, Papa, you startled me," said Albert. He was reading an illustrated magazine dedicated to sugarhouse lamps, lanterns, and other accessories when Jean entered the tiny, dingy room at the sugarhouse where Albert lived during grinding, without knocking. Jean had decided to share with his son his excitement about Banker Plantation before he returned to the City later that afternoon.

Tired and perspiring, Jean removed his gray suit coat and tried to get comfortable on Albert's cot of rusty iron springs. He noticed the wall beside him was marked with the blood of squashed mosquitoes. Overalls, a plaid flannel shirt, and a wide-brimmed planter's hat hung in a row on hooks above the cot. An ashtray filled with cigarette ashes was on the bedside table.

"You know, son, it's hard to explain how one man's failure can be another man's triumph," referring to George Banker's bad luck growing cane.

Albert did not reply. Instead, he thrust a cigarette between his lips, his lips hardened around the tiny protrusion, and he inhaled, emitting a deep hacking cough that reddened his face.

Nerves, perhaps Albert's nervous about getting the rest of the '97 crop to market . . . he never smokes in front of me, out of respect . . . seems his asthma is getting worse.

And Jean wondered what the brandy he smelled on Albert's breath meant to his son.

I could be setting up our household for an indefinite stay, away from Third Street at my newly purchased summer home on the Mississippi Gulf Coast, maybe for the rest of Stephanie's life. I'll never forget the awful, sinking feeling I had when Dr. Gonsoulin first suggested that a change of scenery for Steph might be the only remedy—away from the noise, open canals, and routine of the City to the quiet life and clean air of a smaller town. The important thing now is I believe I've provided Steph with an environment—the new summer home—as close to what the doctor had ordered, and I feel assured about the effects of the Gulf Coast on her health. Seeing a sparkle in her eyes and a flush rise in her cheeks gives me such a great lift, however short-lived; her health seems to improve in the salty air. Yet, I will never stop worrying about her. I might be rich and powerful with a lot of money but I really can do nothing to save my beloved wife.

Jean Baptiste Levert
1898

CHAPTER 61

DURING THE CHILDREN'S Easter holidays, Jean, Freddy, Jean, Jr., and Daniels proceeded to the large covered passenger station at the foot of Canal Street to catch the L&N train. It was the same train that carried the crates and boxes of the Leverts' effects, possessions Jean had decided the family needed to set up their household in regular fashion indefinitely at his newly purchased summer home in Biloxi, Mississippi.

Jean knew it was more than the usual departure for a few weeks from Third Street, for he was taking Stephanie to the Coast for an indeterminate stay, maybe for the rest of her life. He knew Dr. Gonsoulin would have it that way; he was putting them in touch with Dr. George Martens, an old classmate of his at Tulane Medical School and heart specialist whose office was in Biloxi. So Jean and Stephanie expected a visit from Dr. Martens after she was moved in.

Jean often thought that his life had progressed from problem to problem, each resolved by himself just in time to be succeeded by a new one. St. John's troubled grinding season and his business for the present settled, Jean had turned all his attention to the family's move to the Gulf Coast.

To Jean the trip to Biloxi was always slow: The train passed the Old French Market and U.S. Mint after leaving the depot, taking hours to chug through low swamps that encircled the Crescent City before it reached Chef Menteur. When the engineer opened the throttle, the train skimmed over undulating, polished rails at almost sixty miles an hour, frightening birds from their perches on telegraph wires and sending them scuttling for cover. Then the L&N took a more eastward turn toward the narrow Rigolets strait and onto English Lookout, where the Pearl River emptied into the Mississippi Sound, its rippling surface now dotted with white sailboats and dingier sails of commercial ships. After several more stops, the train arrived at Bay St. Louis, crossed the Bay of St. Louis bridge to Pass Christian, passed through Long Beach, and finally came to Biloxi.

Jean ordered Freddy and Jean, Jr., with help from Vic and Daniels, to set up Biloxi house for occupancy. An extensive undertaking, he knew. But they succeeded in filling cabinets and closets with all the transported goods. Vic lost count of the sheets and counterpanes she put on beds. Daniels visited the shops and markets, stocked the pantries.

Jean had purchased a new carriage and a pair of roans, which were ready to meet the L&N upon the family's arrival. And so Daniels drove them up the shell drive near dark on a chilly Monday evening. Jean, who had been standing on the front porch with Freddy and Junior watching for them, walked rapidly to the carriage. Stephanie, Stephanie Marie, Beatrice, Lawrence, Robert, Ella, and Stella, all holding small valises, were in it. Their trunks and large pieces of luggage were delivered by wagon at 8 o'clock the following morning. By 10 o'clock all the children except Stephanie Marie were on the two-story Levert pier. Freddy, a good swimmer, took charge, at his father's insistence. Vic and Daniels quickly set the household in motion, and they got Jean's permission to hire additional help.

On Wednesday at 10 o'clock, Dr. Martens, armed with a complete file on Stephanie given to him by Dr. Gonsoulin, called on Jean's wife. After a few amenities with Jean, the doctor examined Stephanie, taking her blood pressure and pulse rate, looking into her throat and ears, listening to her heart. Jean was impressed by his grave but pleasant manner, but he had no new information. He prescribed the same powders ordered by Dr. Gonsoulin. He assured Jean that he was available day and night, not only for Mrs. Levert, but for the entire family.

A short, doughy man with a pale complexion, Dr. Martens put on his hat and said, "Mr. Levert, there is no doubt that your wife has a seriously enlarged heart. But let her do what she feels like doing. I do not think her limited energy will allow her to overdo. Send for me when you need me. Meantime, I will drop in for a brief chat with her once a week." He nodded politely to Stephanie Marie, who stood beside her father. Then he stepped off the porch, walked to his black buggy where he deposited his medical case on the seat, and unhitched his horse from the post. He turned the buggy around and shook the reins over the horse's rump, the wheels crunching on the shell drive. For Jean, confidence in Steph's doctor was important, and he felt very well about Dr. Martens.

*   *   *

On the following Sunday morning, Jean sat in the parlor, holding his hat and cane, waiting for Stephanie and the children to finish dressing for church. He marveled at how smoothly a large household had been transported, in action so to speak, from one city to another. A light breeze off the water swept through the front screened doors and through the wide center hall dividing the house down its middle front to back. He called it the sitting room. But Jean looked about and realized that someone must redecorate it. The dark, heavy hangings depressed him, and so did the furniture. He wondered how the great room would look with all the woodwork painted white or pale gray and the wallpaper replaced by something light-colored. Wouldn't the furniture be better in wicker or some cheerful upholstery. After all this was a vacation home, not a mausoleum. Perhaps Stephanie Marie, recently returned from Paris, could take on that responsibility.

Tomorrow he planned to leave early for New Orleans to board the Illinois Central for a two-week trip to St. Louis and Chicago. He hoped to find good prices on a long list of tools and supplies needed on all his plantations. And he needed to meet with brokers and sugar buyers. These were dealings he had always done in person; he knew Steph understood.

Ah, here they were, dressed in their best, the younger boys pulling at their ties, the girls carefully lifting their skirts above their slippers.

"You look very lovely, today, my dear," Jean said to Stephanie. She wore a beautiful dress, a rust-colored taffeta trimmed in matching velvet piping, with a large hat to match. He thought her color was not good. Perhaps that would improve when the weather got warmer and she could go out on the pier and sit in the sun. She smiled at him and took his arm.

The boys stood aside while Jean assisted their mother into her seat in the four-wheel, two-horse barouche. Then the girls climbed aboard, and the boys squeezed in where they could. Jean sat on the driver's box with Daniels.

"I think the boys can begin walking to church, it isn't far," Jean muttered to Daniels.

"They probably be glad to. It ain't far, Mister Levert. All boys like to run and cut up."

"I'll instruct them to walk home today. Now, if they come out protesting, just tell them they must do what their father said. I don't want any argument."

Daniels' face split into a wide conspiratorial smile. "I tell em, Mister Levert." And he did. By the time Jean and Stephanie walked up the aisle and out the door, their sons were on their way home, walking along the land side of the beach road.

Jean and Steph had chosen for regular Sunday Mass a small white frame building known as the Nativity of BVM (Blessed Virgin Mary) church. Its age, nearly sixty, its smallness, and location in downtown Biloxi all appealed to their sense of history, love of modesty, simplicity in religious matters. And they liked Father Bernard Tormey, an Irish priest whose long, rambling sermons were not too stirring, not likely to disturb one's peace of mind. Yet, they were certain of the priest's sense of purpose and his great faith, and these qualities could be quite comforting.

The priest stopped them at the door after Mass. "One moment, please, Mr. Levert. I want you and Mrs. Levert to meet someone."

Jean and Stephanie stood aside, somewhat puzzled, as the first of the small congregation shook hands with Father Tormey.

As they waited, Jean noticed a woman standing at the foot of the short steps. She seemed to be waiting for someone. She was very pretty and blonde. As was his wont, he stood for a brief moment summing her up: Mature but youthful looking—full bosomed, straight shoulders, full lips, and a slimness that he likened to the sleek yachts anchored in the Sound—under layers of fabrics that cloaked her body. Yes, she was a good-looking young woman with a chin that told a great deal about her determination, and she carried herself with a sense of pride that would have been cockiness in one less graceful. He saw that Stephanie, too, was studying her. Here was Father, now taking their elbows, and ushering them down the wood steps, right into this lovely girl's face.

"Mr. and Mrs. Levert, allow me to present Mrs. Lila Beaugez. Miss Lila, I want you to meet the Leverts. They have bought the Judge Brown house, and we hope to count them among our parishioners." Jean could tell that Stephanie was instantly charmed by Lila Beaugez, who was about ten years younger than she. The two women clasped hands and smiled at each other like old friends reunited. Jean bowed politely. She returned his courtesy with a wide smile, revealing white teeth and blue eyes bright with cordiality. Jean was fascinated, to say the least. He swallowed and tried not to look enchanted.

Father Tormey waved to the last few worshipers leaving the church. "Well, sir," he said, turning to Jean, "this is a case when introductions seem scarcely needed. The ladies obviously are charmed with each other." He turned his back to them. "I had a reason for securing this introduction. Miss Lila is a trained nurse. Not only is she in possession of an admirable disposition, but she is well informed on medical matters. You mentioned to me that you were thinking of seeking a helpful companion to Mrs. Levert, and it occurred to me that you might want to interview the lady. Let me say that I have not mentioned this to Mrs. Beaugez."

"This could be fortuitous, Father. Look at them. They seem already to be acquainted. Is Mrs. Beaugez married?"

"She is a widow. She and her late husband come from fishing families on the Coast, people who emigrated to this area long ago. I know of nothing negative about her character or her personality. She is a member of this church in good standing."

"Thank you very much, Father. I will speak to Mrs. Levert about this, and I will let you know if we make a decision to interview Mrs. Beaugez. By the way, may I ask how old she is? And does she have children?"

"Of course, she is thirty-seven years of age, and she has never had children."

"Excellent. I am about to leave for points north for two weeks. You will hear from me promptly upon my return."

Jean lifted his hat and bade Lila Beaugez farewell as he took Stephanie's arm. "Daniels is waiting for us," he said to his wife.

"I think we made a good choice in this church, *cher*. The people are very nice, and I've said before, Father Tormey is a good priest."

"I fully agree."

Then, as they neared their home, Jean said, "How are you feeling, *ma chèrie?*"

"I am short of breath," she admitted, a small gasp escaping from her throat.

"Are you all right, Steph?"

"Yes, I think so."

Jean looked at her. Her face had taken on that worrisome gray color. Daniels turned the horses into the driveway. Soon, Jean gently assisted Stephanie. They could not hurry, but he took her toward their bedroom where she had a powder that usually helped with these symptoms. Stephanie Marie had hurried ahead to get the powder and water ready for her mother. Jean left the room while their daughter helped Stephanie out of her corset and other clothing so she could lie down in comfort.

When Jean went back into the room, she put her hand out to him, and as he held it, she smiled at him. "I'm fine now, *cher*. Please don't worry."

But he did worry, and he never stopped worrying. *I am a powerful man with a great deal of money, but I can do nothing to save my beloved wife.*

Chapter 62

JEAN LIKED TO think of the Mississippi Sound, with the newly risen sun reflected in glittering splinters, as the sea. His expansive view of the horizon from the front porch of his new house on Front Beach Drive in Biloxi seemed infinite. Occupying such a home affected him differently from any others that he owned, and he knew it was partly due to this euphoric sense of limitlessness he experienced when he turned his gaze over the water. He had not, so far, lived through a hurricane here, or even a bad storm, only squalls that came up in the afternoon in great billowing clouds low over the water, and quickly exhausted themselves without harm to people or their property.

A deeper satisfaction, of course, came from knowing he was providing his unwell wife with an environment as near to what the doctor had ordered as he knew how. Stephanie seemed happy here and functioned here more normally than she was able to in New Orleans. The children were happier, Jean concluded, because she was available to them here in a way that apparently was impossible at Third Street. But he and Stephanie agreed the children must continue their educations in the Biloxi schools while on the Coast. What was it? He couldn't say for sure, but he was willing to agree with Dr. Gonsoulin that the air on the Coast was different. Perhaps the easygoing days in the sprawling house provided Stephanie with a more relaxed state of mind, thus, easing the body, specifically the heart. His own fears for her eased somewhat in Biloxi.

Jean understood that Vic and Daniels made it possible for him to stay anchored to his business in New Orleans and to spend every moment possible in Biloxi with his wife. Jean had found a girl to assist Vic, an ignorant, untrained creature who had come from the piney woods of upstate Mississippi. Ivory had behaved like a wild thing, who could scarcely speak understandably, but Vic was training her, and already the girl was dusting the entire house, polishing silver, and doing other chores. Daniels, too, had found a boy to do most of the yard work. Jean expected Willie to keep the enormous front lawn well tended, and behind the house a barn and storerooms to be maintained. The servants had arranged comfortable living quarters for themselves in rooms behind the kitchen, and after Vic was convinced Ivory was a satisfactory servant, she fixed a room for her there.

Jean turned as Vic came out onto the porch with a large cup of coffee and set it on a table by his rocker. He nodded thanks and put his finger through the cup handle, his gaze still on the water— the sea. The big house had most of its beds filled for the weekend. And though all guests were still sleeping, he looked forward to his friend Colonel William Behan appearing on the porch. The Colonel, his wife, and their daughter Bessie were guests until Monday afternoon.

Elizabeth Behan was a close friend of Stephanie's, the friend among all Steph knew in New Orleans who seemed to understand best how to maintain a normal relationship with a seriously ill woman. Elizabeth had wit and intellect, she amused Stephanie, and knew when and how to stop a conversation or a walk or a drive before Stephanie became tired and short of breath. Of course, Jean was fond of William Behan, whom he still called Colonel. Bessie, whose marriage engagement had been announced to New Orleans Society, was Stephanie Marie's best friend from their early childhood.

Jean realized such favored house guests imposed no stress on Stephanie, for the ever competent Vic and Daniels could have run a small hotel with no more help than Ivory and Willie. Whatever marvels Vic accomplished in her domestic management, her

primary concern was for *Madame Levert's* welfare. No card game
in the sitting room ever got noisy enough to be heard in the master
bedroom on the far side of the house; and no running, shouting
children were allowed to play on that side of the yard. There was
more than enough room elsewhere. Guests of whatever age learned
the ground rules of behavior at the beach house, and they learned
them from Vic. So, the children's young New Orleans friends were
welcomed in Biloxi; they had a wide sandy beach on which to
run out their energies and a whole Mississippi Sound in which to
swim, go boating, fish, and crab.

Provisions for a houseful of people could have come from
Mars. Stephanie never put on an apron; she'd never known what
it was like to cook and serve meals or perform the myriad chores
called for in usual housekeeping. Both Jean and Stephanie took
servants for granted. Considering his hectic life, Jean lived a very
good life. Jean thought vaguely of all these things as he watched
blue jays bickering and chasing each other through a large oak; he
clapped his hands in delight. Being born and reared on sugar
plantations, the great racket they made from dawn to dusk never
bothered him and Stephanie.

Jean saw Willie coming up the drive, carrying the *Biloxi Herald*.
He walked down to meet the gangly boy, who somehow reminded
him of his boyhood friend Isaac at Golden Ridge.

"Good morning, Willie."

"Good morning, Mister Lavare." He handed over the dewy
newspaper.

"Willie, I want you to do something for me before Daniels
gets you lined up for the day. Gather up all the folding chairs you
can carry and take them out to the end of the pier for me. How
many do you think you can carry in one trip?"

"Oh, they light, Mister Lavare. 'Bout six, I reckon. But I make
two trips. Daniels ain't that rushed. I done cleaned gutters and
swept out here yest'day."

"Good. We've got a houseful in there for the weekend. We'll
need a lot of chairs." He stroked his moustache as he watched the
boy lope off toward the porch.

Willie hurried back past Jean, the wood frames of lawn chairs hanging over his arms. Jean watched in amusement as Willie lifted his knees high as he ran gingerly across the shell road in front of the house, over a broad grassy area laden with sharp stickers, to the sandy beach, and up the steps onto the pier. The soles of his feet must be tough as whitleather.

Jean followed Willie out onto the pier. He walked slowly, his hands clasped behind him. He paused and took out his watch. Eight o'clock. He replaced the watch and stood looking at the curving coastline, which appeared softly scalloped with soft oak treetops. It was, he reasoned, foolish to expect his city guests to rise with the sun when they had come to the beach for a long restful weekend. But he was impatient to see Colonel Behan.

Jean wondered when Stephanie Marie might marry. She was twenty-two, two years older than Bessie Behan, and there were young swains of whom he was vaguely aware among her friends. But he had never heard her speak of any one young man, being steadfastly attached to her mother, and since Stephanie's health had become a serious issue, more vigilant than ever, eager to be by her mother's side.

The Behans would no doubt be having a grandchild after a year or two. Mathilde had been married for two years, but there had been no suggestion yet that she might be expecting. Albert probably would be his first child to bring home a grandchild. He was courting a girl from a prominent family in New Iberia. *This sort of thing would bring more happiness to Steph.* He shook his head. *Stephanie, a grandmother! It seems only . . .* The frightening idea suddenly struck him that she might lose her life before she could ever know that joy. He called to Willie:

"That looks nice, Willie. Later, bring out some more chairs, but no hurry. Go on in and report to Daniels. In fact, ask Vic for another cup of coffee for me."

Jean sat down, not on a canvas chair, but on one of the long benches that bordered three sides of the pier's lower deck. He looked down into the dark green skiff moored to the piling beneath him, its oars crossed primly over the middle seat. He watched the boat bob gently, its bow bumping the wet black creosote post. Whatever else was afoot, he must not falter in his vigilant provision for Stephanie. What else could he do? Gonsoulin was noncommittal except to urge Jean to keep her in Biloxi. One time he was encouraging and the next his implications were more negative. Jean's state of anxiety was now constant. One thing he must do was talk to that attractive young woman Father Tormey had introduced them to at Nativity church several weeks before. He had suggested to Stephanie that he arranged for her to act as companion to Stephanie while he was occupied with business in New Orleans and other distant places, and Stephanie seemed pleased. He discussed it with Father Tormey to see if the priest for any reason thought it was not a good idea. Stephanie had sent her a note of invitation, and it had been returned with an exuberant, "I accept with pleasure!" Jean had looked at the note in Stephanie's hand and smiled to himself. *Lila was charming, all right.* He recalled how shapely she was from the rear and with only a hint of a bustle.

Jean had hoped Albert could come over for the party for family and friends, but he declined, stating business at St. John as the reason. Jean had also invited the Morvants but they had to attend the christening of a grandchild and could not come. We have enough, he thought.

Jean heard the peculiar sound of steps on boards over the water. He turned around and saw Colonel Behan approaching with a light step. Jean realized he had never seen the usually formally attired war hero without a tie, in such relaxed dress.

"Colonel! Good morning! Come on out and join me. I have just sent for coffee." Jean stood and held out his hand.

"Senator! I just met your boy headed out here with a steaming cup for you, and I sent him back for another for me! How bracing this air is!" The two friends shook hands.

Colonel Behan walked about the platform, hands in his trouser pockets, looking out at the water, examining the appointments of the pier, and breathing deeply of the salt air. He twirled his long handlebar moustache, now snow white.

"I must say, Jean, this is a fine way to greet a beautiful morning. I can imagine your quitting the dirty city and retiring to all this."

Jean smiled and raised his eyebrows. "It's very nice, and I believe it will become more and more important to us as a home. Stephanie and I are very settled in here."

Willie came with a tray holding two cups of black coffee.

"You gentlemens don't want no cream o' sugar?"

"Where'd this boy come from, Jean? Sugar and cream, boy? We're from New Orleans. We drink our coffee black and hot. Except for *café au lait* for breakfast." Behan joked good-naturedly with Willie, lifting the cup and saucer from the small tray.

"Thank you, Willie." Jean took his cup.

As Willie headed for shore, Colonel Behan remarked, "These Negro boys have come a long way from their Reconstruction rags. Look at this boy. He's too young to know, though."

The men sipped hot coffee, quietly enjoying each other's company in a setting far different from the usual French Quarter restaurants of New Orleans. Both seemed to savor the pleasure.

"Jean, I can't imagine a more satisfactory place for you and your dear Stephanie than this marvelous summer home. Just look at it. The house is very large, the play area for the children almost unlimited, and this pier! What could you do to improve it? Surely nothing. You know, I'm tempted to look for a place for us over here. Elizabeth loves it."

Jean relaxed in his chair. "I wish you would, Colonel. There is no comparison between my wife's condition here and in New Orleans. She relaxes here. Just look at those whitecaps! I can sit here all day watching the rhythmic motion. The seafood in our kitchen is fresh daily, caught right in our front yard, so to speak."

The waters of the Sound made soft lapping sounds on the pilings beneath the men as they chatted, a brisk breeze cooling their sun-warmed faces.

"Well, if that breakfast Vic served me just now was a sample of your front yard, you have the finest menu in the South. Such a crab omelet!" The Colonel pulled his straw hat down to shade his blue eyes. "You know, Jean, I feel that these years since Reconstruction troubles have been filled with blessings for you. I mean, beyond Stephanie's illness, which is certainly the major concern of you and your children, you have made a great place for yourself financially and in every other way. My God, man, you came to New Orleans fresh from the plantation, a recent prisoner of war, not thirty years old. You set off on your career with confidence and you've never faltered."

Jean looked at his friend and listened to his assessment in some wonder. "It's true, Jean. I'd be interested to know what your real estate holdings amount to. How many sugar plantations do you now own?" Colonel Behan leaned forward, resting his elbows on his knees. "Can you name them?"

Jean smiled, realizing that he probably could not; he owned too much now. But he said, "I can certainly tell you what sugar plantations I own now. You know that I sold my third interest in Golden Ridge, Willow Glen, St. Delphine, and St. Mary's to my brothers, and they operate independent of me. I used those proceeds to buy some property across from my office at Baronne and Poydras streets." He shrugged, then looked out at Deer Island. "Not a bad move at all." He told the Colonel already some of the apartments on Baronne were bringing quite handsome revenues.

"But let's see, Colonel, I own St. John, of course, and Chrétien; they were part of the payment when Bush and I foreclosed on General DeClouet. There's Davis down in St. Charles Parish; Catahoula, which I bought with Colonel Bush in '82; Rienzi over at Thibodaux, which I own with my partner Morvant. He and his family live there, and I think I will probably buy him out one day. That is *entre nous*, however." Then he told him about his latest prize, Banker, which bordered on St. John. Oh, yes, and two other plantations in St. Martin Parish, which he had named Stephanie and Stella for his wife and daughters. "There're close to St. John. I believe those are all the plantations at this time."

"But in the city you also have acquired such valuable property . . ."

"Yes, and I probably cannot name all of it. There's my home on Third Street, and I have bought up all the property in that block, all but one with improvements; some lots facing Third and St. Charles, and lots with houses on Fourth, directly behind my home." He said he bought a nice parcel of lots on Henry Clay Avenue, which he intended to hold awhile. "And the Garden District as an investment area, Colonel, is not going any way but up."

"I agree," said Behan, shaking his head. The Behan home was on First Street in the Garden District, two blocks from the Leverts and closer to the river.

"I also have several parcels of commercial lots on St. Charles; warehouses on Camp; an apartment on Freret Street. And, of course, Colonel, this Biloxi house."

"Several acres, I'm sure," said Behan, his gaze sweeping the beachfront before the house. A pair of swooping seagulls wheeled overhead, crying lustily.

"Five acres."

"That much?" The Colonel's thick eyebrows went up. "Well, aside from its value as a home, there's no question about it as a good investment. Is that all?"

"Probably not, but all I can think of at the moment." Jean folded his arms across his chest with a chuckle. "Oh, I almost forgot. I bought several thousand shares in Biloxi's first bank, The Peoples Bank. Believe me, Colonel, I sense great demand for land in this town and I intend to invest in its real estate when the time is right."

"You must be very proud. You should be, my friend. But do you ever think of slowing down and taking things easier?"

"I have no plans, but my family would certainly be glad to see me do it. Stephanie has been very patient. For thirty years of marriage."

They heard light steps on the upper deck of the pier. It was their daughters, their soft voices audible but barely discernible over the wind on the water:

"Bessie, you must be excited beyond description. Life in Paris is still to me a wonderful dream," said Stephanie Marie. "The year I spent there studying with Professor Moret now seems like just that—a dream."

"Did you want to stay longer?"

"I did. But I was anxious about Mama; I thought about her all the time, and you know if anything had happened to her while I was so far away, I'd never have gotten over it. She and Papa were so wonderful to let me go to stay in Europe for a whole year. I learned so much. I have had a good many invitations to play here and there, to join at least two performing groups in the city. With Rene Moret's name as instructor beneath mine, I seem to find doors opening for me as a musician. But Paris is so wonderful, so beautiful in all seasons. Spring! Autumn! Bessie, you are going to fall in love with the city. But you are already in love, aren't you!"

"Oh, yes! Yes! After the wedding ceremony Henri and I will come to the Gulf Coast to the Montross for our honeymoon, as you know." She told Stephanie Marie that they plan to go by train to New York and from there sail for Le Harve on the *Il Trovetore*." She smiled at Bessie; scattered freckles dotted Bessie's cheeks and the bridge of her nose.

"That is an Italian liner, is it not? Why did you choose that?"

"That was my parents' choice." Bessie said that her parents had crossed on that ship five years before. Henri knew its reputation, and he was completely agreeable. In fact, he was thrilled. He said it was the most luxurious ship afloat and the safest. "And June is supposed to be a good time for crossing the north Atlantic, isn't it?"

Jean and Colonel Behan listened contentedly, smiles of amusement coming and going on their faces, as the young ladies chatted on, anticipating Bessie's trousseau, which she planned to complete after she arrived in Paris. The ladies compared dressmakers in New Orleans—*Madame Derouche* was to make the maid-of-honor dress for which Stephanie Marie had already been fitted.

"I wish she were not going half a world away," muttered the Colonel. "We will never get used to our Bessie not being with us. She has been a wonderful child." He shrugged. "But we cannot keep them forever, can we, Jean? Henri Latour is a fine man, a good French Catholic, who will be good to our daughter. And of course, he is quite well off."

"He sounds like a prince," conceded Jean.

Jean could see Stella and Ella playing on the lawn, now. Ella continually ran up and down the steps of the shoefly. They had two playmates with them. For the life of him, Jean could not recall who the little visitors were. From New Orleans, probably. Freddy had brought Robert and another boy out to the pier to fish. Jean patted the arms of his chair. Apparently his handsome home away from home was functioning just as it was intended. He looked closely; there was Daniels coming down the front steps with iced drinks, headed for the pier. He looked at his watch. Why, it was ten o'clock. Of course! Everyone was ready for a cool drink.

CHAPTER 63

JEAN WAS SAYING, as he parted his coattails to sit down at the dining table at the Boston Club: "Colonel, I'm returning to Biloxi as fast as I can get there." He turned away from Colonel Behan with an inward moan, cursing himself for not being there with Stephanie this instant. For a moment he stared vacantly at Perelli's colorful paintings of fish and game on the walls.

"Is Stephanie not doing well?"

"That's it. I'm worried, more so than usual. She looks bad; she did Monday morning when I left for the city. She was so pale."

"I'm so sorry to hear it, Jean. I must say Elizabeth is quite worried about her since our last visit."

Jean had asked Colonel Behan to meet him for lunch on May 25, a lovely early summer day in New Orleans. The two men had entered the club through the first-floor parlor, with its deep, plush leather chairs, high-backed rockers, and large bay window overlooking the side yard, and were seated at the damask-covered table that, two years after Jean's election as a member, they could count on being reserved for them. A fresh bouquet of rosebuds sat on their table on the second floor of the men's social club on Canal Street.

"Excuse, me, Mr. Levert." It was Bainerd, the head waiter. He carried a small silver tray on which lay a thin yellow envelope.

*   *   *

Jean felt slightly seasick as the commercial vessel *Eau Salubre* steamed its way out of Lake Pontchatrain and into Lake Borgne and finally the Mississippi Sound. He had never traveled by water between New Orleans and the Coast. But after consulting an old L&N Railroad map of the Gulf Coast, he calculated that the steamship, even with its stops at towns and hotels, wouldn't take any longer than the train.

The steamship, which transported tanks of spring water from Ocean Springs, Mississippi, to New Orleans, was sailing empty. It was part of a small fleet operated by New Orleans Marine, a company owned by a business acquaintance, Armand Sonnier, who happened to be sitting within earshot of Jean at the Boston Club when he sprang up in alarm at the news of Stephanie's collapse. Immediately, Jean had left the club to catch the steam locomotive *Smokey Mary*, which carried him and other passengers from downtown New Orleans and the French Quarter, five miles through swamps to the ship landing at Milneburg on Lake Pontchatrain, for departure. Captain Sonnier had commanded his ship to be detained for more than an hour to allow Jean to get aboard, and Colonel Behan had urged Jean to try the water route.

Jean was grateful to Captain Sonnier but he was uncomfortable and nauseous leaning over the rail of the *Eau Salubre* as it swayed and bounced over choppy Lake Pontchatrain. He felt the waters begin to calm as the ship chugged through the Rigolets and into Lake Borgne, then onto Bay St. Louis, the first of many stops. If his mission had not been so desperate, he would have found it intensely interesting.

Only a hundred feet long, the *Eau Salubre* had a draft suitable for Lake Pontchatrain, a body of water Jean knew was notorious for its shallow depth on which severe storms quickly developed. But the Mississippi Sound waters, to his relief, were calm for the remainder of the trip. After nearly ten anxiety-filled hours, a weary Jean worried about locating a hack for the ride back down the beach road to the house after midnight. But to his relief he saw Daniels and Freddy waiting for him. Colonel Behan had telegraphed

Daniels that his employer was scheduled to arrive at Biloxi about midnight, a vague estimated time of arrival, indeed, but as it turned out remarkably accurate. The L&N did not arrive in Biloxi until almost one in the morning.

*   *   *

"Mother's condition is very bad!" Freddy said, as his father climbed hurriedly into the carriage. "We've had Father Tormey."

Finally at Stephanie's bedside, Jean took her hands in his. "Steph, Steph, *ma chèrie*. Can you hear me? Do you hear me, my dearest." His voice was soft, but urgent. Her face was dry and gray. Her hands were limp and without warmth.

"Mister Jean, she been like this since yest'day mornin," said Vic. "Will you excuse me, Mister Jean. I been in here since daylight when Daniels took Miss Lila Beaugez home about 6 o'clock to get some sleep. She be back this afternoon."

"Freddy said Dr. Martens was here at eight."

"Yes, Mister Jean."

"What did he say?"

"He told chilren we must wait and see. He be back this afternoon, too."

"Has she waked up at all since her collapse?" Jean said, his voice tight with fear.

"Kind of, a few times. She opened her eyes some time ago. She look at me like she know me. We just pray, Mister Jean." Vic wiped her eyes on her white apron.

Jean stood up and removed his coat. "Just a minute, Vic." He went into the bathroom and splashed cold water on his face. He washed his hands. He laid the linen waffle towel on the corner of the marble lavatory. His heart lurched as his eyes caught Stephanie's heavy scroll monogram on the towel. It looked so like her, lying there among her most personal things, her hairbrush . . . *Steph, Steph. Don't leave me.*

"Go get some rest, Vic. You must. I need you to stay strong."

He sat down on the bedside and held Stephanie's hands again, rubbing them, trying to stir some life in them. He said her name again and again.

"I'm here, *ma chèrie*. Don't you hear me? I've come home. Oh, *ma chèrie*, I want you to open your eyes for me . . ." He was very tired and sleepy. His heavy eyelids burned. "Steph . . ."

Her hand moved in his. Her green eyes opened slightly.

"*Cher* . . ." Her voice was barely audible.

"*Chèrie* . . ." He kissed her fingers.

She spoke to him in French, asking if he were really there, and he replied in French, saying that he would stay with her forever, that he should never have left her. A tear appeared in the corner of her eye and trickled back into her hair. Jean rejoiced that she was responding.

"Let's not talk now, *chèrie*. You must rest. You will be fine. Be very quiet, and I'll be right here."

The smallest smile pulled at the corner of her mouth, and she seemed to be sleeping again. Jean lay down beside her and fell asleep.

When Jean awakened, Stephanie Marie and Dr. Martens were in the room. Jean rose hastily, adjusting his clothes—tie, cuffs. "Doctor . . ." He touched his moustache and smoothed his hair.

"How do you do, Mr. Levert?" Fine creases, once transient and now indelible, traversed Dr. Martens' forehead as he tried to put Jean at ease with his voice and gesture. "I know you have had a tiring journey. How do you feel, sir."

"I am quite well, Doctor. I am concerned only with my wife's condition. Before I fell asleep, she awakened briefly and talked with me. I take that to be a hopeful sign." The men spoke in low voices.

Stephanie lay still now.

Dr. Martens drew Jean to the other side of the room near a window. He looked out toward the Sound. "Mr. Levert, your wife has almost certainly had a severe coronary thrombosis. She is very ill. Very low. I must advise you and your family to prepare for the worst. I am very, very sorry."

Jean pressed his face into his hands, and muttered, "No, no. I can't stand this. I cannot let her go. Oh, Doctor, you must do something."

Dr. Martens laid his hand on Jean's shoulder. "You must bear up, sir." He bent over Stephanie and held her wrist briefly. He shook his head.

Jean tried to control himself, but he was completely distraught. *I am helpless. I can do nothing. Nothing.*

"Shouldn't she have nourishment? Some broth, perhaps? Perhaps that would . . ."

"If she should rally and ask for food, by all means give her some broth. But do not disturb her about it." The doctor sat down in a chair, watching his patient while Jean paced the room. Finally, he took out his watch, then rose to leave.

"I will be back tonight. I understand your excellent nurse, Mrs. Lila Beaugez, will be back here about five. Try to get some rest when you can, Mr. Levert." He picked up his black bag and his hat. "I'll see myself out."

Jean returned to Steph's side. As he sat watching her, she opened her eyes again.

"Jean, *cher*." She spoke slowly, plainly. "Promise me, *mon cher*. Be good to our children. Especially the young ones—little Robert and little Ella; they are so tender. Be patient, *mon cher*. They all need your love and patience."

"*Ma chèrie*, I shall. Fear not. I shall. You must not leave us. They need you more than they need me. I need you." Jean knew he was frantic, and he remembered the same panic he had felt when he and Stephanie were losing their little Lucie to yellow fever. So long ago. But such a vivid memory. "You know that I cannot possibly live without you."

He saw she was having trouble breathing. Her thin chest heaved as she struggled to inhale.

"Steph!"

The door opened behind him, and Lila Beaugez entered. She walked rapidly to the bed. "We must raise her head, Mr. Levert. Like this." She put strong young arms under Stephanie's shoulders and pushed an extra pillow beneath her. Stephanie's gasping eased, and she lay still. Seeing Lila, Stephanie whispered, "Lila, my dear friend. Jean, she has . . ."

"Shh," whispered Lila. "Save your strength, my dear Mrs. Levert. You must rest."

Jean watched the younger woman. She wore a long starched white apron. She looked like an angel. He marveled at her gentle competency. He felt much more encouraged with her here.

"Lila." He didn't know what to say. "Lila, you are a gift from God. Look, my wife is breathing much better."

"Mr. Levert, please go into a quiet room and get some rest. Vic has some hot food for you. You must maintain your strength." She took his arm and escorted him into the sitting room and returned to the bedroom.

The children huddled in various rooms. He could not bring himself to gather them together. He knew Stephanie expected him to embrace the younger ones, comfort them with words. *Not yet. Later.* He went into the kitchen where he found Vic making two large chicken pies. She pushed the rolling pin over a thinning mound of dough. White flour covered her brown hands and wrists.

"Vic, have the children all been in to speak to their Mother?"

"Yes, Mister Jean. Chilren all tow up. Mister Albert and Miss Mathilde they on their way. They be here tonight or in the mornin." And any moment, Jean was expecting Jean, Jr., home from Mount St. Mary's College.

"Vic, I can't give her up." Jean took out a handkerchief to wipe his reddened eyes.

Vic, too, began to shed tears. "I know, Mister Jean, I grievin. I been with her bout twenty-six years. She been so good to me."

"But Vic, we must not give up."

Vic looked sorrowfully at him, then lifted a large sheet of dough and laid it over a pan of chicken, vegetables, and dumplings. She shook her head from side to side and moaned as she opened the door of the oven and slid the pies into the chamber.

"We just got to pray, Mister Jean."

"Freddy told me that Father Tormey had been here."

"He came last night. Gave her benediction." She ladled gumbo into a soup plate from a large pot on the back of the stove. "Now, here, Mister Jean. You eat some of this hot gumbo." She added a scoop of rice. "You got to have somethin to eat." She leaned across the kitchen table and handed him a soup spoon and a napkin.

"I'm not hungry."

"No! Now don't say that. Eat this hot food. Sit right down here. And tonight you come to the dinin room with whole family and have chicken pie, fresh green beans, and cornbread. That's what Miss Stephanie want you to do."

Jean tasted the gumbo. *No chef in New Orleans can outdo Vic's gumbo.*

"You need to talk to these chilren, Mister Jean. You know they all hurtin."

"I know. I will."

Jean lost count of the days. Perhaps the children really had said goodbye to their mother. Stephanie Marie, Beatrice, Albert, and Freddy went in to see her every day. Mathilde was reserved; she seemed unable to face the prospect of her mother fading away any better than her father could. Jean was glad to see the younger ones resume play on the pier. When he came near them in the house or on the porch, they sobered and looked sad as though he reminded them that death hung over the house and would not go away.

Every day Stephanie spoke a few words weakly to Jean, always asking him to care for the children. On Tuesday afternoon, she spoke only in French, reminding him of their wedding and the honeymoon boatride downriver to New Orleans and the day she arrived with baby Albert at Third Street. Just a few words. Jean sat by her and replied in French. He was exhausted with grief and lack of sleep, but he clung to the hope that she might rally and improve.

Through it all, Lila sustained him. He waited for her arrival each day. He responded to her nearness, her youth, her faint perfume. Occasionally, she brushed close to him and her hand or arm touched him. He was amazed at her power to arouse a lively warmth in his body. And she was genuinely devoted to Stephanie. *Thank God we decided to engage her.*

*   *   *

Lila was with Stephanie on Wednesday morning, May 31, when Jean entered the room. He noticed Stephanie's breathing was quite labored.

"Let's try to raise her up higher on her pillows, Mr. Levert," Lila said. Together they succeeded in doing so. This time it did no good.

"Jean," gasped Stephanie faintly. *"Mon cher."* They were her last words.

He clasped her in his arms. "Steph, Steph," he whispered.

Lila left the room and called for Vic. "Go fetch all the children. Quickly. Mrs. Levert is dying. I hear the death rattle."

Jean heard Lila. He heard Vic sob: "Oh, no!" Quickly she and Daniels located all the children who then began to file into the bedroom. Lila returned to the bedside where Jean was trying to control himself as he held his dying wife. Her body thrashed as she struggled for breath, the entire room of people stricken with the cruel sight. Dr. Martens and Father Tormey had come in.

The scene lasted forever, thought Jean. Then Stephanie stopped her struggle. Her body relaxed in Jean's arms, and peace settled over her face. Jean buried his face in her hair. Dr. Martens stepped forward and took his arm as he laid Stephanie down on the pillows.

"She's gone, Mr. Levert." As Jean stood there, the priest intoned, "In the name of the Father, the Son . . ." Jean heard the scrape of the trowel at his father's burial.

"Is our mother dead?" asked Robert. Vic put her arms about his slender shoulders.

"She gone, son. Your mother gone to heaven to be with God."

Lila led Jean from the room. He felt that he might not stay on his feet if she were not there to sustain him, one arm around his back, as she guided him to a chair on the porch.

*   *   *

Next morning Father Bernard Tormey offered up prayers for Stephanie at a special Mass at Nativity church before her body was returned to New Orleans by train for a high funeral Mass at the Jesuit church, near Jean's office. Jean, Stephanie, and the Levert children attended Mass regularly at the Jesuit church and Mathilde had taken her marriage vows there two years earlier.

Beside Jean and his children and his brothers and their large families, many of Jean and Stephanie's social and business friends and acquaintances attended the services. Mourners included Celeste Bush and her son Reuben; the Behans and their daughters Bessie and Katherine; Emile Morvant and members of his family; Molly Groeble, who had aged so that Jean almost failed to recognize her; numerous members of the Pickwick and Boston clubs. Many of Jean's clients, planters over southwestern Louisiana traveled long distances. Like the mayor, who was present, and Jean, many of the men wore morning coats and striped trousers, warm clothes indeed for a June midday in New Orleans. To his surprise, at home Jean had been handed a long telegram of sympathy from Annie Blanton Kleinpeter. Telegrams also came from Chicago, St. Louis, and Memphis, all the pale yellow sheets lying in their crisp folds on the card tray in the foyer at Third Street, where Stephanie might have walked in a pale green faille dress that matched her green eyes to see who had called.

The long religious service in Latin by priests and choir seemed endless to Jean. At times he felt strangely elevated in mind and body—dazed—and at others acutely aware of his grief and honored by the presence of some of New Orleans' most prominent civic and professional leaders, who came to show their sympathy and respect for Jean Baptiste Levert.

On the sultry morning of June 4, after the benediction, half of the four hundred persons in attendance followed the horse-drawn hearse in a slow procession from the church in downtown New Orleans, past tree-shaded residences along Canal, to Metairie Cemetery outside New Orleans. Jean and his family, chins touching their chests, prayed in silence as Stephanie was laid to rest in the family's above-ground granite tomb. In honor of Stephanie's last wishes, Jean had the remains of their daughter Marie Aloysia and those of her mother and father, Virginia Aloysia Viel and Gideon Octave Dupuy, transferred from St. Gabriel church cemetery, where the parents had rested for about forty years, to the Levert tomb for interment.

*   *   *

When he returned to Third Street after Stephanie's funeral, Jean walked straight to the liquor cabinet in the dining room and grabbed a large unopened bottle of Benedictine. Unaware of the people in any of the rooms, he walked trancelike through the kitchen, out the back porch door, and to the gazebo located in the middle of the backyard. Clutching the handrail, he mounted the steps and entered the miniature chalet. He opened the bottle.

For a moment the stricken man stared at the walls of the gazebo lattice above and gingerbread openwork below. Then he turned the bottle up and drained several great gulps of the strong brandy into his throat. He knew what he sought; he sought escape from his crazed grief. Oblivion. That is all he could hope for now. There was no comfort anywhere else.

The interment had been too much for him. Seeing the polished, mahogany coffin pushed slowly into the Levert vault in Metairie Cemetery climaxed five days of increasing sorrow and stress for all of Stephanie's survivors. But Jean was certain that no one suffered as he did. Since that horrifying moment when his wife had died struggling in his arms in the bedroom at Biloxi, the awfulness of his loss seemed to hit him like wind gusts, ever harder; and it had seemed much worse since the long service at the Jesuit church this morning. Again and again he said to himself: "I cannot go on without her. I cannot possibly get up day after day and face this painful existence. More than I knew she was my life. My beautiful, green-eyed girl—brought down by death so untimely." And inevitably would follow: "Brought on by my neglect. Yes, yes,

yes. It's true. I was away too much when she needed me." He
believed his grief would never subside.

Frustrated at still being too sober for relief, Jean poured down
more brandy. He looked around the small hexagonal building.
White benches had been built as part of the walls, but Jean sat in
one of two dark green rockers, his hand clutching the bottle on a
tabletop of cast-iron grape clusters. He felt the late-afternoon breeze
that drifted through the lattice. Now, his head seemed to bulge
slightly and grow lighter at the same time, as if it might float up to
the roof. He heard a strange sound, at once far away and familiar.
He looked dully through the lattice toward his chickenhouse—
one of his hens was making slow, lazy clucking sounds as she
settled onto her roost. He drank more brandy, wondering vaguely
how he happened to have taken Benedictine and thinking of the
size glass in which it was usually served. The bottle was almost
empty. With a tremulous sigh of relief, he acknowledged that he
was quite drunk.

But the light weight of the bottle told him he must go back to
the liquor cabinet. There were many people in the house—his
children, family, and friends from out of town, his brothers and
their wives. Their carriages lined Third Street for several blocks.
He wondered how he might get through to the dining room
without attracting attention. *Hell, it doesn't matter. Let them stare.*

Starched collar undone, formal dress shirt sleeves rolled to
the elbow, Jean Baptiste tried to stand. Halfway up, he lunged, his
head seeming to dive into the opposite wall. Angrily, he seized a
chair, raised it over his head, and attempted to throw it against the
wall. When it fell behind him, he cursed the chair in French and
clung to a post in the wall, swaying, trying not to fall. At the
entrance of the gazebo, he looked up at the back of the house.
There were faces at the open windows. *"Mon dieu,* there is young
Robert, his face pressed against the screen. And leading the boy
away, who is that? Albert? Let them look. Let them all look. They
know nothing of my suffering."

Griping the railing, Jean managed to put one foot down on
the top step. He must go into the house for more brandy. His

head spun, and he stumbled. He felt very sick. *Mon dieu. Mon dieu.* He tried to cling to the rail as he went down. He fell into the grass, snagging his clothing on one of Stephanie's prize climbing rose bushes, where he lay heaving. He moaned.

Someone was there. He feared opening his eyes. *Who is it? Vic? Daniels? Dieu merci!*

He opened his eyes as William Behan lifted him by his elbows. "Come, *mon ami.* Let me help you. Please, Jean. Come old friend. You have suffered enough. Believe me, I understand. I want to help you to your bed."

"*Mon dieu, Colonel* . . . I am . . . so ill. My poor Steph . . . gone . . . gone . . . ."

Together the two friends struggled up the back steps of the Third Street house, half-dragging, not unlike one soldier helping a wounded comrade from the battlefield.

Chapter 64

JEAN BELIEVED THAT Stephanie's many illnesses, associated with so many difficult pregnancies over twenty years, had been, literally, caused by him. She had suffered alone much of the time when she needed him, and he had not been there for her. With several of the pregnancies, Jean had feared the worst. He had fought off guilty reflections that certain freedoms would come to him if she had died after childbirth. He had felt especially guilty when Mathilde stopped breathing, as Stephanie nearly died giving birth to her, and while still weak from that birth Stephanie had become pregnant eight weeks later with her fourth child, Freddy. He knew her strength had been weakened in her loss of two daughters in infancy and Freddy nearly dying of yellow fever.

Jean had not written in his journal for several months. But on June 10, 1898, eleven days after Stephanie drew her last breath, he made this grim entry: "Births, deaths . . . Marie Aloysia born in Iberville Parish, La., May 19, 1869, died there Feb., 1871; Mathilde born in N.O. April 25, 1872, not breathing. Marie Lucie born in N.O. April 10, 1877, died Oct. 10, 1878. Stephanie Dupuy born June 1850, died . . . ."

*　　*　　*

Three weeks after his wife's death, Jean returned to work on Factors' Row with a firm optimism about the future, to expand his clientele, to wait patiently for the right deal to come along. Once again he began improving his holdings, trying to squeeze out as much profit as possible and, at the same time, continue his search for a new partner with whom he could work and be comfortable and who might compare with Colonel Bush.

While many men might have married again to provide a mother for their children and to satisfy personal needs, Jean built defenses against such temptations. Even after the official year of mourning, he stayed away from large parties; he attended few Carnival balls. Stephanie Marie and Beatrice especially made certain that their father honored their mother's memory. Because of his strong Catholic faith and their indelible recall of their mother, they endeavored to convince Jean that it was wrong for him to remarry. Jean wrote in his journal his thoughts on remarriage and why he believed that Stephanie and Beatrice had been adamantly against it:

"Never did I understand why my children had vetoed my marrying another woman. I find it unfathomable that they have been rendered so sad by such an act, that my remarrying would have been a selfish gesture on my part, that I would have thought less of their Mother—and would have tried to replace Steph with another woman. Never! Never! What of my happiness? Did my children not understand or appreciate my needs and wants? And were they so narrow-minded by a craving for their rightful inheritance that they would have felt slighted by my affections for another woman? Ridiculous! I have not forgotten their Mother nor neglected my religion nor my faith. Perhaps Bea and Steph will come to me in time and reveal their reasons and fears, but it will have to be when they are ready and not because of any urging on my part."

Jean remained in his office on Perdido Street at the end of many work days long after his secretary and the brokers who worked for him had left. He paced for long periods and occasionally lay down on a pallet that had been brought into the office when he had felt faint. He was thankful that no one witnessed his solitary bursts of grief over the loss of Stephanie. His melancholic memories of gambols with her along the banks of the Mississippi River before their marriage, their horseback rides through lush green cane fields at Dupuy and Golden Ridge plantations at the height of harvest, only saddened him; they never left his mind.

Still, he felt a strange fear he had never before experienced close in on him after her death, the fear that he would be alone forever. He feared that he might not be able to comprehend, let alone penetrate, the hidden haven that was now reserved only for Marie Stephanie Dupuy Levert.

*   *   *

It didn't take Jean long to realize that Stephanie Marie Eulalie Levert was totally devoted to lessening his sorrow and anguish, and that she had become his shadow after the death of her mother. As Jean began getting about again, he often took his brunette, freckle-faced daughter with him, relying on her, confiding in her, as suggested in a letter he wrote to her from St. John Plantation:

July 1898

My dear Steph—

I know not what moans in the air or in the soul . . . I came to take of your letter which reached me yesterday, the last day of June, as if to tell me that just one month since your Mother was no longer on earth, one month since from our home in Biloxi she had ascended heavenly to be among the blessed! I am sure she is in heaven, and yet I am sometimes seized with terror in reflecting upon that awful eternity. While speaking of the dead, you said in your letter that you and Bea go to Mass every morning for her. You and your sister are more pious than I, and are doing all you can to help her, and I bless God for it! I am writing this from my room above—that room we occupied much of last summer while you sojourned in Chicago . . . my heart wanders off in the direction of Biloxi . . . crops are doing nicely, growing fast. I mean to leave Sunday for the city.

Adieu, my dear one, and to each and all my tender love
and a kiss. My regards to all our friends in the city.
                                    Your heartbroken Papa

But neither Stephanie nor her brothers and sisters mourned their mother with visible displays and uncontrollable crying, which at times bothered Jean. Ella Marie and Robert denied their mother's death with fantasy daydreams of her return someday. Stephanie Marie's help in caring for the younger Levert children during her mother's long illness and periods of convalescence had suggested to him that she was well equipped to be a surrogate.

Albert continued to live at St. John; Mathilde, married to Dr. Francis Kearny, lived at Plaquemine; Freddy, who was graduated from Spring Hill College in Mobile, became engaged to marry a girl from Birmingham; Jean, Jr., was close to graduation from his father's alma mater, Mount St. Mary's College; and Lawrence planned to enter Tulane University, formerly the University of Louisiana, in the fall. So, Jean knew that left Stephanie Marie to care for him and her younger siblings: Bea, Stella, Ella, and Robert, especially Robert. Stephanie Marie had grown very protective of her baby brother since last Christmas, and Jean thought it was a good thing. While the Leverts were spending the holidays at St. John, Robert, after an early morning ride in the cane fields with his father and Albert, was kicked in the right leg by his horse, leaving him severely crippled.

Chapter 65

ANNA BEATRICE LEVERT, Jean's twenty-two-year-old daughter, grasped a *Cosmopolitan* magazine from the table before the parlor sofa at Third Street; something caught her eye.

"Oh, here's an interesting question—what is a gentleman?" she read aloud, sipping her *café au lait*. "How would you answer that, Steph?"

Seated next to her on the chintz sofa, Stephanie Marie chuckled. "Well, the creature wasn't invented at the time of Adam and Eve. He's a product of civilization, I guess. Primitive man could hardly have been a gentleman, you know."

It was the humid Sunday morning after Jean Baptiste had received the highest honor a Louisiana Confederate veteran could be given—commander for a year of the Louisiana Division of United Confederate Veterans with the honorary rank of major general. From that moment Jean's friends and business associates addressed him as General Levert, and his children, who continued to call him Papa, began referring to him as the General. Jean's station as a gentleman was much emphasized when he was honored; the *Cosmopolitan* article was timely in the Levert household. And Jean's acute grief for Stephanie had eased; again he was giving his attention to dealmaking and business challenges. As he did long ago after Marie Lucie died, he poured himself into his work, bringing much of it home to his Third Street office.

"There's the beginning of the definition ready-made for you, Steph," said General Levert, entering the discussion. Usually, he was not a game player with his children, but he warmed to this discussion. Dressed in a dark blue smoking jacket to replace the morning coat he had worn to church, but still in his starched collar and cravat, Jean stared out of the front window at two similar graystone mansions across the street. Both had towers and spires, not typical of Garden District homes, that reflected the morning sunlight.

"As I have said many times to your brothers, good breeding is natural, instinctive," emphasizing the two words. Jean rubbed his moustache and temples, both turning white, feeling every bit the part of a gentleman general, and added, "It must come from a person's nature, not from cultivation. So, let's make a definition for ourselves, shall we? What does the immortal Webster say about the word *gentleman?*"

"He's quoted right here in this article," said Bea. "He says, 'a man well-bred; one of good family, one above the condition of a yeoman.'" She looked up briefly at her sister and father. Then: "Oh, here's more: 'one of breeding, refined manners.' But breeding alone, that is, birth, doesn't make a gentleman, does it? Look at Harvey Michelle; he is certainly well born, and he is no gentleman."

Stephanie laughed. "Let's make our own definition."

"Go ahead, Steph," commanded her father, enjoying the repartee. He tugged at his high tight collar and cravat, then removed the smoking jacket. Moisture from three days of heavy rain had concentrated in the air until the humidity was unbearable to him; temperature inside the house this midday was a steamy ninety-three degrees. "I'd like to see what you two ladies come up with."

"Well, let's ask why we say such a man—Papa, for instance—fits the description of a southern gentleman."

"Why, because Father always acts like a gentleman." Bea shrugged, turning to her sister. "That's why we say he is one."

"Exactly. A gentleman is known by his acts, yes, and by all his conduct all the time," Stephanie countered.

"That's true. But what makes his conduct? How does it differ from the conduct of a cad?" asked their father. He waited while Stephanie pondered the question.

"Well, Papa is always respectful," said Beatrice.

"Yes, respectful. You mean respectful to others?" her sister answered.

Jean interjected: "He couldn't be that unless he first respects himself. A gentleman is marked by his acts, by all his conduct." He stopped. "Now, that's a good start on a definition. Why do you think a gentleman respects himself?"

"It's a matter of heart and head," exclaimed Stephanie.

"Mostly of the heart, I feel," Bea said.

"It's a matter of feeling—respect is," added Jean confidently. "Respect comes from the heart. A man respects another because he feels with him what his position or nature is. A gentleman, then, is a man who respects himself and others from a kind and true heart."

"All right, Papa, and if he respects himself in the right way, he will have natural dignity. Am I right?" asked Stephanie. "I've seen laborers as dignified as professional men, as full of simple courtesy."

Jean thought for a moment, then said, "They have the essential things, the laborers. But I should stress, just as old Mammy Bébé had them. Dignity and courtesy are outward signs, then, they are the outward signs of an inward character."

Beatrice looked through the sunlight into the parlor and gently rubbed her eyes. "Now, is there something else needed to complete our definition, Father? Shouldn't something be made of habits and customs? Would we be pleased if Papa or our guests came to supper dressed in gardener's clothes or rags?"

"That's the point," said Jean. "If polite society dresses in coat and tie for supper, we shall do so and we would expect, yes, require, our guests to do so at our table. A bicycle-riding outfit would not be acceptable. Clothes stand for something, and guests must feel comfortable. Bébé would probably have enjoyed a carnival ball, but she would have been out of place."

Jean smiled at Stephanie and Beatrice. "Well, haven't we arrived at our definition? Surely we have. You state it, Steph."

Stephanie's head was bent over the *Sunday Picayune* story of her father's honor, and she didn't hear him. Jean repeated his demand.

"Oh! A gentleman respects himself and others with a kind and true heart and conforms to the customs of his class." Then she asked her father how well she had done so far, and he winked at her. She beamed.

"That definition would accommodate Bébé," Jean said, emphatically.

"And most of your friends, too, Papa, I should think," said Bea.

"I guess our definition doesn't leave out any of the Levert children, does it, Papa?" ventured Stephanie. "I hope not."

Chapter 66

JEAN ROSE EARLY on this Saturday morning in late September. On the porch outside the bedroom at Biloxi house, a refreshing Gulf breeze cooled his face as it whipped long green banana tree leaves near the corner of the house. He caught sight of a fisherman making his way up the beach road. Beggarly looking, his broad back bent by the weight of heavy nets rolled on long poles, the man headed across sand and shells and weeds into the Sound. He waded out waist-deep and clambered aboard a boat. Idly, Jean figured he was getting ready to head out beyond the barrier islands to seine for shrimp—a familiar sight in the Mississippi Sound and Gulf of Mexico.

Jean was not long distracted by the coastal scene. Yawning, he returned to the bedroom and sat at a small desk near a front window. He glanced toward the sleeping Lila Beaugez and silently took up a pencil. As he often had done to help ease his deep sorrow after Stephanie's death, he began jotting down some honors and tributes that had been bestowed upon him:

> "—Member, Tulane University board of administrators since 1892.
>
> "—Served one term in state senate . . . played big part in ridding state of infamous lottery.
>
> "—Received highest honor in 1903 given to Confederate veteran, with honorary rank of major general.
>
> "—Represented Louisiana as delegate at 1904 St. Louis

World's Fair . . . presented model of the original state capital,
the Cabildo, and workings of a prototype sugarhouse.
    "—Helped establish Louisiana State Museum . . . on its
first board of directors."

He laid the pencil down and gazed out at the water for a moment. The mantel clock proffered a tentative whirr, wheezed twice, and began to chime the hour of seven. He retrieved the pencil and under his breath he began counting, tapping his fingers on the desktop. He was listing the property holdings he had acquired over the last dozen or so years—St. John, Davis, Rienzi, Banker plantations—to begin with. The more he amassed, the more pleasure he found in reviewing the list, counting up like a scrooge might count his pennies.

Jean listed his holdings whenever he might settle down for an hour or a day—at his Perdido Street office, at Third Street, at St. John, or on a train. When it was quiet, out came a pad and pencil. He sometimes counted on his fingers or wrote in little columns. It was very satisfying, very private. More often than not it was thrilling; he sometimes likened it to holding a woman. A chill would tickle his spine. This morning his spine tickled.

He turned when he heard Lila stir. He watched her reach for the silk coverlet folded at the foot of the heavy sleigh bed, with its oversized headboard of inlaid wood rolling back in a bulging curve. The coverlet lay over her body in delicious outline. But he wasn't ready to wake her. He pulled a small leather trunk from beneath the bed and took out a thick folder. Leafing through its papers, he made neat stacks of land documents, sorted by parish: St. Martin, Iberville, Orleans, St. Charles, Lafourche. He placed his St. Martin and Orleans land abstracts and deeds directly in front of him in a special pile, because he considered them his most valuable, most profitable properties.

After making the stacks, he removed a suede bag from the trunk and gently emptied a heap of gold coins on the desk, then counted them, estimating their value by gold's current prices. In recent years, he had come to love the glitter and glamour of gold.

He scribbled a few figures in an account book, fingered through some other papers, then carefully repacked the trunk. Satisfied once again that these possessions were secure, he dressed quietly and left the room.

Jean had come to Biloxi alone, as he always did when he wanted to see Lila—see her alone. Vic and Daniels were understanding and they were discreet, but he couldn't risk letting them know of these trysts. They wouldn't approve, and he did not like to think what Stephanie Marie and Beatrice especially would say or do if they found out. So, he had no servants to wait on him and Lila.

He went into the kitchen and turned on the electric light, a glass dome hanging by a chain from the high ceiling in the middle of the room. It made more light than Jean once would have believed possible. He made coffee, sliced an orange and some bread, and took butter and milk out of the ice box; also blackberry preserves. He walked to the front lawn and picked up the Biloxi *Daily Herald* and put it on the kitchen table. Then he walked to Lila's bedside and waked her. Smiling, he gently pulled back the coverlet, revealing her small shapely satin-clad body. She opened her eyes. Instantly, she sat up and put her arms around him.

Overjoyed at her warmth and eagerness, he spoke against her ear, "Your breakfast is ready." Together they ate hungrily at the kitchen table.

Later, after a dip at the end of the pier, they sat in rockers on the porch. Jean gently raised Lila's left hand to his lips and kissed her cool salty skin. She wore a ruffled black wool bathing dress, piped in red, a matching brimmed bonnet with a deep crown. Jean wore a red and white striped suit, his legs daringly bare below his knees. They had been in the Sound and on the pier for nearly three hours, and their bodies tingled from the salt and wind. Finally, they had tired of watching oyster schooners glide beside Deer Island in front of the house and returned to the porch, which was cool and private, far back from the beach road.

"This is a lovely time, but I am uncomfortable in this scratchy wet wool," said Lila. She rose and gave him a languorous smile and went in for a bath and dry clothes.

Jean sat on the porch, imagining her disrobing and stepping into the tub, foamy with soap. But not for long. He stood up quickly and walked to the bath on the other side of the house, where he had deposited his own fresh linen last night. Lolling contentedly in the warm water, he thought that barring a surprise visit from Steph and Bea, he believed life could not be any more delightful than this.

He took Lila to the Montross Hotel for luncheon. He knew she loved it, considered it a treat and a compliment to be taken there and to be seen with him there. He also knew that sooner or later they would run into someone he knew, Father Tormey or Dr. Martens perhaps. He had practiced what he would say:

"How are you, Father? Miss Lila and I were just talking about the church. She says you are in need of some, uh, prayer books, and I want to provide some new ones. Or linens for the sacrament table." *Ridiculous. Absurd.* He didn't have to think like this; he wagged his head and shrugged. *Perhaps Father Tormey could indeed use a nice check for linens or something.*

Well, he thought, I am a free man, as free as any man alive. He could take a lady to lunch if the lady wanted to go and if she liked the Montross' splendid white lump crabmeat sprinkled with lemon juice and a few drops of the finest olive oil. Meanwhile, he reveled in the secrecy of his affair with Lila Beaugez. He felt youthful, strong. The satisfaction of hoodwinking his vigilant daughters amused him. It scared him a bit, but it did amuse him.

*   *   *

Jean returned to New Orleans with a light heart, ready to go to work in earnest on several projects about which he felt optimistic. To his surprise he found that Mathilde and Dr. Kearny were lodged in the guest room on the second floor at Third Street. Dr. Kearny, of considerable height, came to his office before Jean could find Mathilde and give her a warm greeting.

"Mr. Levert, it is urgent that I speak with you as soon as possible." There was no cheer on the doctor's face.

"Of course, Doctor. There need be no delay. Please come in and sit down. I trust all is going well with you and Mathilde in Plaquemine." Indeed . . . Seeing the doctor more closely, Jean knew that things definitely were not well. "Sit down, sir."

"Mr. Levert, I will not attempt to soften this blow. Mathilde has been told by Dr. Gonsoulin that she has a malignant tumor in her left breast. I am ill with the news of this terrible diagnosis. I brought her to him yesterday, and with only his preliminary examination, he seems certain that he is correct."

Jean sank into his desk chair, his mouth open, his face suddenly slack.

"Cancer? My God! No! Mathilde? We must get another opinion. Is he sending you to someone else?" Jean gripped the leather arms of his chair.

"Yes. We will see a Dr. Martineau Tuesday. Poor Mathilde. She is scarcely over the stillbirth of our baby . . ."

"Oh, my God. Is there no end of sorrow for us? Surely . . . ."

Mathilde had lost her baby girl about two years earlier. Jean knew that her case had been especially poignant, because there seemed little chance that she could become pregnant again. The child had been full term, a beautiful baby that Mathilde had named Katherine. The family had become used to her references to Katherine. Jean pressed his hands to his temples. *Poor Mathilde.* He must get himself together and do something to help her, to save her. He would talk to Dr. Gonsoulin tomorrow about specialists, not just in New Orleans, anywhere. Anywhere on earth. He had expected to write Lila tonight one of his love letters that she had grown to expect soon after they had been together, an anonymously signed *billet doux*, that he knew was silly, but which amused him as well as it did her. For the time being, that must be put behind him. Perhaps he would wire her; she would understand.

"Shall I go up and speak with her, Francis?"

To his relief, Dr. Kearny said in a soft but firm voice, "Mr. Levert, my wife is quite undone, tonight. I believe we would do well to wait until tomorrow. I have given her a powder that should allow her to rest. I hope she is asleep for the night."

"Yes. Quite. Well, I am tired, too, so I will retire, and try to be refreshed in the morning. Before I go to my downtown office, I will want to speak with my daughter." He rose. "I am grateful to you, Doctor, for coming in to see me. I know Mathilde is in good hands with you. Thank God for your professional training. I will join you immediately in seeking the best of medical talent. I am prepared to go wherever in the world we have to go for help. We must set our sights on nothing less than a full cure." His voice rang with determination and conviction.

Dr. Kearny raised his hand. "Mr. Levert, please sir, I must . . ." He dropped his hand in resignation. Jean's chin was up in his most determined pose. "Good night, Mr. Levert."

Next afternoon, Mathilde and Dr. Kearny retreated to their home in Plaquemine, hoping to keep her comfortable and, of course, with Jean burning candles at the Jesuit church and praying for a miracle.

CHAPTER 67

JEAN AWOKE EARLY on Christmas morning beset with mixed feelings—at once joyous and apprehensive. He sat up in bed and ran his hand through his silvery hair. Of course, he anticipated with pleasure a day with all his children. It was Mathilde about whom he felt distress. She and Dr. Kearny had decided to come down from Plaquemine on the early train to join the family for Christmas dinner and return home the following day.

By long-distance telephone call, Dr. Kearny told Jean that Mathilde, "Wants very much to go to New Orleans for the holiday celebration . . . although she doesn't feel well, and there is no improvement in her condition, she is determined to make the trip." Of course, Jean and the family were glad to learn that she wanted to be with them, though each of them thought sadly that this would be her last Christmas. Jean wondered how happy the gathering could be. He sighed and rubbed his eyes; it was not easy to suppress a houseful of Leverts. He rose to dress, for he intended to ride down with Daniels to meet the Kearny's train.

After her father returned from early Mass, Stephanie Marie walked with him to his carriage waiting in front of the house and kissed him goodbye. With tears in her eyes, she said, "I pray, Papa, that Mathilde will find pleasure here with us for a couple of days. God is good . . ." She pressed her lace handkerchief to her mouth and turned away.

Jean patted her shoulder. "There, there, my dear. We should be back by one o'clock. I know that you and Vic are preparing a handsome feast. We must be cheerful."

He stepped into the large family carriage, and Daniels clicked to the horses. Jean settled back and rested his hand before him on the gold head of his cane, caressing the acanthus leaves beneath his palm. He had been seeing the new electric carriages and reading about them, but all the models appeared too small for a man with so many children still about. And the contraptions were ridiculously expensive. He intended to wait for the ideal machine, and in the meantime, perhaps the prices would come down. Life was moving apace in this new country—electric lights, telephones, and even underground plumbing running all through the City, available to any and everybody. In his sixty-six years on this planet, Jean thought he had witnessed uncanny miracles, that things had surely gone about as far as they could go.

At the train station, Jean embraced his daughter in an emotional display that he certainly would not have indulged had she not been terribly ill. Mathilde felt thin and fragile in his arms. He had not seen her for several weeks, and the feel of her upper torso was alarming. Dr. Kearny shook his head, lifting his derby with his left hand. And the aging Daniels, in his late sixties, bowed to the Kearnys with extra solemnity. Jean was glad no other family members had accompanied him. To have the others there would have magnified the sadness in Mathilde's arrival.

"Merry Christmas, Papa," Mathilde said, and smiled. Jean swallowed hard and turned to see the porter place two bags in the carriage. Dr. Kearny lifted Mathilde into her seat.

Mathilde enjoyed the ride through the Garden District toward home, Jean saw. St. Charles Avenue's mansions were festive with green wreaths and streaming red ribbons on their heavy paneled doors and in their gleaming windows. In the sunny weather, a soft breeze ruffled the ostrich feathers on Mathilde's large hat. On broad verandas families were gathered for the holiday, ladies in colorful, fashionable dresses and gentlemen in their finest suits. Several groups recognized the Leverts and waved to them. Mathilde waved back, commenting on the decorations of the most elegant area of New Orleans.

"Yes, indeed, my dear Mathilde. Yes, indeed," said Jean, and the austere Dr. Kearny agreed. The City was splendid today.

Despite the presence of an ill member, the Leverts celebrated in their typical, noisy fashion, as Jean knew they would. At two o'clock, they sat down to roast turkey, ham, and countless dishes of vegetables, fruits, and desserts at the long dining table that was covered with one of their mother's fine white cutwork linen cloths and centered with a linear arrangement of roses, red tulips, large rose and white peonies, sprays of Stephanotis, and fern. No one questioned the source of such a magnificent, out-of-season bouquet. Jean realized that he was likely to rant when he received the bill from the florist with whom Stephanie Marie shopped on St. Charles, but she had learned how to forestall his wrath about some expenses, wrath that sprang from his stinginess.

Into the family's conversation, Steph remarked, loudly enough to be heard by everybody at the table, that their mother would have loved the flowers, especially the roses, and how elegant they were in her solid silver container, long, low, heavily embossed around its base, edges, and over its classic Grecian handles.

Albert's wife Louise, awed by the elegant bouquet, declared, "No such flowers are available for any occasion anywhere near St. John," and she stated that to live so splendidly one had to live in New Orleans. Then she, too, invoked her mother-in-law's sainted contributions on this Christmas day.

"Yes," added Beatrice, "wouldn't Mother have loved the exquisite flowers! The Dupuy bowl is perfect for them."

Jean studied the dozens of imported blossoms ruefully. After such tributes to their mother, to fuss at Stephanie Marie over the extravagance would be judged a sacrilege. He murmured in agreement and patted his moustache with the white linen Dupuy napkin. *These children think money grows on trees.*

After dinner, the ladies drifted to the veranda overlooking the backyard; they were served small tarts and demitasses. Servants followed Jean and the men to the gazebo, about twenty feet away, with mints, cigars, brandy, and coffee. The gazebo bore a fresh coat of white paint, and new rustic shingles had been laid on its steep circular roof. Ella and Robert had draped garlands of glossy magnolia leaves along its eaves. Christmas fireworks echoed throughout the neighborhood. To Jean all cares seemed forgotten as the family enjoyed the beauty of the lawn from the porch and from the wrought iron balcony across the second floor above, the tasteful treats and decorations, and perfect weather. The balcony had been the setting for many family portraits; a portrait of Mathilde in her elaborate Comus ball gown had been painted there a decade before.

Suddenly, Jean heard what he thought was a shot; he saw Stephanie clutch her waist. At first, he wasn't sure what was happening—Stephanie Marie had been shot in her side. No one knew where the bullet came from, but Jean was certain his daughter was hit from somewhere in the direction of Fourth Street. Bea, Mathilde, Stella, and Ella turned as one to their elder sister in surprise, wanting to help her. Stephanie held onto her wound, her hand filling with a great deal of blood.

Seeing blood coming forth in profusion, Bea screamed, "Oh, God," and motioned to Dr. Kearny. "Doctor! Doctor! Come quickly."

The men rushed up the steps to the veranda to help Stephanie Marie. The family now in the throes of shock, Dr. Kearny, in his reserved manner, took charge. As Jean looked on in alarm, Albert and the doctor carried Stephanie into the parlor. As they let her down on the sofa, the quick-thinking Vic hurried in with a sheet from the laundry and spread it in several thicknesses under Stephanie, preventing the upholstery, an imported French brocade, from being ruined.

"It is a flesh wound. It is only a flesh wound," said Dr. Kearny to the room full of people. "It appears the force of the bullet was spent penetrating her undergarments. I'm no authority on clothing, but I suspect her corset saved her life."

"Thank God," echoed among them, women's and men's voices.

"Is she all right, Doctor?" asked Jean.

"I do believe so, sir. My first observation is that Miss Stephanie is not mortally wounded, or even seriously. I believe we should get her upstairs to her bed. Albert?"

The two men carefully carried Stephanie up the stairs. Still not satisfied that her injuries were minor, Jean followed closely behind them. Eventually, convinced by Dr. Kearny that her wounds were not serious and could be disinfected and bandaged by himself, Jean and the doctor came back downstairs and sent Stephanie's sisters up to be with her, except for the exhausted Mathilde. Dr. Kearny took his wife to the guest bedroom and coaxed her into taking a small amount of morphine and lying down.

After Mathilde fell asleep, Dr. Kearny joined Jean and the other men in the parlor where Daniels boosted spirits and morale with more brandy.

Jean sighed. The apprehension that had nagged him when he had awakened early in the morning had been more than fulfilled. The fears he'd had for one daughter had been realized by two of them. He felt that he must find a source of relaxation soon, for he was exhausted.

Angered about Stephanie's close call, and before the afternoon was over, Jean excused himself and went into his office, where he composed a letter to the editor of the *Picayune,* which he sent directly out to a post box on the corner of Fourth and St. Charles so that it could appear in the paper as soon as possible: "When the laws are suspended to give the people full opportunity for a season of debauchery and crime, the occasion is by no means neglected. One of the outrages most indulged in is the firing of pistols and guns loaded with ball . . . one person was shot while standing in the doorway of her own residence, and a young lady, with her family and father taking tea in the garden, was the recipient of a bullet fired by some man . . . everything goes when laws are suspended! Never have firearms been handled so recklessly as this Christmas, and citizens have begun to feel that there is little safety to life where drunken hoodlums can shoot and carouse at will!"

*   *   *

Jean greeted the new year, 1906, with lingering foreboding. The year just past had held more trouble than he thought any man could live through sanely; such a threat in one's own backyard had been horrifying. Jean declared it to have been infuriating and ridiculous in a civilized city where law and order should be taken for granted by a tax-paying populace.

Although Stephanie Marie's mysterious injury on Christmas day had turned out not to be seriously harmful, Jean and his family still faced Mathilde's almost certain death. It was a terrible blow for Jean—a blow to anticipate the loss of a beloved and talented daughter—and to realize that he faced such an inexorable and uncontrollable defeat at times drove him to distraction. For Jean death was the one enemy over which his determination and hard work became powerless. Facing death, he became outraged and a frustrated idiot, pawing the earth, restrained to impotency by fate. Power and money that enabled him to shape and mold his destiny in so many ways became inadequate in his most critical challenges. He had been powerless to save Lucie; he could not hold onto his mother and father; he stood by helplessly as Colonel Bush faded into death; he had to bow to death with his beloved Stephanie. And now he must standby and watch cancer, that unmentionable and filthy killer, carry away his beautiful daughter, the very presence of which was an insult to decent citizens— Christians. *What is God about, anyway.* But the pitfall of such blasphemy was not lost on Jean, and after such a private outburst he turned himself back—he went to church and prayed and burned candles.

*   *   *

In the midst of his troubles, Jean's youngest daughter, Ella Marie, twenty, was planning her debut and, as Mathilde had done more than a decade earlier, reign as a queen of Carnival—this time at the ball of the prominent krewe of Proteus. The festivities anent the great event fell into place—shopping; dressmakers with their pincushions and tape measures; parties; visits from out-of-town relatives.

Albert and Louise took a rented house on Constantinople

Street in the Garden District, two blocks off St. Charles. Louise remained there for the Carnival season, perhaps, Jean observed dryly, the most enthusiastic celebrant. It occurred to Jean that Albert might never give up the city house. His wife had no love for farm life, no matter that the "farm" was St. John Plantation of St. Martin Parish or that her husband was fast gaining renown as one of Louisiana's best sugarcane growers. Louise was determined to raise their daughter in New Orleans Society, not in a rural town surrounded by cane fields. Jean understood his son's fascination with his wife, for Louise was exciting, young, slender, and lissome as a green reed. She would be hard to say no to.

Dr. Kearny brought the worsening Mathilde down from Plaquemine, and the former queen, pressing her every resource for strength, attended the Proteus Ball enough to see her baby sister sparkle in the glamor of one evening as she herself had done. As soon as she had seen Ella glide one full circle around the ballroom on the General's arm, the exhausted Mathilde and her husband departed to spend the night in Albert's nearby house.

Jean had invited Lila to attend the ball; to his relief, she was welcomed and treated warmly by his daughters. When Albert told his father that he and Louise intended to invite Lila to stay with them in their house, Jean realized that Albert knew of the affair. Not at all dismayed, he found himself relieved. The other sons likely knew, too. Men talked . . . intimately, confidentially. But he knew his sons would never tell his daughters.

Jean thought Lila looked quite lovely in an ice blue satin gown, simply cut, embroidered with seed pearls and brilliants, which he had bought for her along with a matching blue velvet cloak and white kid gauntlets, at Kreeger's. The store had sent several ensembles to Biloxi, and she had made this selection. Jean was pleased with her tasteful choices. If Stephanie Marie guessed where such obviously expensive clothes had come from, thought Jean, she betrayed no such suspicion.

Lila was no longer young, but dressed so beautifully that she held her own among the City's young beauties and a phalanx of bejeweled dowagers. Jean beamed as lorgnettes went up when the

General led her onto the ballroom floor, and he danced with her at every opportunity. He was careful not to downplay his fascination though he wanted to be at her side all evening. Seeing her looking so feminine, so lovely, fired Jean's determination to follow her back to Biloxi as soon as he could get away and spend a restorative vacation with her. The exciting thought caused new life to throb within him, and fears for the days ahead dimmed—at least for the night of Fat Tuesday. He couldn't wait to be with her again in the Biloxi house.

CHAPTER 68

JEAN LOOKED TOWARD Lila through eyes squinted against the late afternoon sun. She lay beside him in a canvas reclining chair on the Biloxi pier, the Gulf breeze blowing her hair gently, cooling his own scalp after two hours in the hot sun. He wondered how much in love with him she was. From the things she repeatedly said to him, he saw no reason to doubt her love.

"My darling, Jean, I adore your thick, wavy hair, the cut of your moustache. Surely no man in New Orleans wears such beautifully tailored clothes or wears them so well. Your posture! There can be no businessman in the city who is so capable of enriching his properties . . . your hands are so pretty, such tapered fingers you have. No man was ever such a lover. Why a gentleman of your gifts and attainments chooses to be with me, I do not know, but I thank God for it. I want to be your lover forever . . ." Such things, when heard often enough, did become convincing to him.

Lila had told him many times, "The first thing that attracted me to you was your tender devotion to your dying Stephanie, the woman who became my truest friend in the last weeks of her life . . . whatever the circumstances of our love affair, I have found real happiness in the weekends we've had together, and I hope nothing ever comes between us." She paused to pull back her wind-blown hair with both hands. The wind had dropped and a thin fog was closing around them, swathing the end of the pier and the distant shoreline of Deer Island. "I would rather have an occasional few days with you than be with some less charming fellow day after day." Jean laughed at that; but he loved to hear her say it. He particularly liked when she finished the statement with a bold assertion about his prowess as a lover. *Wives just didn't talk that way.*

Finally he sat up and gathered towels onto his chair. "I have had enough of this heat, my dear." He pushed his feet into rubber shoes to guard against sharp shells and rocks on the beach and stickers on the grass that must be crossed to get to the house. Lila did the same, mopping perspiration from her face. He could tell she also longed for a cool bath.

*   *   *

That night, Jean stood beside the half-drawn drape in the bedroom that faced the beach, gazing through the window into the wide sweep of the moonlit lawn. Perhaps eight feet away from the bed. He turned to watch Lila, sitting up, take off her earrings and place them on the bedside table, then slide her brassiere over her shoulders; he was imagining that this was the first time he'd seen her like this. He regarded her as a beautiful woman with a graceful body, a profile with proud lines, and fair hair that suggested a sensuous beauty. Slowly she leaned back against a bank of pillows.

"Jean, I want to take us away from everything."

The cloud slipped away, and the moon filled the bedroom with a silvery light. Jean's shadow came toward her. He made no sound; there was no sound. Face-to-face with her, he saw how dark her eyes seemed. Then Lila groaned. She was in some pain; they had not made love in weeks. And everything he did was right, even his silence, as he filled her—nothing held back. She moaned again and wept in passion and in ecstasy, realizing that he was at this moment a part of her. As his senses heightened, he lost himself in the sweet scent of her embrace. For a long time, neither spoke. Finally, his mouth began moving across her stomach . . . again in the quiet of passion and release that followed, Jean at last forgot all sad thoughts of Mathilde.

They slept, but in the darkness before dawn, once again, wearily, happily, he pressed her close, his fingers clutching her buttocks, digging into her flesh. His sudden cry of exhilaration was muffled by her moans of excitement and release. When they parted, daylight streamed into the room; he knew she liked to make love in the morning, because Jean talked to her more than in the dead of night that preceded sleep. As he did now. He praised her body, part by part. He told her what he wanted to do to her before he did it. He spoke in French as well as English, constantly employing different rhythms in his speech.

This younger woman, he told himself, was like a fountain of endless marvels, and he never tired of possessing her. Age flew out the window; he was, if not young, ageless and ever strong. She remained a perfect lady in his mind, no matter how unrestrained her passion. She was a dear girl, and the erotic matter was what he called lagniappe. *Life is good.*

At the Biloxi train depot the next afternoon, Lila stood on her tiptoes to kiss Jean gently on his cheek. But there was hardly a response from him; his heavy concern about Mathilde had returned in full force. He said goodbye to her with a droopy smile that she loved and climbed aboard the L&N bound for New Orleans.

Chapter 69

"POOR MATHILDE," JEAN mumbled, "Poor Mathilde."

Two days after the death of Mathilde Levert Kearny, he read her obituary in the *Sunday Picayune* over and over, ill with sorrow but approving her identification as the daughter of a prominent and wealthy father. Again he had been thrown into soul-wrenching grief. He laid the paper aside and turned to Stephanie Marie.

"And THAT is the end of it all. Her whole existence has been a waste, a failure, because it was silenced so damned early. All her gifts and so little opportunity to use them. Even denied motherhood, all her affections cut short, death with regret. Poor Mathilde."

He stood. "But what right have I, Steph, to call her existence wasted?" Jean walked to the fireplace in his office at Third Street and leaned against the mantel, weeping uncontrollably, now. "I watched her pain-wracked body diminish to seventy pounds after three years of suffering. Even as I took her to the best specialists in New York City three times, her condition continued to worsen. Her case was especially virulent and all the specialists told us her case was 'out of hand.' Your Mother's death at forty-seven was cruel, I thought, but thirty-three! Steph! Thirty-three!"

"Papa, Papa, stop this! What good is this sort of talk going to do anybody? It won't bring Mathilde back." Completely dedicated to her father and the rest of the family for the past eight years, Stephanie could no longer stand to see him like this. She had witnessed enough of it after her mother's death. And Jean knew it was not Stephanie Marie's way of dealing with grief: One pushed on, one did not dramatize one's feelings, one grieved privately.

Jean paid little attention. "Poor, poor Mathilde. Some people are fortunate enough to enjoy growing old, others are never young; Mathilde was that way. She was born mature, sensible, charitable. She was our beauty, she became well-loved in society. Her life seemed to be a constant fight between seeking happiness and finding heartache . . ."

And on he went, reviewing the familiar account of her near death at birth, along with her mother, her pulmonary weaknesses, her nose colds and coughs in the fall of the year. Despite it all, Jean intoned, her disposition remained loving.

"Go on," said Steph. "Is there more?" Stephanie's own grief was deep, her father knew, for her sister was fun-loving and a happy, loving person. She wearied of her father's endless harangue.

Startled, Jean gazed for a moment over Stephanie's shoulders, as though he had just seen Mathilde passing the office door. Turning sad eyes to the window, he saw that a light rain had begun to fall, cooling the steamy April morning.

"No father could have been so proud as I was celebrating the last night of Carnival when she was queen of Comus. What a night that was. Just think, Mathilde's dear mother had only four years to live." He took out a fresh handkerchief.

Stephanie drew a deep breath; steady-eyed, she looked around his office, where they had been alone since breakfast. "Where are the other family members?" she muttered. Everyone had attended 7 'o'clock Mass. The grandfather clock in the hall chimed 11:30.

Jean continued to talk about Mathilde, her beauty, accomplishments, modesty, her superiority over "all her little butterfly friends the night of her reign."

*   *   *

An exemplary mourner to the black band around the gray sleeve of his morning coat, his bearing and behavior in perfect accord with everyday dignified manners and attitudes, Jean watched Mathilde's body placed in the family tomb at Metairie Cemetery on ground where the Metairie Race Course grandstand used to be. The large tomb was embellished with a gable in the roof section and a thick granite cross on top. She was placed among some of the most prominent men and women in business, cultural, political and social life of New Orleans.

William Claiborne, the first American governor of Louisiana during its territorial period and after it became a state in 1812, was buried there. So were Republican Governor Henry Clay Warmoth, whose inauguration in 1868 ushered in Louisiana's darkest political period of corrupt state legislatures during Reconstruction; Percy Benton Stewart Pinchback, Louisiana's only black governor, who filled Warmoth's office for a month after Warmoth resigned in late 1872 to avoid impeachment; Confederate Generals P.G.T. Beauregard of New Orleans, who ordered bombardment of Fort Sumter, and Richard Taylor, son of Louisiana's only president, Zachery Taylor. Jefferson Davis died in the City and his remains were entombed temporarily before being transferred to Richmond, Virginia.

After burial, Jean returned to the Jesuit church and prayed for several hours, his face concealed in a white handkerchief. Then he walked along Baronne Street and over to St. Charles toward Third Street at a solemn, funereal pace, his cutaway flawless, his chin up, his face a mask.

Now, looking into Stephanie Marie's eyes, blinking his own streaming tears, Jean said: "Poor Mathilde. She was so happy in life, so brave in death. Was her uncomplaining life of devotion to her family, to Dr. Kearny, to her God a wasted existence? Was it really?" Jean pulled the clipping of the obituary from his cutaway pocket, unfolded it, and stared for a few moments at the date at the top of the page: "April 9, 1906."

"Father . . ." Stephanie was perplexed as he again posed this question. She remained silent.

"If it were possible, I should attempt steps with the Vatican to have her canonized."

Stephanie emitted a gasp.

Jean walked slowly to the back of the house. Wearily, he took a bag of cracked corn from the pantry to scatter in the chickenyard. He knew he would smile again. Work was his refuge, as it had been through all his griefs and losses. Ambitions and challenges that both pushed and pulled Jean Baptiste Levert to action soon stirred his instinctive urges to get up and go again. And of course, he reminded himself, in Biloxi there was Lila, who could transform his despair and dejection into strength. While he pictured her firm and youthful little body, the barred rock rooster lowered his head and ran toward a generous spray of corn on the bare earth of the chickenyard.

CHAPTER 70

JEAN BAPTISTE STEPPED onto the front porch at Biloxi house, shaded his eyes, and studied the horizon beyond Deer Island, which was located several hundred yards in front of the Levert pier. He did not feel right about this Friday afternoon. Dark, ominously heavy clouds had built up. The sky had grown so dark and gloomy that the oil lamps inside had been lit.

He turned to Lila, sitting in one of the tall rockers, "This weather does not look good."

"It does look unusual, not like one of our afternoon squalls."

"I've always hoped I never witness a Gulf hurricane in Biloxi. My dear Lila, I pray no such misfortune is about to occur." He bit his lower lip, reflecting on the grim possibility of his words.

"Willie!" he called to the black man sweeping the curved brick walk near the porch, "run down to the newspaper office and tell Mr. Harkey that I want to know if he has received any wires about a storm in the Gulf." Jean paused, still studying the horizon, as if he were waiting for some sign the weather was about to improve. "If a storm is coming we need to begin preparations to ride it out now. So be gone. Hurry!"

"I go right now, Mister Lavare," said Willie. He gave a muttered "yessir" and went off, shoes crunching on shells in the driveway. And Jean watched him fly down the front beach road toward Biloxi's business district.

Jean had anticipated a great gathering with his family this Labor Day weekend, and he'd asked Stephanie Marie and Beatrice to make detailed plans for the gala. The entire family had not gotten together at the house in three years, since Mathilde's death, and new in-laws and grandchildren had swelled the ranks in the meantime. The thought of getting control of Rienzi and all of its surrounding property, to take over its operation and finances, had helped lift him from his obsessive grief over Mathilde. Through all his distractions from business, Rienzi and Emile Morvant had lain in the back of his mind.

Jean's party, the largest, had arrived on the L&N at noon Thursday. He had reserved an entire all-steel Pullman car nearest the diner, and Stephanie Marie, Ella, Stella, Lawrence, and Robert traveled with him. Lawrence's fiancé Amelie Gauthier, called Lulu by the family, was ill and remained in St. Martinville. Jean had been thinking about grooming twenty-eight-year-old Lawrence to handle farming operations at Banker Plantation, with Albert's assistance. The former George Banker house, which Jean had purchased at auction a decade or so before, had burned to the ground. He had decided to build a house on Banker as a surprise wedding gift for his son and Lulu, who planned to marry later in the year. Jean, Jr.'s wife, Julia, and their year-old daughter, Elizabeth, and seven-month old son, Jean III, traveled with Jean as his guest, because Jean, Jr. couldn't leave the City until Friday evening.

Later on Thursday Freddy and Molly had arrived from Birmingham with their eight-year-old son, John Bertels, and Albert and Louise were coming from St. John with their two daughters, Stephanie, nine, and Sylvia, one. Jean sent the Levert carriage to the depot to meet every train, including that of Beatrice and Dr. Kearny, who arrived late Thursday night from Plaquemine via New Orleans.

Jean regretted that the Colonel and Elizabeth Behan could not come for the holiday, for he counted the Colonel as his best friend. He thought of his brothers, who had never managed to afford for their families the luxuries that he provided for his. He knew Amèdèe was having trouble keeping a roof over his wife and children; they remained at Golden Ridge. Jean might have invited Augie and Aurelie this weekend, but Augie was not well enough to make the trip from St. Delphine. Most of Augie's recent letters to Jean had told of Amèdèe's financial problems, hinting that Jean might bail out the youngest brother, as Augie had been trying to do for several years. But Jean did not respond to such thinly veiled pleas; he had long despaired over Amèdèe's lack of acumen as a businessman. Lending him funds, Jean reasoned, would be throwing good money after bad. Worse, Jean didn't like Amèdèe's stubborn streak and that he ignored his judgments and advice. However, Augie's health concerned him, and he meant to visit his brother as soon as work permitted.

Jean had made sure the house help from the City had put every bed in readiness, oversaw much cooking, and readied extra rooms for nurses and servants in the rear of the house and in the caretaker's house in back before the family members arrived.

Growing more anxious about the weather, Jean paced the length of the porch several times before sitting down; the drizzle had changed to rain. Beatrice and Freddy had joined him and Lila. Albert came out with a silver tumbler of bourbon on crushed ice, chilly rivulets of condensation rolling down the tumbler's sides into his hand.

"Papa, may I serve you a little toddy?"

"No, thank you," said Jean curtly. Seeing Albert drink always annoyed him; his son liked drinking too well. So much depended upon his farmer son, and any threatening weakness made Jean nervous, irritable.

"I'd like one, Albert," said Freddy. "Who is not here, yet, Papa?"

"Everyone is here except for Junior. He will arrive on the late train tonight. It's due about 12:20, isn't it, Bea?"

"Yes, sir. It's the train Dr. Kearny and I came out on last night." She shivered. "It's a scary trip—so dark out there in the Rigolets." She hugged her arms. "I closed the curtains and pretended we were on dry land."

Jean glanced at Bea's slightly protruding belly; she was pregnant, though neither she nor Dr. Kearny had mentioned it to him. Then he realized he had not seen his daughter in two years, since she had been established in marriage to Dr. Kearny, his former son-in-law and a man he knew well and trusted.

Soon Willie, who had worked for Jean since he bought the house, came loping back through the rain across the grassy lawn. "Mister Lavare! Mister Lavare! Hur'cane in Gulf. Mr. Hahkey, the man down at the paper, done got messages from boats trying to take cover. They say it a big storm, gonna hit long abouts here." He handed Jean a copy of a telegram.

"Tropical storm centered in Gulf of Mexico, moving slowly north northwest . . . winds approaching 60 miles per hour . . ." Jean folded the flimsy yellow paper and pushed it into the pocket of his shirt he wore under his mackintosh, and gazed out at the Sound where the dark sky and black-brown water met with no perceptible boundary. *Nothing particularly worrisome for tropical storms come ashore every summer, bringing wind and rain, even flooding; damage is rare. But if this storm were to stay on its current track . . .* He paced the porch some more then stopped and tapped the glass to read the barometric pressure, but muttered that it was not working.

"I am concerned about Junior," said Jean. He looked at Lila. "Those tracks in the Rigolets are very low." He turned to find Julia, but she was evidently inside the house.

Stephanie Marie came through the screened doors. "My goodness! Look at those clouds, Papa!"

Beatrice hurried to her older sister. "A bad storm is coming, Steph. Mr. Harkey at the paper has received wires. Junior is on the night train coming through the Rigolets."

"Oh, I know it. Poor Jean. Poor Julia. She will be frantic. There is nothing we can do."

Stephanie's voice reflected the fears of all the family. Even as they stood there, a strong wind gust swept over the lawn and whipped banana trees and fat arborvitae shrubs about.

Jean glanced at his watch—five o'clock. *Hours to wait for Junior's train.*

"Willie, you and Diggy be down there when that train arrives tonight. Bring Mr. Junior right on home as soon as he gets off." Jean decided he would have a little drink of bourbon after all. He felt he needed it.

In the kitchen he found Ella Marie and Stella breaking ice with the ice pick. He was shocked to find his daughters making alcoholic drinks for themselves. *The younger generation observes few restrictions about anything.* "Young ladies don't drink whiskey, daughters! I don't approve of you behaving like common hussies." Two years older than Ella at twenty-six, Stella loved to talk, but she was speechless, now. An expression of embarrassment crossed Ella's face as she nervously rubbed her hair pulled back in a bun like Bea's. He watched the girls set their glasses on the drainboard and leave the kitchen seemingly chastened.

After they left, Jean put their ice into his own tumbler and poured a generous amount of bourbon over it. He studied its golden glow before taking a sip.

Outside, the storm continued to grow in intensity, as gust after gust slammed into the house. Jean felt the house tremble, but it remained firmly anchored on its foundation. Suddenly the sound of waves crashing against the beach frightened him. On most days, he knew the Mississippi Sound was as calm as a big lake, that swells did not crash but rather played themselves out on the sand. Jean swallowed more bourbon. He was glad that Lila was here. As the bourbon warmed his throat and stomach, he wished that only she was here with him.

Jean had continued to see Lila Beaugez as often as his busy schedule allowed, relying on her for romance as well as for comfortable companionship. He found ways to include her in the family's frequent gatherings at the house, which had become a year-round mecca for various branches of the growing family, making their trysts more difficult to arrange.

At 10 o'clock, Willie and Diggy went to the barn to try to hitch the horses to the carriage as they had been told. Jean heard a great commotion and went out to find the horses rearing, whinnying, their eyes rolling in fright. Jean quickly closed the barn doors.

"Them horses ain't goin nowhere, Mister Lavare. Look at em. Look at they ears laid back. They scarit to death. Look at em!"

Willie held to the reins, but he was clearly terrified himself. Diggy cowered in a corner.

Jean shook his head. "No, you can't go out in this. Try to quiet them and leave them with some oats and water." A blast of wind hit the barn and the frightened horses reared again. As he hurried past the barn, Jean heard the extra servants whimpering inside. But as strong as the barn was, he knew they were as safe there as they would be anywhere. He rushed on past.

Ella waited for her father in the kitchen. "I'm frightened, Papa. What are we going to do? What about Jean? I'm afraid this house will blow away." As the sound of the wind grew louder, she and Stella clung together near the sink.

Jean summoned everyone to the center sitting room and urged them to sit down and try to be calm. He was not calm himself, but he hoped that was not evident. He was the head of this household, and it was up to him to prevent panic. More and more he took pride in having a large adult family. He often remarked to Colonel Behan that he felt like a potentate when they were all with him. There was strength in numbers, Jean believed, and he drew himself up with dignity anytime he walked down a church isle with his children behind him; watched his handsome sons in white tie and tails and their richly garbed and for the most part pretty wives at a brilliant Carnival ball. Electricity and the telephone had gone out, so Jean ordered Willie to bring in more oil lamps from the kitchen. Jean's greatest fear was for his son on the train, struggling through the marshes between New Orleans and the Mississippi Coast. *Mon dieu. Mon dieu.*

He walked over to Julia, who sat in a corner holding her sleeping son. She looked up at him with large fearful eyes. *Mon dieu, how appealing this girl is.* He laid his hand on her shoulder.

"Mr. Levert," she faltered. "I am afraid for Jean." She laid the child gently on the soft chair and stood up. Her eyes were level with his. He put his arms around her to comfort her, and she melted in his arms. *"Mon dieu! Mon dieu!"* He could tell his son's wife was terrified. He stroked her shoulder. "Poor girl. Poor girl."

He gently lowered her into the chair beside her son. He backed away and looked around for Lila, and he found her dozing in a large chair. He walked over and stood by her chair as if for protection.

"Stella, perhaps you and Ella should bring in some sandwiches from the icebox. Where is Vic?"

"Vic is in New Orleans, Papa," said Stephanie tensely. "Come on, girls. Come with me into the kitchen." She took a lamp. They met Albert at the swinging door, carrying a tray of glasses, ice, and a bottle of liquor, and a candle that provided enough light for him to make his way.

Jean stopped him and poured himself another small drink as the house shuddered under the blow of a violent wind gust. Jean and Albert heard the beams, posts, and joists of the fifteen-year-old house creaking. They swore at the same time; both found some comfort in the rapport. Albert smiled.

"My God, Papa, I believe we will blow away."

"No, we won't. Get over there and comfort your wife and children, Albert. You will be no help to anyone if you are drunk. You have had enough!"

Jean reminded Albert of the hurricanes they had lived through at St. John.

"This is worse than St. John!" said Albert, moving toward Louise.

"We're completely exposed here," said Jean. "This is quite different from the wind that loses strength as it blows across a hundred miles of land before it gets to St. John."

"What about the barrier islands, Ship and Horn? I expected them to give us some protection."

"I'm sure things would be worse without them."

Jean imagined all the houses along the Gulf Coast to be in much the same state of fear and suspended activity as Biloxi house. The long stuffy sitting room that smelled heavily of oil lamps, their flat pinkish light burned dully, steadily, in the sooty chimneys. Outside he could hear everything being slung about out of control in the fierce, roaring wind. Occasionally, Jean saw a parent take a child out of sight for a dark trip to the bathroom. He knew no one was comfortable; certainly no one was relaxed.

* * *

At 8 o'clock Saturday morning, after the wind had died down, Junior threw open the front screened door and staggered into the wide hall, filthy and wringing wet. Jean noticed that his hair was plastered to his head, his eyes wild with fever. All Jean could say was, "Oh, my God! Oh, my God!"

"Quickly!" Stephanie Marie guided her dripping brother to a bathroom. "Freddy! Julia! Undress him." She drew a tub of hot water, and as quickly as possible the others bathed him and got him into the bed and covered him. Stephanie brought more blankets in an effort to ease his trembling, but his teeth continued to chatter audibly. Albert brought whiskey.

When Junior awakened hours later, he told his father and the family that great wind-driven waves had overturned the train, undermining the Bay St. Louis rail bridge and spilling passengers onto the narrow land fills and islets that bore the low tracks. "I have no idea how many miles I struggled, at times trying to swim through the wild weather before I reached Pass Christian. Thank God a doctor on his way to deliver a baby in Biloxi, picked me up in his chaise and put me out on the shell road near the house. Many, many passengers must have drowned . . . people were screaming and slashing about in the dark howling night . . ." Jean saw that his son was too ill to talk further.

Jean found Willie trying to clear twigs and branches off the front porch. Some window panes were shattered, shutters hung awry. A large limb from one of the great oaks in front was on the roof, hanging over the eaves. The shoefly was splintered.

"Willie, I want you to go down the beach to Dr. Martens' surgery and tell him my son needs attention."

"I can't go nowhere, Mister Lavare. Them pine trees from next door layin across the driveway. I can't get no horses through there."

"I don't mean on a horse. I mean on foot. You can get through the beach road. Go on, now." He turned to Albert. "Don't we have a saw?"

"No, sir, but we have an axe. I'll get Freddy to help me, and we'll begin moving those pine logs."

Soon Jean began to realize the heavy damage to the property. He assumed the whole coastline must be brutalized. *Thank God this house doesn't appear structurally damaged.* He didn't learn the full extent of the storm's damage until he had read the Biloxi newspaper a few days later: " . . . Hurricane that skirted the Gulf Coast with 85 mile winds became one of the deadliest storms ever to strike the United States, unleashing its greatest fury on Louisiana and the town of Grand Isle, with winds of 125 miles an hour . . . 350 deaths were reported . . . ." But Jean was worried about Junior. All the way from the porch he could hear him coughing.

CHAPTER 71

EVEN WITH THE illness of Jean, Jr., and the serious damage to Biloxi house from the hurricane, Jean returned to New Orleans on Wednesday feeling uplifted by the family holiday. He felt a renewed sense of unity as a result of their shared experience of the frightful hurricane; it had shored up and strengthened the family, member to member. Riding to New Orleans alone, he leaned his head back on the freshly laundered antimacassar of the train seat and acknowledged a sense of security. *What was it that made this family comforting to him now when he had had so little enthusiasm for them as they were growing up? They had been Stephanie Marie's care.* From day to day, he had scarcely noticed them. There were business matters from which he preferred to keep them excluded. Yet, by and large, he continued to learn, a large family was of value, and Jean was ready to acknowledge to himself that he was fortunate.

He had left Jean, Jr., and his family at the summer home under the care of Dr. Martens. Beatrice and Dr. Kearny remained to see to Junior's return to New Orleans by train when Dr. Martens agreed to it, and Jean asked Dr. Kearny to deal with a contractor he'd hired to repair the house. Jean and Dr. Kearny stayed in close touch by telephone, that invention now installed in all of the houses and at Jean's office. Jean was still concerned about his son, for Dr. Martens and Dr. Kearny agreed that he had pneumonia in both lungs. But Jean was encouraged by both doctors about Junior's prospects for recovery because of his youth and general good health.

*   *   *

A week after Jean returned to his office, Amèdèe and his wife, Ernestine, paid him a surprise visit at Perdido Street. They presented themselves unannounced, and in a desperate manner Amèdèe pleaded his case for a large loan. Jean was most uncomfortable to be faced with such a request, and he had no intention to give his brother money or to sign a bank note for him.

"But Jean, if you cannot help me now, I'll lose everything. We'll lose both plantations. I don't know what else I can do, who I can turn to. You know Augie kept his interest in the plantations after you sold yours to us, but he says he can no longer help me. He is old and ill; I think he is not long for this world, frankly."

"Now, Amèdèe, I am certain you remember that I told you not to mortgage both your plantations. What was it for? Twenty-two thousand dollars, wasn't it? What happened to all that money?"

"Jean, that was in 1901 and 1902, six, seven years ago. I retired some debts. I met payrolls and bought new equipment and plant seed. I managed well for awhile, but expenses were too much, and I fell behind on mortgage payments. Especially after two bad hurricanes caused me to go into what meager savings we had for repairs to the houses and cane fields. Now the Plaquemine bank is threatening foreclosure. I don't have any money left. I still have a large family at home that I am responsible for. Let me tell you, I have done my best."

"Obviously, your best was not good enough," said Jean, coldly. His voice was edged, his mouth took on a half-mocking twist. "I must remind you that I carried you on and off for years. But you always ignored my advice. You are a pretty good farmer, Amèdèe, but you have no business sense, and I have no intention of going on. I must say, too, that my cash is tied up right now with recent purchases, and I really have no options."

He did not add that he had recently learned that a considerable tract of downtown real estate, including a prominent New Orleans hotel, was almost sure to go on the market soon, and that he planned to invest heavily in it, if not get a controlling interest, if he could make a good deal. He knew the deal required all the ready money he could come up with. He realized adding a large hotel to his already impressive slate of real estate holdings in the City would increase his stature mightily in financial circles there. He did not intend to miss an opportunity for such growth if he could manage.

There was a long silence, broken by cooing pigeons on the sill of the open office window, by shouts and clatter of vehicles rising up from Perdido two stories below. Amèdèe's seedy appearance and that of his dowdy wife made Jean more uncomfortable. He thought his brother's flaccid face, with dark circles under both eyes, might be from lack of sleep or worry over his finances or both. *Damn Amèdèe. Damn him. I can't support the whole world. I'm responsible for my own army of Leverts. Most of my children rely on me for something. They're due my first consideration.*

Ernestine's voice interrupted his thoughts. "Do you plan to pick up our plantations when the bank puts them up for auction?" A few years younger than her husband at sixty-three, she patted her fat cheek and gave her brother-in-law a stern glance.

"What? Certainly not!" He tightened his jaw. *The nerve of the woman. No doubt she's heard talk about me from the spinsters in Emile Morvant's family.* Having learned from Emile how aggressive Jean could be in his business moves—a joint venture with him often ended up with him owning the business—the spinsters had accused Jean of deliberately tricking Emile into forming Levert and Morvant Company in 1907 to incorporate Rienzi, Webre, and Orange Grove plantations, the latter a three-hundred-acre estate with fields and sugarhouse located behind Rienzi; so Jean could gain majority control of the Thibodaux properties; so he could ensure his own upper hand. He turned to Amèdèe.

"I'm sorry, Amèdèe. I simply do not have the cash to bail you out this time. Perhaps there is someone else you can call on." He clasped his hands behind his back and began to pace in front of his desk, frowning. He wanted them to leave; he had things to do today. Many things.

But Amèdèe persisted: "Jean, I am talking about Golden Ridge, our ancestral home, where we were all born and reared, *Père and Mère's* plantation, the place they put their hearts and lives into. You know it's been my home for so many years. And Willow Glen was part of your wife's inheritance. They're the only properties I've ever owned in my life. I've never owned any other property, not one inch of land. I'll sign a promissory note to pay you back in three years. Anything you demand."

The more Amèdèe begged, the more resolute Jean became. He stood up. "The answer is no, Amèdèe! At this time I simply do not have that kind of money available." He might have added, "And if I did, I have lost whatever faith I had in your abilities to run these large plantations."

He bowed slightly to Ernestine. Why say more? He knew he wouldn't bother himself about it. He watched them leave his office with stricken expressions on their faces; there also was anger.

*　　*　　*

"Junior has tuberculosis," advised Dr. Gonsoulin, who was visiting Third Street a few days after Jean's encounter with his brother. "I strongly recommend that he be transported to an elevated location with a dry climate, such as Denver, Colorado, or Santa Fe, New Mexico. Both are infinitely more healthful for TB patients than New Orleans, where the heat and humidity are suffocating and breathing is not easy for anyone."

To Jean and the family, Denver seemed more remote and colder than Santa Fe. Much colder. Stephanie Marie argued most strongly for Santa Fe for Jean, Jr., because she had a friend living there and her friend might be of some assistance in getting her brother settled. Jean knew Junior did not have strong feelings about the choice; Junior only agreed that Denver might be too cold, too snowy in wintertime.

Immediately Jean began to make plans to move the young family. He thought it best if Stephanie accompanied Julia and her two children and with the help of Stephanie's friend, could find the best housing for them. Then he decided that Lawrence should also go along. Jean knew accommodations likely would be primitive, for New Mexico, still a territory, had not yet been admitted to the union as a state.

"What would we do without you? I truly believe this change will make my husband well," said Julia, with tears in her eyes, holding Jean's hand. Julia had come into Jean's office at Third Street on the night after the decision to go to Sante Fe.

Her words touched him, a slight smile appearing at one corner of his mouth. He encircled his pretty daughter-in-law's shoulders as he walked her to the door and bade her goodnight. But he could not help but be fearful for Jean. Jr., for tuberculosis was a fearsome, contagious disease, one that claimed the life of many of its victims. He was worried because Junior couldn't seem to throw off the debilitating symptoms that had hung on since his frightful night of exposure during the Biloxi hurricane. He thought his son did not look well at all, and he coughed continually, pressing a handkerchief to his mouth as he did. He figured the rest of the family would be safer with the young man gone. As it was, they had moved him to a back bedroom upstairs where he was isolated, and Jean made certain all visitors washed their hands in a bowl of disinfectant near the door as they departed, and did not touch him.

*   *   *

Jean was pleased when he learned that his secretary had made complete arrangements for transportation by the best available accommodations on the Southern Pacific train from New Orleans to Santa Fe. When the day of departure came, he bade Julia, Junior, and their two children farewell from the front gate at Third Street. Jean only crossed himself and said a prayer as he mounted the steps and reentered the house. *My son surely will return home in restored health.*

*   *   *

The day after his family left for Santa Fe, General Levert joined Colonel Behan for lunch at Galatoire's in the French Quarter. The General clipped on his pince-nez to study the menu, but he did not have to study the hand-penned parchment for long; he dropped the spectacles on their black silk cord into his breast pocket. He could never resist Galatoire's crabmeat ravigote with French bread and butter. The Colonel joined him in his choice, and with glasses of Chardonnay, the two old friends toasted Jean, Jr., and his return to good health.

Chapter 72

AS JEAN WALKED out Magazine Street toward home, he hoped that most of his children were there. He seldom knew for sure who would be at the supper table. He had some good news and he was eager to go home to tell them.

Well, Freddy was there, home from Birmingham to confer with his father about the burgeoning real estate market there; Jean was thinking of opening a real estate office in the Alabama city, with his son as manager. Lawrence, Robert, Stella . . . oh, yes, Bea was in town, and perhaps Dr. Kearny, though the doctor could not leave Plaquemine for New Orleans as easily as his wife could. Perhaps everyone wasn't present tonight—Albert could not be—but he would announce his triumph to those who were. Jean was excited as he placed his furled umbrella in the stand near the front door at Third Street.

Ah! There's Dr. Kearny. And Stephanie! And there are Ella Marie and her husband, Mr. Gore. Nice fellow, Gore, insurance and real estate.

"Well! I am glad to see you all," Jean declared. His arrival interrupted animated conversation around the long mahogany dining table. He bowed slightly. "Dr. Mr. Gore." He drew his chair, with an elaborately embroidered cushion, out from the end of the table. His children and their spouses occupied the other nine chairs. A mahogany sideboard for silverware stood in one corner, with two silver service sets on top. Beaming, Jean sat down and pulled a white napkin across his lap by one corner; he cleared his throat.

"I have an announcement to make that should come as very good news to you all."

"Papa . . ." Stephanie Marie spoke tentatively.

Jean was annoyed to have her interrupt him. In his excitement, he forgot that Stephanie, upon whom he depended for so much, had arrived home today from Santa Fe. It never crossed his mind.

"Yes?"

"Excuse me, Papa. Perhaps you did not notice that I am back. I arrived on the noon train from Santa Fe."

"Oh, Stephanie, my dear, welcome home. I want to talk to you later about that. But right now, I have something of great importance to say." Dressed the way he always dressed for supper—business suit with starched collar and cravat—he rose and stood at his place to command more attention. He thought his military posture still was a perfect fit for his clothes and that his honorary title of General fit him fine. He had become used to wearing only the finest fabrics, and a piece of cheap material offended him. Finally, they all laid down their forks and listened.

"Today, children, has been a productive day." He told them that he was one of the agents in the liquidation of La Baronne Hotel Realty Company, which owned prime real estate in the central corridor of the New Orleans financial district of Poydras at Baronne streets; it also had built the hotel there. "The newly chartered Hotel DeSoto Company has purchased all of La Baronne's physical properties and assets, including the hotel, and has assumed many of its debts and mortgages . . ." He paused and looked around at the faces turned toward him. Still a handsome and impressive gentleman at seventy-four, he ran his hand through his hair, thick and wavy, almost white. He smoothed his full, expertly trimmed moustache. He realized that they weren't listening; no one spoke. Unmoved by their lack of enthusiasm, Jean added, "It is going to be a great long-term investment for every one of you."

Finally, Ella's husband, Joseph Maybin Gore, responded: "How very interesting, Mr. Levert. Are we to be privy to any of the details of the transaction?" A balding man of thirty, with ears measuring four inches in length on a rather large head, Gore knew the La

Baronne properties were to be liquidated and sold. Jean knew that he knew, for they had discussed their value. Jean respected his son-in-law's judgment of investments, but he had not sought his approval or advice in the matter.

"Joseph, I'll be delighted to discuss more details with you, presently. The deed is done, so I'm not looking for counsel. However, I am about to buy some warehouses downtown and also a tract of land at Broadway and Freret Street, then maybe improve the land and build some houses and several duplexes on it. I'll be interested in your opinion of these purchases." Ella smiled at this manifestation of confidence in her young husband. They had been married recently at the Jesuit church, where many important family occasions had been observed, in a major social event of the season.

Other than Joe Gore's response, Jean's children showed no interest. Finally Freddy stood and proposed a toast. Jean, who had not seen Freddy for several months, noticed that he'd put on weight, had drooping bags under each eye. Jean also saw that his son was not altogether sober.

"Here's to . . . what hotel is it, sir? You haven't told us what hotel it is." His stemmed glass, half raised, was suspended before him, his wine atilt.

"It's the DeSoto! Used to be the Denechaud, built in 1905, nine stories high," said Jean. "But the hotel's only a portion of the valuable properties. I'm proud to say that I am now one of the owners of the Hotel DeSoto Company as well as the hotel, with thirty shares, and I was elected to the first board of directors. I mean to keep buying up shares of this new company until I have controlling interest." A slow "aahhh" sounded among the diners. "And I was very pleased when I learned the hotel had the first hydraulic elevator ever to be installed and the first basement ever built in this city."

"That's near your office, isn't it, Father?" asked Stephanie. "I daresay it will make you lots of money. Do you plan to remodel, redecorate?"

Jean smiled gratefully at his daughter. "There's been no decision about that. But it is a functioning hotel, earning good revenues without remodeling, so it may be that I will begin making money out of it without further ado." Quickly he went on:

"The other day I signed papers to buy, for a good price, about 900 acres from a Mr. Sam Burton, after his properties were seized and put on the block." He said there was no manor house but a small home for an overseer on the property in St. Martin Parish, and that he planned to continue growing cane there. "I am eager to get over there and make some changes. In fact, I need to be there before the week is out."

Beatrice's eyes swept up and down the table. "Oh, Papa, do you have to go on buying like this," she said in a harsh voice. "These new properties will keep you gone all the time. You'll never be at home with us at night for supper. You're seldom at home as it is."

"You exaggerate, Bea," he said, brushing her negative response aside. *Why must she always seem negative?* He was unmoved. He pressed on, continuing some exchange with the men at the table. He knew most women hardly discussed or knew nothing about business. He lifted the heavy silver soup spoon to his lips. *Besides I don't need my children's applause to justify anything I do.* His deep pleasure in owning more and still more land and buildings was at base a private feeling. Beyond the joy of acquisition, it was reassuring to him to make so much money, for he never doubted that he could meet the heavy costs of his family and the upkeep of his plantations and homes.

Little was said about the DeSoto during supper, but Jean knew he would have further discussions with his sons and sons-in-law.

Finally, over demitasse, Jean addressed Stephanie: "Now, tell me about Junior."

"I left them all in good spirits. Jean is comfortable at Sunmount Sanatorium. He will be confined and treated there as needed. It is a large, spread-out building, very airy, bright and complete with every comfort and convenience for the patients. You and Dr. Gonsoulin will receive letters describing Jean's prognosis."

She told her father the sanatorium was about four miles out

in the desert, where the "air seems perfectly clean." She said the patients lie in the sun for hours at a time. On cool days they are covered with soft white blankets. "Junior is doing a lot of reading, for he has nothing but time. I have been telling everyone tonight that the most cherished gift you can send him is a good book. On most any subject. You know Jean's interests are almost limitless."

"I'm glad to hear that he is in such good care," Jean replied. "Now tell me about Julia and the children. Are they situated to your satisfaction?"

"I must say they are not. My friend Margaret and I helped Jean and Julia search for a small house. We finally found an adobe on a ranch near the edge of town, but it is very primitive. None of you could believe what a hard life Julia is going to have. She has no running water."

"What!" Jean was dumbfounded. "No water!"

"She has to go outside to a well and bring in water in a bucket and boil it on an old wood-burning stove. With this she cooks and fills a bath in the kitchen for her and the two children to bathe."

"What about a bathroom?"

"There is none. They have what is called a two-holer in the backyard."

"Oh my God!" Jean's chin had sunk to his chest and his reply seemed muffled, as if he were speaking to himself.

"I think Julia must be the most courageous woman I have ever known. She is being an absolute heroine, doing things she has never had to do in her life and bearing up without a word of complaint." Stephanie glanced at her father.

Jean was almost speechless. "Why, why, she must have some servants. Her health will not stand up under these straitened conditions. Whatever it costs, Steph, I'll take care of it. That goes for the house, too. I've already told you this. They'll no doubt need money for living expenses, of course. Junior has very little money." His left hand clutched his napkin on the tablecloth.

"Servants!" There are none of the sort you are thinking of, Papa. Let me say that I found a Mexican woman who will come every day and help with cleaning and laundry. Margaret was a great help with this. She is going to keep an eye on the family, and if this Mexican woman doesn't work out, Margaret will do her best to find another."

Lawrence, who had remained silent, added, "Miss Margaret has a car and she is going to take Julia out to the sanatorium occasionally so she can visit Junior. Somehow, Junior bought an old buckboard, but it is little more than a wagon, and the road is no road at all, just a sandy trail. I don't know what Julia needs most, an indoor toilet or a flivver." But he added, "Julia is a rock. You'd think she'd been raised way out in the sticks."

Jean noticed that everyone at the table had glum looks over the living conditions of their sister-in-law and the children. He could not imagine civilized people existing under such circumstances. He asked some more questions before he pushed back his chair and excused himself. He had had a strenuous day, and he wanted nothing more than to go to bed. He thanked Stephanie for her report and both her and Lawrence for their efforts in Santa Fe.

"Goodnight," he said to everyone. As he departed the dining room, Beatrice was at the sideboard, setting out a tray of tiny crystal glasses and a bottle of Benedictine.

When Jean got into bed, he thought briefly of his young Stephanie Dupuy, with her blonde hair and green eyes, as he often did late at night. She seemed so long ago and far away most of the time, but tonight as he lay in her girlhood bed, she seemed nearby. He fancied he smelled the faint carnation sachet she kept among her nightdresses.

He turned out the lamp and settled into the down pillows. He began to make plans to do something about the living conditions in that faraway adobe. But not so far away when his daughter-in-law and his grandchildren were in it. And having to go out behind it, God forbid. He turned on his side and fell asleep with visions of tumbleweeds blowing across a vast dusty tract.

CHAPTER 73

SITTING AT HIS office desk at Perdido Street, Jean drew up a list:

One cast iron enameled bathtub, one porcelain commode, one porcelain pedestal basin, one cast iron enameled kitchen sink, and necessary attachments for all these fixtures. He stroked his moustache and studied the list for a moment, then added: Four towel racks. He could think of nothing more that he needed to upgrade living conditions for his family in Santa Fe. Stephanie Marie had seen to the purchase of all the linens they could expect to need. He rose from his desk and stepped into the outer office.

"Miss Fortier, I want you to call Laborde Wholesale Plumbing over on Tchoupitoulas Street and order the items on this list. Just a standard grade. Don't let him sell you something fancy. Have everything billed to me here at the office. I want these things properly crated for shipment by rail to Santa Fe, New Mexico. Please ascertain how quickly Mr. Joseph Laborde can prepare this order.

"Now, I must go to Santa Fe to make certain that Jean, Jr.'s family is properly housed. When you are certain of a date, I want you to make a reservation for me to Santa Fe, best Pullman accommodations they have. Have these crated fixtures shipped on my ticket." He checked the list again. "Miss Fortier, please keep me informed as to your progress so I can plan accordingly. I have much business going on here, and I want to be gone only for the time necessary for me to stay long enough to get these improvements accomplished. I dare say it will take a few days."

He slipped his watch from his vest pocket, the heavy gold chain arcing out from the other side of his broad front. "I must get to the Boston Club for a luncheon engagement." With his thumb, he slipped the watch back into the small pocket. He returned to his private office for his hat and cane.

"I'll attend to this immediately, Mr. Levert. Enjoy your lunch."

*   *   *

Jean rose as Colonel Behan approached the table in the club dining room. "Colonel! I must say you're looking fit." He clutched his napkin in one hand. "I've signaled for your drink." Jean chuckled as they sat together. "Not that I need to tell Boudreau after all these years." He noticed the lines in Behan's aging face creased more deeply in a warm expression as he faced his old friend across the table. Both men took careful sips of their whiskies.

"Now tell me, what is on your mind?" Colonel Behan asked finally. "What has you so intense today?"

"I'm going to Santa Fe. Junior's family is living under uncomfortable and unsanitary conditions out there. I'm having modern fixtures shipped out, and I am going to have plumbing installed in their house. Junior's provisions at the sanatorium are excellent, but Julia and my grandchildren are living in an unhealthful environment. I don't know how better to correct the situation than to just go out there and see to it myself. Stephanie Marie represented me well, but a woman can only do so much."

Colonel Behan cleared his throat. "Well, sir, I'm sure this is the most effective step you could possibly take." He patted his mouth. "It will be a rough trip, but I tell you, General, I rather envy you the adventure. When will you go?"

"As soon as my secretary can make all the arrangements."

"Where did you order the fixtures? Laborde?"

"Yes. He has the best and he will make me a good price. I've bought much from him for Third Street and for Biloxi, even for St. John, as we have remodeled. And I think he will get to it promptly. I want to get it done and get back." He told the Colonel he had some important legal matters in the works with his lawyer that must be completed as soon as possible. He sipped his drink again. "How are things with you? Are you and Elizabeth going to Europe in June?"

"No. I think we have made our last trip abroad. I hate to admit it, but neither of us feels up to another crossing. It's very wearing, you know. Elizabeth is quite undone about it. Hates to give in, you know. Paris is quite beautiful in the spring. Breathtaking . . ." His voice trailed off as the waiter served them salad and gumbo.

"Well, I'll be glad to get this business taken care of and get back to New Orleans. I have no curiosity about New Mexico."

"It has a harsh kind of beauty, about as different from New Orleans as you could find."

On the way back to his office, Jean stopped by his bank, New Orleans Canal & Banking Company, the Canal Bank, and asked to have an ample line of credit established for him at the Santa Fe National Bank Company. From there, he walked to Perdido Street.

He was amazed that the efficient Miss Fortier had gotten assurance that the plumbing order would be at the train station in one week, and that his train compartment was reserved. He complimented Miss Fortier, something he typically forgot to do, and she smiled in surprise. She wasn't the most beautiful thirty-five-year-old Jean had ever seen, but she had good looks, was a stylish dresser, and had a better-than-average figure. Jean returned to his desk to study drafted papers of incorporation that Fernand Dansereau had sent over by runner that morning. Dansereau was a highly respected corporate lawyer with whom Jean entrusted the legal organizing of all his companies. He considered his fees devilishly high, but he believed he was worth it. He never feared signing any final papers that Dansereau had drawn up. Jean studied the preliminary papers diligently and prepared to return them to the lawyer well before he left for Santa Fe.

*   *   *

The Colonel is right. This country is harsh, desolate. Texas had seemed endless to travel across, and it appeared more unsettled

and desolate as the train chugged through the long miles. Jean
continually opened and closed the window of his compartment as
he tried to adjust the income of hot dry wind. The arid heat by day
was severely uncomfortable for him, but the low humidity made the
night air seem pleasant, even cool, for August. Whatever the
temperature and humidity of air blowing in, it was laden with soot.

Within a day's ride, Jean felt filthy with soot, and his collar
and cuffs were dingily smeared. He could hardly bear to think
that at the end of this journey there would be no large warm tub
of water in which to clean himself. Even in the prewar days at
Golden Ridge there had been bathrooms and excellent baths in
copper tubs that were filled by slaves. He shook his head and
resolved to step out at the next station of any consequence and
buy a newspaper. He had finished reading the *Picayune* the first
hour out of New Orleans.

Toward evening, after four days of travel and changing trains
several times, Jean finally arrived in Santa Fe. The trip north from
El Paso on the Atchison, Topeka & Santa Fe seemed particularly
hard. Although exhausted, he was more resolute than ever to make
life more comfortable for Julia, whom he loved more than any of
his children-in-law. Also, he felt certain that this would be his
only time to make this long arduous rail trip to see his son and
his family, so he intended to do everything that he could toward
making it an effective mission.

He was surprised to find Santa Fe located so high in the Rocky
Mountains. The exceptional and exotic scenery, which Jean in no
way discounted, did not fascinate him as it might have someone
whose visit was not so dedicated. The first thing he noticed in the
little train station, a mustard-colored clapboard structure trimmed
in dingy red, was a sign that announced: BATHS FOR
GENTLEMEN. He followed an arrow that pointed across the street.
When Jean walked out of the bathhouse, where he had experienced
a surprisingly satisfying, if crude shower, he now felt renewed,
ready to do whatever he might have to do. He had taken a fresh
collar and shirt from his small valise, and felt that his appearance
was rejuvenated.

Back in the train station, the station master assured him that the crates of plumbing fixtures, which now sat on the station platform, could be taken by wagon out to the ranch the following morning. Jean was about to ask that the man get a taxi of some sort for him when a large vehicle was upon him, its loud horn blowing.

"Mr. Levert! Mr. Levert! It is Margaret, Stephanie's friend. I'm sorry I'm late. But here I am to take you to the ranch!" A tall handsome woman with rich auburn hair, olive skin, and a slim, lithe figure, stepped down from a Model T Ford. Jean stared in amazement. He could not remember having seen a woman driving an automobile, but this one seemed to be in full command of the elevated black machine with its canvas top folded back. Quickly, he got himself together and smiled, removing his hat to nod at the same time shifting his furled umbrella to his left hand.

"How do you do, Miss Margaret, Miss Margaret Gelpi. My daughter says you are originally from New Orleans. How kind of you to come for me. I expected no such courtesy. I was prepared to rent a cab."

Margaret laughed. "We have no cabs as you think of them in New Orleans, just a few buggies around town that meet trains and go to and from the sanatorium. Come. Toss your valise onto the back seat and get in. The trip is not long. We can get there in twenty minutes." She walked around to her door and turned the handle down sharply.

Jean followed her lead and climbed into the front passenger seat. He now owned an automobile, and he had hired a chauffeur-valet to drive him around New Orleans in the new Buick Touring car. Not that Jean wanted to be driven anywhere that he could walk, and that was considerable. But automobiles were no longer exotic creations to him. In New Orleans, one had only to look out one's window to see one rolling noisily past.

Now, he sat in the Model T and slammed the door smartly. To his shock and before he could speak, this lovely creature, who was Stephanie's age but looked younger, jumped down, hurried to the front of the automobile, and cranked the engine into action.

Just as quickly, she trotted around to the car door, climbed in, stepped on the foot pedal, and took off down the road, stirring clouds of yellow dust and blowing her horn loudly at two swarthy men in enormous hats and wrapped in striped blankets. She looked over at Jean good-naturally and smiled with her large, full mouth, which was the color of a certain large plum that grew on Golden Ridge before the war.

Mon dieu. Jean's gloved right hand gripped the door beside him. *Mon dieu.*

When Margaret stopped the car in a sandy yard before an undistinguished adobe dwelling, Jean's heart sank—the house was indeed a poor hovel. Julia and her two children came running through the low door screaming his name before he could exclaim over it. He clasped his daughter-in-law close to him and kissed her soft cheek; he patted his grandchildren on the head. His grandchildren, Elizabeth and Jean III, hugged and kissed their grandfather excitedly. To his surprise, he noticed that Julia was expecting another child.

"Please come in, Papa, Juana has prepared a lunch for all of us. Considering our primitive kitchen, we think we have done quite a good job." Jean entered the hut with trepidation. The luxurious accommodations that he was accustomed to in New Orleans seemed a world away. When Julia offered to take his coat, he let her have it without protest, for the temperature was high. He sat down at their table in his shirt sleeves, something he had seldom done in his adult life. After they enjoyed a simple meal served by the silent Mexican woman, who padded back and forth between the table and an open hearth, passing bread and rich stew, Julia led her father-in-law into a small back room furnished with a narrow bed, where his valise now lay. A table held a washbowl and a soft thick towel monogrammed with an elaborate *JBL*. Julia indicated an enameled chamber pot beyond the bed. She left him in the room and closed the door behind her.

Mon dieu. He felt desperate, as though he must rush right back into Santa Fe and locate a plumber before nightfall and get him out here immediately to begin work on the installation of the modern fixtures he had brought from New Orleans. *This state of affairs simply will not do.* He knew Julia was strong-willed and came from good stock, the Buckners of New Orleans, some of whom were bankers and brokers. But he wasn't sure if she could endure and survive primitive conditions in the desert.

He washed his hands. After he returned to what Julia called the parlor area, he sat down with her and Margaret. The space was a corner of the larger room that included the dining table. Both children leaned against their mother's knees and looked at their grandfather.

"Mr. Levert, I'll come back early in the morning and drive you into town to talk with a plumber I know. I'm not certain he is what you want, but it is worth a try. I understand you have brought quite a number of nice appliances and fixtures that will transform the house into something quite comfortable. Then day after tomorrow I'll drive you out to the sanatorium for a visit with your son."

"You are very kind. I hardly know how to thank you, but I do thank you, and I'll be eager to get started tomorrow if it is possible. I am eager to visit my son."

When Margaret stood, Jean rose politely and as fast as a man half his age might, for the presence of a handsome woman always inspired him. And out here in this Godforsaken desert he found himself in the company of two extraordinarily attractive ladies. As Margaret took her leave, Jean smiled and bowed.

*   *   *

Two Mexicans unloaded the plumbing fixtures after they were delivered the next morning and set them behind the house. Jean made a note to have the plumber bring a crowbar to open the crates; plumbers were noted for failing to have the required tools to complete a job, or in the case of the crowbar, bringing it.

Margaret arrived early and got out of her car wearing rough clothes, long brown suede culottes, a tan duster of ordinary cloth,

wide-brimmed hat, and dusty western boots. He looked at her in
wonderment as she greeted him and Julia with her wide smile.

"I keep a crowbar in my car," she said, swinging the tool
against her dark skirt.

"Well, thank you. How did you know. . . ?"

"I know you'll have to get into those crates with something."

"*Mon dieu.*"

In Santa Fe, Margaret drove to a small, dilapidated building
where she spoke rapidly in Spanish with a man whom Jean took
to be a plumber. His hair and his moustache were shaggy and as
black as coal. He had long white teeth, and after a short time, he
bared them in a big smile and began to bow repeatedly. Jean felt
sure that this indicated a satisfactory agreement for the job.

Jean did not get out of the car, and Margaret returned to assure
him that the plumber had had experience with such installations
that Julia needed and that he would be out this afternoon to open
the crates so that he could begin work early the next morning.
Jean could hardly believe his good fortune. *This woman is a
wonder.* He was embarrassed that he knew nothing about her
except that she was a good friend of Stephanie's. They had become
roommates and close friends the year that Stephanie had spent in
Paris, but Jean did not recall what Margaret was doing in Paris.

"I operate a sheep ranch," she told him as they drove back to
the ranch. "I'm surprised that Steph has not told you."

Mon dieu.

Next day they drove out to Sunmount Sanatorium, where Jean
had an emotional reunion with Junior. He met his son's doctor, a
tall handsome man with silver hair, who spoke with guarded
optimism about Junior's prognosis. The sanatorium was generally
luxurious, Jean saw. Almost everything was white, rooms and
porches spotless, all visible linens immaculate. Beds and reclining
chairs on the porches appeared comfortable, and Junior had
nothing but praise for his treatment by all the attendants. He was
looking forward to going into town for a furlough, as he called it,
at home with his family.

"Thank you, Papa, for all you are doing for us. I suppose that if it were not for you, I would die." He said this simply as an obvious fact, but without emotion. He smiled slightly when they shook hands and parted.

As he stepped out of her car, Jean said, "Thank you again, Miss Margaret. Nobody ever had a finer friend than you."

Early next morning the plumber brought a helper and began work in the bathroom. Jean was surprised at his diligence and abilities. He had expected much less, but he did not want to leave until the job was completed, and Julia, Junior, and the children had modern facilities. He was also pleased with the housemaid, Juana. She was smarter then she looked and obviously had developed great loyalty to Julia. He had not thought so at first, but things could be worse here.

While the plumbers worked inside the house, a well was dug, and a septic tank was put in place. Ditches were dug, and in less than ten days Jean was happily looking forward to getting back to New Orleans. The bath was the first room to be made usable. Stephanie had sent more sumptuous linens, including a small rug. As the kitchen facilities neared completion, Jean felt that he had never enjoyed helping anyone so much as he had in assisting his daughter-in-law. She and Juana could hardly stay out of the kitchen as that work neared completion. Junior came in for an overnight visit, and Juana prepared a fine dinner of chicken and rice and beans and tomatoes. She brought to the table a long crusty loaf of bread with butter. It was nothing like a New Orleans meal, but Jean found it quite tasty.

*   *   *

On the night before his departure, Julia and Jean sat under the stars in small chairs near the front door, talking more intimately than he had ever talked with his own children. Jean decided he must be filling an empty role in her life. She shared her fears that Junior might not return to good health. She thanked him for his help in a most touching manner and told him she loved him as though he were her own father.

Jean felt his eyes sting as he reached for her small hand. "My dear child. It gives me nothing but pleasure to be able to make things more comfortable for you and your husband and the children." He cleared his throat. "Now tell me, Julia, will $150 per month be enough for you to run your house? I based that amount on rough estimates . . ."

"Oh, Papa, yes! We can live handsomely on that. It's perfectly wonderful . . ."

"Well, now, I have a little surprise for you, my dear. I have purchased a car for you, and Miss Margaret has agreed to teach you to drive it."

Julia gasped. "A car! My goodness. The children and I can go out to see Jean whenever we want to. Thank you."

"It isn't brand new. I did not find a new car dealer in Santa Fe. But Miss Margaret learned of this nice Buick being for sale by the owner. She will see that it is driven out here tomorrow afternoon. It is a very nice car and only two years old. But if you have any problems with it, I will expect to pay for whatever maintenance you are faced with."

To his dismay, he realized Julia was weeping softly into her handkerchief.

From somewhere, the face and voice of Colonel Louis Bush came to his mind. What he was doing for Julia and Junior was a small thing, but perhaps it fit into the Colonel's suggestions that he do something for others. Jean had mystifying feelings about his new role.

But *mon dieu*, how he longed to get home to Louisiana, lush and green. To Third Street. To Perdido Street. To St. John. And Biloxi. He had not seen Lila in a month.

CHAPTER 74

"SEVEN, PLEASE," JEAN said excitedly to the uniformed elevator operator in the Carondelet Building at Carondelet and Gravier streets. He had just turned into the building after walking there from his office on Perdido, a few blocks away. But he wished he'd waited to see his attorney, perhaps tomorrow morning when he knew it would be cooler for a walk.

The late August heat on this afternoon felt intense, and he could not have been more uncomfortable in his white linen suit that he usually wore through the summer. But, as Beatrice had told him at breakfast, he looked "cooler in the light wool and extremely well-groomed." Jean often admitted to certain vanities, and he preferred linen, blue and white stripped seersucker, or poplin, as a uniform for summer in the City.

Jean liked to ride the elevator. They were not numerous in New Orleans, but he knew this one had been one of the first installed in the City. It had a soft rug and mirrors all around. He gripped the polished brass bar on the wall beside him after stepping into it. At the seventh floor, the car came to a shuddery stop. The operator opened the heavy door, then the elaborate brass folding gate that guarded against an accident at the threshold, which could be a fall of thirteen stories in this building. Jean stepped out safely, with an invariable small thrill of survival in his spine. He always got it upon leaving an elevator unharmed. Several passengers stepped in, the doors closed again, and the trip below began.

Fernand Dansereau's receptionist was homely, but she was pleasant enough as she invited Jean to be seated while she announced him. He thought she looked much better from behind, and he could see her ankles, and her derriere was charming. *Thank God women no longer wear bustles, their skirts dragging behind.* She reappeared and asked him to enter Dansereau's private office, which he found to be smaller than his Perdido office, but more elaborately furnished: Two oriental rugs; a large oil painting of a famous Louisiana plantation house that covered the wall behind his mahogany desk; smaller paintings of landscapes and French Quarter streets; a curved-back, leather upholstered sofa; sturdy wooden shelves along one wall holding legal books and briefs; and a grandfather clock in the corner about to chime two o'clock.

Jean met Dansereau's private secretary, Adair Gautreaux, in the door's confining space; she no doubt had been in to lay all the papers of incorporation on the desk. She was another story, thought Jean, a beautiful young lady with a winsome, even alluring, smile. He exhaled sharply as they faced each other in the doorway. He sighed.

Dansereau looked up from his work, squinting through the cigarette smoke that wreathed his head. "How are you, General?" the forty-three-year-old lawyer said. "I hope you were able to accomplish what you set out to do in Santa Fe?" He rose and walked from behind his desk, hand extended. After shaking Jean's hand he smoothed his prematurely gray hair.

"Very well, thank you, Fernand. A bit overheated from my walk over here. I did achieve my goals, thank you, but I'm glad to be back from the desert." He waved aside the cigarette smoke.

"Forgive me, sir, but you should have taken a cab."

"Oh, no. I never do that."

The lawyer sat for a few seconds, dragging on his cigarette. "Why not?"

"It's too expensive, for one thing."

Dansereau chuckled, for Jean was one of his most wealthy clients. He drew his dark brows together, studying Jean as if reassessing him.

"Also, mainly, because I like to walk. I walk the twenty or so blocks from my home on Third Street to my office as often as possible, summer and winter. I just enjoy the exercise." Dansereau shrugged, apparently ready to let the matter drop. He snuffed his cigarette.

"Well, sir, I have the articles of incorporation for Levert St. John for your review and signature. I found no serious notations on the copy I sent to you to read before you left for Santa Fe." Dansereau waited for Jean to remove his copy from his briefcase, then he flipped through the lengthy document to make sure all the pages were in order. "It has been notarized, but let's go over most of it together."

He read fast and monotonously, covering every possible endeavor relevant to agriculture, even animal husbandry, in southwest Louisiana. But Jean listened carefully, intent on missing nothing. "General, you are chartered 'with capital stock fixed at two hundred and fifty thousand dollars, to do just about any imaginable business related to sugarcane . . . to buy, sell, plant, cultivate, produce and harvest cane; to manufacture, refine, buy or sell, and generally deal in sugar, molasses . . . to acquire, own, and operate sugar plantations and factories, and other works necessary therefore . . .' The corporation is domiciled in New Orleans, as you requested . . . ."

Jean gave Dansereau a slantwise look that held grudging admiration, for he was pleased with the masterly document designed to cover his seven plantations in St. Martin Parish, including St. John, Banker, and Catahoula; to protect these extensive holdings and keep them thriving for generations.

No one who knew much about Jean was surprised at the share distribution: Jean, 1,488 shares. Everyone else on the board of directors, including his children, Dr. Kearny, Joe Gore, and Jack Swanson, Stella's husband, were granted one share. *I know exactly what I'm doing. I've worked too hard, too long, and with too much success to let my children, none of whom have thus far shown any special talent for business or respect for money, become empowered to undo my ingenious achievements.*

Dansereau interrupted his thoughts when he handed the original copy of the document to Jean for all the signatures. "And how about the realty business in Birmingham?" Fernand rubbed his neatly cropped beard and moustache, which had a reddish tinge to them. "Are we to incorporate in Birmingham?"

"What? Oh, yes, well yes. Freddy insists that real estate has a great future in Birmingham, and as far as I can tell, he is right. He's making an excellent living selling real estate, as I have told you. Commercial, residential, even industrial in the mining business. Still, I am not sure just what I want to do about that yet. Now that I have St. John properly incorporated, I can turn my attention to Birmingham and other things that I have mentioned to you—a plan for some gifts—Tulane, perhaps. Later. Have I signed everything necessary here?" Jean uncrossed his legs and rose. "How is your father? I haven't seen him since the June party at the Pickwick. He seemed well."

"Oh, yes, thank you. He and Mother are well."

Jean took his cane, hat, and linen jacket from the brass tree near the door. "Give him my regards." He smiled slightly, and walked through the door toward the elevator.

CHAPTER 75

JEAN BAPTISTE LEANED lightly on his gold-headed cane and studied the changes in the flora at St. Delphine Plantation. Since he was here for his father's funeral years before, he saw there had been many changes. Countless forest trees were gone from the front and back lawns, victims, he had learned, of a ruinous hurricane six years earlier that ripped through the river parishes from the Louisiana gulf coast. New magnolias and oaks and wild shrubbery were growing up and by now did not look altogether new. Still, he thought that the old contours had changed greatly. As he walked over to Aurelie to wrap his arm around her shoulders, a ray of sunlight pierced the gloomy midmorning.

"I wish I could have gotten here before he died, Aurelie. The train seemed to take forever. I loved Augie and had great respect for his abilities as a farmer and as a businessman and public servant, serving his parish in the Louisiana house as I served mine in the state senate. My great hope is that he left you with funds that will provide comfortably for you for the rest of your life."

Aurelie looked at him in some surprise. He thought she showed little appreciation for his words. Well, she was in the shock of grief. Jean had to acknowledge that she had never been blessed with much personality, almost no passion for any interest, but a nice woman of good background, who certainly had maintained St. Delphine in good taste. She was surrounded by eight children and twenty-odd grandchildren. Knowledge of the world was not one of her burdens. He patted her plump shoulder again and walked toward the front lawn.

He remembered the day he was here for his father's funeral—he had spoken the eulogy right about here. The place was filled with local farmers and planters, carriages, buggies, wagons everywhere. His father's respected place among the area's planters was obvious. Jean looked around; there was quite a crowd. Apparently his eighty-four-year-old brother enjoyed the same respect.

And the manor house had changed. No doubt the hurricane damage necessitated carpentry that altered details. The wisteria vine no longer clung to the tall chimney at the end of the gallery. In fact, much of the gallery had been removed. *The widow Delphine Daigle wouldn't like these changes that time and circumstance have made in her picturesque plantation house.* It all left him slightly disoriented, and he didn't much like the feeling.

Ah, there's Henri Bourgeois, Augie's lawyer. They saw each other at the same moment and moved to shake hands.

"Bourgeois!"

"Levert!" Then the burly, red-haired man added, "Very, very sorry, Jean." He looked around at faces in the crowd. "Where's Amèdèe? I've looked everywhere for him. He's here, isn't he? I know he moved to New Orleans. Did he come up with you?"

"No, no. I offered to bring him, or to pay his fare on the train. But Amèdèe fell out with me, I'm afraid, back when he lost his plantations, our ancestral homes, to the Plaquemine bank four years ago. Yes, I understand my brother, his wife, and a number of his nine children moved to New Orleans to live with one of Ernestine's relatives. I've wondered about his situation, Henri, but I've never pursued it. But to answer your question, I think that pride made Amèdèe say no to my offer to pay his way."

Bourgeois stared at Jean, but said no more about Amèdèe.

"I'm interested in Augie's will. I'm concerned that he has left Aurelie comfortably off and I'd like to discuss it with you. Augie was a much better farmer and businessman than Amèdèe."

"I don't think you have anything to worry about, but I'll be glad to talk to you within a week or ten days."

Jean tipped his derby. "Thank you." He bowed slightly and continued to walk among the guests.

Burial was beside their mother in the church cemetery at Brusly Landing near Plaquemine. As Jean stood behind the widow, he remembered the scraping sound of the mason's trowel as the man spread wet concrete and sealed his father's tomb. He had known then that he would never like the memory of that sound.

He walked rapidly to his Buick, where Bailey, in black livery, stood waiting by the door. Soon they were on their way to New Orleans.

Often Jean made small talk with Bailey, who had a wide smile on a round face and youthful Negro wit that he thought made him a good companion from time to time; he could break the monotony of the long rides to Biloxi, for instance. But today Jean was silent, and after a few tries, Bailey gave up any attempt to talk.

Jean gazed out the window into the swamp. He had attended many family funerals. He was thinking that, except for Amèdèe, he was the last of the Levert family. There may be no one of his generation to attend his funeral when he died. Even if Amèdèe were alive, he might ignore Jean's rites. Although Jean seldom thought of it, he knew that he had offended his brother forever by refusing to help him financially anymore. He seldom thought of it because he didn't care. But today, he was engaged only by the past, and the past included Amèdèe.

Rain forced Bailey, who could barely see ten feet in front of him, to drive the car into the weeds along the road. When it stopped, he got out and polished the windshield with a large chamois, wringing it dry several times as he worked. Jean had no idea what life the young Negro had, if any, other than driving him all over the City and state and to the Gulf Coast. But he was glad Bailey was available day and night and seemed eager to wait on him as valet as well as chauffeur.

*   *   *

A week later, Jean returned to St. Delphine amid his brother's large family. Henri Bourgeois was in the large parlor. "Actually," the lawyer said, "your brother died intestate."

As soon as he said it, the room fell silent. Jean smiled sardonically.

"But his heirs are his wife and the children she bore him. The deceased left an estate consisting of property real and personal, all of which was acquired by him during his marriage . . . petitioners show that there are no debts, and an administration of said property to be divided according to Louisiana law among the survivors . . ."

Bourgeois talked on in his dull legal language, but Jean concentrated on reading the long list of Augie's holdings. He was amazed to discover that Augie's stock portfolio was worth about $200,000. The portfolio included bank, oil, and railroad stocks; real estate mainly in Iberville Parish; several mortgage bonds worth $65,000; personal mortgage notes valued at $20,000 from which he received interest; stock valued at $26,000 in the Auguste Levert Planting Co. in Plaquemine, the company in which Jean had owned a third interest before selling his shares to Augie and Amédèe many years earlier. *Mon dieu. I had no idea he was such a businessman.* Of course, he knew Augie's estate was modest compared to his, but on its own it was impressive. *Look at this! The Canal Bank! My bank!* He looked at the list again to be sure he had read it correctly: "Ten shares of stock in the New Orleans Canal & Banking Co., valued at $1,700."

While he read he heard soft exclamations from heirs seated around him reading their own copies of Auguste Levert Jr.'s investments that, he hoped, would make them all comfortable for life, if they were prudent. Augie's oldest boy looked like Auguste Sr., Jean noticed, and that bode well.

Before he joined Bailey for the long ride back to New Orleans, Jean tried to express warmth as he told his sister-in-law farewell: "Aurelie, I am pleased to know that my brother was so clever a maker and manager of money. Let me assure you that I am most happy for you. And now, I must bid you adieu." He bowed over her hand. "Till we meet again." He nodded pleasantly toward Augie's children. He thought one of the girls was rather pretty.

Somewhere during the long ride back to the City, Jean told Bailey that he wanted to go to Biloxi next week, to spend several days at his summer home.

"I enjoy that, Mister Jean. We not been over there in while. Yes, sir, I just get this fine car all clean and ready for the trip."

*   *   *

Early the following year Jean was back in Dansereau's office to sign incorporation papers establishing Levert Realty Company, Inc., in Birmingham, Alabama. From the long ornate mahogany desk, Jean smiled down at his attorney, who, to his surprise, had rolled his shirt sleeves to the elbows and removed his cravat in the noonday heat.

"I think we made a wise choice in naming Freddy president of the corporation and I am so pleased you accepted the position of secretary," said Jean, after he signed the papers and returned them to Dansereau. "Again, thank you for your usual thorough document. I feel very optimistic about the future of my first out-of-state venture, and I have high hopes for Freddy's success."

Freddy had married Molly Jordan, daughter of a Birmingham doctor, and Jean believed that their active participation already in the social and business life there was a great asset to the new company.

*   *   *

Several days after Levert Realty was chartered, Jean arrived home in late evening to find stacks of letters, sugar trade journals, and newspapers that he received almost daily at Third Street. A story on the front page of the Baton Rouge *Morning Advocate* caught his eye: "Annie Blanton Kleinpeter, widow of wealthy sugar planter, Edwin Kleinpeter of this city, died in her birthplace of Shelbyville, Kentucky, after a brief illness . . . active in social, civic, and charitable organizations in Baton Rouge for many years, Mrs. Kleinpeter was seventy-four . . . ." Although Jean had not heard from Annie for several years, the news shocked and saddened him deeply.

Chapter 76

NOVEMBER 18, 1918. Seventy-nine-year-old General Jean Baptiste Levert stood curbside of the corner of Canal and Royal streets with seventy-seven-year-old Colonel William Behan. Pictures of sartorial elegance, the men leaned on their canes and watched the Armistice Parade—World War I was over.

Jean and the Colonel could not talk over the noise of the cheering, applauding crowds on either side of Canal, which they considered the widest boulevard in the world. Rows of mufti-clad soldiers home from Europe were marching behind a military band playing George M. Cohan's *Over There*, and Jean began tapping his foot as the band passed in front of them. He moved close to the Colonel's ear and said, "I wouldn't have missed this opportunity to be among the celebrating hoards of happy Orleanians for anything."

Later, in the cushioned quiet of the Pickwick Club, the two old warriors agreed that the war in France just ended lacked the military profundity and drama of their war of the Sixties; there would never be another war like their war. Training was different, more stringent; soldiers were different; their cause was different; more local—was that the word?

Colonel Behan shook his white head over a bowl of crab bisque. "Well, I suppose Bessie and our grandchildren can safely return to France before long. And of course that is for the best, but really, General, I don't know what Elizabeth and I will do without them."

Jean placed his spoon next to his bowl of gumbo, blotted his lips and white moustache with a napkin, and nodded sympathetically.

Abruptly changing the subject, Jean said, "Colonel, this may not be the time or place, but I wonder if you'd do me the honor of critiquing an early draft of my speech to the Pickwick in January. Actually, it's more like a letter than a speech to be read at the club's annual banquet. As you may know, facing audiences no longer gives me the satisfaction that it once did. In fact, speeches make me nervous, now."

Colonel Behan's nod was barely perceptible. "I'd be glad to, my friend, I haven't even begun drafting what I'm going to say. I must get moving, I suspect, since it's only a few weeks before the club honors us as its oldest members."

Jean reached into his jacket pocket, removed two folded sheets of yellow paper, and handed them to Colonel Behan. "Seems like I'm always writing notes to myself about one thing or another, and speech drafts are no exception."

Silence of the next few minutes, as the Colonel read Jean's letter, was broken only by clanking of coffee cups on their saucers and the drone of voices rising from tables around them:

Dear Fellow Pickwickians:

With keenest regret, I find myself unable to be with you tonight. But I would be untrue to myself and my long membership, were I not to express my appreciation of the honor that is to be conferred on the "Ancients" . . . it seems but yesterday my good friend Lafayette Folger introduced me to your ranks. But recently returned from the Civil War, with life before me, it meant much to be welcomed to your exclusive ranks. Ourselves and the Club have had our ups and downs together, these six glorious decades. War, pestilence, flood, fire, and commercial ruin have assailed us, and again, the fruitful harvests, the brighter political day, the rising tide of a nation's prosperity, have alternately sounded their knell, and their

> *jubilee, in these treasured precincts . . . of all the young bloods*
> *that made life hum in half a century of the history of the great*
> *South, only two of us remain—the two "Ancients," as they*
> *style us, Behan and myself. Much as we would wish it, we*
> *cannot be here another sixty years, so let me appeal to you,*
> *you who are not "Ancients," to support the traditions of the*
> *Club. Keep it as you found it, keep it a place where any gentleman*
> *will feel at home, and where only gentlemen will be found . . . and*
> *when forty years from now, these halls echo with the celebration*
> *of our first centennial, may the Pickwick Club be still what it*
> *is now, and was always—THE club of New Orleans.*

"Excellent, first rate, Jean! You always did have a way with words, whether in writing or in your speeches. I wouldn't change a thing. The members certainly will appreciate your kind, thoughtful words."

Jean beamed at his friend, who was seated across from him at their regular table in the club dining room. Of course, Jean knew he would never forget the cheers and applause at his first address to the Pickwick members when he was a young man, eager and ambitious to command the attention of his elders, eager to inspire them to stand up for their beliefs in the southern way of life and to fight the evil Louisiana Carpetbag government that ruled the City then. But now, he considered speeches tiresome.

After an hour or so the men shook hands and parted, the Colonel taking up the *Picayune* in the reading room and Jean heading for his office.

The crowds had dispersed, and Jean enjoyed a stroll along parade-littered Canal Street. He glanced into Coleman Adler's window, which twinkled with gems of many sorts. In the center of the exquisite display Jean saw a watch, a small diamond encrusted timepiece with tiny emeralds for numerals. The round watch hung from a heavily engraved gold bow. The piece's delicate femininity instantly reminded him of Lila. Impulsively, he entered the jewelry store. Mr. Adler, in his frock-tail coat and winged collar, greeted Jean with a warm handshake.

"Come in, come in, Mr. Levert. How are things at the exchange these days? Will war's end have great effect on the commodities market, eh?" Adler's German accent reminded Jean that the respected jeweler was, in fact, German, something he had never thought of since the United States had entered the war.

"We'll see. We'll see," Jean responded amiably. "I'd like to see that little jeweled watch on the gold bow pin in the window, please."

"Certainly, sir." Adler opened the small door into the display window and produced the watch in its open black velvet box. Ah, the little diamonds and emeralds glittered in his eyes. He pictured the bauble on Lila's plump bosom. *It's made for her.*

"I'll take this, Mr. Adler." Jean got out his checkbook while the owner handed the watch to a clerk for wrapping.

Coleman Adler opened the door, and the gentlemen genially bowed to each other. Jean walked toward Perdido Street, his right hand in his overcoat pocket, holding the little box and thinking of Lila.

CHAPTER 77

IT'S SETTLED . . . I'LL go to St. John early tomorrow morning. I just need to get away.

It was past two in the afternoon when Jean, looking out his office window, decided to treat himself to a belated eightieth birthday present with a visit with Albert. For a few seconds he watched three men, dressed in dark business suits and derbies and carrying canes, scurrying in a southerly direction on Baronne Street toward Hotel DeSoto. Jean did not like the idea of being dispensable at Perdido Street, but he needed some special diversion that might relax him. He found himself increasingly worried and depressed about Jean, Jr., who was not making the progress he and the family had hoped for.

Recently Junior's doctor had written to Jean and to Dr. Gonsoulin, making carefully worded reports. Jean did not feel up to another trip to Santa Fe, though he did not admit it to anyone. He was glad Stephanie continued to make trips out there as often as she could. She returned with ambiguous conclusions, and gradually Jean had begun to believe that his son's condition was hopeless. He and the family kept up a dialogue of optimism despite the poignant tone of Junior's letters to his sisters and brothers and to the family nurse, Mary, who had attended him in New Orleans while he lived at Third Street. Jean feared for Junior. As much as anything he thought the birth of his and Julia's third child in Santa Fe had fostered hopes for the young man's future.

Jean had received two documents from Fernand Dansereau, sent to his office by messenger several hours before he caught the train to St. Martinville—one to incorporate all his real estate holdings in New Orleans, including Davis Plantation in St. Charles Parish; the other to cover a large tract upstate near Alexandria that he'd purchased after World War I.

As the train rattled through the Louisiana swamps, seated in his sleeping car, Jean lifted the thick document marked "J. B. Levert Land Company, Inc." from his brown, gold-edged briefcase; and he liked what he was reading:

" . . . Capital stock fixed at four hundred thousand dollars . . . the following named stockholders shall constitute the first board of directors, to be elected annually: J. B. Levert, Miss Stephanie Marie Levert, Robert L. Levert, Dr. Francis Kearny, and Albert O. Levert . . . officers of the corporation and the number of shares of stock, at one hundred dollars each, subscribed by each are as follows: J. B. Levert, president, 2,980; and Stephanie Marie, vice president; Robert, treasurer, Dr. Kearny, and Albert, all with five shares . . . ."

Jean knew his children were blasé about their positions on the rim of power. *To them money is just something to spend. Functions of earning it and making it grow bore most of them.* He thought his sons-in-law, on the other hand, were conscious of their roles, albeit small, in a large organization. He made Stephanie, who he regarded as bright and level-headed, vice president, because she listened and asked sensible questions, and he made Robert treasurer, hoping that the top designation might inspire his son.

He set the papers next to his briefcase on the seat in the Pullman. He removed the thinner document his lawyer had prepared to incorporate Levert-Shirley Company, Inc. " . . . To be domiciled in New Orleans . . . to cover and protect a large tract of land near Alexandria that included two plantations, Shirley and Ellen Kay, situated in Rapides and Avoyelles parishes, respectively . . . ."

A wide grin covered his face, and he pumped his right fist in the air several times. He let out a small breath, feeling relief flood through him, and muttered aloud, "Yes, yes, Fernand, you've done it again . . . excellent work."

Finally, after he replaced the documents in his briefcase, he reached into his coat pocket and removed Junior's letter to Nurse Mary that Stephanie had put there before he left for the office earlier that morning. "Thank you for sending me nice things and also your kind thoughts . . . ." But at this point, Jean was not hungry for words from his son's pen. He dreaded any hint of impending doom from his ailing son. Whatever he feared to be the truth, he did not want to face the loss of a fourth child. Mathilde's death remained acutely painful in his memory, and even the heartbreak of tiny Lucie's death at times haunted him. He thought his wife's death was cruelly premature, and the memory of Aloysia's death so long ago still saddened him. With the addition of his parents' passing and Augie's recent demise, he believed death had become a specter to him—one that too often and too depressingly knocked at his door.

*   *   *

The country air at St. John invigorated Jean. It always lifted his spirits. *There is just something about this place.* Jean did not want to part with it, ever. He did not want his heirs to sell it, ever. It was called St. John, but it was the Levert Plantation. A singular comfort was in his knowledge that Albert had proved to be an able farmer and that he loved St. John possibly as much as he did. Jean disapproved of Albert's conduct—he still seemed a wild boy at times—but their common love of St. John bound them in a comforting way.

Jean knew cutting time was upon them. Albert's crews had been up since dawn ready to begin the great chore of cutting thousands of acres of as fine a crop of sugarcane as Jean had ever seen—sun and rain had cooperated in growing and making the stalks rich in sweet juice. The cane, as much as fourteen feet tall, was magnificent, its wide grassy leaves blowing in the hot October wind, waving with that certain rhythm that made Jean imagine the ocean's waves on a perfect day at sea. This day in the fields was brilliant, and Jean decided he needed a sun hat. The old one that he always took down from a hook in his first-floor back bedroom was not there, and a half-hearted search with Dottee did not locate it. "I need a new one, anyway," he said as he spurred his horse, Sailor. The thick-bodied, dark brown animal leaped forward, and Jean reined him toward Levert Mercantile, the company store, near the front lawn of the Big House.

A decade earlier, Jean had incorporated Levert Mercantile, Inc., the first of three companies that made up the Levert business domain: "With fifteen thousand dollars in capital and stock," the company, domiciled in New Orleans, was formed to serve sugar farmers and their field laborers, white and black, throughout St. Martin Parish. "Of the total one hundred and fifty shares of stock, Jean owned 98 shares, Sidney Gonsoulin owned 50 shares, and Albert and Lawrence each owned one share . . . ."

Jean looped the reins over the porch banister. He looked up as Sidney Gonsoulin, his store manager and brother of Albert's wife, Louise, came through the door, a broad smile on his tanned face. A distant relative of the Levert's physician in New Orleans, Sidney was a big man with thick black hair, eyebrows, and moustache. He wore a plaid shirt, brown trousers, and laced knee boots. He greeted Jean in his thick Louisiana French accent, a speech characteristic that Jean never had. Plaquemine was on the eastern rim of Acadian Louisiana, and although Amèdèe and Augie had a tinge, it was nowhere near so heavy as that of the people of St. Martin and other largely Acadian parishes. Jean had begun to detect a bit of "Cajun" in Albert's speech soon after he moved to St. John. He thought schooling at Sophie Newcomb College in New Orleans had smoothed Louise's speech somewhat, but it amused Jean to hear their young daughters speak their mix of English, French, and Acadian, each tongue flavoring the other. Gonsoulin's chatter was sometimes difficult for Jean to understand.

"Come in, come in, Meestair Lavair! You have not visit us in a long time, yeah!" He was cordial as always.

Jean's spurs rattled on the porch floor. "Sidney, I need a good sun hat. I hope you have a good wide-brimmed one that will save my face from burning out there. I plan to be out in the fields for several days."

Jean was pleased to see the shelves and walls in the white wooden frame store lined with a great variety of necessities for plantation families: Horse collars, oil stoves, slopjars, chewing tobacco, kitchen staples that included barrels of flour and even sugar, rope, cooking pots of all sorts, leather harnesses, and bolts of piece goods. There among all that and more was a stack of big straw sun hats. Gonsoulin lifted the top one and handed it to his boss of bosses.

"How dat do, yeah? It do fit, no? I b'lieve it do, yeah."

"It does indeed, sir!" Jean took out his wallet.

"Combien de, Sidney?"

"Eh? Oh, yeah! Tirty five cents, yeah! For you, Meestair Lavair, we make good price. Dat what it cost us."

"Well, no profit for the store on this sale." Jean laughed his country laugh, realizing he responded a lot less formally over here than in day-to-day conversations in the New Orleans financial district.

Putting the hat on his head, he bade Gonsoulin good morning and mounted Sailor again. The hat had a strap under the chin, and Jean felt like a gaucho as his horse trotted off toward the south field. The day brought back boyhood memories from long ago at Golden Ridge, when he worked hard from daylight until dark. He recalled coming home in the early season, tired and hot, stopping by the iron water kettle in back of the Big House to splash water on his head and arms, passing time with Bébé, who often sat on the kitchen steps back there, shelling peas, shucking corn, snapping beans, talking to him—always talking. He looked up and saw Albert approaching on a chestnut mare he'd named Ajax. *Damn, Albert rides a horse hard.* He reined abruptly.

"Papa! What do you think?"

"Never more beautiful, Albert. I believe this is a perfect crop." He rubbed his hand across his moustache. "Let's hope we don't have one of our hurricanes."

"The sky looks clear." Albert scowled as he looked at the sky in every direction. "I believe we will make it. I am proud of this crop."

"You should be. You and your people may bring in the finest ever for St. John."

"I see you bought yourself a hat. I'm sorry about your old one. I know how you hate extra expense. I hope Sidney gave you a good price."

"He did," said Jean.

They had ridden across the field to a large live oak, where they dismounted and walked about in the shade of the spreading tree. The hanging Spanish moss raked Albert's forelock back from his forehead. He took a package from behind Ajax's saddle.

"Dottee sent us a lunch. Just look at this." He unfolded a table cloth on the ground and spread papers for fried chicken, biscuits, ripe tomatoes from the garden, and large slices of pecan pie. "Depend on that Dottee. She sends good things down to the sugarhouse at night for me."

Despite some rheumatism in his knees, Jean got down to the ground to sit at the edge of the cloth, where, picnic style, he hungrily ate his share of Dottee's lunch. *Somebody in that kitchen is a good cook. I've never eaten food at St. John that was not delicious.* After eating, they walked about briefly, stretching their legs, then lay down on the grass under the oak, where both fell asleep.

Jean bathed at five o'clock and then joined Albert in the dining room. Louise and her two daughters had moved to their rented house on Constantinople Street in New Orleans for the grinding season, as they did every fall, staying there through the Carnival celebrations. Jean repeatedly dismissed the matter from his mind, reminding himself that whatever he thought of such a wife's conduct or a husband's tolerance, it was their business. Of course, he knew, basically, that no son of his lived a monk's life. Never mind. The two men were beginning a superb supper of broiled red snapper, smothered corn, sliced tomatoes, and buttered biscuits, when the phone rang in the hall. Dottee rushed through the dining room to answer it.

"Probably Louise," said Albert. "I hope nothing's wrong."

But Dottee came back and told Jean it was for him. "It Miss Stephanie Marie, Mister Jean. She sound sorta upset, yeah."

Jean passed the napkin across his mouth, pushing his chair back as he did.

He picked up the receiver from atop the telephone box where Dottee had left it. "Hello."

"Papa, this is Stephanie."

"Yes? What is it, Stephanie? Is anything wrong? Not bad news from Junior, is it?" This concern was never far from his consciousness.

"No, Papa." Stephanie was shouting over the miles. "It's Dr. Kearny."

"Kearny? What's wrong. Is he ill?"

"No, Papa. Dr. Kearny died this afternoon." She began to cry. "He was duck hunting near Plaquemine. He had a heart attack, Papa. He died right there in Bayou Marigouin before they could get him back to town."

Mon dieu. Mon dieu.

"Papa? Are you there?"

"Yes, Steph, I'm here."

"Papa, poor Bea. She is just out of her mind. Bailey is driving me up there tonight. Lawrence and me. We are leaving immediately. I was only waiting until I could call you."

"All right, Steph. All right. I will leave here as early as possible, in the morning, Albert and I will. We'll get over there as soon as we can get out of here." *Mon dieu. What will happen next.* "Give Beatrice my love. Get her priest over there if he is not there already. Tell her I am coming. *Mon dieu.* "And have Bailey get out my funeral clothes and bring them. I have only rough clothing with me."

"I have already done that, Papa."

"Thank you, my dear. Goodnight."

"Goodnight, Papa."

By seven o'clock, a balmy breeze cooling their faces through open windows, Jean and Albert were speeding in his son's old Ford on a narrow dirt road—a shortcut Albert had found—toward Plaquemine. They could talk little over the clanking of the engine; there was nothing to say. Thought Jean: Dr. Kearny, husband of two of his daughters, a good family man. Poor man, strickened while hunting, taking time for a little recreation. Poor Bea, with two children. Poor Bea . . . .

Albert adroitly avoided several deep potholes in the dirt road. "Watch it, Albert! Take it easy, son! You're driving like a wild man!" was all Jean could say during the two-hour trip. When they reached the Kearny home in Plaquemine, the car was so splattered with khaki-brown Louisiana mud that they couldn't see through the windshield.

Stephanie rushed out to meet them. She clung first to her father, then her brother. "Oh, Papa. Bea is in terrible shape. She is in shock. The children are bewildered. Their father is dead, but they do not understand. Their mother is almost incoherent with grief.

"Is her priest here?" asked Jean.

"Yes, he is with her now. They are in Dr. Kearny's office."

"Then I will go to them." Jean was not as serene as he sounded.

Beatrice screamed when she saw her father, rushing into his arms. "Papa, Papa, Papa." She wept into his shoulder. It seemed to Jean that she would never stop sobbing. But when she did, finally, she was more calm. And soon, with Stephanie, Albert, and Lawrence, she made the arrangements for her husband's services at the St. John the Baptist church in Brusly Landing and his burial in the Kearny family tomb at Metairie Cemetery outside New Orleans. Jean escorted his daughter down the aisle to the very seat where he had guided his father at his mother's funeral in that church.

Funerals, funerals. Jean went through it all again, this ceremony of loss. Forever. It was terribly sad. But Jean Baptiste discovered something about his daughter. Beatrice had been madly in love with Francis Kearny, her dead sister's husband. Somehow he looked at Bea with a special new regard. He had not known that she held such a passion for the man. *What a happy marriage they must have had.*

After the funeral Stephanie told her father that she would return to Plaquemine with Bea and help her pack. "She must come home with us to Third Street, Papa. She cannot stay here alone with these children. We simply cannot leave her. Can't we make room for her for a while?"

"Well," began Jean, wondering just where they would put a mother and two growing children.

"What about the big room over the kitchen. Nobody is using that. It's a lovely room. They can stay in there and have plenty of room. Bailey and Jenny can move things out and bring in another bureau."

"Of course, Stephanie. We will make space. You know I will make a place for my own daughter."

"Oh, Papa," cried Stephanie, and rushed into his arms in a fresh flood of tears.

"There, there, my dear. You must be calm. You have quite a bit ahead of you. Beatrice will be depending upon you altogether. Let me send Lawrence with you girls. You will need him, and we can spare him. Yes. Bailey will drive all of you back to New Orleans, and I want you girls to call me when you are packed, and I will send him back for you."

"Yes, Papa. Thank you." Jean looked at his eldest daughter, tiny, dark, beautiful. *What a woman she is.* He thought she couldn't have looked less like her mother, but she was a lot like her— unselfish, always kind to others.

CHAPTER 78

JEAN DECIDED NOT to return to St. John to continue his visit with Albert; he had no heart for it. He was grieved over the death of Francis Kearny, and he was apprehensive about Beatrice's moving into his house with two children. It occurred to him that Jenny, who had assumed household chores at Vic's retirement, might quit, just walk away when she learned of the enlarged household and additional duties.

"Don you worry, *M'sieu Levert*, we manage," said Jenny, conferring with Jean in the Third Street dining room after he had returned from Plaquemine. "Now, you jes hire me a little maid to hep. Me and Bailey and a little maid can do everthin." Jenny smiled confidently.

Jean was surprised. He had not thought of hiring another full-time servant. "Well," he began, "I . . ."

"You jes don worry, *M'sieu*, leave it to me. I get somebody good, yeah. Jes leave it to me. I gets somebody." Without waiting for his response, she padded through the swinging door into the pantry. He'd always enjoyed listening to Jenny speak in her Cajun *patois*; it reminded him of his easy conversations with Dottee and especially Bébé.

Jean sighed. *Perhaps this is the answer.* Stephanie was constantly hiring temporary help for special occasions; she'd be glad to hear that there would be more regular help. *Yes, this is the answer.* He sighed again and opened the morning paper which lay, as always, parallel to his damask napkin on the breakfast table.

*   *   *

A week later, after he had been back at his office and into the
relaxing routine of lunch at his clubs, Jean sent Bailey to Plaquemine
to fetch Stephanie and the Kearny family. Jean seemed happy with
Stephanie's choice of an upstairs bedroom for Bea and her ten-
year-old daughter, Beatrice. With the addition of a daybed, their
mother's old sewing room across the hall was now suitable, thought
Jean, for Frank, Jr., Bea's five-year-old son.

Stephanie helped Bea put away her things, complimenting the
servants. "Jenny, there are two lovely old needlepoint pillows in
the top of the first-floor linen closet. Please bring them up for the
window seat in Miss Bea's room."

Stephanie Marie urged her father to come upstairs to see what
they had wrought. He thought it was nice, but poor Beatrice looked
terrible—sad and dismal in her black dress. The sight of her
depressed him. "Bea, my dear, I know you are in grief, but we
hope to cheer you up in your old home. As you feel like it, please
come down to meals. You know that is what Francis would want
you to do."

But Beatrice remained in a black gloom, Jean saw, spending
hours in prayer or weeping. She depended on visits from Father
Patrick Gaspard of the Jesuit church, a long-time family friend
who had married her and Dr. Kearny at Nativity church in Biloxi.
Heavily veiled in her black garb, Jean and the family could not get
her to go to church, and she showed almost no interest in her
children. The children were dependent on Stephanie and Jenny
who already had their days filled with responsibilities. Soon, to
his utter disgust, Jean arrived home early one evening, tired, and
carrying his briefcase filled with business to complete, to find his
home in chaos. His grandchildren, who had been at Third Street
for a month, were sliding down the banisters and running and
shouting through the house. He did not know how to cope with
them; he had never trained or disciplined his own children, and
he had no intention of doing so with them. But if running and
shouting were not enough, he found his prize hens running loose

on St. Charles Avenue. *Mon dieu. Mon dieu!* He rushed into the kitchen.

"Bailey, Bailey. Hurry! Those brats have left the chickenyard gate open! My hens are out, running all over the neighborhood! Get out there and try to run them into the backyard. I'll try to herd them into the chickenyard. Please hurry!"

Stephanie had never heard her father curse. When she heard him screaming, "Goddamn those brats. Damn their black little hearts . . . ," she rushed out to him, with Jenny trailing close behind. They found him disheveled, his face flushed, his hair standing on end.

"Papa! What on earth? What has happened?"

"It's those children, Stephanie. The little devils have let my chickens out. They've run out, all the way up on the Avenue."

"Good God," gasped Steph. "But, Papa, you must calm down. You'll be ill. Please, let Bailey handle this. Let Jenny help. Come back in the house, please!" She put her hand on his arm.

Jean acquiesced. She was right. He knew he was completely undone. He tried to smooth his hair, straighten his tie. Stephanie picked up his cuff link from the ground.

In the parlor, Steph persuaded her father to sit down; she brought him some brandy.

"Thank you, dear."

Finally, Beatrice appeared for dinner in her widow's weeds, looking forlorn and vague. Her children were behind her. Jean swallowed hard and excused himself.

"What's wrong?" asked Bea.

Stephanie directed her sister to a chair. "Sit down, Bea. We have to talk." She pointed to the nearby sofa in the corner of the dining room. "You two children sit there, too, and do not move."

After that evening things improved, and Jean allowed Stephanie full rights to discipline the children. Though she was new to the role, he thought she became quite forcible. When Jean came in at night, the children had eaten their supper at the kitchen table and been spirited upstairs, where they were seldom heard from until he was gone in the morning.

To Jean's pleasure Beatrice began to dine with him and Stephanie and whatever family members might be present. After dinner Bea read to her father from daily newspapers and important business letters and documents. He welcomed her in his home office, and they developed a rapport. But she never departed from mourning; she abandoned society altogether, and hers was a slavish role that Jean had never anticipated in his once lively and outgoing daughter.

Jean credited Stephanie Marie with transferring Bea's children into "tolerable, civilized youngsters." But he knew he would never forgive them for the loss of his five fine-laying hens—golden Buff Orpingtons from eggs that Dottee had hatched in an incubator at St. John.

*   *   *

In late May, Stephanie received a letter from Jean, Jr. That evening after dinner, she took it into her father's office and read parts of it to him: "I have been feeling so very punk . . . I had an attack of appendicitis. I don't know whether it is really my appendix or my stomach. I cannot get much out of Dr. Mera, and Dr. Patton says it is gas, but it is very painful and has been going on for nearly three weeks, and I admit that it is making a bad situation much worse . . . Did Papa tell you I am getting ready to write my will and very soon? I could use your advice about naming Julia administratrix. She has had no business experience, and I fear that she might be taken advantage of by unscrupulous people. I need your advice about this right away."

Stephanie's hands, clutching the letter, dropped below her waist. She looked down at her father.

Jean threw back his head and stared at the glass bookshelves for a moment. He bounded from his desk chair. "He thinks he is dying."

She shivered at the thought. "I fear that, Papa," her face pinched with worry. Her father moved to put his arm around her.

Appreciative of Stephanie's countless trips to Santa Fe to try to help and encourage Junior through his fight against tuberculosis, Jean, his eyes still on the bookshelves, said: "Unfortunately, I must settle a business matter first. I am closing an important deal for some prime real estate on Jackson Avenue in the Garden District. If there are no problems, it shouldn't take more than a day, two at the outside. Then I'll be on the next train to be with Junior." He paused, looking reflective. "You don't know how happy it makes me feel that you're about to make another trip to see your brother."

After she arrived in Santa Fe, Stephanie posted a letter to her father, reporting on her brother's rapidly deteriorating condition. But it arrived in New Orleans the day after Jean Baptiste, Jr., had died at Sunmount Sanatorium—and before Jean could see his forty-two-year-old son again. Once again, Jean felt death's shadows falling on him and his family and he felt deep remorse for having allowed his business to take precedence over all else; his mother's death flashed through his memory.

Almost daily, Stephanie wrote long letters to her father. She described the funeral service and burial in the stark cemetery near the ancient adobe church where the family had worshiped. She reported about the business of selling the ranch and the old Buick: "The Buick should be easy, but the adobe house poses a larger problem." She told Jean there were many repairs to be made to the ranch, trees had to be sprayed and pruned again, and the ditch repaired, having been washed out by heavy rains. "If Julia could stay on indefinitely and wait for a rich man to come," she wrote, "I think she'll wait forever for $15,000 for her ranch. She should get $9,000 . . . ."

In another long letter she mentioned meeting a Mrs. Fories. "She asked about you and to my surprise seemed to know all about you. She is from Shelbyville, Kentucky, and she knew a Mrs. Kleinpeter from there—but who lived for many years in West Baton Rouge Parish—and Mrs. Kleinpeter claimed to have known you quite well. Do you remember such a person? Mrs. Fories just happened to mention Jean Baptiste Levert, Jr.'s name to Mrs. Kleinpeter . . . apparently Mrs. Kleinpeter knew you during the war."

Jean's face wore a quizzical expression as he re-read the paragraph about Annie Blanton Kleinpeter several times. *Small world.* He had not thought of Annie since he had read her obituary in the newspaper.

Several weeks after Junior's death, Stephanie wrote her father that the ranch "finally was sold, and that she and Julia sold all the furniture, packed their personal belongings, and with the three children, planned to board the next available Achison, Topeka & Santa Fe train for the circuitous route back to Louisiana . . . ."

*   *   *

Two days after Stephanie's final letter from Sante Fe had arrived, Jean received word from Lila that she was ill and wanted to see him as soon as possible. He considered boarding the L&N for the Gulf Coast, but instead asked Bailey to drive him over in the new 1922 Packard. With its smart styling and elegant features, the car was Jean's choice from among the automobiles built following World War I.

Because of Julia's affinity for the Coast and her not wishing to return to live in the City after her husband's death, Jean had agreed to settle her and the children in the two-story caretaker's house located behind Biloxi house. Jean looked forward to seeing Julia again; he also wanted her to accompany him to see Lila, and he was pleased that Julia had accepted his invitation. He had Bailey bring in Sookey, the Negro girl who had been a housemaid for the family for several years, to cook and clean for Junior's family. Jean knew that for however long their sojourn might be in Biloxi he and Julia would be comfortable with the vigilant Sookey watching and entertaining his grandchildren.

Upon arrival, Jean called Lila to set an hour to see her. He was dismayed to hear how weak her voice sounded over the telephone. He had not seen her for too long, and he was extremely anxious to get to her pretty cottage, a house he had bought for her years earlier and where she had lived within walking distance of the beach and her beloved church.

At ten the next morning, Bailey drove him and Julia to see Lila. Jean was stunned at her appearance. In less than two months her health apparently had collapsed. She was abnormally thin, and her face was gray. He tried not to show his shock as he introduced Julia to her. *Poor little Lila.* He sat by her bed and held her hands. As he stroked her graying hair back from her forehead, she smiled her sweet smile and her eyes brightened. She had Julia sit on the side of her bed. Soon, Julia left them alone and walked out to the small fall garden of asters, sweet williams, and daisies. Jean could see her walking slowly among the flowers, her head lowered as if she were in deep thought. He and Lila talked until he realized that she was too exhausted to continue. He kissed her goodbye. Near the door, she called his name softly, and he returned to her side; her eyes glistened. He leaned down and kissed her warmly on her lips, once, then again. She kept her hand on the back of his head briefly.

"Please take care of yourself, dear Jean."

He smiled and left the room. He felt certain he would never see Lila again.

That night he and Julia sat on the porch at Biloxi house. They talked very little but finally Julia spoke.

"Papa . . ." She faltered, then began again. "Papa, I didn't know you had someone . . . someone you care about." She looked at him. "Someone who cares for you."

Jean did not answer immediately. "Yes," he said sadly. But he was glad Julia knew.

*   *   *

It helped Jean when Father Tormey rang the doorbell at Biloxi house two days later.

"I must tell you, Mr. Levert, that Miss Lila passed on to her reward last night. I was with her." They sat down together on the porch. "I am very sorry, sir. I know she was a dear friend, and you have been so kind to her for many years."

Calmly, Jean told the priest that he wanted Lila to be buried in the cemetery behind Nativity church, near the spot where he first set eyes on her. "See that she is laid to rest in the best manner that the undertaker here can provide. You say the Mass, Father. See that there are many flowers. She loved her flowers."

"Yes, yes, Mr. Levert, I'll see to everything."

"Now, did you ever replace that stained glass window that was blown out in the last bad storm? The one on the west side of the sanctuary?"

"No, we have not. It will be very expensive, you know. Our committee has one picked out, but it will take years for us to collect that amount of money."

"If it is what you want for the church, Father, I want you to order it and have it installed, all at my expense. It is to be in Lila's memory, anonymously, of course."

Jean was quite moved as he ordered the memorial for Lila, but he spoke firmly and with purpose. Suddenly he liked very much what he was doing. He wished she could know about it. And Colonel Bush might approve.

"You are most generous, Mr. Levert. Our congregation will be happy to hear this, happier than I can tell you. They have wanted to replace the beautiful window so badly. Thank you so much, sir."

"What was the scene, Father? I confess I do not remember all the windows, though they are very beautiful for so small a church."

"It was taken from one of Raphael's Madonnas, mother and child, not so, eh, exquisite in glass as oil, but, yes, it was beautiful and quite an ambitious work—from a glass studio in Venice. Quite expensive, Mr. Levert."

"I am sure it is, Father. Please send me a base figure, and I will send you a check as soon as I get back to my office." Jean stood.

"Yes, sir, I will, very soon. You have my sympathy, Mr. Levert, and my gratitude. You can be sure that I will not disclose the name of the donor. And shall we attach a plaque identifying the one honored?"

"By all means. And Father, when is the funeral?"

"Tomorrow afternoon. Three o'clock."

As Jean watched Father Tormey disappear down the shell road, Julia came out on the porch. She had heard the priest's news.

"Julia, I must return to New Orleans in the early morning. Just don't feel I can stand up to another funeral, not even for a special, dear friend, especially not this soon after Junior's passing."

"Yes, Papa, I understand perfectly well. It is not easy to let go of someone forever . . . When do you think you'll be returning to Biloxi?"

"As you know, my dear, I want to come back soon with . . ." Suddenly Jean stopped. He clutched the back of a tall rocker. He was losing his balance. *Mon dieu.*

Julia rushed to him. He leaned heavily on her as she helped him to sit down.

"Papa! What is it!"

As he regained his equilibrium, he shook his head. "I'm sure it's nothing. I was just dizzy there for a moment." He shook his head again as if his balance were not quite back to normal.

Julia sat quietly beside him, her hand on his arm. Finally, he said, "I'm all right, Julia. I must be a little tired. I'm fine."

"Now, Papa, you're forgetting you are eighty-two years old. You can't be fine if you are about to fall down from dizziness. You must get to a doctor when you get back to the city. Has this happened before?" A small line of worry formed between her brows.

"You are very kind, Julia. But I am all right. Really. Now, please do not mention this to Stephanie or Bea or their sisters." But Julia made no promises.

*   *   *

In the back seat, Jean Baptiste clutched the velvet-lined loop on the door post, his thumb firmly pressed into the outer brocade, as Bailey drove the shiny Packard slowly down the curving, oyster-shell driveway. Its sturdy support seemed an object of importance to his comfort and certainty. An early morning shimmer of light played on the gentle ripples of the Sound, a sight that usually stirred his imagination, inspiring little phrases of description. But he did not feel his usual interest in the weather developments on the Coast.

When Bailey turned to the right, toward New Orleans, Jean laid his head on the back of the leather seat and closed his eyes. He was tired, and he knew the drive ahead was many hours long. Depending on weather and road conditions, the drive could take up to ten hours. He wished he could sleep all the way to Third Street. He felt that this was a cowardly way to face the coming days, not his usual attitude, he hoped, but his world on which he had most of the time held a tight rein seemed in danger of falling into other hands—doctors? children?

He picked up a copy of the Biloxi newspaper that lay beside him on the seat and, scarcely reading, looked over the front page. There in the lower right-hand column was Lila's brief obituary. Disbelief swept over him all over again. The article was modest, as Lila was. *Mon dieu*. Jean laid the paper back on the seat and closed his eyes. *Lila. Lila.* He acknowledged that for more than twenty years Lila had been one of his most steadying anchors. Whether with him or not, she was always there for him. Her comparative youth and geniality had made him feel ageless. She never asked anything—never pressed him about marriage, a step that would have caused trouble between him and his children.

What will life be without her, her patience, her unquestioning support. The future looks uncertain. I feel rudderless with her gone. He opened his eyes as the car swerved sharply on fresh oyster shells spread over rutted Front Beach Drive to keep from hitting a cat. For a moment he had feared he was having a dizzy spell, but looking out the windows, he got his bearings. *Dieu merci!*

Soon after they crossed the Mississippi line into Louisiana, after passing through Poplarville and Balltown, where they crossed the Pearl River, Bailey pulled off the unpaved road onto a grassy spot. He lifted a large basket from the front seat to show Jean that they had a lunch. They agreed that it was a good idea to eat and rest before encountering the treacherous Honey Island Swamp.

The swamp area was rolling, hilly country, but the low spots today were virtual quagmires, having been torn up and filled with deep holes caused by recent rains and constant traffic of ox teams with heavy loads of timber.

"You hungry? Look here what Miss Julia done fix us." Bailey opened wide the hinged top of the basket and lifted up samples of their food. "Now, look here, a nice big fried chicken bress."

"Very well, Bailey. Hand something over to me. I'm not hungry, but it must be one o'clock." He looked at his watch. "*Mon dieu,* it's 1:30."

"I not hurry you 'cuz you had such a big brakefast. I know you not like to rush it."

"You're right, Bailey."

Bailey handed him a napkin. Then he filled a dinner plate with fried chicken, sliced tomatoes, and a ham and cheese sandwich. Jean took the plate and settled it comfortably on his lap. He had felt no hunger, but he found himself eating the delicious food, of course.

"Do we have any lemonade?" he asked.

"Oh, Mister Jean, scuse me." Bailey poured a full glass of the cold drink and passed it carefully over the seat to his boss. "Scuse me, Mister Jean. I just step out here."

Bailey took his plate of lunch and walked to a large pine stump not far from the Packard to eat his lunch. Then Jean opened the car door and stepped from the high running board to the ground. He walked into the thicket of swamp myrtle and wild huckleberry to relieve himself. Returning to the car, Jean noticed the Packard was mudded almost beyond recognition. Soon they were on their way again, bumping along on muddy roads that took them to Covington, Ponchatoula, and Hammond—the regular route by land to New Orleans.

"How you feelin, Mister Jean, fellin pretty good?"

"Fine, Bailey. Fine, thank you."

Bailey knew better. He had learned all the signs of his boss's moods. Jean knew this. Through their days at Third Street or getting about in the automobile, the white man and the black man lived many of their waking hours together, side by side, often as parallel as railroad tracks, but like the tracks, ultimate convergence was illusory.

"I'm going to try to take a nap, Bailey," said Jean. He thought of Daniels and how faithful and dependable he had been to his white family. Bailey was the same. Jean did not think it ironic at all that white people simply had to have good Negroes to make life worth living. He fell into a deep slumber that lasted until Bailey stopped at the small hotel in Ponchatoula.

"Would you like to get out and stretch your legs, Mister Jean?"

The Ponchatoula Hotel was a regular rest stop for the Leverts traveling by car between Biloxi and New Orleans. When Bailey opened the car door, Jean stepped out and walked stiffly into the lobby and into the public men's room. Inside the small confinement, he became very dizzy and had to hold onto the lavatory to keep from falling.

Bailey was waiting for him beside the car, but at the hotel's entrance, Jean called to his driver that he was going to have a cup of coffee in the coffee shop. Bailey waved back to him.

While Jean sat at a round, oil-cloth-covered table, a thin young woman drew coffee from an urn and brought it to him. Watching her return to her post behind the counter, he stirred the black brew. The coffee was not the chicory blend that Jean was used to in the country or in New Orleans, but it was hot. He sipped a few spoonfuls before he lifted the thick white cup to his lips. He couldn't help but wish that he were home.

On Highway 51 again, heading for Hammond, Bailey drove the car as fast as he could on the wavy swamp road. Jean's mind wandered to business.

Levert-Shirley Co., Inc., was doing well up near Alexandria, but he wished he could interest one of his children in this land. There were other acreages adjacent or nearby that would almost certainly produce good revenues. He wanted to buy additional properties if he had closer managerial ties, but Alexandria was far from New Orleans, and he had been unable to convince either Robert or Lawrence that he should move upstate. These two, he knew, doted on the social life of New Orleans, and did not want to leave. So, he had decided against buying more property. He did have an idea for Lawrence, and that was management of Rienzi. He had decided to foreclose on the Morvant family.

In the decade after Emile Morvant's death, Jean had advanced large sums of money to Morvant's heirs for operation. They had mortgaged their shares of stock in Rienzi to Jean in exchange for sixty thousand dollars for operating expenses. As security, Jean had received several promissory notes, dated one year from execution of the lien. Finally, after several more liens were executed in exchange for money from Jean, coupled with the inability to repay the money on time, the Morvants were heavily indebted to Levert and Morvant Company on notes now totaling more than a hundred and sixty-five thousand dollars.

Jean looked out of the car window, watching the swamp vegetation go by and knew that he had made up his mind to transfer Rienzi to J. B. Levert Land Co. later. *I will definitely foreclose. I've gone as far as good business practices allow. Walter Morvant and his family will have to seek another home. Their very good luck had run out.*

*   *   *

At Third Street, Bailey drove into the driveway, stopping outside the barn door. He hurried out of the car to assist Jean. He was close at this elbow as they climbed the steps and entered the kitchen. As soon as Jean saw the faces of Beatrice and Stephanie, he knew Julia had telephoned them. He also had a severe head-swimming episode and had to clutch the edge of the kitchen table for fear of falling. *Mon dieu.*

"Papa! Papa!" cried both of his daughters. Stephanie commanded Bailey to get him up to his bedroom. Bailey complied, talking all the while to his boss. He helped him undress and put on a nightshirt. Once in his bed, Jean commanded Bailey to go take care of the car and to bring in his luggage.

"Go on, now, Bailey. If I am not safe in my own bed, we'd better just give up."

"Whatever you say, Mister Jean."

Within half an hour, Jean was amazed to see Dr. Gonsoulin at his bedroom door with Bea and Steph close behind him.

"*Mon dieu.* What is this fuss all about? Doctor, I was planning to call you from my office in the morning. There was no need for you to come over here at your dinnertime." Jean looked disapprovingly at his daughters. They stood by silently while Dr. Gonsoulin examined Jean and asked questions. He listened to Jean's heart, his lungs; he looked into his ears and down his throat with a flashlight, noticing his throat was red. Jean complained he was having some pain swallowing. He also took his temperature. Finally, he stood aside and clasped his hands behind him.

"General, I strongly suspect that you have mastoiditis. It will surely make a man dizzy, and it is a dangerous disease. My nurse will make an appointment for you with Dr. Homer Dupuy the first thing in the morning. In my opinion, he is one of the finest ear, nose, and throat specialists in the south. Valedictorian of his medical school class at Tulane, I believe. Excellent reputation. He will give you his opinion and tell you what to do. Now, this is serious, General Levert, and you must follow his recommendations to the letter."

Jean appeared subdued. "I will do as you say, Doctor. Thank you for coming at this inconvenient hour. Girls, see Dr. Gonsoulin out. Bea, bring me my briefcase as soon as you are free to do so, please."

Bea and Steph followed the doctor out and closed Jean's door.

As he waited for his briefcase and the folder on Rienzi and the Morvants, he stroked his moustache. Well, he would see Dr. Dupuy. He knew him slightly, a fellow Tulanian. He did have a good reputation. A man of about fifty, maybe more. But Jean had a busy week with many things to tend to. He must see Fernand Dansereau and get this Rienzi matter settled. He also had an important social engagement, the annual awards dinner for the Board of Administrators of the Tulane Educational Fund on Thursday night at the Roosevelt Hotel ballroom. He did not intend to miss that.

CHAPTER 79

JEAN FELT MUCH better after he bathed and dressed the next morning. With the usual attendance of Bailey, he went downstairs looking his natty self, and experiencing no dizziness. Jenny was serving crab omelet from a chafing dish on the sideboard, and Lawrence, who had dropped by for breakfast, was beside her, asking for a second helping of her small flaky biscuits that dripped butter.

"Papa!" all three chorused, "how are you feeling this morning?"

"If I felt any better, I don't know how I'd deal with it," he replied solemnly. "I am glad you came by, Lawrence, I have some very important business to talk to you about. After we've had breakfast, please come into my office, and we'll discuss things before I leave for Perdido Street."

"Yes, sir!" said Lawrence in his customarily affable tone. In a half-joking voice, his round-faced son said, "I hope it's not about Alexandria and those two plantations, Shirley and Ellen Kay."

Jean shook his head negatively. "No. No. It has nothing to do with Alexandria. I am not cruel enough to drag you that far from the bright lights." He was not smiling.

"How is your dizziness, Papa?" asked Stephanie.

"It's gone. I was just tired from traveling."

"But Papa, you must see Dr. Dupuy. Dr. Gonsoulin is making an appointment. You must see the specialist."

"Oh, I'll get over there. Don't worry. I have some business to tend to today. Things I cannot avoid. Serious matters."

"But Papa, I know Dr. Gonsoulin intends for you to see Dr. Dupuy as soon as possible . . ."

"Steph, eat your breakfast." Stephanie Marie lifted her coffee cup to her mouth and looked at Beatrice across the table.

In his office after breakfast, Jean told Lawrence about his plans to take over Rienzi completely and that he wanted him to move to the showplace manor and manage the agricultural business going on there, which included Orange Grove. For the past decade or so, Lulu and Lawrence and their two sons had lived on Banker Plantation and, with capable assistance from Albert, Lawrence had managed farming operations for his father. "I want the Morvants to continue managing daily operations at Webre, their ancestral place, as they have been doing at Rienzi for more than fifteen years. But I want you to report to me regularly about the operations there just as your brother is still reporting to me from St. John after thirty years." Jean said the Morvants own an Acadian-style house on Webre—not as large or elegant as Rienzi—where the family probably will move after leaving the Rienzi manor.

"I hope you are prepared to accept this responsibility, Lawrence. Including Webre and Orange Grove, it's over four thousand acres under cultivation. It's an opportunity many, many young men would envy, and Lulu and Lawrence, Jr. and little Edward should love it. But before I send you there, I want you to continue working with Albert at Banker to learn everything you can about farming. Don't be afraid to ask your brother or me questions. When Albert and I feel confident you're ready for the challenges and responsibilities of the Thibodaux properties, I want you to move to Rienzi. Albert will take over at Banker, and I hope Walter Morvant will run things for me until then." He told him that Walter Morvant, his late partner Emile's son, had assumed control of Webre and day-to-day operations at Rienzi after Emile's death.

"I know Lulu and the boys will love it, Papa. Thank you, Papa. I want to go, and I thank you for this job. I hope I will do well at it and will cause you no disappointment. I'm not the farmer that Albert is or the businessman that Fred is, but perhaps, with advice from them and from you, I can become pretty good at it." He reached to shake hands with his father.

Jean was surprised at his son's enthusiastic response. "Wonderful, Lawrence, I am delighted with your attitude. I intend to get Dansereau on this as soon as possible, and I'll let you know when the Morvants have been notified and are out of the way at Rienzi."

"How long do you think this will take?"

"Probably not long, if Walter gives me no trouble. I'll keep you informed."

"Has Morvant done a poor job, Papa?"

"He has done fairly well, matter of fact. In truth, I cannot fault the man's farming abilities—a better sugar grower than businessman. I have sixty per cent majority interest in Levert and Morvant Company, which Emile and I formed many years ago to incorporate Rienzi, Webre, and Orange Grove. But now I want complete control. I want all the revenues I can get out of the cane fields, that's all."

Jean smiled to himself as he recalled what Stephanie Marie had told her sisters and brothers when she learned of her father's advantageous plans and that he would have majority control in the company: "Papa is a benevolent sort of man who wants to help people out of their financial problems; he just buys them out."

Lawrence murmured a soft sound that his father did not bother to interpret. It didn't matter. All that mattered was that his son was willing to take the job. Jean knew Robert would never have been able to handle it; he still limped noticeably from the horse kick at St. John and he was not physically able to be a cane farmer. So among his family members, Lawrence was his only hope. He told Lawrence good-day and prepared to leave for Perdido Street.

Taking his cane and hat, he departed. Two blocks from home, as he crossed the street, he saw, through the corner of his eye, that Bailey was following him in the car at a discreet distance.

Damn. He is in collusion with Bea and Steph. Intriguer! In annoyance, he struck a small tree with his cane. At that moment he felt dizzy. He steadied himself by taking hold of the tree. *Damn. Please, God, don't let me fall.* The Packard glided up beside him, and Bailey jumped out to take his elbow.

In his frustration, Jean could say only, "Thank you, Bailey," as he was helped into the back seat.

In his downtown office, Miss Fortier informed Jean that Dr. Dupuy was expecting him at 2 o'clock on Friday for consultation. He thanked Miss Fortier and told Bailey to pick him up at the Pickwick at 1:30.

"What time you want me to pick you up to go to the club, Mister Jean?"

Jean realized that he had better not try to walk the few blocks, so grudgingly, he said, "At noon, please," and closed the door of his private office behind him. Alone, he sat at his desk and thought that his family and his employees were actually trying hard to help him. *I must try to help by cooperating. Well, what else could I do.* On the interoffice, he asked Miss Fortier to call Fernand Dansereau for him. *First things first.*

*   *   *

As Jean Baptiste entered the ballroom at the Roosevelt Hotel near Canal Street, he thought the Christmas decorations were more beautiful than he could recall. Focal point was the enormous Christmas tree in one corner, a shapely fir trimmed with glittering ornaments. Nearby was Stephanie's harp, for as had become the custom, she had been invited to favor members of Tulane's board of administrators and their guests with a program of Christmas music.

Jean, in evening dress as were all the men, his hand in the bend of Robert's arm, thought he must be one of the last to arrive. He saw so many familiar faces already there—Rudolph Matas, world-renowned physician and specialist on yellow fever who originated vascular surgery, and his revered former partner's son, Reuben Bush, who for a time had been a partner in the Bush & Levert brokerage firm. Jean raised his hand in salute to Colonel and Elizabeth Behan. Even Dr. and Mrs. Homer Dupuy were there. Dr. Dupuy was looking at Jean as he talked with Stephanie Marie and Beatrice; he knew Stephanie and the doctor had had a crush on each other when they were younger; they were social friends, now. At forty-eight, Stephanie was still beautiful and had left quite a few broken hearts behind her among New Orleans swains. Tonight it did not seem so amusing, for he believed Stephanie should have a life of her own. Jean thought of the passion Bea had developed as the wife Dr. Francis Kearny. As usual when his family appeared with him, Jean felt pride in their number and in their good looks. Lawrence's wife, Amelie, looked stunning in a black silk sheath. She wore a choker and earrings of pearls, diamonds, and opals that had come from the Dupuy family. All of Stephanie's family jewelry was kept in Jean's bank box, and his permission was required for a loan for special occasions. Jean had made Stephanie Marie the keeper of the key, and it was she who must go to the bank and fetch the pieces. Among his daughters and daughters-in-law, Jean was generous with his late wife's baubles, but he had forbidden Stephanie Marie to lend anything to Robert's wife, Olga. He told Stephanie frankly that he thought Olga was a schemer after the Levert money. Privately, he thought of her as spiteful, unpleasant. But he often acknowledged that they couldn't all be like Julia.

Tonight Beatrice was dressed in black, as always, but in a becoming gown with a border of jet beads around her neck. Stephanie wore a pale yellow gown that set off her dark skin and hair. She sat in the gilt chair beside her golden harp and began to play "Adeste Fidelis." The familiar air had an obvious spiritual effect on the crowd, and it made Jean forget his problems for the nonce. Lawrence came up and took his father by the arm.

"May I cut in?" he laughed, excusing Robert. "There is someone over here who wants to meet you, Papa."

Lawrence guided Jean to a small group that included Reuben Bush. Bush stepped forward and greeted Jean cordially, then announced, "Mr. Levert, may I present Mr. and Mrs. Louis Guidry. Mr. Guidry is a sugar broker and realtor, and although he has seen you at the exchange, he says he has never had the pleasure of speaking to you."

Jean studied the fleshy face of the man with reddish hair parted in the middle, clinging to a high forehead. Guidry stepped forward, extending his hand; Jean took the hand in handshake. His posture had a kind of sloppiness to it, as if in defiance of his slender body, and his eyes were hazel and questioning. Guidry presented his wife, Pauline, but Jean scarcely looked at her. Later, he would remember her as thin, sharp featured, with, alas, a certain similarity to Olga.

To Guidry he said, "How do you do, sir? What firm are you with? Could it be Trosclair and McCloud? Trosclair told me they have recently brought in some young men."

"Oh, no, Mr. Levert. I am working on my own. Not that I wouldn't like to be part of an established firm, but I am doing very well as things are. My business is going strong. I'd be eager to talk to you sometime about some of my plans and methods."

Methods, plans. Somewhat taken aback by Guidry's cocky assertion and his casual address with his elder, Jean looked at the man he estimated to be in his mid-forties. Although Guidry stared straight into his eyes, annoying him, Jean found himself not offended, but fascinated. Something about the man reminded Jean of himself as he was beginning his career as a sugar broker in New Orleans. Jean knew he had been brash and had offended many of his clients and elder colleagues in his determined drive for success. It had been his good fortune to become the partner of two highly respected, established brokers who tolerated his "methods." Not that he was humbled by the rigid honor codes of Harry Groeble and Colonel Louis Bush. He favored Guidry with a friendly smile.

"We must have lunch," said Jean, continuing to smile.

"I'd be delighted, sir. Perhaps the Pickwick? I am a new member there."

Really. Jean bowed slightly, biting his lip. "I'll have my secretary call you." He turned to greet Colonel Behan and his wife.

"Elizabeth, my dear. You look ravishing."

At seventy-five, Elizabeth Behan was still tall and straight, with an impressive cloud of white hair framing her classic features. She laughed good-naturedly at Jean's extravagant compliment.

"I saw you talking to Louis Guidry," said the Colonel when they were out of earshot.

"Yes, do you know him?"

"I know some of his people. They're New Orleans. I hear he is quite a comer, a go-getter, as they say. I've also heard that he is rather pushy. Tries a bit hard. He is said to have pulled a couple of ruthless tricks."

"Who is his wife?"

"She is from up around Ponchatoula, an Italian family. Name of Cashio, I think."

"Italian!" Jean Baptiste looked surprised.

"Now, General," smiled Mrs. Behan, "you know we cannot all be French."

Stephanie was playing what turned out to be her last number—"Jingle Bells," which she performed on an instrument designed for less jaunty compositions. The sedate crowd began to sing along with some gusto. When Stephanie pushed back her little gold chair, Dr. Felix Larue, Jr., and Dr. Homer Dupuy and his wife almost collided in Larue's effort to escort Stephanie to dinner. Finally, Larue seated Stephanie and himself where Jean could not see them for the centerpieces of red roses and tulips.

Midway through the sumptuous meal of gumbo, shrimp remoulade, crabmeat ravigote, and assorted vegetables, Eustis Kelleher, outgoing chairman of the Tulane board of administrators, recognized and toasted Dr. Matas, Dr. Larue, a protégé of Dr. Matas and prominent New Orleans surgeon, General Levert, and other distinguished guests. Kelleher acknowledged Jean for his thirty years as a board member, "one of the longest terms in the history of the university," and for his "generosity in support of many Tulane fundraising efforts." The chairman announced that the campaign to raise money for Tulane's new football stadium was a "resounding success thanks to men like General Levert." Jean, whose son Lawrence had attended Tulane and played football and baseball there, beamed at Kelleher's comments; he was proud of his contributions over the years to the stadium fund.

*   *   *

"I was impressed with Mr. Louis Guidry," Jean began.

"Hmmm!" grunted Lawrence. "Don't be fooled by that smoothie, Father. I don't know him well, of course, but my impression is that he would cheat his grandmother. I'm not alone in this assessment. He has a reputation."

"I am not likely to be fooled, Lawrence. I am a good judge of character. I did notice a certain eagerness about him, but that doesn't mean he would cheat his grandmother!"

At the breakfast table the next morning, Jean found the usual family drop-ins. He was glad, for it was always entertaining to him to gossip after an important social evening. It didn't take long to get to the subject of Louis Guidry, either.

"I wouldn't trust him as far as I could toss him, Papa," said Robert. "I'll tell you one thing, that wife of his is a pushy flirt." Robert, easily intimidated by his father, seldom spoke his mind in his father's presence.

Jean started to laugh, then stopped, intrigued. "Boys!" he chided. He seldom called his sons "boys." But he thought they were acting like haughty children.

"Let me tell you, she is a mess." Jean was surprised to hear Stella speak up. Nearly forty and something of a gabber, she had until now remained silent. "I knew Pauline Guidry at Louise McGhee School. She was caught cheating on a French test." Stella's eyes flashed. "Her people are not from New Orleans originally. She set her cap for Louis Guidry and really went after him. She thought he had money because he is Old New Orleans. She got him, and if he cheats his grandmother," she laughed at Lawrence, "it's probably because Pauline drove him to it. Her clothes and jewelry speak loudly."

"Well, Steph, Bea, do you girls have anything to add? I am amazed at what I have heard so far."

Bea shook her head, and Steph said, "I don't really know them."

Jean felt dizzy, almost falling, when he attempted to leave the breakfast table. Robert, who was seated next to his father, despite his crippled right leg, moved quickly to steady him.

"Papa, Louis Guidry can be found at the Fairgrounds most afternoons. Those people are usually over their heads in debt to the bookies in this town . . ."

Jean rose before his son finished. After regaining his balance, he thanked his youngest son and excused himself to freshen before leaving for the office. His carriage erect, he was determined to give his children the impression of strength and self-possession as he walked away from the table.

*   *   *

Jean stepped from behind the screen in Dr. Dupuy's examining room in his spacious Medical Building office on Baronne Street. He had put his clothes on his upper body, after weighing in at a hundred and forty-five pounds, five pounds more than he had weighed when he was fifteen. Taking off most of his clothes was a demand he had not anticipated from an ear, nose, and throat doctor. The nurse entered and asked him to step into Dr. Dupuy's office. He found the doctor at his desk, writing in a folder.

"Have a seat, General Levert." Solidly built, with thick black eye lashes, the doctor did not look up and continued writing. Jean sat in a leather chair facing him. There was something almost ceremonial about this, and Jean did not like his role—taking commands from a doctor and nurse.

Presently, Dr. Dupuy closed the folder and rose from his chair. He walked around and took a seat in a chair near Jean. He removed his pince-nez, pushed back his dark hair, and cleared his throat.

Mon dieu.

"General. I feel certain of the diagnosis. You do indeed have mastoiditis, and in both ears. You are facing a serious situation. Mastoiditis in the ears of a patient of any age is serious, a major cause of death among children. But for a man of your age, it is even more critical. I will be quite frank and direct. Your condition demands surgery and without much delay."

Stunned, Jean's face went almost white. "Surgery?" His large eyes were fixed unwaveringly upon the doctor's face and he sat stiffly erect, gripping the arms of his chair with both hands, as if to keep from fainting. "What about medication, bed rest, something less heroic?"

"I regret, sir, your trouble is beyond those measures."

"Mon dieu!"

"Permit me to describe what you face, what the operation amounts to. But first let me assure you that I know this is shocking to you, and you have my most sincere sympathy for your alarm. For assurance, I can tell you that I have done a good many of these surgeries and with good results." He explained there were several particular risks—infection, of course, as in all surgery, presenting in such a case as this the threat of encephalitis, a dread brain inflammation, that could lead to subsequent brain abscess, even death, if not treated immediately. He told Jean another risk was an occasional complication from the anesthesia. He said the mastoid was a bone behind the ear and that infection began with a sore throat, which went directly to the mastoid bone. "Mastoiditis is one of the most dangerous conditions that an ear, nose, and throat doctor ever faces."

Dr. Dupuy looked down at the folder for a moment, then continued: "The scalpel necessarily must pass very near to the brain. With the best of luck, you, as an otherwise healthy man, have a good chance to avoid these complications. You will be under anesthesia for more than one and at least two hours because I must deal with both ears." He told him that Dr. French, a highly skilled anesthesiologist, will be at his side throughout the surgery, that a heart specialist will be on hand; that the accommodations at Hotel Dieu were as adequate as any in the city; that the Sisters of Charity ran an immaculate and efficient hospital. "I must say, I am more completely comfortable at Hotel Dieu."

When Jean remained silent, Dr. Dupuy went on. "I will be glad to try to answer any questions you have, sir. Also, I urge you to feel free to seek a second opinion."

Finally, Jean found his tongue. "Dr. Dupuy, of course I am surprised to hear from you that I must have such risky surgery. I am eighty-three years old. The risks sound worrisome to say the least. How many years do I have left. I mean I am thinking this. But whether I shall live another year or another ten years, I seem to have little choice. It all seems, well, frightful, but apparently, I have no options. Be assured that I feel no need for further diagnosis beyond yours. When must this be done? I am in the midst of certain important business transactions. Do you think we could delay this operation for a few days until after my business is completed? It is uncommonly important to me."

"General Levert, I must insist that you enter the hospital almost immediately. I shall schedule your surgery for next Monday morning at Hotel Dieu. I want you to check into the hospital by mid-afternoon on Sunday and be prepared to remain there for two weeks, assuming there are no complications. You will need the care of a private nurse for the first week or so. If your family prefers the services of registered nurses whom you know, you may engage them. If not, our office can locate excellent private nurses for cases like this."

"Well, we do call on a Miss Ida Colee. She has served our family several times. For others, I shall have to depend upon you, sir, thank you." Suddenly, it occurred to Jean to ask: "Dr. Dupuy, what are my chances? Can you reckon in percentages?"

"I don't deal in percentages. But I can tell you the sooner you have the surgery, the sooner the mastoid bone is opened and the infection cleaned out, the better the prognosis and your chances for a full recovery. The longer the surgery is delayed, the chances of more dizziness and falls are increased."

Well, he had asked. The answer shook him. He looked at his hands clasped in his lap thinking of the positive and the negative. The negative seemed in command at the moment.

"My family, my daughters, especially the two who live with me are going to be very concerned . . ."

"General, if you wish, I'll be glad to telephone Miss Stephanie and give her some idea of what has come about. Would you care to have me do that?"

"I would be most grateful, Doctor. I'm sure you will be gentle with Stephanie. This is going to be difficult for her."

"Oh, yes, of course. By the way, General, I believe I am distantly related to your late wife, Stephanie Dupuy. I believe my grandfather and Mrs. Levert's father were second cousins."

"Indeed. Well, I shouldn't be surprised. The Dupuys are not so numerous among the existing French families in Louisiana. A quite distinguished clan."

"Thank you."

In parting, the two men shook hands. For the brief moment of the surgeon's genteel gesture, Jean felt the irony of Dr. Dupuy's slender, long-fingered hand holding life or death for him.

"Take it easier, now, in your business pursuits . . . it's just time for you to begin giving something back." I think a lot about the advice Colonel Bush gave me many years ago, before he died, yet, I've never really heeded it. It's been hard for me to stop the business wheeling-dealing and accumulating money—until now. There's a good chance I could be leaving this life prematurely because of my serious ailment . . . I intend to give fifty thousand dollars to the hospital if my life is spared, if I am able to resume my normal life. Hell, I have too many unfinished plans and my children aren't ready to take full control of my businesses. What I did for Julia and Junior was a small thing, compared to the hospital pledge. My son was dying in a sanatorium way out in the desert and could no longer support his family. And there were donations of land and money for St. Martinville's first high school and gymnasium and for a red brick schoolhouse on St. John for all the children of my farm laborers and those of nearby plantations, white and black. I still have mystifying feelings about my new role—doing something for others. Perhaps I will establish a foundation to fund my gifts to schools, institutions, and churches in all the towns my companies do business.

Jean Baptiste Levert
1923

Chapter 80

JEAN BAPTISTE WAS alone in his room at Hotel Dieu—that's how he wanted to be. Stephanie Marie, Freddy, Albert, and Lawrence had escorted him to the hospital at three o'clock on Sunday afternoon. Not to mention Bailey. He was pleased that his out-of-town sons came for the operation, but it made him nervous to have the whole family in a tumult.

Jean insisted that no nurse come on duty until his surgery was over if, indeed, he was still there to be nursed. Wearing his own white linen nightshirt, he looked about the room. His robe lay across the foot of the hospital bed, his slippers were parked neatly on the floor beside the bed. It was a nice hospital room—large, on a corner, with two windows, tastefully draped icons on the walls, but he thought the wood floor needed polishing. It had a private bath and an anteroom where a family member could sleep. Dr. Dupuy told him, sotto voce, that it was a room reserved for important people. Well, he saw nothing inappropriate about his occupying the room for he was an important person. But he was denied supper.

To Jean the whole building, occupying a block on Tulane Avenue between Bolivar and Johnson streets, smelled of ether. From the entrance off a bricked courtyard, up eight granite steps, through the halls, and all the way to his room on the third floor. An awful smell. *If I live, I'll never enter another hospital. I'll stress that to Steph and Bea. I intend to die in my own bed.*

After a discreet knock, his door opened, and a nun entered. She looked crisp and in control in her habit. When she came into full view, he saw that she was the Mother Superior. She glided across the room under the full sail of her wimple to his bedside, looking authoritative. She had a serious expression on her face, yet Jean could see a steely gentleness in her expression.

"Good afternoon, Mr. Levert."

"Good afternoon, Mother. I do have the honor of addressing Hotel Dieu's Mother Superior, do I not?"

"You do, sir. Let me welcome you to Hotel Dieu." She glanced around the room. "Are you quite comfortable? This is our finest guest room, you know."

"Someone has said as much. Yes, it is very comfortable. That is if one must . . ."

"Of course. None of us wants to be sick in a hospital." She cleared her throat and pulled in her breath. "Dr. Dupuy tells me you are to have a very serious operation tomorrow morning. I hope your mind and heart are at ease about the outcome. God is always with us, as you know. We are ever in His hands no matter the state of our health or circumstance. He is our comfort and our strength."

She lightly stroked a heavy silver cross that hung on the starched white bosom of her habit. As she looked at him, a softness crept into her blue eyes, and Jean knew the elderly nun felt deeply for him. Indeed, he was in need of comfort. Listening to her spiritual consolations, he felt his deepest fears take shape in his mind as they had not before. Until now he had had diversions to absorb his fears. At this moment, facing this holy woman, he realized that he faced the formidable likelihood of departing this life in the morning.

"Mother . . ."

"Yes, Mr. Levert?"

"Mother, I must not die tomorrow or at any time as a result of this ailment . . . I must get over this. I have many unfinished plans, projects . . . My children are not ready to take over the full reins of my businesses. I have grandchildren I scarcely know . . . What I'm trying to say . . ."

"I understand, Mr. Levert. I know what you are trying to say. You don't want to die, and you have been told you have a good chance of doing just that. How may I comfort you? I am eager to speak to Our Lady. She holds you in her arms as she did when you were an infant. That never changes for a good and true Catholic. May I? . . ." She clasped her hands in supplication beneath her chin and closed her eyes.

After a few moments of silence, Jean said, "By all means, Mother, do pray for me. Speak to Our Lady. But also I want to speak to you about a more worldly matter. Worldly but not unreligious."

"Yes?"

"I want to make you a promise. If in this hospital tomorrow and the days following, my life is spared and I can resume my normal life, I promise you that I will contribute the sum of fifty thousand dollars to this institution to be used as you and your board deem most appropriate."

Mother Superior gasped as the amount of the pledge sunk in. She took a step back and laid her hands on her face. "Mr. Levert! Fifty thousand dollars!"

"Absolutely."

Mother Superior got over her shock and calmly said, "Now, Mr. Levert, you know you cannot bargain with God."

"I'm not talking about bargaining. I'm talking about gratitude. Appreciation. Whatever you might want to call it. If I survive, I will be in the debt of everyone who cares for me in this hospital. I will want to say thank you in the best possible way."

"I believe I understand, Mr. Levert. God will surely bless you. I shall beseech him to do that."

"To what order do you belong, Mother?"

"We are the Sisters of Charity. Our order was founded by Mother Elizabeth Ann Seton at Emmitsburg, Maryland, in the very early part of the nineteenth century."

"Mount St. Mary's! I was doing graduate studies there when the war broke out."

"I know that."

Really. Jean wondered how she knew where he got his education. But now she was bowing her head again, praying for him and for the salvation of his soul. Then she excused herself.

In a short time, Jean found himself being blessed again. Father Patrick Gaspard from the Jesuit church came in with what Jean regarded as enthusiastic and encouraging blessings. Actually Jean was expecting the priest, for they knew each other well. They had become good friends after Father Gaspard, as a young priest, had celebrated Marie Lucie's funeral mass.

"Mr. Levert, I have never really taken the occasion to tell you how much I respect you and your splendid family. Forgive me, but I must say you and your children represent all that is best in strong Catholic families. Our church has benefited in many ways as we have observed so many of the sacred rites of the Levert family over the years. The saddest of times, the happiest of times, burials, marriages, christenings. I call it epic participation."

Jean caught the old priest's enthusiasm, and his eloquence impressed him. Some of the epic participation flashed through his memory. Steph's funeral, all those christenings, that morning he and Mathilde arrived there for Mass to begin Lent after her debut at the glittering Comus ball. He had never forgot the spiritual leveling they both experienced that morning in the old Jesuit church, surrounded by other revelers, eager to come to terms with real life and mortality after the wild celebrations of Mardi Gras. He had learned something about Mathilde that night, his beautiful daughter long passed on among his dead children. Perhaps he was about to join them. *Little Lucie? Junior?*

"Mr. Levert? Mr. Levert?"

"Oh, yes, Father. Thank you for your blessings. I think I need them more than ever. I . . ."

"I will bid you good night, sir. You will be in my prayers and in the prayers of all the religious of this city. All who know you and your good works." The priest slipped out of the room. *A good man, hard working,* thought Jean.

Soon a young nurse entered and gave him a small white pill.

Shapely and smiling in her starched white uniform, from the cap on her dark curls to her quiet white oxfords, he scarcely noticed the youthful charms that usually caught his imagination, or at least his eye.

At six the next morning, he had no recollection of the young nurse or going to sleep. The little white pill . . . .

*   *   *

Upon awakening about noon on Monday, Jean's first thought was a surprised, "I am alive. I did not die." But his thoughts made little difference to him; he was more ill than he could remember. A nurse pressed a basin to his cheek and he retched until he thought his body would be torn apart. Bea—he thought it was Bea—laid a cold cloth on his forehead, then on his throat. The misery seemed to go on forever. It did last all day. That and the smell of ether were almost as bad as any of the horrors of his imprisonment at Fort Delaware. He wished he had died.

To his annoyance, Dr. Dupuy came in and told him that the operation was a success, and that he would be feeling fine soon. *Feeling fine! This man does not know what this dreadful nausea is like.* Jean felt no inclination to talk to anyone, either in good spirits or bad. He wanted everyone out of there except the apparently competent nurse. His greatest relief was in the naps that gave him temporary respite. When he waked, retched, felt the cool cloth, he only wanted, mercifully, to go back to sleep.

By noon Tuesday, propped up on pillows, Jean managed to have a conversation with the select few allowed in his room. Dr. Dupuy, his earliest visitor, came in looking rather elegant in his street clothes. Jean realized that the doctor was quite handsome.

"*Bon jour, Monsieur Levert.*"

"*Bon jour, Monsieur le docteur.*"

The two men spoke French throughout the doctor's visit. Jean was feeling so much better that he fully appreciated a conversation in his ancestral tongue, a pleasure he did not enjoy often enough. During Jean's entire stay at Hotel Dieu, he spoke only French with

Dr. Dupuy. Soon Mother Superior discovered her patient liked to converse in her native language, and between them also English was dispensed with.

Jean knew that he was healing faster than his surgeon had anticipated, and feeling better, he became bored. Sometimes he closed his eyes and thought of Lila. He thought of the erotic dream he had had about her during one of his drugged sleeps . . . *her daintiness, her velvet voice, a touch or two, that evening at her house. Oh, that special evening.* Each night he fell asleep wishing he could have the dream all over again.

In another dream he was with Colonel Bush, and the Colonel spoke as if Jean were the older man's son, citing again the rewards of sharing one's wealth. It seemed strange to realize that he was now much older than the Colonel was when he died. Nevertheless, the avuncular tone remained. Louis Guidry, the young broker he had met at the Tulane board of administrators' dinner, appeared briefly in a dream, but Jean could not recall what the man was doing or saying.

These perplexing dreams and thoughts filled his mind; Jean became weak lying in the hospital bed. The relief he felt upon going home to Third Street was tempered by his impatience to get on his feet again, specifically to walk to his office on Perdido. But soon Bailey was driving him for half a day's work, then adding to that lunch at one of his clubs, and in a matter of three weeks, Jean was working a full day. Work had piled up because he had lost his most competent sugar broker. So Jean replied to letters, made inquiries by letter and telephone about available property, dunned his clients for delayed payments, dealt with such matters as removing the Morvants from Rienzi, this latter with Dansereau. And he realized that he must find someone to join J.B. Levert Land Company who, without a long training period, would assume responsibilities equal to his own. An associate with a solid reputation on Factors' Row, who would bring to the table good business connections and extensive knowledge of the real estate market. Although Robert had become treasurer of the Levert companies, Jean knew he could not rely on his son to handle every type of business—to travel for him, to deal with his important clients in St. Louis or Memphis, but especially to handle real estate ventures he was thinking about pursuing in earnest.

Already a large property owner downtown, Jean had become interested in several residential and commercial properties uptown, in upper St. Charles Avenue from Lee Circle to Jackson Avenue. After careful analysis of the earning potential there, he was convinced that upper St. Charles one day would become one of the finest retail and apartment thoroughfares not only in New Orleans, but in the United States. He was already prepared to spend large sums to purchase several tracts along St. Charles, preferring corner lots. His plan: Buy land and clear it for construction of duplex apartments and two—and three-story houses, rents from which he knew would yield large profits.

Louis Guidry telephoned for a business appointment before Jean mentioned his intentions to anyone. Jean was about to invest heavily in real estate along St. Charles. Perhaps Guidry knew this, saw his opening, thought Jean. But what did Guidry really seek? What was he after? Jean detested causeless affection, just as he despised unearned wealth, and he knew that Guidry had inherited all of his wealth. He professed to care for Jean for some unknown reasons. What were they?

After one office interview and, later, lunch at the Pickwick, Jean offered Guidry a job. Within days, after approval of the majority of the firm's board of directors, Dansereau drew the necessary papers for signature making Guidry an associate. Jean had his lawyer add two clauses to the contract: First, Jean would receive a promissory note from Guidry for five thousand dollars, dated one year from execution of the lien, securing a certificate of fifty shares of J.B. Levert Land Co. stock at a hundred dollars per share; second, "If Jean Baptiste should become mentally or physically incapacitated or if Guidry should leave the firm for any reason, Guidry shall not sell his shares to anyone outside the company or outside the Levert family without first offering his shares to the firm or to a family stockholder, giving him ten days within which to purchase those shares at market value."

Jean realized he probably made a hasty decision, but he judged Guidry competent. If he had discussed the decision with Colonel Behan, Reuben Bush, or any of his business associates, they might have talked him out of his action. So he decided to bring Guidry into the firm, then tell them.

CHAPTER 81

STILL THE PRINCIPAL in J. B. Levert Land Co., Inc., Jean thought that he had at last found an associate capable of assuming most of his work and responsibility that he was admittedly no longer able to handle himself. Men had come and gone during the past four years or so, since the company was formed, but none had filled the bill to his satisfaction.

As Jean regained his health and overcame the shock of serious surgery, Louis Guidry had taken over all long-distance travel. Several times in Jean's stead he had gone to check the Levert-Shirley Company-owned plantations, Shirley and Ellen Kay, near Alexandria, and Jean was satisfied with his reports. Guidry had traveled the St. Louis, Chicago, and Memphis circuit, renewing and maintaining important and historic alliances Jean wished to continue profitable associations. After Guidry returned from travels near and far full of enthusiasm and showing aggressive attention to all areas of the brokerage business to which he was exposed, Jean judged him confident and enterprising. Yet, he noticed that although he returned to the City full of plans and good reports, he sank into a less happy state of mind within days.

Jean began to study his associate, trying to figure out what was wrong. Were his gambling debts out of hand? Or was something wrong at home? Recalling things he had been told about Pauline Guidry, he decided that, gambling not discounted, she was his basic problem; she was a "driving woman," he was told. Too many afternoons Guidry was away from his desk, sometimes making up obvious lies concerning his whereabouts.

Several times Robert told him he had seen Guidry at the Fairgrounds when Louis told a different story, told him that the bookies to whom Guidry owed large sums of money were not forgiving types.

The difficult situation frustrated Jean. At eighty-five, he was remarkably strong, but he was an old man; to himself he admitted this. Since his surgery he had fallen three times, once at Biloxi house and twice at Third Street, bumping his head seriously enough on one occasion to miss a day at the office. But mentally, he felt fully capable of running his businesses. He just realized it was time to shift some responsibilities. Increasingly, Jean lay the blame for Guidry's behavior at the feet of the shrewish, rapacious wife, Pauline. As increasing money flowed in from the thriving business, Guidry asked for a raise in salary, and Jean was certain the man was spouting lines given to him by Pauline.

Then Elizabeth Behan called. She asked Jean to stop by the Behan home in the Garden District one afternoon for a cocktail. The Colonel was not well and for several months had not been able to go downtown for lunch with Jean. Jean thanked his friend's wife and said he would be delighted.

That afternoon at five, he was met by a servant and taken to the library where the Behans awaited him. As the three of them exchanged warm greetings, the servant came from the next room with a tray of drinks—bourbon and soda on tinkling cracked ice for all. After they began sighing and relaxing, Colonel Behan, dressed in a tweed jacket with leather elbow patches, spoke: "General, we must inform you of some unhappy news. To get directly to it, your associate Louis Guidry is planning to do you in."

"Do me in?"

"Do you in. Yes. Elizabeth has an almost incredible piece of information that she stumbled upon entirely by accident. Tell him, my dear."

Mrs. Behan cleared her throat and looked quite uncomfortable. She fixed her large brown eyes on Jean. "Well, General Levert, May de la Houssaye and I went down the Avenue for lunch at

Delmonico's yesterday. We were seated in a secluded spot, our table invisible behind a bank of palms and other plants. Soon a man and woman were seated quite close to us, but as invisible to us as we were to them. It did not take long for me to realize the two people were Pauline and Louis Guidry."

Jean raised his eyebrows. *What is so strange about that?* But he began to have apprehensions.

"Almost immediately the Guidrys began to argue quite audibly. May and I were dumbfounded. We couldn't resist listening to what was being said. To sum it up, Mrs. Guidry was furiously accusing her husband of not acting as they had agreed. To put it bluntly, Mr. Guidry had gone with your firm deliberately planning to try to take over your business as she had instructed him." Mrs. Behan hesitated and turned her head aside before she continued. "She said he must now get a court interdiction, I believe that is the phrase she used, against you, proving that you are unable physically and mentally to manage your brokerage business. She intends for her husband to have control of J. B. Levert Land."

Mrs. Behan frowned. For a moment she looked as if she might decide not to go on. "Mrs. Guidry told her husband that he was weak, addicted to gambling, and unable to act. He told her, his voice rising in pitch, she was a spendthrift, building up debts for clothes, jewelry, entertainment, and other things, making it impossible for him to take care of their finances . . . she threatened to leave him if he did not turn their allegations over to the court within a week."

Colonel Behan looked almost ill as his wife told her story; he removed his tweed jacket. Elizabeth looked as though she might weep. Jean himself felt downhearted disappointment such as he had never experienced. Though he knew that Guidry had been behaving strangely, this disclosure of the row in a public restaurant shocked him. In the past several months, Jean realized that, compared with Pauline, Louis Guidry cut a pathetic figure. Utterly dominated by his wife but basically good-natured, Guidry had long since given up thought of making himself heard even in his own home. Jean knew Pauline controlled everything, watched over everything, gave orders to everyone.

Mrs. Behan came to Jean's side and laid her hand on his shoulder. "Jean, William and I feel that you must know this so you can take appropriate action, head him off, so to speak. I must tell you that we are just sick about it. Still, we must be thankful that you know and can defend yourself."

Suddenly struck by the awful significance of her words, Jean bounded from his wing chair in front of bookshelves along a wall. His face red with anger, he looked at both of them. He smiled wryly. *These are the best friends I have in this world, friends enough to let me know what a terrible error I made in taking in Guidry. And being taken in by him.* He shook his head.

"I can only say, thank you. I will call Dansereau at his home tonight. I will not wait until Monday. But I think Guidry will get nowhere. This charge is ridiculous, of course. I'm as sharp as he is. And that is pretty sharp. I knew something was wrong in his life, and frankly I suspected that his wife was back of it. I never liked her looks or her pushy, forceful manner, from the first night I met her at the Tulane dinner at the Roosevelt Hotel. Remember?"

"Oh, yes," they said at once, and the Colonel added, "We never knew what attracted you to him."

Jean sighed. "I think it was the little bit of myself I saw in him. Young, brash, ambitious, hard worker . . . like Narcissus looking into the pool. My children certainly warned me about both of them. *Mon dieu.*" He shook his head again. "Could Eli drive me on home? I believe I don't feel like the walk."

"Of course, General," said Elizabeth, and she leaned from her chair near the fireplace and gave the bell pull a light yank. When the butler appeared, she told him that he would be driving Mr. Levert to Third Street presently and to bring the car to the side entrance. To Jean she added, "Now, don't rush off."

"I must go. I want to thank you both for telling me this. I'm shocked and yet not so shocked. I'm angry. Not only must I start looking for another experienced broker to assist me, I must defend my sanity."

"Well, you know there are many younger men who would welcome an invitation to join your company. Capable, honorable men," said Colonel Behan. "And perhaps all this idiocy will come to nothing. Try to stay calm and watch out for yourself, old friend. Dansereau is a good lawyer, and I know you are capable of putting up a fierce battle, war hero that you are, but it's time you and I should be able to lay our weapons aside."

The men shook hands. Jean was tempted to kiss Elizabeth on the cheek, but he didn't like kissing a woman who was taller than he was. So he squeezed her hand. From the door, he turned back to them.

"I don't want my children to know about this until absolutely necessary."

"Of course," they said together.

*   *   *

Jean stepped off the Carondelet Building elevator at ten o'clock on Monday morning and turned toward Fernand Dansereau's office. He hadn't liked calling his attorney late last night, for he knew sleep had been hard for Dansereau recently. He had several other clients awaiting trial on charges ranging from misdemeanors to income tax evasion.

"First of all, Mr. Levert, let me ask for some frank answers. Do you believe that you are in anyway diminished mentally and physically? Do you even sometimes suspect that you are no longer able to keep up with each day's demands in business? Please be completely frank with me."

Jean pursed his lips, as if trying to form a distasteful reply delicately. Finally, he said, "Fernand, if I am diminished mentally, I am too diminished to know what's happening. But let me assure you, I do know what is happening—all around me, at work, at home, among my friends, socially. I am alert. No man can run a mile when he's eighty-five years old. But I just don't know what to make of all this except that Louis Guidry is driven by an avaricious wife. From what I know of the man, he would never dream all this up on his own."

"Well, if he goes through with it, we'll be getting a summons to a hearing. You'll be called upon to show beyond doubt that you are completely competent and you will probably need testimony from others—your family, your doctors, friends, business colleagues. Naturally, he is going to point to your age, probably to your serious surgery."

"*Mon dieu.* This is all so ludicrous. Perhaps Louis will back out. He might come to his senses. From what you've told me about this interdiction procedure, it can be very costly. I just can't understand why Louis would go to such lengths considering his financial problems, unless the man's plain desperate or a damn fool, or both. There is one thing for certain; whatever he does, he is going to be out on his ear with no job as soon as I can manage it."

"Well, we must be ready for papers. I have a lot of material on file here about your conduct of business. And already my clerk has uncovered some relevant information about Guidry. His Napoleon Avenue home is already mortgaged; obviously the bank has been overly indulgent. He is in debt to most of the bookies in the city. His relatives have all but abandoned him. These are indisputable facts. If some lawyer goes for an interdiction of you, I can't imagine we'll lose. Meanwhile, be careful of your health." Dansereau half-smiled. "Don't take any risks that might cause another fall. By all means let your chauffeur drive you to work and to other appointments."

*　　*　　*

Although Guidry was out of the City, traveling in the interest of J.B. Levert Land Company, Jean received a copy of Guidry's petition for interdiction the day after his visit with Dansereau, as he was leaving his office in early evening. Immediately he returned to his office with the paper to read it. *The bastard didn't waste any time, did he?* One paragraph summed up the allegations:

> *In the matter of the interdiction of Jean Baptiste Levert—*
> *now comes Louis Edward Guidry and files this petition . . . the*

petitioner is an adult and a businessman in partnership with
Jean Baptiste Levert. Petitioner is of the belief that by reason
of advanced age and physical incapacity, Jean Baptiste Levert
is unable to manage his own affairs without assistance, and
further a curator should be appointed to aid in the
management of the properties and holdings of Levert . . .
attached hereto as Exhibits A & B are affidavits of two
reputable physicians authorized to practice medicine in the
State of Louisiana, certifying as to their examination of Jean
Baptiste Levert and the results thereof, one of which is from
the physician who performed the serious surgery two years
before on the person of Levert . . . that the best interests of
Jean Baptiste Levert could be served if the Court appointed a
curator . . . the petitioner leaves to the sound discretion of the
Court whether a curator should be appointed.

Jean read with disbelief and increasing bitterness. He paced up and down in his office, cursing the "damnable henpecked, rascal, the *cochon.*" He stopped pacing. He walked to the wash basin and pressed his forehead against the mirror, trying to force his mind not to think—the only way he thought he could get through this absurdity. He returned to his desk and called Dansereau, who hurried to his office for consultation. After reading the petition, Dansereau called it fairly routine and declared that it did not seriously threaten Jean. It did not demand total submission of his business responsibilities, of operational power. But it did call for Jean to be assisted, as needed, by Guidry in running the business.

"He's maneuvering himself into position to rob you blind."

With guarded confidence, Dansereau, who could be abrasive, but was quick-minded, a real charmer for the most part, advised Jean to be optimistic. He also advised him to control himself no matter how outrageous Guidry's claims were before the judge. Show no anger, he admonished.

Now, Jean had to tell his children what he faced; he knew they would be called upon to attest under oath in Civil District

Court for the Parish of Orleans that their father was competent. When he spoke to them face-to-face at a Third Street conference, he was thankful, even touched, by their completely supporting response. No one said, "We told you so," and all were angry and vociferous in their disgust with and rejection of the cur Louis Guidry.

*   *   *

The scene in Judge Horace Parmley's airy courtroom, in the white marble edifice known as The Civil Court Building on Royal Street, seemed surreal to Jean. The elderly robed judge sat at a bench of dark wood on an elevated platform and surveyed the people seated before him in a cluster behind a railing. Jean was pleased to see many members of his large family—middle-aged children and their husbands and wives, a number of adult grandchildren, eight or ten distinguished citizens, his closest friends and colleagues. A dignified, well-off set of prominent New Orleans citizens.

The clerk of court, a stenographer, and other court officials sat at a long table in front of the judge. With Jean at one of the counsel tables were Fernand Dansereau, Albert, Lawrence, Freddy, and Robert; and Jean's secretary, who had a stack of files before her. At the other table sat Louis Guidry, his wife, and a countrified-looking fellow, who never spoke, but who Jean learned later was Pauline's cousin from Ponchatoula. He was not Guidry's attorney, for Guidry had declared himself to be his own counsel.

Dansereau leaned into his client and whispered, referring to the old saying that the man who represents himself in court has a fool for a client. Jean tried to smile, but he was too stricken at the sight of the Guidrys to be amused, especially Pauline. *Look at that woman! Diamonds on her earlobes at ten o'clock in the morning! And she's dripping silver fox. Such vulgar taste! And all at my expense, she thinks. Well, Stella said she was caught cheating on a French test. Mon dieu. I should have listened.*

The courtroom had a row of large windows down the lefthand

side overlooking the French Quarter; the windows looked like milky glass that blocked the view of the outdoors, but still let in a lot of light. The room was quiet and tense. Judge Parmley sat in front of the windows and against the bright daylight; all of the participants appearing no more than black silhouettes. The judge rapped once lightly with his gavel, then cleared his throat with a cough.

"This hearing will commence," he said, peering downward at the petition through bifocals clipped to the bridge of his nose. "Yes, yes, Messieurs Louis Guidry and Jean Baptiste Levert. We shall make every effort to determine whether evidence warrants the establishment of Mr. Guidry as Mr. Levert's guardian."

At the word *guardian*, Stephanie Marie gasped. Colonel Behan said, loud enough to be heard, "Ridiculous! Absurd!" The judge banged his gavel once.

Louis Guidry stood and began by thanking the court and acknowledging the great responsibility of representing himself. Obviously deeming brevity to be admirable in the eyes of the judge, he did not linger in his speech. He told the court he had worked for Mr. Levert for two years, during which time he had been intimately privy to every facet of Mr. Levert's business enterprises. His employer had sent him about the country on sensitive and responsible missions for his companies. Locally, on behalf of J. B. Levert Land Co., Guidry said he had handled the purchase and sale of important New Orleans residential and commercial properties. He outlined his discovery that Mr. Levert, being in his mid-eighties, having had extremely serious and dangerous surgery, and—here his voice became more ominous—having had some bad falls wherein he bumped his head, had convinced him that Mr. Levert was no longer capable, physically and mentally, to conduct his vast businesses alone, as he had been doing for so many decades. He also argued that his intentions were designed *only* to protect Mr. Levert from being exploited by "ertswhile business partners or clients he had foreclosed on or bought out, from being possibly ruined financially."

Angry as he was, Jean could not help admitting to himself

that Guidry was speaking rather well, better than he would have expected. Yet, he repeatedly looked down at his wife as if for approval or prompting. The man was pathetic, a pawn in the hands of his wife, if Jean ever saw one. No members of Louis's or Pauline's immediate families were present. Dansereau had told Jean that gossip had it that their families strongly disapproved of his actions and the court petition.

Once, Guidry paused and took a sip of water. Inadvertently, his eyes locked for a moment with Jean's. The younger man's face turned brick red, and he looked away. After that, his delivery seemed less poised. For witnesses, he called Stephanie and Bea, both of whom took the oath and indignantly denied that their father had ever faltered in any way except when he was confined to a hospital room. Dr. Dupuy and Dr. Gonsoulin testified that they had never "at any time observed any lack of judgment on part of their prominent patient." To Jean's shock, Bailey was called into the room and questioned.

The faithful servant, his round face happy of expression, stood clutching his peaked cap, his eyes large with awe. But he testified glowingly to his boss's "generosity, kindnesses, and fineness." Jean almost chuckled aloud at his chauffeur's blandishments, compliments that Jean never heard from anybody other than committee members accepting large philanthropic checks. The judge excused Bailey in the midst of singing the praises of Mister Jean.

Dansereau whispered to Jean before he stood to speak for his client, "This is a farce. Will you join me for some wiener schnitzel at Kolb's over on St. Charles Avenue?" Jean smiled wryly, but gave no answer.

Dansereau attested to his client's capabilities, which, he said, were as sharp as they were when they began their relationship years before. Then, one by one, he called witnesses who gave eloquent testimony in Jean's favor—his children, the two distinguished doctors, Colonel Behan, three long-time colleagues at the Louisiana Sugar and Rice Exchange. Finally, after his artfully constructed questions had evoked just the answers he desired, Dansereau addressed Judge Parmley:

"Your honor, we have more witnesses, but with your agreement, we will stop here. If it pleases the court, we believe we have given more than adequate evidence of the sanity and judgment of the honorable gentleman, General Jean Baptiste Levert, and request that this hearing be dismissed and that the General be allowed to return to his busy workday."

A soft murmur emanated from Jean's cluster of supporters. But Judge Parmley rapped the gavel. He brought the hearing to a close but stated that he would announce his decision about the petition in one week after he had time to study the court stenographer's records in the silence of his chambers. "This hearing will convened at ten o'clock the following Monday, whereupon I will pronounce my decision in the matter," the judge added.

Dansereau stopped and said gravely, "Thank you, Your Honor." Louis Guidry, not acquainted with courtroom etiquette, merely followed suit. He looked down at his bejeweled wife, it seemed to Jean, for approval. But Pauline Guidry sat stoneyfaced. Obviously she did not want to be put off for a week. Besides, everyone present could see her husband had scarcely made his point. Later at Kolb's, a German restaurant, Dansereau declared his surprise that the judge did not rule Guidry out of order on the spot.

After a week, when the principals assembled in the courtroom, Judge Parmley ruled in Jean's favor, but not before he reviewed Guidry's petition and argument with more credulity and respect than any of Jean's family, friends, or his lawyer could understand. The ordeal had tired Jean, and he knew he would look back on it with sorrow and distaste for the rest of his days.

*   *   *

That evening, Jean remained late at his desk in his office. The window overlooking silent Perdido Street showed outer darkness weakly diluted by a distant lamp on Baronne Street. He was waiting.

Waiting.

Sure enough, after nightfall, he heard the doorkey's metallic turn, and his Judas entered the dark outer office; so dark within that Louis Guidry reached for a match in his jacket pocket and lit it, striking the match on the sole of his shoe. As soon as the door closed, Jean turned on his desk lamp. Louis Guidry stood before him, his breath frozen in his throat, looking stunned, horrified, at the sight of his benefactor staring at him in the lamp's soft glow. In the drama of Jean's staged scene, Guidry instantly saw all the condemnation, disappointment, and anger on the old man's face, an old man who once again held all the cards and knew it.

Guidry turned abruptly and entered his own small office, which was adjacent to Jean's. Jean sat silently and listened to the beaten man—the loser—gathering his possessions in the next room. *He thought he would sneak in and sneak out under cover of darkness. But I even headed that off.*

Suddenly, Guidry appeared at Jean's office door wild-eyed, clutching its facings. Jean stared at him.

"Why, Louis? Why did you do this? Was it your wife's idea? Did she do the scheming?"

Guidry burst into a flood of hysterical tears. Between sobs, he gasped, "My son! It's my boy and my little girl! She is going to leave me and take them from me! I can't live without them. I didn't know what else to do. I owe more money to the bookies, the banks, even to my own sisters and brothers than I can ever earn. I . . . I . . . ." He jammed his hat on his balding head and rushed out of the office into the chilly night.

"*Mon dieu*," murmured Jean. "*Mon dieu*." Finally, he began to relax. There was the answer. Jean knew it was the wretched, greedy woman, but he hadn't fathomed the cruel threat of Guidry's losing his children. Bailey, who had driven Jean to his office, stood silently in a corner.

"Come on, Bailey. Take me to Third Street."

"That some mizable white man, Mister Jean. I seen some mizry in my time, but I ain't never seen no mizry like that."

"You're right, Bailey. I hope the poor fool doesn't kill himself."

CHAPTER 82

"ALL ABOARD!" THE conductor yelled, and Jean, a small valise in his right hand, climbed aboard the L&N bound for Biloxi. As the train pulled away from the station at the foot of Canal Street, chugging eastward along the river, he sat at the window, his head thrown back, not moving and wishing he would never have to move again. Slowly he turned his head and fixed his eyes on glass-front restaurants, outdoor cafes, and the French Quarter's produce market teeming with housewives and cooks filling baskets with fresh fruit and vegetables—seeing nothing. On this warm Friday in March, Jean didn't even want to hear the train wheels knocking in an even rhythm. All he wanted was to move the whole experience of Louis Guidry into the back of his memory, to put his painful ordeal behind him once and for all.

Painfully, he had acknowledged his error in allowing Guidry into his company, and the extreme misfortune of the man's suicide. He had read in the newspaper that Guidry—his wife and children gone from him, no friend or family left, his creditors hounding him—blew a large hole through his brain with the pistol that his father had carried at the battle of Chattanooga in the Civil War. But ugly as the episode had been, he knew that he must not let it do him in; his life had become precious. Besides he had dealt with suicide before—his pathetic partner, Harry Groeble. It seemed to be capitulation of a destitute spirit, and it did not evoke sympathy in him. He did not completely forget Madelaine de la Croix's dreadful end. Well, that was different.

Jean had struggled to regain his strength through walking near his house, but he could not walk as much as he had before the mastoiditis surgery. If he walked to Perdido Street, Bailey followed him in the car. Much of the time, to avoid argument, he got into the Packard at home and let Bailey drive him to the office. He knew it calmed Stephanie and Beatrice, who were convinced that he was going to fall and break his hip, or worse. "That will be the end of you, Papa," one or both of them warned him if he slipped unnoticed out the front gate for work. He was never without Bailey; if the chauffeur was not at his side, he was within calling distance.

Jean enjoyed riding alone in the Pullman, which was located behind the diner. Bailey rode in the coach for Negroes, the first car behind the engine and coal car. At noon, as the train was steaming through the low-lying Rigolets marshes, Bailey returned and assisted his boss to the diner, then came back for him at one o'clock.

He was glad he came to the Gulf Coast, and he was happy to see Julia, who with her youngest son, Jimmy, met them at the Biloxi station in the Buick that Jean had bought for her. He thought the summer house looked beautiful, the lawn breaking out in spring grass and azaleas.

Still, even in the company of his beloved daughter-in-law, things were not the same. *Lila is no longer here.* He realized how much more he missed her in Biloxi, where she was a part of his days. He had always called her soon after he arrived, and nothing ever prevented him from seeing her at her home or his. *Now that long, comforting custom is over. I can do nothing to restore it in any way.*

For several hours on Saturday morning Julia and Jean rocked on the porch. Later, Bailey followed them out onto the pier where Jean sat quietly on an upper deck bench, a strong breeze whipping his thinning white hair about. For a long time they listened to the raucous shrilling of gulls swooping over small swells in the Sound. Soon a bell rang announcing lunch, and they returned to the house. Within seconds of their return, Julia's servant, Sookey, produced platters of shrimp and crab, broiled red snapper and crispy fried speckled trout.

In the afternoon Jean worked from his briefcase on the porch, pouring over reports from Lawrence. His son was learning the many ins and outs of guiding three plantations through spring costs, losses, profits, weather frustrations or blessings, and he was proud of him. Week by week, all of his son's reports focused toward the fall and production of cane—a large crop of juicy sugarcane that father and son hoped for. Jean thought Lawrence looked forward to the operation of Orange Grove sugarhouse with special enthusiasm. It had been a reasonable moneymaker under Walter Morvant's management, and he believed his son could increase its efficiency.

All in all, Jean felt he had made no mistake in placing Lawrence in charge at Thibodaux. But, he reminded himself, it was too soon to tell for sure what kind of a farmer-businessman Lawrence would make. He also reviewed the usual reports from Albert regarding operations at Catahoula, Burton, Banker, and St. John. Jean believed it made no sense to compare Lawrence to Albert, who was unusually capable at the hard and demanding occupation. The thing that the sons had in common was a love of parties— partying somewhere as often as possible and savoring all that went with them, most especially liquor—and at times it distressed him.

Jean tapped the gold clip of his fountain pen on the last page of Lawrence's reports. Again he reminded himself that he was Lawrence's employer, and as long as Lawrence did his job well, was honest, and did a good day's work, his personal peccadillos were irrelevant. Almost irrelevant, anyway.

Rocking on the porch the morning before returning to New Orleans, Jean glanced toward the long, wide front sitting room when he heard Julia answer the telephone.

"Oh, my goodness," he heard her say. "Oh, dear, oh, dear me."

Jean set his coffee cup in its saucer on the table beside him. Although he could barely hear her, he sensed that she was not happy about the news coming over the wire. Soon his daughter-in-law was pushing a rocker next to his and sat down.

"Papa, I fear you have some bad news, here. It's Stephanie."

"Stephanie! What? What is wrong?"

"I don't mean something is wrong with Stephanie. She is calling to tell you sad news. Your brother Amèdèe died last night in New Orleans. Please come in and talk to Stephanie."

Julia took his arm to help guide him to the telephone. Jean did not push her away, but he took his cane and relied on it to steady him. He did not need a woman to hold him up.

"Yes, Stephanie. What is it? Has Amèdeè died?"

"Yes, Papa, he died last night. We learned about it too late to call you. The funeral is day after tomorrow at Our Lady of Lourdes in uptown New Orleans. Will you plan to attend Uncle Amèdèe's funeral?"

Jean thought only a few seconds: "No, my dear, I cannot attend. Funerals are just more than I can handle these days. Send a bouquet of flowers to the church with my card. That will have to do. I couldn't even attend the funeral of my sister, Euphrasie, God rest her, who passed away last year. It was too much for me then. The poor thing had never married, and she had been bedridden with chronic rheumatism the last twelve years of her life."

"Well, Papa, Bea and I can go. We will go. It just doesn't seem right, I mean polite, for our family not to be represented. We will go." She seemed resolute. "We will give your respects to Aunt What's Her Name. By the way, how old was Uncle Amèdèe?"

"Well, that will be just fine, if you want to go. I think he was eighty or eighty-one, Steph. Besides I am expecting Fred to arrive in New Orleans tomorrow. He is staying at the Hotel DeSoto, as usual, but I imagine he will have supper with us most nights that he is in town."

"Yes, Papa. Then, we will expect you on the evening train day after tomorrow. I hope you have had a nice time in Biloxi. Is the weather nice?"

"Yes, very nice. Thank you, my dear." Jean hung up the black receiver on the wall telephone. Julia stood nearby. She folded her arms across her chest and looked at him with sympathy.

"I'm so sorry, Papa."

"I know, Julia. It seems that death follows me from place to place. But do not grieve. My brother and I have not been at all close. To be truthful, I scarcely ever think of him. He did not like me very much. He certainly had no respect for my judgment about farming and business management."

Instead, he said, "Fred is coming down for a few days. I am thinking of grooming him to take over management of J. B. Levert Land Co., or possibly the others as well, St. John and the mercantile companies."

"You mean he and Aunt Molly might move back to New Orleans?"

"Perhaps. I'm not sure. He might be a successful chairman of the board in charge of operations by long distance, making only occasional visits to my office. I'm just feeling my way along. Actually he is my only hope, with Junior gone. Poor Robert's affliction makes it impossible for him to work that hard. Lawrence seems to be working out too well so far at Thibodaux to take him away from there at this time. And of course, Albert is permanently established at St. John. I can never take him away from there. So, as you can see, Fred will possibly be holding two big jobs."

"Gracious!" said Julia.

"Yes, we shall see what we shall see."

*　　*　　*

Jean sat alone in the parlor at Third Street, waiting for Beatrice and Stephanie to return from Amèdèe's funeral. He tried to imagine the youngest son of Auguste and Eulalie Levert being interred in a New Orleans cemetery, his grave encircled by his impoverished family—except for Bea and Steph, of course—the child of a successful planter, brother of a successful planter, and, of course, brother of one of Louisiana's wealthiest men. Jean had no vivid memories of Amèdèe as a young boy on Golden Ridge, and he could recall few details of his brother's service in the Civil War. Was it he or Augie who was taken prisoner in New Orleans? Well, it didn't matter.

Jean did regret that Amèdèe had died dependent on his wife's people and more or less in poverty. *Part of my success was surely due to the fact that I married a beautiful and charming wife, who at all times was a source of pride and rich inspiration to me.* And he did admit Stephanie had a great deal of money, especially for postwar times in the South. Alas, his brothers had not been so fortunate in their selections of wives.

He heard the back door shut, and in moments his two daughters burst into the room. Their animation suggested they might have been to a bridal luncheon, not a funeral. Bea was still in her mourning black, but of late she had a smart wardrobe, and today, she looked particularly fashionable in a short dress and a black straw cloche. Both daughters were pulling off kid gloves.

"Papa, it's just too bad that you could not go with us," said Stephanie.

"Oh? A small attendance; I knew I'd be needed."

"Oh, no, Our Lady of Lourdes was filled, and most people went on to the cemetery. No, I mean that you would have been pleased to see how many friends and relatives were there. Uncle Amèdèe had made many friends and apparently was important in his church. There was a sea of flowers honoring our uncle, and the priest gave a most moving eulogy before the Mass."

"Yes," said Bea, "and we enjoyed meeting Aunt Aurelie again and some of her children and grandchildren. They are a lovely family."

"Aurelie was there?" Jean did not hide his surprise, barely nodding.

"Yes, indeed, Papa, she is in her eighties, but seems well. Aunt Ernestine told us of her generosity since Uncle Augie's death," said Stephanie. She pulled two hat pins out of her large leghorn straw. She still had her long gleaming, almost-black hair, today done in a chignon to accommodate the crown of her hat. She laid the hat on the sofa table with a slight flourish. "The two ladies have become good friends, discovering they have much in common."

Stephanie told her father Uncle Amèdèe and his family have lived in a lovely though modest home on Vendome Place uptown, that for the past decade her uncle worked for one of the large sugar refineries out on River Road along the Mississippi, and that he had a good job. She said all of the children of both brothers were successful in some pursuit; Uncle Augie's son Charles, was a doctor. "Really, Bea and I were very proud to be part of this charming branch of the family. We enjoyed talking with relatives we have scarcely known."

Jean tried to accept the surprising news of Amèdèe's apparent good fortune, or good luck, without a show of total incredulity. His daughters were surprising him on several fronts. *Obviously, I've been wasting my pity. Or sympathy. Well, I am glad for my brother and my two sisters-in-law.*

Beatrice was saying: "Did you know Aunt Aurelie inherited a portion of Uncle Augie's estate that was a long time being settled? I never heard of that. But obviously she became very well off, and she had been very kind and generous with her money. This has been such an interesting day, hasn't it, Steph?"

"*Oui, oui, Soeur. Très intéressant, Père.*"

"I am sure your relatives were proud to have you among them. Remember, you are among *the élite, the crème de la crème,* of New Orleans society. Do not discount their fascination with you."

Beatrice and Stephanie Marie looked at each other. Jean saw their exchange, and he knew what it meant—they were shrugging off his claims of their social prominence. But he also knew that they knew what he was talking about; they were proud of their position in the City.

"By the way, Stephanie, Dr. Felix Larue called while you were out. He left his card and told Jenny that he would call again tomorrow."

"Didn't he come in to speak to you?" asked Steph.

"No. Why should he? He is an estimable gentleman but not one who calls on me," Jean Baptiste said, smiling to himself. It had become obvious to him that Dr. Larue, a widower for many years, had eyes only for Stephanie. But with her many social and professional engagements, Stephanie seemed only minimally responsive to the doctor. He was an impeccable escort for the opera and other important social occasions. Beyond that she seemed to have no serious interest.

Stephanie looked archly at her father. "Actually, Papa, Felix does have cause to visit you."

"Well, I don't know whatever for."

Bea threw back her head and giggled. "Papa! Felix Larue wants to ask you for Steph's hand?"

Jean stood up so fast it made him slightly unsteady. "Marriage! Stephanie, if you want Dr. Larue, you shall have him." He smiled broadly and put his arms around her.

"Now, Papa, I don't want you to buy him for me." She, too, giggled like a girl. "But I do care deeply for Felix, and do want to marry him."

"*Étonnant!* I am happy for you, my dear. I know you have given too much of your life to my care. I have often wished you could have a life of your own, a home of your own." His face saddened. "Ah, but you will take your magic harp with you! I don't know if I can live without your beautiful music, Stephanie."

"Thank you, Papa. Let me play one of your favorites for you right now." She sat down at her golden instrument and played *Clare de Lune.* Jean concealed his emotions with great effort, for Chopin's rich and tuneful composition was indeed his favorite.

Her father was more pleased with Stephanie's choice of a husband than he had been with any of his daughters' mates, even the late Francis Kearny, who had twice been his son-in-law. He knew Dr. Larue would bring nothing but additional luster to the Levert family's name. Dr. Larue had been graduated from Mount St. Mary's, Jean's own graduate school. He had studied medicine in Paris, and he had done residency in New Orleans under the great Rudolph Matas. The two men remained associated in medical practice, and they seemed to enjoy great accord as members of Tulane's board of administrators.

*   *   *

At nine o'clock the next Monday morning, Jean met Dansereau in his office in the Carondelet Building to discuss the widening range of his philanthropies. He felt he was ready to establish a J.B. Levert Foundation to fund his major gifts to various institutions, churches, and schools, especially Tulane and Hotel Dieu Hospital, in all the communities in which his companies owned property and did business. The lawyer called his secretary, Miss Gautreaux, to bring in two black coffees with warm milk.

Jean was saying, "I want the foundation heavily endowed with carefully invested sums that will bear fruit for many decades to come . . . I want the foundation board to consist mostly of my sons and sons-in-law, to whom I am now preaching what Colonel Bush preached to me many years ago—slow down buying and selling and begin giving something back; there's great responsibility and reward in discreetly sharing one's wealth for the betterment of the community."

Jean shook his head, grinning. "I've never told anyone this, Fernand, but there is irony in all this—preaching the same things to my sons and sons-in-law that Colonel Bush preached to me shortly before he died. It took me nearly twenty years before I began to heed his words, to give something back to society. It just wasn't easy, as you know, to stop the business dealing and accumulating money.",

Jean went on to mention the first philanthropic moves of significance that he had completed more than a decade earlier: Three-thousand-dollar donation for construction of a brick schoolhouse on St. John for children of his farm laborers and those of nearby plantations, black and white; donation of land for use as a public school building; and a ten-thousand-dollar contribution for construction of St. Martinville's first high school, including a gymnasium that bore his name.

After sipping his *café au lait* gratefully, Jean changed the subject. "Fernand, there's nothing quite like having your own hotel or least having majority ownership. The foundation board and the corporate Levert boards now can meet at Hotel DeSoto to conduct business and my sons now have a place to stay when they are in the city. Oh, if I haven't mentioned it before, I've started grooming Fred to run my real estate businesses, Fred and my son-in-law Joe Gore."

Dansereau nodded approvingly. "Yes, sir, you told me recently." The lawyer had several stacks of papers before him on his desk. "You will have a nice addition to the foundation money from the sale of Levert-Shirley."

"Indeed, I know that." Jean, with his lawyer's help, had found a buyer for the two plantations after several years of being unsettled about the operations. He believed the properties were too far away; he was never comfortable there. Besides, he knew none of his sons wanted to leave the City and move upstate to rural Bunkie, Louisiana, to manage the properties for him; Bunkie was like a foreign country to an Orleanian. *That rascal Guidry could probably have done well with the operations. But that is all in the past.* "Oh, Fernand, did you know that after the new owner took possession, there were pumping oil wells all over both plantations!"

He knew Dansereau was not listening because he didn't answer. He was staring at the papers before him on his desk, making mental notes, Jean assumed, of how to distribute his client's gifts.

"Fernand, for as long as you are secretary of this foundation board, I want you to remember how important my gift for the chapel at Hotel Dieu is to me. The fifty thousand I pledged is in escrow . . . I want to help build a permanent shelter for the Sisters of Charity. They just move those poor nuns from pillar to post, trying to accommodate a growing number of hospital patients. I think they are in old basement rooms at present." He paused and set his coffee cup on the butler's table in front of the curved-back leather sofa. There was a space of silence. At last, Jean continued:

"And let me reiterate—I want funds given to the stadium fund, until the stadium is completed. They'll never stop enlarging that Tulane stadium, I'm afraid, not as long as they have football stars. Howard-Tilton Library and the university scholarship fund must have regular sums . . ."

"Yes, sir," said Dansereau, who had all these preferences well noted among his papers. "Keep reminding me of your desires, for I am eager to do your wishes and prepare that they shall be carried out after you and I are long gone."

When Jean remained silent, Dansereau added: "This is off the subject, but I believe Albert or perhaps Fred told me not long ago that a big reason you wanted the Hotel DeSoto, besides as an investment, is because it's across the street from your office and to have a place to eat your lunch. Is that true?"

Jean merely smiled at the family joke, then said: "When I was your age, I never gave a thought to being 'gone.'" He chuckled. "Let's walk over to the Pickwick for a nice cocktail, then some ice-cold oysters on the half-shell. After that, perhaps a Spanish mackerel broiled in lemon. Yes!"

"*Oui, Monsieur.*" Dansereau smiled. "*En idée excellent.*"

Chapter 83

JEAN WAS DELIGHTED to have Fred and Fred's son, John Bertels, accompany him to celebrate the first step of construction on the J.B. Levert Chapel at Hotel Dieu Hospital. Major contributor to construction of the ornate building, General Levert turned the first spade of soil at the ground-breaking ceremonies on this cool autumn day in New Orleans, assisted by Archbishop John Shaw of New Orleans. At eighty-five, knowing he was no longer hale and hearty, the General was glad that his grandson walked with him and stood beside him as he held the shovel and posed for newspaper pictures of the event.

Jean talked in a low voice to John Bertels during the ceremony, whom he believed to be a likely eventual successor as chairman of the board of J.B. Levert Land Co.—after Fred retired and also Albert. Jean could not see his hard-living sons surviving at the helm, as he had, until they were in their eighties. He'd always kept his eye out for promising men in the third generation, and he considered twenty-six-year-old John Bertels bright and handsome. Although his background was more Alabama than Louisiana, he knew his grandson liked New Orleans and was interested in the Levert businesses.

Now, John Bertels held his grandfather's elbow as he assisted him back to his seat on the platform of dignitaries at the Hotel Dieu site on Tulane Avenue. Jean enjoyed the kudos and applause, as always, but he remained quite conscious of his grandson at his side, for he never lost sight of the future. Most of the General's family were seated before him in front of the dais.

Mother Superior sat between Jean and the architect who had designed the chapel, a beatific smile on her pale, plain face. As priests, doctors, and the mayor made short speeches, she turned toward Jean and nodded seriously. Jean took that to mean that she was pleased that he was keeping his end of the bargain with God, though he knew she did not like the term. In his own mind, that was exactly what he was doing, and it felt good.

Later, with all of the family gathered at Third Street in their never-ending desire to get together for talk and drinks, Jean had to excuse himself and lie down on his bed to rest. Bailey went with him and removed his shoes and talked with him for awhile.

"Now go on down and help Jenny and Ruby, Bailey. I'm all right, and I'm sure they can use some help. There are quite a few extra people down there."

"I be back to see about you, Mister Jean."

Jean was glad to be alone and quiet. He had felt dizzy at the ceremony. He considered that particular symptom to be most annoying after his dangerous but supposedly successful mastoiditis surgery, which was supposed to have corrected that problem. He knew he must keep his cane handy and not ever be without it. He dozed.

But the next week, Jean attended the dedication of Tulane University's new football stadium on Willow Street for much the same sort of ceremony, but with quite different edifices to celebrate. Bleachers, which rose on either end of the playing field, were filled with alumni and other staunch supporters of Tulane and its increasingly acclaimed football team. When Coach Clark Shaughnessy ran out onto the field, followed by his uniformed players, some of them helmetless, the crowds rose and cheered so loudly, thought Jean, that they could be heard all the way to Third Street. To him, it was a thrilling sight—Orleanians at their heartiest. Honored guests were recognized in the dedication ceremony at halftime. Jean was quite moved by the applause he received when Tulane President Albert Dinwiddie cited his many generosities to the university, and especially for the stadium. "Funds," the president assured the crowd, "that made the extent of growth and improvements to the stadium possible—and without which, the addition of the second tier of seats would not have been possible."

John Bertels Levert again assisted his grandfather to the platform to receive a parchment scroll and what Jean described as a "thundering ovation" from the crowd. He insisted no other person honored that day received such shouting and clapping.

*   *   *

Not long after these two triumphs, Jean received an early morning call from Elizabeth Behan, telling him that her eighty-eight-year-old husband evidently had suffered a stroke and was in critical condition. Jean insisted that Bailey drive him immediately to the Behan house so that he might be of help to her and perhaps be able to have a few last words with his oldest and dearest friend.

"No, General, no," said the Colonel's wife. "No," she said again, "you must not put such a physical and emotional strain on yourself. Everything possible is being done for William. He is comfortable and at peace. His doctor does not expect him to regain consciousness. He says it is only a matter of hours." Her voice broke, and the servant Eli took the phone to say she could not continue.

"She say she want you to hear this sad news from her, Gen'ral Lavare. She say Colonel would want her to let you know."

"Thank you, Eli," said Jean, and hung up the phone.

*   *   *

After Colonel Behan's burial in Metairie Cemetery, Jean, again on the arm of John Bertels, moved to speak to the Colonel's widow, who sat among her relatives at the flower-banked bier before the Behan tomb. Eli stood beside his longtime employer's widow. When Jean bent slightly and kissed her gloved hand, he did not try to hide the tears that welled in his eyes. Then he and his family, all of whom were present, walked away through the throng of Orleanians.

Stephanie Marie and Dr. Larue led them toward the Levert tomb that Jean had purchased in Metairie Cemetery when the doctors convinced him that his wife's death was imminent. Today, Jean realized, was the first time the entire family had gathered there to pay respect to their deceased members since Stephanie's death thirty years earlier. Her children were now middle-aged with grown children who never knew their grandmother. For a moment, standing on the well-tended expanse of lawn, he had a stirring recollection of his life with his beloved Stephanie, a fleeting image of her youthful face with her clear green eyes and fair hair.

Beatrice was reading aloud the names of family members whose remains had been interred in the large granite tomb, some of whose dust had been removed to this site years after burial elsewhere:

"Marie Stephanie Levert, born June 18, 1850, died May 31, 1898.

"Gideon Octave Dupuy, born July, 1832, died September 13, 1858.

"Marie Virginia Aloysia Viel Dupuy, born March 9, 1831, died February 14, 1853.

"Marie Lucille, born April 10, 1877, died October 10, 1878.

"Mathilde Marie Kearny, born April 29, 1873, died April 9, 1906."

"Some dates and names are wrong, Papa," exclaimed Stephanie, studying the marble plaque on front of the tomb. "It should be Lucie, not Lucille, and Mathilde was born on April 25, 1872, not April 29, 1873."

"I know, my dear," said Jean, "but these things I'm afraid do happen sometimes. There's nothing we can do about it, now."

Jean, silent for a moment, was deep in thought. Then he leaned forward, his eyes alight, studying his children as they stood in their best clothes listening quietly, reverently, as Beatrice enunciated each name and the dates of birth and death. He knew that in this tomb so close before them lay the dust of those who had gone before them, that none of his children knew the grandparents buried there—the Dupuys—but they knew a lot about them from their mother's accounts of her early childhood. A soft breeze passed through the cemetery on the late autumn afternoon, with no effect on the ranks of surrounding marble statuary and classic marble facades on tombs that housed New Orleans' most prominent dead. But the pleasant air was especially cooling to Jean. Jean put on his fedora, and the other men followed suit, a signal that this formal ritual, far different from a gathering for the usually fun-loving Leverts, was over.

"It's time to go," said Jean, and they began to walk through low-hanging oak limbs toward the drive near the funeral home where their automobiles were parked. "Wait," he said. "Here we are at the Kearny tomb. I had forgotten it was so near. Would you like to read these, Bea?"

But Beatrice shook her head and looked away. "I cannot. Stephanie, will you, please?"

Stephanie stepped closer to the plaque on the tomb and read softly, as if to ease the sound of the words that Bea did not like to hear:

"Dr. Francis J. Kearny, born June 2, 1860, died December 2, 1920." And then she read the names and dates of Dr. Kearny's mother, who was also entombed here: "Mary Annette Finn, 1837-1876."

Jean looked at Beatrice's sorrowful face; she was dressed in her fashionable black outfit. Almost ten years, and still she mourned for her dear husband. He took John Bertel's arm and continued to lead the way to the drive. Jean was relieved to see the familiar face of Bailey, who stood by the open door to the gleaming Packard, ready to help him into the back seat.

As the Packard's engine roared, Jean looked toward the site of Colonel Behan's tomb, where masons worked at sealing the vault. Jean knew that sound.

*   *   *

At Third Street spirits soon lifted. After settling his boss comfortably in the parlor, Bailey assisted Robert at the bar on the sideboard in the dining room. The ladies removed their hats, and the young people went to the gazebo in the backyard to chatter and giggle.

"Papa," said Albert, coming in to sit beside his father and express his sympathy concerning Colonel Behan's death. "I know you are going to miss your old friend. He was a fine gentleman."

"Yes, indeed, son," said Jean. Then: "Albert, tell me how you think Lawrence is doing at Rienzi. How you really feel about him as a planter. Is he still enthusiastic? Ella and Joe Gore drove over to see him at Thibodaux. Ella tells me he was asleep on a bale of hay at two o'clock in the afternoon. He was probably drunk."

"I couldn't say, Papa. Could I have a drink?"

CHAPTER 84

JEAN BAPTISTE COULDN'T remember when the heat and humidity of August in the City felt so oppressive. Electric fans in the Third Street parlor whirred, but they only stirred the hot sticky air. Despite the heat, dressed as always in coat, high collar, and cravat, Jean appeared cool and comfortable, but all through his afternoon visit with Marie Stella, she never stopped complaining of her misery in the heat. His daughter had brought Mary Bell, eighteen, and Jack, Jr., a year older, to the house to visit their grandfather before they left for a year's study in London. Jean had told Stella that he thought it was "a wonderful opportunity for them."

"My dear child, how old are you?" He had to suppress a chuckle.

"Why I am forty-seven, Papa."

"Do you mean to tell me that after living through forty-seven years of New Orleans summers you still cannot tolerate our incomparable heat?" Jean couldn't help from laughing now, and he looked at Mary Bell and Jack, Jr., as if to say he despaired of their mother.

Jean tried to divert Stella with repeated mention of other subjects. His mention of having survived the '29 stock market crash and come through the first year of the Great Depression in better shape than any of his associates and friends, got no reaction from her, not so much as a raised eyebrow. Neither did the fact that since all his children's incomes depended on him and his corporations, their fortunes also managed to escape severe loss.

Jean had just completed, with an assist from Fred, what he regarded as his last business deal: Acquiring Webre Plantation in May, 1930, in a foreclosure suit against the Morvant family, on notes of more than thirty-five thousand dollars. Mentioning that achievement didn't even stop Stella from her bellyaching.

"Stella, I know your Englishman husband, Jack Swanson, a pretty good broker himself, is pleased as punch about his own survival of the crash," said Jean, beaming. He knew that a large part of his own survival was because his investments were not all in stocks and bonds, but in the rich, black cane-growing soil of southwest Louisiana and in prime real estate of New Orleans and other parishes. That his sugarcane plantations continued to produce sugar and its by-products, and with lowering overhead. "The fact that your husband's securities didn't take a hard hit is one of the reasons you are able to send my grandchildren to England for a year, is it not?"

Stella did not respond to any of her father's remarks. She looked bored, and Jean stared at her, frowning. He assumed it was because she was still rather blasé about how money was made, where it came from, or didn't care one way or another.

Now, Beatrice joined them in the parlor. Jenny followed close by, carrying a sterling silver tray with coffee, brown raw sugar from St. John, and cream, all in their proper silver containers, for Stella, Bea, and Jean. The servant brought vanilla ice cream and chocolate cake for Jean and his grandchildren.

"Oh, I lost money in the crash, don't misunderstand me, a large amount, matter of fact," Jean continued. He picked up his cup, sipped his coffee, and set it on the silver tray. "But I think what save me—I know it's what saved me—is I don't have all my eggs in one basket, as they say. I have different kinds of investments, I am well diversified." With a slight smile, he rubbed his hands together.

What he didn't tell his daughters and grandchildren was that on the morning after Black Thursday, he had nimbly removed, not pondering for long his options, thousands of dollars from several banks, including Canal Bank. And unbeknownst to anyone other than Fernand Dansereau, he had for years kept large sums in a safe—a heavy iron vault—in his Perdido Street office and in a wall safe in his Third Street office. Although he had never spoke of these things or of impending doom to any of his children, not even to his lawyer, Jean knew that he was well-prepared for it. He had always felt uneasy about banks, and he had never totally trusted Wall Street.

Finally, Stella and her children rose to leave, and Jean began to heave himself out of his deep leather chair. Beatrice hurried to his side and helped him to stand.

"No need, Bea, I'm perfectly capable to getting out of my chair without help." His daughters smiled at each other. "I am so pleased to see you young people traveling abroad. I remember when your Aunt Stephanie sailed to France to study with the great maestro—what was his name, Bea?" Not giving Bea time to reply, he continued, "We did miss her, but she came home a finer musician. Now, Bea, turn loose of my arm. I just want to walk out front with them to wave goodbye."

"Take good care of yourself, Papa," said Stella, as Mary Bell kissed her grandfather on the forehead and Jack shook his hand. Jean, holding on to one of the veranda columns, took a white handkerchief from his breast pocket to wave to them.

"*Au revoir*," he called, "*au revoir*."

Suddenly, Jean lost his balance and away he went. He fell forward, rolled down the six steps, and landed on the brick pavement.

"Bailey! Bailey!" screamed Beatrice and Stella in unison. "Come quick . . . hurry! Oh dear God!"

He lay on his back, quite still, moaning, until a weeping Bailey and a shaken Jack, Jr., lifted him up and carried him into the house and up the stairs to his bedroom.

CHAPTER 85

JEAN WAS ALERT as he was laid carefully on the smooth sheets of his four-poster. Obviously, he had created a stir among the family members who were present. He knew he had fallen down the front steps; he did not know why. He recalled no dizziness or other problems. So he lay in his bed silently with his eyes closed.

Beatrice, Stella, and Bailey were moving quietly around his room. They whispered to each other; they thought he was unconscious. He knew it was only a matter of minutes before his old friend Gonsoulin would be at his bedside. Bea had called Steph; Steph would have come; and they would have called the doctor no matter how much he protested. *These girls have grown bold. Well, that's all right.* He just prayed to God that he had broken no bones. He believed he had not. He wanted to go to an auction tomorrow—the sale of what looked like a great buy on Baronne Street, an office building with excellent occupation—professional people who should be able to keep up with their rent. *Maybe. This Depression was no respecter of persons.* He lay still. *Four stories. A nice classic facade. The owner is desperate . . .* Before he had any more thoughts, he fell asleep.

*   *   *

Jean was grainy-eyed when the woke the next morning. He'd not gotten a lot of sleep. He groaned loudly when he tried to move. Pains in his chest felt like he was being cut by a sharp knife. *Mon dieu, mon dieu. Au secours!* He tried to bend his knees, lift his arms. When he attempted to raise his head he screamed, *mon dieu, mon dieu.* He felt a warm, gentle hand on his arm.

"General, General Levert, lie still. I'm afraid you have had a bad fall."

"Is that you, Dr. Gonsoulin?"

"Yes, sir."

"I can't move without pain. What has happened? Have I broken my back? My legs? Help me. I tell you I cannot move. I need to go to my bathroom. Quickly!"

"Bailey," said the doctor, "bring General Levert the urinal I set on the basin in his bathroom. Ladies, excuse us, please."

There was a rustle in the room, and the door shut quietly.

"Everthin gonna be all right, Mister Jean. Don't you worry none." Bailey awkwardly maneuvered to help his boss, who was groaning as the servant had never heard him.

"What in God's name happened to me, Bailey? Were you there? What happened?"

"I feedin them chickens of yours. I'm sorry, Mister Jean. I thought Miss Stella and Miss Bea was lookin after you. I shoulda been there."

"No, Bailey. It's not your fault. I'll be all right in a little while. I must have slept a long time. I believe it's getting dark outside. Or are the draperies drawn?"

"It gittin dark, it nearly six o'clock. You done slep nearly all day. Dr. Gonsolly, he give you a shot so you can rest."

"So that's it. Thank you, Bailey. You can take that thing away."

"Wash it well, Bailey, and keep it handy. General Levert will not be able to walk to the bathroom for quite a while."

"Have I broken a bone?"

Dr. Gonsoulin cleared his throat. "I don't think so. Your blood pressure is high. It's hard to tell, but you might have suffered a small stroke."

"A stroke! My God. How bad is it?"

"I'm not sure that you have had one. We'll just have to watch you. You may take these little powders for rest every two hours.

Don't allow yourself to become upset, now. I know you to be a man very much in control of himself. Be calm and have faith in your God. We'll hope to have you up and around in a few days."

"I need to attend an auction tomorrow . . ."

"You must forget that, General Levert. There is no chance."

The two men fell silent. Jean dozed. When he awakened, Dr. Gonsoulin was gone, and Stephanie Marie sat beside his bed.

"Steph?"

"Yes, Father."

"Open the draperies."

"Yes, Father." She rose and swept back the heavy brocade. Evening light filtered into the large bedroom. Jean felt more sure of himself. Familiar shapes became softly visible: All of the Dupuy walnut furniture that Stephanie had loved so, her odds and ends of porcelain, silver, and rare antiques sat about on chests and tables. There was a mahogany fireplace screen with an oak tree carved in the center. The small oil portrait of Stephanie, painted when she was seventeen, shortly before she married Jean, hung on the wall above the lowboy. *What a comfort to be in these familiar surroundings. I must die here.*

"Steph?"

"Yes, sir."

"Promise me, Steph, that I will not be taken to a hospital."

"How can I promise that, Father?"

"Just do it. I am your father, and I command you. I intend never to be a hospital patient again."

"Not even Hotel Dieu?"

"Not even Hotel Dieu. Did Dr. Gonsoulin leave something for the pain. I hurt terribly in my chest."

"You may have a cracked rib. He says there is not much we can do about that but keep you still. But I can give you another powder for pain and it will help you sleep."

Jean did not answer, but with great effort he swallowed the powder with as much water as he could gulp down his throat.

"Is your chauffeur here, Stephanie?"

"No, Papa. I sent him home to serve Felix's supper." Stephanie had married Dr. Felix Larue in one of the smallest Levert family weddings—only family members and a few close friends—at the church of the Holy Name of Jesus on St. Charles Avenue.

"Then I want Bailey to drive you home. I'm sure you have been here all day, and you must get some rest and be with your husband. I have plenty of help here. What time is it?"

"It's ten fifteen."

"*Mon dieu*. It is far too late for you to be out. Bailey will see you to your door. Now I insist that you go right now."

"How is your pain, now, Papa?"

"The powder has helped. I can move my arms without it hurting my chest so much." He cleared his throat. "Thank you for coming, my dear. I am going to be all right. You must not neglect your husband to stay here with me. *Croire moi, chérie*."

"Very well, Papa. Let me call Bea. She is taking a little nap in her room." In seconds, Stephanie was back at his side with the faithful Bea. Stephanie kissed her father on his forehead, then rubbed his white hair with tenderness.

"*Bon soir, mon Père, a demain*."

During the next week, the General received many messages from friends in New Orleans. Elizabeth Behan visited him for a few moments. She stepped inside his large room looking tall and regal. Jean was glad to see her, but he discovered that the slightest conversation tired him, and he asked his daughters not to allow anyone other than his family to see him until he was much improved.

"But there is one other person I must see, Bea, and that is Fernand Dansereau. Please call him for me."

Dansereau arrived at Third Street the next morning, and Jean summoned enough strength to speak with him. Finally, the old man said, "I have a question to ask if you can answer it, Fernand. Can you tell me how much I am worth? In homes, real estate, investments, what do I have?"

The lawyer set his coffee cup and saucer on the bedside table, opened his briefcase, and thumbed through some papers Jean had asked him to bring with him. He scribbled a few numbers in the margins. "Your holdings now total three and a half to four million, General. That's my best estimate since there's no official inventory of all your effects and property."

"Thank you, Fernand. That is really what I wanted to know. I appreciate your coming here at this early hour." His lawyer remained at his bedside for a good while, taking a second cup of chicory coffee, trying to lift Jean's spirits. Suddenly Jean's eyes grew moist as Dansereau rose to leave to catch the St. Charles Avenue streetcar for his downtown office.

Albert and Louise had come from St. John and Lawrence and Lulu had come from Thibodaux. Fred and Molly had come from Birmingham and, of course, Stephanie and Dr. Larue and Robert and Olga lived in the City. Stephanie and Robert were at Third Street everyday. Julia lived in New Orleans now, and she wanted to see Jean everyday, but even with someone so favored as Julia, he could not tolerate conversation for long.

Dr. Gonsoulin visited him every afternoon. After several days, he brought a cardiologist in to see his patient. Dr. Carl Woolrich, a young man, was a Yankee, he told Jean, but apparently a gentleman. He tested the strength in Jean's limbs, and he pronounced the General to be discernibly weaker in his right side. The two doctors stepped to the other side of the room, each holding his pince-nez by its rim, and spoke in low voices. Such secrecy annoyed Jean; but he could hear something of what they said. After a brief conversation the two medical men came back to his bedside, where Beatrice stood silently by her father.

"General Levert," said Dr. Gonsoulin, "we believe you have suffered a stroke. It would seem to be the cause of your fall and of the obvious weakness on your right side." He nodded toward Dr. Woolrich.

"Well, sir, I would say that this is a small accident in the left side of your brain, which, as you probably know, affects your right side. Since it appears not to be a massive affair, I think you would do well to get up, with assistance, and begin to walk about your room, perhaps sit on your upstairs balcony here outside your room, and enjoy the autumn sunshine. For the time being, be sure that you have someone with you when you stand or try to walk." He turned to look at Dr. Gonsoulin as if for approval.

Jean had not felt so helpless since his dysentery in prison during the war. Reactions raced through his mind. He would have guessed his loss of balance was due to some remaining effect of the mastoiditis. Dr. Gonsoulin added before he could speak:

"General, I expect you to be taking drives through the Garden District within a few weeks. Would you not agree, Doctor?"

"Barring further trouble, I agree," replied Dr. Woolrich. "Continue your quiet, peaceful regimen. Eat the good food that I am sure is brought up from your kitchen. Very gradually increase your movement on this level of your home, and we'll see how you progress. I can promise nothing, but your chances of returning to a quiet, enjoyable life look good to me."

Jean realized that Bea was holding his hand—his right hand. He believed it was slightly numb, but he said nothing of it.

"Have you any questions, Mrs. Kearny?" asked Dr. Gonsoulin kindly.

"Thank you, Doctor, I believe I understand. We will keep him quiet, well fed, and begin a bit of physical activity. Perhaps his valet can get him up this afternoon. The veranda is lovely today, Father. Bailey has recently swept it clean and brought up two rockers from the lower veranda."

"Mrs. Kearny is the widow of the late Dr. Francis Kearny, a highly esteemed Louisiana physician, Dr. Woolrich," said Dr. Gonsoulin.

Woolrich bowed. "Delighted, Madam."

As soon as the doctors departed, Bailey knocked on the door.

"Now, Beatrice, I want you to leave me to Bailey. Go get some rest. We'll see if I can stand on my feet." He got out of his bed, leaning heavily on Bailey, alarmingly weak, especially his right leg.

"Come on, Gen'l. We walk to foot of the bed and back. Then lie down again. We do this every day for an hour." After that, leaning on his man for all duties, Jean began to walk about his room. He was surprised and much encouraged at his increased strength. On the third day, he sat on the veranda facing Third Street. He thought the view was lovely, and he realized he should have been enjoying this spot for many years. He even warmed to the sound of traffic over on St. Charles Avenue. He turned to Bailey:

"We must plan a trip to Biloxi as soon as I am able."

*   *   *

On September 14, Jean celebrated his ninety-first birthday quietly in his bedroom. The family had assured him that they were planning a party downstairs as soon as he felt like it.

"We'll all get together when you feel like it, Papa," said Albert, who had entered his room to check on his father and to see if he needed anything.

"Yes, okay, yes." The General looked at the mahogany-encased clock on the fireplace mantel after his son left; the hands stood at five minutes to eight in the morning.

After Bailey helped him dress he took Jean for a drive out to Lake Pontchartrain. Beatrice and Stephanie went with him. They didn't stay long, but the old man seemed to enjoy what was one of his favorite drives with the chauffeur.

Later that afternoon, Bea and Stephanie suggested that he might feel able, belatedly, to celebrate his birthday by taking a longer drive and staying downstairs for supper. Bailey and Albert supported him as he came down the winding staircase. He sat on the back seat of his Packard with Beatrice, Julia and Robert. Bailey drove them over the newly constructed levee, then up a narrow grassy ramp to top of the levee where Jean exclaimed over the view of the river. He drove them through Audubon Park and along St. Charles. Jean's and his late partner Colonel Bush's support of the City's building of a public park there, on property formerly owned by Étienné de Boré, flashed through his mind. Jean asked Bailey to stop at a shop near the park and buy a fine box of chocolates for after supper that night; he was thinking of the candy as a birthday lagniappe. Fred was still in the City, and he knew others would be at Third Street for supper with them.

At home, having complained of being tired, Jean lay down on the sofa in his downstairs office until supper. Left alone, he realized his breath was coming in rather short, shallow gasps. But he fell asleep for a while, and when he awakened he felt rested, to his relief. Bailey sat in a straight chair by the window.

Jean spoke in a tense voice, "Tomorrow I want you to drive me down to Perdido Street, Bailey."

"Oh, Mister Jean, Miss Bea ain't gonna let you do that. He bent close to his ear. "Don't ax me to do nothin like that. I couldn get you up them stairs."

Shaking his head stubbornly, Jean said, "I don't want to go upstairs to my office. I just want to drive by there. Maybe we could stop at Hotel DeSoto. I could have lunch with Mr. Fred."

Bailey rose from his chair and turned around more than once as he considered his boss's ambitious plans.

"Bailey, sit down. You remind me of an old dog getting ready to lie down for a nap." He and Bailey laughed together. He was not unaware of the good companionship he shared with the faithful colored man. He added, "We've been a long way together, Bailey."

"You right, Mister Jean, we really has."

The supper bell tinkled. Bailey disappeared into the kitchen after he seated his boss comfortably at the head of the table.

Not only did Fred, Molly, and their son, John Bertels, join them, but also Stephanie and Dr. Larue; Julia; Lawrence; Stella and Jack Swanson; Olga, Robert, and their children, Olga and Robert, Jr.; and the Gores—Ella and Joseph and their daughters, Virginia and Marie Ella. After birthday toasts and polite inquiries of their father about his outing, the Leverts chatted away together as they dined on roast pork, mashed potatoes, and assorted vegetables from Jenny's kitchen, including a glittering birthday cake. Jean felt sure that none of them had any idea how thankful he was to be once again with them at his place at the table. Well, perhaps Beatrice and Stephanie. And perhaps Julia.

*   *   *

Jean did not mention a drive to Perdido Street again to Bailey. He hardly thought of it. He felt bad the day after his birthday party, and asked not to get up for his walks. He claimed it was too cold to sit on the veranda, though the October temperature was mild and comfortable. Bea tried, but the only response was: "I'm just too tired, dear."

On the next afternoon, Dr. Gonsoulin stopped by. He was baffled by his patient's lassitude.

"His vital signs are not bad," he told Bea and Stephanie. "Perhaps he overdid it yesterday. Let him rest for a day or two. But not for too long, for he will grow weak if he doesn't walk about every day."

Beatrice followed the doctor down to the front door. She confided that she was worried; was there any further advice that might help her better care for her father?

Putting on his felt hat, Dr. Gonsoulin reminded, "Your father is ninety-one years old, Mrs. Kearny. That is a very great age. It's quite possible that after rest he will be up and around, feeling better. But I can promise nothing. Remember he has had a stroke." There was a moment's silence, then he smiled kindly at her. "Good evening."

Beatrice leaned on the door for a moment. She was glad Albert was coming back tomorrow. She wanted her father to see all his children as often as possible, now.

*   *   *

Jean had been in a coma for four days. His doctor came and went. Father Albert Biever of the church of the Holy Name of Jesus, devoted to Jean and his family and who had married Stephanie and Dr. Larue, called and said prayers. Jean's children came back from out of town and began a vigil with their New Orleans brother and sisters. Julia stayed, sleeping wherever she found a space. The sight of their father lying so still and pale on his bed visibly upset Steph and Bea, for Jean's breathing became more labored. Several times he had stirred and shown signs of consciousness, but not for long. They could not be sure how deeply comatose he was. Their nerves were frayed and they found little solace for their grief, for they had been closest to their father.

Feeling guilty, Steph and Bea talked in the sickroom of their possible error in letting their father know that they did not want him to marry again. "And look at me," said Steph, as the sisters stood together at the foot of his bed. "I married when I was fifty. Papa was not much older than that when Mother was taken from us."

"We were all selfish," said Bea. "I always wondered if he might have found some happiness with Lila."

"Who knows," said Stephanie. "We'll never know. Papa was a youthful widower, younger than Felix was when we married. I know he liked Lila, and she was a lovely little person, quite inoffensive."

Jean stirred, and Beatrice put her finger to her lips. Perhaps he could hear them after all, she thought. The two elder daughters looked at each other.

"Do you think?" said Stephanie.

"No, I'm sure not. Dr. Gonsoulin says he hears nothing." Bea began to cry. "If only we could do something. What will we ever do without Papa? He has been our mainstay for all of our lives." She sat on the side of her father's bed and held his hands. "His hands are cold," she said.

Stephanie gave a sob. "Oh, Papa, Papa, Papa, don't leave us."

Their brothers quietly filed in to look again at their father. Except for Robert, they were departing for Hotel DeSoto to spend the night. They said little. Albert patted Stephanie's shoulders. Robert was staying to sit beside his father through the night, so Beatrice could get some rest and Stephanie could go to her home to sleep.

After lunch the following day, Steph and Bea returned to their father's room to keep vigil. Both were tired, and for the first hour they said little to each other, but took seats in chairs that had been pulled near his bed.

Beatrice studied the elaborate tester over the bed—fine brocade gathered to the center in the walnut frame which she judged to be ten feet high. Her mind wandered in thoughts of their large family. Sometimes she thought she knew little of some of her siblings. It was true that they had good times together at Third Street and in Biloxi and at St. John, especially during the Christmas holidays; she acknowledged that they were rich, privileged in many ways. They did not always do just what they should.

"Steph," she said softly.

"Yes, Bea."

"Have you ever lent money to Robert?"

"Oh, yes. Haven't you?"

"Yes. His gambling debts are absorbing all his investments that Papa made for him. I wonder if he owes the others."

"I suppose so," sighed Steph. "There's no telling what he owes or to whom he owes it. I just can't turn him down. I feel so sorry for him. Poor boy."

"I do, too. His accident with that horse kicking him was terrible. But a lot of sick and injured people don't let that kind of bad luck make them irresponsible. He has been fortunate in many ways—all the finest doctors, you know. This gambling is like a terrible disease. He told me that he owes his family and the banks thousands of dollars."

"I know. I sympathize with Robert for a lot of reasons. He was only ten when our dear mother died—a lonely frightened little boy. Then, let us be honest, he married Olga. She has never been a valued part of this family. She is, in fact, a shrew. Robert admitted to me that he thinks she was after his money. I really don't know how she keeps spending on pure luxuries with Robert so bad off financially. It's perfectly awful. As long as I live, I will never turn my back on him. As long as I have a dollar, I will help him, even if it means leaving part of my inheritance to him." Stephanie was weeping.

"How much does he owe you?"

Both sisters looked at each other in stunned silence. Their father had spoken to them.

"Papa!" They rushed to his side. "Papa," said Bea breathlessly. "You're awake. You have been—asleep—for so long. Speak to us."

In a weak, faltering voice Jean said, "I could hear you. How much?" He was speaking hoarsely between short breaths. "How much does he owe you girls? Who else?" Then he closed his eyes, trying to sort through the dire misadventure when he had fallen down the front steps. He opened his eyes, and in the sky outside his room he saw lightning flicker. A cold wind was blowing, bringing with it the first spits of rain.

"Please, Papa," said Bea, "please don't think of what we were saying. It's all right. Robert just owes a little money. You know he loves to go to the Fairgrounds and bet on the horses, and sometimes he loses a little more than he can afford. Don't worry yourself, now. Can we get you anything, Papa? A sip of water?"

There was no answer. He was not smiling, rather, he was thinking with despair about his youngest son's financial plight. Jean stirred restlessly a few times, then fell into unconsciousness again. Bea called Dr. Gonsoulin, and he promised to come in later. At five o'clock he came into the bedroom. Robert had come back after a nap, and Albert and Lawrence had returned, gratified to hear that their father had appeared to be rallying. Both declared that they must return to their plantations; grinding was in full swing.

"General Levert?" Dr. Gonsoulin called his name several times. He felt the pulse and listened to the faltering heartbeat. He shook his head.

Early next morning, Father Biever and Dr. Gonsoulin arrived together, coming through hard rain. The doctor examined the General and pronounced the pulse and heartbeat to be very weak. He walked around the room shaking hands with the sons and patting the daughters on the shoulder, silently showing the family his sympathy. Then he nodded toward the priest and left the room.

As the storm grew worse, with lightning flashing wildly through the bedroom and thunder crashing noisily and continuously, the old priest gave the last rites to Jean Baptiste Levert:

"Through the holy anointing, may the Lord in his love and mercy help you with the grace of the Holy Spirit. May the Lord who frees you from sin save you and raise you up to everlasting life. God our father, we have anointed your son Jean with the oils of healing and peace. Caress him, oh, Lord. Shelter him and keep him in your tender care."

Jean's children joined the priest:

"In the name of the Father, the Son, and the Holy Ghost, amen." It was late morning, October 15, 1930.

When the priest left the room, Jean's children remained on their knees around the bed in the darkened room, a dull lamp casting soft shadows. Stephanie and Beatrice, who held his hands, raised themselves and kissed his cheeks, their tears spilling into the deep creases of his aged face. Ella, Julia, and Stella leaned across the other side of the bed. Suddenly, a violent gust of wind struck one of the tall windows on the side of the house. Glass shattered and fell on the floor. Several large oak limbs snapped and crashed to the front lawn outside the window, the frightful display freezing the kneeling Leverts in stunned silence. Then for one brief moment Bea and Steph were transfixed as their father gripped their hands tightly and opened his eyes.

"Is it another hurricane, Albert?"

"Father!" They all screamed and gathered closer. "Father!" Albert repeated.

Beatrice held his face in her hands. "Papa? Are you gone, Papa? Papa?" She began to weep aloud. All of the children sobbed almost hysterically. Finally, they all stood, and Albert, after finding no pulse in the old man's neck, spoke to them calmly.

"He was born in a hurricane, you know. Many times *Grandpère* told me about the terrible wind that nearly destroyed Golden Ridge on September 14, 1839. Many times he told me about the day that Papa was born." Albert's voice faltered. He bent and touched his father's hand, choking back tears. After regaining his composure, he continued: "As you know, Papa and I weathered three hurricanes together that laid waste a big part of St. John. We finally lost Junior after the terrible Biloxi hurricane. I found out how he hated and feared a hurricane. I think a hurricane is the only thing Papa ever feared."

The storm had subsided. The only sound was Bailey sobbing audibly outside the bedroom door, mourning the loss of the General.

Epilogue

ON THE PAGES of an historical novel, I want the same weaknesses and strengths, hopes and fears, dreams and regrets of General Jean Baptiste Levert, my great-grandfather, to become evident to us all. Many of the essential facts presented here are faithful to the memories of three of his daughters, Stephanie Marie, Anna Beatrice, and Ella Marie, my grandmother, and to the memories of many of his grandchildren and great-grandchildren: General Levert's appearance, personality, Civil War experiences, business conduct and relationships, love for his wife and children, his love of money, and the Mardi Gras. His daughters began to recount memories of their father in the 1950s when I spent summer vacations with them at St. John Plantation.

I sit now in the front parlor of St. John house on an overcast September morning, seventy-three years after my great-grandfather's death. I can feel the General's presence—the deep-set blue eyes of his portrait, painted circa 1870 when he was thirty-one years old, watching me from above the fireplace.

In back of the house, tractors pull cartloads of harvested cane stalks from the fields to the sugarhouse for start of another grinding season at St. John. Drivers who pass by the house slowly in their noisy automobiles stare across the expansive front lawn shaded by giant oak and magnolia trees. Perhaps the drivers imagine shiny black barouches, string music, dancing in the grand ballroom, belles fanning themselves on the front gallery; perhaps they believe they hear the ghosts of a bygone time. From the parlor I can see thousands of acres of sugarcane. I can visualize my great-grandfather on horseback in the fields, dressed in billowing khaki trousers, high black riding boots and planter's straw hat, observing his overseer and field hands at work, as he often did.

Later, I climb the curving staircase to the widow's walk atop the white-columned house to glimpse the sugarhouse, as charcoal-colored smoke rises from its tall chimney. Inside machines crush juice from cane stalks and the stalks into almost dry fragments, evaporate water from the juice until it becomes a thick syrup— unrefined brown raw sugar. The same sugarhouse where General Levert and his eldest son, Albert, refined their skills of sugarmaking.

Now it's quiet where I sit. I can only hear the sound of the wind as it stirs the tops of the sugarcane, pushing yellow-gold, twelve-foot stalks into whispers with memories of a long time ago. I believe the ghost of my great-grandfather will forever stroll this manor house and plantation, now almost a hundred and seventy years old. For it is the ghosts who have really told the story on the pages of this book.

Ira Brown Harkey
St. John Plantation
Levert, Louisiana
September 2003

AUTHOR'S NOTE

THIS HISTORICAL NOVEL, which differs from a biographical novel in that it introduces some fictional characters and probable events against a background of history, tells the story of General Jean Baptiste Levert based on the surviving facts of his life and through the actual people who helped make it happen—his parents, his children and grandchildren, descendants of his brothers, descendants of life-long friends, house servants, business associates and their descendants, admirers and detractors alike.

Names, characters, dates, places, and events connected with the General's life are as factual as I could make them to be. Many thanks to the following state and national institutions and agencies and to their archivists, curators, and reference librarians for allowing me to peruse certain material for background and private research use only: National Archives and Records Service, Washington, D.C.; Library of Congress Genealogy Department, Washington, D.C.; National Archives of Quebec, Montreal, Canada; Department of the Archives, Diocese of Baton Rouge (Louisiana); Special Collections and Louisiana Divisions, Tulane University Library, New Orleans; Department of Archives and Manuscripts, Troy Middleton Library, Louisiana State University, Baton Rouge; Archives and Special Collections House, St. Joseph's College and Mount St. Mary's College, both of Emmitsburg, Maryland; Archives and Records Service, Louisiana Secretary of State, Baton Rouge; Sons of Confederate Veterans, Louisiana Division, Baton Rouge. Also: The Historic New Orleans Collection; Louisiana State Museum, New Orleans; Notarial Archives, Orleans Parish, New

Orleans; public libraries in New Orleans, St. Martinville, Plaquemine, St. Gabriel, and Port Allen, Louisiana, and Biloxi, Mississippi; Orleans, St. Martin, Iberville, and West Baton Rouge parish and Harrison County (Biloxi), Mississippi, courthouses. For advice and suggestions during early stages of my research, I am grateful to the Catholic parish priests in New Orleans, St. Martinville, Baton Rouge, Thibodaux, Plaquemine, and Donaldsonville, Louisiana; editor and publisher, Plaquemine, La., *Post and Iberville South;* and publisher, St. Martinville, La., *Teche News*.

The principal characters did exist. Others are necessarily made up for purposes of the storyline and either are a product of my imagination or are used fictitiously. Any resemblance to actual persons, living or dead, is purely coincidental. All the dialogue is invented. But in every instance it is based on my knowledge of the characters' personality, temperament, and spoken in the language of the day, which was more formal than it is today. All the diary entries by General Levert and by his Acadian grandmother, Anna Comeaux Levert, are created by me. House servants from the Louisiana Acadian parishes, such as Bébé and Dottee, speak in their local Cajun dialect, or *patois*.

Furthermore, as much use as possible is made of authentic historical data. I have included references to real historical figures, dates, places, and events for purposes incidental to the story, and such references are made without the knowledge or cooperation of the individuals referred to or involved.

I acknowledge the constant help and encouragement afforded me by so many during this undertaking. Foremost, I owe a profound debt of gratitude to Martha Lacy Hall Shelton, my editor, who took countless months away from her own literary pursuits to tackle difficult creative reading and editing of the manuscript. Her sensitive, imaginative and enthusiastic editing improved significantly the final product.

My father, Ira B. Harkey, Jr., author, newspaper publisher and editor, and Pulitzer Prize winner, was my most helpful critic, preserving many of the Levert family stories and sharing them with me. His knowledge of the history and culture of New Orleans and Louisiana was invaluable. I thank the following people who helped me in ways out of the ordinary: Pamela Tapie, Robert Becker, Charles LeBlanc, my cousin, L. C. "Boo" Levert, III, Wiltz Duplantis, and the late Ramon Billeaud, all current and former officers of the Levert companies. They turned me loose in the St. Martinville, Louisiana, office and in the New Orleans corporate office, where boxes of General Levert's business papers, records, and personal correspondence—many of them dated from Reconstruction until his death—are stored.

Jean Baptiste Levert, III, deceased, shared many intimate details about his grandfather, particularly how his father, Jean Baptiste Jr., became ill after the Biloxi, Mississippi, hurricane circa 1909, and succumbed 12 years later to tuberculosis. I am most thankful to other descendants who not only shared entertaining anecdotes and stories, but allowed me to use as I saw fit any contents of personal letters and scrapbooks in their possession: Mary Bell Swanson Mayer, granddaughter; and Marie Ella Levert Gore Harkey, Virginia Gore Friedrichs, Beatrice Kearny Couch, Sylvia "Bootsie" Levert Cunningham, Frank Kearny, Jr., and Jack Swanson, all deceased grandchildren; Frances Haley Levert and Margaret Wright Levert, grandchildren by marriage; Virginia Friedrichs Burke, "Winnie" Levert Goulas, Jane Cunningham Legier, Stephanie Levert Musser, John Bertels Levert, Jr., J. Alfred Levert II, Harvey Couch, III, Albert Lamar, and the late Thomas J. Martin, Jr., all great-grandchildren.

I am especially grateful to Dr. Homer J. Dupuy, Jr., of New Orleans, third cousin of General Levert's wife, Marie Stephanie Dupuy. Because of his vast knowledge of the family, I interviewed and corresponded often with Dr. Dupuy. Also of great help were Constance Benton, through marriage a descendant of the General's business partner, Colonel John Louis Bush; Clifton Morvant, descendant of Emile U. Morvant, another of the General's business partners; the late Lamartine "Shorty" Lamar; son-in-law of the General's; the late John Wilds, author, newspaper writer, editor, and former newspaper colleague of mine, and Ronald Levert, descendant of the General's brother, Auguste "Augie" Levert, Jr., all of New Orleans; the late Harold Aubry of New Iberia, Louisiana, who as a young chemist worked for General Levert at the sugarhouse on St. John Plantation; the late Mae Gauthier of St. Martinville, Louisiana, a relative who as a young woman worked for the Levert family; the DeClouet family, especially the late George DeClouet of Lafayette, Louisiana, descendant of General Alexandre Étienné DeClouet; Mrs. Pat Daly of Ft. Myers, Florida, great-granddaughter of Annie Blanton Kleinpeter; and Faye McLeod of Escatawpa, Mississippi, my computer guru/typist.

I would be remiss if I didn't thank my wife, Helen, for her patience and understanding during the creation process and writing of initial drafts of the manuscript, all done in longhand. I took over our dining room for about four years, forcing my family to eat in the kitchen. I owe her a great debt of gratitude.

Ira Brown Harkey
Ocean Springs, Mississippi